RUNELIGHT

I

FROM THE KEEPERS LIBRARY
THE AENIGMA LIGHTS

JA ANDREWS

For Jason.
Thank you, and
I love you.

PRINTABLE MAPS

You can find printable maps at
https://www.jaandrews.com/printable-maps/

WHITE WOOD
HOME
SEE INSET BELOW

RULLDUIN RIVER (SUBTERRANEAN)

KEEPER STRONGHOLD

MORROW

RULLDUIN (TUNNELS)

BARREN HIGHLANDS

QUEENSLAND

THE WHITE WOOD
AND SURROUNDING AREA

WHITE WOOD

HOME

RAVINE

RULLDUIN RIVER

EASTERN QUEENSLAND
AND THE WESTERN EDGE OF THE
OLD KALESH EMPIRE

the ravine

Reston Ridge

to Home

heavy forest

rock shelf

cave

camp

road

Surn river

SKETCH FROM BO'S JOURNAL

DATED 17TH MADNEY

PART I

THE BELL

It's been seven decades, and I've still never written it all out.

I should have, right when it ended. Not because it was fresher in my mind, but because the true tragedy of it all didn't hit as hard back then. For all my thirty-two years, I'd yet to experience some of the truly heart-breaking things in life. Back then, "heartbreak" was just a word I thought I understood.

The tragedy wasn't the full story, of course. That makes it sound like there was no adventure or mystery. No friendships deep enough to feed the soul. The tragedy was only on the peripheral. Like a mist you can see through the trees around you but can't tell that it's also touching your skin.

But I'm getting ahead of myself.

It all began with the bell.

The first time I heard it, I was only twelve. It's fitting (although I didn't notice at the time), that it always tolled out in a vast, lonesome darkness—No, that's not entirely true.

The first time I heard the bell, there was nothing but light.

CHAPTER ONE

AGE 12

"Do you smell that?" Kate dropped the handles of the heavy wheelbarrow and straightened. The disorienting scent filled the air, and she grabbed the corner of the horse stall to steady herself. Splinters dug into her palm, and the sharp, tangible pain chased away the elusive smell.

The sound of her younger brother tossing straw inside the stall stopped, and she regretted her question immediately.

Evan's eyes, half covered by his mop of curly red hair, poked around the end of the wall. "Smell what?"

Of course he didn't smell it. No one ever seemed to.

Although, if anyone were to notice something strange, it should be her ten-year-old brother who was endlessly amused by anything odd.

"It's…" Kate turned and stepped toward the open barn door, trying to recapture the peculiar scent—one of the few that kept plaguing her. It was like the bright scent of the evergreen boughs her mother hung on the lintel in Midwinter, blended with the smell of the woods after the rain.

Except there wasn't a pine tree in sight. Nothing but bare oaks and maples covered the hillside next to the barn, their branches dusted with the light green of early spring.

And above them, the sky stretched over the valley in a clear, cloudless blue.

"I cleaned out all the dung, Katria," Evan declared. "I swear."

"Not that kind of smell." Her words were quiet enough even she could barely hear them. "Pines…after a rainstorm." She shook her head at how poorly that captured it and sniffed again.

It was gone, though, leaving only the warm scent of straw drifting out of the barn.

"Never mind," she said, but the rustling sounds of her brother working drowned out her words.

She pushed her long auburn braid back over her shoulder and was turning back to the wheelbarrow when a strange sensation prickled at her. She took a tentative step out of the door and stopped.

The whole world felt…off.

The morning air was chilly, but a slight warmth pushed against her cheek from the nearby rows of green shoots growing in the wheat field.

On the other side of the barn, the forested hillside was bright enough that she squinted against it.

Except it wasn't bright. It was the same bare branches and hints of spring green from yesterday.

She shrank back into the shadow of the barn. Just some trick of the light? The sky was clear, the sun its usual self. Her eyes traced the shape of the bright-but-not bright hill, finding everything about it both ordinary and foreign at the same time.

She peered down at the river running past the end of the farm, and her shoulders relaxed.

The water level was high on the rocky riverbank, churning white and foamy over huge submerged boulders, but the light green current, browned a little from the rush of spring rain, looked completely ordinary.

She soaked in the familiarity of its rapids and ignored the unnatural warmth and brightness of everything else.

A flicker of motion caught her eye from the hillside past the water. A strip of red fabric fluttered from the branch of a dead tree.

She clutched the doorframe next to her.

"Evan!" She stared at the little flicker of scarlet, as though it were another trick that was about to shift back to the usual blue. "A red flag at the mine!"

"Red?" Evan scrambled out of the stall and around the wheelbarrow, skidding up next to her. "What's Bo doing there? Ma sent him to the market!" He tossed the pitchfork into the corner and ran out the door. "C'mon!"

"Wait…" Kate glanced back into the barn. "The chores…" But the flag was red, and no signal flag in all their years had ever been red. Not from the tree fort near the river, or the rock fort up the hill, or in the months since they'd discovered the mine.

Her feet stayed locked to the floor for a breath before she shoved away from the door and ran after her brother.

Evan was two years younger than her, but his legs had grown like weeds in the past year, and his long strides ate up the distance to the river. Kate stretched her shorter legs to catch up. The wheat field crowded close to the path, little waves of warmth rolling off the rows of green. She pointedly ignored them, focusing on the fluttering bit of red on the hillside across the water.

What called for a red flag? Since Bo had turned sixteen, Ma had taken to sending him on longer errands. "Because he never gets himself into trouble he can't get out of," she'd say with a pointed look at Evan. But Bo shouldn't be back yet, and why would he go to the mine alone?

The twinge of disappointment at being left behind was quickly overrun by a picture of him bleeding in the dark of the tunnels, and she ran faster.

Evan reached the rope bridge strung across the river a dozen paces before her. He slowed as he stepped onto the wooden slats, setting the bridge to rocking.

Kate's foot hit the first plank before he was halfway across. She paused, wrapping her hands around the rough rope that was knotted into a tall net-like railing. It rose above her elbows like a barrier between her and the rushing water, and she gripped it, forcing herself to wait until he was only steps from the far side.

He wasn't quite off before she started. The wood shivered and shifted under her weight, but she slid her hands along the scratchy rope and used the smooth, rhythmic pace that kept the bridge from swaying erratically.

The rapids swirled beneath her, wild and fast. Pools of rusted green spun between roiling patches of froth. The rushing of the turbulent water blocked out any other sounds.

The cool air over the river blew away the last of the strange heat from the field, and she jumped over the last few slats onto the other bank. There was no sign of Evan, and she raced down the short path that ran along the riverbank.

Her feet pounded around the turn as the trail veered sharply uphill, narrowing until it was nearly choked out by the tall scrubby bushes of the steep hillside. They nagged at her with a barely perceptible warmth, but she shook away the sensation.

A branch scratched against her arm as she ran around the first switchback and caught sight of Evan, rounding the second.

Her legs burned and her breath came fast before she reached the third turn and the black opening of the mine came into view.

"Bo!" Evan shouted, ducking under the thick beam that ran over the entrance.

She reached the mouth of the mine, and the scent of rain-drenched pines swirled past her again. Spinning, she cast a wary look over the valley.

There was nothing. No pines, and definitely no rain.

"He's here!" Evan called. "He took one of the lanterns."

Kate pushed away questions about irrational smells and hurried into the mine without needing to even dip her head under the beam. The floor of what they'd dubbed the Entrance Hall was worn nearly smooth, and the walls were speckled with familiar shadows and wooden beams. A half-dozen tunnels wound out of it, disappearing into darkness.

"Bo?" Kate called, her voice echoing back high and frightened.

"Maybe he found a way to see how deep Shadow Grave Shaft goes." Evan knelt to light the remaining lantern.

"That's hardly a reason for an emergency flag. What if he's hurt? Stuck somewhere?" Kate moved to the first tunnel on the left. "Bo!"

"If he were stuck somewhere, he wouldn't have been able to put up the red flag," Evan pointed out.

Kate paused. "That's true."

"He must be fine, and seeing the bottom of Shadow Grave would call for more than the usual blue 'I'm at the mine' flag." Evan took his lantern to the second tunnel on the right. "Maybe it really is a grave and he found skeletons at the bottom!" He started down the tunnel, and his lantern cast dim golden light on the slats of wood bracing the Western Wing Passage. "Or it's a pit where goblins were thrown!" He turned around a corner, and the lantern light disappeared

Kate leaned into the second tunnel on the left, straining to see any light from Bo. "Goblins?"

"Goblins!" Evan's voice echoed slightly muffled from behind her.

The enthusiastic tone in her brother's voice drew a huff of

laughter out of her as she headed toward the next tunnel opening in the dim recesses of the Entrance Hall.

"There have never been goblins in the Wildwood," she called.

Her brother didn't answer, and the idea made her pause.

Goblins didn't smell like pines after the rain, did they?

The tunnel Evan had disappeared into was utterly black, and the silence of the mine settled around her like a blanket. Nothing but dim sunlight filtered to the back of the Entrance Hall, and the mouths of two tunnels gaped open in front of her, thick with shadows and darkness.

What if Bo had found goblins?

In the closer of the two tunnels, a trace of light caught on something claw-like and sharp.

Rocks skittered behind her, and she whirled around.

Instead of goblin teeth, Bo's wide, crooked smile greeted her as he stuck his head out of the first tunnel. His dark hair stood up on his head, a sure sign that he'd been excitedly running his hands through it. He raised an eyebrow. "What's got you so jumpy, Ria?"

The familiar nickname was like an extra bit of light dribbling into the mine, and her shoulders loosened.

"Goblins!" Evan came back into view with a grin. "From Shadow Grave Shaft."

With both brothers there, the Entrance Hall fell back into its familiar shapes.

Kate cast another glance toward the dark tunnel, but the claw shape was nothing but a jagged bit of stone. "There are no goblins," she said, trying to make her voice firm.

She turned back to Bo, searching him for any signs of injuries. "Why the red flag?"

"Because!" He flashed a smile at Kate that was both nervous and exhilarated. "We're almost out of time! They could be here at any moment!"

CHAPTER TWO

"Who could be here at any moment?" Kate asked.

"Goblins?" Evan offered with a grin.

Bo let out a laugh. "I think goblins are small. These were full-sized men."

Evan crossed the Entrance Hall to where Bo stood. "Who?"

"Foreigners." Bo cast a look outside. "Two men were at the market today with strange clothes and strange accents asking questions about Kyrost's Tunnels."

"Who's Kyrost?" Evan asked.

"No idea. But do you know of any other tunnels around here?"

Kate walked back to the mouth of the mine. Below her, the rocky valley was empty. Across the river, there was nothing but the wheat field, the barn, their small home, and a few sheep grazing in the pasture. "What are they looking for?"

Bo let out a laugh. "Well, what would bring you all the way to a foreign land to search an old mine?"

Kate turned to find Evan staring at Bo.

"You think they're here for treasure?" her younger brother asked.

"Don't you?" Bo turned to the tunnel he'd come out of. "C'mon! Black Rat Tunnel is the only part we haven't searched. This could be our last chance!"

Kate's worry dissolved in the face of Bo's familiar enthusiasm, leaving a knot of anger in its place. "Bo, you scared me. I thought you were hurt."

His smile turned slightly abashed. "Sorry. I didn't have a faster way to get you two here."

"You could have come to the barn," she pointed out.

He shifted. "I didn't think of that."

"You went down to Black Rat by yourself, didn't you?" Evan asked, his voice caught between annoyance and admiration.

A smile quirked up the edge of Bo's mouth. "I found a room. And there is so much stuff in it! I think miners lived there once."

"What are we waiting for?" Evan pushed past Bo and started down the tunnel.

Bo turned to Kate, and his smile shifted to a wince. "I'm sorry I worried you, Ria. I…got excited."

"You got stupid." She pointed a finger at him. "If we find treasure, I get part of your share."

He grimaced. "That's fair."

She sighed and dropped her finger.

His face split into a wide grin. "It's *when* we find treasure, not if. There's something in Black Rat Tunnel, Ria. I can feel it!"

She let her own smile grow. "You say that about every tunnel."

"Which means I'm gonna be right someday!"

She walked over to him, her feet crunching on the bits of gravel littering the floor. "I don't think it works like tha—"

A new scent rushed into her.

Summer. Late summer…That wind that came tumbling over

the southern hills in late summer, golden and wild, bringing air from some distant, exotic place.

She stumbled to a stop as Bo started down the tunnel. It wasn't the smell of the wind, not really, but it was somehow like it.

She hunched her shoulders, refusing to look out the entrance of the mine. It was months until late summer.

Bo kept moving, and Kate's eyes locked onto his back.

With each step he took, the scent receded.

She started after him, slow and hesitant.

Evan and Bo waited at the first turn, their voices tumbling over each other in the echoes of the mine.

She held her breath as she approached them, but the two scents seeped into her anyway, not actual smells, but impressions springing up in her mind. Late summer wind and rain-soaked pines, all jumbled together.

Bo glanced at her and paused, waving for Evan to be quiet. "What's wrong, Ria?"

"I..."

Evan paused when he saw her face. "Did you smell the thing again?"

"What thing?" Bo asked.

"Ria smelled something weird in the barn."

Bo stepped toward her. "Are you all right?"

She swallowed but couldn't bring herself to nod. "I keep smelling..." She couldn't say people.

Evan's eyes widened. "Is there bad air in here?"

Both boys looked around warily as though they might see a cloud of poison hanging over their heads.

"It's not bad air," Kate said.

Evan spun back to peer down the tunnel. "Is it goblins?"

"No!" She let out an exasperated breath. "It's you!"

They both turned slowly to look at her.

"I do not smell bad," Evan objected.

"Not bad." She paused. There was no way to put it into words. It was like trying to catch the sparkle on the top of the river water. Nothing was going to explain smells that weren't smells, but both boys were looking at her expectantly, so she gave a twitchy sort of shrug. "You smell like pine trees after it's rained, and Bo smells like that hot wind that blows over the hills in the summer."

They stared at her for a moment, and she waited for them to laugh. Or tell her she was lying. Or crazy. Evan looked as though he were waiting for the rest of the joke, but Bo's brow drew together in concern.

Finally, Evan leaned toward Bo. "You smell like air," he whispered loudly.

Bo elbowed him in the side. "Shut up. You smell like wet trees." He came over to Kate, raising the lantern so he could look at her. "What do you mean we smell like that?"

There was no mockery in his face, just curiosity, and something inside her loosened at the fact that he believed her. "It started a few weeks ago. Just a bit here and there, but it's happening more and more. I didn't realize until just now that it's from...you." She glanced over Bo's shoulder at Evan. "I think maybe I can smell Ma and Dad, too."

Evan's usually wide smile seemed caught between laughter and worry. "That's crazy."

She flinched at the word.

Bo shot him a scowl. "She's not crazy."

"I didn't say she was crazy," Evan protested. "I mean...it's Ria. You drag us into crazy places like this, I get us into trouble, and Katria fixes it all. The weird smells are probably..." He cast around the tunnel, swinging his lantern wildly. "Fixing something that we don't even know is wrong." His eyebrows shot up, and he peered at her. "Or it's magic!"

"No one has magic in their nose," Kate said, shifting under the scrutiny of both boys. "It's not... Can we stop talking about it? We're running out of time."

Bo hesitated, but then gave her his crooked grin and patted her on the shoulder. *"Prapiro thesaur!"*

Speed to treasure, a phrase he'd stolen from an old story and made into something between a blessing and a battle cry.

Kate forced a smile despite the scent of summer swirling around her. *"Prapiro thesaur!"*

Bo headed down the tunnel, and she followed. Evan fell in next to her, and she waited for him to make a joke, but he just walked beside her, quieter than usual.

She caught him watching her out of the corner of his eye. "You think I'm crazy."

"No. A little weird, maybe," he said with a smile, "but not crazy."

"It feels crazy," she admitted.

He nudged her arm with his elbow. "At least I understand why you never want to explore Shadow Grave Shaft." His smile grew. "You're part goblin."

"What?"

He tapped his nose. "Goblins can smell gold."

"I don't smell gold." She shoved her shoulder into him. "I smell you."

He rubbed his arm with a chuckle. "I've been called a treasure."

"Only by Ma."

They wove quickly through tunnels while Evan recited the tale of the goblin princess who couldn't smell gold and got lost in her own royal warrens. His voice echoed through the tunnels as he proclaimed the lines of the nasal goblin king or belted out thundering voices of the troll who'd come to rescue the princess.

By the time Bo's lantern light fell on the familiar dark, rat-shaped rock that stood guardian in front of Black Rat Tunnel, Kate's cheeks were tired from grinning and the strange scents felt, if not normal, at least less frightening.

Bo let out a whoop of excitement at the mouth of the tunnel and hurried into it, with Evan speeding up to follow. Kate trailed behind.

She adjusted her pace, falling back a little or catching up to them. Every time she drew near one of them, beyond their smell, she caught faint sounds. Evan's like tumbling, burbling water, and Bo's like an indrawn breath, or maybe a huff of laughter.

She followed them around more turns before they spilled out into a cavern large enough that she could barely see the far side. To their left, the lantern light fell on the dusty remains of a tattered blanket, a broken pickaxe, and a spindly wooden stool that looked like the slightest weight would crush it.

"I bet Dad's right," Evan said, moving toward it. "It must be a hundred years since miners were here."

"I didn't look through any of the stuff without you two," Bo said over his shoulder, "but I explored the tunnels a bit. The one to the left connects back with the Sandy Path." He held his lantern up to show a few dark holes in the walls. "And this one leads to the base of Little Rock Wall. Not sure where the rest go."

Evan peered around the room. "This is central enough that they might have actually lived here."

"I agree." Bo walked slowly to the right, his lantern held out, casting a glow over small dust-covered piles of things left behind long ago. "And where they might have kept their valuables!"

Kate leaned against the wall next to the tunnel and let them both wander away with their strange smells, trying to make out the shape and size of the cavern.

With both boys moving away, the world felt normal again, and she watched their lanterns shine light over old dusty things. They'd come across enough caverns like this that she'd given up hope of finding anything more valuable than rusting mining tools, and she just wanted to stand in the unscented quiet for a moment.

Something past Bo caught her attention. A bit of light. Not the wavering reflections of the lantern light, but a low, steady glow. She crossed the cavern but found only a rotted wooden crate and a pile of rubble against the wall.

"Find something?" Bo brought the lantern over. He paused near the wall. "There's something here!" He dropped to his knees, facing the rubble.

Evan ran over, dangling his lantern over Kate's shoulder. "Is it gold?"

She pushed the lantern away from her face. "It's not gold. He's looking at the pile of rocks."

"Not the rocks." Bo crouched down and pulled the stones away, revealing a few slats of dried wood covering a deep nook.

Kate knelt next to him, pebbles jabbing into her knees as his fingers pushed the last of the stones away from the boards. The lantern light fell on something smooth barely visible between the gaps.

His breath came quick and shallow, as though he was afraid breathing too deeply would shatter the moment. He wiggled a finger into one of the larger cracks and pulled. The slat came free with a dry crack, and Kate flinched.

They sat perfectly still for a breath before Bo looked over at Kate.

"*Prapiro thesaur,*" he said with a nervous smile.

She managed a tight one in return. "*Prapiro thesaur.*"

They leaned forward, shoulder to shoulder.

Bo drew out a leather-wrapped bundle and unfolded it to reveal a box made of age-worn wood. He brushed his hands over the surface, wiping off a thin layer of dust and revealing hammered metal straps that wrapped along the corners. Small nails studded the corners, dinged and rounded with age.

"We found something!" Bo whispered. "We actually found something!" He grinned as he turned the box over, his movements reverent.

He wiped his sleeve over the lid, revealing a series of arcs and lines laid out in precise, complex runes that caught the light and seemed to hold it for a moment.

Kate felt a momentary annoyance that a medallion covered the middle of them—until Bo brushed the dust off it, revealing a tarnished gold coin stamped with an intricate image of a dragon coiled around a sword.

"It *is* gold!" Evan breathed.

The dragon was so detailed that its tiny scales shifted and flickered in the lantern light.

Bo fiddled with the box, trying to lift the lid, pulling on the front and the sides, wedging his fingernails into anything that looked like a seam, but nothing moved.

Kate leaned forward to see it better, and Bo handed it to her.

"Maybe it's solid," Evan said.

The box fit easily in her hands and was light, like the tiny wooden chest her mother kept coins in on the mantel. Kate ran her thumb over the age-darkened metal along the edges, considering the box. There was a sense of vastness to it. She brought it close to her ear and knocked against the top. "It's definitely hollow."

She caught the faint smell of something odd. Something spicy but cold and somehow very, very slow.

Before she could sort out the fact that almost none of those were smells, it was gone.

"Even if it's just a fancy bit of wood with a piece of gold on top," Evan said, "it's better than anything we've ever found. I wonder what else is around here?" He headed across the room to another dusty pile.

Kate touched the medallion, running her fingertips over the sinuous dragon and the vicious sword. It was elaborate, but it merely felt like cold metal.

Her eyes were continually drawn back to the carvings surrounding it, though, and she moved her fingers to trace one of the lines.

The box, or her fingertips, or maybe the air around her, hummed.

The spicy smell filled the air around her again, sharp in her nose and crisply cold in her lungs.

Somewhere, a bell rang out, haunting and lonely and nearly lost in an unimaginably vast darkness.

The note thrummed deep in her chest. She twitched her hand away, but the humming grew. Racing through her ribs and up her spine until her skull buzzed with it.

In another heartbeat, it blossomed out to her skin, stinging every inch of her with the prickle of a million tiny needles for an instant before it shot out into the air with a glitter of silvery light that was gone almost before she saw it.

The bell sound faded, but everything else around her bloomed into light and sound and smell.

Next to her, Bo's scent flared vibrant and clear, rustling with breathy laughter. His body sent off waves of heat like a fire. Something about him brightened, even as he stayed barely visible in the lantern light.

Kate shoved the box away and scooted back, spinning to take in the rest of the cavern. Evan stood a dozen paces away, glowing brightly, his rainy-pines trail floating behind him like a mist.

"What is it?" Bo asked.

She looked back at the box. "That's more than a fancy bit of wood."

"I knew it!" Bo said, his voice full of certainty. "I think it's a puzzle box. An aenigma."

"What's an aenigma?" Evan called over his shoulder.

"Something hard to understand," Bo answered.

"Like Kate's weird nose thing?" His grin flashed from across the room.

Bo picked up a pebble and threw it, bouncing it off Evan's back, making his laugh echo off the walls.

Kate's eyes traced the markings on the box again. They seemed to speak of something, as though she could almost read them.

She focused on the spicy-cold scent, trying to decipher what it actually was.

The hint of a different scent jabbed into Kate like a knife, and her hand flew up to cover her nose. But it wasn't a real scent, and it seeped into her anyway, rancid and caustic with a grating, scraping sound in the background.

She leaned away from the box just as Bo leaned closer.

"How does it open?" he mused.

A scuff sounded from the mouth of the cavern, the real sound so jarring that Kate whirled toward it.

The rank stench grew stronger as two men stepped into the cavern, their faces cast in stark, harsh shadows.

The taller man fixed his gaze on the box. "It doesn't."

CHAPTER THREE

KATE SCRAMBLED TO HER FEET.

Bo shoved himself up almost as fast, pulling her behind him as he faced the men. She grabbed the back of his shirt, steadying herself against the barrage of smells and sounds and the strange heat emanating from him. Over his shoulder, she saw the men move closer until they stopped only a handful of steps away.

The man who'd spoken was older, his white beard and hair cropped close. A step behind his shoulder, a younger man, shorter but broad enough to be part bear, slowly drew a dagger.

Evan stood frozen on the far side of the cave, his eyes shifting between Kate and Bo, the men, and the exit they blocked.

The stench cut through the room, and Kate crowded against Bo's back. His windy smell saturated the air around her, but it did nothing to drive away the new foulness.

The older man held a candle sheltered inside a glass lantern, the flame so small it showed little more than their blood red tunics.

They could almost be the sort of men who had important jobs in a city, combed and clean and busy. But either because of the stench or the shifting shadows of the lantern light, Kate kept catching cruel shadows slipping around the edges of their mouths.

"Give me the box," the older man commanded, holding his free hand toward Bo.

The strangely accented words echoed harshly in the cave, but they filled the air, and a strange numbness wrapped its fingers around Kate's mind.

She fought the sudden urge to push Bo and the box toward the men.

"No," Bo said from between gritted teeth, even as one foot slid forward.

At the sound of her brother's voice, her mind cleared slightly.

"Do not speak," the man commanded, the words rich and deep, "and give me the box."

Each of his words crowded around Kate, humming and drowning out every thought except the urge to obey. She tried to shake her head to clear it, but her neck refused to move.

"Why—?" The rest of her question was strangled out after the single word, and her voice echoed thin and small in the cavern, but just that single sound dispelled some of the fog.

The younger man stepped forward, and the candlelight revealed black embroidery on his red sleeve. A dragon coiled around a sword. "Because it is ours. Bring it here, slowly."

The embroidery matched the medallion on the box, and the man's request felt suddenly, utterly rational. A nagging voice shouted something in the back of her mind, but the box obviously belonged to these men, and Kate couldn't think of any reason to keep it from them.

Bo took a step toward them, and the acrid foulness of the men swirled into the space behind him, catching in Kate's throat. She coughed, and the haziness in her mind cleared.

She grabbed Bo's shoulder. "Don't," she whispered. "They smell—"

"Silence!" the first man snapped.

The command tried to wrap its numbing tendrils around her mind, but the abrasive smell sliced through it, too sharp to be ignored.

"No." Kate pushed the word out with as much force as she could, and Bo twitched.

Across the cave, Evan straightened and drew back from the men.

The older man's eyes focused on her, cold and calculating.

Kate looked around the cavern for some sort of weapon, anything that would move the men away from where they stood, blocking the exit.

Her eyes caught on the black tunnel opening just past Evan, and she paused.

The men were blocking one exit.

"Don't be stupid," the younger man said. "There's no need to hurt any of you. Just hand over the box."

The words slid off her, but Bo started forward.

Kate dug her fingers into his shoulder, clamping down until he hissed in pain.

"You know what's stupid?" She pushed as much volume into her words as she could, and Bo glanced at her, looking slightly confused. "Coming into a mine you aren't familiar with, and bringing only one tiny, weak candle."

Across the cavern, Evan let out a little huff of laughter, and the men shifted, their faces growing bleaker.

"If your light goes out," Kate said, looking between Evan and Bo, "you'd have to restart it in the dark—which is harder than it sounds—or find your way out without it."

A small smile curled up the side of Bo's mouth. "True. Unless you've practiced navigating in the pitch black, you should always bring an extra light."

"That's just common sense," Evan agreed. He edged toward the tunnel nearest to him. "This leads to Sandy Path?"

Bo nodded.

"Don't move," the knife-wielder snapped.

Evan's step faltered. His brow creased in concentration, and with a grunt of effort, he lifted his lantern and flipped open the side. Giving the man a glare, Evan blew out the flame, dropping his side of the cavern into shadows.

Kate leaned down and picked up the lantern by her feet. The metal handle was cold in her hand, but the tiny flame inside felt hotter than usual. She glanced at the foreigner's candle. It wasn't too far away.

Bo twitched the box slightly and looked across the cavern at Evan. "We'll need our hands free for Little Rock Wall," he told Kate.

Evan set his lantern down, turning to face Bo.

"It's been a while since we did Little Rock Wall in the dark," Kate murmured.

"I know," Bo answered with a strained smile. "Should be fun, huh?"

"More fun than staying here," she admitted.

"Put the lantern down!" The older man strode toward her. "Give me the box now, or things are going to go very badly for you."

Bo tensed at his command, but Kate shook her head. "You smell too bad for your crazy word thing to work on me."

The man paused, studying her as though trying to figure out her words.

Bo shifted his weight. "Ready?"

Kate opened the lantern. *"Prapiro thesaur."*

He let out a tight laugh. *"Prapiro thesaur."* Before the older man could speak again, Bo tossed the box toward Evan.

The men shouted something in a language Kate couldn't understand, and their eyes followed the box as it arced through the air. A soon as Evan's fingers closed around it, Kate blew out her light, plunging the cave into shadows.

She aimed at the tiny flame held by the older man and, with all her strength, hurled her lantern. It crashed into his chest, and he dropped his candle.

Glass shattered, and the cave guttered into blackness.

CHAPTER FOUR

HARSH FOREIGN SHOUTS filled the cavern, echoing back harsh and furious in the utter darkness.

Bo's fingers wrapped around Kate's. "This way!" he hissed, pulling her toward the nearest passage.

"Stop!" one of the foreigners shouted, but his voice was battered by too many echoes to carry the weight it had before, and it didn't even slow their steps.

Her free hand scraped into the wall, and she followed Bo along it until he turned into the tunnel.

Their palms were slick with sweat, but his grip was solid and steady, and she tightened her fingers. Running her other hand along the rough wall of the tunnel, she tried to keep her balance in the blackness. She slid her feet forward in slow, shuffling steps, searching for anything that might trip her.

She'd been the one to insist they practice getting out in the dark, after Evan's lantern had run out of oil deep in a tunnel one day. Eventually, it had become a game with blindfolds and attempts to confuse each other. But now, with no lantern in reserve, no flint and bundle of kindling in Bo's pocket, no Evan laughing and attempting to give her bad advice, the blackness was like a solid thing. Something to work through, swim through almost.

Kate's eyes stretched open, straining for any sign of light around her, but they were utterly encased in darkness.

Except…

Her gaze slid to Bo, walking a step ahead of her. The blackness was absolute, and she couldn't see him at all, but…he was there. Like the echo left after looking at something bright, the vague shape that lingered behind your eyelids. Somehow, she could see the shape of him moving, even while she saw nothing at all.

Or maybe she could feel him. He was warm. Like he was made of smoldering coals.

But how could she feel the shape of his warmth?

On top of all that, the windy smell of him filled every breath she took, so intensely it would have been terrifying if it weren't so reassuring.

She fought to move silently, but her heart pounded and every breath came fast and deafeningly loud.

The men's shouts grew fainter, though, with each bend of the passage.

"Who were they?" she whispered.

"And why did I keep wanting to do what they said?" Bo slowed and worked his way around a turn before picking up the pace again. He squeezed her hand. "Did you say they smelled?"

"Awful!" She blew out a breath as though she could drive away the memory of it. "Like rancid meat."

"What does that mean? They're evil?"

"I don't know." Her hand ran into a rough beam rising toward the ceiling, and she dragged her fingers across it and back to the rough earth wall. "But let's never be near them again."

"We'll be out soon enough. There's a fork up ahead, and Little

Rock Wall is off to the right," They continued on in silence until he gave a low laugh. "Nice throw with the lantern back there. They'll have trouble backtracking in the dark."

"Except their path is shorter than ours."

"Only if they can do it without any wrong turns."

They shuffled forward in the black until they reached a spot where their tunnel butted into another.

"Turn right," Bo said, nudging her in that direction.

Kate paused, listening behind them, but the tunnel was silent. "How far to the wall?"

"Just a little ways." He pulled ahead until he was a half step in front of her. "At least it was when I had a lantern."

Time stretched on interminably in the blackness before Bo gave an approving hum and stopped. Kate reached forward and found the rough rock wall. This ledge of rock, which would have been light grey if there were torchlight to see it in, jutted up as far as Kate could reach until it ended at the edge of another tunnel that continued back to the Entrance Hall.

"You climb first." He took her hand and put it against a wide hand hold.

With light, this was a simple climb, but in the darkness, her other hand fumbled against the surface until it found something to hold.

"Close your eyes," he said, quietly. "You know the route. The foothold is near your right knee."

Kate took a deep breath, trying to absorb his calmness. She closed her eyes. Somehow the blackness of her eyelids made the tunnel feel more familiar, and she lifted her foot until she found the thin shelf that served as the first foothold. Bo kept his hand on her back as she climbed, groping for handholds and footholds, until she climbed too high for him to reach. She scrambled over the top and crawled away from the edge, breathing heavier than the little climb warranted.

Bo followed with enough grunts and gasps to let her know that it wasn't any easier for him. When he reached the top, he rustled around until his hand touched her arm. He pulled her to her feet. "Not far now."

She didn't point out to him that she knew how winding the walk was from Little Rock Wall to the Entrance Hall and that she'd never call it "not far."

But the good thing about walking in the pitch black was that long before they reached the Hall, the faint traces of light that managed to wind into these endless tunnels were easy to see. The tunnel began to lighten, almost imperceptibly at first, then more and more until they stood in the shadows of one of the tunnels in the back of the empty entrance cavern.

"Do you smell them?" Bo whispered.

Kate leaned forward and sniffed. "No, but I don't smell Evan either."

He looked toward the entrance where Evan's route would bring him. "He'll make a run for it as soon as he gets here. Maybe he's outside already." He glanced at her. "Whatever happens, you keep running until you get home."

"I'm not going to leave you and Evan—"

"Ria," he said, taking her shoulders and looking down into her eyes. "I don't think these men would flinch at hurting a girl. You need to get away from them, and someone needs to get to Ma and Dad. Evan and I will be right behind you, but promise me you'll run. No matter what."

She frowned at him but nodded. "Don't do anything stupid."

He flashed her a smile. "Wouldn't dream of it. Now, we'll move as quietly as we can across the Hall and then run for the bridge."

They listened another moment but heard nothing. She slipped out of the tunnel, gripping his hand and hurrying across the Entrance Hall, squinting against the bright sunlight. The familiar cave seemed to stretch with each step, and she found herself holding her breath as they hurried toward the outside world.

Kate ran out of the mine, and a wave of heat and blinding brightness slammed into her. She stumbled to a stop, letting go of Bo and throwing her hands over her eyes.

Bo grabbed her elbow and yanked her to the side, out of view of the cave.

"Your eyes will adjust." He tugged at her elbow. "But we need to move."

The light and heat surged against her.

She pressed her hands harder against her eyes, but she could still see the bush next to them blazing brightly. Tufts of grass growing at the edge of the dirt and tumbling down the hillside were like glowing coals spilled out of a fire.

The chilly spring air brushed across her skin, making her shiver after the warm stillness of the caves, but at the same time waves of heat rolled against her from every direction, doing nothing to actually warm her.

"Ria!" Bo pulled her forward. "We need to move!"

Kate cracked her eyes, and the real, physical brightness of the world was bearable if she squinted.

She cast around for Evan but saw no sign of him.

"Go!" Bo gave her a push toward the trail down to the river. "Run!"

She stumbled forward, then broke into a run, hunching down against the barrage of light and heat.

Her feet slammed down onto the hard dirt, and she slid around the first corner, almost losing her balance and tumbling into the blazing scrub brush next to her.

She locked her attention on the trail in front of her and stretched her legs to run faster.

A searing light the size of a pebble buzzed in front of her, and she skidded to the side, ducking under it, just as she recognized it as a honeybee. A glowing, hot honeybee.

Bo's footsteps pounded on the path behind her, but even more, the rush of heat from him pushed her forward.

It was living things.

She tore her eyes away from the bee and raced down the path.

It was living things that were bright and hot and strange. Grass, bushes, bugs…Bo.

Turning the last corner, she burst out of the bushes onto the trail along the riverbank.

She looked back over her shoulder just as Bo raced out after her. Up on the second switchback, Evan's wild curls flashed past a gap in the brush.

Up at the mine entrance, she caught sight of a red tunic.

"Go!" Bo yelled.

She sprinted the last few steps to the bridge, her breath heaving as she grabbed the post at the end and tore onto the wooden slats.

The rope bridge bucked under her heavy footsteps, and she forced herself to slow, grabbing the ropes to brace herself.

Beneath her, the river swirled and frothed over rocks, and she moved forward more carefully. The air was mercifully cool, the green water was merely water, speckled with sunlight and frothing eddies of foam. Whatever living things were beneath the surface, their light and heat were hidden.

She'd barely gone a handful of steps when Evan broke out of the brush with a burst of heat and light and ran toward the bridge. His body glowed brightly, his red hair bouncing like strands of burning embers on his head. Bo stopped on the end and Kate picked up her pace, rushing to get off so the boys could cross.

"Stop!"

The word rang out from the hillside, harsh and accented,

snapping around her like a rope. Kate's foot caught on a slat, and she crashed to her knees.

The bridge lurched to the side, and she fell into the netted rope. Beneath her, the water churned and swirled, spraying drops into her face.

Clutching the rope, she dragged her eyes to the shore.

Bo stood frozen at the end of the bridge.

Evan, his legs locked in mid-stride, pitched forward. The box flew out of his hands and tumbled onto the path. He slammed into the ground at the edge of the riverbank, his body staying rigid as he twisted and rolled down the slope.

His shoulder smashed into a sharp rock, and he plunged into the surging water.

"Evan!" Kate screamed, and the word loosened her body.

Bo gave a strangled yell, but his feet were locked in place at the end of the bridge.

Evan's head bobbed the surface, gasping. His arms flailed against the rocks, grasping for purchase and finding nothing.

The current shoved him over a rock and sucked him into a swirling mass of foam, and the water closed over his auburn hair.

CHAPTER FIVE

THERE WAS NOTHING BUT CHURNING, foaming rapids between the rocks where Kate's brother had been.

"Evan!" she shouted again.

A strand of pale green light spun out through the water from where he'd disappeared, then another. A half dozen, then a dozen twisted away, mapping out the chaos of the current, rising to the surface before plunging back down into the depths.

Kate's hands clenched the rope as more and more light snaked out.

For a heartbeat, Evan's auburn curls broke the surface, plastered to his forehead. Streams of light bled out of him, splaying across the river. The current dragged him down again, leaving nothing but strands of pale green swirling through the water.

"No!" Kate reached her hand out as though she could stretch over the water and shove all that light back into him. "Evan!" She leaned on the rope rail of the bridge until it tipped forward. Ignoring the water below her, she focused on the threads. A bit of warmth rose out of them, a swirl of heat in the cold river.

Her arm was far too short, but she imagined it longer, reaching all the way to him, and, somehow, she could feel the strands. There were more roiling beneath the surface. She grabbed at them, feeling their heat, sensing the brightness her eyes couldn't see. She raced along them, down under the water, until she found the fiery knot at their center.

Evan's body spun in the depths, shoved down by the current and trapped in a hollow between three huge cold rocks.

Kate gripped the rough rope of the bridge with one hand and thrust the other toward Evan. Her mind shoved at the threads, and they shifted. A sharp pain flared in her palm, but she clenched her eyes closed and sought out Evan's heat, reaching under it, gathering all the threads of light and warmth and shoving with all her might toward the surface.

Heat ripped out of her hand, and agony sliced across her palm. Her eyes flew open, and she cried out.

Evan's body burst out of the water. Glowing green threads bundled under him, flinging him up onto the shore. He landed hard, coughing and gasping for air.

With a shout, Bo lurched forward and staggered toward him.

Kate sank against the ropes, still clinging to them with one hand. A wave of dizziness rolled over her, and she slid down onto her side on the wooden slat, exhausted as though she'd just swum across the river and pulled him out of the rapids herself. Her palm was seared and blistered, and she cradled it to her chest.

A blur of red made her look up as the broad young foreigner ran out of the bushes. His eyes fell on Evan, collapsed on the bank, and the box lying near him.

Around the edges of Kate's vision, shadows gathered. Her arms and head were too heavy to lift.

Bo, still struggling to move, stumbled to the top of the bank above Evan. The foreigner stepped into his path, and when Bo tried to shove him away, the man grabbed him by the throat, lifting him off his feet as though he weighed nothing.

Bo pounded his fists against the man's chest and stomach, but the foreigner merely leaned closer, his face brutal and cold. His mouth moved, but the words were lost over the tumult of the water.

He finished speaking, and Bo's body went limp.

The man tossed him aside.

"Bo!" Kate called, but the word came out weak.

The taller foreigner ran out of the brush and raced for the box where it lay at the top of the riverbank. He dropped down on his knees next to it, pulling a small pouch out of his tunic.

Just like the men and Bo and Evan, a hazy light emanated from the box. Unlike the people, though, misty tendrils also stretched out into the air around it, waving like thin strands of hair.

She stretched her mind toward it, as she had with Evan, and when she brushed against it, a surge of smells and sounds rushed into her.

The sharp, spicy scent, now richer, more toasted and pungent.

The coldness, numbing her face like frosty-laden wind in the dead of winter.

The sound that was not a sound. Vast and empty. A silence that spoke of enormous space.

And somewhere in that vastness, the haunting, lonely bell tolled again.

Kate gripped the railing with her unhurt hand. The note vibrated the wood beneath her body, thrumming up into her until she felt it in her bones.

The red-clad man pulled a jagged shape out of his pouch. The edges were irregular and clear, like rough, broken glass wrapped around a tumult of light.

It was like a sliver of the full moon on a snowy night. Or the brightest star. Even in the clear afternoon sun, it shone like a beacon.

The man crushed it between his fingers with a crack like a brittle bone snapping, and shimmering liquid spilled onto the box.

He tossed away the rough empty husk and began chanting something rhythmic and harsh.

A rush of sounds and images pushed past every other sensation, flooding Kate's mind.

Bo's face and her own, lit by torchlight, leaned forward and peered back at her with the ceiling of the mine in the background. Just as they'd peered down at the box only a few minutes ago. His dark hair tousled, his eyes wide with excitement. Kate's own bright red braid was dulled to a deep amber in the darkness of the mine, but her freckles stood out in bright relief against her pale skin.

The view shifted, and she was looking up at an old man, his beard long and dirty. He held a torch, and she was in his arms, being carried. Above him, the ceiling of the mine moved slowly past.

A dizzying shift of the light made her squeeze her eyes shut, but the pictures continued. Snippets of forests and cities. Faces and voices.

A younger man's face flickered into view.

The foreigner's chants changed, slowed, and the image slowed with it.

Kate was small like the box, being clutched in the young man's arms, looking up at his close-cropped beard. It was shaped into a point at his chin, but on his cheek, the dark hair was cut through with swirling scars that looked as though they'd been carved purposefully and precisely into his skin.

The world around him was shrouded in smoke. He hurried

under a line of trees and turned back, revealing a small complex of stone buildings, their wooden roofs engulfed in flames.

Black-clad soldiers ran through the smoke, shouting and swinging curved swords at anyone who crossed their paths. Dark, unmoving lumps lay on the ground, and she tried not to look at the bodies.

The man turned away and ran into the woods, and the image faded to blackness.

"*Deb z'Kyrost!*"

Kate's eyes flew open as the foreign man on the shore pushed himself to his feet, holding the box.

"*Deb z'Kyrost!*" he repeated, and his companion let out a triumphant laugh.

The shadows were growing darker on the edges of her vision, but she saw the stockier man move to a path leading deeper into the hills. He lifted one of two heavy packs off the ground and slung it over his shoulders, rattling off excited words Kate couldn't understand.

On the riverbank, Evan pushed himself to his knees, then shoved himself up and crashed into the older man, sending the box tumbling to the ground. Evan grabbed for it at the same time as the foreigner, and they grappled for a breath before the man drew a dagger out of his belt.

Kate stretched out her burned hand toward them. The man's red tunic nearly glowed in the midst of her darkening vision. The black embroidery on the sleeve shifted with his motions, and for a heartbeat the dragon slithered around the sword.

She blinked, and it was nothing but a normal sleeve.

Evan caught sight of the knife and ducked, still pulling at the box.

"No!" Kate called hoarsely. She flung her other hand through the ropes, reaching over the water as the dagger rose above her brother. "Get away from him!" The words seemed to rip out of her palms. Fresh pain shot through her wounded hand, just as she felt her other palm split open. She shoved toward the man with nothing more than a furious need to have him gone.

Bone-deep exhaustion filled her, and her arms went limp, but Evan and the man stood unchanged.

The foreigner shouted something, bits and pieces of the guttural words tumbling over the water to Kate, incomprehensible and harsh. His words, unlike her own, brought a rush of air. A ripple that was both cold and warm at the same time, and it rolled over her like she was nothing.

Through the rising shadows, she saw Evan stiffen and his head twitch as he looked around. His eyes grew wide and unseeing. He looked toward Kate for the briefest moment, terror creeping across his face, before his gaze slid away.

He shouted something, his voice hoarse and distant.

Kate sagged against the bridge, the hard, rough wood of the plank jabbing into her cheek as the bridge rocked slowly over the water.

The foreigner's blade paused, glinting in the sunlight.

Everything was too bright, or too dark. Too close to splintering apart. The tall bushes behind Evan were glaringly green, each leaf shivering with a motion that she couldn't understand. But the dirt under his knees grew darker by the second, and the light drained from the sky, pooling in the people on the shore, who trembled in her vision.

Kate groaned, trying to focus, but the light shot into her skull, and her vision blurred.

The foreigner spun his glittering dagger in his hand so the hilt pointed down and grabbed Evan's shoulder with his other hand.

Evan cried out something as the hilt came slamming down on his head.

Evan crumpled as the two of them, and the entire world, exploded into a blinding light.

Pain lanced into Kate's eyes, and her vision shattered. Glints from their glowing shapes burst into a thousand shards of light, and she tumbled into darkness.

CHAPTER SIX

THE BRIDGE SWAYED beneath her and the breeze dragged a lock of hair across her cheek like a feather.

Kate groaned and shifted, prying her eyes open. Her lids were heavy and gritty, and she squinted into the afternoon sunlight.

The riverbank was empty of everything but dampness where Evan had knelt.

She forced her head to lift. It felt as heavy as a boulder. Not far from the edge of the bridge, Bo was sprawled on his side, perfectly still.

There was no sign of the foreign men, or the box, or Evan.

She lifted her arm, heaving it up to the nearest strand of netted railing, and grabbed the rough rope.

Pain lanced through her hand, and she yanked it back. A wide blister stretched across her palm, the roof of it torn off by the rope. Blood oozed out of it, dribbling up her wrist.

Her other hand ached just as much, and she shifted to look at it, finding more blistered skin, red and shiny and ready to burst.

She curled her fingers around the burns, hissing against the motion, then shifted onto her stomach. Using her elbows and knees to push herself up, she struggled to her feet and moved toward Bo, her legs heavy and slow.

Her eyes raked across the hillside and the riverbank, searching for any signs of Evan. There was nothing but the brush-covered hill and the flicker of the red flag above the mine. She looked down the edges of the river too, trying not to imagine her brother's body shoved up along the rocks, but there was nothing there either.

Stumbling off the bridge, she reached Bo and fell to her knees next to him.

He was so still she froze for a moment, afraid to touch him

But then his shoulder rose, and she let out breath that was nearly a sob.

"Bo?" She pushed the back of her hand against his back, leaning over him, trying to see his face.

He groaned, and she dropped her forehead onto his shoulder, tears springing to her eyes.

"Ria?" He shifted and she pulled back. With another groan of pain, he pushed himself up to sit, twisting to look at her. His eyes widened when he saw her tears, and he spun back around. "Where's Evan? Where's the box?"

"Gone," Kate gasped, trying to stop the tears. "He hit Evan on the head! They're all gone!"

"Evan!" Bo called, scrambling to his feet and running to the riverbank. He spun in place, searching the rocks. "Footprints! The men!" He started forward, his eyes down on the soft earth near the top of the bank, following the prints. He stopped at the rocky trail leading up the valley past the mine. "Evan!"

Kate let her hands lie heavy on her lap, her burned palms facing up. She stared down at them. Everything about her felt dull and exhausted. The living things around her were still slightly bright and warm, but not as jarring as before. She could feel Bo walking onto the trail, somehow warm despite the fact that she couldn't actually feel him at all.

She closed her eyes against the other obvious fact.

There was no one else nearby.

No warmth or heat beyond the grass and the brush.

No scent of pines after the rain.

No stench of rancid meat.

Bo's footsteps and warmth came closer, and he dropped to his knees next to her, reaching toward her hands before he stopped himself. "Ria," he breathed. "What happened?"

"He fell in the river," she said, the words not sounding like her own. "I..." She lifted her eyes to his and found his face pale, his eye wide and frightened. What had happened? "I...pushed him out...I think."

He blinked at her words and studied her face for a moment. "And then...they took him? With the box? I see their footprints until the rocky path, but I can't see any sign of Evan—did they carry him away?"

She closed her eyes, seeing again the brightness that grew in her brother. Hearing the foreigner's fierce chanting, seeing the dagger fall and Evan crumple—

She shook her head. "They...He..." She swallowed. "They hurt him," she whispered. "I wanted to stop them, but..."

Bo leaned forward and wrapped his arms around her. She buried her head in his shoulder, holding her hands gingerly between them, letting him block out the world.

"It's not your fault, Ria."

She shifted her fingers, and pain arced across her palms. She did it again, letting the pain dig into her.

She'd shoved him out of the river all the way from the bridge. And yet, in the end...

"I couldn't..." She closed her fingers slowly, her nails pressing into the burns like knives. "I should have..."

Bo pulled back from her and set his hand gently around her fingers. "Ria, please stop."

The warmth of his hands sank into hers like a soothing balm, and she loosened her fingers, hissing in pain as they pulled away from the split blisters.

"They took the box," she said numbly, leaning against Bo in her exhaustion. "And they took Evan, too."

PART II

THE WAITING

It took twenty years before the story resumed. It was threaded through all those years, of course. Years of studying and searching.

Years of refusing to give in to the fear that I was already entangled in the tragedy.

And maybe I wasn't. All my fears back then were off base. I was missing too much of the story to know where the real sorrow was.

The slicing fear of what Evan could be going through aged and shifted into an endless gnawing. The hole left by his absence stayed dark and quiet, but it took up part of me. Every day of every year.

When I left Bo to join the Keepers, and they welcomed me with their own burned and scarred palms, he began to wander. Farther and farther. Searching for the box, or Evan, or eventually searching for anything interesting he could find. I sent him maps and information. He sent me trinkets from more and more distant lands.

But the trinkets always told me less than they could have, because I didn't have the right tools.

I thought about the liquid those men had poured onto the box until it *became almost an obsession. To feel the remnant and memories of an object...*

Some ingredients I found easily, but the final essential element eluded me. I searched all the wholesome places, but it was at the edges of the darkness I finally found the piece I needed.

I was so close when everything fell apart.

CHAPTER SEVEN

TWENTY YEARS LATER

"It's the hole in the story that's the problem," Kate explained, grateful for something to take her mind off the incessant waiting.

She carefully folded the worn letter she'd been reading and set it aside along with her journal, which was opened to a page with a profusion of small notes connected with arrows and questions and short lists. Beneath them, two maps were laid out on the age-darkened tavern table. The parchment on the right had elaborate, hand-painted framing, detailed drawings of cities, and a massive network of roads and ports along the waterways.

Kate traced her finger over the red and black symbol embossed and painted into the corner.

A dragon coiled around a sword.

"This map is what the land looked like four hundred years ago." She touched the corner of her letter to the sparsely labeled one next to it, heavily notated in her own hand, with only a few large cities in isolated, disconnected territories. "That is what it looks like today."

"Ahh." Pella tapped her washrag against her flour-dusted skirt and peered at the maps. "Where abouts is Brenlen?"

"Oh, no. We're not on this. This is... well, it doesn't have a name today. Not as a whole. At one time it was the Kalesh Empire, but it's months of travel away from here. Far to the east."

"Ahh," the innkeeper repeated with more politeness than understanding. "An' it has a problem?" She stood next to the table, her greying hair swept back in a tired bun. Layered on top of the physical smell of stew simmering somewhere in the kitchen, Kate could sense the more elusive scent of yeast touched with honey. The homey, welcoming scent the woman's remnant had carried for years. It had grown thinner over the decades, a bit wearier, but still inviting, which was the reason Kate always chose this tavern when waiting to meet someone in Brenlen.

Kate scanned the vast sprawl of the ancient land. "It had a problem. Centuries ago, it was a thriving Empire, dominating everything it touched." A lock of auburn hair fell into her face, and she tucked it behind her ear before glancing at Pella. "They almost conquered us, you know. Issable, the first queen, fought them off just barely—"

Movement across the small common room caught Kate's eye, and her attention snapped up to the door.

But it was still closed, as it had been all afternoon, the flicker of motion nothing more than the shadow of a tree shifting across the front window.

The tavern sat quiet and nearly empty, which wasn't unusual this far from any trade route. The only other patron was a man slouched in the far corner who'd been drinking ale at a trudging but determined pace all day. His remnant filled the cracks of his chair, settled deep into the grooves and scratches of the table, and clung to the walls around him like soot around a fireplace. It might once have been solid, like rich earth, but now it was hollow, eaten away by...a plea. Or maybe the absence of one.

His eyes moved slowly through the empty space in front of

him, tracing unseen memories. From the lines on his face and the bow of his shoulders, those memories were well worn.

Kate's thumb rubbed over the edge of Bo's letter in her hand. She knew those sorts of memories. The ones that felt like this old letter, too often held, faded and soft, grown weak at the folds until the merest breath would crumble away a bit more of the crease. The paper that had grown ragged from fingers brushing the edges and tracing the words, fingers that were afraid to hurt it but couldn't resist one more touch of the only thing they could hold. The only thing left.

Kate shied away from the familiarity of it. Metal dug into her other hand, and she realized she was gripping her locket.

Letting go, she glanced back at the door. "If Wolff doesn't show soon, I may need to stay another night. I can tell the story of Queen Issable and the Kalesh Empire this evening, assuming anyone shows up to hear it."

"It's already too late to leave if you're going as far as your Stronghold," Pella said, a note of disapproval in her voice. "An' judgin' by the little faces I keep seein' pressed up against my windows, the children know you're still here, so sure 'nough, everyone else will too. No one misses a night with a Keeper in town." She gestured to the map. "Can you get t' there from 'ere?"

Kate set down Bo's letter and leaned over to put a crumb from her lunch on the far left edge of the table. "This is where we are in Brenlen. To get to the map, you have to go south"—she traced a path over the worn tabletop—"across Black Hills and out of Queensland altogether. Then you'd round the southern end of the Marsham Cliffs and travel all the way across the moors." Her finger reached the southwest corner of the elaborate map. "Which would only get you here. It would take weeks, months maybe, to cross it and reach the far edges of what was once the Empire. You could spend years exploring it and not see it all."

Pella looked between the crumb and the parchment. "An' people live that far away?"

"Three hundred years ago it had far more people than we do in Queensland. Until Emperor Sorrn—their last Emperor —disappeared."

"Killed?"

"That's the hole in the story. No one knows what happened to him. He was here in his palace"—she pointed to an enormous city along the Southern Sea—"then he was gone." She pushed Bo's letter off the top of her journal and pointed to different notes. "Some records say he was murdered and his body was thrown into the ocean. Some claim he inexplicably snuck out of the city with a retinue of soldiers under the cover of night. Some claim his advisor, a man fabled to have magical powers, transformed him into a great serpent who slithered through the land, killing his enemies." She breathed out a sigh that held years of questions and looked back at the map. "Whatever happened to him, he had no heir, and his disappearance broke the entire Empire." She tapped the symbol of the dragon and the sword. "That was the emblem of his family."

"An' they don't use that symbol there now?" Pella asked.

Kate paused. "Well, they shouldn't. There is no empire any longer. Just weak, warring territories. But…when I was young, I saw someone who was still using it."

"Who?"

"Another mystery among many. When Emperor Sorrn disappeared, so did reliable records. The next accounts we have are sixty years after his death, and by then the land had been broken, ravaged by disease and famine. Most of these cities were deserted or destroyed." She looked over the modern map. "It never recovered. The last two hundred and fifty years have been riddled with wars and death. The land has barely a tenth of the population it once did, no huge cities, no safe trade routes."

Her eyes strayed to the man in the corner of the tavern, still lost to whatever memories haunted him. "Nations are a bit like people. They can lose something and never recover. Sometimes you know exactly how it was lost."

She touched her locket again. "But sometimes, even though it disappeared without a trace, you wonder if it's really gone. Maybe there are clues that were missed. Maybe someone remembers something that can show you how to find it again."

"Yer lookin' to find an emperor that's been dead for three hundred years?" Pella asked slowly.

Kate laughed and dropped her hand. "I doubt there's much of good old Sorrn left to find. But I would like to know what happened to him. What was so pivotal that it destroyed an entire empire thoroughly enough that centuries later we can barely find a trace of it?"

Pella ran a finger over the dragon and sword on the parchment. "It's all a bit sad, t' be honest."

"Not entirely. The Empire was militaristic and brutal and controlling. The world might be better off for it being gone. Still, whatever happened when Emperor Sorrn disappeared, the human cost was staggering."

"What do you think happened?"

Kate picked up the letter. "My brother Bo is there trying to find that answer, among other things. He digs around in the ruins of ancient places and sends me interesting things he finds." She used it to tap her journal. "And I'm trying to make sense of it all and working on a way to get more information from the items he unearths." Kate pointed to a small town near the center of her modern map. "This last letter, which was from six months ago, put him here, digging through the ruins of an old city."

Pella looked at the spot on the map with interest. "His job sounds more fun than yours," she said with a smile.

Kate traced Bo's recent route through the last two ruined cities from the Imperial age and the remains of an enormous monastery. The small notations on the map didn't do justice to the piles of papers he'd written, recording the things he'd found, or the two small boxes of relics he'd sent her. "Sometimes," she agreed.

The door of the tavern opened, and a long slant of late afternoon sunlight sliced across the room. A man with a sapphire blue cloak came into the light, tinting the tavern blue for a moment. His beard was trimmed close and shaped to a point, even more narrow than his face. The blustery wind of early fall jostled past him before he closed the door, and Kate caught the scent of Wolff's greasy remnant. He flashed her a smile with all the warmth of a snake, held up a small pouch, and started toward her.

Kate let out a breath somewhere between relief and disgust and instinctively pulled her papers closer.

"I'll meet you over there, Wolff." She motioned to the bar and closed Bo's letters inside her journal. "Stay away from my things."

"I'm insulted," he said in an unruffled voice and ambled toward the counter.

Pella hurried over behind the bar and swept up the few coins sitting out before he could reach them.

Kate moved over to him, tamping down the hope stirring inside her. "Are you ever not running late?"

The trader held out the pouch, his fingernails yellowed and crusted with dirt. When she didn't reach for it, he set it on the counter and gave her a smile that was probably meant to look amiable. "Do you have any idea how far I had to travel to find this?"

Kate took the seat next to him, trying to ignore the stench of his remnant. He was like oil that had gone rancid, and it stung in the back of her throat.

She took the pouch and drew out a small vial filled with milky white liquid. Trying to keep her expression detached under Wolff's scrutiny, she held it up, but the serum caught the light from the window and shimmered, and she drew in a breath. She tilted it, and the viscous serum flowed slowly, clinging to the glass like thinned honey.

Tenea serum.

The blood doctors in Napon clarified it from the blood of a spiny sea creature. They used it for interrogations, but not in this unstable form. It was nearly useless like this. The Naponese solved the problem by stabilizing it with a flesh-eating acid that burned the fingers off their prisoners—a use so barbaric she'd almost ignored the potential the serum held. But if she could stabilize it with something less dangerous...

The fluid sparkled, and all the hopes she'd been cradling for months, afraid to even look at them too closely for fear they'd disappear, crystalized in the tiny, fragile specks of light.

The vial trembled in her hand, and Wolff's smile grew more complacent.

She forced her fingers to loosen their grip as she studied the scarlet wax sealing the cork, stamped with Naponese runes. "Could I get more light?" she asked Pella.

The innkeeper lit a candle and brought it close, and Kate examined the wax for signs of tampering. There were traces of Wolff's remnant everywhere. The bottom of the wax was thick with it, as though he'd tried to peel it away from the glass. A flicker of irritation rose at the idea of him polluting the serum, but she tilted the glass and found his remnant reached no farther than the edge. The seal itself remained unbroken, the symbols stamped across it undamaged.

"I paid the blood doctor eighteen silver." Wolff pointed to the largest of the runes, which resembled the number eighteen. "Plus the cost of travel means you owe me twenty-four."

"Six silver for a fortnight's travel?" Kate slowly turned the vial, reading the next set of runes. Mind syphon. A fair enough description of the fluid.

Just past that was the small mark she was looking for.

"Took quite a bit longer than a fortnight," Wolff pointed out. His yellow nails scratched absently at a dry rash on his hand bearing the telltale pattern of itchweed.

Everything about the trader irked her. He was greedy and dishonest, he never did anything without swindling, and right now he was flat-out lying.

She tapped the seal thoughtfully. "Just needed to check whether they put anything special in the wax. A deterrent to anyone who tampers with it."

Something in Wolff's posture shifted almost imperceptibly. "A deterrent?"

"Blood doctors have been known to enchant things. If the wrong person opens it, they break out in boils or worse."

"Did they enchant this?" Wolff's ever-present smile was still there, but the edges looked strained.

"I suppose it doesn't really matter. The vial was intended for me, so I'm safe." She glanced at the trader's itchy hand. "You didn't try to open it, did you?"

"Of course not," he answered smoothly.

"Just looks like itchweed on your hand, anyway." She turned back to the vial, adding almost absently, "Good thing too—the only treatment I know for magical rashes is urine."

"Urine?" Pella swatted at Wolff's hand with her rag. "Stop touching my counter."

"My hands are clean," he said defensively. "It's just itchweed."

"Nothing about your hands is clean." Kate set the vial down gently and faced him.

"The only problem with my hands is that they're empty of twenty-four silver pieces." He leaned closer, and the feel of his oily remnant thickened. "If you're unwilling to part with that many coins, we could agree on something else. That locket must be worth something."

His filthy fingers reached toward her.

She grabbed his bony wrist, and, with a flick of her other fingers, she sent out a lash of *vitalle* and tore the flame off the candle, yanking it into her palm. She poured more *vitalle* into it from her own body, and the fire flared up until it filled her hand.

Pella shoved back from the bar, and Wolff froze, his eyes wide.

Kate leaned forward. The flame blazing above her hand bathed the weathered lines of his face in firelight. One of the stray hairs of his beard smoked, and he drew back, but she kept her grip on his wrist.

"Nineteen silver," Kate said, her voice flat.

Wolff kept his eyes locked on the fire. For once, there was no slimy smile on his face. "Keepers aren't supposed to bully people out of their honest money."

"Honest?" Kate's palm began to burn, both with the heat of the flame and the *vitalle* she was feeding into it. She held it near his face for another breath before slowly closing her fingers and snuffing it out.

She released Wolff's wrist, and he jerked it back.

Picking up the vial, she pointed to the first symbol. "This doesn't say eighteen. The price is this small mark in the back, which says fifteen."

Wolff hesitated. "Ah, yes, fifteen. Now I remember."

"And where's the other vial?"

"I don't—"

"The marks you assumed were the price actually say 'first of two.'"

Wolf glanced between her and the vial, then reached into a pocket in his cloak. "Right. Forgot I took this one out of the pouch. Didn't want them clanking together and breaking."

She plucked it out of his hand and examined the seal, but this one appeared unmolested. "What were you going to do with this? Sell it? Unless you found another Keeper, no one could do anything with it, and the other eight Keepers know I'm the one who sent you to find it."

Wolff shrugged. "There are always buyers."

"Someday you're going to try to swindle the wrong person." Kate pulled a coin purse from one of the pockets in her black Keeper's robe. "And the world is going to have one less dishonest trader."

Pella grinned and leaned her elbows back on to the counter. "I think he almost just did."

Kate set nineteen silver on the bar. "Fifteen for the serum and four for your services."

He looked at them with a pained expression. "This is robbery." But his thin fingers swiped up the coins.

"If your business with Keeper Katria is finished," Pella said, "get out of my inn."

"I need a room for the night," Wolff objected.

"Absolutely not."

He opened his mouth again, but Kate leaned forward and touched the unlit candle wick with her fingertip, pressing a tiny bit of *vitalle* into it until a new flame burst to life. "She told you to leave, Wolff."

The trader watched the flame warily.

Kate glanced at him. "You should probably see to that rash, anyway. Don't forget the tip about urine."

Pella wrinkled her nose at the idea.

Any pretense at friendliness dropped off Wolff's face as he stood. "Always a pleasure to work with the Keepers."

Kate let all the distastefulness of his presence fill her expression. "A delight." She watched him until the door closed behind him. Letting out a long breath, she shifted her shoulders, as though she could shake off the lingering residue from his remnant. The pouch was saturated with it, and she pushed the leather toward Pella. "I don't want anything of Wolff's. Keep it, or burn it, whatever you like."

Pella glanced at the candle, then back at Kate a little warily. "I guess I can stop worrying about the way you travel everywhere alone."

Kate rubbed her palm. "Sorry about the fire. That man puts me on edge."

"That man puts everyone on edge." The innkeeper eyed the vials. "Did the wax really give him that rash?"

"No. He tried to open it, but the wax looks normal. I would guess Wolff's just stupid enough to stick his hand into itchweed."

Pella raised an eyebrow. "Urine will make an itchweed rash worse."

Kate allowed herself a small smile. "I know. I guess Wolff's level of discomfort tonight is going to depend on how nervous his guilt makes him." She turned back to the vials, letting her smile grow. Two whole vials of tenea serum.

She walked to the table with all her papers. "I'll have to tell the story of Queen Issable and the Kalesh Empire another night. I can reach the Stronghold well before midnight if I leave now."

"Midnight!" Pella said, aghast. "Katria, please stay! It's too late. Folks've seen wolves in the woods lately. An' those are worse than the human Wolff."

Kate glanced up from folding her maps. "Fire will scare those off too."

"But there are rumors of raiders in the forest. Dangerous ones. Farther east of here, a few of the outlying homesteads have been robbed, and I heard two farmers a bit to the south were killed.

They said the Snares from the south have been coming farther north and stealin' people."

Kate paused. "They have? I'll send word to the palace. Duke Ruslin needs to get control of those Snares. Brigands like that can't be allowed to spread." She tucked the last of the maps into her pack.

The innkeeper twisted her washrag in worry as she looked about for inspiration. Her gaze landed on a stack of bowls on the counter.

"Will you join us for dinner?" Pella asked quickly.

Kate gave the innkeeper a slightly exasperated look. "Pella..."

"You can't refuse the invitation to a meal, can you?" the innkeeper said with a triumphant smile. "I know you folk from th' Wildwood still follow that old elven tradition. An' after dinner, it will definitely be too late t' leave."

Kate crossed her arms. "That was devious, Pella."

The older woman shook her head. "It's true about the wolves and the brigands." She paused, then let a small smile cross her face. "And having a Keeper in town for another night is like an unexpected holiday. You can have your room again, of course."

Kate dug out another silver and set it on the table. "I'm not as bound to that tradition as the elves were. If you invite me to a meal again, and it's inconvenient, I will refuse you. But for tonight, I'll stay." She picked up the serum. "I'll be in my room until dinner."

"You know you don't have to pay, especially when it's at my invitation. You're giving more than enough by entertaining us for the evening."

"I'm using your best room for another night. Keep the coin." Kate turned away before the woman could argue.

Kate held the liquid up to catch the sunlight. The milky fluid shimmered slightly, and the hope she'd been trying to stifle surged up. She moved quickly toward the stairs.

Maybe there were clues she'd missed.

Maybe there was someone who remembered something.

Her hand gripped the glass.

Maybe she could find him again.

CHAPTER EIGHT

KATE SAT at the small desk upstairs, rubbing her finger across the runes stamped into the wax. She held the vial up to the fading evening light and leaned closer, swirling the serum and trying to capture a glimpse of the light dancing in the shimmering sparkles.

"Glimmering dust of the stars..." she whispered. Pinnren the Scribe's description of tenea serum had always stuck with her, but she'd assumed it was just more of his overdramatization. Glimmering dust of the stars capturing memories and dreams in their dance of light.

"Not a bad metaphor, Pinnren," she said quietly.

In truth, it was an excellent metaphor. The kind that captured all the right aspects of its subject. Dust and stars and dreams and dances.

She turned the vial slowly, and the shimmering lights wove around and past each other, floating in currents she couldn't see.

If the glimmering was real, maybe the rest was too.

It'd been two years since she'd first heard of the serum. Two years of searching and waiting, and here it was, shimmering just inside the glass.

It would only take a moment to test, to get the first hint of whether all this was even possible.

And yet she hesitated.

The vial trembled in her grip. She set it down and rubbed her palms together, trying to banish the tingly stream of nervousness threading down her arms and into her hands.

She pulled her locket forward so she could see the metal pendant. The interwoven runes stamped onto the surface hummed quietly with *vitalle*, sealing it shut. She pressed a tiny bit more out of her fingertips, breaking the seal and letting the door at the front hinge open.

A small amber stone lay inside, and she searched for the remnant.

A hint of pine trees after a rainstorm fluttered across her mind, but it slipped away before she could be sure it wasn't just a memory. She snapped the door shut and pushed *vitalle* into the runes, locking in whatever echo of remnant remained.

Letting the locket fall to her chest, she picked up the vial again.

Even if this worked, it was just one small step toward the actual goal of drawing memories out of an object.

"It's stupid not to try, isn't it?" she said finally.

She pulled a glass of water closer and broke the wax on the vial. Twisting out the cork, she measured two fat drops into the water, watching the shimmering white serum disperse until the solution was uniformly misty.

Setting the vial aside, she searched for a recent vivid memory.

The broken man in the corner downstairs came to mind, but she shook the thought away.

Nothing broken. Not for this.

Instead, she brought up the memory of Wolff. The slant of the light through the door, the whispery dry sound of yellow fingernails scratching his rash, the rankness of his remnant.

Unpleasant to be sure, but vivid and short.

"All right, let's see what you can do." She dipped her finger into the serum and pushed the memory into it.

A thin trail, barely brighter than the rest of the liquid, snaked out from her fingertip. When it stopped, she pulled her finger out and leaned closer to the glass.

The brightness swirled through the fluid, growing hazy and breaking into a handful of fuzzy threads. Each piece slowly rose to the surface. One touched the air and disappeared.

Before the rest of it vanished, she pushed her finger back into the liquid. Each sliver of light moved toward her as though drawn by invisible strings.

She closed her eyes and heard a faint, dry scratching, then smelled rancid oil, then saw a sharp line of sunlight before all three sensations faded.

Hope flooded into her, painful and sharp.

She sat perfectly still, her eyes closed, her fingertip in the cold serum. "You work," she whispered, almost afraid to say the words out loud.

She opened her eyes. The shimmers hovered in the serum like glittering slivers of possibility.

Pulling her finger out, she wiped off the wetness and let a giddy smile spread across her face.

She rubbed her hand over her mouth and tried to calm her thoughts.

"You have the potential to work." Her correction sounded enough like Keeper Mikal's elderly, chronically unimpressed voice that she sobered.

Potential wasn't enough. Scattered, jumbled memories that

evaporated into the air would never be able to do what she needed.

She tapped the locket at her neck thoughtfully. Everything she needed to work on the serum was back at the Stronghold, but that was hours away, and the golden light of the setting sun dampened any lingering desire to leave. She felt a hint of gratefulness at Pella's invitation to stay and eat.

It wasn't walking alone at night or wolves that were the true worry. It was the final bit, the path to the Stronghold itself. She glanced at the vial of serum. "That's not something any of us want to face in the dark."

A roll of laughter came through the floor, followed by a swell of voices from the gathering town. The idea of telling the tale of Queen Issable and the Kalesh Empire tugged at Kate. It was a good story. A complete story with no gaping, three-hundred-year holes.

She stood and slipped her arms into her black Keeper's robe, allowing herself a small smile.

It had the potential to work, and that was closer than she'd ever gotten before.

A ceiling of featureless grey clouds pressed down over Kate, so low that the tops of the pines along the King's Highway looked as though they might pierce it.

She pulled her robe tighter against the chill of the mid-morning air. "There's no reason you can't hold off on the rain a little longer," she pointed out to the sky.

The clouds did nothing but loom heavily above her, so she shifted her pack and picked up her pace.

She pulled up her hood when the drizzle began. It quickly shifted to a persistent, dreary rain, and she moved to the side of the road where she could walk along the grass instead of through the steadily softening mud.

When her stomach prodded her for lunch, she started searching the edge of the forest for a sign of the path to the Stronghold. The Marsham Cliffs towered just beyond the forest to her right, or she assumed they still did, but any familiar landmarks they had to offer were as hidden as the sky.

She moved carefully along the edge of the trees until something prickled the back of her neck and she caught sight of a thin trail winding into the woods toward the cliffs.

Pausing at the mouth of it, she slipped her hand inside her hood to rub the tingling off her neck, not quite banishing the foreboding that came with it. This path wasn't much better in the bright light of day.

Trying to ignore the trail itself, she concentrated on the Stronghold. Past the Wall that would keep the rain and the path and everything out, Gerone would have a hot fire burning in the kitchen, and there'd be the smell of baking bread and the scent of the white stones of the tower itself, which seemed to have their own remnant, rich and old and steady.

Only four of the eight other Keepers would be there. The rest were busy at court, but even half empty, it called to her.

"Just a short walk." With a bracing breath, she stepped onto the path. "'Grounds us in our humanity,'" she muttered in a poor imitation of Keeper Mikal's voice. "'Fosters community by reminding us of our fears and weaknesses.'"

The rain lessened under the trees, shifting from a steady patter on her hood to louder, irregular drips from the high boughs. Between the clouds and the dense trees, the path was shrouded in shadows, and she paused as it disappeared completely into a patch of ferns.

"You're off to a difficult start this morning." She searched the ground before catching a glimpse of the trail ahead to her right. "More difficult than usual, which is saying something."

Even with the prickle drawing her on, she lost the path twice and had to backtrack. There was never any familiarity about this part, no matter how many times she traveled it. The trail itself seemed to want to stay unknown.

She reached a fork she'd never seen before and considered the two paths.

A howl tore through the air from the righthand trail, close and menacing.

She took a half step back. "Wolves?" Her voice was less steady than she'd hoped. "It's been a while since you used those." She turned toward the sound. "Did I insult you in some way?"

She paused. If Pella was right, maybe that wasn't merely a disembodied sound set to scare away anyone who came too close.

Kate cast out, sending a wave of awareness into the woods. The trees around her sprang into pillars of heat, *vitalle* flowing slowly up their trunks in a thousand tiny streams. Thin snips of energy threaded through the blades of grass at her feet, dotted with small insects and grubs, little bundles of life going about their business of foraging and growing. The wave spread like a ripple across a pond, revealing an ever-widening, ever-dimming sense of the life of the forest until it faded away in a few dozen paces, having found nothing larger than a mouse. Certainly nothing near the size of a wolf.

She moved in the direction of the howl, studying the trees lining the path ahead of her. There were no real wolves, but at some point, the trunks would show signs of—

A tree ahead of her flashed a warm patch of *vitalle* at about eye level on its trunk, and her steps faltered to a stop.

She gripped the vials of tenea serum in her pocket, trying to drag up the hope they stirred in her. Trying to cling to it.

Nothing moved in the forest. No more wolves howled. No

little creatures scurried or chittered. There was nothing but the trees, tall and solemn and marked.

No voice slithered out of the silence to gnaw into her—not yet, but she felt her hope tremble anyway.

"I hate being grounded in my humanity." She cast out again, feeling the life energy of the trees next to her blaze up into a tower of warmth. The runes carved into the trunks ahead flared like torches.

Straightening her shoulders, she started forward again, her eyes locked on the tree where the first rune waited.

As she approached, a milky figure slid out of the trunk, its gauzy face lit with a dim light. An older woman with a faintly disapproving expression. "Such a waste," she whispered, her raspy voice sliding across Kate's skin like a shiver. "They all know it."

Unwilling to decipher who "they" were or what exactly they knew, Kate moved quickly past the ghost. There was no remnant in the apparition. Nothing to it beyond a bit of magic anchored to the tree trunk, and Kate tried to focus on the ground ahead and keeping her feet moving forward.

An older man appeared a few trees farther down. "You are alone."

Kate let a little breath of laughter out. "You'll have to try harder than that. Being alone is lovely."

"You're alone," a young man's ghost agreed from the other side of the path, "because you failed them all."

Her smile dissolved, and she pointedly didn't look at him as she passed.

"He's been a slave for years," another young man whispered. "Don't try to deny it."

"He died that day, and you know it," a young woman said, and the words stabbed into her, the fear so familiar she couldn't push it away.

Kate started to shake her head, but the woman continued, "You pretend he didn't, but you know the truth."

"I know no such thing," Kate said, keeping the words firm.

The drawn, exhausted face of her mother slid out of the next tree, her skin aged and wrinkled, her hair lightened with streaks of grey. An empty, hopeless look in her eyes. "You're never going to find him."

Kate flinched at the perfect inflection in the whisper. "I…"

Another face slipped into view on the other side of the path. His dark eyes caught her attention, and she stumbled to a stop. The years had made him more rugged. A short scar marked his cheek, running into the edge of his dark beard. His hair was curly and a bit wild, like the last time she'd seen him. But his crooked smile hadn't changed since they were children, and it rooted her feet to the ground.

"Ria," Bo whispered warmly.

She stood even with the tree. The heavy drops that pelted her hood passed right through his face.

A voice in her mind screamed that it was always a mistake to linger.

But the eyes and the face and the voice were so achingly familiar, and the way he said her name felt like a shelter she could step underneath and rest in. She let go of the vials in her pocket and raised her hand, stretching her fingers out as if she could touch him.

His mouth twisted into a mocking curve. "You'll fail again."

Her hand froze an inch from his cheek. These words weren't whispered. He spoke them, low and blunt.

"It's what you do," he continued as a drop of cold rain dribbled past her wrist and up into her sleeve. "You hide behind your books, and you fail at everything that's important."

She closed her hand and forced her feet down the path again, holding his gaze as she passed him, unable to look away from the contempt in his eyes.

A root caught at her foot, and she spun forward to find her father's face, creased with disgust. "He's gone because you failed when he needed you." His voice dripped with revulsion, and she stumbled back.

"All you ever do is fail," her mother's voice agreed from across the path.

Kate didn't look at her. She ducked her head, keeping her eyes on the trail as she broke into a run.

A huge tree reared up in her path, and she skidded to a stop, throwing her hands up to catch herself. The wet, rough bark dug into her palms, and she leaned close, her breath coming in gasps.

Evan's face eased out of the trunk, only inches from her own, and she jerked back. Her brother's skin was pasty white, his hair bleached to milky silver. He looked young, exactly as he had that day outside the mine, but his eyes glittered with a perfect comprehension of who she was and what she had done.

Kate froze.

His expression shifted to one of loathing.

"Give up the hope of finding me." His words pressed down onto her with an inexorable, unavoidable weight. With the grim impartial march of winter ice, smothering the lapping ripples of a lake, or the slow approach of inevitable death. "I did. Long ago."

The simple declaration tolled out like a death knell, and she shoved away from him, shouldering past the tree. She ran through the last of the forest and out into a gloomy clearing at the foot of the cliffs. Stumbling, she crashed to her knees.

Her breath came in gasps, and she curled forward, pressing her palms to her eyes, trying to push away the white faces seared into the black behind her eyelids.

She opened her eyes and groped for her pocket, fumbling the vials before she pulled them out. Even in the gloom, a few sparks glittered in the liquid, and she clutched it to her chest, clinging to the hope that maybe this time, things would work.

She cast a glance over her shoulder, but the forest lay still, the ghosts sunk back into their runes, their voices only echoing in her mind.

CHAPTER NINE

KATE LET the rain patter down on her shoulders and hood for a long minute before she took a shuddering breath and turned away from the woods. The towering Marsham Cliffs reared up in front of her, their top disappearing into the low clouds, their base covered by a segment of stone wall set directly onto the face itself.

The rain caused ripples in the pools forming around her knees. The damp and cold seeped through her pants, her boots, her robes, bringing a chill that pulled her attention away from the gnawing words of the ghosts. Kate tucked the vials into an inner pocket of her robe and stood. The rain-sodden ground quickly filled each of her footprints with little pools as she stepped closer to the wall.

The wispy, glowing tangle of remnant lay thick and layered on a particulate stone just to her left. Kate approached the stone and traced the lines of the ancient runes. The remnants of current and previous Keepers mingled together, wrapped around each other, gave Kate a sense of distant lands, forgotten times, memories of lives long ago forgotten.

"Hello, again." She set her hand on top of the mixture of

scents and sounds, and it felt like the first breath of home. "Aperi." A pulse of *vitalle* flowed out of her palm, and the stones beside her shifted.

The Wall opened to reveal a long tunnel boring straight through the cliff. She stepped in, pressing her palm to matching runes inside. "Cluda." The surge of energy was stronger this time, and she winced at the burning heat in her palm.

The stones shifted back, blocking the silent forest. She rubbed her sore hand and started toward the sunny bit of valley at the far end.

The Marsham Cliffs sat above her like some eternal, unmovable guardian, blocking the rest of the world out of the Stronghold valley, and, in the case of days like today, also blocking out the low-hanging clouds. Kate stepped out of the tunnel into an entirely different day—a different world.

The sky high above her shone with an untamed blue, and the sun flung down light as liberally as the clouds outside poured down rain. The valley itself, more aptly called a rift in the high desert above, stretched away peacefully to either side.

Ahead and a little to the left rose the round white tower of the Stronghold.

The stones reflected sunlight, casting brightness onto the handful of low buildings around the tower, but they gave off more than light. The closer she came, the richer the air felt. Warmer, without actually being warm. It wasn't quite a remnant, but there was a sound—a thousand sounds, echoing quietly. The rush of a distant river or a crowd of people, still far off.

And the smell…

She breathed in deeply, as though it really was a smell that could be captured. It was the impression of warmth and food and hearths and thunderstorms and a hundred scents that couldn't be named.

There was a slight disorder to it, though, and she traced the different rocks as though she could sort it out.

When she'd first seen the Stronghold, twenty years ago, it had been a pile of enormous white rocks splayed across the valley floor. It had taken a team of dwarves and the magical assistance of every living Keeper over three years to rebuild it, block by block. While the others claimed it was nearly identical to what it had been before, she thought it felt jumbled. As though its stones had built up a story over centuries that had been shattered and put back together slightly out of order.

A light flashed on the ceiling of the covered balcony at the top, bright enough to see even in daylight, and she paused to watch as glitters from the Wellstone skittered over the stones.

If she could get her serum to hold memories a tenth as well as a Wellstone—a hundredth as well—it would do everything she wanted.

Kate was almost to the low wooden kitchen extending from the first floor of the tower before she noticed the smell of real, physical bread. She pushed the door open and stepped in to find two elderly men sitting at the enormous table that filled the center of the room, cutting up apples and dropping them into a huge pot.

They looked up at the same moment.

Keeper Gerone's white curly beard split apart to show a wide smile. "Kate!" He pushed himself to his feet and let out a little huff as he slowly straightened his back. "Come in! Have some apples."

She shrugged her pack off onto the table and gave the old man a hug. Gerone was like baking bread through and through. Yeast, warmth, flour, sugar. She could taste it in the air around him. His remnant was infused with it, and, as the dusting of flour on his cheek showed, his clothes and hair were too.

"Did you get it?" Keeper Mikal asked, still seated. His steely-grey beard was straight and combed smooth, his hair short and tamed, giving him an instant air of sophistication that the disheveled Gerone completely lacked. Still, there was a small smile on Mikal's face, which was as much as Kate had ever seen from him.

"I did. Two vials of tenea serum." Kate moved between the two men's chairs and set one hand on Mikal's shoulder, smelling the dark red berry ink that he used to shade his maps, which mixed seamlessly with his remnant. A slight sweetness mixed with the tang of vinegar. She leaned down and kissed his head.

"Don't be so emotional," he said. "You were only gone a few days." But he patted her hand before picking up another apple. "Is the serum pure?"

"It appears to be." Kate chose a slice of green apple from in front of him and took a bite. It was crisp, and her lips puckered at the tartness.

"We're making applesauce and tarts and green apple pies," Gerone said with a smile. "Tomorrow, I'll make puffy apple cakes for breakfast."

"Stop chattering at her," Mikal said, tapping his knife on the table. "Are you going to show us the serum or not, Katria?"

She pulled the two vials out of her pocket, handing one to each of them.

Gerone lowered himself back into his chair, and both men held the vials up, peering at them closely.

"Beautiful," Gerone said quietly. "I did wonder if it would really shimmer."

"The color is good." Mikal tilted the vial, watching the thick serum flow to the side. "Viscosity looks right."

Gerone nodded "Like silver honey."

"Thinner than honey." Mikal carefully pulled out the cork and set his fingertip into the fluid. A delicate stream of light flowed into it, breaking into pieces. In a breath, it rose and disappeared. "They were right about the instability."

"It held a memory," Kate said. "Not for long, and it ends up tattered and out of order, but..." She smiled at them and picked up another slice of apple. "It works."

"It has the potential to work," Mikal corrected her.

She laughed, and he looked up sharply. "It does," she agreed.

Gerone gave a hum of agreement and handed back the vial. "But it's a step in the right direction."

"If she can stabilize it." Mikal offered his back as well. "Even with her remnant amplifier, this is a far cry from a unified *solus* potion that draws both remnant and memories from an object."

Kate tucked the two vials back into her pocket, unable to argue with him.

Gerone shrugged. "Whatever those men used long ago, Kate, I have no doubt you can recreate it and improve upon it."

"No one is doubting her capabilities," Mikal said. "I'm just pointing out there's a lot of work left to do."

"Which I have the utmost faith that she can do," Gerone said with a note of finality. "And then she should go find Bo and help him dig up all the things she wants to use it on."

Kate shifted at his words.

"If she goes, who would stay in the world's largest library and research things that same world needs to know?" Mikal said, a note of exasperation entering his voice.

Gerone turned his face up toward Kate, pointedly ignoring Mikal. "Time goes faster than you think, my dear. I see the way you look at those maps. You should go."

Kate set a hand on his shoulder, ignoring the complicated feelings that rose up from his words. "*Solus* potion first."

"To tempt you a little more," he said, pointing to a small desk tucked in the corner, "mail came from the palace for you while you were gone."

"Finally!" Kate crossed the room. "I expected something from him a month ago."

"Stop trying to make her leave," Mikal said sternly.

"I'm merely encouraging her to follow her heart," Gerone said mildly.

"Katria is a Keeper, and her heart is in research. In digging out the bits of story then weaving them together into something glorious. She provides a crucial service to the queen, and the entirety of Queensland, and she's among the best of us at it. Which is why she should stay."

"Your heart is in research," Gerone corrected him. "Thankfully, because you look into all the things that bore even the rest of the Keepers." He leaned toward Kate. "Like the variability of the textile trade from year to year for the queen."

Kate started toward the desk. "Why—"

"Don't ask!" Gerone said quickly. "He's been researching it for days, and every bit of it is utterly boring."

"It is not boring," Mikal said mildly. "It is more useful than researching a way to combine a cherry tree and a pear tree to create a new kind of berry."

Kate moved to the counter with the mail. "That sounds delicious."

Gerone grinned. "More importantly, I think it will grow fast and need little space. Possibly something that could be grown even in small garden spaces in cities."

Kate flipped through the stack of papers until she found a cream-colored letter addressed in Bo's familiar hand to Keeper Katria, Royal Palace, Queenstown.

Trying not to think of his ghost on the path, she slid the paper closer, touching just the very corner.

It was light and thin. Curiously thin considering the thick bundles he usually sent. She searched for any sign of him after weeks of travel, but among the disjointed bits of remnants she found on it, there was only the faintest trace of summer wind, the quietest waft of breath. She flipped it over, but there was nothing there either, except around the very edges of the silver wax, stamped with the familiar shape of the aenigma box.

With no remnant to disturb, she picked up the letter and tucked it into her pack.

"We have cheese and smoked fish," Gerone said.

Kate spun to look at him, holding up a finger. "Don't you dare invite me to eat with you. The library is calling."

"I wouldn't dream of keeping you, my dear," the old man said with a smile. "But take some food with you if you're about to disappear for hours. I will invite you to a dinner tonight, though. Finding the serum calls for a celebration. Let's open one of the Naponese wines."

Kate grinned at him as she made herself a plate of food. "I'd be happy to join you for that. I'll pick out a bottle." She started down the short hall leading into the Stronghold tower.

"A celebration?" Mikal's voice drifted down the hall. "There's nothing to celebrate yet. Whoever made the serum has done all the work so far."

"We're celebrating the hope, Mikal," Gerone said patiently.

"Hope should be nurtured quietly and carefully," the other Keeper said, "not scared away by loud celebrations."

As she opened the door into the tower, she heard a snort of amusement from Gerone. "You can stay in your room nurturing quietly, then. The rest of us will celebrate."

She smiled at their familiar tones. They'd been Keepers for decades, spending years at court or traveling Queensland recording local legends and histories. They'd written dozens of books, developed treaties with neighboring countries. The two of them, together, had once formulated a cure for a wasting disease that was ravaging both Queensland and Coastal Baylon to the south. The two old men were as intrinsic to the Stronghold as the stones themselves.

Kate stepped into the Stronghold, and the presence of the building wrapped around her. Her shoulders loosened. A handful of steps through the tunnel brought her out into the center of the main white tower, which opened to a tiled ceiling far above. A ramp beside her spiraled up, passing door after door until it wound through a hole in the ceiling and out onto the balcony.

She crossed to a hallway that led into the rich wood of the library. This shorter tower was also round and walled with books. Shelf after shelf, from floor to ceiling, broken only to allow space for desks and comfortable chairs.

Kate moved to the railing that overlooked the open center. Just like in the white tower, ramps connected the different levels of the library. Three stories above her, a glass roof poured in sunlight, warming the wooden railings, casting plenty of light on the tables set along them. Four levels below her, dug deep into the ground, lay the tiled floor, swirled in a mosaic of blues and greens, like eddies of water, with bits of gold and silver glittering through it.

The library didn't have a remnant, but that didn't matter because it smelled of books and ink and stories.

She turned toward the ramp, but a skittering of light caught her eye.

"Most of the library doesn't have a remnant," she said quietly to the display mounted on the railing. It held a creamy yellow dragon scale set on a pitch-black pillow. The sunlight skipped across the ridges and dimples of the scale, flowing in frosted ripples. "But you do." She brushed her fingertip over the scale and found the faintest echo of a remnant so vast it could encompass the entire valley. She paused, trying to explore the extent of it. Beyond the fact that no animal she'd ever encountered had a remnant, there was something strange about this one. It was alien, inhuman, and there was something permanent about it. As though the remnant would still be clinging to it in a thousand years.

She glanced up at the library roof where, out of the corner of her eye, she sometimes caught a glitter of yellow in the glass. Stretching her awareness toward it, she searched for traces, residual essence that had been pulled from the scale and infused into the glass years ago, but found nothing.

She moved to the nearest ramp and headed down.

As she passed the next floor, she caught the fresh, healing scent of tree sap. In the shadows between two bookshelves, she saw the youngest Keeper's back, hunched over a desk with nothing but a dim bluish light sneaking over his shoulder. Her pack thumped against the rail, and the light winked out as he glanced back, his shaggy hair hanging in front of startled eyes.

When Kellen saw her, though, his shoulders relaxed and he flashed her a grin. "Welcome back, Kate."

"Thank you." As she crossed to him, his remnant fleshed out to include a brightness, a spark of curiosity. She looked over his shoulder at the book he had spread out before him. "Is that Mikal's treaty on the history of southern trade routes?"

His smile widened. "It is."

The page had Mikal's uniform, neat handwriting filling the bottom half, but the top half was blank. Kate could feel the thin trail of *vitalle* hovering at Kellen's fingertip, poised above the first visible word, which was already half-erased.

"...Are you erasing it?"

"I'm rewriting it." Kellen tapped a black inkwell sitting next to the book.

"In *verus* ink?"

His grin turned downright devious, and he touched the wick of the unlit candle next to him. "*Verus elucida.*"

A burst of *vitalle* shot out of his fingertip, and a ball of bluish-white light flared on the candle. Silvery words sprang into view on the page, written in Kellen's less uniform, less neat script.

Kate blinked at the page. "Why?"

"Yesterday," he said with an irritated tone, "Mikal left a note telling me to research these monumentally boring trade routes, focusing, yet again, on the textile trade. So I did. And I wrote a summary, which was vastly more interesting than his work. But, when I handed it in, he told me I'd done the wrong work. Told me he'd written more of the assignment in *verus* ink on the bottom of the note."

"He left you a secret message?"

"'A true Keeper,'" Kellen said in a remarkably good imitation of Mikal's voice, "'can sense *verus* ink immediately.'" He shot a glare in the general direction of the kitchen. "He threw my research in the fire and told me to redo it, on top of the new assignment for today."

Kate glanced at the book. "But instead you decided to spend the morning rewriting a page of his book in *verus* ink?"

"Not a page." He thumbed back through the book.

Page after page of silvery writing shimmered as they flipped past, and Kate's mouth dropped open. "You did all that? This morning?" She glanced at him. "I know you can move a lot of *vitalle*, but this... How are you not exhausted? That should have taken days."

He smiled. "I was only going to do the cover page, but then I realized that it's the beginning of each word that's hard in *verus* ink. Once you get the ink started, and you've begun to trickle the *vitalle* into it, it's easy. So I just didn't lift up my quill." He held the light closer to the page, showing the thin lines of silver connecting one word to the next. "If I need to, I leave a little dot of extra ink, and as long as I don't wait too long, I can just set my quill in it and continue. Which means I only have to infuse the ink at the top of each page."

Kate looked between him and the book. "That's brilliant!"

"Thank you." He pushed his hair out of his eyes. "Do you think Mikal will think so?"

"No." She laughed. "At least not at first. You realize you're going to be up most of the night finishing two assignments for him, even if you start now?"

Kellen flashed another smile as he picked up his quill. "Worth it for the few seconds of stunned silence I'll get out of him the first time he opens this book."

"I hope I'm around when he does." Kate patted the young man on the shoulder and left him to his mischief. She headed down another level until she reached the long table spread with her research, overlooking the center of the library. The near side of the table was covered with maps of the Kalesh Empire and lined with stacks of books and paper.

She put her pack down on the floor and dragged her chair to the far end, where a latticework of glass vials and flasks and syringes and funnels glittered in the sunlight like a crowd of shining faces welcoming her home. Most sat in neat rows on a series of shelves along the railing, but a few pieces perched on a thin metal stand, connected by thin copper piping or poised over unlit lamps.

The pipes were mottled with the browns and greens of aging. The only coppery bright part was the topmost curve, which glowed like it had captured a bit of the sun.

Kate rubbed her fingers over the curve. "*Prapiro thesaur*," she murmured and settled down into the padded chair.

Everything was exactly where she'd left it, every familiar piece of glass and the open journal filled with lists of mixtures to attempt. She pulled the vials of tenea serum out of her pocket, and the entire table suddenly felt different. The ingredients she'd gathered based purely on hope suddenly felt purposeful. The glass jars were no longer merely empty—they were waiting to be filled. The entire table felt expectant.

Breathing deeply to dispel the bubbling nervousness in her gut, she set the serum vials in a wire frame to keep them upright.

"All right, no need to rush past things that could tell me something."

Kate reached over and opened the lid of a wooden box carefully tucked against the end of her row of books. Inside, a firmly corked, wide-bottomed jar held a fluid so vividly blue it looked like liquid sky.

The color was fitting in some way she couldn't describe. A mixture that amplified remnants should be like the sky.

Using a dropper, she extracted a small amount and closed the box quickly before the sunlight could break it down. Carefully, she let a drop of the amplifier fall on each vial of tenea serum.

The blue fluid began to dissolve into a sky-colored mist the moment it touched the air, and Wolff's rank remnant flared into her senses. She forced herself to lean closer, sorting through it for other scents or sounds. A faint, dry hiss sounded, like scales slithering across rock. She grimaced at the unpleasantness of the sound and strained to hear more, but there was nothing else.

The last of the amplifier dissipated into the air, and the remnants faded. It was slightly unnerving that the other people using tenea serum were all corrupt.

"Nothing unexpected there, though." Kate wiped her hands on her robe, as though wiping off the unpleasant remnants. "Let's use you for something better than torture, shall we?" she said quietly to the vials. "And once you're a nice, stable memory serum, we'll see if we can mix you with the amplifier to create…"

The memory of the Kalesh man standing over Evan, dripping the liquid onto the box and chanting, surfaced, and she pushed it away with a sigh. "A single *solus* potion that both shows memories and draws out remnants, which I have very little idea how to make." At least the chanting didn't matter. Words were a tool to focus *vitalle*, but hardly necessary. Whoever that man was, no matter how he'd appeared to her back then, if he'd needed to chant, his powers had been very limited. If she could make the liquid correctly, she wouldn't need chants or magical words. It would just need a little infusion of *vitalle*.

She reached for a basket tucked under the table. "But that's a future problem. First, the tenea serum." Without bothering to reference her journal, she gathered ingredients. This first part was the one thing she was confident of. It wouldn't fix everything, but if she could keep the memory from breaking into pieces, it would be a good start.

Picking up one of the tiny spoons laid out in a neat line, she measured out powdered sap and brought it toward her flask. Evan's face from the tree outside came back to her mind, and her hand twitched, spilling half the spoonful onto the table. She pushed the thought out of her mind, focusing only on the process and remeasuring the sap precisely before stirring it into her mixture.

When the flask was half full of a hazy brown liquid, she leaned forward and held it in the sunlight, examining the color.

Earthy and thin. No hint of granules. No oily film on the surface.

She lit an oil lamp and set the flask on a metal rack above it with trembling hands. Uncorking one of the vials of tenea serum, she carefully measured two drops into her liquid. The silvery serum caught at the sunlight, glittering as it slowly sank.

Wiping her sweaty hands on her robe, she picked up a single smooth renberry pit from its bowl and dropped it in.

For a dozen heartbeats, the solution did absolutely nothing.

Another dozen heartbeats passed.

She sank back and let out her breath.

No change was good. A properly measured solution should take hours to dissolve the pit, then hours more to reach the consistency where she could test anything.

"Tomorrow morning, then," she said to it, rolling her shoulders, torn between satisfaction and impatience.

A small box sat among her books, and she pulled it closer. The tight joints on the corners were coated with wax. More wax sealed a glass lid shut, keeping every bit of air and remnant trapped. Inside, on a piece of black silk, sat a gold medallion, stamped with a dragon coiled around a sword.

Except for the scalloped edges, it was identical to the one from the aenigma box long ago. And it matched the mark on Kate's map. The symbol of an empire that had ended three hundred years ago. Yet neither this medallion, nor the one on the box, were terribly old.

"I'm getting closer," she said quietly to it, rubbing her thumb over the corner of the box, "but yes, there's still a lot to do." Like figuring out how to stabilize her memory serum, then how to combine it with the remnant amplifier to create a *solus* potion that could finally tell her who had touched this, finally show her the memories objects held. Finally give her some clue to what the medallion meant, why Bo had found it in a burned-out fort, and why there'd been a nearly identical one affixed to a curious magical aenigma box.

And maybe some clue as to how to find her brother.

For now, though, there was just a little more waiting.

That, at least, was something she was good at.

CHAPTER TEN

KATE SLID her chair to the other side of the long table. The research she was working on for the northern duchies—looking into which of them, historically, had owned a certain mountainside where some interesting mineral deposits had recently been found—was far too boring to pick up. There was no mystery there, just a cross-referencing between maps, following the trail of name changes that the small towns in the area had gone through over the last four hundred years.

She reached into her pack for the one thing that would be a pleasant diversion from the waiting.

Bo's letter.

The thinness was disappointing, but also curious. Just a single folded piece of paper, not his usual packet of notes and maps. Her name was written in his familiar hasty hand—maybe more hasty than normal—and there were none of the sketches or quirky puzzles that usually decorated the outside.

She broke the seal and unfolded the letter carefully, touching only the edges, trying not to disturb any echoes of his remnant that might still linger.

There it was, the summer wind across the hills and a quiet breath, although whether it was a bit of laughter or a gasp of wonder, she'd still never been able to decide.

It was dated six weeks ago from "The Spire outside Morrow," and the writing scrawled across the page.

> *Ria!*
> *I know. You're waiting for a follow-up of my letter from a fort-night ago, and I have one partially written, but it's back in town, and, for obvious reasons, it's very long.*

"That would be, what? Eight weeks ago?" Kate glanced around her desk. "I don't have a letter from a fortnight before this one, Bo."

> *But there's a merchant here at the Spire, waiting (impatiently) for me, who is heading all the way to Greentree, and that is not an opportunity I can pass up.*
> *I'm up to my neck in fascinating books in the Spire library—so many tales of monsters! You'd be so amused. They almost didn't let me in it, and that would have been awful. This place could fill another letter, or ten. It's small, but what a library! A literal trea-sure trove of monsters.*
> *And Ria! It opens!*
> *I think by moonlight? And maybe…hope? That alone deserves a monumentally extensive letter, and I swear one is coming.*

"Or just a little clarity in this one," she muttered. "You opened a treasure trove of monsters?"

> *But there's more! That note from the exiled scribe? It's true!*
> *I know where Emperor Sorrn died!*

Her fingers tightened on the paper, and she leaned forward. "What?"

> *Home!*
>
> *Or at least in the vicinity.*
>
> *I head north to follow the trail as soon as I pack!*
>
> *Ria! Maybe some answers are finally within our reach!*
>
> *Wish me prapiro thesaur! If there's more treasure here, some speed in finding it would be nice for once. I hear snow comes early in the north.*
>
> *Yours, with even more enthusiasm than this deluge of exclamation points expresses,*
>
> *Bo*

"What?" she repeated, flipping the page over. Everything else was blank.

She reread the letter, but nearly every word remained nonsensical.

"Where is Morrow?" Pulling the modern map of what had been the Empire's lands from her pack, she ran her finger over the area where Bo had last been, slowly widening her search. All the way over on the western side, only a day or so from the mountains that bordered the land, she found the small town. Weeks farther west than she expected him to be.

"Why are you there?"

A pile of papers sat at the edge of her desk, and she flipped through it in case any mail had been left while she was gone. Finding none, she turned back to the letter. "I would love to be excited with you, Bo, but this is the stupidest thing you have ever written me. How about less exclamations and more sense? What's the Spire library, why does it have a treasure trove of monsters—which I assume you do not mean literally—and how does it open by moonlight? And, as much as I would *love* to think you found where Sorrn died, he never lived more than a day's walk from the Southern Sea. So his home is *not* north of you."

She pulled out her journal and opened it to a new page. Referencing the strange letter, she listed the main points, spreading them out on the page: *Morrow, the Spire library. Sorrn's home, treasure trove of monsters.* A few of the ideas were obviously connected, and she drew lines between them, creating the beginning of a web for sorting out whatever this story was. She listed her obvious questions and searched for more connections.

There were no more.

This was like having a few shards of a full story and not a hint of context for any of them.

She drummed her fingers on her desk, looking at the books stacked along the railing as though one of them could explain any of this. It was the collection of every book she'd found in the Stronghold that mentioned the Kalesh Empire, but not one discussed the area around Morrow.

She reached out to the oil lamp with a small finger of *vitalle* and pulled part of the flame into her palm. Sitting back in her chair, she rolled her fingers, shifting the little tongue of fire from the pad of one finger to the next, feeding it a thin trail of *vitalle* to keep it lit. It danced across her skin, the warmth of the fire flitting past like the brush of soft fabric.

Her gaze traced the bookshelves around her. Most books on foreign lands were here, on the second level, but searching for a place as blandly named as the Spire was an effort in futility.

She turned her hand over, letting the flame slip up to dance on the back of her knuckles.

The flickering light reflected off the nearest glass flasks on her desk in little glints of light. "Yes, there's a slim chance the Wellstone might have something," she admitted to them. "But an even slimmer chance that I'll find it based on"—she glanced at the letter—"this."

The candle flame danced over her fingers in unconcerned frivolity, and the glass beyond it cheerfully reflected each movement.

"I know." She flicked her fingers, and the flame winked out. "There isn't anywhere else to look."

A cough sounded from high up in the library, and she leaned forward, craning to see the top floor. Nothing moved up there, and she couldn't feel his remnant from this far, but that cough meant the tiny wizened leader of the Keepers must be up at his table, researching some odd thing or another.

"All right, there is one more place."

She picked up one of the tenea serum vials and Bo's letter and headed up the ramp.

Sunlight poured into the top floor of the library, just under the spiderweb of arched wooden beams that held dozens of panes of glass. She followed the railing around to where several tables had been pushed together, blocking the aisle and creating a little nook.

Towers of books crowded every surface and every bit of floor, nearly all of them topped with a volume spread open, often holding papers with scribbled notes. A small path wound through the books to a chair piled high with pillows and holding the little form of the Shield himself, currently fast asleep on a stack of papers on his desk, his bald head shining in the sunshine, and his tremendously bushy eyebrows glowing white.

Every shelf seemed to hold his remnant, not just because it had rubbed off him over time, but because it was infused into the wood, the books, the panes of glass above him.

Kate stood in it for a moment, closing her eyes and probing it. The Shield's remnant felt...unusual. It was *more* than any person she'd ever met. Stronger, thicker. Fiery. It smelled like warmth in an undefinable way, and she could almost hear crackling flames. Except there was even more than that. It was inquisitive and golden. She had never met anyone whose remnant had a color. Not a color she could see, of course, but a color nonetheless.

The strangest part about it though, was the extra bits, the bits that made his presence somehow an intrinsic part of the Stronghold. Occasionally, she smelled flowers or spices or a salty scent that she imagined the ocean might smell like. And there were sounds—whispers, faint bits of song, rustling, shushing. These bits weren't well attached to him but seemed to trail away into the walls of the Stronghold itself.

He stirred, and she opened her eyes to find him blinking at her. He pushed himself up with a grimace and a quiet hiss of pain. Kate's fingers twitched toward him, but she pulled them back. He'd just wave her off and mutter that anyone who'd lived one hundred and fifty years deserved to fuss over a bit of pain.

"Katria," he said kindly, smoothing his face into a smile. "You look like a woman who found what she went searching for."

"I did." Kate held out the vial.

He let out an appreciative hum as he took it and inspected the serum. "And do you feel hopeful?"

"I do. A renberry pit is currently dissolving, so I should know more by morning." She couldn't keep herself from smiling. "You're invited to a celebratory dinner tonight. We're opening a bottle of Naponese wine."

"I wouldn't dream of declining an invitation from you," he said with a smile. "Especially if Naponese wine is involved."

She looked over the assortment of books on his table. Unlike most times, when every book within arm's reach was on a certain topic, these books were such an eclectic mix that she didn't see any commonality. "What are you looking for?"

A small crease appeared between his brows, and he looked over his desk. "I'm not sure yet."

Kate reached over and picked up *Hidden Caves of the Scale Mountains*, revealing the next book titled *Historic Trails of Baylon*. "Then how do you know what books to look in?"

"That *is* proving to be a bit of a puzzle." He sighed and set down the vial. "I have managed to find two different references I was searching for years ago, though, and one book on building secret passages, misshelved all the way over in the forestry section, if you can believe that." He scanned the bookshelves around him. "A library where every book was shelved properly, now that would be a magical place."

She set the book down and handed him the letter. "Speaking of puzzles, Bo's latest letter is mostly nonsense."

He read it, then flipped the paper over as though he'd find more. "That's both more enthusiastic and less clear than usual. What's the Spire?"

"I was hoping you might know. I found Morrow on a map, but it's quite a bit north of any home Sorrn ever lived in, so I don't understand Bo heading farther north either." She shook her head. "I was going to look in the Wellstone for any references, but this is very little to go on."

He blinked thoughtfully, considering the letter. "I'm afraid this means nothing to me," he said, handing it back to her. His fingers brushed hers, and his eyebrows shot up. "It's you!"

"What's me?"

He took her free hand in his knobby fingers, which were colder and more papery than the feel of his remnant would suggest. After a moment's thought, he blinked up at her with a wide smile. "I'm supposed to find something for *you*. The answer to something, but I'm not sure what the question is. What questions do you have?"

Kate blinked at him. "The same ones I've had for years. How

can I make a *solus* potion that will show me remnants and the memories tied up in them from all the strange objects Bo sends me?" She paused. "And where is Evan?"

He nodded sagely. "Both excellent questions. All wrong for this, of course, but still excellent questions." He sighed. "The library's been nagging at me for weeks, but it's been so vague."

"The library?"

"Or the tower." He tilted his head. "Do you think they're the same thing?"

"The library and the tower?"

He let go of her hand. "I am inclined to think they are, even though they're made of vastly different stone. The white tower is obviously special—they knew that four hundred years ago when they used the priory stones to build it, and while the library is just regular rock, it *is* old, and it's been connected to the white stone for so long, maybe the voice of the tower has rubbed off?"

"The tower has a voice?"

He gave her a mildly confused look. "I assumed you, of all people, knew that."

"It has a remnant. Or something like one."

"How could it not? After all these years?"

No other ancient buildings she'd ever seen had remnants, but she didn't point that out. "And you think the library wants to tell me something?" It was odd how nonsensical things seemed to almost make sense in the presence of the Shield.

He nodded. "What do these books make you think of?"

She scanned the titles she could see. *Mining the Northern Slopes of Gulfind*, *Baylonese Coastal Cities*, *What's Beyond the Reaches?*, *Precious Gems of Napon*. A whole pile of books Will had written about the Roven Sweep were stacked near the rail, bookmarks poking out of each.

She picked up one titled *The World's Best Wine.* "That's quite a claim."

"A somewhat metaphorical title," he said with a sad smile. "That is the story of a man who left his small unsuccessful winery on the moors—and left his family with it—searching for better wine to increase their fortunes. Which he found, deep in Napon, but he was gone so long that his wife died and his children grew up and left. When he returned, imagining all he could do with his own winery, it was abandoned and overgrown."

"Is it a satisfying sort of tragedy?"

The Shield shook his head. "Merely a tragic one."

Kate set it down gently. "The only thing I see about these are that they're all about foreign lands, but none are the Kalesh Empire."

"No, but that is the right track!" He looked thoughtfully out the roof. "We don't have many books about the Empire."

"I'm acutely aware of that fact," she said with a smile. "What sorts of things does the library care about?"

He gestured up at the panes of glass above him. "Well, once it cared that the roof wasn't strong enough to withstand a dragon. Twice it gave me ways to help the forest at the north end of the valley. Once for tree rot, once for an invasive beetle." At Kate's raised eyebrow, he shrugged. "It likes that forest. Once it had me send a book to the dwarves in Duncave about some rare stone called viren, for reasons unknown. And once…" He gestured to a small green book at the end of a nearby shelf. "I spent over two years searching for that book. I still have no idea why."

She stepped closer. "*Lost Things*?"

"I'm not positive it's not the tower's idea of a joke."

She almost laughed, but the remnant of the tower was so strong that the idea of it joking might not be entirely unbelievable. She studied the way the Shield's remnant snaked out of him and connected with the building. "Why are you part of its remnant?"

"Am I?" He looked pleased at the idea.

"You are, and you're growing more connected to it."

His smile faded and he turned his face toward the ceiling. "Ah," he said quietly.

"*Ah* is not an answer."

"Your last words weren't a question." He looked out of the glass above them at the side of the white tower soaring up above them. "I believe that the spirits of the Shields who have gone before me are still here."

"In their memories?" Kate asked glancing up with him at the side of the Stronghold, as though she could see the sparkling light at the top. "In the Wellstone? I suppose every Keeper is still here, in one sense, in the memories they left us."

"No, I mean in the building itself. The longer I live here, the more often I think the Shields are speaking to me, but I don't quite know how to listen."

"And you think you're becoming part of it too?"

His eyes lit with amusement. "I guess we'll find out." He climbed out of his chair and walked to the railing, standing on his tiptoes to look thoughtfully over it at the lower levels. "When are you leaving?" he asked, almost absently.

Kate paused. "I didn't know I was."

He turned and blinked up at her for a heartbeat. "Oh. For a moment it seemed like…" He trailed off absently. With a shake of his head, he said, "When you go to the Wellstone, focus on the Spire Bo mentions. I have a niggling feeling I heard something about that once."

"I will." She picked up her vial of serum and headed down the ramp.

She was on the floor below him when his bald head popped over the railing. "Katria! See if the Wellstone knows what I'm looking for, too."

"I'm already trying to connect a letter I don't understand to information I don't have, and you also want me to find the answer to a question you don't know?"

He beamed down at her. "Exactly! I have the utmost faith in you!" With a wave, he disappeared from view.

She looked up at the empty railing and sighed. "People keep saying that."

CHAPTER ELEVEN

THE ONLY NOISE in the tower was Kate's footsteps, echoing across the open center in a muffled, disjointed jumble. The sound played as a familiar backdrop to the myriad of quiet sensations emanating from the white stones around her. She trailed her hand along the top of the railing, brushing her fingers through the remnant that hung in the air around it like a mist. She probed it, searching for anything that reminded her of the Shield, but there was nothing that specific.

It was like standing in a crowd of quiet conversations, every voice pitched just too low to hear. Or entering a square on market day and having to weave through the ever-changing motion, passing through countless smells that wafted past before she could name them.

Whether from twenty years of familiarity or from the nature of the remnant itself, the rich complexity of it was as soothing as dragging her fingers through warm water.

Her legs burned from the climb by the time she reached the top of the ramp, emerging into the cool shadows of the covered balcony at the very top of the Stronghold. Leaning her hand against one of the chilled stone columns that held up the roof, she paused to catch her breath. A swirl of breeze blew up the valley and brushed past her, carrying the distinct crispness of fall.

A sparkle of light caught her eye, and she leaned against the low wall between the columns, facing the glittering Wellstone. She crossed her arms and studied it. It sat on a small table, deceptively small and docile. No bigger than a melon, its hundreds of facets flickered with bits of color or motion or slivers of images. Every single flash like a shape in the corner of the eye, gone before it was really seen.

"I have questions for you," she said firmly to the stone, "and they're vague, so if you could pay attention for once, that would be helpful."

Nothing changed in the erratic skittering of light, and she pushed off the wall, crossing to sit in the chair next to the table. She set both the vial and Bo's letter down between the roots of the tree-shaped stand that held the stone.

Light shot out in all directions, skipping across the table, the columns, and the ceiling above her, blithely tumultuous and wild.

"Fine." She rubbed her hands together. "We'll do it your way."

Setting her palms on either side of the stone, she closed her eyes and let her mind step into the swirling chaos of the stone.

Disjointed memories battered her. Faces, voices, smells, wide vistas and small spaces. Candlelight, sunlight, darkness. Victory, crippling pain, boredom, frustration, serenity. Each memory hurtled through the stone, trailing faint lines connecting them to other memories, each thread holding a bit of remnant. As always, there was a sense that these memories were continually sorting themselves in a way she couldn't understand.

It tossed her about, like a small boat in a storm, and she wondered if every Keeper felt this insignificant amidst the maelstrom.

The chaos buffeted against her until she reached out and ran her awareness over the different remnants, tracing their connections. The web of memories encircled her, and she could almost make out patterns before they shifted again and she lost them.

The Wellstone slowed, seeming to turn its attention to her. Further away, memories still churned in an undecipherable pandemonium. Around her, though, things calmed and the stone pulled at her, stretching fingers into her mind, searching for new memories it hadn't seen yet.

There weren't many, since she'd come to the stone the night before she'd left to meet Wolff, but it found them quickly and drew them out, splitting them into individual ideas and sending them spinning away.

She watched her own experiences flow past and scatter. At first, the stone jumped from moment to moment without any particular interest. When Wolff handed her the tenea serum, though, the flow slowed, centering on the glittering bits in the fluid.

It didn't take long before the first spidery thin, silvery connection appeared, snaking between her memories and distant things lost in the chaos.

The threads, instead of being things in themselves, were like drawn-out strands of the memories, pulled out the way a strand of honey clung to the spout of the honeypot after you'd poured a little on your bread. Kate's memory of Wolff stretched away, trailing his rancid smell, until it intertwined with another memory—Alaric's, judging by the inky remnant—of the trader in a different tavern.

The Wellstone quickly drew to the end of her most recent memories, finishing with her walk up the tower just now, and turned away. The surging tumult closed in on itself, pushing her to the outskirts.

"No," she said, pressing her palms tighter against the stone.

"You got what you want. Now it's my turn."

She reached out into the swirling motion, catching a glimpse of her recent talk with the Shield. She drew it closer, concentrating on how his remnant had merged with the walls around him.

The swirling around her slowed.

"You like him, don't you?" Kate drew her attention down to the books on his table.

"I'm supposed to find something for you," the Shield said. *"The answer to something, but I'm not sure what the question is."*

Kate pulled away from the image, tracing out the connections the Wellstone was making between it and other bits of memory. They ran to other scenes of the Shield at his desk, a few of the books placed somewhere else, but nothing particularly useful.

More and more threads appeared, hundreds of memories of the Shield and the library connecting with each other. Thousands, maybe, each thread saturated with his remnant.

Kate stared at the massive tangle of connections.

The strands began to stretch, and Kate refocused on her own memory of the Shield just as it sped up. Kate dug into it, trying to get the Wellstone to pay attention to the books and the question, but the scene merely raced ahead, and she was pulled along with the memory of herself, leaving the library and climbing up the tower. The memory ran on, immune to her attempts to stop it, to the point where she sat down at the Wellstone. With no new memory left, the Wellstone turned back on itself, and the conversation with the Shield disappeared into the storm.

"That was incredibly unhelpful." The churning memories ignored her. "All right, let's try something a little more...well, it's not more specific, but you should have less connections to it."

She pushed some *vitalle* into the stone along with the idea of Bo's letter.

For a moment she fought for the attention of the stone,

pressing in more *vitalle* until it noticed her and stilled. She gripped the memory of the letter and the map for a moment before she found a few small threads branching off it. They were short, and she caught glimpses of other letters from Bo, but she poured more energy into the stone, looking for anything connecting to the word "Spire."

She held the stone's attention for another heartbeat before everything around her sped up again.

She let out a sigh and was starting to loosen her hold on the letter when she caught sight of a hair-thin thread stretching away from Bo's writing and snaking into the Wellstone.

She grabbed at it and pulled herself along, moving deeper into the turmoil, following the thread until the sense of Bo's remnant faded and another one took its place. Something like a small stream, but salty.

The thread carried her to a room in some run-down tavern. She sat looking across a table at an old, weathered man with a quick smile and worn traveling clothes. There was a scar across his temple that disappeared into his grey hair, and the hilt of a longsword leaned against the table next to him.

Resting in front of Kate were the aging hands of another man spinning a silver coin, the cuffs of his black Keeper's robe hanging around his wrists. The likeness on the coin made her draw the memory even closer. King Ryke's knife-sharp nose was impossible to miss. This conversation couldn't be more than sixty years old. She spared a moment to wonder who the Keeper was before the words of the memory caught her attention.

"Got as far north as Morrow's Spire," the man said. "The towns-people say it's full of books, but only the local holy man is allowed in. I tried to sneak a glimpse inside, but there were no windows. Just a squat little tower with a shaggy thatched roof and ribbons hanging down from the eaves to ward off evil spirits. Thought you'd want to know there might be a library there."

"Doesn't sound much like a spire," the Keeper said.

"A ridiculous name," the man agreed. "The first snow fell that night. It wasn't much, but they assured me more was coming, and the only thing north of there was the elven White Wood and monsters." He shrugged and lifted a roughly carved wooden mug. "It seemed like a good time to turn around and come home."

"Monsters? You're not one to be scared off by folktales."

The man took a long drink, then wiped his mouth with his sleeve. "There are places with folktales, and there are places with monsters. You don't live to be my age without knowing the difference." There was a moment of silence, and the old man gave a small smile. "Doubt all you want, but whatever's north of Morrow, it's frightening enough that people will suffer through a lean winter rather than hunt in those woods." He shook his head. "When the men of the town won't go there to find food for their children, it's a safe bet the monsters are more than tales."

"The elves of the White Wood aren't monsters," the Keeper pointed out.

The man shrugged. "Supposedly they help keep the monsters contained, but I'll tell you, the townsfolk are as frightened of the elves as they are of the monsters."

A barmaid appeared with bowls, and the two men shifted to discussing an upcoming dinner. The memory grew hazy and faded away.

There were a handful of connections leaving the memory, each with the Keeper's remnant, but they slipped out of Kate's grasp before she could follow them. The Wellstone went back to its own business and pressed Kate smoothly and inexorably to the edges.

She opened her eyes into the bright sunlight of the Stronghold valley and pulled her hands off the Wellstone. She glanced down at Bo's letter, a knot of worry forming in her stomach. "Maybe Morrow's stories weren't supposed to be amusing, Bo. I hope you didn't really head north."

CHAPTER TWELVE

KATE SWORE, slamming her lantern down on her desk, rattling the glass jars that glinted at her in the darkness like a dozen surprised eyes.

The flask in the center of her desk was filled with something sludgy and dark.

She shoved it away and sank into her chair while the silence and darkness of the library pressed around the island of light on her desk.

Six days and eight mixtures, and still the serum didn't work.

Her first attempt to keep the memory from breaking into pieces had been a success, but no matter what she added to that basic liquid, nothing stopped the memory from fraying and dissolving almost immediately.

She sank back in her chair, closing her eyes. "I need..." She rubbed at her exhausted face. "What do I need?"

Her voice faded away in the quiet library.

"I need a serum strong enough to hold memories together, but still active enough to combine with the remnant amplifier and make a single potion." She dropped her hands and drummed her fingers on the book. Past her circle of candlelight, there was nothing but blackness. "I need something as solid as stone, that still lets light and *vitalle* move. Like…glass." Of course, if glass had ever shown any inclination for amplifying or affecting *vitalle*, it might be worth testing.

The thought made her pause. "Actually…*our* glass…"

She pushed away from her table, grabbing her lantern and running up the ramp.

The library glass wasn't normal glass. It had been strengthened by something harder than rocks and very happy to let light move.

A glint of creamy yellow light skittered across the dragon scale sitting on its black pillow.

She brought the lantern closer, and the flame sent ripples of frosty light racing over the dimples like glittering sunlight on a lake.

"Yes." She picked up the scale. "You are exactly what I need."

Her footsteps rang out as she hurried back to her desk. She poured herself a new portion of the serum and dipped the edge of the scale into it.

Closing her eyes, she cast out toward the thin scale. It didn't hold *vitalle* like a living thing, but it was filled with the crystalline structure of its own essence. Billions of tiny nodes, intrinsically dragon-scale-ish, lit up in her mind, linked together in complex layers and shapes.

Slowly, she stretched out a thread of *vitalle* and brushed against the nodes, knocking a few loose. They sank into the liquid until they gathered a cluster of sparkles around themselves like a web of glitter. She held her breath, but they didn't break apart. They drifted toward other clusters, joining and growing.

A gust of air escaped her, half laugh, half shock, and she opened her eyes. The jumble of nodes was like a speck of sand in the jar, and she took in the volume of the fluid, doing a quick calculation. "This is going to take a long time..."

She tapped her finger against the edge of the scale. "By lunch, do you think?"

Neither the scale nor the candles nor anything else in the library answered her, but she nodded. "By lunch, I think."

Holding the scale over the serum, she drew another feather-light brush of *vitalle* across the dragon scale.

<hr />

Midday sunlight streamed down into the library before the entirety of the serum was gathered around nodes. Kate rolled her shoulders and set the dragon scale carefully to the side. There was no sign on the scale itself that she'd taken anything from it, but the serum glowed with a delicate, luminous yellow tint.

She held the serum up into the sunlight, and ripples of frosti-ness moved through the golden sparkles. Allowing herself a small smile, she brushed her finger along the side of the jar. "*Prapiro thesaur.*"

Movement on the roof caught her attention. The midday sky was a brilliant blue, holding nothing but the crescent moon creeping into view, but on one of the roof beams, a hawk shifted, perching for a breath before launching into the air.

Looking back at her desk, she dipped her finger into the fluid and pushed in the memory of the hawk.

A thin strand of white light slid out into the mixture, smooth and clean and bright. The edges shone like silver moonlight and lit the glittering particles floating in the serum.

Kate pulled her finger out, and the thread of memory swirled, coiling and twisting but remaining perfectly defined.

A moment passed, then another.

She let her breath go, silently and carefully, barely daring to blink.

Slowly, like a feather rising instead of falling, it moved toward the surface. When one loop reached the air, it faded away, and Kate put her finger back in before any more could disappear.

The beginning of the memory soaked into her finger.

The image of the hawk appeared, its wings flapping. The smell of ink, the feel of her chair.

The full, ordered memory lay neatly over everything she could see and hear around her, with a slight gap at the end where it had touched the air. It faded from her mind as the last of it sank into her skin, leaving the serum empty.

Her hand shook, hitting the side of the jar and sloshing the serum, almost spilling it over the side. She twitched away from it.

It worked.

She searched for a longer memory to test. Her eyes fell on the box with the medallion.

Finding the aenigma box. That was long, detailed. Perfect.

She set the paper aside and dipped her finger into the serum, bringing the spring day from her childhood to mind.

She'd been kneeling shoulder to shoulder with Bo in the dusty mine, full of excitement and wonder.

The strand of light slid out of her, glowing softly, lengthening until it coiled in the jar.

She pulled her finger out before the foreigners appeared and wiped off the wetness.

Without waiting, she dipped back in. The memory snaked toward her, sinking into her skin.

Closing her eyes, she let the memory flow. The empty darkness of the cavern, the small pool of lantern light, the dusty air, the press of rocks against her shins. The play of the light off the wooden box. Bo's excitement. Evan's curiosity.

The box, or her fingertips, or maybe the air around her, hummed.

The spicy smell filled the air around her again, sharp in her nose and crisply cold in her lungs.

Somewhere, a bell rang out, haunting and lonely and nearly lost in an unimaginably vast darkness.

The memory faded, and she opened her eyes. The fluid, now empty again, shimmered gently.

Across the library, something moved, and she looked up to see Kellen walking up the ramp, a stack of books in his arms.

"Kellen!" Her voice rang out so loudly that the young man jumped. "Come here!"

He came over, setting his books on the corner of her desk.

"Want to see a memory?" She pushed the jar over until it sat between them. "About finding a treasure?"

Kellen grinned at her. "Always."

She dipped her finger into the liquid and pulled up the memory of the mine again. When she was done, the trail of light curled around itself, long and winding. "Stick your finger in before any of it touches the air."

Kellen set his finger gently into the jar and closed his eyes. The beginning of the memory seeped into his skin.

He let out a little gasp, then stood very still.

Her hands gripped the edge of the table as she watched flickers of curiosity and interest cross his face.

When the light disappeared, he opened his eyes and stared at her in wonder. "Where were you? What was that box? What did the runes say? Something about a king?"

A laugh tore out of her, and she stood, shoving her chair back. "It was an abandoned mine, and those runes were partially covered. I haven't translated all of them. The top one says 'a bowing king.'" She laughed again and grabbed his arm. "The memory was clear? You could see Bo? And the box?"

He smiled widely at her excitement. "See it, feel it, smell it."

He paused. "There was a smell that didn't fit though. Like....dry wind. Or a hot summer day or something."

"That's Bo's remnant!"

"Really?" His expression grew curious. "Then the box had a remnant too?"

"Of sorts. Or maybe it holds them from people who've touched it?" The idea dragged at the other, more painful memories of that day, and she sighed. "It was a strange box." She searched through the collection of glass on her desk, looking for a small clean vial.

"I've never had any sort of adventure like that," Kellen said, his voice tinged with wistfulness. "Why aren't you with Bo, looking for things like that?"

Kellen ran his finger over the embossed symbol of the dragon and the sword on her map. She let her gaze travel along Bo's most recent route, lingering on the notation of the abandoned monastery he'd recently discovered. "I didn't show you how it ended." She turned away and sorted through her glassware. "My magic was just waking up."

"I could tell."

"I had no idea what was going on, but men wearing that Kalesh symbol showed up to take the box, and we ran from them..." Every detail of that desperate flight played out in her mind. The terrifying sounds and smells, the painful brightness, the utter vulnerability. "At least one of the Kalesh men could move *vitalle*, and he made my younger brother fall into the river." She turned her hands over, showing the old scars on her palms. "Evan's remnant was pouring out into the water, and I was too far away to reach him, but...I grabbed his remnant, and the *vitalle* that must have been mixed with it, and shoved him back up onto the shore."

Kellen's eyebrow rose. "Impressive. Sounds like you saved his life."

"No." The word slipped out on a ragged breath. "Because then the Kalesh man began chanting. To this day, I don't know what he said, but he traced runes in the air over Evan. I tried to use *vitalle* to shove the man away, but I couldn't, and...everything started glowing..." She closed her eyes, but she could still see Evan's bright form seared into her eyelids. "I tried to..." She looked back at her burned palms. "But everything went black. When I woke, the men's trail led into the wild hills, and Evan was gone without a trace."

Kellen rubbed his own scarred palms. "That wasn't your fault," he said quietly.

"No," she agreed. "I was only twelve. I didn't stand a chance against them. But I never want to be there again, in that place where someone else's safety is in my hands. I'm not that person. I'm..." She looked around the library. "Bo is that person. Being here, I've learned the Kalesh language and history, I've found ancient maps to help him, I'm close to recreating the *solus* potion those men used so I can learn the history of the box from the remnants it held." Her gaze fell back to the maps, and she sighed. "So, as alluring as Bo's life is—and sometimes it is very alluring—I'm..." She gestured to the desk. "This person."

He opened his mouth as though he'd argue, but she reached into the collection of glass and pulled out a clean vial. "I want to show the serum to the Shield."

He hesitated only a moment. "I'm headed up to take these books to him anyway."

Kate poured a little serum into the vial and, trying not to look at the maps as she passed, followed Kellen up the ramp.

"Will it run out?" he asked over his shoulder. "If you share too many memories?"

"I think so. I think the tenea serum in it will deteriorate over time. And the more memories it tries to hold, the faster that will happen." She held up the vial. "But this only used two drops of the serum, and I have two entire vials. So I can always make more."

They found the Shield leaned back in his pillow-filled chair. When Kellen came close, the old man glanced over and his eyes widened.

"Books!" He was reaching for them when he noticed Kate and stopped. "Katria! I found it!" He rummaged through the stack in front of him. "I found the book for you!"

"I don't need it anymore." She held out the vial. "It works!"

He stopped, his eyes lighting. "Really? Well done, my dear! But the book isn't about the serum." He pulled out a small brown volume.

Kate traded him for the vial of serum, which he held up toward the light.

She flipped the book open. Every page was blank. Except it didn't feel blank. "This is…"

Kellen looked over from where he was situating the new pile of books. "That has a lot of *verus* ink in it."

"Indeed." The Shield set an unlit candle on a stack of books near Kate.

She touched her finger to the wick. *"Verus elucida."* With a surge of *vitalle,* the flameless blue-white light appeared.

Silver ink shimmered into view. A diagram of a fat nine-pointed star was on one side, each tip labeled with a short paragraph. The other side was filled with slanted, elegant script.

"This is…" Kate's finger trailed over the words. "A poem? Or a riddle?" She glanced up at the Shield. "In some dialect of Old Kalesh?"

"My conclusion as well."

"How…?" She turned the page. "I had no idea we had another Kalesh book."

The Shield sighed. "Misplaced books plague my very existence. That little treasure was actually pushed to the back of a shelf behind a set of puzzle books on the fourth level. Which isn't terrible, since it does seem to contain riddles and puzzles, but its language demands it be shelved on the second floor, don't you agree?"

"I do."

"Especially since the part I believe you will be most interested in is not a riddle at all." He reached over and flipped to the inside of the front cover. The moment the *verus* light shone on it, a map glinted into view. "Although it is, in fact, the answer to a riddle you have."

Kate moved the book closer to the light. "The northwest corner of the Kalesh Empire." She took in the familiar hills and mountains wrapping around the western and northern edge of the map. The main river split where it flowed out of the northern mountains, an odd enough thing for a river that Kate had spent a decent amount of time wondering why. Most turned east and flowed toward a series of lakes. The rest wound south along the base of the mountains that headed that direction. One of the smaller tributaries was missing but, aside from that, it held everything she expected.

Morrow, where Bo had written from, was marked with a very small dot near the bottom, along with quite a few other small cities. The elven forest called the White Wood was tucked into the corner between the mountain ranges, and—

"Home!" She looked up to find the Shield smiling. "Home is a city!"

"Indeed," the old man said, picking up the top book from Kellen's pile.

"The emperor died near *Home*!" She looked at the map. "Why on earth was Sorrn all the way up in this corner of the Empire? Was he going to the White Wood? Did something happen with the elves?" Kate's gaze snagged on a note near Morrow. "What does 'last safe town' mean?"

"Maybe it literally is the last safe town. Aren't those little drawings of monsters around the White Wood?"

On the next page, the title of the book was written in large letters. "*Monsters of the North*."

The Shield gave her a pleased hum. "Possibly not meant as metaphorically as other—"

The old man drew in a sharp breath, and both Kate and Kellen looked up from the book.

The Shield's eyes were unfocused. "Someone opened the door…"

Kate glanced around the library. There was not a single door. Several floors below them, the hallway to the Stronghold did have a door, but she'd never seen it closed. Much like the front door of the tower itself, unless some unusually strong storm was blowing. "What?"

"The door," the old man said, looking out the window. "Someone is at the door, and it's open." There was a note of uneasiness in his voice.

"What door?" Kellen asked.

Kate followed the Shield's gaze out the window. The tunnel leading out of the valley was just barely visible at the edge of her view. Her hand tightened on the book. "The door at the Wall?"

Kellen straightened. "Were we expecting anyone to come home?"

The Shield shook his head slowly. "I don't think they're human."

CHAPTER THIRTEEN

A CHILL ROLLED across Kate's back, like a draft of winter air had slipped through the library. She dropped the book and ran for the ramp. "Kellen!"

His heavy footsteps pounded behind her, and he caught up as they ran out into the Stronghold. "Who's ever opened the door besides us?" he shouted as he sprinted past her.

She ran out the front door after him into the brisk afternoon. "No one I've ever heard of!"

The shadowed mouth of the tunnel was empty.

Empty and alarmingly vulnerable.

The familiar passage that had always been the first breath of home suddenly felt like the single chink in the valley's armor.

She ran down the front steps two at a time, scanning the rest of the valley. The white-wooled sheep grazing in the grass along the valley floor were isolated and exposed. The tower itself rose high above her with no walls or battlements. Surrounded by nothing but empty air.

Just as she leapt onto the gravel path, Kellen cast out, and the pressure sent her stumbling to the side. His wave surged out like an explosion, racing through the valley ten times farther than hers would ever reach. The snips of *vitalle* in each blade of grass lit into a smoldering blanket. The round shapes of sheep grazing flared up, and farther out, smaller things like rabbits were revealed, tucked unseen in the grass.

Kate followed the path of the wave all the way to the edge of the valley, where it lit even the distant trees before it was corralled by the cliff walls.

Kellen slowed at the entrance to the tunnel, and Kate stopped next to him, her breath coming fast.

The tunnel was empty, but a patch of green forest was visible through the open door at the far end. A breeze pushed against Kate's cheeks from the outside world, and she shivered.

Shadows filled the woods between the trees at the far end, and Kate's gaze shifted among the dark patches, trying to make out any shape. "Can you make out things at this distance?"

The young man cast out, not in a circle, but in a tight path down the tunnel. It rolled out like a silent thunderclap, passing nothing but cold rock and earth until it burst out the far end and swelled into the trees, turning them to hot pillars of life.

Whether there was anything else among them was impossible to say at this distance.

"Well," Kate said, wiping her damp palms on her robe. "The door didn't open itself." She started forward, and Kellen stayed at her side.

"What's out there, if not a Keeper?" His hands were clenched into fists, held up at his chest as though he expected a brawl to break out.

"I don't know," Kate admitted.

"Maybe it *is* a Keeper. It's been five years since I came. It's nearly time for a someone new to appear."

"If the next Keeper is capable of both finding and opening the door without training, I'm scared of them already."

"Still better than the other ideas coming to my mind," he answered.

"Like what?"

"Rhundenn."

Kate let out a breath that wasn't quite relaxed enough to be a laugh. "I doubt there's a mythological reptilian creature out there."

"Then one of those...what are they called? The ancient Naponese mages who absorbed each other's powers?"

"Syrapten. Let's hope there's not one of those."

She stretched her mind forward, searching for a remnant. She caught a whiff of something foreign. "There's someone there, and they're definitely not human."

A breeze swirled into the tunnel, and a rich remnant flooded in with it. She stopped and grabbed Kellen's arm.

The scent encompassed an entire forest with needles and leaves and mossy fallen logs crumbling into the soil. The leafy green of a lakeshore. Ferns and streams and leaves. Layered amidst the smells, it held the shushing of the wind and the patter of the rain into water and the chittering chirps of countless creatures. But every bit of it was tainted with an unusual spice and the prickle of some needly sound.

"Kate?" Kellen asked, his voice thick with wariness.

"That remnant is..." She shook her head to clear it, letting go of Kellen's arm. "Huge."

"What? What has a huge remnant?" he whispered.

It reminded her very vaguely of... "A dragon."

Kellen's eyes widened. "A dragon?" he mouthed.

"This isn't a dragon," she clarified, "but it's more than us. More magical than us. More..."

"Powerful?" Kellen asked. "Dangerous?"

She shook her head. "I don't think so. A bit wild, maybe, but not habitually dangerous."

Kellen cast out a third time, and his wave surged out of the tunnel and into the clearing, where, just out of their view to the right, a single shape flared up at the edge of the forest against the background heat of trees. Human sized, but blazing far brighter than a human. "If it is a dragon," he whispered, "it's a small one."

The warmth of the trees began to fade, but the shape lingered a little longer. "An elf?"

"Just one?" Kellen whispered. "Are the elves in the Greenwood old enough to travel alone?"

"Not according to Douglon." Kate frowned down the tunnel. "And they're not that tall. But there haven't been elves in the Wildwood for over two hundred and fifty years, so I don't know where else one would come from."

Kellen leaned forward. "I've never met an elf."

"I've only met baby ones." Kate started cautiously toward the open door again. She shifted to the left side of the tunnel so she could see off to the right, past the entrance, and squinted against the sunlight shining into the clearing. Green and brown shadows speckled the forest beyond, and at first she saw nothing.

Until, against one of the larger trunks, a figure shifted, making itself barely distinguishable from the mottled woods around it. She was tall and lean and elven, and she slumped against the thick pine. Her hair hung over her shoulder in a thick braid, burnished with reds and golds, like a maple in autumn. The worn brown of her leather vest mirrored the trunks around her, and her long sleeves and pants were subtle greens. A small knife was sheathed in the strap of a worn pack lying diagonally across her chest.

Kate stepped forward, and her foot sent a pebble skittering across the ground. The elf shoved herself away from the tree, and her arm shot up. A small crossbow mounted on her forearm aimed a dart at Kate's chest.

Kate held her hands up, and the elf blinked at her, her large eyes bright. Almost feverish.

"Hello," Kate said warily, watching the tip of the dart. She probed the elf's remnant, sifting through the complexity of it. Under the surface, a metallic taste slid past, the sound of a whetstone along a blade, the coiled, latent feel that warriors always carried.

Everything about the elf was steeped in foreignness. Every scent too strong or slightly off. Every sound shifted to a subtly different—

A familiar scent tickled the edges of Kate's mind.

She yanked her eyes away from the sharp metal tip and studied the elf's face.

There was nothing familiar about her, but she did not look well. Disheveled strands of hair fell loose from her braid. Her skin was a faded, pale brown except for two flushed splotches on her cheeks. Dark smudges of exhaustion lay under her eyes. She blinked at them, and the crossbow pointed at Kate lowered.

The elf didn't spare a glance for Kellen. "I'm looking for Ria," she said in a voice both severe and ragged.

Kate's hands dropped. "I'm Ria. How do you know that name?"

A flicker of relief crossed the elf's face.

"No one calls me that," Kate said, "except—"

The familiar thread of remnant came again, sharp in her nose and crisply cold in her lungs.

In the vast emptiness of a place she couldn't see, a bell tolled.

Kate's gaze caught on the object clutched in the elf's other hand.

A box, its worn wood edged with metal straps. Its corners studded with small aged nails. The medallion on the top partially covered by the elf's long fingers.

"Wait," Kellen said, shifting closer. "Isn't that—"

"Where'd you get that?" Kate demanded, striding toward the elf.

The elf's shoulders loosened, and she held out the box with a grimace. "Bo asked me to bring it to you." Her accent pulled at the words strangely. The vowels were too long, the consonants all softened, and there was something low and angry running beneath it.

Kate stumbled to a stop, her gaze torn between the elf's face and the box, her mind desperately trying to understand her words. "Bo?"

The elf jiggled the aenigma box impatiently, and Kate took it, feeling the roughness of the metal straps against her fingers. The medallion sat affixed to the center of the lid, partially covering the runes carved beneath it. She ran her fingers over the carved lines, and the box hummed.

Tearing her eyes away from it, she looked back at the elf. "Bo had this? Where is he? Who are you?"

The red-haired elf sank against the tree again. The ferocity drained from her face, and her paleness took on a sickly cast. She had the ageless sort of looks elves were reported to have, but she didn't have the weight of centuries around her. If she were human, Kate would put her near her own age. Certainly younger than forty.

Regardless of her age, she looked ready to collapse.

She watched Kate closely with exhausted eyes, as though gauging something. "My name is Venn. I met Bo near the White Wood. He asked me to bring you this." Her tone bordered on belligerent.

Kate gripped the box so tightly that the edges dug into her fingers. She could feel Venn's remnant on it. New, fresh smudges, not worn into the box the way it would have been if the elf had touched it often. Bo's remnant was there too. Faded, but caught in crevices and cracks, worked into the runes.

A flood of questions built up in her like a tidal wave, and she took another step forward. She settled on the simplest. "You came from the White Wood? That's over a month away."

Venn's expression flattened. "I'm aware of that." Her honey-gold eyes flittered between Kate's face and the box. "You have the box," she said, as though defying Kate to disagree. "My task is complete." She started to turn away but stumbled and caught herself on the trunk.

The swirling questions in Kate's mind turned desperate. "Wait!"

Even propped up by the tree, the elf swayed slightly. A gash in the shoulder of her tunic lay open, revealing bright red skin beneath it.

"You're exhausted, and wounded, and..." Kate glanced down the path leading into the forest. "Oh...Did you come past the ghosts?"

Venn twitched.

"Ah," Kellen said. "That's explains how awful you look."

Kate gave him a quieting glance. "He means that's a hard way to end a month-long journey when you're wounded. Why don't you come to the Stronghold and rest for a night?"

"A guest?" Kellen asked slowly. "Do we usually invite guests in when they're angry, and we have no idea who they are?"

"She can open the door. What's the point of leaving her out here?"

He frowned. "Yes. How did you do that?"

Venn squeezed her eyes shut with a grimace. "The trees told me how."

There was a moment of silence as Kate glanced at the tall pines surrounding the clearing.

"They didn't tell you how to get around the ghosts, though?" Kellen asked, sounding almost hopeful.

Venn didn't open her eyes. "They said there is no way."

"That's...too bad," Kellen said quietly.

"Please come in," Kate said to the elf, trying to keep her voice patient.

The elf kept her eyes averted from the tunnel. "I don't go underground."

Kate's desperation shifted toward irritation. "It's just a tunnel." The words came out more condescending than she'd intended, and she took a breath. "There's a valley on the other side. Kellen can stay at this end and keep the door open. You'll be able to see both ends. We'll walk fast and be through it before you know it."

"My task is done," Venn said tiredly. She pushed herself off the tree and took a step back, then another. Her eyes locked on the box in Kate's hands. "You agree I gave you the box?" she demanded.

Kate glanced down at it. "Yes…"

Venn shook her head, as though trying to dislodge a thought. "I was just supposed to bring it to you."

Kate held out one hand, her irritation flaring into something hotter. "Wait!" The word snapped out like a command, and the elf stiffened. "You haven't told me where Bo is!"

"I have no idea!" Venn spat the words at her. "He called for me, and when I reached the clearing where he'd been, there was nothing but the box and this." She pulled a folded slip of paper from her pack and thrust it at Kate.

It was a torn off bit of paper with Bo's writing scrawled across it. *Take this to Ria at the Keepers' Stronghold—please.*

Kate turned it over, but there was nothing else. "But where was he?"

Venn managed a shrug.

Kate's fingers tightened on the note, crumpling it. A dozen questions crowded her mind, and she grabbed at one. "You didn't look for him? Just ran off on a month-long journey because he left you a note?"

"I looked," Venn said flatly. "He was gone."

"I thought elves could track anything through a forest."

Venn shoved herself up from the tree and pointed a finger at Kate. "I could follow every track leaving that clearing. Elven, human…" Her jaw twitched before she continued, "But none of them were Bo's."

"You mean someone carried him away? Why? Who? Elves?"

"I don't know." Venn bit off each word. She swayed slightly and raised her hands to scrub at her face. "All he asked was that I bring it to you!"

Kellen shifted and reached a hand toward her. "I think you should sit down."

Venn glanced at the tunnel, then up at the towering cliff above them, and she shuddered. She turned away and fell to her knees. "Too heavy," she murmured.

She grabbed for the tree trunk next to her, struggling to rise, but only managed to shuffle one knee forward before she collapsed face down on the ground.

Kate ran over and knelt down, rolling the elf onto her back. Venn's breath was shallow and slow, her skin flushed, her forehead hot under Kate's hand.

"I thought elves could heal themselves," Kellen said, standing uncertainly at Venn's feet.

"So did I." Kate set her palm on Venn's arm and cast out. The elf's *vitalle* was stronger than any human's Kate had ever felt, but it moved sluggishly, and there was a bundle of heat in her left shoulder wrapped around a cold knot deep in the wound. "There's something in there. We need to get her to Gerone. Will you carry her?"

"She said she didn't want to go," Kellen objected.

"By the time she wakes up, she'll be in the valley, and she can leave the moment she wants to."

Kellen's brow creased. "I don't—"

"What else are we going to do?" Kate interrupted. "Ask Gerone to walk all the way out here with all his herbs and stay with her overnight while she recovers?"

Kellen sighed and picked up the elf. "She's not going to wake up while I'm carrying her in the tunnel, right?"

"I don't know about elves," Kate said, "but if she were human, I'd be worried she might not wake up at all."

"It's just…" He gave Venn a nervous look. "She's already angry."

"Well, I'm angry too."

Kellen glanced at her. "But you're not scary."

Kate waved him toward the tunnel. "Come on. She needs help. And then she's going to answer a *lot* of questions."

CHAPTER FOURTEEN

KATE'S EYES stayed locked on Venn's feet, hanging limply over Kellen's arm, as she followed him into the tunnel. His pace was so fast that the elf's legs bounced and swayed.

Questions swirled in Kate's mind, spinning in a growing pool of frustration.

Signs of travel hung on Venn like moss on a tree. Her leather boots were splattered with several different colors of mud under a thin layer of dust. The cuffs of her pants were frayed, the elbow of her tunic ripped. There was dirt under her nails and in between her fingers.

Kellen's sappy remnant threaded through the rich tapestry of sensations from Venn, and Kate waded into them, parsing out the individual pieces. The scents of the forest were so strong they were like burying herself in a pile of autumn leaves. Underlying it like a rock shelf beneath the earth was the metallic taste of someone who'd known fighting, though it lacked the wet coating of brutality that some warriors carried.

She caught an impression of open space, a grand vista. Vastness.

It felt like wandering and traveling and curiosity, and Kate ran her senses through it like a comb. Even here, boxed in by the tunnel walls, Venn's remnant somehow wended its way through distant lands.

Something about it reminded Kate of Bo's blustery, windswept scent, and the similarity irritated her, like an itch under her skin.

Bo had never mentioned an elf. What possible reason would Venn have to travel over a month just to deliver a box for him—based only on a note?

None of the answers that sprang to her mind soothed the itch.

"Isn't that the box you found in that mine?" Kellen said over his shoulder.

Kate dragged her gaze back to the box, hardly believing she was clutching it in her own hands.

It *was* the box.

Even in the gloom of the tunnel, she was sure of it.

Except…it couldn't possibly be *the* box.

Not here.

Without Bo.

Carried by some strange elf.

There was no sense in it. No reason.

Twenty years of searching and it was just…here?

She'd imagined holding the box a thousand times. Each time, Bo had brought it, and she'd been thrilled. Fascinated.

But at this moment, she didn't feel anything like that.

The aenigma box sat in her hands, and it wrung something inside her.

"It is the box," she answered him finally, brushing her thumb across the side, feeling its strange remnant. All the things she'd sensed long ago in the mine were still there—sharp spiciness, frigid cold, even the echo of a distant bell.

A smear of Venn's remnant smudged one corner, new and thin

and invasive, but the traces of Bo's windy, wild scent were caught all over it. He'd touched every surface, prying into cracks, running his fingers over the carvings until the grooves were lined with his remnant.

It was faded, matching Venn's claim that she'd had it for a month.

Kate's mind jumped to the next glaring question, and a tingly stream of nervousness threaded down her arms and into her hands.

The answer was already blatantly obvious, but she still forced herself to search for traces of anyone else.

They were nearing the end of the tunnel, and the growing light showed the dings and scratches where remnants might hide.

"Did you know Bo had found it?" Kellen asked.

"I had no idea he was even close. He wrote a letter eight weeks ago that I never received, though." She probed each crevice in the wood, her heart sinking further with each one.

Kellen turned to look at her, his eyes wide. "Do you think he also found your younger brother?"

She tore her gaze away from the box, swallowing down the disappointment that flooded her. "There's no sign Evan touched this. At least not recently. Only Bo."

Kellen made a sympathetic noise as they hurried out of the tunnel. Under the open sky of the valley, his shoulders relaxed a little, but he kept a quick pace as he strode toward the Stronghold. "Do you think Bo's in trouble?"

She grimaced at the question. "He's often in trouble." Which was true. She just usually didn't find out about it until he'd gotten himself out of it and was safe enough to write her a letter. Which felt far preferable to this. "He probably has a hundred friends near the White Wood by now and got help from them." Her voice didn't sound particularly reassuring, even to herself. "He makes friends everywhere he goes."

Kellen looked down at Venn. "Clearly. But why'd he send the box?"

Kate blew out a breath. "That is…odd. Although, his plan was always to find the box and send it to me. We'd hoped I'd have the *solus* potion ready by then, though. Maybe he had something else keeping him there and thought Venn was the fastest way to get it to me, and the safest. Sending it by elf isn't a bad idea, really."

Kellen glanced at Kate. "You could go find out…"

"Where? To the White Wood?" She shook her head, still gripping the box tightly. "No. We'll see what Venn has to say when she wakes. Until then, I'm not going to let myself worry."

Kellen gave an unconvinced hum and hurried through the kitchen door. Kate followed him to the sickroom in the back, where there was a clatter of activity.

Both Gerone and Mikal were there, clearing off the table in the center of the room, pushing tea pots and powders and drying herbs to the back of the counter that ringed the room. Their breaths came quick, as though they'd rushed to get there.

Mikal stopped in the act of setting a small crucible on the counter. "An elf!"

"How did you know to come here?" Kellen asked, carrying Venn to the table.

"The Shield said we were needed." Mikal hurried over to look more closely.

"How did he know?" Kellen asked.

"Apparently the tunnel told him." Mikal shrugged and reached out to help Kellen extricate his arms from under Venn. "Watch her feet!"

One of Venn's legs slid off the side of the table, twisting her body. Kellen leaned over to grab it, pulling his arm from under her shoulders and dropping her head to the table with a thunk.

"And her head!" Mikal chided.

Kate set the aenigma box out of the way on a counter and

opened the drapes further. A sheen of sweat glistened on Venn's forehead, and the splotches of red on her cheeks were stark against the sunken greyness of the skin under her eyes.

"She collapsed outside the wall," Kate said. "There's a wound in her shoulder that's closed, but I think there's something in it."

Kellen was sent to the kitchen to mix a poultice for the wound, and Kate stepped closer to the elf, letting the complex remnant flow around her, blocking out the other sensations from the room.

A thread of cold silence wound through the remnant, and Kate closed her eyes, drawing it out.

It reminded her of winter. Of standing in the woods, the air bracingly cold in her lungs, huge, soft flakes drifting through the air around her. The world muffled in white, the silence so thick it felt like a sound.

Stillness and freedom and solitude.

"You're right, there's something in there," Gerone's voice said from so close that Kate's eyes flew open.

Both Gerone and Mikal bent over Venn's head.

Kate set her hand on Venn's unhurt arm and cast out into her body. The swarm of energy in the elf's shoulder was clustered around something dark. "Maybe a bit of thorn?"

"It's deep for a thorn," Mikal said, "but it's either that or some kind of stinger. Her body has been working hard to heal, but based on how exhausted she is, I think she pushed herself too hard to get here." He glanced at Kate. "Any idea why?"

"Not a clear one." She was about to pull her hand off when she noticed a hum of energy on Venn's forearm under the crossbow. Kate unbuckled the small weapon and pushed the elf's sleeve up. Complicated runes were tattooed on her skin. "What's this?" A trickle of *vitalle* moved in the runes, very slowly seeping into Venn's body. "I didn't know elves used runes."

"Neither did I." Gerone set a hand on Venn's arm near the

tattoo, and Kate felt a delicate, searching wave as he cast out. "It's tethered to her *vitalle*. Although I'm not sure exactly what it's trying to do. Whatever it is, it's taking the little reserve she has to keep working."

Kate traced a finger over it, and the markings pulled a whisper of *vitalle* out of her fingertip. The tattoo pushed it into Venn's arm, and it was absorbed into the elf's body, lost in the sluggish attempts she was making to heal herself.

"Mikal," Gerone said, "I'll need your help pulling out whatever's in here." The biting scent of vinegar and spirits cut through the room as he cleaned her shoulder.

When Gerone made the first incision, Venn didn't move. Working quickly, he cut into her shoulder, and Mikal used a small set of tweezers to draw out something small and black. Gerone started to clean the wound while Mikal moved closer to the window.

"Strangleweed thorn, I think," he mused.

Gerone took out a bandage and began to wrap the wound.

Venn's tattoo was dark against the paleness of her skin, and Kate studied it more closely. The complexity was impressive. The most pronounced mark was an ancient form of the rune for *hinder*. Or maybe, more accurately, *block*. But the runes around it were harder to translate. They intertwined with each other in a circle, and Kate's eyes traced around them. It was an unending path, a continual working of…something. She brushed the tattoo again, and it pulled a breath of *vitalle* out of her and pressed it into the elf's body. Not toward her wound, though. It kept the heat in her arm.

Gerone looked at the marks with curiosity.

"Whatever it is," Kate said, "it takes a small flow of *vitalle* and keeps it right here."

He made a thoughtful hum. "Does the tattoo feel depleted?"

Kate set her palm over the runes. Venn's arm was hot with

fever, but the warmth of the *vitalle* was an utterly different sort of heat, and Kate followed it as a thread seeped out of her hand and into Venn's arm. "It feels...hollow. A bit hungry."

"You should keep feeding it," Mikal said from where he stood, cleaning the knife. "Even from here, I can see it speaks of holding things back. It'd be a shame to heal her shoulder just to have her die of...whatever she's been stopping with that."

"I agree." Gerone turned back to the bandage.

Kate left her hand on the tattoo. The marks never pulled anything more than a whisper of *vitalle*, but they kept up the draw and slowly grew more satisfied.

Venn let out a groan, and Kate glanced up at her.

"Venn?" Kate asked.

The elf opened her eyes, and her gaze darted around the sick-room. "Where am I?" she demanded, her voice low and rough with pain.

"In the Keepers' Stronghold," Kate answered. "You collapsed. There was something embedded in your shoulder. Gerone removed it."

Venn's face curled into a scowl, and she yanked her arm away from Kate's hand. The movement jerked the bandage out of Gerone's hands. Venn hissed in pain. "That was unnecessary," she managed between gritted teeth. She shoved her sleeve down, covering her tattoo. "I can heal myself." She slid her legs off the table and pushed herself up to sit, glaring at Kate. "It would already be done if I hadn't needed to travel for weeks on end."

"I'm sure," Gerone said kindly. "Such a wound would be deadly to a human, but I doubt it would be the end of you."

"It would not." Venn stood, staggering before she got her footing. Kate reached out to steady her, but Venn gave her a fierce look. "It would *not* have killed me," she said, as though daring anyone to disagree.

Kate raised an eyebrow. "I believe you."

Venn scrutinized her, as though searching for some trick in her words, then gave a tight nod.

"I can finish off the bandage, if you just allow me a moment," Gerone offered, but she waved him off.

"How did the tip of a strangleweed thorn get so deeply embedded in your shoulder?" Mikal asked.

"An accident." Venn pushed away from the table and crossed the few steps to the counter holding her personal effects. Her last step stumbled, and she grabbed the counter for support.

Kate took a step toward her. "Maybe you should lie back down."

Venn pulled her bag closer. "What is the payment?" she asked, the words not particularly warm.

Gerone looked at her curiously. "No payment is necessary. You were hurt and we could help."

Venn pulled a small pouch out of her pack and fished out a foreign-looking silver coin. She set it on the counter and pushed it toward Gerone. "Thank you," she said brusquely. Sliding on her leather bracer, she began attaching the small crossbow to it. A trickle of blood dripped down her shoulder from her wound.

"Keepers aren't known in your part of the world," Mikal said, "but we never require payment for helping—"

"I know who the Keepers are," she interrupted.

"Oh?" Gerone exchanged glances with Mikal. "That's...good."

Venn leaned her hip on the counter and squeezed her eyes shut for a moment before continuing to work on the crossbow.

Kate folded her arms. "How do you know Bo?"

Venn gave his box a cold sidelong glance. "I don't, really."

Kate watched her fumble with the buckle for a moment, trying to keep a rein on her rising irritation. "You need to come up with a better answer than that."

The elf finished with the buckle, adjusted the crossbow on her forearm, then lifted her pack and settled it on her unhurt shoulder. "Is the only way out of here through that tunnel?"

Kate moved to stand between Venn and the door. "How do you know Bo?" she repeated.

Venn gave an exasperated sigh. "I don't," she repeated, enunciating each word.

"Yet you went on a month-long errand for him?"

"He asked." Venn sidestepped Kate and headed for the door.

Gerone frowned after her. "Some rest would help you feel stronger. You're welcome to stay..."

Venn ignored him and moved down the hall, running one hand along the wall to steady herself.

Kate started after her. "Wait!"

Venn didn't slow.

Kate cast about for some way to stop her. What would stop a belligerent elf?

"Will you join us for dinner?" she called.

Venn jerked to a stop but didn't turn.

Gerone let out a small chuckle. "I'm not sure that tradition is meant to be used as a weapon," he said quietly.

Venn turned slowly, her expression irritated.

"Please," Kate said, not bothering to make the entreaty polite, "would you join us for dinner?"

Venn's jaw twitched, and her hand gripped the strap of her pack so tightly every knuckle stood out white against her skin.

"Once," Kate said, holding Venn's angry gaze, "elves considered an invitation to a meal to be so great a favor, they wouldn't dream of refusing. How do they feel about it these days?"

Venn exhaled a long, tightly controlled breath, her gaze gouging into Kate. "I would be honored," she said coldly. "But then I'm leaving. I'll heal faster if I sleep among the trees."

Gerone clapped a hand on Kate's shoulder. "Excellent! There's soup cooking and bread baking, and everything can be ready in an hour." He held up the coin. "Since you overpaid for my services, Venn, would you allow me to even the scales by patching you up?"

Venn's eyes were still locked on Kate as though she'd rather throttle her than eat dinner with her. "Yes," she said firmly. "Even the scales."

"And Katria," Gerone said mildly, "the sickroom is generally a place where we keep animosity to a minimum. Perhaps you could wait outside while we finish with Venn." Kate started to shake her head, but he squeezed her shoulder. "Let everyone rest and heal for an hour, then we can find a more congenial tone over dinner, don't you think?"

"Fine." Kate picked up the aenigma box and strode into the hallway, where Venn still stood.

The elf's eyes locked on the box, and she shifted out of the way, as though trying to avoid it more than make room for Kate to pass.

Kate didn't bother to make her smile look genuine. "I look forward to hearing your answers to so very many questions at dinner."

CHAPTER FIFTEEN

KATE STRODE into the kitchen and caught the smirk on Kellen's face. "Dinner?" he asked.

She allowed herself a small smile. "It was the only idea I had." Setting the box down in a bright spot on the table, she sat. "All right, what's going on?"

Her memory serum wasn't enough. She needed the full potion the men had used. The liquid that drew out not just the remnants in the objects, but the memories of what had happened to it.

She tapped her fingers onto the table. It would be days until she had that, even if her first ideas of how to fuse the remnant amplifier and the memory serum worked.

"How did Bo find you?" she asked the box, studying it as though the answer were marked into its surface. "*Where* did Bo find you? And why didn't he tell me?"

As a child, she'd merely thought the box looked old, and yes, the wood was scratched and marked with age. It was worn to a smooth honeyed brown wherever fingers had rubbed it over the years, the grain only growing darker and more textured near the edges of the metal straps that protected the corners. But every edge and every seam were still tight. The metal was dinged, but each strip was straight and whole, each small nail along it placed precisely. The box was old but incredibly well-made.

The gold medallion was exactly as she remembered it. Intrusive.

Shoved onto the center of the top, it was too large and too pretentious for the box. Three clusters of runes were carved into the lid, set in a triangular shape, but the medallion covered enough of each that Kate could only make out bits and pieces.

"Who put the ugly gold emblem in the middle?" Kellen asked, leaving the pot of herbs he was simmering and coming to examine the box.

"It's the Imperial Seal of the last dynasty of the Kalesh Empire." She grabbed the medallion with her fingertips and tugged at it. It wobbled slightly, as though it was only affixed in the very center. "They liked to confiscate valuables and place their seal on them."

"Whoever put that on is an idiot."

"Or at least couldn't read runes," Kate agreed. "I imagine they thought the marks were just decorative."

"Is that the bowing king?" Kellen pointed to the top group of runes.

She nodded. "And this one is something about standing at the wall."

"I don't recognize any of the third," he mused.

"Neither do I." She crossed the kitchen to Gerone's basket of utensils, searching for something thin but sturdy.

"Do they still hum like they did in your memory?" Kellen asked.

"Touch them and see." Kate pulled a small dull knife out of the bottom of the basket.

Kellen drew in a breath, and she turned to find him running his finger over the runes.

"Can you hear the bell?" she asked.

"No, it just vibrates." He picked up the box, examining it from every angle. "It's lighter than it should be, don't you think? Even if it's empty?" He shook it, but there was no noise. Looking unsatisfied, he set it back down. "How does it open?"

"The man who took it from us said it doesn't." Kate worked the knife under the medallion, trying not to scratch the wood as she pried up gently on the disk.

"It feels like it should open," Kellen said. "It feels like it's meant to hold things."

"I agree." The medallion shifted, and Kate rocked the knife back and forth until the gold disk popped loose and tumbled onto the table, landing on its face and revealing the short nail embedded in its back.

It left a small pit in the center of a lighter circle of wood on the lid, and Kate drew in a breath at the intricacy of the runes that ran through it.

Kellen let out an appreciative "Oooh…"

The three main clusters of runes were definitely set in a triangle around the center, but they were not separate from each other.

Strokes from each stretched through the center, connecting to other runes, arcing and crossing in a star-like pattern, or maybe like a flower with nine petals. It wasn't quite regular, but it flowed in a way that drew Kate's eye from one rune to the next like she was being pulled down a path.

Kellen studied the topmost rune. "That doesn't say *a bowing king*."

"No." Small lines crossed it, shifting the meaning to a more violent one. "*A king brought to his knees*." The root of the *king* rune trailed down through the central star and connected to the lower left group. "This one isn't about standing at the wall either. I'd say it's *the wall cannot stand*."

"There's an accent on it," Kellen said. "Maybe battlement instead of wall?"

"Yes, *the battlement cannot stand*. Although the reason why is blank." She pointed to a gap in the rune.

"Maybe the important part is that the battlements fail?" Kellen mused. "Not why?"

The gap where the cause should stand was odd, though. Too empty. The rune could easily have been formed with the causation left blank and not needed such a gaping hole in the strokes.

Tiny scratches and dings covered every surface of the box, some deep enough to be called gouges, but most were featherlight scuffs. Fewer marks were visible where the medallion had protected it, but there were still a few faint lines.

Several of them fit the star too neatly to be merely scuffs. "Look. The rune clusters are connected in other ways, too." Kate traced a thin line that began in the gap of the battlement rune and curled up into the king.

"Is the king the wall?" Kellen asked. "Is he protecting something?"

"No, it's connecting the cause of the battlement's failure to the reason the king has been brought down." The thin lines linked portions of the complex runes to each other in unexpected ways. "There are a lot of connections here."

"What's the third cluster mean?"

Kate pulled her attention to the group of runes at the bottom right. "Solace?" The largest one was something like that. The marks around it were unclear, but there was an impression of loss and hollowness. A broken finality, hopeless—except for the small symbols of light and life entwined with it.

Each time she focused on a part, trying to tease out a firm meaning, her eyes were drawn away along paths leading to other runes or through the central star to one of the other clusters.

The hopelessness in the runes tugged at her. Even without

fully understanding them, she knew they were written by someone who'd lost something precious. Everything about them echoed the empty space inside her still left by Evan's absence.

"These thin lines remind me of the way I connected the *verus* ink words," Kellen said thoughtfully. "Maybe they're for letting *vitalle* flow from one to the other more than connecting their meanings."

Kate pulled her eyes away from the mournful runes. "Maybe it's doing both." She touched the center of the star and pressed some *vitalle* into it.

Strands of fiery heat burst out along the star and flowed into each rune cluster, setting them ablaze. The pronounced shapes turned to molten streams, the smaller symbols intertwined with them like glowing threads, and behind it all, a net of hair-thin scratches lit like a spider web in the firelight, tying the runes together with intricate connections that layered one on the next.

"Well," Kellen said, his voice quiet with awe, "I guess we know which are runes and which are scratches."

Kate funneled more *vitalle* into the design to keep the lines glowing. "The thickest lines are the main connections, but each smaller line adds nuance."

"Don't tell Mikal how many of these are unfamiliar to me."

"They're ancient." Kate pointed to the small barbed line near the top of the *king* rune. "They put more amplifiers into the main rune than we do today. For instance, this denotes something small. The king of a small land, even while this arc over it means wealth. Great wealth, considering how thick it is. I'd say these runes are at least three hundred years old. Possibly as much as five."

Kellen glanced at her. "Why is the box still in one piece, then?"

"I'm not..." A faint reflection of light caught in a scratch on one of the metal bands. "Maybe because of these." She moved her finger to the metal and pressed *vitalle* into it. A lattice of runes blazed into light, racing across the strap and spreading out onto each bit of metal it touched. In a heartbeat, the entire box was outlined in tiny glowing runes. Protection from rust and water and fire and dozens of other things she couldn't quite make out.

Kellen let out a huff of breath somewhere between amazement and shock. "What was this box made to hold?"

Kate pulled her finger off the box, and the runes faded back to dull scratches on the surface. She stepped back and considered the box. "And is it still in there?" She crossed her arms. "I've been waiting to find this box for twenty years in the hopes it would tell me something about where Evan is, and now that it's here, I'm suddenly more worried about Bo."

"Kellen," Mikal called from the sickroom, "where's the poultice?"

The young man pushed away from the table and picked up the now steaming pot. "It has to open," he said, heading toward the sick room.

"Oh, it opens. I can feel that it opens…"

The words lingered in the empty kitchen, feeling oddly familiar.

Kate straightened, Bo's cryptic letter echoing in her mind.

"It opens! By moonlight and hope! Bo, *this* is what you meant! The box opens!"

CHAPTER SIXTEEN

KATE SPUN to look out the window. She'd read that letter so many times, she had it memorized.

Ria! It opens! I think by moonlight? And maybe...hope?

The moon was out now—just a crescent, and it was still afternoon, but if the moon was in the sky, there should be a tiny amount of moonlight.

She grabbed the box and ran out into the cool afternoon. There, hanging high in the sky, was a waxing crescent, pearly and distant, and she struck out across the grass.

Moonlight and hope...

Those were two very different things.

Moonlight might hold some *vitalle.* Sunlight did, anyway, and moonlight was just a reflection of that.

But hope? Hope was...different. Hope was a thought, an emotion. It was confined to a person. You couldn't pour hope into a box.

She reached a small table situated in the sunshine and sank

onto a bench. There were no trees to block the light, and she cast out toward the moon but felt nothing. Sini was the only Keeper who could feel the *vitalle* in sunlight. Even though she was currently at court, Kate could almost hear her describing how much *vitalle* rained down in the sunlight. Kate situated the box in whatever moonlight there was and set her hands on its sides, imagining the top soaking in the *vitalle*.

"But how am I supposed to give you hope?" she asked the box.

Emotions resonate, Keeper Will had told her years ago when he was exploring whether the way she could sense remnants was similar to how he could feel people's emotions. *If you're angry, you can make the people around you angry. If you're happy, that's contagious too.*

"All right. What do I hope for?" She tapped a finger on the smooth old wood. "I hope Venn explains herself." That particular hope felt more like irritation, but she watched the box closely. Nothing changed.

"I hope..." She rubbed her thumb over one of the dinged, rounded nails holding the metal strap onto the edge of the box. "I hope I can figure out Bo's clue." She pushed the idea of hoping out through her palms, but *vitalle* flowed out instead, lighting the runes along all the edges.

She paused.

Bo couldn't move *vitalle*. Almost no one could. The nine Keepers currently alive were most likely the only people in Queensland who could. There were a few others who could sense *vitalle*. Keeper Will's wife, Sora, couldn't manipulate it at all, but she could feel when living things were near her. Bo couldn't even do that. If he'd managed to open the box, it wasn't by channeling the *vitalle* in the moonlight or putting anything of himself in the box.

A thought struck her, and she let her hands fall from the box.

Leaning on her elbows, she fixed it with an irritated look. "Did you say *moonlight* just because you're obsessed with the moon, Bo?"

But the moon is out, Ria, Bo had written once at the end of a letter from a ruined Kalesh temple where he'd failed to find anything interesting, *and...if I could just see the world from where she does, if I could just step away from all of this, could I have faith that everything is moving as it should? That the sun and the moon and even this mess of a world are moving as they should? That there's an order and a purpose forging ahead, unhurried and unbattered by all our failures? I ask her, but she does nothing more than slip slowly through the sky. Somehow, silently, she gives me hope, though. So tomorrow I'll start toward the ruins at Kelchren. Someday, Ria, I may actually find something.*

"Moonlight and hope are the same things to you, aren't they?" she asked. "But I'm not feeling particularly hopeful. An old man in the Wellstone said there were monsters in the White Wood, and so did a map that apparently the Stronghold wanted to give me, and now you're..." She blew out a breath. "Your cryptic elven friend says you're gone. But you sent the box here, so..." She rubbed her hand across her mouth, as though that could stifle her next question. "Are you coming too?"

There was no logic to the question, but the idea laced its fingers into her. He wouldn't have sent the box if he were coming himself, but she clung to the idea anyway, hoping it could stave off her growing worry. "That man in the Wellstone took the first snow as the sign to come home."

She rubbed her thumb along the corner of the box and looked up at the moon. There was something about it, suspended in the blue, pitted and scarred, yet still serene. Unruffled by anything happening below.

She lingered on the idea of Bo sitting here with her, actually here, with that steady solidness he always had. Offering his crooked smile as he spoke too fast, his words tripping over each other like they still did when he was excited, explaining where he'd found the box, how he'd opened it, telling new theories about where Evan might be…

"Maybe you thought the same thing," she whispered, "that it was time to come home." Even though the thought was foolish, it felt like cool water on a parched tongue.

Kate dropped her eyes to the box and drew in a breath.

On the front, a shallow drawer sat open, just a hair. She grabbed the edges with her fingernails and scrabbled at it until it opened.

Summer wind wafted out, tumbling and rolling over distant hills, full of wandering and curiosity and the shushing exhale that spoke of amusement and wonder.

Bo's remnant swirled around her as strongly as if he stood in front of her, and she stared into the drawer for a long moment before she saw what was in it.

Folded neatly to fit inside the drawer was a small stack of paper covered in Bo's handwriting with her own name at the top, dated *26th of Madny, Spire Library at Morrow.*

She pulled it out and did a quick conversion from the Kalesh lunar calendar that still existed in that part of the world. Madny was the Dry Moon, so the full moon at harvest time. "Two months ago?" She glanced over the first few paragraphs, which spoke of him arriving in Morrow and gaining access to a strange little library in a squat tower called the Spire. "Ahhh…The longer letter you were writing when you dashed off your cryptic, nonsensical one."

The first page was filled with nothing more interesting than a few quirky stories of the local people, and she glanced back into the drawer.

Settled in the bottom was a thick, well-worn journal.

She pulled it out and flipped it open, finding it full of Bo's writing, small and cramped as though he had striven to fit as many words as possible onto each page. On the final used page, she found a few tightly written sentences.

> ...*definitely Kalesh. You'd love one item in particular. It's a medallion from a necklace. There are words on it—I just can't make out enough of it after all this time to figure out what it says.*

She paused at how normal and unflustered he sounded. No mention of aenigma boxes or new clues about Evan.

Or references to red-haired elves.

She flipped back a page to see whom he was writing to.

Her own name was written at the top, dated five weeks ago.

> *Ria,*
> *I made it as far north as the White Wood.*

She felt a chill at the words. "Tell me there's nothing troubling there," she whispered.

> *You'd like it. The elven wood fills a huge valley between the northern mountains and the rocky hills that run south, and it's full of pine trees. The trunks are white, though. Bone white, if you want to be chilling. Except the needles are too green to be chilling. I can't find the words to tell why it feels so...off. Of course, maybe it's not the trees—maybe it's the people. They're terribly superstitious about the woods.*

She thumbed through the rest of the journal, finding each entry addressed to her and filled with descriptions of places he'd explored, small sketches of interesting finds, maps of a town or some ruins.

On the first page, she found one dated three years earlier from the town of Norserin in Gringonn.

Ria, if I ever die and this (or any of my journals) finds its way to your hands, you're probably going to think it strange that it's all addressed to you, but the truth is I need to talk things out some-times, and in all my travels, I've never found anyone easier to talk to than my little sister. You'd be surprised at how many puzzles you've helped me solve by being a page in my book. Maybe I should have asked your permission before dragging you into all these riddles, but you've never minded before, and I suppose if you ever get tired of all my letters and thoughts, I don't want to know.

CHAPTER SEVENTEEN

KATE CLOSED THE JOURNAL, feeling oddly intrusive, despite it being addressed to her.

She set it down and something about it looked odd. It took her a moment to realize that it looked too thick to fit inside the shallow drawer.

She set it back in, though, and it fit with room to spare. Tilting the box, she let the journal slide over and thunk against the side.

There was so much extra room that it was shocking she hadn't heard the book clunking around.

She tilted it again, and the drawer started to shut. She grabbed it and pulled the journal out. "I think I'll keep this where all I need is curiosity to read it, thank you," she said. "Not where I have to use hope and moonlight."

She set the book down on the table and was going to pick up the letter again when she stopped.

The top of the journal sat even with the top of the drawer.

Except the journal was sitting flat on the table, and the bottom of the drawer was at least a finger's width above that. There was no way the book should fit.

She cast out as she tucked the top end of the journal back into the drawer. She caught no sense of *vitalle* moving, but when the top edge of the book slipped into the drawer, it...shrank. Or the drawer grew. Somehow, the journal fit. She felt unsteady for a moment, like she sat on a rocking boat instead of a stable bench. She pulled the book out and watched the box warily, but it did nothing aside from sit on the table.

Bo's letter caught her eye, and the normalcy of it felt like an anchor against the unmoored feeling of the box. The paper and his handwriting were just like dozens of his letters. The only unusual part was the strength of his remnant.

"Please tell me you're going to explain things, Bo. Where you found the box. Where you think Evan is. Actually, I'll take any information at this point."

The first page told only of reaching the town of Marrow and trying to gain access into their library. She skimmed, looking for any reference to an elf or the box or Evan. She found it in a new section on the second page dated six days later.

> *6th of Zemny, the Spire Library, Morrow*
>
> *Ria! It opens! Last night, I was sitting out under the moon—nearly full, and I was looking at the box. It was dim and so much like the first time we ever saw it that...for the first time in years, I felt hope. I looked up at the moon and wondered if Evan was nearby. If the box got here, maybe he did too, right?*
>
> *And when I looked back at the box, there was a little drawer partially opened. It was empty, but it didn't feel empty.*

The next section discussed his fiddling with the drawer, discovering how things bigger than it seemed to fit easily inside. He moved on to his searches in the library at Morrow, and she jumped ahead, landing on the description of records that Emperor Sorrn had passed through the area just before his death.

But Emperor Sorrn could wait. She turned to the next page, searching for any reference to what he was doing, or any mention of Evan.

Instead, she found more records of Bo heading farther north.

12th of Zemny, The Blind Pig Tavern, Home
I made it as far north as the White Wood. You'd like it. The
elven wood fills a huge valley between the northern mountains and
a line of rocky hills that run south, and it's full of pine trees. The
trunks are white, though. Bone white, if you want to be chilling.

That was the same as the journal entry. She glanced back at his book, wondering how many entries would match letters she'd received from him.

Skimming past what she'd seen in the journal, she continued.

I'm staying in the town of Home, which is small enough that
"town" may be too big of a word. It used to be larger, as the ruins
outside it indicate. The people are on edge, but I think they're prone
to wariness. They have more stories about monsters in the moun-
tains north of here than even they can keep straight. You'd love it.
Maybe you could make sense of which stories are based on truth and
which are tales made up to scare children.
I was afraid by the time I reached this far north that the
language would be more based off Old Kalesh than our common
tongue, but the old Immusmalan settlers and gold merchants must
have made it this far. There are a few Kalesh words sprinkled into
the local dialects, and the accent is strongly eastern, but everyone
here could easily be understood in Queensland. Which is good, since
my Kalesh is very rusty.
But, on a more interesting note, there's something to the rumor
that Emperor Sorrn died here. The town believes it, at least. There's
a ravine south of Home that they say is cursed. Long ago, it was the

main route into town, but the ravine is prone to massive rockslides (the supposed curse), and so they built a longer road by another path and still avoid the ravine.

I found the old road, though, and it had cracked paver stones from the quarry at Elheim!

Despite the gnawing worry in her stomach at the fact that he'd gone near the White Wood, Kate let out a little laugh.

Don't roll your eyes at that, Ria, the Empire used these pavers all over for the better part of a century. The marbling pattern is easy to recognize. I know you don't believe me, but it's more obvious than the way you think you can tell a true Atticus play from an imitation.

"I doubt that."

18th of Zemny, The Blind Pig tavern, Home

I'm close Ria! Really close! In the bottom of the ravine, I found the rim of a wagon wheel! Stamped! Empire! Third Era! Sized for an imperial governor's retinue!

Now I just need the weather to hold. There is already snow on top of the mountains to the north, even creeping down into the tree line. I've hired five men from Home young enough to brave the "cursed" ravine, and they're making good progress clearing the road.

There are actually the remains of an imperial battalion.

We also discovered some caves near the road. There are signs that they were mined, although so long ago that the tools I found were rusted to almost nothing. Were the imperial soldiers here for the caves?

All sorts of things have been found along the road, including three metal insignia, two captains and a general. It's all Kalesh.

You'd love one item in particular. It's a medallion from a necklace. There are words on it, I just can't make out enough of it to figure out what it says.

> *21st of Zemny,*
> *Ria, I'm writing all this to you just in case something...*
> *Well, just in case.*
> *We were attacked.*
> *I was deep in one of the caves when the ground started shaking. I wasn't even to the exit when I heard the first screams. By the time I reached the entrance, three of the men I hired lay on the ground not far away. The last two were facing off against...Ria, I don't know what it was. A tree? It moved on long, snake-like legs, its body was rough like a trunk, and there were branches...or arms that reached out with this horrific groaning.*
> *Two knives were stabbed into it, farther than a knife should go into a tree, and a half-dozen arrows.*
> *Ignoring the men, it shoved its branches down into the ground and twisted, making the whole hillside shake.*
> *They shot at it again, and two more arrows sank into it before it stretched a branch with a dozen gnarled fingers toward them. There was a light and...*
> *Ria, the men just collapsed.*
> *Dead. In an instant.*
> *The hillside shook and the tree thing started toward the cave. I had nothing with me but some paper and a charcoal pencil. No knife, no...anything.*
> *Maybe it was cowardly, but I hid.*
> *The creature came in, not far from me. It didn't move easily. Each shuffle forward on its roots seemed tortuous.*
> *Something dark and wet dripped from each wound, leaving a smear on the ground behind it like blackened blood. It had a face, of sorts. A slash through the bark for a mouth, dark holes for eyes. A*

moan tore out of it, like some plea I couldn't understand, and it stumbled to the far wall, where it crashed to the floor with its back to me.

It kept…speaking. At least I think it was speech, but it was pained and not a language I understood. It didn't notice me, but as it lay on the ground, I saw something glint in its branch—the weapon that had killed the good men outside.

The ground stopped shaking, and I began to think I might sneak out behind it—until its roots stretched toward the entrance and burrowed into the rock.

The creature gave a cry, and cracks shot through the wall. The entire cave shuddered, and I thought the roots were going to tear it apart.

But then the creature went limp. Unconscious or dead, I don't know.

The cave shook again, and a rock the size of my head fell onto the creature. It still didn't move.

I risked stepping out of my hiding place and was sneaking toward the door when something bright rolled out of its grasp.

The weapon.

As I write this, it sounds foolish, but I couldn't leave it there. Whatever the creature was, if there was a chance it was still alive, it couldn't keep such a thing.

So, even though the cave shook like a leaf in a storm, I snuck over and took it. It was…some kind of uncut gem. The extra time almost cost me my life. I was barely out of the cave before the entrance collapsed.

The entire hillside shook, and I spared only a moment to be sure the men were really gone before I ran.

This was two days ago. I haven't been able to write of it until now. The people of Home risked the ravine to gather their dead. They blame me, of course, for waking the curse. I blame myself as well.

*There's more to tell, a lot more, but I'm coming home, so I'll tell
you in person. I don't have the heart to write it out.*

*Winter is nearly here, and something has changed in the woods.
It's full of movement and…a shadow. I don't know what else to call
it. There's a patch of darkness that moves through the trees. I catch
glimpses of it on the nearby hills.*

*I've told no one that I took the weapon, but…I think the shadow
wants it. I think it's tracking me.*

*I suppose that doesn't sound any crazier than anything else I've
told you*

*I'm sitting on an outcropping of rock and losing the light. I can
see down the ravine to the rockslide that now covers the caves. A bit
of the work we did along the road is still unharmed, but without
help, I'll never make progress on it. At this moment, it doesn't feel
like the work will ever continue.*

His writing was interrupted by a sketch of the view from
someplace high. A thick forest of pine trees sat below, dropping
down into a valley, but the hillside across from it was rocky and
barren. A jumbled rockslide poured down the center of it. About
two thirds of the way up, a sharp horizontal line crossed it,
distinctly a road carved into the slope.

*The White Wood is to my left, filling the long, wide valley with
a ghostly aspect. Bone-white suddenly feels like a fitting description.
The world feels large and lonely, if I'm being honest.*

*I can see a few lights from the outskirts of Home, but I can't go
back there. I'm not even sure they'd allow me shelter for the night. I
stayed for the funerals of the men and gave the families three times
what I'd offered to pay their sons and husbands, but I think they
only tolerated me because it was a day of mourning. Now that the
men are buried, the townspeople might kill me on sight.*

I'm high above my camp. It's on this side of the valley but not terribly far from the bottom of the rockslide. Right now, that feels like a long way to go, and I can't shake the feeling that the shadow is somewhere in the woods.

There's a cave along the rocks I'm sitting on, and I contemplated staying in it tonight, but—maybe it's everything else that's happening, but it feels…wrong.

Actually, do you know what it feels like? It feels like the old mine. There's a thick timber set over the opening and…

There's nothing else really. Nothing I can put my finger on. But I stood at the entrance and all I could think of was Evan.

Tonight does not feel like the night to recall such dark memories.

So I'll say goodbye and head downhill. One more night of camping, and I'll start for home at dawn. At least we have the box. Maybe you can learn more from it than I can. Some link to Evan I can't find.

I admit I am anxious to see a familiar face, Ria, even though I have weeks to travel before I reach you.

Yours always,

Bo

Kate gripped the edges of the paper, rereading the attack.

He'd told her of plenty of dangers over the years. A bear that had crashed into his campsite, a mountain cat that had stalked him for hours, a band of raiders who'd nearly killed him, but never once had he sounded like this. Uncertain. It was there, hidden between his words. He was scared, and it sent a chill down her spine.

She thought back over the monsters she'd read of but couldn't think of a single one that had been described as a shadow or a tree. Elves could turn into trees, but when they did, they were just trees. Lodged into the ground by their roots. Aside from a few moments immediately after the change, they couldn't move at all or even change back into elves without assistance.

The idea of elves made her glance up at the date. This must have been only days before Venn had found the box, and yet no mention of her. And obviously Bo hadn't started home.

"What else happened?" She turned the page over and found another piece of paper stuck to it with what looked like a smudge of sap. The bottom was torn off it, and she carefully peeled the two pages apart.

Scrawled across the torn page was writing she could barely read.

The shadow is coming. How does it know?
Ria—Keep this saf—

The word ended in a sharp slash that gouged into the paper and ran off the torn edge.

The strokes were messy and fast, each one dug into the paper as though Bo had jabbed the pencil into the page.

She ran her fingers over the indentations, her alarm rising. She stared at the page as though she could drag more information out of it by sheer will.

Her thumb brushed over the jagged tear.

A torn edge.

Kate dug in her pocket and pulled out the note Venn had found with the box. *Take this to Ria at the Keepers' Stronghold —please.*

She lined it up with the other page. The two edges matched perfectly, and the slash from Bo's letter ended on Venn's note.

Kate shoved herself up, grabbed the papers, the journal, and the box, and ran for the Stronghold.

She raced into the kitchen. The scent of fresh bread and savory potato soup felt jarringly calm compared to the swirl of dread inside her.

Venn sat in a tall-backed chair at the end of the table, turned sideways so she could stretch out her feet. She leaned her head back, her expression weary.

Kate dropped the box and most of the papers onto the end of the table, and Gerone's spoon paused in the soup as he looked over his shoulder.

"What happened to Bo?" Kate demanded.

The elf's face hardened, and she opened her mouth.

"Don't tell me you don't know!" Kate slammed the last page of his letter down next to the elf. "I opened the box and found a letter from Bo. He was being tracked by something when he disappeared."

Venn's eyes dropped back down to read Bo's quick writing. "A shadow?"

"That's what he says."

When Venn looked up, Kate couldn't read her expression.

"There are many strange things near the White Wood," Venn said, "but I haven't heard of one called a shadow."

"Did Bo strike you as the sort of man who makes up monsters and runs from them?"

Venn considered her words for a moment. "No."

"He's not." Kate jabbed her finger at the page. "Take me to where he disappeared."

Venn shook her head, still reading the page. "I travel alone," she said, absently.

Kate set her hand on the arm of Venn's chair. "I don't care."

Venn lifted her gaze slowly, looking unimpressed.

Kate gripped the chair until the edges dug into her fingers. She stared into Venn's indifferent eyes, wanting to shove her own fury into them. "You don't like to owe people, do you, Venn?" She didn't bother to keep the anger out of her voice. "That's why you brought this box all the way here—you owed Bo something. Something big. And now we helped you, which is why you insisted on paying us for cleaning your wound. Except...you still owe us."

"I paid silver for your services," Venn said coldly.

"For the cleaning and stitching of a wound, yes. But you owe more than that, don't you? That infection was troublesome, but that tattoo on your arm...that was the real problem, wasn't it? It was failing."

Venn twitched.

"I think you could have taken care of the infection," Kate continued, "but not before your tattoo was too depleted to work. I don't know exactly what it's doing, but it would be very, very bad for you if it stopped, wouldn't it?"

The elf's hands tightened into fists on her lap, and she stared at Kate, unmoving.

"I thought so. You owe us."

A deep, fiery outrage flickered to life in Venn's eyes, but she didn't disagree.

Kate leaned closer. "So you will repay us by taking me to where you found the box and telling me every single thing you know about Bo and the White Wood."

CHAPTER EIGHTEEN

A THROAT CLEARED behind Kate just as a tangle of remnants from Kellen, the Shield, Gerone, and Mikal flowed around her. She stayed leaning on Venn's chair, holding her gaze.

Finally, the elf gave an angry twitch of her head, enough like a nod that Kate pushed herself back and straightened.

"Good." Kate grabbed the box and the rest of Bo's writing and moved to the other side of the table.

Kellen's eyes shifted between Venn and Kate, his eyebrows raised, while Mikal stood next to him scowling faintly.

The Shield stepped past them both and gave Venn a bow. *"Ilidris solestra,"* he said warmly.

A flicker of surprise crossed Venn's face at the Elvish words, but she inclined her head toward him. *"Illidris solestra."* She glanced at the other Keepers. *"Yl illuci nic ellian Keeperi velucia."*

"Most of us speak a little Elvish," the Shield answered. "But not enough to converse easily."

Kate sank into a chair across from Venn and dropped her head into her hands, her mind spinning.

The White Wood was easily a month's travel away, and a

month had already passed since Venn had left it. Whatever trail Bo had left would be long gone. She dug her fingers into her scalp. How would she track a two-month-old remnant?

The amplifier serum should work. If she could keep it well protected from sunlight until she got there—

The thought of her work in the library brought her up short.

She was close. Maybe. The memory serum worked, and the first idea she had of how to mix the two was complicated but should only take a few days. Until that was made, she'd have no way to see the memories from an object…

She looked between her hands at the aenigma box. If she could get the *solus* potion finished, she'd have access to everything the box had experienced. She could follow the men who'd taken Evan across the entire world if she had to.

Maybe tonight, if she could gather the right ingredients, she could work on the mixture as they traveled…

She let out a breath. It was unlikely she'd get the mixture right in the controlled, calm setting of the library. There was no way she'd accomplish anything on the road.

Gerone set a steaming pot on the table and pulled out a chair beside her. Kate looked up and found him offering her a basket of freshly baked honey bread.

"I know some Elvish," Kellen said, taking a seat. He looked up toward the ceiling for a moment, then spouted off several lines of the flowing language.

Kate kept her eyes fixed on Venn as Mikal dropped his head into his hands with a groan.

The elf's mouth fell open, and she let out a little huff of laughter, and the first smile Kate had seen tugged at the corner of Venn's lips.

Kellen grinned. "Did I say it right? When Will was trying to teach me about cadences, he made me memorize that Elvish poem. It's what Aderen of the Greenwood said to the human woman he was enchanted to fall in love with. I believe it translates to *I love you more than my own soul, though your nose is fat like a mushroom and you smell like an old horse.*"

"A musty horse," Venn corrected him, but the ghost of a smile stayed on her face.

Venn unbuckled her pack and pulled out a small box. Setting it on the table, she opened it to reveal a half-dozen small purple fruits. She took in the Keepers around the table, avoiding Kate's eyes. "I'm honored to share a meal with you." The words sounded almost sincere.

"Blood apples!" Gerone's eyes lit. "From the moors! I haven't had one in decades!"

"That's a disconcerting name," Kellen said.

"Cut one open," Gerone said, passing out bowls.

Kellen did and let out a low whistle. The flesh inside the apple was deep, dark red. He sniffed it, then took a bite. "Tastes like apple," he said around a mouthful.

"Astounding observation," Mikal said.

Kate tapped her fingers on the table as they all talked. She couldn't just walk away from the *solus* potion. Not after all this time.

Gerone set a steaming cup in front of Venn. "Some tores tea. Should help with the inflammation and the pain."

She sniffed the tea, then nodded her thanks and took a long sip.

Kate picked one of the soft, warm slices of bread, keeping her eyes on Venn. "You're from the White Wood?"

Venn met her gaze over the top of the mug but didn't hurry to set it down. When she did, she shook her head. "Not exactly. My people live along three lakes a few hours' walk from the Wood."

"To the east of it?" Kate asked. "Along the larger branch of the Surn river?"

Venn's hand paused in the act of picking her own slice of bread. "Yes," she answered cautiously.

"Katria has studied the lands of the old Kalesh Empire extensively," the Shield said.

"Much like Bo." Kate leaned forward. "But he wasn't near the lakes, was he? He was near Home, just outside the White Wood."

Venn inclined her head slightly. "I met him near the Wood, not far from Home."

"Home?" Mikal asked.

"A small town where Bo believes the last emperor died," Kate said, without looking away from Venn. "Do elves from the lakes frequent the White Wood?"

"Not many." Venn took a bite of her bread.

"Why are you so reluctant to answer my questions?" Kate asked.

"I've answered everything you've asked," Venn said, taking another bite. She gave Kate a humorless smile as she swallowed. "Maybe you ask poor questions."

Kate dropped her bread onto her plate and opened her mouth, but Gerone spoke first.

"You seem comfortable among humans, Venn," the older man said, his voice pointedly polite, handing her a bowl of steaming soup.

Venn turned to him, and her expression softened. "I've met plenty in my life."

The amiable expression on Venn's face made Kate pause with a ladle of soup halfway to her own bowl.

"Do elves and humans interact often in your part of the world?" Gerone asked curiously.

"Most don't, but for years, I've facilitated trade between my people and the nearby human settlements."

"Really?" Mikal said. "We've never managed to do that here."

Venn gave a hum of agreement. "No, when we lived in the Wildwood, we stayed separate from the humans."

At that, everyone in the kitchen stopped and stared at her.

"You used to live in the Wildwood?" Mikal asked. "Our Wildwood?"

Venn glanced around the table at the shocked faces. "I was born there."

"How old are you?" Kellen said in a hushed voice.

"Kellen!" Mikal said disapprovingly.

"What? The elves left at least two hundred and fifty years ago, and she doesn't look any older than Kate."

"We left just over three hundred years ago," Venn said to Kellen. "The humans were encroaching, so we went east to live near the White Wood."

The Shield studied her curiously. "All we knew is that the Wildwood was emptied."

Kate's hand tightened on the ladle. "Three hundred years ago?"

Venn ignored her and continued to address Kellen. "This is my three hundred and forty-seventh year. My people left the Wildwood when I was still a child. But I have fond memories of it."

"You were a child when you were forty years old?" Kellen asked. "How long are elves considered children?"

"Nearly a century," she answered.

Kellen opened his mouth to ask another question, but Kate held up her hand to stop him. "You were in the Kalesh Empire before it crumbled?"

Venn glanced at Kate and managed a cold, brusque nod.

A thousand questions sprang into Kate's mind, but Venn ate the last piece of her bread, then closed the box of apples, latching the final two inside, and tucked it back into her pack. "Thank you for dinner. It was delicious." She glanced at the Shield. "And thank you for your hospitality."

"We're leaving now?" Kate asked. "There's only an hour or two of sunlight left. You could rest here tonight and heal—"

"You don't need to come," Venn said curtly. "But the healing I need will be found in a night with the trees."

Kellen glanced at Kate. "You're leaving?"

Kate hesitated. "I…" She dropped her eyes to the aenigma box. The *solus* potion would tell her so much.

Maybe.

If she could get it to work.

Which could take months of experimenting.

A surge of frustration rose in her. There had been no clues when Evan was taken. None. And now this was in her possession and it held everything. Clues from twenty years ago were right there if she could just unlock them.

The thought brought her up short.

The one ghost on the path outside always brought up the same fear. Maybe she would do all this and the box would show her that the Kalesh men had killed Evan that day and tossed his body in the river.

Twenty years of searching, and maybe all this time she'd been searching for a ghost.

But Bo wasn't a ghost. And the clues about him were…well, not fresh, but two months old was better than two decades.

She could investigate the box in other ways as they traveled, but she could hardly stay here, looking for Evan, whom she might never find, when Bo needed help now.

She looked up at Venn. "Yes, we're leaving. Let me grab some things."

CHAPTER NINETEEN

KATE STRODE out the hallway into the Stronghold, and footsteps rang out behind her, surrounded by Kellen's remnant.

"Are you really going with her?" he asked in a low voice. "She's..."

"She knows where Bo is. Or where he was." Kate started up the tower ramp.

"But...isn't this all weird? How does she know Bo? What if she's the one who stole the box, and..."

"And brought it here? No. Somehow she ended up owing Bo something. She obviously didn't want to come here, and I think she just wants to be done with all this. But I intend to find out as much as I can from her about what is going on." She reached the door of her room and pushed it open.

Kellen stayed on the ramp, looking worried. "Well, be careful. I don't trust her."

"Neither do I." Kate grabbed her pack from where it hung on her wall. "But her remnant isn't..." She blew out a breath. "She's too hostile for her remnant. Whatever's making her angry right now, it's not habitual." Kate glanced at him. "And she's only really hostile toward me."

"Which isn't comforting."

Kate set a hand on his shoulder. "Thank you for your concern, but I don't think she's terribly dangerous."

Kellen frowned at her. "I'll believe that when you're back safely."

He headed down the ramp, and a little niggling worry crawled up Kate's neck at his concern. Maybe leaving with Venn was a bad idea.

A hint of summer wind rolled off the aenigma box, and Kate's fingers tightened on it.

She gave her pack a quick check to make sure her supply of blank journals was adequate, along with the little tin of char pencils and ink and quills.

A breeze with a wintery bite in it wafted in, and she crossed her room to the window. The sun was decidedly farther south than it had been even a week ago, reaching the top of the western cliffs earlier and earlier each day. The first dusting of snow would probably come to the valley in the next fortnight, and the White Wood was considerably farther north than the Stronghold.

She pulled the window closed and latched it. "This is going to be a cold trip,"

It took a matter of moments to pack warm clothes and exchange her usual Keeper's robe for the wool-lined winter cloak.

She tucked in Bo's journal and letter. The aenigma box waited on her bed where she'd dropped it, every surface clinging to remnants and memories she couldn't reach. "Don't look at me like that. Of course I wish I had the *solus* potion made. You didn't give me enough time." She shoved the smug box into the pack. "Yes, I realize it's been twenty years. Do you think it's easy to create something like that?" She flipped the top of her pack closed, shutting the box inside. "Of course I'll take what I have."

Buckling the belt that held her small hunting knife at her waist, she slung her pack over her shoulder and headed to the library, where she gathered maps, her research, and two small tightly corked vials. One of the memory serum and one of the sky blue remnant amplifier. She wrapped each carefully in thick, soft cloth and tucked them into a protected pocket on the side of her pack.

Gerone met her outside the kitchen with a bundle of food. "Be careful, my dear. Stay warm and remember to eat."

"Detailed notes on the White Wood!" Mikal called from the kitchen. "Don't get so caught up in the history of the Empire that you don't learn about the elves!"

Gerone sighed and gave Kate a quick hug before disappearing back into the kitchen. "Who could possibly forget the elves?" His voice drifted out.

"Someone obsessed with an Empire," Mikal retorted.

"She'll be traveling with an elf!"

Kate walked to the front door and stopped next to the Shield. Here in the main tower, his remnant was like a living, fiery mist, stretching out tentacles that seeped into the stone around them.

Outside, the world lay in shadows. The sun, hovering some-where below the western cliff, only lit the very top of the eastern edge of the valley. Kate sighed. If they had an hour before sunset, they'd be lucky.

She shifted her pack and followed the Shield's gaze to where Venn rested against a maple that stood a short way down the path to the tunnel. The lower branches were still green, but the crown of the tree glowed a vibrant red in the autumn evening light, similar enough to the red woven through Venn's hair that the elf looked like she was a part of it.

"Think she'll ever give me straight answers?" Kate asked the Shield.

The Shield shrugged. "People don't like to answer questions that make them feel vulnerable."

"That's hardly the kind of question I'm asking."

"She seems to think so."

"Well, if normal questions about what happened are too vulnerable for her, how am I supposed to find out anything?"

He tilted his head, and his expression turned to a grimace. "The only key I've ever found to getting someone to trust me is to trust them first." He glanced at her. "Not the easiest solution, since it requires genuine vulnerability."

"She has hardly earned my trust or my vuln—" Kate stopped with a self-conscious laugh. "I see your point."

He smiled up at her before his expression turned serious. "Be very careful with her, though."

Venn leaned against the trunk, her head tipped back. She'd braided her hair, washed her face, and stitched up the rip in the shoulder of her shirt, making her look less travel-worn and disheveled, but her eyes were closed, and her shoulders bowed with weariness.

"You think she's dangerous?" Kate asked.

He shook his head as he considered Venn. "Not dangerous. Well, maybe to some. I meant you could hurt her a great deal if you're not careful. She's..."

"Too sick to travel?"

"I think she's mending from that. She's just...a bit fragile, don't you think?"

"Fragile? No. She seems quite sturdy."

He took Kate's hand with both of his. "We're all fragile in some ways, aren't w—" His eyes grew distant, and he cocked his head as though listening. "You're taking the book the library gave you?"

She paused at the change of subject. "I am. It's all children's rhymes about the White Wood. The first rhyme was utter nonsense."

He beamed at her. "My favorite kind." He patted her hand. "Well, your new friend seems anxious to be off, so I'll wish you safe travels."

Kate watched Venn shift and grimace under the tree, rolling her shoulder in small circles. "Friend is a bit of an overstatement."

"As Flibbet the Peddler says," he answered cheerily, "'A friend is merely a soul in whom we see our own reflection.'"

"You see my reflection in the surly, secretive elf?"

He raised his bushy eyebrows. "Don't you?"

Kate let out a laugh. "No."

"My vision must be going, then," he said with a grin. He glanced back at Venn, and his smile turned into a more serious, troubled expression. "Do stay safe, my dear." He gave her hand a squeeze before dropping it.

Kate shifted her pack on her shoulder. "I'll do my best,"

"It was lovely meeting you, Venn!" the Shield called, raising his hand. "Safe travels!"

The elf gave him a polite nod but crossed her arms as Kate approached. Venn's brow drew down fiercely, and her muscles tightened until she nearly hummed with resentment and vexation.

Kate stopped in front of her. "This would all be less frustrating if you were more of an open book."

Venn pushed herself off the tree. "I am not a book."

"Metaphorically, you're a very closed book. Sealed tight shut. Refusing to give up everything but the smallest amount of information."

"Metaphors are limiting and simplistic. And I've told you everything that matters."

"No, metaphors are powerful and clarifying and glorious. But you haven't told me everything that matters. I'm going to need more clarification about it all, if you don't mind."

"Actually, I do mind." Venn studied her for a moment. "What do you think you'll find in the Woods that I couldn't?"

Kate started walking toward the tunnel. "People leave trails. Remnants." *Which will have faded by now*, her mind reminded her. She ignored it.

Venn fell in next to her. "Bo didn't leave anything."

"Not that you found."

The elf let out a derisive breath.

Despite the fact that Venn was a little taller than Kate, there was a slight strain to her strides, and Kate slowed her steps, glancing toward the stable. "Do we need horses so you can keep up a good pace?"

Venn gave her a withering look. "I do not need a horse."

"Really? Because we have one named Molly who'd be perfect for you. It's short for Mollify, because she manages to calm even the most irritable riders."

Venn's mouth twisted up at the edge. "I'll ride her if you ride one named Silence."

Kate let out a laugh. "We'll walk, then. Try to keep up."

Venn's eyes locked on the huge cliff. She clamped one hand around the strap of her pack, and the muscles of her jaw clenched, but she didn't lag behind.

"Don't worry," Kate said, "when we get out, there won't be any ghosts. They're not there to keep people from leaving. Only to keep people from finding the wall." She glanced at Venn. "Which obviously doesn't always work."

Venn shuddered. "I was under the impression that Keepers were kind, generous, helpful..." Venn waved her hands as though more such words applied.

"Is that not how you found us?"

The elf gave her a gauging look. "The others were, at least.

But I don't understand the ghosts. Are you so desperate to keep people away that you torture them with their fears?"

"The first Keepers made them. There's a quote carved into the library wall that says, 'What are you afraid of?' It's from an old prioress the first Keepers knew. She thought the one thing that ruled everyone more cruelly than almost anything else was their own fears. And she believed the only way to weaken those fears was to face them."

Venn gave a disbelieving look. "So the ghosts are to help you grow?"

"Mostly they make me want to run, and they definitely make any stranger want to run." Kate frowned at Venn. "Most strangers, anyway. But yes, every time we come home to the place we are safe, we have to get past our own fears. To see, right in front of us, the things that are holding us hostage. The things that shape our actions and decisions.

"When we're out in Queensland, people treat us with great respect. It can get almost intoxicating. These woods remind us that we're still fragile, frightened creatures, just like everyone else."

Kate looked ahead as though she could see through the closed door. "I don't know everything the other Keepers see, but just knowing they see something brings us closer. Mikal always says it reminds us of our shared humanity." Glancing at Venn, she added, "Which I suppose doesn't strictly apply to you, but you get my meaning."

The tunnel mouth was shadowed and dark, and the cliff loomed over them, unimaginably heavy and solid. It had been years since Kate had thought about the massive weight of rock above her. But the hunch of Venn's shoulders and the tension radiating from her made Kate rub the back of her neck to banish the creeping, heavy feeling pressing down on her as they walked under the stone arch.

The light disappeared behind them, and the sound of Venn's short, tightly controlled hisses echoed oddly in the darkness.

"We're halfway through," Kate said, more to break the silence than to reassure Venn.

At the end, Kate set her hand to the rune on the wall. "*Aperi*," she said, shoving *vitalle* into the stone. Heat seared through her palm, but the rocks shifted.

The moment there was enough room, Venn strode out. Kate let the door open fully, then followed and closed it from the other side.

She turned to find Venn pressing both hands to the nearest tree, her head bowed, her shoulders rising and falling with her gasping breaths.

Kate stepped up next to her. The elf's skin was deathly pale, and her brow was contracted as though she was in pain. She clenched her fingers into the bark so tightly that the tendons stood out on the backs of her hands.

Kate reached out but stopped shy of the elf's shoulder. "Venn?"

There was no answer beyond deep, shuddering breaths.

"This is a mistake," Kate said quietly. "We should go back. You need rest."

The elf straightened her shoulders and lifted her head but didn't release her hold on the tree. "I don't need rest. I need the trees and—" She hissed and turned outraged eyes on Kate. "You brought the box?" It was less a question than an accusation.

Kate let her hand drop, her sympathy evaporating. "Of course I did."

"Why would you do that?" Venn demanded.

"Why wouldn't I?"

Venn shoved herself off the tree and took a step away from Kate. "Because I'm trying to get rid of it!"

Kate stared at the furious elf. "What's wrong with it?"

"Something, obviously," Venn said, turning away. "It's too heavy for what it is." Muttering something in Elvish, she started down the path.

"What are you talking about? It's lighter than it should be."

"Maybe for someone like you," Venn tossed over her shoulder. She kept to the edge of the trail and reached out hesitantly to brush the first trunk. No ghost appeared, and her shoulders relaxed as she skimmed each trunk with her fingertips.

Kate rubbed her hands over her face to try to drive away her irritation and followed.

The elf continued for a minute or two before pausing with her hand on a larger pine. She stood still for a moment, then turned and headed south into the woods. "This way," she said, without looking back.

"This way to what?" Kate asked, but Venn gave no indication that she'd heard and continued to move quickly through the forest, touching each tree as they passed. Occasionally, she veered to the side to brush her fingers along a trunk that would have been out of reach. Every step seemed planned to keep her as close to another living thing as possible, as though she'd missed the forest so much in the time she'd been in the Stronghold that she needed to reacquaint herself with it.

They continued in a relatively straight line, and Kate saw glimpses of the Marsham Cliffs to her left. She mulled over which of her many questions was the most pressing and lengthened her stride to catch up. But when she caught a glimpse of Venn's face, the elf's eyes were nearly closed and shadowed with dark circles.

Perhaps it wasn't the time for questions.

Up through the branches, a sliver of orange-tinted cloud was visible.

"We don't have long until dark," Kate pointed out.

Venn turned at a large elm. "This way," she said, angling back toward the cliffs.

She continued to touch each trunk along their path, and an idea grew in Kate's mind. She cast out and felt the little slip of *vitalle* flow out of a tree into Venn's fingertips.

As the wave rolled out, Venn followed it through the trees around them, then looked curiously at Kate. "That's an interesting trick."

"You felt that?"

"Everything alive grew brighter."

Kate nodded. "You're getting strength from the trees, aren't you?"

Venn let out an exasperated breath. "No. I lied that I needed the forest to heal."

Kate started walking. "Well, while you're looking for healing, see if you can also find a more pleasant attitude."

The edge of Venn's mouth quirked up again. "Where will you find one?"

CHAPTER TWENTY

THE FOREST OPENED into a small clearing with an enormous pine on the far side. Venn stumbled to it and sank to her knees, setting both hands against the tree.

Kate looked at the elf for a moment. "I'll get a fire started and warm up some food."

Venn turned to sit against the trunk, leaning her head back and closing her eyes. "I don't need a fire. I have apples in my pack."

Kate pulled out the food from Gerone. "If we have a fire," she said, trying to keep her voice polite, "we can have warm bread with our apples."

"They're my apples, not ours," Venn said, still not opening her eyes. "We've been together all day, so don't bother with an invitation to a meal. We can both just eat our own food in peace. I've traveled for over a month and haven't needed a fire yet."

The elf's limp arms and weary face were the only reason Kate bit back her reply. She gathered dry sticks from under the tree, snapping the longer pieces in half with more force than was necessary.

Kneeling under the branches, she brushed a pile of dried needles together, leaving a bare circle of dirt around them, then arranged the wood on top.

"Don't make the flames too tall," Venn said without moving. "The pine is parched at this time of year."

Kate jabbed her fingertip into the needles. "I know how to build a campfire." She shoved some *vitalle* into it, and a tongue of flame burst to life. She funneled in a little more until it grew into a short blaze. Firelight lit the bottom the branches above, turning it into a living roof while the clearing beyond filled with shadows.

Venn wearily dug an apple out of her pack, eating it without opening her eyes.

Kate stabbed a stick into a chunk of bread and held it over the fire, staring into the flames until the dancing light rubbed the sharp edges off her irritation.

The evening darkened around them while she ate, turning their fire-lit campsite into a small cavern of light in the vast world of blackness. She took a bite and pulled out Bo's journal. The branches were too low to build the fire up bright, so she reached toward the campfire and pulled out a little tongue of flame, feeding it *vitalle* through her fingertips as she held it near the open journal on her lap.

His writing was small, though, and thin. She found the final entry, then moved slowly toward the front, trying to decipher dates and locations. But the flickering light of the flame set the tiny words dancing across the page and left his notes crammed into the margins illegible.

With a flick of annoyance, she snuffed the little flame and let the journal close.

The forest wrapped around them like a thick wall of darkness. Venn lay unmoving against the tree. The fire crackled low and steady, confined to its small circle of earth.

Kate shifted, and a matching fire of frustration flickered inside her, chafing against the inactivity of the evening.

Weeks. It would be weeks until she reached the White Wood. And it had already been weeks since Bo disappeared. She rubbed a hand across her face at the thought.

There would be none of his remnant left. No trace to follow.

Her pack sat beside her, and she cast out toward the aenigma box hidden inside it, but there was nothing to feel. For all the magic the box contained, when it wasn't being touched, it seemed utterly dormant. Her fingers itched to pull it out and examine it again, but there'd be nothing to learn of it in the dark.

She blew out a breath, trying to push away the growing anger at the entire situation.

Venn shifted slightly where she sat slumped against the tree, staring tiredly into the fire.

"How did you meet Bo?" Kate asked, the words sounding more like a demand than a question.

A flicker of something like distaste crossed Venn's face, and she didn't look away from the fire. She was quiet for long enough that Kate thought she was refusing to answer. When she finally spoke, her words were measured. "There had been an early snowstorm. I was above the tree line and..." She met Kate's eyes, her expression edging on defiant. "I hurt my leg. Bo found me and helped me down the mountain."

Kate waited for more of an explanation, but the elf merely looked back at the fire. "I can see how that would frustrate you. Being helped is so awful. How long was that before he disappeared?"

"Two days."

Kate stared at her. "Two days? What exactly did you and Bo do in two days that made you such great friends that you traveled all the way here for him?"

Venn looked over in amusement. "I barely saw him during

that time. Why does it bother you so much that I helped your brother?"

"It bothers me that you won't tell me anything about how you met!"

"I just did," Venn said dismissively, turning back to the fire.

"Fine," Kate said, "then tell me how you found the box. The last thing he wrote was that a shadow was following him. I think he meant an actual shadow, not a metaphorical one."

Venn looked over with a creased brow. "Who's chased by metaphorical shadows?"

Kate gave a short laugh. "A lot of people. Shadows of fear or guilt. Shadows of people they remember. It's the memories of things that haunt them or the shame or anxiety they still live with."

Venn blinked at her. "He said 'shadow.' I think he meant it was a shadow."

Kate let out an exasperated sigh. "That's what I'm saying. A real shadow. And he sounded scared. I have never heard Bo sound scared before. He said, 'The shadow is coming. How does it know?' What does that mean?"

Venn's expression shifted to confusion. "How would I know? What is he talking about?"

"He said he found some weapon. A gem. That a creature like a tree killed the men working for him with something before it collapsed. He took the weapon away from it, and then he thought the shadow was chasing him because of it."

"A tree creature and a shadow that moves? What are those?"

Kate threw up her hands. "You're the one who lives in the White Wood where there are strange monsters all the time—you tell me!"

"I do not live in the White Wood, and I've never heard of a creature that looks like a tree or…" Venn's gaze shifted through the flames thoughtfully.

"Or what? Do you know about the shadow?"

The elf glanced up at Kate, her brow still drawn. "I...maybe. There was a shadow, but I thought it was just a passing cloud."

"Where?"

"In the clearing where I found the box. The trees showed me who had been there, and I saw Bo, and some elves, and another human and..." She frowned. "A shadow."

Kate pulled her pack open and dug out the tenea serum. When she unwrapped the vial, it caught the firelight and glittered like a million tiny stars had been trapped inside the glass. "Will you show me?" She held the vial out.

Venn's hands stayed in her lap. "What is that?"

"Tenea serum. You put a memory into this, and I can draw it out and see it like it was my own."

Venn kept her eyes on the vial, watching it as though it might attack her. "You want to steal my memory?"

Kate shook her head. "No. You'll just share it with me. It won't take anything away from you."

Venn considered the vial. "Like a wellstone?"

Kate brought the serum back to her lap. "I forgot elves know what those are. Yes, this is a very poor replica of a wellstone. The memory deteriorates quickly but lasts long enough to transfer from one person to the next. But seeing as I can't take the Keepers' Wellstone with me when I travel, this is what I have to work with."

"The Keepers have a wellstone?"

Kate nodded. "We store our memories in it and try to use those memories for research when it cooperates."

Venn frowned. "You all use one?"

"We always have. The Keepers have had it for hundreds of years, and it holds the memories of all of us. It draws connections between them. Some of which make sense, some of which seem random.

177

Venn stared at her. "It must be huge."

"The size of a small melon."

The elf's mouth dropped open. "Where did you get one that big?"

"It was a gift from the Greenwood elves. How big are the ones you use?"

"You could hold the largest of ours in your palm, but only a single elf uses each. We use them whenever elves grow old as a memorial of their life." Venn looked between the serum and Kate's face. "You use that first."

Kate hesitated. "That's fair. What do you want to see?" She gave Venn a small smile. "I could show you how irritating you've been all day."

"I've had enough irritating people for one day," Venn answered. "You want something personal from me. Show me something personal to you."

"Finding a box is personal?"

Venn merely closed her eyes again.

Kate rolled the vial between her fingers. Her first thought of something personal was the day she'd found the aenigma box, but that was *too* personal.

The Shield's voice came back to her mind. *The only key I've ever found to getting someone to trust me is to trust them first.*

Not that much, though, she thought as she slid her locket absently along the chain at her neck.

Something personal, but—she glanced at Venn—still on par with the elf finding a box she didn't understand.

Kate tapped her finger on the locket. Venn's eyes followed the motion, and Kate's hand paused. The locket was a good choice.

The very first treasure hunt. A memory with Bo and Evan, a year before the aenigma box. Back when treasure hunting had been merely adventure with no cost.

In many ways, that day had shaped everything that followed.

Kate uncorked the vial and dipped her finger into it, pressing *vitalle* into it as she drew the memory to mind.

Kate stood between Evan and Bo, peering across the street at Old Lady Whiskers' house, which loomed over the shorter buildings around it. Townspeople moved in and out, carrying off parts of the household.

"I heard she was dead three days before anyone found her," Evan said, his boyish face lit with curiosity. "She was only a skeleton, but she tried to bite the butcher's hand when they took her to the graveyard."

"She wasn't a skeleton after three days." Bo inched forward, his nose pointed at the house like a hound on a scent. "Takes a long time for the bugs to eat everything off the bones."

"Gross." Kate shoved him with her elbow.

"It's true!" he protested.

"Maybe Whiskers' house is full of bugs!" Evan whispered.

"She swept every day," Kate pointed out. "She didn't have bugs."

Bo took a step toward the house. "Let's go see."

"What?" Kate asked, but the boys were already crossing the street, and she hurried after them.

No one paid them any heed when they slipped inside.

The house smelled stale, like even the dust had grown old and chalky. Old Lady Whiskers' son stood by the front door, looking suitably sober with his greying hair and furrowed brow. He no longer lived in Welsley, and his clothes were finer than anything Kate had ever seen. He talked seriously with the townsfolk, making a record of what people bought, noting their meager payments.

Bo gave the man a quiet, "Our sympathies for your loss," as they passed.

"Do we have sympathy for mean ol' Whiskers?" Evan whispered.

Bo shrugged. "That's what people say, and he did just lose his mama. Even if she was Old Lady Whiskers."

Kate glanced back at the man. His eyes scanned the ceiling and walls of the old house, and she couldn't decide what she heard in his sigh. Maybe sorrow. Maybe impatience.

"Why are we here?" she asked Bo as he led them through the house.

"They say Whiskers had treasure, and I think I know where she hid it."

"You've never been in this house before."

"Didn't need to be. What's the one thing Whiskers cared about more than anything?"

"Wood," Kate answered immediately.

"Where's my wood?" Evan whisper-shouted in a crotchety voice. "It's midsummer! I need my wood!"

"Exactly," Bo said. "Ma say it's just 'cause she had to spend one winter too cold. Except…she kept her wood in a locked shed." He leaned closer and whispered, "I think she wanted a pile of wood for another reason."

"To hide her treasure!" Kate whispered back.

Bo gave her a crooked grin and stepped out the back door into a neatly kept yard. "But it shouldn't be locked today, because the whole house is open." He slipped over to a large shed and pulled tentatively on the door. It swung open easily, and a stream of sunlight fell in, landing on rows of stacked firewood, filling the shed from wall to wall. A grin spread across Bo's face as he stepped in, peering around in the gloom.

"Probably in the back, where it wouldn't be disturbed." He clambered up onto the wood and crawled to the back of the shed. Evan followed, and, after a glance at the door, Kate grabbed the rough, dry wood and started to climb.

Bo dropped into the small gap between the wood and the back wall and began rummaging. Before Kate could even reach the back, *he let out a gasp and held up a small honey-colored stone. It was the size of a blueberry, smooth and translucent. He moved it into the line of sunlight, and it glowed.*

"Gold?" Evan said. "She had gold!"

"It's not gold." Bo looked down into the wood. "It's a stone. It must be amber, which is very rare. There's more of it here!"

Bo pulled out two more stones, nearly as large as the first, handing them to Kate and Evan. Voices floated in the open door, and Kate froze. The voices faded away, and Evan peered down into a gap in the wood. "I bet there're tons buried here."

"Probably," Bo agreed, climbing back up on top of the wood, "but we don't really want to steal it all from Whiskers' son."

"So you're just stealing a little?" Kate asked, trying to sound disapproving.

Bo's eyes glinted with excitement. "Just taking a little proof that we actually found treasure." He held out one of the amber stones to her.

It was like golden honey hardened into a gem. She reached out to take it and couldn't hold back her own smile as she met his excited grin. "I think it's still stealing."

He held a finger to his smiling lips. "Shh. Let's keep calling it proof."

Kate pulled her finger out of the vial, smiling at the memory, and handed it to Venn. "Just set your finger in, and it will come to you."

The elf touched the serum cautiously, then she straightened. "Is that Bo?"

Kate nodded. "He was fifteen. And my other brother, Evan, was nine."

Venn closed her eyes. Kate took the last bite of her bread as the bright thread sank into Venn's finger.

Venn looked at her when the memory ended. "You stole dried tree sap?"

Kate laughed. "My father found us when we got home and asked why we were so excited about sap. Bo was so mad he hurled his into the river, sure he'd missed the real treasure. I lost mine somewhere, but Evan always kept his in his pocket. He used to rub his thumb along it when he was thinking, eventually smoothing it out a bit."

She opened her locket, looking down at the small amber piece of sap sitting inside, slightly flattened. An echo of remnant trickled out of the little chamber. Crisp pines and tumbling, wild mischief.

"You carry an old piece of sap from your brother in a locket?" Venn asked slowly. "Clearly, there's more to that story."

Kate tried to breathe in Evan's remnant, but it was so faint she wasn't sure it was real. "I'll tell you all about it in exchange for you explaining your tattoo."

The side of Venn's mouth twitched up into a humorless smile. "I'm not that curious."

Kate snapped the locket shut. "Then it's your turn to share a memory."

CHAPTER TWENTY-ONE

VENN CONSIDERED THE SERUM. "Are all memories that hazy?"

Kate paused. "Hazy?"

"Everything looked a little vague. I could hear everything clearly, though, and feel things. I could smell the wood."

"Nothing was hazy," Kate protested.

"Maybe humans have bad memories." Venn looked into the sparkling serum for a moment. Finally, she gave a slight nod and set her finger in the vial. "I'll show you when I found the box, but remember that trees don't care about time like we do. There's no sense of today versus yesterday. There is only recent or long ago. Keep that in mind."

Before Kate could ask what that meant, Venn closed her eyes. A trail of light seeped out, brighter white than Kate's.

When the memory ended, Venn handed the vial to Kate.

Kate put her own fingertip in, and a rush of light filled her mind, tremendously vivid and bright.

Venn strode through a forest, the evening light slanting through the trees to land in bright splashes among the deepening shadows.

Tall trunks towered around her, infused with heat and light. The bark of the nearest pine emanated a smooth, warm golden glow. The oak's ahead was threaded with strands of molten copper. A slender pine shoot radiated a faint green in the growing shadows.

Something pulled her forward. Something strong, drawing her through the crisp twilight toward the clearing ahead, throwing fuel on the edges of the irritation burning inside her. She tried to fight against it, but there was no way to push it back. No way to give herself room to breathe. She picked up her pace, running out into the wide glade. The evening sunlight blinded her for a moment, and she spun, taking in the emptiness around her.

The gnawing urge dragged her across the clearing to a low spread of juniper bushes clustered between three aspens whose leaves were just beginning to be kissed with the gold of autumn. She stared down at the juniper branches stretching along the ground, each tiny needle edged in a soft blue glow.

There was no one here.

She braced against the compulsion that still pulled her forward. "Bo?" she called.

Her voice was quiet and tense, and she spun to take in the clearing. It was totally empty.

She let out a frustrated breath. With effort, she stopped shoving the pressure back and let it rush into her. It yanked at her so roughly that she stumbled farther into the juniper.

Her foot struck something, and she looked down to see the edge of a box.

She froze, her breath coming faster than it should. She glanced around the clearing again. Without touching the box, she moved to the nearest aspen and set her hand on it.

A surge of warmth and affection flowed into her from the tree. Its leaves, which shimmered with a silvery green light, trembled and brightened. An impression of sunlight and a small nest of birds. Venn pushed the ideas away, gently but firmly.

"What happened here?" She didn't ask in words, not precisely, but the question was put to the tree, and the tree, after another impression of leaves quivering in a breeze, showed her.

Everything was fragments. Slivers of motion and change.

A lone elf moved through the clearing in noonday light, his steps purposeful and quick while wind blew from the west. He followed a game trail out.

Three deer ambled past on a still morning, stepping carefully through the dew-covered grass, their heads low.

A human entered, some grey-haired stranger with a long beard and worn clothing, and stopped to eat while sunlight poured down on the aspen's summer-green leaves.

Heavy, cold rain pelted down, thrumming into the ground and shaking branch and leaf.

A pair of elves skirted the edge of the clearing on a clear dawn. More deer. Strong wind. A fox.

Then Bo ran into the clearing along the game trail. The world was steeped in the blues of late twilight, and he looked over his shoulder, gripping his box in both hands.

"This," Venn said firmly.

The image slowed as Bo ran to the juniper and knelt, shoving the box under some branches. The memory flickered for a moment to a fox darting past, then back to Bo. He hunched over something on the ground, then twisted to look over his shoulder again.

The image disappeared as a wind blew Venn's hair against her face. The tree's branches stretched, and it lost itself in the dance.

"The man," she reminded it.

Bo appeared again, then the bearded man eating lunch, then an elf, then a flicker of Bo standing in the dusky light with a knife held out toward the game trail on the far side of the clearing, taking a step away from the dark shadows under the trees.

Then Bo was gone, and there was nothing but sunlight and a soft breeze.

185

"Show me the man," Venn repeated, the biting compulsion making the words snap with anger.

The image returned to Bo facing the shadow.

"What happened?"

But Bo was gone again, and a small party of elves moved through, following some tracks along the ground that took them quickly away.

Venn dropped her hand and stepped back from the tree. Kneeling, she moved the juniper branches to the side.

There was Bo's box, carved with ancient runes, each surface humming with power.

There was a sense of loneliness about it. A solitary feel that left her cold.

She squatted down, and her thin elven fingers reached out to touch it. The moment they brushed the wood, it yanked her forward, and she crashed down to her knees. She pulled her hand back, and a bit of torn paper fluttered in the shadows next to it, caught in the tiny juniper needles.

She turned it over warily, revealing quickly scrawled words: Take this to Ria at the Keepers' Stronghold—please.

The writing weighed down the page until she could barely lift it. Staring at the words, she sank back on her heels.

"No…" She breathed the word out with a shudder. Her fingers gripped the note. It was merely a slip of paper and a small wooden box, but they pulled at her until her whole body curled around them, until the weight of the entire forest dragged her toward them.

She grabbed the box and clutched it to her chest. "Bo!" Her shout disappeared uselessly into the forest.

She rose and stumbled to the aspen to her left. "Show him to me," she demanded.

Flickers of the same scenes passed through her mind. She ran to the next pine. "Show me."

The evening sunlight left the ground and slowly moved up the trees as she worked her way around, stopping at each trunk, setting her hand on bark that glowed silvery or green or a subtle red, coaxing out who had passed. With a patience that took all her will to hold, she sorted out the paths that had led everyone into and away from the clearing. The route of the band of elves was easy to follow. The bearded man left an obvious trail to the south. The lone elf she watched several times. He'd come from farther down the hill, following the game trail north.

She reached the tree Bo had been facing with the knife and lingered, but there was nothing new. The game trail Bo had entered the clearing on ran between this tree and the next, and she caught one glimpse of a darkness filling the space, black as the deepest shadow. Its edges were ill defined. The bottom pooled on the ground and seeped into the dark crevice between two tangled roots, the far side stretched into the evening gloom of the forest.

Then it was gone, and the lone elf paused close by where the shadow had been, stopping along the trail. His eyes assessed the woods around him, flitting from the ground at his feet to the edges of the brush. He knelt for a moment at a small branch, the tip broken and hanging limply.

His brow creased in a frown, and Venn reached out, but he moved on.

Venn continued along the edge of the clearing until she came to the juniper again and dropped her gaze to the box and the note clutched in her hand. She looked north toward the White Wood, down the path the lone elf had traveled, and she crossed the clearing and took a few steps after him.

The compulsion from the box reached bony fingers into her chest and tightened around her lungs. She stopped, and it didn't grow worse. She took a hesitant step south, and the pressure loosened, but the tugging on her mind pulled her on with the relentlessness pressure of a river.

That path she knew. It would lead south for days, then west across the moors, then north again, past the home she'd left long ago, to some elusive valley where the Keepers lived.

She rubbed her free hand across her face. Glancing once more over her shoulder toward the north, she swore, then she shoved Bo's box and the note into a small pack hanging at her side and started south with long, steady strides.

The evening woods faded, and Kate blinked at Venn, speechless for a moment. "There was...There was a shadow. A literal shadow!"

Venn nodded. "But just a shadow. The trees are aware of living things, as you can see. But that darkness was like any other patch of it. It was nothing. Just a lack of light."

"Bo didn't think so."

"Obviously, but...it had no path. The forest is vast, and it knows what moves through it, but it pays no heed to shadows that appear and shift with the clouds. That darkness was odd, but...the trees didn't..." She exhaled and shook her head. "If it had been a living thing, they'd have remembered its path. The trees thought it was merely a shadow."

"Did it take Bo?"

"I don't know!" Venn said, exasperated. "It wasn't substantial enough to do anything to anyone."

"Then the elves took him?"

"They'd have no reason to. They'd have no use for him. Those were all rangers from the White Wood, tasked with scouting the woods for creatures that have descended from the northern ranges. They watch for threats. A human like Bo is not a threat. He's...nothing to them."

"That one elf seemed interested in where Bo had walked."

"Ayen," Venn said. "He's a captain in the rangers. And that was both the trail Bo came down and where the shadow stopped." She raised a hand. "Before you spoke of a shadow, I hadn't even paid any attention to it."

Kate studied the elf for a moment. "The shadow is what we need to find."

Venn rested back against the tree and closed her eyes. "I have no idea how to find a lifeless shadow." Her face was drawn with weariness, but her words sounded honest.

Kate corked the vial of tenea serum and rolled the little glass container between her fingers, watching it glitter in the firelight. "Is that what it feels like to you when you owe someone? That compulsion you had?"

Venn's brow twitched into a scowl, but she didn't answer.

"Then I understand why you like to keep things even." Kate packed the serum back into its box. "Do you think Bo's..." She hesitated, unwilling to finish.

Venn cracked one eye. "I don't think he's dead, if that's what you're asking. I wouldn't take you all the way back there if I did."

"But how do you know?"

Venn closed her eye again and was quiet for a long moment. "There was no sign of a struggle."

Kate let out a short laugh. "What does that matter? Are you saying you couldn't harm me without leaving signs of a struggle?"

A smile curled up the edge of Venn's mouth.

"Because I could hurt you without leaving signs of a struggle," Kate pressed.

This earned her a direct look. "I believe I'd like to see you try."

"Bo ran into that clearing," Kate said, leaning forward, "and left the box we've searched for our whole lives, left a message about being chased by a shadow—which you and I both saw—and then he disappeared. Yet you seem unwilling to believe it was the shadow that took him. Why would he say any of that if it weren't true?"

"I don't know," Venn said in a level voice. "I hardly know the man."

"Well, I know him. I've known him my whole life. If he said the shadow was after him, that's what we need to find."

Venn shifted lower until she was nearly reclined against the trunk, between two large roots. "I'm sure you believe that. When I met him, he told me he was from Queensland, and we discussed Keepers. He told me you're his sister." She gave Kate a searching look. "And yet in the past fifteen years, he's only seen you four times. He said he writes you letters regularly, but you never write him."

"I can hardly get a letter to someone who's constantly traveling."

Venn shrugged. "Relationships, even with family, aren't magical, eternal things. At this point, I'd imagine you're merely something of a muse to him. He can't really know the person you've become. And you can't know him either."

Kate shifted at how uncomfortably plausible the words were. "That's a very cynical view."

"You were close as children, but childhood ended long ago, and time changes things."

"Not for us," Kate said firmly.

A derisive breath was her only answer as Venn rolled to her side, her back curled against the thickest root. "I'll take you to where I found the box, but if you're looking for someone who lived fifteen years ago, don't be surprised when you don't find him."

CHAPTER TWENTY-TWO

THE NIGHT GREW COLDER, and Kate added a few sticks to the fire, listening to Venn's breathing grow steady.

The walk through the forest had taken a toll on the elf. Her skin was pale, even in the firelight, and though Venn appeared to be sleeping, her brow was creased. A wind blew through the clearing, and she shivered.

"Venn?"

The elf didn't answer.

Kate moved over next to her, kneeling and shaking her shoulder, but Venn didn't stir. Instead of feverish, her skin felt chilled, and Kate shook her again. The elf's slow, long breaths didn't change.

Kate sat back on her heels. "I only have one blanket, Venn, and you need something." There was still no answer, so with a murmured apology, she opened Venn's pack. It was nearly empty. The box of apples was near the top. Below it were some tightly rolled clothes and one larger bundle that turned out to be a blanket, thin and made from something that shimmered in the firelight. Where Kate's hand touched it, the fabric warmed. Kate closed up the pack, then spread the blanket over Venn. Within a few breaths, the crease in the elf's brow smoothed.

Kate cast out at the blanket, hoping it wasn't taking *vitalle* from Venn to stay warm, but it didn't seem to be doing anything but reflecting her own heat back to her. There was, though, a gentle flow of warmth from the tree seeping into Venn's body.

Pulling her wool blanket out of her pack, Kate wrapped it around herself and sat down by the fire. The forest was hushed and still. No wind ruffled the trees. Venn's breathing continued slow and steady, but her face stayed pale.

Kate added some more wood to the fire, trying unsuccessfully to warm the small space.

"I think you might need more than a night with the trees, Venn." Kate cast out toward the fire. The flames themself were bright and hot, nearly a solid thing she could have picked up if she'd wanted. The heat above it was more elusive. More slippery. "It's easier to move flames," she said, "but I'm guessing you don't want to be set on fire."

She stretched her hand forward and pushed out a thin sheet of *vitalle*. It grew slowly, fed by her own energy and the warmth of the campfire. She unfurled it like a tent over the flames. Her fingertips tingled as she extended the shell, bending three sides down around the fire and stretching the fourth to the tree trunk above Venn, creating an invisible tunnel. The heat of the flames rolled up against the shell-like smoke trapped by a roof, and Kate hunched a little lower in her blanket as the warmth was cut off from her. She funneled it to the side until it reached Venn and pooled around her.

Kate's fingertips began to burn, and her palm prickled as she kept the wall in place. It absorbed some of the heat like a blanket, the rising warmth pushing at the fabric of her shield, soaking through and pulling strands away. Instead of using *vitalle* from herself, Kate drew some out of the burning fire and pressed it into the tunnel, mending the tiny rents.

When Kate cast out again, Venn, her blanket, and the tree roots around her were bright with warmth.

Twisting her hand, Kate turned the tunnel until it funneled toward herself. A wash of heat rolled over her, like she was stepping into hot summer sunshine, accompanied by the familiar smell of the river from her childhood and the wheat field in the spring. The smell of her remnant was never noticeable until it was trapped beneath a shield.

When her blanket was warm to the touch and her cheeks tingled with the heat, she cut off the *vitalle,* and the shell dissolved into the cool night air.

She lay down, casting out every once in a while to measure how fast Venn was cooling off.

When her eyes grew heavy, she slipped a hand out of her blanket to create another shell, guiding the heat over to warm Venn again, then dragging some over to herself. She fell asleep before her own blanket had even begun to cool.

She woke sometime later to see Venn curled into a ball, her blanket pulled tight. Kate added some wood to the fire and pressed some heat toward the elf and herself before falling back asleep.

A shuffling noise woke her, and she found Venn standing and rolling her blanket into a small bundle in the grey light of early morning. The elf's skin was a warm golden brown, her eyes clear, her motions effortless and smooth.

Rubbing at the grit in her eyes, Kate sat up. "You look better." Her breath clouded in the air, and the chill slipped beneath her blanket. She wrapped it tighter around her shoulders.

"You don't," Venn answered.

"I wonder why." Kate reached a hand toward the fire. The heat seeped into her fingers, and she shifted her whole body closer, opening the blanket to the warmth. She was halfway through a yawn before she realized the fire should be dead instead of blazing brightly. She glanced at Venn's back as the elf squatted down to tuck her blanket into her pack. "I thought you didn't need a fire."

"I don't," Venn said without turning. "But I know what you did last night, and I appreciate it."

The fuzzy edges of sleep clung to Kate's mind, and she blinked at the friendly sentiment. Maybe the tree *had* taken away Venn's animosity while it healed—

"It was unnecessary," Venn added, shooting a pointed look over her shoulder, "but I acknowledge your attempt to make me more comfortable."

"Ah, there it is." Kate stood, pulling off her blanket and shaking it to scatter the dew beaded on its surface. "And now you've made me a warm fire first thing in the morning, also unnecessary but appreciated, so we're even."

Venn didn't bother to nod as she pulled on her pack. "We have a long way to go."

The sky above them was shifting to a bluish grey with only a few thin strands of clouds strung across it. Kate slung her pack over her shoulder, then wrapped her blanket around herself again, warding off the chilly air. Venn started out of the clearing without waiting for her to finish.

"Yes," Kate said under her breath, "by all means. Let's get this trip over with."

Venn settled into a comfortable pace, and Kate followed, letting the crispness of the morning clear away the last of her drowsiness. The forest was damp and chilled, but the sky above was a light, crisp blue, and her vague annoyance with the elf cleared away as well.

Despite moving as though she were perfectly healed, Venn continued to brush the trees they passed and drag her fingertips through the leaves of every small bush. Yesterday, the motion had held an undertone of desperation, but this morning it seemed habitual.

They reached a stream and knelt to fill their waterskins. When Venn finished, she moved to an oak and set her hand on it. Above her, most of the leaves were specked with golds and oranges, while some clung to their summer green.

"Are you still tired?" The air was growing warmer, and Kate folded her blanket and tucked it into her pack.

"Who could be tired after a night in the woods?" Venn asked, her tone dismissive.

"I don't know. Maybe the elf who spent weeks sleeping in the woods before collapsing outside the Stronghold?"

Venn waved her words away and cast a dark look at Kate's pack. "That was different. I'm merely saying good morning and seeing what they have to say."

Kate corked her waterskin. "And?"

Venn looked curiously at her. "I thought Keepers could speak with the trees."

"We can tell they're alive," Kate corrected her, "and give or take *vitalle* from them, but we can't talk to them."

"*Vitalle?*"

"The energy that exists in all living things. The warmth and light of life."

"Ahh. The *iza.*"

"Is that Elvish?"

"Yes. *Ael'iza.* The fire of life. You cannot hear the trees' voices?"

Kate shook her head.

Venn looked up into the sprawling branches. Between the golden light filtering through the trees and her tranquil expression, she looked like a different elf from the one who had shown up at the Wall.

"Do you have to be touching them to hear their voice?" Kate asked.

Venn gave a hum of agreement. "He likes the feel of his leaves changing and drying. They're loosening, and he can tell that they'll whisk away on a breeze soon, leaving his branches almost weightless. Free."

Kate moved up beside her and set her palm on the rough bark. "I had no idea they could speak that clearly. Or that it was a he." The *vitalle* of the tree was warm beneath her hand, but she felt nothing beyond that.

"Not everyone listens closely enough to hear them. Not even elves. Even they often hear only the whole forest speaking together, telling of creatures who've passed." She looked into the woods. "There are a lot of deer and squirrels nearby. A fox and many rabbits." A flicker of uneasiness crossed her face and vanished so quickly Kate wondered if she'd imagined it. "A pack of wolves as well. Although they're far south of here. No people close enough for us to meet today." Venn dropped her hand and struck out through the woods again, and Kate fell in beside her.

"When your people first went to the White Wood," Kate asked, "did you see any of the Kalesh Empire?"

"We didn't go to the White Wood," Venn corrected her. "We went to the lakes. Most stayed there, but Evay used to go exploring into the Empire. She'd take me on trips with her to nearby towns."

"Evay?" Kate stopped in her tracks. "Evay from the old stories? The elf who helped Issable become the first queen of Queensland? The queen the entire country is named after?"

Venn paused. "She knew your first queen. Called her Sable."

Kate stared at the elf, her mind reeling. "Of course she would! I...I love Evay in those stories! She's how we know the White Wood exists! Can you tell me about her?"

"No." Venn started walking again. "But I'll introduce you to her. She loves meeting humans, and she'll be thrilled to meet a Keeper." Kate opened her mouth, but Venn held up her hand. "I said I'm not going to talk about her. You can pepper her with questions when you meet."

Kate swallowed back all her questions about the famous elf and returned to the earlier subject. "So for the last three hundred years, you've traveled to human towns?"

Venn nodded. "There are five that are within a week's walk of the lakes. I visit each in the spring and again in the fall."

"Are they large towns? The maps I have show nothing particularly populous."

"They're larger than they were. Healthier."

"Than when?"

Venn's brow contracted. "There was a time when they were dying. Starving. Poor and sick and barely surviving. That was over two hundred years ago. Several nearby cities disappeared altogether. Either abandoned or an illness swept through and turned them to graveyards."

"That's after the Empire fell?"

Venn gave a hum of agreement. "When we first got there, the human cities were enormous." She looked ahead into the woods, her eyes unfocused. "They sprawled over hills and valleys, stretching into farmlands. Roads ran out of them like strands of a spiderweb. At night, they were full of light and sound." Her voice sounded disapproving, but there was a note of something nostalgic in it. "Evay hated the Empire, though. She refused to go near any of the cities large enough to have imperial garrisons, so we stayed with the small towns on the outskirts."

"Then how did you see the large cities? Were they close to the lakes?"

Venn shook her head. "The nearest was a ten-day walk."

"But you saw it?"

"Once with Evay from a very distant mountain, and once I went there without her, just to get closer."

"Will you show me?" Kate unbuckled her pack to pull out the serum.

"We have a month's walk ahead of us," Venn said, irritation creeping into her voice. "We're not stopping to swap memories every time I know something you don't."

"I can take the memory and walk," Kate said, hoping that was true. "It'll be...mulling an idea. Or daydreaming." Venn started to shake her head, and Kate added, "You agreed to tell me what you know of the Empire."

The elf sighed and held out her hand for the serum. "All I did was get close. I didn't go into it." She uncorked the vial and thought for a moment before pushing her finger into the fluid. The memory threaded out, bright silvery-white, curling through the gold specks of the serum, turning them to glitter. When the long strand ended, she pulled her finger out, leaving the memory floating like a curl of moonlight in a sea of golden stars. She handed it to Kate without meeting her eyes. "If you walk into a tree while you're watching this, I'm not helping you up."

Before any of the memory could float to the surface, Kate stuck her finger into the glowing serum. A scene overlaid itself across her vision, and she started forward, paying vague attention to her path while keeping the stunning images in her mind.

Venn lay on her stomach on a grassy hill, her chin resting on her folded hands, overlooking a vast sprawl of a city. It covered three hills like a rough grey blanket that bristled with rooflines and chimneys. On the farthest hilltop, a thick wall encircled a stone complex of squat towers and red-tiled roofs. Flowing out from that fortress, the rest of the city poured down the hillside, pooled in the valleys, and crawled back up the adjoining hills. A wide river ran through it, spanned by countless stone and wooden bridges, its water nearly choked with boats.

Roads wound through the mass of buildings like grey brambles, twisting and interlacing in a chaotic tangle. The largest stretched out of the city, carving paths through the countryside, leading to smaller clusters of homes or shops.

To the left, in the far distance, snow-capped mountains lined the horizon, but here on the hillside, the air was warm. A few large chimneys released clouds of dark smoke, but most only let out small trails, gathering in the sky. The evening sun was slowly changing it from a dingy grey haze to a warmer brown.

She peered over the tops of the blades of spring-green grass, watching the subtle shifts of movement along roadways and the river. The thick plait of her braid lay over her arm, bright with strands of reds and oranges and golds, like she'd drawn the colors from an autumn forest and woven them together.

"There are so many of them," an awed voice said from the grass beside her.

She glanced over at the young elf staring at the city. "Thought you said humans were never surprising," she said with a small smirk.

"I was wrong." He lifted his head higher, his eyes tracing the long line of the river that meandered off to the south. He was brighter than the grass around him, his arms glowing slightly. Her own elbow seemed mundane next to his, just a smooth light brown compared to his coppery flush. His hair was a deep russet that glowed like there were tiny coals interlaced with each strand.

"Evay says this isn't even that big. Far to the south, their capital city sits along the sea, and is ten times bigger. She says you can't walk across it in a day."

He pulled his eyes from the city and gave her an incredulous look. "What do they all…do?"

A small wagon train moving into the city caught her eye. "Build things. Buy things. Sell things. Transport things to other places." She shrugged. "The larger the city, the busier they are."

He was quiet for a long moment. "You've never been in there, have you?"

The edge of her mouth curled up. "I wish. You're so impressed you're glowing."

His eyes widened, and he glanced down at his arms. The brightness faded quickly as he clamped down on it, giving a self-conscious smile.

"No, I've never been in any city nearly this large. Evay says mobs of humans are unpredictable. They are generally calm, but when violence erupts, it spreads like fire."

"She's been in some?"

Venn nodded. "She's been in the capital. Says it's amazing and smothering. Said my parents would kill her if she took me somewhere like that."

He gave a short laugh. "Wonder what my parents would do."

Venn grinned and went back to watching the city. "Just wait until it gets dark. There are so many torches it looks like a pool of fiery stars."

The memory shifted, and the world grew dusky. Light after light flickered to life among the buildings. When the world was shrouded in deep blues, she sat up. In front of them, the city turned to a thousand pinpricks of light, rolling over the hillsides and drifting along the river.

The boy had grown very still.

"You're never this thoughtful," she said.

He didn't look away from the city. "We should come here again."

She let out a short laugh. "Sure. Next time you have twenty days when no one will notice you're gone."

He turned to her, his eyes drawn with seriousness. "I would like to come here again."

She searched his face, but there was no sign of humor. "All right."

Looking down on the sprawl of lights, she felt like a bird sitting on the outskirts of an unknown world. She wanted to slip down the long hillside and into the shadows of the city. Move among the humans. Wander the knotted streets between all those buildings. And she also wanted to stay right where she was, not stepping one foot closer to the strange commotion that filled the city like a foaming swirl of water among the rapids.

"Whenever you want," she answered.

Kate pulled her finger out of the vial, blinking to clear the last of the memory from her view. "How long ago was that?"

"Two hundred…" Venn looked up into the sky. "No, nearly three hundred years ago." She gave a nostalgic smile. "We sat there for the entire night until the city woke the next morning. I never saw a bigger city than that. We went back twenty years later, but it was in ruins."

"Who was the glowing boy?"

Her smile faltered. "A childhood friend. He had a tendency to lose track of the light when he was shocked." She took a deep breath, and her face grew sober. "He's…been gone a long time."

"Oh," Kate said, "I'm sorry—"

A shriek rang out ahead of them, muffled by the trees, a faint echo bouncing off the nearby cliffs.

Kate jerked to a stop.

Venn lifted the arm with her small crossbow mounting on it and pressed her other hand onto the tree trunk next to her.

The cry came again, like a woman or a child screaming in pain, ahead and off to their right.

Kate gave Venn a sharp look before breaking into a run. "You said there were no people nearby!" she yelled over her shoulder.

Venn pushed off the tree and sprinted after her. "There *are* no people!"

CHAPTER TWENTY-THREE

THE CRY SOUNDED AGAIN in front of them, quick and pained. Kate raced toward it, casting out. Each tree around her warmed with *vitalle.* The wave rolled on in a widening circle, giving impressions of more trunks than she could see. It lit the shapes of a few small animals scurrying away from the screams but faded out before reaching anything bright enough to be human.

Venn ran past her, a dart loaded in her crossbow. Sticks littering the forest floor caught at Kate's boots, rolling or snapping or twisting sharply as her feet landed on them. The next shriek rang through the trees much closer and much weaker, but another sound tickled at Kate's ears. Low and indistinct.

She cast out again.

Venn's blazing form ran ahead of her, twice as bright as a human, and in a gap in the trees just past the elf, an enormous cloud of *vitalle* exploded into light and heat. It swirled and shifted, nearly filling the clearing and rising high into the branches around it.

There was absolutely nothing human about it.

Another scream pierced the morning air, this one ending in a whimper.

Venn skidded to a stop a dozen steps ahead.

A low buzzing sound filled the forest, and Kate drew up next to Venn.

The clearing was full of golden light, or hundreds of golden lights, spinning and churning and humming in a massive cloud.

"What are..." Kate cast out a third time, and every single point of light flared even brighter, putting out a wave of heat as though each were a tiny searing fire. She took a half step back. "Are those...vimwisps?"

Venn's eyes traced the motion of the swirling swarm, and she nodded.

These weren't normal vimwisps, slow bumbling thorn-shaped bits of light, barely the length of a fingernail. Those were sent out by a hive to buzz around flowers and fruits like glowing bumble-bees, drawing out tiny drips of *vitalle*.

These vimwisps were as long as her thumb and swirled through the air in a seething cloud. Normally, they let out a faint shushing noise like wind fanning a flame, but these crackled and snapped and hummed. The leaves of the nearby trees trembled with the sound.

"What is wrong with them?" Kate whispered.

A whimper came from the ground at the base of the churning swarm, and Kate caught sight of red fur between the lights. A fox lay curled in a tight ball. She cast out toward it, and below the brightness of the vimwisps, she found its small form, weak and leaking *vitalle* from a thousand punctures.

The bright light of a stinger drove into its back, and the fox let out a yelp that sounded like a child's cry. Another stabbed into its neck, and it flinched.

Kate took a step forward.

Venn's hand snapped out, grabbing her arm. "Don't—"

But Kate's motion had sent a ripple through the edges of the cloud, and two vimwisps swirled away from the others, diving toward her.

Immediately, a dozen more followed.

As if a gate had opened, more wisps spun out of the swarm and raced after them.

Before the first wisp was halfway to Kate, it turned and veered toward Venn, maybe drawn to the elf's massive amounts of *vitalle*. Venn dropped Kate's arm and started to lift her crossbow in a gesture that looked habitual before letting it fall. "Run!"

"Wait! They're just *vitalle*—" Kate stepped closer to the elf.

The first vimwisp sliced down toward Venn's chest, and she threw up her other hand to block it. The tiny dagger of light stabbed into her forearm, and Venn hissed.

Kate flung out a shield of *vitalle* wide enough to cover herself and Venn. Heat shot out of her palm as she shoved the shell wider, forming the thin layer faster and broader than she'd ever tried, and the next stinger slammed into it in front of Venn's shoulder. A starburst of light exploded across the shell as the vimwisp shattered with a crackle like lightning. The impact tore into the surface, ripping open a gap and sending a prick into Kate's palm. She shoved more *vitalle* into the shield as the next vimwisp hit and burst into a spray of light.

The next four wisps drove at them, slamming into the barrier with harsh crackles, tearing into it. Kate ignored the jab of pain in her hand at the damage to the shield and syphoned the energy blasting out from their impact to strengthen the shell.

The stream of wisps flowing toward them spread out, and Venn swore, putting her shoulder to Kate's. "They're going to get around your shield."

"Back to back!" Kate turned her shoulder toward the wisps and felt Venn back up against her.

More stingers barreled into the wall, crackling and humming, and Kate grabbed their *vitalle* and fed it into the shell, stretching it around herself and Venn, arching it overhead and drawing it down toward the ground.

Kate caught the scent of her own remnant before Venn's flooded the small space.

A vimwisp darted under the edge and stabbed into Kate's calf like a tiny dagger.

The shield wavered. A biting cold spread from the half-buried vimwisp, and it pulsed with a glaring light that matched her racing heartbeat as it bled *vitalle* out of her.

Venn let out a grunt behind her. "Doesn't seem to be working perfectly," she shouted over the sound of the bursting wisps.

The circle of cold on Kate's leg grew wider, and the wisp grew brighter until it burst apart. A dozen more hurtled into her wall. She swept their *vitalle* into the shield, slamming it down to the ground.

A steady stream of wisps swirled around them, the buzzing hum growing steadily louder. They darted against the shield and ricocheted off or exploded into light that shredded holes into the wall.

"What does the nest need this much *vitalle* for?" Kate yelled.

Despite the fact that she could catch energy from the wisps to strengthen the shell, Kate's own reserves dwindled. Holding a shield was easy. Mending one required a push of concentrated *vitalle*, and even with the heat in her palms, her forearms grew increasingly cold as the life energy leached out of her bones.

She needed *vitalle* from something else. Kate glanced at the nearest tree, but it was too far to reach. Thick brush covered the ground at their feet, a sprawling, twisting tangle of branches and dark green leaves spreading all the way across the clearing. One thin branch was close to Kate's shin, and she shoved her leg closer until it jabbed her and she drew the *vitalle* up out of the brush and into herself, funneling it toward her hands. It reached her forearms like a little river of warmth, and she thrust it into the shield.

The leaves nearest her leg curled and browned, but *vitalle* continued to flow from the next branch.

"How long can you keep this up?" Venn yelled over the noise.

Kate had both hands pressed against the inside of the shell, and her palms burned as she focused on repairing the chinks from the barrage of wisps. "I don't know! If we can get to the fox, I can protect him too!"

"Why? So all of us can die when your shield ends?" Venn shifted, craning to see through the wisps. "We need to find the nest!"

A handful of wisps slammed into the wall next to each other, and a small hole ripped open, sending a slicing pain across Kate's palm. Two stingers darted in, straight toward her neck.

Venn twisted and flung her arm up, blocking the wisps with her forearm.

"Thank you," Kate yelled between clenched teeth, dragging the hole shut again. "How are we supposed to stop them?"

"They're controlled by the hive. I can put it to sleep—" Venn hissed as the two stingers pulsed in her arm. "If I knew where it was!"

The swirling cloud of vimwisps obscured most of the clearing, but there was a knot of *vitalle* high in one of the trees past the fox

"It's in the pine across the clearing." Kate jerked her head toward it.

"Are you sure?" Venn shifted and loaded a small dart into her crossbow.

"No, I thought I'd just guess," Kate snapped, sweat beading on her forehead at the effort of keeping the wall whole, "because this seems like the sort of thing we want to be uncertain about!"

Venn stretched to the side. "I can't see the nest!"

"See that broken branch on the skinny pine? Like a pig's snout?"

"A pig's snout?" Venn demanded, shifting to stay close to Kate while raising her crossbow toward the tree. "In a tree?"

"Not a real pig! A branch that *looks* like a pig—"

Venn loosed the dart.

A needle of pain drove into Kate's palm, and the shield shuddered as she tried to keep hold of it. "What are you doing? I didn't say shoot the broken branch! The nest in the large pine next to it! On the trunk! At the same height as that broken branch! It's in a fork in the trunk!"

"You said the pig branch!" Venn snapped another dart into her small crossbow. "I can't see the big pine through the swarm!"

"That's why I pointed out the pig branch!" Kate shifted toward the clearing. "We need to get closer. Head toward the fox!"

Venn swore but stayed against her as they pushed through the swarming, crackling cloud. The *vitalle* pressing out of Kate's hands to feed the shield burned, and hot blisters rose on her palms.

Her fingers trembled, and she felt the bottom edge of the shell begin to tatter. "Faster!" She broke into a shuffling sideways run and Venn kept with her, back to back.

They were nearly at the fox when Kate's foot caught on the brush and she crashed to her knees.

Venn dropped down next to her. "I see the nest!" She leaned hard against Kate's shoulder as she craned to peer around the swirling wisps.

A yelp came from the fox, and Kate shuffled closer until her leg pressed along the fox's back. She stretched the shield, enveloping it inside the barrier.

Outside, the wisps flung themselves wildly against the shell, their motion growing more frantic. Tiny holes appeared, and Kate tried to seal them, but they came faster than she could fix.

"Are you waiting for some kind of invitation?" Kate yelled.

The crossbow twanged just as three small holes tore into one large gash.

Vimwisps dove in through the gap and ripped into Kate's shoulder and neck, bursts of icy cold spreading instantly as the stingers drew out her *vitalle*. Venn grunted in pain behind her.

Kate's hold on the shield faltered. The edge of the gash unraveled. She grabbed at it with her mind, drawing more *vitalle* from the brush beneath her, but the shield disintegrated from a thousand places at once, like a tattered bit of smoke blown away by the wind.

Vimwisps surged toward them. Venn shouted something in Elvish and curled forward. Kate threw herself over the fox, squinting over her shoulder into the cloud and bracing against the stings plummeting toward her.

A dozen hit, driving into her skin like icy needles.

One dove for her face, and Kate flinched, but instead of a sting, a breath of air puffed at her.

The roaring buzz of the vimwisps shifted to hundreds of tiny pops.

The wisp nearest her burst into sparkling dust. With a deafening rush of airy explosions, every wisp fractured and disappeared.

CHAPTER TWENTY-FOUR

KATE STARED up into the empty clearing, her breath heaving in her chest. Pain radiated out of her palms, and the wisp stings on her shoulder and neck burned with an icy chill.

Behind her, Venn sank back on her heels.

The buzzing roar of the vimwisps was gone, leaving nothing but the breeze in the trees and the chatter of a squirrel. Venn's remnant fleshed out the smells and sounds of the forest, and, aside from Kate's heavy breathing, the only other noise was a low, barely discernible rumble. Like thunder from a distant storm.

Up in the pine, an enormous yellow bundle was tucked in the fork of the trunk. The other vimwisp nests Kate had seen were small enough to sit in the palm of her hand. This was twice as big as her head. "Why is it so huge?" she asked, letting her hands fall to her lap with her palms up. "And how long is it going to sleep?"

"If I hit the heart of it, we should have hours." Venn pushed herself to her feet and walked to the pine, studying it. As she stepped away, her remnant receded, and the rumble of the hive sounded more clearly. It was a remnant, of sorts. A strange one, though. Remote. Detached somehow.

"And if you missed?"

Venn squinted up into the tree, her eyes probing the nest. "Let's hope I didn't."

Kate's head drooped forward, heavy enough that she'd have liked to lie down and sleep. Her hands sat limp in her lap. Both palms were covered in blisters, two of them split and leaking, but she turned her attention to the fox.

Its pelt was slick with blood. More trickled from tiny punctures in its muzzle.

She glanced down at her palms. "I suppose I can't hurt them worse," she muttered, reaching toward the fox. It took more willpower than she'd expected to press one hand down on the creature's side and the other into the brush beneath them. Refusing to acknowledge the blazing pain in either hand, she funneled a small amount of *vitalle* out of the brush and into the fox. It would normally only be enough to barely warm her skin, but it burned across her blisters like liquid fire.

Gritting her teeth, she syphoned *vitalle* into the little creature, giving it strength to heal its wounds quickly. Its fur was thick, but she could feel the punctures across its skin, and she directed the energy there.

From near the pine, Venn gave a hum that sounded like some sort of confirmation. She pointed to a rough vine snaking up the trunk. "I found the problem."

"A sap vine?"

"The biggest one I've ever seen."

"Isn't that tree big enough to handle a little sap being drawn out of it?"

"Yes, but it's wrapped around the hive too. Cinched into it. Probably draining it faster than the vimwisps can refuse it."

"No wonder they were so…hungry."

"Maybe I can untangle it while the hive sleeps." Venn climbed quickly up the rough trunk.

Kate let her eyes fall closed, fighting off a wave of dizziness as she probed the fox. The burning in her palms had become like a background of pain that she tried to ignore along with the strange thundering remnant from the hive.

"They weakened you quite a bit, didn't they?" She worked her fingertips into the thick fur at the back of its neck as though it were a dog, trying to focus on his coat and the fact she was actually touching a fox, rather than on how even the soft tufts stung her palm. "Just between us, they weakened me, too." The wounds on its side were almost healed, and she turned her attention to its muzzle. A trickle of blood fell from a puncture near its eye. One eyelid was swollen and red, except near the wound, where it was a sickly grey. "I'm not sure I can get you feeling normal, but if we can get these healed, maybe you can go find a place for a long nap—"

The fox twitched. Its swollen eye slit apart as it scrambled to its feet with a small whine of pain. It spun to face her, its body crouched with wariness.

Kate sat perfectly still. "It's all right," she said, her voice low. "You're—"

"We have a few hours," Venn shouted from up near the nest.

The fox flinched at the sound, then spun and raced off into the forest.

Kate let her hands drop to her lap again, leaving her burned palms facing up. "You're welcome," she called as the creature's tail disappeared past some brush.

Pushing herself to her feet, she moved over to the pine. A thick vine crawled up the trunk, about three fingers wide. Its surface was a dark greenish brown, speckled with black spines.

"This vine..." Venn's voice was somewhat muffled as she leaned awkwardly around the hive. "It's embedded in the hive, and I think that..." She gave a growl of pain and muttered a string of angry-sounding words too low for Kate to hear.

Kate drew her small knife out of her belt, holding the handle gingerly with her fingertips, setting the tip between the needly thorns. "We could just cut it and pull it off of the tree, couldn't we?" She pressed gently into it.

"Don't touch the spines!" Venn warned. "They're—"

The knife tip sank into the soft flesh.

Spines shot out in every direction, stabbing into the fleshy side of Kate's hand and along her forearm. She jerked away from the tree.

Branches thrashed, and Venn swore loudly in a long stream of Elvish. "Stop touching it!"

Kate groaned. "Sorry!" Gingerly using only her fingertips, she took hold of one lodged in the side of her hand. She pulled, but it merely tugged against her skin. She yanked at it, and a little chunk of flesh ripped out with it, and she hissed in pain.

"Don't pull them out! They're barbed!" Venn's voice snapped down from above.

"I figured that out!" Kate yelled through clench teeth.

"Twist it like a corkscrew!"

Kate backed away from the tree and turned the next needle slowly. It slid roughly, but twisted out, only taking a tiny bit of skin with it. She sank down against a nearby tree, working her way up her arm, twisting out spine after spine.

In a few minutes, Venn climbed gingerly down, holding her head at an odd angle to the side and favoring her right arm. She dropped down the last few feet with a grimace and turned to glare at Kate.

At least a dozen spines were embedded in the side of her neck. "I almost had the nest free before you attacked the vine."

Kate winced. "Ah...sorry. I can help you get those out."

Venn gave her an annoyed look but dropped to the ground in

front of her. The back of the elf's right shoulder bristled with spines that stretched nearly down to her elbow, and they went up her neck almost to her ear.

"How on earth were you situated up there?" Kate reached for the ones stabbed through the fabric of Venn's shirt, each surrounded by a spot of blood. Kate forced her aching hands to grasp a needle and spin it slowly, working it out of Venn's shoulder. The elf's remnant swirled around them again, overlaying the normal scents and sounds of the forest.

"Uncomfortably." Venn let out a grunt of pain. "And that was before you did this."

"I am sorry." Kate grimaced and moved to the next one. "I've never seen a sap vine shoot spines."

Venn unbuckled the crossbow from her forearm so her sleeve would shift more easily, then set it carefully on her lap. "Seems that drawing life from a vimwisp hive altered it." She rubbed her other hand across her face and let out a long, controlled breath. "Your shield was impressive."

Kate raised an eyebrow at the compliment, even if it sounded a bit begrudging. Venn held out her hand, looking at a vimwisp welt near her wrist. "Except for when it frayed at the bottom and all the holes it kept getting, it was fairly effective."

"Fairly eff—?" Kate bit down on her response and set her fingertips on the next spine. "Well, your shot at the nest was also impressive." She gave a slightly quicker twist of the needle, and Venn twitched. "Once you finally aimed for the right place."

"You mean once you finally communicated clearly," Venn said between clenched teeth.

"Just stop talking and stay still." Kate spun out three spines in quick succession while Venn pinched her eyes shut.

There really were a lot of spines, and Kate winced with the elf at the ones embedded in the skin on the back of her arm. With each spine, her irritation shifted closer to sympathy. "How did you put the nest to sleep?" she asked finally, trying to keep her voice friendly.

"Can you not put something to sleep with your *iza*?"

"If I touch them. I couldn't do it from a distance."

Venn used her other hand to pull a dart out of her quiver. Just behind the tip, a small nut-shaped bulb was fixed into the shaft. "That holds a small amount of *iza*. I merely sent my wish for the hive to sleep up with the dart."

Kate cast out toward the arrow and felt the knot of *vitalle* sitting on it. "That's clever. Can you do other things with it as well?"

"All these just put things to sleep." Venn slid the dart back into her quiver.

Kate pulled out the last spine. "Done." She dropped her hands to her lap. The small wounds on her forearm still beaded with drops of blood, but the ones on Venn's neck were already closing.

"I see you're healthy enough to heal yourself again," Kate said, standing.

Venn pulled her sleeve up, exposing the tattoo that had been under her crossbow. She looked it over, but none of the stingers or spines had gotten near it. She glanced up to see Kate watching and lowered her sleeve, buckling the crossbow back on. Her gaze caught on Kate's palms, and she stopped. "Do you have bandages for those?"

Kate nodded and tried to unbuckle her pack, but her fingers fumbled with the strap.

"Here." Venn knelt next to her and unbuckled it, opening the top.

"On the right side, near the bottom, is a burlap pouch."

Venn rummaged for a moment before pulling out the little medicine bag Gerone always made sure was stocked.

"There's a jar of yellow salve." Kate gingerly opened her waterskin and began to rinse one palm.

"Let me do it," Venn said, the words more commanding than an offer to help should be. "You're wasting water." She took Kate's hand and cleaned it, thoroughly if not gently, applied a glob of yellow salve, and wrapped it with one of the small bandages. "You're remarkably well-prepared for treating burned palms," she noted, working on the second hand. "I didn't realize Keepers' magic was so harmful to them."

"If I'm doing something small enough that I only need a little *vitalle* from myself, it doesn't hurt. But when I need to draw from outside things, that's when it can cause trouble."

Venn glanced down at the withered brush. "I didn't realize you could take so much from other things."

"Can't you?" Kate asked.

"I can take in *iza* from a tree if I'm touching it. Or push a little into it. But everything is subtle. I can influence a tree to grow a little, or bend. I could calm a creature if I touched it. Put it to sleep or wake it up. But nothing like…" She gestured to the shriveled plants.

Kate stretched her fingers on her bandaged hand. "I can take *vitalle* from fire or anything alive, and it doesn't hurt if done in moderation. But the wisps pushed me a bit past that point."

Venn squinted at Kate's hand as she tied a knot on the second bandage. "This looks like more than a bit."

Kate looked at the elf to see if she was joking, but she seemed serious. "I didn't mean it literally. By 'a bit' I meant 'very far past.'"

"Then why didn't you say that?"

Kate let out a tired breath. "I don't know. Irony seemed easier. Before I knew I'd have to explain it to you."

Venn tucked the pouch back into Kate's pack. "Can you take *vitalle* from another human?"

"Yes," Kate answered honestly, "but no Keeper would. We don't believe it's our right to take energy from another person.

Fire is my favorite source, then plants. If I needed to take from an animal, I might, but the need would have to be dire."

Venn studied her. "And if we end up somewhere dire, would you take it from me?"

"Not without your permission."

Venn held her gaze as though gauging the truth of the words, then gave a slow nod. "Your shield *was* impressive. Thank you." She held out a hand, and when Kate raised hers, the elf grasped her forearm and pulled her to her feet.

Kate wobbled slightly.

"Can you walk?" Venn asked dryly. "Or do we need to find some horses so you can keep up a good pace?"

Kate rolled her shoulders. "I'll be fine." The exhaustion from using *vitalle* was real, but not exactly physical. She flipped open her pack and took out the last of the raisin bread Gerone had packed for her. "A little food will help."

"Good." Venn started toward the tree with the broken branch. "I need to find my other dart that you wasted by telling me to shoot a nonexistent pig."

Venn's remnant faded as she walked away, and the forest around Kate grew quieter. She glanced up at the nest.

The thundering sound was gone. She cast out toward it, and it blazed up brightly.

Kate frowned. Remnants didn't disappear just because something was asleep or wasn't in pain any longer. Of course, things like nests or animals, even distinctly magical ones, didn't usually have remnants at all.

Venn rustled around in the brush, and Kate followed her, casting out in the general direction the dart had flown. Among the trees, a handful of small mice warmed up, and one little knot of bright *vitalle* was lodged under a fallen stump. Venn headed for it.

Kate leaned her shoulder against the nearest trunk. Her arms still felt heavy and her palms ached. "Do many elves use cross-bows like that?"

Venn shook her head. "Only the royal guard. I trained with them for a time."

"The royal guard?"

Venn plucked the dart up from the ground. "We should keep moving."

Kate took a bite of bread and pushed herself off the tree. "While we walk, want to share a memory of the guard with me?"

Venn stalked into the woods, heading south. "Not even slightly."

CHAPTER TWENTY-FIVE

A LOW RUMBLE of distant thunder tickled her ears, and Kate glanced over her shoulder at the pathless forest growing darker in the ruddy evening light. A hint of breeze wafted past, pulling gently on the strands of moss that hung from the branches, but the rest of the woods were quiet.

But it had been there again. The strange remnant.

When she'd heard it around midmorning, there'd been no obvious source. The second time, a twitchy grey bird had watched her for a breath before darting away. Or maybe it hadn't been watching her and she was just imagining things.

She cast out. A bird flitted through the branches, but not close. A few squirrels or rabbits gamboled across the ground. There was no sense of a vimwisp nest, though, especially not one huge enough to thunder. And…a nest couldn't follow them.

From somewhere low to the ground, so faint it might have been her imagination, she heard the rumble.

"Are you always this jumpy in the woods?" Venn asked, not bothering to stop.

"Can you hear the thunder?"

Venn looked up at the slivers of blue sky through the trees. A few wispy clouds trailed across it, tinged orange with the sunset. "Why would there be thunder?"

Kate glanced behind them again. "I don't know."

Venn squinted at her for a moment before shaking her head and starting forward.

Kate cast out once more, but there was nothing unusual. The only remnant was Venn's.

"Earlier," Venn said without looking back, "you said Keepers were respected in Queensland. Is that because you wield magic? Almost no humans near the White Wood can. I assume it's as rare here."

"That's part of it. Usually a Keeper appears every five to ten years, around the age of twelve, because their magic has awakened. But we don't just train to use *vitalle*. The first Keepers gathered the powerful magic wielders together in order to create an order of men and women who were committed to protecting the land. At the time, the great enemy was the Kalesh Empire, a people who destroyed any history or stories that didn't fit their own goals. So the early Keepers dedicated themselves to recording and protecting the history of the land. Political history, folktales, small personal stories. We've almost always had a close relationship with the monarchy of Queensland and offer counsel or research."

"Then why do you stay locked up in a tower that no one can reach?"

"That's where our library is," Kate said, "and where the older Keepers settle to train the youngest ones. Right now, four of the other eight Keepers are scattered around Queensland. Alaric and Sini, both of whom are good at research, currently sit on the queen's council at court. Zander is seven years older than Kellen and is working as the ambassador between Queensland and the dwarves in Duncave. Will, who is unquestionably the best storyteller in generations, travels the land collecting tales and entertaining everyone with his own."

"My aunt says there are few stories as good as a Keeper story." Venn glanced at Kate. "Do you tell many?"

"I do," Kate admitted. "I'm not as gifted as some at storytelling, but I'm good at gathering seemingly confusing parts of a story, fitting them together, and discovering the truth."

"Like figuring out why a grown man was afraid of a shadow and thought a tree attacked him?"

"And why an elf who is supposedly familiar with that area wouldn't believe either. Yes, that sort of thing."

A distinct chill filled the darkening forest by the time Venn stopped in the shadow of a huge oak tree. The tops of the branches blazed with bright oranges and reds even as the lower leaves held on to their summer green. She dropped her pack to the ground and put her hands against the trunk, closing her eyes.

Kate followed, looking curiously up into the thick canopy. "Do you expect rain?"

"This is the oldest tree nearby." Venn glanced at Kate. "Despite your fear of thunder, I don't think there's any chance of rain tonight."

"It wasn't fear." Kate pulled her own pack off, trying not to let anything press against her bandaged palms. "It was—"

Quiet thunder sounded from her right as a flash of motion whipped past.

A squirrel's tail disappeared under some brush, and the sound faded.

"Did you see that squirrel?"

Venn nodded slowly, looking cautiously back at Kate.

"Did you hear it?"

Venn folded her arms and put her back against the tree, studying Kate. "Did you hurt your head as well as your palms earlier?"

Kate flicked her hand dismissively at Venn. "Of course you didn't hear it." She crossed the clearing to peer after the squirrel.

"I'm sure I can hear more than you," Venn said, her voice vaguely insulted.

Kate knelt down near the path where the little animal had run. There were faint hints of sound. Maybe thunder, maybe wind. And an impression of...

She ran her fingertips over the ground. An impression of emptiness. Like the night sky. She sat back on her heels, searching the forest. "It was a remnant."

"I have no idea what that means," Venn said, "but the oak says it was just a squirrel."

"It had a remnant." Kate stood and walked to her pack. "And it sounded like the vimwisp nest, and a bird earlier." She reached into the side pocket of her pack and pulled out her vial of serum, uncorking it. She turned to find Venn looking at her with a suspicious expression.

"Is this like the metaphorical shadow you thought was following Bo?"

"I think a *literal* shadow was following Bo," Kate corrected her, "and this is a literal sound as well. But you won't have heard it." Kate pressed her finger into the serum and pushed in the memory of the thunder from the nest before Venn had pulled the vine off it, then the times in the woods, and finally the squirrel. She handed the vial to Venn.

The elf took it with narrowed eyes but set her finger into the fluid. Her eyebrows rose as the memory spooled into her. "Do animals usually sound like that to you?" She pulled her finger out and wiped it off.

"Those are remnants. Sometimes they're sounds, sometimes smells." Kate took the vial back. "Animals don't have them. Only people do." She poured the memories of Kellen's remnant and Gerone's into the serum, then added Venn's for good measure. "Everyone has one, and everyone's is unique."

Venn took in the memories, then looked at Kate inscrutably. "That's an interesting skill. Why is mine so different?"

"I assume because you're an elf, but you're the only one I've ever met, so I don't know if you're normal."

"And people leave them behind? Like a trail?"

"If they've been past recently, it's a very obvious trail." Kate glanced back to where the squirrel had disappeared. "It starts to fade after a few hours, and by a couple of days it's totally gone."

"Those remnants…" Venn handed the vial back to Kate thoughtfully. "They fit Kellen and Gerone."

"They always fit. They're a manifestation of who the person is. They can even change a little over time if the person does." She wrapped the serum and tucked it into her pack. "But I've never known an animal with one. Except a dragon, which is so strong it lingers in its scales for…centuries, maybe." She nodded after the squirrel. "That was not the remnant of a dragon."

"No one needs your skill to know a dragon didn't just scamper by." Venn's eyes traced the branches above them. "Maybe this forest is different. This is the edge of the Wildwood. I can feel it in the trees. Especially right here. The power of the elves still lingers. Maybe the animals here remember being more."

"I'm aware this was part of the Wildwood." Kate pointed toward the southwest. "I grew up not far from here. My brother and Bo and I spent our days exploring the woods, finding the few trees that still felt …"

"Alive."

"More alive than other trees, but I assure you, the animals here don't have remnants."

Venn's mouth quirked up in a smile. "Do you think it's a dangerous squirrel?"

Kate shook her head. "Remnants of dangerous people are very easy to pick out."

The distant chitter of a squirrel made them both twitch toward the woods.

"That remnant wasn't vicious. It was…" Kate tapped her fingertip against her leg, but the motion made her palm ache. "I would say it was lonely."

"I don't think of squirrels as getting lonely. Or nests."

"Remnants aren't from current emotions. It's more of who they are in their core."

Venn studied her for a moment, not looking particularly convinced. "So you're saying the squirrel, and the bird, and something else earlier, are all the nest? Or are all the same as the nest?"

"It seems that way."

Venn squinted at her. "Literally? Or metaphorically?"

Kate let out an annoyed breath. "I don't know! I've never found two things with the same remnant, never mind four things, none of which should even have one."

"Well"—Venn turned back to the huge oak and set her hand on its trunk—"none of those things seem particularly threatening, but if anything else thunders at you, and you think we're literally in trouble, let me know." She glanced over her shoulder at Kate. "If it's all metaphorical, don't tell me. I can't make something stop thundering at you."

Kate ignored her, sat against the oak, and let her eyes run over the forest.

There were no landmarks, but Venn was right. They'd reached the old Wildwood. There was a bit of brightness in the air that had nothing to do with the setting sun. A light that was always just out of the corner of her eye. A vividness to the colors around them. The vividness that had surrounded Kate's childhood and left all other forests feeling slightly hollow.

"Tomorrow we'll pass near a group of..." Kate hesitated. "'Towns' is too generous of a word. They are three little settlements run by self-proclaimed warlords. They're petty and ineffective everywhere but in their own lands, but the local duke refuses to do much about them." Kate squinted toward the south. "Actually, I think the duke is corrupt and being paid to look the other way, but regardless, tomorrow we should stay closer to the cliffs. The settlements have a reputation for kidnapping travelers and selling them to slavers in the southern lands." She worked the buckle open on her pack and pulled out her medicine pouch.

Venn pressed her palms to the trunk of the oak and looked up into the branches. "I didn't know Keepers were scared of common rabble," she said distractedly.

Kate's fingers paused in trying to untie the bundle. "They travel in bands of four to six men they call a Snare, which would be an inconvenience, even for you."

"Four to six barely qualifies as an inconvenience. Ten is an inconvenience."

"Even when Snares use poisoned arrows and blades that will dull your mind and your reflexes? Add to that the fact that they are expert trackers?"

Venn spared a quick glance at Kate's hands. "Are you worried you're too wounded to help fight them off?"

Kate dropped her head and took a deep breath, searching for patience. "Having my palms burned makes any magic I try more difficult. So yes, it would be mostly up to you to fight them. Are you saying that four to six men trying to capture us wouldn't even be a nuisance in our day tomorrow?"

Venn's attention was back up in the branches, and her lips moved silently.

"I realize you don't give my opinion any weight," Kate said, attempting to keep her voice polite but failing, "but I've traveled these particular woods a hundred times, and I'm saying we should stay near the cliffs."

Venn gave a small shrug. "It's as good a route as any."

Kate finished tugging on the tie of the pouch and opened it gingerly, pulling out the burn salve. A chilly wind blew against her and pulled her breath away in a cloud. She glanced up into the sky.

The coming night had the feel of a cold one. She sighed and set down the salve. No point in tending her bandages if she was just going to dirty them again while gathering firewood. There was a low branch above her. It wouldn't be terribly hard to put up a shelter against that to keep in a little heat. She let out another sigh at the thought of work Venn probably wouldn't be interested in sharing and stood.

The low branch creaked and dropped. She ducked and scrambled toward the trunk, kicking up a spray of leaves. "Watch out!"

Venn stood against the trunk, her eyes closed, while the three lowest limbs bent lower, creaking like they were being pressed by a strong wind.

Kate stayed low, staring up into the tree. "Venn?"

She didn't answer. The boughs of the oak lowered until their tips brushed the ground, forming a sloping wall of living branches.

The evening wind rustled the leaves outside but only snuck through in tiny tendrils.

"That's…" Kate stared into the leaves. The sunlight set the

higher ones glowing with golds and reds that filtered down through into the gloom beneath the branches. "How did…"

Venn dropped her hands and surveyed her work with an approving look.

"I knew elves could convince trees to shelter them, but…I swear I read that it took several elves and at least a full day."

"This oak is old. He remembers the elves from before."

"Before? As in three hundred years ago?"

Venn looked up into his branches. "He's *sol'veluce*." She glanced at Kate. "Elf touched. They woke him, long ago. There were…" Her eyes grew distant. "Meetings here, councils. Bindings and blessings." She blinked and smiled into the leaves. "I could feel him getting closer all afternoon."

"So you couldn't do this with any tree?"

"I could. Talking with trees is as easy as breathing. Younger ones just take more prodding." She sat down next to the trunk and pulled three pears out of her pack. She tossed one to Kate.

"Where did you get these?"

"There was a pear tree near our camp this morning. I picked them while you slept."

The fruit was soft, a bit past its peak, but Kate's first bite was juicy and sweet. She stood and looked around at the wall of branches. "Is your *sol'veluce* tree going to mind if I build a fire?"

Venn took a bite and leaned back against the trunk. "Can you keep it under control?"

Kate headed out of the gap at the side of the branches. "Controlling a fire is as easy as breathing." She glanced over her shoulder. "And it doesn't even have to be an old one."

She stepped out into the blue-tinged evening. The wind shoved against her, and she pulled her lined cloak closer. Working quickly, trying to pick up dead branches without letting them jab into her bandaged palms, she gathered an armload of firewood. Before she was done, the shadows had grown to broad pockets of midnight blue under the trees. The sky above was a richer cerulean, just light enough to make the gloom of the forest floor more impenetrable.

The chill seeped into her fingers, making them clumsy and making each jab of rough bark or pine needle ache more than it should.

Before she stepped under the shelter, she cast out again. There were bundles of brightness and warmth nestled among the smoldering pillars of trees, but nothing unusual.

She ducked back inside, out of the wind, and felt her way through shadows so deep she could just barely make out Venn's shape still leaning against the trunk. Kate knelt and set the wood down. She scooped up the crunchy fallen leaves from a wide circle and piled them into a heap. Finding bits of kindling by feel, she piled them on top, then set her finger against the leaves.

With a whisper of *vitalle*, she lit it. The leaves were wet enough that the flames merely slid along the edges with bluish hearts and thick swirls of smoke, but she kept her hand nearby, funneling more *vitalle* into the fire, encouraging it to grow and spread to the other leaves, leading it to the smaller pieces of kindling, then to the larger, until a blaze flickered cheerily on the ground.

The shelter emerged from the shadows into the golden light, the roof of leaves lit with reds and yellows and greens like some lavish tapestry.

Carefully, Kate broke off larger bits of wood and fed them to the fire, spreading it out to the sides, keeping the flames from rising too close to the branches overhead.

She held out the back of her hands toward its heat, protecting her palms, until her fingers finally warmed. Outside, the wind grew fiercer, tearing through the leaves high in the oak, but only short blusters of wind snuck into the shelter, and the space warmed steadily.

Between the sap vine thorns and the vimwisp stings, every motion brought little jolts of pain. None were terribly sharp, but each was a small leak, draining away her hope that she'd find Bo quickly. It had been a single day of travel, and the dozens lying ahead stretched out depressingly far.

She pulled some *vitalle* out of the fire and fed it along her arms and into the rest of her body to help heal the stings. When they were only minor aches, she pulled the bandages from her hands, treated each palm with her burn salve, and rewrapped them both.

Gingerly, she took out the last of the sharp cheese from Gerone and held out a chunk to Venn. The elf only paused for a moment before nodding.

Kate tossed it to her and took a bite. Her eyes traced the pathways of branches above them, moving among the different-colored leaves as her mind flitted from questions about Bo to ones about the box. Curiosity about the Kalesh city from the memory earlier vied with the oddness of the thundering remnant that followed them. She wondered briefly whether the fox was healing. Her tired mind refused to settle on one thing, moving restlessly from question to question.

Venn sat against the trunk with her eyes closed, her posture decidedly uninviting.

Kate shook her head, trying to clear it. But, aside from talking things through with an interested partner—she shot an annoyed look at Venn, which was entirely wasted on the resting elf—there was really only one way to quiet the swirl of thoughts.

Rummaging inside her bag, she found one of the blank journals and a charcoal pencil. She ran her finger over the tightly wrapped string around the rod of charcoal as she tried to sort out where to begin. Finally, tilting the first page toward the fire, she started with the easiest idea: a quick list of everything that had happened since Venn had appeared at the Stronghold.

The soft pencil scribbled out dark lines as the list of events grew. She added small notations alongside them, questions to consider or references to check, and her mind slowed as the words spilled out.

On the second page, she drew the old, thriving Kalesh city Venn had shown her, noting the rivers, hazarding a few guesses as to which city it might have been, listing the maps she'd want to cross-reference once she was finally back at her desk.

The notes were sparse and the drawings merely quick sketches, which would most likely look even worse in daylight. The char pencil would smudge a bit, but it would be enough to remind her of the details when she wrote out her full account. In ink. In a clean book. Somewhere with a nice flat table and good light.

On the third, she made a rough map of the clearing where Bo's box had been found.

On the next, she wrote out every idea she could remember from Bo's letters and journal and Venn's memories. The box, the library, the rockslide, the walking tree, the shadow, the other elves, Venn's actions. She scattered the words across two facing pages, connecting them with lines or arrows to their detailed descriptions and the other ideas they were related to. Between them all, she threaded in the questions each raised.

When she was done, a strange sort of map filled the pages. The most interconnected questions—like "What is the shadow?" —stood out prominently merely from the sheer number of lines stretching out from them.

Connected to more ideas than any other were the words "Where is Bo?"

"What is that?" Venn asked.

Kate glanced up to see her looking at the page, her arms folded across her chest. "An old habit. I call it a story map. I try to see how the seemingly unrelated parts fit together. And then I can write out the true story in a way that hopefully captures the essence of what it was really about."

Venn's eyes locked on Bo's name. "Why does he call you Ria?"

"My full name is Katria. Everyone's always called me Kate, except my brothers. We used to play games in the forest, pretend we were great adventurers. We had forts and hideouts and secret routes." She ran her finger over the thin white scar over the bone on her wrist. The path through the scarletberry brambles had been a tight fit, even back then. Her arms and shoulders had been scratched every summer, but this was the only one that had scarred. Bo had a similar one on his elbow. She let a little smile cross her lips. "Bo thought Kate sounded like the name of someone who stayed home, but Ria was brave and wild."

Venn was quiet for a moment. "You call yourself Kate."

Kate looked up from the scar with a flicker of irritation. "And?"

"Just making an observation."

"That I'm not the person Bo thinks I am?"

Venn shrugged. "You seem more like a Kate than a Ria." She closed her eyes and leaned her head back. "But I hardly know you."

"It's foolish to step into something when you don't know what's happening. That's when people get hurt. And it's hardly a bad thing to stay home and research to understand the truth of things."

"Unless you're doing it because you're scared to leave."

Kate let her pencil drop onto her journal. "I walked out of the Stronghold with you, didn't I?"

Venn gave a grunt that was almost an agreement. "Shall I start calling you Ria?"

Kate picked her pencil back up and flipped to the next page with enough irritation that the bottom of the page ripped. "Until you know me as well as my brother does, you can stick with Kate."

Venn gave a short laugh. "Feels like a low bar."

Kate took a deep breath and turned back to her journal. Gripping the pencil, she scrawled notes and thoughts about the vimwisps and the fox until her irritation ebbed. The swirling mass of questions drained from her mind, slipping out her fingers and spreading onto the page in thin marks of charcoal.

What is carrying the thunder remnant? She scrawled the question at the bottom of the fourth page, then underlined *What.* She pondered a moment before crossing it out and writing *"Who."*

She let the journal close and caught sight of the corner of the aenigma box in her pack. She reached in and pulled it out, searching for the elusive hum of *vitalle* it held.

Venn shifted, and Kate glanced up to find the elf paused in the act of unbuckling her crossbow, giving the aenigma an irritated look.

Kate ignored her and refocused on the box. It had opened last time when she'd been stirred by the hope, as irrational as it was, that maybe Bo was on his way home. That hope had faded, replaced by the cold certainty that something had happened to him. That at the very least he was on the run, and more likely, caught by...something.

She pushed the fear away. Every thought in that direction was heavy with dread and a sort of creeping grief. The first hints of a loss too deep to even brush up against.

No, this box wanted hope, and she'd found one. An idea she'd barely acknowledged, because the spark of yearning it created was so strong that it stopped her breath. An idea that was easier to push aside until there was reason to really believe it might be true.

But that wasn't how hope worked.

Kate closed her eyes, gripped the side of the box, and let the hope she'd been shoving down unfurl.

Evan had touched this box.

Pain, thick and sharp and desperately hopeful, rushed through her. Something between terror and joy. Something so tangled in loss and anticipation and despair that she'd never unwind it. Something so good it threatened to break her heart.

It was only in her imagination that she could feel his remnant on it—she knew that with a certainty as solid as the unmoving Marsham Cliffs. But he had touched this. Just moments before they took him, he had touched this box, and that meant that after twenty years, she had a clue. A connection.

She could picture his smile, his unruly auburn curls. For the first time in years, she could picture him away from that horrible moment when the man had taken him. Picture her brother, his laugh, the mischievous glint that lived eternally in his eyes.

This box still existed, and whether it made sense or not, the hope that Evan also still existed bloomed into an aching fire.

She opened her eyes.

The small crack was there, crossing the front of the box.

Kate pulled the drawer open with her fingernails and angled it until the firelight lit the empty interior. With Bo's journal and papers out of it, there were only the slightest traces of his remnant, rubbed into the wood at the bottom of the drawer, but not strong enough to drown out the other, more elusive, impressions.

She closed her eyes and probed into it. There was another remnant here. An unfamiliar one. Perhaps more than one. A hint of metal on her tongue, a snapping sound.

The crackle of the fire faded into the background. The remnants were old. Older than maybe any she'd ever felt, and she studied them, wondering what gave her that impression. They weren't worn out, not really. Not thin, the way an elderly person's grew. They were…just old. There was a sense of another time, when the world itself was younger. Or at least different.

She brushed a finger across the inside of the drawer, and the impressions sharpened. Bo's rollicking wind filled her senses, but she sorted past it, looking for the others. There was the metal. Not the steel of a blade, though. The greenish patina of copper. Soft and malleable.

The snapping sound wasn't really a snap. It was a strike. Wood against wood, perhaps.

She was about to pull her finger away when she heard it.

The low toll of a bell.

She stopped, diving after it, sorting through the other sensations. It sat beneath them all. The other remnants were rubbed into the surface, but the bell was infused into the wood itself.

Opening her eyes, she reached in the pocket of her pack and pulled out the sky-blue remnant amplifier that was tightly wrapped in black fabric to keep any trace of sunlight away. She uncorked it, and a mist of silvery-blue rose immediately from the liquid. Working quickly, she tipped a single drop into the drawer and corked the vial.

Bo's remnant burst out so strongly that for a moment she was overwhelmed with the summery scent of southern wind, the indrawn breath as loud as if he sat next to her.

Mist rose from the drip as the amplifier evaporated, shrinking smaller with each moment. She tilted the drawer, and the drip rolled to the back corner where the other remnants lingered.

The sharp tang of copper covered her tongue, and she flinched at the crack of a stick striking some surface. Each remnant grew stronger and fuller. The copper gained a shushing sound, like wind. The crack let out the smell of icy mint.

She pushed past them both, letting the drop settle into the corner, letting it slowly seep between the tightly joined pieces of wood.

After a heartbeat, the bell rang out rich and full, vibrating through the bones of her hands. She probed at it, but there was just a bell, the sound rising or falling in volume but never totally fading away.

Wherever it was, the space was vast. So vast it felt limitless. There was no echo, no walls to reverberate off of. No end.

There was just the bell. Remote. A continual ebbing and flowing of hope, tangled with an endless, gnawing grief.

CHAPTER TWENTY-SIX

THE LAST OF the amplifier dissolved into mist, and the remnants all dwindled back to their subtle impressions.

Kate opened her eyes to find Venn watching her closely.

"Does the box speak to you?" the elf asked, her tone lighter than her expression.

"It has remnants." Kate wrapped the amplifier vial and tucked it into her pack. "A few different ones, but aside from Bo, I don't know who any of them are."

The small drawer only filled the bottom third of the box. Slowly, she pushed it shut. For a moment when it closed, she could see the edge of it as an incredibly thin line. Then there was the smallest flicker of *vitalle* across the surface, and the drawer was gone.

There was plenty of room for another drawer above it, still allowing the lid to open into a shallow compartment.

Kate focused again on the hope of finding something about Evan, but the fierceness of the feeling had faded. She tried for several minutes, but no drawer appeared.

She almost put the box back into her pack, but there was

something soothing about holding it. Letting it rest in her lap, she trailed her fingertips over the runes.

Venn settled back against the oak as she probed the two healing vimwisp stings near her tattoo with a finger. She tilted her head, as though listening, then glanced up into the branches with a small smile.

In the flickering firelight, the detailed runes of the tattoo were merely a dark impression around the thicker, central ones. The way the larger runes were placed became suddenly obvious, as did the way they connected with each other through the smaller markings around them.

"How long would you have?" Kate asked.

Venn's finger stopped. "What?"

"If something happened to your tattoo. How long until whatever it's stopping kills you?"

The elf didn't move.

"The runes are old," Kate continued, "but I can read enough to know they're holding something back. It's cleverly done. There's no end to it, just a constant cycling of energy into a barrier."

Venn's expression shuttered.

The purpose of the surrounding runes became clear. "The smaller runes around it keep it efficient, don't they?" Kate asked. "I was having a hard time placing them because I expected them to do something healing or empowering. But they're layers of control. Keeping *vitalle* from escaping the main runes through heat or from trickling into your body to be merely absorbed. But how do you fuel it? Do elves just have enough *vitalle* that you can afford…" She paused. "Ahh. You use the trees. You don't brush past every single trunk because you are enamored with the forest. You're pulling traces from a hundred living things all day long. You sleep against a tree at night." She let out a breath that was almost a laugh. "No wonder you didn't like being inside the Stronghold."

The corner of Venn's mouth twitched up, but there was no humor in it. "If I'd been in there any longer, I would have had to pull from one of you."

"We would have given *vitalle* willingly." Kate gestured at the tattoo. "Especially the small amount that needs. Gerone had already poured plenty into you while working on your shoulder."

"That was not something I had to ask for."

"So you were just too proud to ask?"

Venn's shoulders stiffened, and she tugged her sleeve down, covering her tattoo. "It was not pride."

Kate let out a short laugh. "Seems a lot like pride. And you haven't answered my question. How long would you have if that tattoo was damaged?"

Venn's only answer was a flat look.

"It feels like something I should know." Kate set the aenigma box aside and turned her full attention to Venn. "If tomorrow, some raider shoots an arrow into your forearm—"

"My forearm is protected," Venn interrupted.

"*If* it's not," Kate continued, "and something stabs into your tattoo, how much time would I have to solve that particular problem? Would you be dead in an instant? An hour? Do we have days?"

"*We* don't have anything."

Kate crossed her arms and waited.

Venn huffed out a breath and rubbed her hand over her sleeve. "I was bitten by a red-backed spider when I was young. On my smallest finger." She held up her hand, and in the firelight, the inside of her finger looked wrinkled, almost withered.

Kate studied Venn's palm and other fingers, but the rest

241

appeared healthy. "That would kill a human in a matter of minutes."

"It takes longer for an elf, but the spread is inevitable. It kills faster than our bodies can heal. As long as someone was actively working to heal me, they could hold it back, but as soon as they stopped…" Venn dropped her hand and looked into the fire. "My aunt knew runes humans used, and she created this." She gestured toward her forearm. "It draws life from things I touch, just the slightest amount, and keeps the venom from spreading. If…" She let the words dwindle, keeping her eyes on the fire.

Venn rubbed her thumb over her sleeve. There were a few records of people tattooing runes onto their skin, but never for any reason as complex as what Venn's was doing. It wasn't merely a barrier. It had to hold the venom back while still allowing blood and *vitalle* to flow in and out of Venn's hand, somehow keeping the smallest finger both isolated and connected.

"If it were damaged," Venn said quietly, and Kate's gaze flicked up to find the elf looking at the aenigma, an unreadable expression on her face. "I don't know if it would reach my heart or my brain first. But neither would take long."

She met Kate's gaze with an edge of defiance, and Kate curled her own hand into a fist. Imagining her finger cold, constantly waiting to leech venom into her body. "Does it hurt?"

Venn's eyes dropped, but she didn't answer.

"And cutting off the finger isn't an easier solution?"

"The venom is up past the wrist," Venn said, her voice as unemotional as if she were discussing the coolness of the night breeze. "I'd have to remove my arm at the elbow. The shoulder if we wanted to be sure to catch it all."

Kate sat for a moment, watching the elf. "May I see it?"

Venn shoved her sleeve up. Kate moved over next to her.

"These are early monarch runes from not long after Queensland was formed."

A hum of agreement came from Venn. "Evay learned the runes from the first Keepers."

"You must be close to her if you traveled with her and she healed you."

Venn pulled her sleeve back down. "There are connections between my people and the elves of the White Wood. Evay is my mother's cousin, although a very distant one. She's always been like an aunt to me."

Kate set aside more questions about Venn's tattoo. "Did she return to the White Wood when your people left here? In the old stories, she was…banished from there or something."

"She would never go back there."

Kate opened her mouth to ask what would get an elf banished, but Venn raised her hand to stop the question. "I will not share stories that are my aunt's to tell. She lives with my people on the lakes when she is feeling settled enough to stay in one place." The side of her mouth curled up. "Everyone always said I was too much like her, but I understand how she feels. I love the lakes, but if I'm there too long, I feel restless."

"And none of the other elves mind that you two travel so often?"

Her smile faded, and she pulled her thin blanket out of her pack and settled back against the tree again, closing her eyes. "No more stories tonight. Healing the vimwisp stings has been more tiring than it should be." She cracked one eye and looked at the welts visible on Kate's neck. "You should sleep too. And heal however much you can."

"So they do mind that you travel."

Venn rolled away, putting her back to Kate. "Don't burn the oak."

Kate tossed another stick onto the fire. "You're welcome for the warmth."

Venn didn't answer, and Kate watched the flames for a long moment. Her hands ached, and the stings scattered around her body burned with an icy sort of pain. Her legs and arms felt heavy, but her mind spun between thoughts of elves and puzzle boxes and Bo. Her hand strayed to her locket. Wherever Bo had found the box, had there been no sign of Evan? No clue?

She wrapped her own blanket around her shoulders and pulled Bo's journal out of her pack. Tilting it toward the firelight, she flipped to the newest entries, shifting closer to the flames to read the small writing.

Two weeks before he opened the box with "moonlight and hope," she found the answer.

A sketch of the box filled the lefthand page. Notes were scribbled around it, describing the color and condition of the sides, the size of the medallion, the lightness of the box.

Ria,

I found it. I actually found it. It is the same box, I swear.

The monastery itself is nearly in ruins, but it was burned recently enough that the grain sealed in the cellar is still in reasonably good shape. I would guess it's been a few years. The walls are all stone and standing, although most are blackened by the fire that took the roofs and the interior.

I almost didn't find the shrine in the back. I'll call it a shrine because there was a terribly ugly statue at one end. The entire room was stone, no bigger than a large closet and protected because it was roofed with a dome of stone instead of the thatch the rest of the buildings had. The door to it was wood, but rubble had fallen across it, protecting it so that only the top was charred by the fire. It took me all day to clear it, but I could see the room from all sides. It was centered in the monastery and accessible only by the one door placed at the end of what had once been a wide hall with elaborate stone floors.

Obviously not something I could just walk away from.

Ria, you would not believe what it held. Piles of silver coins stamped with the ancient Imperial emblem. Three books, each in Old Kalesh, each depicting military campaigns from the last dynasty, complete with maps and population counts and estimated values of each territory. More than triple the amount we've ever managed to learn before.

And there, on a shelf in the center of the far wall, nestled between a very old, rather cloudy spyglass and a ring with the Imperial signet, was the box.

Holding a place of honor in a Kellrhean monastery.

But I know that's not what you care about right now.

To answer your question, I spent three days searching the ruins, turning over every stone I could find. On the third, I found the stairs to the underground cells where they would have kept their slaves.

I started thinking about Evan. About how I didn't protect him that day at the mine. How I've failed over and over to find him. How scared I am that this search can never end well.

I stood at that entrance for ages. It was too much. If I found his remains…

It was one of those moments that always feels too big for me. I'm paralyzed by my own weakness. By all the times I've failed before.

A month after Evan was taken, I tried to go back into the mine. I didn't take you with me because I didn't want you to see how terrified I was. From the entrance, the blackness was a wall, and I wasn't enough to pass through it. I couldn't be brave enough or strong enough.

It was you who finally got me to take a step. How would you ever overcome your fear of the mine if I couldn't? When I thought of you—of who you were, of what you needed—then I could take one step.

So I thought of my little sister who walked into a pitch black mine with her brothers, completely undaunted by the unknown. The girl who faced down grown Kalesh men and crippled them with darkness.

"I was more ignorant than undaunted," she whispered.

That's always what those One Step moments need. Not a huge goal or feat of strength or brilliant answer.

They need a small push, a real push. Driven by something outside of me. Something I love.

And then I can see the best decision, and I can take one step. And then I can take another.

In the monastery, it was you again. You deserved to know what was in those cells, and that's what helped me move down the stairs.

There were two bodies there, or what was left of them. One was far too small for Evan, the other…It was barely more than a pile of bones.

I won't lie to you. The femur was about the size of my own. Which narrows it down to any average-sized man, but doesn't rule out Evan.

The back of the cellar was open though. A wall had collapsed and there was a way out. Two other cells were missing both the chains that should have shackled the slaves to the wall and any sign of a body.

I buried the bones I could find under an elm. Whoever those poor souls were, they at least deserve a more beautiful place to rest than a dank underground cell.

Tonight I am camped on a hill above the monastery. I have searched every inch of it for a sign of Evan and found nothing more. And yet I'm loath to leave. If the box came here, did he? If he was

*among the slaves, are those his bones under the elm? If he escaped,
where did he go? From the exit of the cellar you can see a valley full
of trees with a clear stream running into it. If I were to crawl out of
a dungeon under a burning monastery, that's where I would go.*

*Tomorrow I'll follow the valley. Perhaps there is a homestead or
a villager nearby who knows something of the monastery or of some
poor slaves who escaped the terrible fire.*

The next entry held only somber reports of finding nothing, and she flipped ahead until she reached the part about him getting to Morrow and discovering the emperor had gone to Home.

Letting the journal fall shut, she set it on top of the box next to her pack and lay down, staring into the fire. Exhaustion from the day rolled over her, and when she closed her eyes, it felt as though she were sinking into the hard ground.

High in the oak, the wind blustered at the leaves. Their shelter shuddered, but most of the chill was held back by the fire, and Kate's eyes grew heavy.

When I find you, Bo, she thought, *you'll take me to that monastery. Maybe there's some remnant I can find…*

A strong gust of wind pushed past her, grabbing the thought and pulling it away, unspooling it, jeering at the levels of implausibility it held.

The leaves rustled like a thousand whispers above her.

Evan is gone, the wind said. *There is no trace left. You lost him long ago.*

She pulled her blanket up over her head and tried to ignore the next obvious thought.

A breeze shimmied in through a gap and dragged cold fingers along her neck. *And now Bo is gone too. You were ignorant as a child. But you're not now, and you know how these stories end.*

A coarse, grating cough dragged her out of dreams of fire and stone and twisting mazes of dank prison cells.

She jerked her blanket down from her face, and her breath blew out in a cloud.

The air was so thick with the scent of roasting pork and spiced ale that she could taste it, but the fire was merely a bed of glowing coals.

Something small shifted in the dim light near the embers. It swelled and let out a sharp croak.

A toad.

Kate blinked at it, trying to grasp the complexity of the remnant filling the shelter and the fact that the fat, bumpy creature was staring at her.

The wind howled in the tree above her, and the toad croaked again, louder than before.

Behind it, she heard something else. A distant rumble of—

Something big swore under its breath from behind her head, and her pack lifted off the ground.

Kate shoved her hand toward the fire and poured *vitalle* into the coals until flames erupted, flooding the shelter with light.

Venn shot to her knees, her crossbow aimed at a second stocky figure hunched near her.

In the crackling firelight, two dwarves stood frozen, each holding a pack. Their small dark eyes, nearly hidden between brows and beards, flickered between the toad and Venn and Kate.

The nearer of the two smelled like roasted pork. The remnant of the other bit into the back of Kate's tongue like spiced ale.

The one holding Kate's pack flashed some teeth through his beard. "Two Dwarves Complimentary Pack Removal Service. Sorry to disturb you."

"Two Dwarves," Kate repeated slowly, staring at them, "Complimentary Pack Removal Service?"

The toad croaked again, and Venn's dwarf glanced at it. "Two Dwarves and a Toad."

"No," the one holding Kate's bag said, his eyes narrowing, "I don't want the toad."

The other dwarf shrugged. "Just Two Dwarves, then. Please return to your night of slumber. We'll be out of your way in moments."

CHAPTER TWENTY-SEVEN

VENN ROLLED up onto her feet, her crossbow aimed at the dwarf who held her pack half raised. "Drop it."

The two dwarves glanced at each other, identical black eyes glittering out from under bushy black brows. Identical black beards covering their chests and stomachs.

"An elf!" the one near Venn whispered loudly to his twin, seemingly unconcerned with the crossbow.

"Unexpected," the dwarf holding Kate's bag agreed. "It looks angry."

Venn took a step toward him. "Drop my pack. Now."

The dwarf blinked at her in confusion for a moment. "I'm holding it..."

"And I'm going to shoot you if you don't stop holding it."

Her dwarf held up his free hand in a placating manner.

Kate drew a handful of flame from the fire and held it in her cupped hand, rising to her feet. The burns on her palm flared at the heat, but she pushed *vitalle* into the fire anyway until it was the size of a torch. She brought it toward the nearest dwarf, whose remnant smelled so strongly of roasting pork it was like standing in a tavern. The top of his head was at her eye level, and she brought the fire closer. "Drop mine, or I'll find out if dwarven beards burn as fast as human hair."

His mouth dropped open in indignation, and he covered his beard with his free hand. "You will not!"

Venn's dwarf scowled. "I don't like either of these two."

The other nodded vehemently. "Burn my beard? Who threatens that?"

"Monsters. That's who."

Venn's crossbow let out a quiet twang, and her dwarf jumped back. A small dart quivered in the thick leather of his belt, right in the middle of his stomach.

"That's your last warning." Venn had a new dart loaded before the dwarf even looked back up.

The two dwarves stood as casual and relaxed as if they were chatting with old friends. Each had a thick axe on his belt, and a long, curved knife, but they made no moves toward the weapons. Venn's shifted his weight with a lumbering sort of motion. "But these aren't yours," he protested.

She pointed the dart at his chest.

"Dwarven law states," the other said hurriedly, "an item belongs to whomever holds it."

Kate cut off the fire in her hand with a flick of her fingers, stepped up to her dwarf, and grabbed his forearm. Her fingers didn't even wrap halfway around it, and he gave her a vaguely amused expression. "The law is for objects, not dwarves. What are you going to do, little twig?"

She smiled back and funneled a trickle of *vitalle* into the muscle under her palm.

The dwarf raised an eyebrow, but Kate kept the *vitalle* targeted under her hand until the muscle softened.

His arm went limp, and the bag dropped to the ground.

Kate picked it up. "Now it's mine again."

The dwarf shook his arm, which flopped uselessly. His face curled in anger. "You killed my arm!" He lunged with unexpected quickness. His other huge hand stretched toward her neck.

Kate leapt back as Venn's crossbow twanged again, and a dart sank into his shoulder.

He stumbled forward, his hand dropping to clench around Kate's arm with an iron grip as he fell to his knees. Kate yanked away, but he held her arm fast until his eyes glazed, his fingers loosened, and he toppled face-first onto the ground.

"Tribal!" The other dwarf took a step toward him. His casual stance evaporated, and he spun to face Venn, the motion smooth and dangerous. His thick, wickedly curved knife hissed as he slid it from his belt. "Did you just kill my brother?" he asked quietly.

"He's only sleeping." Venn snapped another dart into her crossbow.

"As was his arm." Kate glanced over to where her pack had sat, but aside from her blanket, the ground was empty. "Where's my box? And the journal?"

"That's it." Venn raised her arm. "I'm shooting this one too, and then we'll search them for our things."

The dwarf still standing dropped her pack and gave an annoyed growl. "That won't be necessary. Neither of you had anything of value."

"My box?" Kate repeated.

The dwarf squinted at her. "That might be worth something," he muttered as he moved over to his sleeping brother. "Excellent craftsmanship." He rolled Tribal over onto his back with a heave and unbuckled a sack tied to the dwarf's belt.

A crack sounded from deep in the woods outside the shelter, and Venn snapped her crossbow back up to point at the dwarf. "How many of you are there?"

He sat very still, his head cocked in the direction of the noise. "Just Tribal and me."

Kate cast out. Aside from the trees, there was nothing, until more than twenty paces away, it rolled over a dozen blazing forms, fanned out and creeping closer.

Venn stiffened.

Kate met her gaze. "Humans."

Venn's shoulders dropped, and she let out an annoyed breath. "A Snare?"

"I would assume."

"A Snare?" The dwarf kicked at the fire. "Get that out!"

Kate stretched out her hand toward the flames and sucked the *vitalle* out of them. The fire guttered down to red coals, and the shelter plunged into darkness.

There was a moment of silence.

"Who are you people?" the dwarf whispered.

In the scant light from the coals, Kate saw Venn raise a hand and point toward the approaching men. "That is considerably more than four to six, Kate," she whispered.

"I noticed."

"How many?" the dwarf asked.

"A dozen."

The dwarf swore under his breath.

Kate slung her pack over her shoulder and cast out again. They were closer, except for three who were gathered in a knot farther away. "Some have stopped around…something," Kate whispered.

The dwarf swore again, more vehemently. "Our wagon." He grabbed Tribal's shoulders and shook him. "Wake up, you idiot!" he hissed.

"If we leave these two and run," Venn said to Kate. "They'll slow down the raiders."

Kate shook her head. "Only temporarily. They'll track us. And the dwarf has the box."

"Even better." Venn moved toward the side of the shelter.

"And Bo's journal."

"You're right—they'll track you," the dwarf whispered, a frantic note in his voice. He looked up into Kate's face. "Wake up Tribal. We know a place they can't track you."

Kate rubbed away a sudden tiredness that rolled over her eyes and squinted at him. The offer was tempting. Certainly better than running long enough to lose the Snare. "And you'll give me back my box, the journal, and any other thing you took from us."

The dwarf let out an agitated breath. "You can have back all your useless things. Just wake him up!"

"Venn?"

The elf stayed at the edge of the shelter, halfway out into the night already. There was a beat of silence before Venn muttered something in Elvish and strode across the shelter. She grabbed the dart in Tribal's shoulder and yanked it out. His twin grimaced at the motion. Pushing her hand onto his forehead, Venn whispered, "Wake up, you useless thief."

"Thief?" the standing dwarf whispered, appalled.

Kate felt a brief surge of *vitalle* from Venn, and Tribal's eyes flew open.

He shoved himself up and let out a bellow of pain. "Silas! They—"

Silas slapped his hand over Tribal's mouth. "Snare!"

Tribal froze, then muttered something into his brother's hand.

"A big one," Silas answered, "and close." He held out his hand and heaved his brother to his feet, then made a series of hand gestures.

In one fluid motion, Tribal turned and shoved into Kate's shoulder with the force of a charging bull.

She staggered back into the branches of the shelter and fell, landing hard on her back. The sound of Venn crashing into branches was all Kate heard as the two dwarves ran out of the shelter on completely silent feet.

Kate cast out again as she scrambled up. The Snare was only fifteen paces away, spread in an arc around their shelter.

And there were more than a dozen. Several forms she'd taken to be one person had split into two. "Venn?" she said quietly. "Still think this many men is only an inconvenience?"

"That is more than ten," Venn whispered. The dim shape of her arm reached down to the quiver at her belt. She twisted to look down, letting out a vicious string of Elvish. "They took my darts! Tell me you can track the dwarves."

"They smell like a pig roast." Kate stepped onto the trail of the remnant left by the dwarves.

"Is that another metaphor?" Venn hissed.

"No!" Kate gave her an annoyed look. "Their remnants really smell like roasting pig and spiced ale."

Moonlight shone in frosty silver off the leaves high in the tree-tops, but the forest floor was steeped in shadows. Between the edge of the shelter and the nearest trees, though, lay an unbroken pale stretch of grass. "The Snare may be close enough to see us."

"Wait," Venn whispered.

The elf bent down and picked up two stones, then moved swiftly to the opening at the far side of the shelter. She hurled one into the woods, then a second. There was a loud snap where the first stone landed, then a second past it.

Kate cast out, and the hot shapes of the Snare shifted toward the noise. Behind them, where the dwarves' wagon had been, a bright warmth flared up, like it had been set on fire. There was no sign of the dwarves, who must be moving swiftly away.

Venn ran back on quiet feet. "Find the dwarves," she hissed.

Kate waited until the Snare had moved away, then, crouching low, she crept out into the moonlight. She stayed hunched as she ran to the nearby trees. With each step, small twigs cracked loud enough to wake the dead, but the shapes of the Snare continued to move away.

"Dwarves can't run far," Venn said grimly. "We'll catch them when they stop."

Tribal's remnant lay over the ground like he'd dragged a haunch of meat behind him. His brother's overlaid it like sloshes of spiced ale. Kate ran along it until the smell of it grew strong enough that her stomach growled. The sky to the east was more purple than black, and last night's small dinner felt long ago amidst the smells of a feast.

She followed the trail, sorting out the two remnants. They were rich and thick, but there was not even a hint of thunder woven through them.

"Why are there dwarves here?" she asked.

"Because they like to annoy the rest of the world. It's what dwarves do."

Kate glance at the elf. "I mean, why are they on this side of Queensland? Duncave is in the west, and dwarves rarely leave their tunnels to do anything, never mind travel across the entire country to rob travelers."

"Maybe these two are too disreputable for even other dwarves to want to be around."

A few minutes further on, the remnants grew suddenly stronger, and Kate drew to a stop a few paces from a pair of large pines. She cast out, and the shapes of the two dwarves flared up behind the trees. She waited as the wave rolled out behind her as well, but there was no sign of the Snare.

"You have things that belong to us," Kate said.

Neither dwarf moved.

Venn let out an exasperated breath. "She can track you. She doesn't need light or footprints or any physical sign that you've passed. And the trees will tell me where you are."

"The Snare, though, will need light, but they'll be tracking all of us as soon as the sun's up." Kate pointed at the trees. "And you promised us a place to hide where they couldn't find us."

There was still no sound or motion from the trees.

Kate sighed. "Tribal is behind the pine to the right, and Silas to the left. From your postures, I'd say you're both holding axes."

Silas leaned around the tree, studying Kate. "You have some interesting skills."

"You told them we'd find them a place to hide?" Tribal demanded, stepping around the tree and turning to his brother.

"I told them we *knew* a place to hide." Silas looked past Kate into the woods. "Where's the Snare?"

"Back near the camp," Kate said. "They found the shelter by now, and I believe they set your wagon on fire, but"—she gave Tribal a smile—"I guess it wasn't yours anymore."

Both dwarves' eyes widened, and they glanced at each other.

"What?" Tribal said. "Why would they set it on fire?"

"I don't know, but we should leave," Silas said hurriedly, turning away.

"Why?" Venn asked. "What's in your wagon?"

Tribal shot a worried look back through the trees. "Nothing that should be set on fire."

"Quickly, now." Silas started through the woods toward the Marsham Cliffs. "This way."

"We are *not* taking these two with us," Tribal objected, jogging after him.

"They can track us. It's not like we can stop them."

"Where are you planning to take them?"

"How do you two feel about caves?" Silas called over his shoulder.

"No!" Tribal declared. "Absolutely not."

Venn planted her feet. "I hate caves."

"Well, then stay here and be captured by the Snare." Silas

glanced up at the wind-blown trees. "Or choke on the poisonous fumes that will probably get here first. I don't really care which."

"Poisonous fumes?" Kate asked. "Time to move, Venn."

Venn crossed her arms. "How long will we have to stay in caves—away from all living things—before the Snare gets tired of looking for us? Because that doesn't work for me."

Kate glanced at the crossbow covering Venn's tattoo. "I'm a living thing. I'll keep it fueled until we get back out. Trust me."

Venn gave her a cutting look. "I don't trust you. I barely know you."

"It'll be fine. You won't owe me," Kate said quickly. "And the dwarves do have your darts."

Venn turned her glare onto the dwarves' backs.

"You two are very strange," Silas said over his shoulder. "It's this way. Keep up."

CHAPTER TWENTY-EIGHT

THE HEAVY DWARVEN feet ahead of them plodded on at a steady, nearly silent pace as they moved closer to the Marsham Cliffs, and Kate's legs burned with the effort of keeping up. She watched the boots of the dwarves closely, but they made almost no noise, regardless of what they stepped on.

Kate cast out behind them but found no sign of the Snare. "We don't see many dwarves in the forest."

Silas glanced back at her. "We like to visit human villages every once in a while to trade. You people have horrible steel. Tools we'd melt down for parts, you think are masterpieces."

"How many of you come here?" she asked.

Silas waved away the question. "You humans never pay much attention to other races. It's not surprising you haven't heard of us visiting."

"Actually, it is. My particular people keep track of things like this. Barely any dwarves have been in this part of Queensland for several hundred years."

Tribal shrugged. "Then maybe we don't exist."

The sky lightened, and the shadows under the trees thinned

away to blues and dark greens. The dwarves broke out of the woods at the base of the towering Marsham Cliffs and headed left toward an old rockslide that splayed out into the forest.

Silas scrambled up onto the rocks, then glanced at Kate and Venn. "Hope you're up for a little climb."

"This is a very bad idea, brother," Tribal said, clambering up behind him. "Just take them far enough that the Snare will lose their trail, and put them back in the woods."

"They woke you when the Snare was coming," Silas said simply. "We made a deal."

"After putting me to sleep," Tribal grumbled. "And I would have woken up."

The first rocks were knee high on Kate, and she climbed up onto them. "Captured by slave traders."

He ignored her and looked up to where his brother was climbing around a huge boulder, doubling back and angling up the rockslide in the other direction. "You could have handled a few humans."

"There were a dozen." Silas squinted at the cliffs above them.

"Fifteen," Kate corrected him, jumping to the next rock.

"I would have woken up," Tribal grumbled again.

"Not from my dart." Venn stepped lightly from stone to stone, glancing behind them into the woods. "Anyone close? Because we're awfully exposed on this dead hillside of stone, and I can't talk to any trees from here."

Kate cast out, but there was nothing except trees.

Venn waited until the sensation of the wave faded. "Maybe the Snare won't even track us."

"They will," Tribal answered. "That's what they do, and our trail away from that campsite will be so obvious it might as well have a glowing sign pointing the way."

The climb up the rockslide felt like an endless scrambling over rough stones. Kate's foot slipped into a crevice, and she grabbed the edge of the rock for balance, sending a searing pain across her palm.

They climbed long enough that bright sunlight poured over the top of the cliff, and Kate had taken to casting out every few minutes to check for the Snare, before Silas ducked around a boulder and disappeared. Tribal, after an annoyed look at Venn and Kate, followed. Kate slid down the side of the last waist-high rock, sending a skittering of tiny pebbles shooting out below her, and walked around the boulder to where a shadowy gap was nestled between it and the cliff face.

She stepped through and found Tribal and Silas standing in a small cave.

Silas gave her a broad smile. "The Snare can't track us over the rocks. We can wait them out here."

Kate moved in and sat against the wall to catch her breath.

Venn hesitated at the opening before stepping in and holding out her hand to Silas. "My darts."

The dwarf's smile soured, but he pulled the small quiver out of his sack and handed it to her.

Kate looked at Tribal expectantly, and Silas jabbed him with an elbow.

Tribal sighed and drew the aenigma and Bo's journal from his own sack, handing them over with an annoyed expression. "Everything about this situation is wrong."

"Yes, it is," Venn agreed. "You two stay where I can see you. I've rarely met anyone who feels more duplicitous than either of you."

"Duplicitous?" Tribal said.

"How can we feel duplicitous?" Silas asked. "We just saved your life."

"Elves have intuition about people," Kate said, kneeling to tuck the box and the journal back in her pack. "She'll know a great deal about you just by being close to you."

Both dwarves' eyes narrowed, and they shifted farther back in the cave.

Motion at the entrance caught Kate's eye, but it was merely a moth, fluttering into the darkness and landing on an outcropping of stone.

Kate sat and dropped her head into her hands. Remnants crammed into the small space. Venn's vivid forest, Tribal's roasting meat, and Silas's spiced ale jostled against each other like a crowd. She took a deep breath, separating them out, trying to grasp whose was whose in an effort to organize the chaos.

The dwarves sat with their heads together across the small cave, and she focused on Tribal's first, separating out the rich meaty scent, realizing there was a low hum that ran beneath it too. When she'd isolated the remnant, she realized she could taste the spices, cinnamon and ginger, among the fuller malty taste of ale. And he hummed too. A slightly deeper tone that blended with Tribal's almost perfectly.

Venn's remnant was as strong as ever, emanating from near the entrance where she lingered, like the elf had brought the entire forest into the cave with her. From the expression on Venn's face as she let her gaze rake over the lifeless stone walls, she would have liked to.

Venn shifted, and Kate caught a small rumble of thunder.

She twisted, searching the elf, but Venn stepped farther inside and leaned against the rock wall, while the quiet rumbling stayed near the entrance.

The moth fluttered its wings slowly, and Kate rolled up to her knees, crawling toward it. The moth's wings were dusty brown, mottled with darker and lighter patches. Its head was fuzzy and drab, with two feathery antennae sprouting from above tiny black eyes.

A trail of sound came from it, nearly hidden under the other remnants. A peal of thunder, so low and quiet that Kate closed her eyes and tried to draw it out.

It wasn't thunder, not exactly. It ebbed and flowed, rumbling louder and softer. She combed through it, pulling out smaller details. Wind, a bird...

It was the ocean.

She'd seen memories in the Wellstone of Keepers who'd been to the sea. This was the thundering sound of waves crashing against rocks.

Kate opened her eyes and studied the moth. It was only half as long as her thumb, and, judging from the way it had fluttered into the cave, a trip from the ocean would have taken it months.

"Who are you?" Kate whispered.

The moth twitched and took off, flying out of the cave with its erratic twist-turn fluttering, taking its quiet remnant with it.

She turned back to find Venn watching her with a suspicious look.

"It thundered..." Kate said.

Venn stepped over. "Where'd it go?"

"I don't know."

The two dwarves were whispering vehemently in the back of the small cave, Dwarvish words tumbling over each other with sharp edges.

Venn turned away from the entrance and crossed her arms. "So, now that we've trapped ourselves in this little pocket of death, how long will we need to hide?"

Kate pulled her eyes away from the bit of sky she could see out the entrance, which was empty of all moths and remnants. The dwarves stopped speaking and fixed Venn with insulted looks.

"Little pocket of death?" Silas said.

"Hide?" Tribal added. "No one hides in a cave. You live in them, explore them, relax in them."

Silas nodded. "Grow rich from them."

"Grow old in them," Tribal agreed.

Silas jabbed a thumb toward Tribal's gut. "Grow fat in them."

Venn looked unimpressed. "We're definitely hiding in this little pocket. And everything in here is dead."

The dwarves exchanged exasperated looks.

"I'm not dead," Silas pointed out.

"This is not a pocket," Tribal said. "It is an entrance. A secret entrance that no human, and certainly no elf, has ever found." He gave his brother a glare. "One which we'll probably be murdered for bringing you into."

Silas waved off his words. "It *is* an entrance, and it doesn't matter that from this point you could get to the old southern door of Torren, or the watchtower on the Eastern Reaches, or"—he pointed at Venn—"the White Wood itself. You'd never find your way. You'd be lost before lunch and die a slow death of dehydration, even though there is plenty of water to be found if you have half a brain."

"You can reach the White Wood from here?" Kate asked.

"You think we just build tunnels that go nowhere? Under the earth, you can travel fast, without having to follow the land, or be cold, or get rained on."

"Or have your wagon burned by a Snare," Tribal added.

Silas winced. "That's gonna cause some trouble."

Tribal rubbed a huge hand over his face.

"Mostly, though, in caves you can avoid humans all together." Silas glanced at Kate. "No offense."

"How long would it take to get to the White Wood?" she asked.

Tribal glanced at his brother. "Three days?"

"Four the way they'd need to go. Can't exactly waltz past the gov'nor, can they?"

Tribal laughed. "Four days."

Venn stared at them. "You do know where the White Wood is, don't you? Even if you had a tunnel that went straight to it, you'd still need weeks to walk that far."

"Why would you walk when it's all downhill from here to your creepy woods," Silas said, "and you could just take the river?"

"An underground river?" Kate sat forward. "Will you take us—"

"*They* can't take the river," Tribal said to Silas, jabbing a finger at Kate and Venn. "Because *they* shouldn't even be here." He turned to glare at them. "Since you already are, we are willing to stay with you until nightfall when you can leave and continue on your way. We'll even take you down a path that will put you back in the forest an hour south of here, and the Snare should never pick up your trail."

A wave of tiredness rolled over Kate, and she sank back. She looked questioningly at Venn. The offer was tempting. An hour south should put them outside the search area the Snare would cover, and if they kept up a good pace—

The thought felt fuzzy and off.

Unnatural.

Kate straightened. That was the second time an offer from the dwarves had felt tempting. And yet this one shouldn't be tempting at all. An hour south of here was definitely not better than a route through the cliffs.

Pushing herself to her feet, she studied Tribal. "How'd you do that?" She cast out toward him.

Along with the hot, dense core of heat that filled the stocky dwarf, the soles of his boots flared up, and a spot on his chest, hidden behind his beard, burst into light. Silas warmed in identical places.

The boots were steadily warm and answered the mystery of

how the dwarves had moved so quietly. Muffling sound wouldn't take much *vitalle* at all.

She focused on the bright spot on Tribal's chest, and his hand went up to protect it. "What does that amulet do?" The *vitalle* streaming out of it was leaky and rough. She could feel the runes carved into it, blocky and crude, drawing energy from the dwarf himself and spreading out around him. "It makes your offers more appealing, doesn't it?"

"What amulet?" Tribal's hand tightened on his beard over the spot emanating heat.

"It's not even that sophisticated, is it?" Kate took a step forward, and he slowly pulled his knife from his belt. "It just makes me tired, so I don't have the energy to argue with you, and then makes me think your offer might be tempting." She pointed at Silas. "You used it in the shelter too, when you wanted us to wake Tribal."

Neither dwarf answered her.

"So," Kate said. "you travel the human world trading for goods while manipulating people to accept your offers."

Silas glanced at Tribal. "She makes it sound so shady."

"Humans never really understand a good bargain," his brother agreed.

"Let's make a bargain right now," Kate said. "What's the price for you taking us through the tunnels to the White Wood?"

CHAPTER TWENTY-NINE

VENN TURNED to give Kate a disbelieving look.

"There is no price high enough to get you through our tunnels," Tribal answered immediately. "In fact, don't move any farther from the entrance. It's going to be nearly impossible to erase all signs of a human and an elf from what you've dirtied already."

Silas nodded. "You could never afford such a bargain."

"We would never make such a bargain," Venn declared. "Four days? Underground?"

"Four days!" Kate flung her hand toward the back of the cave, where any number of cracks in the walls might lead them deeper into the cliff. "Four days instead of four weeks! Bo has already been missing a month!"

Venn crossed her arms. "Impossible."

"It's not impossible," Kate answered her. "We can take care of —"

"It *is* impossible," Tribal interrupted. "For perhaps the only time in my life, I will agree with the elf. My idiot brother mentioned the path to the White Wood to make a point about dwarven greatness, not as an offer to be your tour guides through the glorious realm of Rullduin."

"Rullduin?" Kate glanced around. "Once this was called Torren."

"If we're being precise," Silas said, holding up a finger, "only the city itself was called Torren. The tunnels have always been—"

"Dwarven!" Tribal thundered. "They are dwarven. For dwarves. And only for dwarves. No dwarf has ever led a human or an elf into these tunnels."

"Humans and a half-elf entered the door at the Northern Corner," Kate countered. "It was four hundred years ago, but Thulan, the dwarf, led them in and—"

"Thulan wasn't real," Tribal cut in.

Venn gave a hum of dissent. "My aunt knew Thulan. Said she was the first dwarf she'd ever met worth talking to."

Kate gestured at Venn. "See? Thulan took them to the dwarven king."

"Where they were captured," Venn added.

"Yes," Kate said, trying to keep her voice patient, "but then escaped with the help of other dwarves and ended up raising an entire dwarven army to help fight off the Kalesh Empire."

Silas shook his head. "We're not taking you through the tunnels."

"Good," Venn said, "because we don't want to go through the tunnels."

"Yes, we do." Kate studied the dwarves. There had to be something to leverage. Her gaze fell on their two thick beards. "Your amulets—how often do they work?"

Silas squinted at her while Tribal pinched his mouth shut and shook his head.

"How often do they sway someone to take to your bargain?"

"Often enough," Silas answered.

"What if they worked all the time, and more subtly than those ridiculous runes can?"

"What runes?" Tribal asked.

"The ones carved into the amulets you're hiding." Kate held out her hand. "It's not a bad enchantment, honestly, but it's done so poorly I can't believe it works even one time out of five."

"You're offering to help them swindle people?" Venn asked.

"They'll never be able to really swindle anyone. But I can make it so that their offers carry enough weight that someone will at least consider it. They'll never convince anyone to do anything they're dead set against. But maybe a dagger they would usually sell for three silver can be sold for three and a half."

Silas was looking at her with a calculating look, while Tribal continued to shake his head.

"Every bargain?" Silas asked.

"In a very small way. Nothing you'd be able to use to actually steal from people."

"Prove it." The dwarf drew a copper amulet the size of Kate's palm out from behind his beard and pulled it over his head.

"Have you lost your mind, brother?" Tribal demanded as Silas handed the amulet to Kate.

"You know these things barely work. Only worked on these two because they were distracted and half asleep."

Venn turned to Kate. "Have *you* lost your mind?"

Kate studied the disk. It was chiseled with a set of three runes, each one messy and blocky. She drew her finger across the soft metal, warming it with some *vitalle* until the edges of the first rune were smooth. She pulled the small knife from her belt and carved in the connections that were missing, adjusting the way the *vitalle* would flow.

Silas moved closer, looking over her shoulder. "How are you doing that?"

"I don't like that she can do magicky things," Tribal said. "We need to get rid of these two now.

When Kate finished, she handed it to him. "Set it back on your chest. Actually against your skin would work better."

The dwarf pulled the leather cord over his head again and tucked the amulet inside his shirt.

"What if she's trying to kill you?" Tribal demanded.

Silas glanced at his brother. "You're right. Let me hold your knife in case she tries anything."

Tribal slid his thick, curved blade out of his belt and held the handle out to his brother. "And step back away from her."

Silas stared down at the offered blade, his mouth open.

Tribal blinked and snatched it back. He flipped it over, pointing the tip at Kate. "What did you do?"

Silas grinned. "She fixed it. Yes, we'll take you to the White Wood."

"Half payment now." Kate nodded to Silas's amulet. "And I'll fix Tribal's once we safely reach the White Wood."

"I am not spending four days with Silas," Tribal declared, "where I'll want to do anything he asks."

"We're not spending four days underground no matter what," Venn said.

Kate waved away her words and turned to Tribal. "Now that you're aware of the amulet, you'll be able to resist it easily. The suggestion of agreement it gives is incredibly weak."

Silas leaned toward his brother. "Can I have your dinner tonight?"

"If I can cut off your arm," Tribal growled.

Kate smiled. "See?"

Venn cleared her throat. "If this conversation continues, I'm leaving. I came for my quiver. A hundred humans couldn't find me in the forest if I didn't want to be found." She glanced at Kate.

"It'll be harder to keep you hidden, so if you're coming, we'll wait until sunset."

"Venn," Kate said, moving over closer to the elf. "We could be at the White Wood in four days." The elf's expression stayed adamant. *"Four days!* You can't tell me you're looking forward to weeks of travel, a huge portion of which is across the edge of a treeless grassland. We'll spend far more than four days crossing the moors."

"The moors are covered with grass."

Kate lowered her voice. "I could give you ten times more energy than grass can every day and still have plenty left over."

Venn crossed her arms. "It doesn't work as well from people. Plants have a more subtle—"

"Four days, Venn!" Kate flung up four fingers. "You could be rid of me and the box in four days. Just get me to where Bo disappeared, and you can go on your way."

"Four days in the tunnels," Silas clarified, "then one more to the White Wood itself."

Venn started to shake her head.

"You owed Bo," Kate said before she could object, "and were compelled to bring me the box. Then you owed me and have to take me to where you found it. But I swear to you, as soon as we get out of here, we'll go straight to that clearing, then you and I are done. I swear on Bo and the box and everything I hold dear that bringing me there will fulfill any obligation you have to me or Bo or anything having to do with this box."

Venn still shook her head.

"Fine. Then you take the long way. I'm going with the dwarves, and I'll see what I can find without you. After you've walked for weeks to catch up with me, you can tell me if I'm in the wrong place."

"You can't go with the dwarves. They're not trustworthy."

Silas gave an insulted huff.

Tribal's bushy eyebrows dove down. "We're trustworthy."

"They're not entirely trustworthy," Kate said. "But neither were you, and I trusted your word. If they vow to help us, in clear language that actually covers them helping, I'd trust them too. And I'm capable of taking care of myself."

"Until you're sleeping and they rob you—again—or leave you to die in some dark tunnel."

"It's not robbing," Silas objected, "it's just taking unclaimed items. And we don't do it to our friends."

"Drunner. And Plot," Tribal reminded his brother in a low voice. "…and Grenley."

Silas's beard split in a grin. "Oh, yeah. Well, we won't do it to you. You have our word. In exchange for two working amulets, we will see you, with all the belongings you currently have, safely through the tunnels and to the White Wood." He raised one hand. "May you cut off our feet and our hands and our beards if anything harms you before we bring you to the White Wood." He spit into his palm and held it out toward Kate.

Tribal's mouth fell open. "You did *not* just swear me to that too!"

"Think how handy the two amulets will be when we have to explain to the gov'nor what happened to the wagon."

Tribal paused.

"Kate," Venn said vehemently, "do *not* shake that hand."

Pointedly not looking at the glistening wetness in Silas's palm, Kate spared a brief moment to be grateful her own hand was wrapped before spitting on the now dirty bandage and clasping the dwarf's hand.

He shook her off, then grasped her forearm instead, his huge fingers wrapping around her like she was a twig. A warm, slimy patch slid across her skin.

Grimacing, she gripped his forearm too, not bothering to try to reach around the thick muscles. "You have a deal, sir dwarf," she managed, trying to hold it long enough to make the deal official.

Tribal buried his face in his hands and groaned.

Silas let go of her, and she wiped her arm on her shirt. He pounded Tribal on the back with a triumphant smile. "Don't worry, brother, this will be quick and simple, and we'll all come out ahead."

Venn shook her head, the motion tinged with desperation. "I can't walk under all that rock while it's just waiting to crush me."

"Crush you?" Tribal pulled his axe from his belt and rammed the handle into the rock. Kate and Venn both flinched, but it did nothing more than let out a dull thud.

"Hear that?" he said. "It's solid."

"Until it collapses," Venn pointed out.

"How could it collapse?" Silas asked, looking baffled. "Does a tree collapse because a bug bores through it?"

"If enough bugs do, yes."

"We're not stupid enough to bore too many tunnels," Tribal said.

Venn gave him a doubtful look. "Are you saying dwarven tunnels never collapse?"

"Of course they collapse." Silas gestured up at the wall. "But not tunnels like this. This one's solid."

Venn squinted at him. "Are we going to travel through any that aren't solid?"

Silas flashed her a grin. "Not really." He turned, walked to a rough part of the wall at the back of the cave, and disappeared behind it.

"Come on." Tribal motioned at them impatiently, his brow furrowed. "Don't look at anything and don't touch anything. The sooner we get this over with, the better."

"I couldn't agree more," Venn said.

Kate moved closer to her. "Just let me know as soon as you feel like you need *vitalle*," she said quietly.

Venn's eyes ran over the stone surrounding them, her face curled in distaste. "I'd rather bring the forest with us."

"How long can you go without touching a plant?"

"Once I went a full day." She grimaced. "I do *not* want to do that again."

"Let's start with every three or four hours, then, and you tell me if we need to adjust."

Venn muttered something in Elvish and, with a determined, angry set to her shoulders, stalked away after Silas.

Kate glanced out the cave entrance. There was no sign of the moth, and as Tribal stepped closer, she could hear nothing but his deep humming sound.

"If you'd rather go risk the Snare, you're welcome to," Tribal said, waving toward the outside world.

"And miss the chance to tour dwarven tunnels?" Kate said, forcing a smile as she pulled her eyes away from the sky outside.

"I am *not* your tour guide." Tribal fell in behind her, close enough that she lengthened her stride. "You're not here, you never were, and, with any luck, you'll leave no incriminating traces of your existence."

PART III

THE KNOTS

The tragedy wasn't a physical loss. That was there, of course, woven through everything long before I could see the threads.

But the heartache that really drove the events near Home—the heartache that had driven them for hundreds of years—was the kind that is tucked away inside each of us. The way the scars life has given us carve into the surface of our hearts, causing the slightest pull with each beat. So subtle and familiar we don't even notice they're there.

It was different heartaches tangled together by strands of obligation or love or betrayal or merely proximity, and every choice and struggle tightened the strands, knotting it all inexorably together.

CHAPTER THIRTY

AROUND THE SIDE of the rough section of wall, a thin entrance to a tunnel wound off into the darkness. There was no sign of either Venn or Silas, and Kate hesitated in the shadows that lay heavy even a few steps in.

"Move on," Tribal said behind her. "Your eyes won't adjust standing out here in the daylight." He gave her shoulder a push. "Go. Go."

She stepped around the corner and faced complete blackness. Keeping one hand on the wall and the other stretched out in front of her, she took a few tentative steps forward. The absolute darkness was as disorienting as the smothering intensity of the remnants around her. She cast out, and Venn's warmth flared up a handful of paces ahead of her, farther than she expected from the vibrance of forest smells and sounds soaking the air. Tribal's dense, almost solid heat came from behind her, and Silas's matching shape waited up ahead, but the dwarves' remnants seemed to echo off the walls, the low hum gaining volume and nuance. It pulsed like a deep, slow heartbeat, each dwarf's shifting and changing in subtle ways that wove together into something rich. And the scents of roasting meat and warm mulled ale almost infused the rocks themselves.

She stretched her eyes wide and made out a faint orange glow. She latched onto it as she stepped forward, and it resolved into light from a small lantern near Silas's stomach. He held a second out to Venn.

"To make sure I barely see the obstacles I stumble into?" the elf asked.

He grinned at her. "Give it a few minutes. You'll see everything you need to."

"They'll see everything they're not supposed to," Tribal grumbled.

"Oh, no," Venn said dryly. "We'll see boring rock walls that all look the same. What amazing secrets we'll have to share with the world."

"All look the same?" Tribal sputtered. "This isn't some forest with a million identical trees being knocked over by slight breezes as they grow old and die. This is the heart of the earth itself. Its soul. Warmed by its life, protected by its bones, which have been steady and unbreakable for millennia. Civilizations have built on it, grown and thrived and died out, and the earth remains unchanged."

Venn turned back around. "You just used more words to say 'boring.'"

"That's it, Silas!" Tribal snapped. "We're leaving these two at the bottom of Pitchem Pit."

"Then you won't get your amulet," Silas said mildly.

"Fine, we'll just get rid of the elf."

"We shook on it, Tribal."

"*You* shook on it!"

"I did. For both of us. Stop whining." Silas hunched over another lantern, and a faint orange glow grew. He closed the little door and held it out to Kate.

Inside the glass housing was a small pile of moss, glowing gently and glistening with water. It didn't provide much light at all. Far less than a candle. More like the subtle light of a hot coal. But Kate could make out the faint shapes of Venn and the dwarves and the jagged wall of the tunnel next to her.

"It'll glow as long as we keep it wet." Silas glanced at his brother. "Want one?"

"We have *three* lanterns already. Why didn't we just bring the sun in with us?"

Silas shrugged and started down the tunnel.

"If only," Venn muttered, falling in behind him.

Whether the mosslight grew brighter or Kate's eyes merely grew accustomed to it, after the first half hour she could make out the tunnel around them reasonably well. It emerged from absolute blackness in front of Silas and disappeared into the same behind Tribal, but the space between was visible. The walls were sometimes smooth and flowing, as though they'd been shaped by water. At other times, the rock was broken off in sharp faces, marred by gouges from tools.

In the mosslight, Venn's braid, leather vest, and pack were all various shades of reddish-orange, as were the walls, the ceiling, and the surprisingly level floors. Shadows in the crevices of the rock were depthless pools of black that shifted and shuddered as the lanterns passed.

The dwarves' boots made almost no noise on the rock floor beyond occasionally sending pebbles skittering over to bounce off the wall. Venn's footsteps were light, too, but Kate's normal footfalls echoed loudly from the walls and ceilings. In some sections, they jumbled into each other until it sounded like a handful of people were walking by, but in other parts they merely thudded dully into the darkness, the sound deadened by the shape of the rocks or maybe the size of the tunnel.

"How far to the river?" Kate asked, breaking the silence.

"Three days' walk," Silas answered.

"Assuming you two can keep up a good pace," Tribal added.

"We'll need to avoid the city and the two outposts and…" Silas took in Venn and Kate. "Everyone. There's not really a precedent for bringing foreigners into the tunnels, so we'll need to take a few detours. But there are plenty of routes that skirt around busier places."

"It sounds like you two spend a lot of time avoiding the governor," Venn said.

"Gov doesn't always appreciate the more nuanced aspects of our plans," Silas said with a grin. "But he won't give us trouble. Not really."

"There's a city? How many dwarves live here?" Kate asked. "I had no idea they'd—"

"More important than that," Venn cut in, "what else lives here? Are there any plants? Or do you eat stones and dirt?"

"There are more kinds of moss underground than kinds of trees in a forest," Tribal answered.

"Where?" Venn raised her lantern to study the rocky wall.

"Well, not *here*," Tribal said, as though the question were ridiculous. "Moss needs water."

"Not far ahead is a cavern with a nice carpet of moss." Silas glanced back at his brother. "We could stop for a bite to eat."

Tribal gave a hum that sounded displeased, and Silas shifted his attention to Kate. "I don't suppose you have extra food? Ours was set on fire by the Snare."

Venn stopped. "You brought us to the land of the dead without any food?"

"Land of the dead?" Tribal demanded.

"There's plenty of food here." Silas gestured at the walls around them.

"It just tastes awful," Tribal added glumly.

Silas grimaced. "It tastes…not great. But it's food. Some of the moss ahead is edible, and there's a pool with blackfish."

"Raw blackfish," Tribal muttered. "This trip gets better all the time."

Kate looked between the two dwarves. "I can start a fire."

"No fires in caves!" Tribal declared. "You'll kill us all with the smoke!"

"All right, then. There are ways to cook things without fire," Kate said.

Silas looked at her suspiciously. "There are?"

She nodded. "How far to the cavern?"

"A few hours."

Venn muttered something and walked after him again.

Kate glanced up out of habit, as though she'd be able to judge the movement of the sun through endless layers of rock. Time felt interminable in the darkness, with only the small patch of tunnel visible around them. They might have been walking for only an hour, or it could be nearly noon. She set her hand on Venn's arm and fed a little *vitalle* into the elf. The small trickle of energy barely hurt Kate's blistered palms.

Venn turned her head and gave a very small nod of acknowledgment.

They walked on in silence, moving deeper and deeper into the dwarven tunnels, the remnants crowding along with them.

Kate glanced over her shoulder at Tribal. The dwarves from Duncave, on the far western side of Queensland, sent emissaries to court often enough that she'd met several. Ever since Keeper Alaric had befriended Douglon, a dwarf with very close ties to the High Dwarf, relations between humans and Duncave had been unusually friendly and open. Several Keepers had spent time in Duncave itself, although Tribal was right—it was highly unusual for foreigners to be allowed into any dwarven realm.

Tribal and Silas, though, looked slightly different from the dwarves she'd met. Broader, which was an odd thing to say about a race that was already twice as broad as she was. And taller, nearly as tall as she was. It was possible the twins were unusually tall, but there was more. Their skin was browner, their beards darker. The differences were subtle, but they were there.

"When did dwarves become interested in these tunnels again?" she asked Tribal.

He gave her an odd look but shook his head. "Not a tour guide."

She glanced past Venn to where she could make out Silas's back disappearing around a turn ahead.

"Neither is my brother," Tribal added. "We agreed to take you through, not give you a lesson on dwarven current affairs. Just walk without talking."

———

"A few hours" might have been accurate, but it felt like an eternity in the darkness before Kate heard the trickle of dripping water through the sounds of the remnants around her. After several more turns, the echoes of her footsteps shifted from close and crowded to distant and hollow, and Silas led them out into a cavern. In the dim mosslight, the low ceiling stretched away into darkness, studded with long, pointed teeth of rock that hung from the roof like icicles. Thin tracks glistened on their surfaces where tiny trails of water dribbled down to the floor.

Venn let out a breath, as though she'd been holding it for hours, and strode deeper into the cavern, holding her lantern up. Out in front of her, a faint green light glowed, stretching out across the floor.

Kate stopped as she caught sight of more and more green. "What is that?"

"Elven gold," Venn said, stepping onto the glowing surface. "It reflects back even the tiniest amount of light."

"It is not elven gold," Tribal said. "That's stone moss, and it has nothing to do with elves."

Kate drew closer, and the extra small light from her lantern sent shimmers of green across the floor around her.

"Mind the ground near the stoneteeth," Silas said, pointing to where a tower of rock grew out of the floor. "It'll be wet and slick."

"Stoneteeth?" Kate asked, stepping closer to it.

"Drus'testlen,"—Silas pointed to the tower on the floor, then to the tooth hanging from the ceiling above it—"and Draiy'testlen, if you're being precise. But stoneteeth works. The water running through the rock above picks up trace amounts of minerals, and when it flows down the teeth, it deposits a tiny bit, and the teeth grow drop by drop. It's fascinating. You can tell what sort of rock lies above us by the gradients in the—"

"Do not teach the human about stone," Tribal interrupted. "Don't even talk to her too much. You'll start smelling like human, and then everyone will know what we've done."

Silas waved off his brother and held his lantern up. Deeper into the cavern, the mosslight glinted back from the other stoneteeth hanging in the darkness. "Some are red with iron deposits. There's one near the far wall that's a beautiful turquoise from an old copper vein that ran above it."

"Can we eat and move on?" Tribal asked, taking Silas's lantern and heading toward where the wall curved down to meet the floor to the left. In a handful of steps, his light landed on the smooth, dark surface of a pond. He pulled a net with a long handle from where it hung on the wall and stepped to the edge, hanging the lantern out over the water. A ripple marred the surface, then several more. With a quick scoop of the net, he caught a half-dozen small blackfish and turned to squint at Kate. "Can you really cook these without fire and smoke?"

"And some of the moss?" Silas added. "It's best boiled for a bit. Actually, a little soup with the moss and the fish is almost tasty."

"Next, you're going to ask her to bake some bread," Venn said, kneeling on the moss and pressing her hands into it.

"Bread is out of the question," Kate said, pulling a small pot out of her pack. "But a bit of soup, we can do." She took a deep breath of the cavern air. In the open space, the remnants of her companions spread out and the emptiness around her felt like a breath of fresh air. They were still more obvious than human remnants would be, but spread out this much, she could ignore them and the damp air of the cavern felt almost normal.

The dwarves made quick work of cleaning the fish and crumbling some moss into a pot. Tribal brought out a savory-scented bundle of dried herbs.

"I thought you didn't have any food," Kate said.

Silas sat. "Tribal always keeps some tastifier in his pockets."

"Tastifier?"

"Packets of seasoning. He usually has several. Savory ones with dried herbs and mushrooms. Sweet ones with crystalized honey and sugar. Eating bland food is not fun."

"Sounds delicious." Kate pulled up a small patch of moss in search of the earth beneath it. "There isn't any dirt. It's just rock."

Venn nodded. "Elven gold is nourished by the air and the water in the caves."

Kate nestled her pot against the rock. The moss around her was made up of tightly packed little stems with flat tops, and each one held only the tiniest bit of *vitalle*, but Kate set her hand into the springy surface and funneled the energy into both the pot and the stone beneath it. The moss slowly browned and withered around her, but there was so much of it, and it was so interconnected, that she found enough heat to make the rock glow and bring the water to a simmer.

A rich scent of mushrooms and herbs wafted out of the pot,

and Tribal gave a reluctant hum of approval and sat down.

Kate moved back, letting the heat from the rock keep the pot warm. The cavern stretched out around them into gloomy dark corners, but her mosslight illuminated the nearby space enough that she pulled her journal and stylus out of her pack. She started a new page with a bullet-pointed list of the toad and the dwarves and the Snare and the bargain before turning her attention to the cave and sketching the way the frozen icicles of rock hung from the ceiling and tried to touch the teeth growing below them.

The smell of the cooking fish grew stronger, and Silas moved over to the pot to peer into it.

Tribal was lying on his side by the fire, his eyes closed, his breathing regular. The leather sheath of his knife had dwarven symbols stamped into it, and she raised her lantern to see it better. Dwarven runes weren't terribly complicated, but these were odd. The main strokes were bold and almost familiar, something about a gift commemorating…something. But smaller flourishes and markings pulled at the symbols, changing them in ways she couldn't put her finger on.

"If you try to touch my knife, Twig, we are going to have a problem," Tribal rumbled without opening his eyes.

"My name is Kate, and the elf is Venn."

"I don't remember asking."

Kate tapped her pencil on her journal. "Is your name Tribal because you're sort of tribal and only like other dwarves? Or did the name make you that way? Your brother is a lot friendlier."

"My brother has a soft spot for stupid creatures."

The handle of Tribal's axe had the same unusual runes. Kate looked closely at the dwarves' faces. "You're not from Duncave, are you?"

"All right, stupid is one thing, but insulting is another." Tribal raised his voice. "Silas, do we have to keep up the deal if they continue to be rude?"

"Insulting?" Kate asked.

"She's not being insulting." Silas dipped a spoon into the soup and pulled out a little chunk of fish.

"She thinks we're cave goblins with no sophistication or respectability."

"I've met several Duncave dwarves," Kate said, "and every one of them was more respectable than you."

Tribal shoved himself up.

"For instance," she continued, "none of them tried to steal from me or made an offer to help me, then tried to run away without fulfilling it."

"One"—Tribal held up a thick finger—"it's not stealing if you just leave it lying about. Two, you tricked Silas into offering help because he was under duress."

Kate ignored him and turned to Silas. "If you're not from Duncave, where are you from?"

Silas opened his mouth, but Tribal interrupted. "Don't chat with the twig. You are too fond of humans in general. She knows nothing, and that is how it should stay."

"She's just a human," Silas said. "They're curious little things. Doesn't hurt to talk to them."

"She's a Keeper," Venn said from where she lay in the moss, one arm flung over her eyes. "Which makes her curious to an extra high, extra irritating level. You've been warned."

Both dwarves glanced at each other, then turned to look at Kate, both their faces suddenly sober.

"I assume by the stunned silence I don't need to explain the name," Venn said, not bothering to look. "You're no match for her, Tribal, I assure you, so you can dispense with the posturing." Venn's lips twitched up in a smile. "She could probably beat both of you in a fight and not leave signs of a struggle."

Kate let out a little laugh.

Tribal shifted to face her more fully. "It's bad enough that you befriend a human," he said to his brother, "but it had to be a Keeper?"

"You're the one who found their campsite," Silas pointed out.

Tribal rubbed his hands over his face. "We're dead."

Kate straightened. "The Keepers have a long history of good relations with both dwarves and elves. We're not going to invade you or anything. I'm just surprised you're here at all. We thought these tunnels were deserted."

Silas scratched at his beard, grimacing slightly. "This might have been a mistake."

"Might?" Tribal ran his hands through his hair. "All right. We'll take the far south route past the old quarry. We can slip through Toothsome Gap to avoid Ruchkton, but we should aim for Purchten Docks, not the old ferry crossing. You're gonna have to get us a boat."

"Me?"

"You're the one who brought her here."

"What's the problem with me being a Keeper?" Kate asked.

Silas sighed. "Do you plan on forgetting that you found dwarves behind your Marsham Cliffs?"

"How could I possibly forget that?"

"Well, that's the problem right there. If you were some random human, no one would believe you or care, but a Keeper..." He sighed again. "And you know where the door is. Soon your queen will know, and then there'll be ambassadors and dignitaries and invitations." He glanced at Tribal. "We're dead."

"We could get these two out of here, then block the entrance," Tribal suggested.

"And lose access to the woods?"

"Better than letting the gov'nor know we told the humans we're here."

"What exactly are you doing in here that's so secretive?" Kate asked.

"It's not secret—" Silas twisted sharply toward the far wall of the cave, and Tribal tensed.

Both dwarves rose to their feet. Tribal moved silently over to stand at his brother's side.

Kate closed her journal and leaned to see around the dwarves just as Venn sat up and shifted into a crouch, facing the same way.

The floor of the cave spread out with a light green glow, reaching nearly to the barely discernible walls. A few black gaps in the wall signified the mouths of tunnels.

Nothing moved in the darkness.

Silas's fingers flickered in a series of signals, and Tribal placed his hand on the hilt of his long knife.

A dim light wavered in the shadows, outlining the mouth of a narrow tunnel.

"Smells delicious, boys." A broad dwarf stepped forward, his lantern setting the moss near his feet into a ripple of green light.

Tribal and Silas stared unmoving at him.

"Maybe he's here alone," Silas said, his voice so low Kate almost didn't hear it. "Unofficially and—"

Two more dwarves appeared, holding their own lanterns.

When a fourth appeared, holding two lanterns, Tribal let out a barely audible sigh. "Looks pretty official."

"Don't bother running, boys," the broad dwarf called, his voice echoing loudly. "No reason to make this hard. With the size of the reward placed on you two, we will track you to"—Venn rolled smoothly to her feet—"the...very ends..."

The dwarf's eyes locked on her as she loaded a dart into her crossbow with a click that echoed in the cavern.

His gaze swung to Kate.

There was utter silence for a breath.

When he spoke again, his voice held a dangerous edge. "What have you boys done now?"

CHAPTER THIRTY-ONE

Tribal and Silas stood shoulder to shoulder, facing the other dwarves. Venn stayed where she was, several paces away, and Kate rose to her feet.

"Silas," Tribal said softly, a note of accusation in his tone.

"Yes, you were right, brother," his twin answered quietly. "This was a mistake." He cleared his throat and raised his voice. "Captain Brustol, what a pleasant surprise." He made no attempt to disguise the unfriendliness in his tone. "I see you brought friends."

"I'm surprised he found friends," Tribal added. "But these guards are ordered to follow him, I suppose."

Silas grinned. "You've walked into something more complicated than you can understand, cousin. Trust me when I say it's in your best interest to take these fine guards, turn around, and forget you saw anything."

"This is your cousin?" Venn asked.

"All dwarves call each other cousin." Kate cast out, and the dense, low heat of the four guards moved closer. Her wave hit the far wall, rolling into a shadowed tunnel, and one more huge form flared up.

Brustol ignored them both. "There is no sum large enough to make me forget that I found the Weasel Brothers clearly returning from another unsanctioned run out of the Slide Door. But…" He continued forward, the guards spreading out in an arc around him like dark, dwarven-shaped shadows. "But this time you brought back—into *our* tunnels—a human? And an *elf*?"

"That's the part you're not gonna be smart enough to understand," Silas said. "Just walk away, Brustol. We don't want to hurt you."

"Again," Tribal added.

"You're outnumbered." Brustol stalked forward. "So this time, you can't cheat."

Tribal glanced at Silas. "There's no logic there at all. More of them means more reason for us to cheat."

Silas motioned to the three guards. "Last chance to walk away, boys. You all know you don't want to do this. Don't get hurt because Brustol is too stupid to stop."

Two of the dwarves exchanged looks, but none of them paused. They set down their lanterns and shifted their hands to the weapons hung at their waists.

Silas glanced over his shoulder at Kate. "Your amulet doesn't work. It's not convincing anyone of anything."

"You're using it wrong. Fewer insults, more friendliness."

He flashed her a grin. "Where's the fun in that?"

Tribal pointed a finger at Venn. "You stay out of this."

"Then *you* take care of it," Venn answered, not lowering her crossbow.

He left his knife sheathed and shook out his hands. "There are only four of them."

"A fifth is hanging back," Kate said. "He's big."

Silas grimaced. "I was hoping he hadn't brought Cren."

The guards drew closer, slipping quietly through the stone-teeth like a pack of wolves, drawing long knives and gripping heavy axes.

A hint of their remnants reached Kate, thick and rich with earthy smells and rumbling sounds. She stretched her fingers, wincing at the pain that the motion shot across her palms. Even something as simple as putting a few of them to sleep was going to hurt.

Tribal and Silas stepped forward to meet them. They separated from each other, but their motions stayed fluid and strangely connected, as though they were one body instead of two. Their shapes blended with the shadows as they moved away from the mosslight.

At a signal from Brustol, the three guards around him rushed at the twins. There was a flurry of motion that Kate couldn't make out in the gloom, and two heavy crashes.

Only one guard still stood, and he took a step back, his attention shifting between Tribal and Silas.

"Never agree to fight with Brustol," Silas told him. "He'll hang you out to dry every time."

The guard nudged one of his fallen companions with his foot, but the lump on the ground didn't move.

"Come help your friend, Brustol," Tribal called. "We'll wait until you're ready. And, Cren, why don't you come out too? It'll feel more even that way."

"Tribal!" Silas objected.

"Better to get it over with all at once," Tribal answered.

"I'm really not sure that it is."

The shadows by the narrow tunnel shifted, and a huge dwarf stepped out, easily an entire head taller than the others. His shoulders were so broad it was shocking he'd fit in the passage, and he dragged something dark and heavy behind him as he walked.

"Oh, good," Silas said, "he brought his club. Do you think his arm has healed?"

Tribal sighed. "Should have. Was a clean break."

With Cren coming, Brustol began inching forward.

Tribal gave the guard still standing nearby an apologetic look. "I changed my mind about waiting, cousin. Sorry." He darted forward, and his elbow shot up and slammed into the other dwarf's face, sending him staggering. Silas followed up with a punch to the ear, and the guard crumpled to the ground.

Brustol hesitated, but Tribal and Silas launched toward him.

Kate missed which dwarf knocked Brustol's axe out of his hand, but it was Tribal who doubled him over with a knee to the gut, and Silas who added a kick to the face.

Before Cren was halfway to them, Brustol lay senseless on the ground.

"Cren," Silas called. "How are you? It's been a while. Your club looks new. What happened to your old one?"

The giant dwarf's only answer was to swing the massive wooden cudgel, smashing off the points of two stoneteeth in its arc.

Tribal and Silas stepped away from each other, and Cren's gaze moved between them, his heavy brow hiding his eyes.

Kate caught the first sound of Cren's remnant when he was only paces from the twins. A drumming sound that made her think of deep caverns and the rhythmic pounding of mining tools.

"We could try Wrap Around," Tribal said.

"He's too tall," Silas answered. "Cat Sneak."

Tribal gave his twin an incredulous look. "Only if you're the cat."

"You're always the cat."

"Not against Cren." Tribal sighed. "Pinch foot."

"His neck is the size of my waist."

"You have a better idea?"

Silas let out a groan. "This is gonna hurt."

They waited for Cren to take two more steps before Silas flicked his fingers and both twins sprang forward. Tribal rushed straight at Cren while Silas raced around the massive dwarf and leapt up onto his back. Cren let out a bellow and swung his club at Tribal, who ducked in close enough to take the blow from the dwarf's arm instead of the weapon.

Tribal grunted and grabbed the huge arm. "Sorry about this, Cren." He slammed his elbow into the dwarf's forearm.

Cren let out a roar of pain, and his club fell from his hand.

"Looks like the arm isn't healed," Tribal shouted.

Cren swung his other fist into Tribal's back and sent the smaller dwarf sprawling on the ground.

Silas shimmied higher on Cren's back and wrapped his arms around the huge dwarf's throat. "Tribal?"

His twin let out a groan and pushed himself up. Cren bent down, ignoring the weight on his back, and grabbed his club with his unhurt hand, swinging it up and over his own shoulder, crashing it onto Silas's back.

"Tribal!" he gasped.

Tribal pushed himself to his feet and ran at Cren again, wrapping his own arms around the massive one holding the club.

Cren dragged Tribal a few steps, then leaned down and bellowed into his face just before slamming his other fist into Tribal's side.

Tribal groaned in pain as Cren pulled his fist back for another punch. "Any time now, Silas!"

"Why is he so big?" Silas yelled, wrenching his arms tighter around Cren's neck.

The huge dwarf shifted his attention to Silas. He flung his fist back, slamming it into Silas's jaw before grabbing the arms Silas had wrapped around his neck, pulling them away from his throat.

"Tribal!" Silas yelled, a note of panic in his voice.

There was a small twang, and a dart sank into Cren's chest, just a finger's width from Tribal's head.

"Stay out of it, elf!" Tribal yelled.

Cren continued to pull Silas's arm for a heartbeat, then staggered to his knees.

Silas anchored his feet on the ground and tightened his choke hold. Cren shook his head, blinking against the effects of the dart, but didn't fall.

"That's not working, Venn," Kate pointed out, starting forward.

"Well, he's ridiculously big." Venn snapped another dart into her crossbow.

With both of Cren's hands busy trying to pry Silas off his neck, Kate ducked around to his side, moving into his drumming remnant. The thrumming was loud enough she could feel it vibrating in her chest, but it wasn't violent. It was almost soothing.

"Get"—Tribal glared at her, trying to pull Cren's hands away from Silas—"back!"

Cren bared his teeth through a thick, wiry black beard. He inhaled, then bellowed at her, blasting hot, humid breath in her face that smelled like musty mutton.

Kate squinted against it and set her bandaged palm on Cren's forehead, shoving *vitalle* into him.

Cren leaned toward her, pulling the twins with him, and snapped his teeth at her. The *vitalle* stung her palm, but she held her hand against him, adding more *energy* until his eyes glazed and he sagged.

Tribal swore and shoved Cren's now limp arm away, scrambling back before the huge dwarf toppled forward.

He spun to face Kate with a blistering look. "We told you to keep out of it!"

Brustol moaned and lifted his head off the floor, and a dart sank into his neck.

"Stop!" Tribal shouted, running at Venn, who was reloading her crossbow. He shoved her arm to the side. "*STOP SHOOTING DWARVES!*"

She snapped a new dart into place and jabbed a finger into Tribal's chest. "You didn't do your job."

"It was perfectly under control! And now, you....you—" He swung around to face his brother, who was climbing gingerly off Cren's back. "Silas!"

"I know," Silas muttered, moving his jaw gingerly. He looked at Kate and let out a sigh. "You did not help matters."

Kate crossed her arms. "Should we have let him keep pummeling you both?"

"Rather than have an elf and a human attack a dwarven guard? Yes."

Tribal stomped over to where the pot of soup was still steaming, the motion made somewhat less impactful with his boots making no noise. "I'll hide our trail." He poured a bowlful of soup and pointed the bowl at Silas with a dark look. "You fix the twig's feet. Then we need to move!" He took a slurp and stormed toward the far wall.

"My feet?" Kate asked.

"They're loud." Silas moved over to Brustol and knelt next to him. He sighed as he yanked the dart out of Brustol's neck and held it out to Venn. "Good luck rolling Cren over for your other one."

Venn squatted down by the big dwarf and heaved at his shoulder. His arm lifted from the floor, but the rest of him stayed face down. "What is he made of?" She let him drop back down. "Rocks?"

Kate wriggled her hands underneath his thick upper arm. "He's a giant."

Venn's brow creased as she hefted his shoulder. "He's too small for a giant."

"Metaphorically, Venn!" Kate grunted, dropping lower and shoving the heavy dwarf up until his chest was off the ground.

Venn shifted lower, planting her shoulder against his side and feeling underneath him for the dart.

Kate's arms shook with the effort of holding him up. "Running out of time here!"

The elf let out a grunt of success and gave a sharp yank, then slid her arm out holding a dart with a bloody tip. Kate let Cren drop back down to the floor and shook out her arms.

Venn gave a small grimace at the condition of the tip and wiped it off on the bottom of Cren's shirt. "That's going to leave a mark."

Kate stared at her. "Is he now bleeding out of a hole in his chest?"

"It didn't go into his heart or anything," Venn said. "If dwarves even have hearts. It barely sank into one of his ridiculous muscles. It'll just be a little blood."

Kate shook her head and walked to the soup.

"No time to eat. We need to move," Silas said quietly, glancing up from where he rummaged through Brustol's pack. One of the other guards groaned. "Quickly. Before any of these cousins wake up."

"I can make them sleep for a bit." Kate knelt by the groaning dwarf and set her hand on his forehead. "*Dormio*," she said, feeding in a little *vitalle*. His body relaxed, and his breathing deepened.

Silas watched her with narrow eyes. "How long will that last?"

She moved to the next guard. "A couple of hours." She

pressed *vitalle* into his forehead, wincing at the burn it caused.

She gritted her teeth before doing the third. All three guards had remnants reminiscent of food and fireside, but she turned toward Brustol and caught a grating sound that scraped across her spine. Something noxious threaded through his earthy scent, like the vinegar tang of rotting fruit. She held back, swallowing down the biting chill of metal that cut across the back of her tongue. Cold and ruthless. "How about your dart, Venn?"

"Should be half a day," the elf answered, "but dwarves are unnecessarily big. I'd say at least two hours."

"We'll leave him with just the dart, then." Kate stretched her fingers and aching palm.

Silas sat with his hand in Brustol's pack, looking between Kate and Venn with a sort of wary appraisal. "All right. If you want soup, eat fast."

Kate moved away from Brustol's remnant and squatted by the pot, pouring out three bowls as Silas joined them, his arms full. He handed her some thick, soft fabric. "Wrap these around your shoes." He sorted through the rest of the things he'd taken, then grabbed his bowl of soup.

The fabric was shaped like huge socks, far too big for her, but each had a pair of long ties. She set them aside and took a gulp of the soup, getting a small chunk of the fish. It was so mild she could barely taste it, but the broth wasn't objectionable. "Care to explain the extreme level of animosity these dwarves have against you and outsiders?"

"There's not really a story there," Silas said easily.

A slight brush of tiredness slid across her mind. Stories about the bickering of dwarves did sound rather dull.

She pushed the thought away with a laugh. "Did you really just try to use the amulet I made? On me?"

He gave her a guilty smile. "Was worth a try."

"It really wasn't," Venn said.

Silas glanced over his shoulder toward where Brustol had come from. "Well, then, no, I do not care to explain. But I will. Just not here. Your involvement in this little skirmish is going to make every dwarf in Rullduin angry to a level Tribal and I have never managed to attain before. We need to get away from here as quickly and as quietly as possible. Sound travels a very long way underground."

Tribal continued to circle the cavern, muttering to himself and occasionally kicking rocks across the floor.

"Tribal's leaving false trails, but it'll only throw them off for a bit." Silas untied a bulky bundle he'd taken from Brustol's pack and gave a grunt of approval. "Only hardtack, but that'll last us a couple days. Brustol always carries too much food."

Kate drank down the end of her soup and pulled the fabric over her boots, securing it by crisscrossing the straps from the top of the socks to her ankle.

"I thought the rule was whoever held something owned it?" Venn said, peering at Brustol's small knife, compass, spyglass, and ring that Silas was tucking into his own pack. "Those things were very clearly still in Brustol's possession."

"Brustol owes me so great a debt," Silas said with a grim smile, "that he should give me every single thing he owns. It's not my fault he refuses to pay me back when he's awake."

"What debt?" Kate asked.

"In the unlikely event we ever become friends, maybe I'll tell you." He took the last gulp of soup and moved to the little pool where he rinsed his bowl and the pot.

Tribal stopped near the far wall and gave a short whistle.

"Time to go," Silas said, handing Kate the bowl and pot.

She rose to rinse out her own bowl in the questionably clean water. The thick fabric muffled her footsteps until they were merely a hushed rustle. Each step was cushioned, as though she walked on thick grass instead of stone. Silas gave an approving nod, then moved among the fallen dwarves one last time, shifting a few of them to positions that looked more comfortable, but leaving Brustol with his arm pinned awkwardly beneath him.

Venn rinsed her own bowl, and Kate tucked everything into her pack.

She glanced at the double mosslight lantern that one of the guards had dropped. The two lanterns were attached to a short pole that split at the end before it curled into two hooks. "That's just lying around—can we take it with us? Double barely any light is better than barely any light."

Silas shook his head. "Only guards carry a forked lantern."

"Because only guards need to see?" Venn asked.

"Because the first dwarven soldier, Turrethlow, carried a forked lantern into the underworld to fight the demon of the deep and wrestle the keys of stone from him." Silas gave the elf a pointed look. "Are you prepared to do the same? If not, no forked lantern."

Venn glanced at the bodies sprawled on the ground. "These guards couldn't handle you two, never mind a demon of the deep."

"No forked lanterns," Tribal declared from across the cavern.

Venn stood looking at the moss floor with a regretful expression.

"Did that hold enough *vitalle* to help you?" Kate asked.

"It's not a forest, but there's enough." Venn looked over to where she'd been lying, and the moss had a wide patch of darkness. "It's the right kind, though. Yours works, but it's...more abrasive. A forest is like being surrounded by a warm pool. It just seeps in."

Kate looked at the dark section. "Does it bother you that you kill it?"

Venn gave a half shrug. "The forest is a cycle of life and death. Things die so that others can live every day." She surveyed the cave. "I wouldn't want to kill it all, but this will regrow. Death is not the enemy."

Kate glanced at her. "What is?"

Venn was quiet for a moment. "Corruption."

Kate let her eyes wander over the carpet of glimmering green that filled the cavern, winding around the stoneteeth and butting up to the edge of the black pool. The blackness caught at her, looking like a hollow pit amidst the light. "I agree, but I still find myself fighting and hoping against death."

Venn followed Kate's gaze to the pool. "My aunt says we were not built for mourning. It goes against everything we want and hope for and need. Even when the death is a relief from the pain of dwindling life. She says grief digs its claws into us, and no matter how many times we wrestle it out, accept what we've lost, and try to focus on remembering the life, another day comes when something catches us off guard, and the claws sink in again."

Kate stared at the pool, her fear for Bo stirring inside her like some creature stretching against its bonds. It tangled with the old, familiar fear for Evan, the grief that couldn't be faced without giving up the hope that she'd find him. She shoved it all back and took a deep breath.

Venn's hand fell on her shoulder. Kate looked up at her. Venn's expression was caught between resignation and something Kate couldn't name. "We should not mourn someone before they're gone."

"And if we don't know if they're gone?"

Venn let out a breath that felt rueful. "Then we try to hope until we know." She dropped her hand and started toward her pack.

Kate's eyes dropped to the glowing moss beneath her feet. "Silas, when we leave this cave, will there be more moss?"

"Every once in a while."

Kate dug her fingers into the nearest thick patch and pulled up a small section. It tore off the rock with only a little resistance, and she grabbed another. She glanced at Venn. "You wanted to bring the forest with us."

Venn looked at the patch of moss. "I meant a literal forest."

"Those are heavy." Kate stacked the little rugs of moss into a pile. "Small slivers of forest life, though, ripped into a convenient carrying size, mean you can bring the life of the forest with you wherever you go. Metaphorically." She paused. "Or symbolically? No, almost literally, really... Anyway, you're paying your way through dwarven tunnels with elven gold. What's better than that?"

"Not going through tunnels at all," Venn said, but she pulled up enough to fill her own pack to overflowing.

Tribal whistled again, and Silas, giving the torn-up moss a curious look, motioned for them to hurry. "This next tunnel is very well connected to a lot of places. No talking."

"For how long?" Kate asked.

Tribal's voice floated quietly back out of the tunnel. "Forever."

Silas blew out a breath and squinted after his brother. "All day would be best."

"Fine by me." Venn walked after Tribal, keeping a dart loaded in her crossbow. "It's Kate who'll have a problem with that."

Kate fell in behind her, her pack heavy with moss. "I can be silent now, but you promised me answers."

"Tonight," Silas said, bringing up the rear.

In moments, the walls of a new tunnel wrapped around them. With Kate's footsteps muffled, the air was filled with nothing but the remnants of her companions, and her lantern lit only jagged rock and Venn's back.

"The gov'nor's gonna figure out where we're headed," Tribal said quietly, his voice echoing dully down the tunnel.

"I know," Silas said grimly. "Let's be faster than him."

CHAPTER THIRTY-TWO

KATE'S MIND returned again to the question of Bo's disappearance as she trudged behind Venn around the thousandth turn in the dreary, monotonous, labyrinthian tunnels. Even with the extra padding on her boots, the constant drumming of her feet on the stone floor had set them to aching hours ago.

She ignored how tired and heavy they felt and thought of the memory of that clearing that Venn had shown her. How had the trees noticed everything except how Bo had left? The obvious answer was that the shadow had enveloped him, and the trees had deemed him nothing but another bit of gloom.

But there was that elf ranger, the one who'd stopped to study where the shadow had waited. That was who Kate needed to talk to. What had Venn said his name was? Ayen? A captain of the rangers shouldn't be hard to track down.

Venn drew to a stop in front of her, and Kate blinked, refocusing on the tunnel.

A quiet rushing sound bled into the tunnel. Smooth, only peppered occasionally with a trickle of water. Tribal held up a hand for them to stop, then sat down and scooted into a hole Kate hadn't noticed along the wall. He disappeared into blackness, and they waited for a long moment before he let out a short whistle again.

"There's a path down," Silas whispered, "but the rocks may be wet, so watch where you step."

Venn held her moss lantern into the hole with a grimace. "Fantastic. A smaller tunnel."

"It opens up just inside," Silas assured her.

Venn sat, stuck her legs in, and scooted forward, holding the lantern in front of her. Her dim light lit a slope of rocks leading down to a low cavern with an inky black stream running through it.

Kate followed, sitting and sliding down the rough rocks that jabbed at her palms through her bandages and scraped along her legs until she dropped far enough to rise to a crouch. She clambered down the last of the slope and was able to stand under the low ceiling of the cavern. It was rounded and mostly empty, with only a small stream running through it. Tribal disappeared into a shadowy nook to her left. She followed and found a small room only a handful of paces across.

Kate sank down, stretching her sore feet out in front of her with a groan. Venn sat with her back to the opposite wall, facing the door, her mosslight glinting off the dart that still sat in her crossbow.

A few moments later, Silas joined them. "No sign of anyone following us. We should be good to sleep here."

"Why in this room?" Venn asked. "It already feels like a prison cell. Won't anyone following us come for water?"

"There are far easier places to get water, and that stream tastes stale. This room is the perfect hiding place because of acoustics." Silas tapped his ear. "The stream jumbles sounds enough that, as long as we use quiet voices, no one out in the tunnels will hear us."

"Excellent," Kate said, resting her head back against the wall. "Then, in a quiet voice, explain what is going on."

"We don't like strangers invading our house," Tribal said. "How hard is that to understand?"

Kate gave him a flat look and turned to Silas. "You explain."

"He's not wrong," Silas began. "We don't like humans coming into our tunnels"—he gestured to Venn—"never mind elves, but the gov'nor is more sensitive than most, on account of the fact that our rights to be mining here are…"

"Fine," Tribal finished.

"They're a bit blurry," Silas continued.

"Because these tunnels still belong to the Duncave dwarves?" Kate guessed.

"They left four hundred years ago," Tribal pointed out.

"Yes," Silas said. "You see, about six hundred years ago, there was a disagreement involving a steelstone deposit and a fire topaz stolen from the High Dwarf Trum's crown, which was blamed on his cousin Reld."

"Dwarves seem to be often troubled by their cousins." Venn pulled a mat of moss out of the top of her pack. It was so dry it crumbled under her fingers. Silas and Tribal studied it for a moment, giving Venn a suspicious look. She set it beside her on the floor and fixed them with a level gaze. "I'm sorry. Did you need that patch of moss for something?"

Silas glanced at the other moss stuffed into her pack, still soft and green. "It's weird that *you* need it for something. Anyway, we call all dwarves cousins, because if you go back far enough, we're all related, but Trum and Reld were actual cousins. Their mothers were sisters, and they'd been like brothers their whole lives. But Trum grew paranoid and accused Reld of trying to steal the throne, and things got worse when the topaz was stolen."

"And then there was a tribe of feral weasels," Tribal added.

"Feral weasels?" Kate asked.

Silas grinned. "Someone released a dozen feral weasels into the throne room when the High Dwarf was announcing his betrothal to Belina."

Kate raised an eyebrow. "That sounds...disruptive."

"It sounds hilarious," Tribal said.

"It was both," Silas continued. "Belina, by all accounts, was very clever and very strong but couldn't shake rumors she had a tail. During the weasel incident, she was bit."

"By a feral weasel?"

Tribal chuckled. "On her"—he glanced at Venn and Kate—"backside."

"It was the proverbial spark in the fire powder." Silas's smile faded. "A lot of cousins died that day, and in the end, High Dwarf Trum exiled Reld to Rullduin." He gestured to the rock around them. "He took his supporters and came here, even though it was minimally developed and barely mined."

Kate rubbed her eyes against the exhaustion creeping up on her. "And they lived here until four hundred years ago when a cave-in destroyed their city, and they moved farther west to Duncave."

Silas nodded. "Leaving Rullduin unoccupied."

"Where do the descendants of Trum live now?"

"Where they always have," Silas answered. "In Muerdus Follen."

Kate looked between the two dwarves. "I have no idea where that is."

"East," Tribal said, a note of fondness in his voice. "Far to the east in the caverns beneath the great forest. Caverns the likes of which your little minds couldn't imagine. Vast galleries with rivers and lakes. The veins of gold and silver are so thick you could never mine them all. The walls are carved by the craftsmen of old with skill that would make you weep."

Venn leaned back against the wall and brushed her fingers

over the living moss on top of her pack. "Being underground always makes me want to weep."

"Even you would like Follen," Tribal said. "The soil from the forest washes down in the rivers and spreads on the shores, and we have trees and orchards and grazing grass for our sheep."

Kate looked between the two of them for any sign of a joke, but they seemed serious. "How far away is it?"

"Farther than we'd ever take you," Tribal said. "And they don't allow humans there, either."

"If you're so happy about trees," Venn said, "why don't you just live in the forest?"

"Live under the giant, empty sky, confined to roaming only the skin of the world?" Tribal asked. "When you can shelter in the very heart of the earth?"

"So your governor," Kate interrupted before Venn could argue, "came here to do...what?"

"There are interesting deposits in Rullduin," Silas said. "Deposits no one was mining, and so Follen's current High Dwarf Bluonren ordered an unofficial survey of the tunnels, and when they were found to be abandoned, he set the gov'nor the *very* unofficial task of mining a bit of it and sending it back to Muerdus Follen."

Kate glanced between the twins. "And you two are part of that mining operation?"

"We were the survey team," Tribal answered. "Got the gov'nor to the right spot, then decided to keep surveying and see what we could find."

"And how does that lead to dwarves wanting to arrest you?" Kate asked.

Tribal shrugged. "No idea."

Silas let out a chuckle. "Some of our surveillance got a little close to some of the gov'nor's secrets, and we may have discovered some things he'd rather keep hidden. Then there's the fact that he strictly forbade us from leaving the tunnels and going into your little land."

"Queensland," Kate said.

"Yes, that. He's convinced there's a Duncave dwarf hiding beneath every stone, and when they hear of the new stonesteel deposit we found, things might get tense."

"How long have you been coming into Queensland?"

"Just since last winter. And like you said, there are no Duncave dwarves anywhere nearby. They're all hiding in Duncave. The humans don't care about our tunnels either. We explained to the gov that there was no risk, but he wants absolutely no one to know we're here."

"Well, that explains Brustol's reaction to you," Kate said, yawning.

"And to us." Venn unclipped the dart from her crossbow and examined it. "How hard is it going to be to get out of here?"

"Assuming we can reach the river before the gov'nor, it should be fine."

"And if not?" Kate asked.

"Then...we'll need to adjust our plans."

"What are the chances we get there before the governor?"

"Reasonably good. We'll sleep a few hours, then move again," Silas said, his voice unconcerned. "We have two days to the river, and they'll be long. But then it's just a leisurely float."

"How do we see to navigate an underground river in the pitch black?" Venn asked.

Silas shook his head. "We don't have to navigate it."

"And 'tain't pitch black," Tribal said. "You'll see."

Kate considered the two dwarves. "Brustol called you the Weasel Brothers." The side of Silas's beard twitched up in a smile. "And you told us a story about feral weasels causing havoc."

Silas's smile widened. "Comparisons have been drawn."

Venn turned to Kate. "You made a deal with two dwarves

who are like feral weasels." The statement bordered on accusation.

"Feral weasels who know a shortcut," Kate reminded her.

"We're harmless," Silas said blithely. He motioned to Kate. "You should try to sleep. We have two long days of walking to reach the river. Tribal'll take first shift scouting the tunnels to make sure no one's near, and I'll take second."

Venn looked at the dwarf as though he was an idiot. "We are not sleeping and leaving ourselves at the mercy of you two."

A yawn pushed its way up Kate's throat, and she squeezed her eyes shut against the exhaustion from last night's interrupted sleep and the long hours of walking.

The remnants of the dwarves filled the room, and she sorted through them again. There were the strong smells that reminded her of hearths and feasts. There was the humming, low thrums that shifted and harmonized with each other. As she sat, the one from Silas shifted up a small amount, and in a moment, Tribal's matched it. With an ebb and flow, the two sounds climbed a little higher or dropped a little lower, staying in tune with each other.

She hunted past the sound, searching for any hint of sourness or the rancid smell of corruption. There was the metal tang on her tongue that warriors often had, but it was like Venn's. A vein running through the larger aspects of their remnants. Contained and isolated, unlike Brustol's, which had permeated the rest of his with a brutality she could taste.

She opened her heavy eyelids. "Wake me when we need to go." She pushed her pack to the side and lay down on it like a lumpy leather pillow.

Venn let out a disbelieving breath. "You trust the lying, thieving dwarves whose own people want to arrest them?"

"It's in their best interest to not let us get caught," Kate said.

Venn flung a hand out, gesturing to the walls around them.

"They could do that by leaving us in a small cave next to a tainted stream to die where no one will find us."

"They could. But they smell trustworthy."

Silas let out a snort of amusement.

Tribal lifted an arm and sniffed his armpit. "I do smell great."

Venn ignored them both, narrowing her eyes at Kate.

"They smell as trustworthy as you do," Kate said. "And they're more friendly—" She glanced at Tribal. "Well, half of them are more friendly than you were when I embarked on a month-long journey with you."

"Next you'll say the giant dwarf who attacked us was trustworthy too," Venn said, pointing her dart back in the general direction of the mossy cave.

"Cren was all right." Kate let her head sink back and her eyes close. "I think he would have rather been mining deep in some cavern than fighting for Brustol."

For a moment there was nothing but the shushing tinkling of the stream in the larger cavern outside.

"That's exactly what Cren would rather do," Silas said slowly.

"Who *doesn't* smell trustworthy?" Tribal asked curiously.

"Brustol," Kate answered. "I would not fall asleep near Brustol. That dwarf is corrupt enough that it's tainted everything about him."

The dwarves were silent for long enough that Kate opened her eyes to find them watching her with unreadable expressions.

Finally, Silas gave a grunt that sounded like an agreement. "No one should fall asleep near Brustol."

Kate glanced at Venn. "Do you trust me?"

Venn's brow creased. "I barely know you. And I definitely don't share your confidence in these two."

"We've already passed two cracks we could have tossed your bodies into," Tribal said.

Venn pointed her dart at him. "Would you trust me to watch over you in the woods?"

He grinned. "I wouldn't trust you to watch over me anywhere."

"Then stop talking and go scout wherever you're supposed to scout." Venn turned back to Kate. "You get some sleep. I'll stay up and keep an eye on the feral weasels." Before Kate could thank her for the offer, Venn continued, "Humans are useless without good sleep." She twirled her dart between her fingers. "I don't want to carry you tomorrow."

"Your concern is heartwarming." In the quiet, it was impossible not to think of the rock pressing down from above and the idea of wandering forever in the dark if the dwarves left them. She resolutely pushed the thoughts away and ran over the history of the dwarves in her mind again, cementing it so she could write it down whenever they returned to someplace with daylight. Or even candlelight.

Partway through imagining a tribe of feral weasels pouring into a dwarven throne room, she fell asleep.

CHAPTER THIRTY-THREE

KATE SHUFFLED backward and pressed her back into the hard stone wall with Venn at her shoulder. She stretched her eyes wide, but her mosslight lantern was smothered under her cloak, and the huge cavern the dwarves had dubbed the Crossroads spread out in front of her in complete blackness.

A breeze blew past from somewhere to the right. It didn't carry the dusty staleness the tunnels had held for the last three days, but the wet mossiness of a river. Venn breathed slow and steady next to her, and the two dwarves shuffled into place ahead of her, blocking off the large cavern.

Kate stifled a yawn into her arm. After two nights of short sleep, today's supposedly short trip had ended up needing two detours to avoid guards and an hour of hiding in a cave that smelled like rotten eggs.

"Our tunnel is over to the right," Silas whispered. "Once we're in it, it's a quick jog to the river, where there should be at least a few boats waiting. We'll grab one and be on our way."

"Are you sure there's a patrol coming?" Kate asked.

"Can't you hear them?"

Kate listened. "No. Can we get to our tunnel before they get here?"

"Not unless you can magically jump from here to there. We only have a few seconds."

Kate strained to hear but still couldn't make out any sounds that indicated an approaching group of guards from any of the tunnels across the cavern. "Venn could step across to it. Elves from the White Wood can cross long distances in a single step. Her aunt Evay is famous among humans for it."

Silas shifted. "Really? You could go make sure our tunnel's empty, Venn."

"I can't step like my aunt," Venn said. "And no one would step in a dark cave when they can't see where they'd land. They could end up inside a wall."

"Is your aunt especially good at it?" Kate asked curiously.

Tribal shushed them just as a speck of light appeared far across the darkness. Then another. In moments, a line of three mosslight lanterns wobbled in the distance, carried by dimly illuminated dwarven shapes.

Kate waited quietly. Maybe this was just a group of random dwarves—

A fourth appeared with the forked lantern, and she sighed.

Snippets of low voices sounded in the cavern as the lights spread out, bobbing into different shadowy corners. The sounds echoed oddly through the space, bouncing off unexpected walls, sounding closer than the guards were or from the wrong directions.

"How thoroughly are they going to explore?" Kate whispered.

"It's third watch," Silas answered, "which means that is either Nurren or Hardd's band. Neither of which are particularly thorough. This side of the cavern is a dead end. Hopefully, they'll just check the other tunnels, then pick one to follow."

"Unless it's fourth watch," Tribal said, "and that's Surrion."

Silas swore quietly. "It can't be fourth watch already."

"You backed us into a dead end?" Venn asked.

Silas shushed her.

The mosslights continued to move in a measured, logical path around the cavern, drawing slowly closer. In the dim light, Kate could make out the outlines of the twins and Venn, whose hand was tucked into her pack where her stash of moss was kept.

Silas swore again. "It can't be fourth watch already."

"We're going to need to make a run for it," Tribal said quietly over his shoulder. "Wait 'til we tell you."

Silas squatted, and Kate heard the faint scrape of a rock. "We could hit the ledge above the Mullduk's Path."

Tribal's dark shape bent over. "Runwater Tunnel slopes down-hill. The rocks would go farther."

"That's a bit close to where we're really headed."

"If it's really only third watch, they'll all run into it like idiots," Tribal said.

His brother let out a grunt. "Fine."

"What if it's fourth watch?" Kate whispered.

Silas stood still for a moment, and she thought she could see him wince. "It's third watch."

He swung his arm and hurled a rock. Tribal did the same half a heartbeat later. Silas threw one more before the first quiet crack echoed from across the cavern, to the right of where the guards had entered. The mosslight lanterns spun around toward the noise.

The second rock caused a skittering of bits of gravel, and the third sounded muffled and distant.

A sharp call sent all the lanterns running toward the sounds. The first three disappeared into the tunnel, while the fourth, the guard with the forked lantern, stayed at the entrance.

"Fourth watch," Tribal muttered.

Silas swore a third time and turned to Kate and Venn. "It

won't take long for them to see no one's been in there recently. We stay along the near wall and make for the river. Quietly. No light."

"I could shoot him from here," Venn offered. "Put him to sleep."

"Are you looking to start a war?" Tribal demanded in a whisper.

"A war?"

"You sneak into our home and keep shooting us with your tiny elf arrows!"

"*You* brought us here!" Venn hissed. "And I've barely shot anyone. They're just darts. They barely hurt."

"You shot *me*." Tribal pointed at his shoulder. "They hurt."

"Shut up and move, Tribal," Silas hissed.

His twin growled at Venn, then spun and stalked out of their nook. Venn followed, muttering something under her breath. Kate stepped out after her, running her hand along the wall and easing her feet over the dark floor.

Silas pushed her in the back. "Hurry," he whispered.

She lengthened her stride, keeping two bits of mosslight across the cavern in sight while also trying to make out anything ahead of her in the blackness. The guard holding the forked lantern shifted, and for a moment she caught a glimpse of his face peering into a dark tunnel.

She stepped quietly, letting the fabric socks muffle her steps, until her foot landed on something that felt like a stick, and a sharp crack rang out.

The forked lantern swung around, and Kate tried to stop, but her other foot came down on the stick, which twisted, slamming into the wall with a dull crunch.

Venn, Tribal, and Silas all froze.

The guard across the cavern spun and hurled his lantern like a lance, sending it soaring toward them in a high arc.

"Run!" Silas snapped, pushing Kate forward.

Tribal broke into a sprint, and the guard shouted.

The mosslight crashed down a dozen paces away, casting the floor into long black shadows, and Kate dashed through them, hoping they weren't hiding anything that would trip her up and send her sprawling.

The guard's shouts echoed through the cavern, joined by others, growing quickly closer. Tribal and Venn hurtled into a tunnel and disappeared into darkness. Kate ran in, pulling her mosslight lantern out of her cloak, trying to shield it with her body and still illuminate the floor in front of her.

Silas skidded to a halt behind her at the entrance, and she stopped.

"Go!" he hissed at her, waving her on as he dropped to the floor and pulled something from his pack.

The tunnel led straight downhill, and the smell of plants and wetness and fish grew stronger as she ran.

Silas came up behind her, and when she glanced back, he flashed a grin. "Don't look that way."

She pulled her eyes forward just as the guards' shouts filled the tunnel.

"Eyes closed!" Silas shouted.

A cry of surprise rang out behind them, and a blinding flash of light exploded.

Kate squeezed her eyes shut, but a purple image of every detail of the tunnel was seared into her eyelids. Behind her, chaos erupted. The guards' shouts were choked out by coughs before they fell ominously silent.

Silas let out a laugh, pushing Kate in the back. "Go! Go!"

Tribal and Venn raced through the tunnel until it came out high in the wall of a huge, bright cavern. Kate joined them, ducking behind a short wall. The path wound away to the left, down a steep slope.

Kate lowered her lantern, which was unnecessary in the bright cavern, and peered over the wall.

Twenty feet below them, glowing moss carpeted the floor in long, cultivated rows, lighting the entire cavern like a dusky evening up on the surface. The center of the cave was full of an inky black lake, covered in tiny wavelets that lapped against the shore.

Their path turned sharply and led down the steep slope to the cavern floor. A few buildings stood near the lake, and four small rowboats bobbed in a line along a pier. Each boat was only large enough to hold a half-dozen dwarves, but each was almost full with crates and barrels and sacks being loaded by six burly workers.

Silas came over and squatted next to Kate, grinning.

"How long did that buy us?" she asked quietly.

"The gas will knock them out for a few minutes. When they wake, they'll be disoriented and still flash-blind, so we should have a couple more before they're in any shape to follow."

"And what about the six dwarves between us and the boats?" Venn asked.

"Silas and I can take care of them." Tribal pointed at Venn. "You stay out of it. Only the first boat is set. You two make for that."

"Set?" Kate squinted down at the dimly lit dock. Something long and thin rose from the stern of each boat, connecting it to a thick wire hanging over the lake.

"They travel down that wire," Silas said. "Keeps them from floundering into rocks in the narrow parts. See how the back three are tied to it with rope, but the lead boat is hooked with a metal rod? They'll all get a rod before they leave, but it's too heavy to have more than one rod hooked to the wire in the span by the dock, so—"

"They don't set them until they're ready to go," Tribal interrupted. "That's the important part. Stop talking."

"We're going through that?" Venn pointed to the right, where the lake narrowed. The stone walls crowded in quickly, sheer and jagged, to fence in a narrow black gap in the cavern wall. The wire ran straight through it, hanging over water that frothed with white-tipped rapids.

"That's the Drain," Silas said. "Don't worry, it widens out quickly. That's not our problem. The other three boats are our problem."

"What if we cut the ropes?" Kate asked.

Tribal shook his head. "They'd float down ahead of us, clog the Drain, and we'd never get out."

"What if the rope didn't break until we were away?" Kate asked.

A muffled groan came down the tunnel behind them.

"Time's up," Silas said. "Wait here until we've started the fight, then run for the lead boat. Hopefully we'll get onto the river fast. It'll take time for them to set the other boats. That'll have to be enough."

Kate nodded toward the workers. "Will those dwarves be on the lookout for us?"

"At this point, everyone will," Silas said, another grin peeking out of his beard. "This definitely tops anything else we've done."

Tribal flashed a smile as he stood and strode down the path, his brother following him casually. They were nearly to the dock when the workers noticed them, and there was a spattering of friendly greetings before one recognized the twins.

"You could step to the boat," Kate said quietly to Venn. "The elven form of stepping, obviously. If you magically jumped over there, I'm the only one who'd have to get past the guards."

Venn shook her head. "Won't work."

"Why not?"

Venn's answer was interrupted by Tribal throwing the first punch.

"Go!" Venn gave Kate's shoulder a push.

Kate rose and dashed down the slope, her feet skidding on pebbles. The trail was steep, and Venn sent a skittering of gravel down behind her. A dockworker shouted and pointed at Kate, but Silas slammed an elbow into his ear, and he crumpled.

"Untie the lead boat!" he yelled.

Kate angled for it, taking in the thick rope connecting the other three boats to the hanging wire above them. She held her lantern out to Venn. "Can you untie the boat? I'll be right there."

Venn gave her a questioning look but took the lantern and headed for the first rowboat.

Tribal smashed his head into another dwarf's nose, sending him sprawling while Kate ran along the pier. Each boat was tied to the dock at the bow and the stern, and she set her finger on each rope, pressing *vitalle* into them until they smoldered and tiny flames licked the rough fibers. When the dock lines of the fourth boat were smoking, she climbed on board.

Above her, the thick wire hung too high for her to reach, but the rope tethering the boat to it ran from a ring in the stern up to a hook hanging over it. Kate set her finger halfway up the rope and pushed *vitalle* into it.

A tendril of smoke rose, and the bristly hairs that jutted out from the rough rope curled in the heat. She turned and climbed over the crates toward the third boat.

"Wrong rowboat, Twig!" Tribal yelled.

She ignored him, setting the tethering rope on the third boat to smoldering before climbing toward the second.

Silas and Tribal faced off against the last two workers as she reached it. But a sharp yell rang out from up at the tunnel mouth, and the band of Surrion's guards burst into the cavern.

Kate clambered onto the second boat, crawling over bundles

and grabbing for the rope at the back. She shot *vitalle* into it just as a tiny four-pointed metal star sank into the wood next to her leg.

She jerked back, and the smoldering rope at her fingertip flared into a small flame.

Another star hit the wood near her, and she scrambled away from it, hurrying along the side of the boat away from the pier, hunching down behind crates and casks.

Tribal dropped the last worker and ran after Silas toward the lead boat, limping and grimacing. "We will leave you behind, Twig! Get to the boat!"

The guards thundered down the slope as Kate reached the front of the second boat. A span of water, about as far as she could jump, sat between her and the bobbing stern of the boat where Venn waited, holding out her hand. Kate lunged for it, but the boat shifted under her feet, and she toppled toward the water.

Venn grabbed her forearm and heaved her forward. Kate's stomach slammed into the stern, her feet slapping into the ice-cold water.

"Tribal! Go!" Silas shouted, climbing over a crate to grab Kate's other arm and drag her on board.

Tribal shoved the boat away from the dock with a long pole, sending the rowboat lurching and rocking as it floated into the lake.

One guard tore onto the dock and leapt for the boat, but Silas rammed a stiff arm into his chest. The guard flailed at him, trying to grab hold, but dropped into the river.

Kate scrambled up and spun to check on the other boats. Small lines of smoke were all she could see. She held out her hand and closed her eyes, searching for the bits of warmth.

"What were you thinking?" Silas demanded.

She ignored him, focusing on the wisps of heat climbing up each rope. They were slowly moving farther away, but she pushed *vitalle* toward them, threading it through the air to feed the embers.

A knot of heat flared up on the ropes of the first boat.

"No!" Silas sputtered. "No fire!"

Flames licked up the rope of second.

Their own boat floated away from the dock, and before the distance to the farthest boat could grow any larger, she shoved a blunt rush of *vitalle* at it. It ripped out of her almost-healed palm with a searing heat, but the last rope burst into flame.

She opened her eyes to see the fires racing up the dry ropes and the boats rocking slowly away from the dock.

Two dwarven guards dragged their comrade out of the water at the edge of the dock. The third, a dwarf with shrewd eyes and a grey-streaked beard, hurled something small that glinted as it flipped through the air. Tribal twisted out of the way, and a sharp metal star sank into the wood where he'd been standing.

"Only a drustkin star, Surrion?" Tribal called toward the dock that was now a dozen paces away. "Am I worth so little to you?"

The dripping wet guard scrambled to his feet with a growl and spun, flinging a short knife end over end.

Tribal merely watched as the knife flipped past him and clattered against the inside wall of the boat. "A Ren blade!" he called out. "Better!"

The wet dwarf raised another knife but, at Surrion's curt command, held on to it. He settled for shouting vicious words in dwarven, which echoed harshly across the ceiling.

Tribal chuckled. "I'm looking forward to it, little pup!" He held up the Ren blade. "I'll bring my new knife."

Surrion seized the wet dwarf by the shoulder and shoved him toward the other boats. Another guard barked out a series of commands, which quickly turned to confused shouts at the sight of all three boats swirling into the lake, trailing smoldering bits of rope.

The rowboat pitched under Kate, and she grabbed the side. Next to her, the surface of the lake rippled into ridges and dips as the current dragged them toward the churning water of the Drain. The guards' shouts grew muffled by the rushing of the rapids. Tribal planted his feet near the front of the boat, his long pole ready as the walls of the cavern narrowed.

Silas sat on the stern, his hand on the metal rod that hooked over the wire above them—a wire which now looked uncomfortably thin. He pushed on the rod and it pulled the wire down, slowing the boat slightly.

"Best to stay low," he called with a wide grin. "The Drain'll toss you about a bit."

Kate sank lower against the side of the boat in one of the few small gaps beside a crate, wedging her knees under the bench it sat on. She looked up to find Venn braced between two barrels, glaring at her.

"If I drown in some slimy black river in the dwarven deadlands"—Venn's shoulder slammed into the side of a barrel as the boat crashed against a wave that felt like a rock wall—"I swear my spirit will haunt you for all eternity!"

"Your people live on lakes," Kate yelled. "How do you not like water?" A spatter shot over the side of the boat, spraying her in the side of the head, the water so cold it felt like shards of ice dribbling into her ear and down her neck.

"I like water! This is not water! This is a slow, cold, sunless death!"

"You'd wash out into the sunlight eventually!" Silas called.

"You'd be bloated and disgusting," Tribal agreed, laughing, "but you'd reach sunlight. And you're already pretty ugly, so it wouldn't make much difference."

The boat rolled to the left, and Venn's retort was smothered under a wave of frigid water that dumped over the side.

"Here we go!" Silas bellowed. "Hold on to your beards!"

Kate wedged herself lower as the rowboat careened forward, twisting and shuddering, crashing her against everything around her, no matter how hard she braced herself. The walls raced toward them until the rock to their right was close enough for Tribal to shove away with his pole.

The bow rose for a breath of stillness, and Kate caught a glimpse of Tribal looking over his shoulder, grinning like a maniac. The mosslight of the cavern lit him in stark relief against the complete blackness ahead. The boat smashed down against the water, sending a shower raining down on them.

The rushing of the water drowned out all but the loudest shouts from Tribal and Silas as they faced down the river, laughing and calling out directions to each other.

A rock wall loomed into view ahead of them, and Tribal jabbed at it with his pole, shoving the boat around a corner and hurtling it into darkness.

CHAPTER THIRTY-FOUR

KATE'S SHOULDER slammed against the crate again as freezing water soaked through her boots and dug icy fingers into her feet. She kept her eyes fixed on the two small mosslight lanterns near Venn, which now sat in an inch of water. Everything else was pitch black as the boat lurched over the rough river, tossing her around like a pebble in a bucket.

The boat gave a final jerk to the side and settled into a low rocking.

"See?" Silas's voice came from behind her. "Not too bad."

"Tell me we lost at least one of them," Tribal called from the bow.

"Looks like they both made it," Silas answered. "Or else we picked up two waterlogged stowaways somewhere."

Venn lifted a lantern and held it over the water. The dim orange light reflected off ripples and bubbles swirling next to them.

"Is this another lake?" Kate asked, shifting and sloshing her feet through the cold puddle at the bottom of the boat as she leaned over the side. The water lapping along the outside of the boat was as black as a pool of ink.

"Just a wider section of the river." Silas's dim form settled down onto the small bit of empty space in the stern.

Kate sat on the hard wooden bench next to the crate and caught a reddish glow moving past. She made out a bit of moss growing on a rocky wall above the waterline. It was out of her reach, but Tribal could have easily touched it with his pole. "The river isn't terribly wide, is it?"

"Wide enough," Tribal answered.

Another patch of moss slid into view, this one yellower. A greenish one caught her eye on the far side of the boat. Upstream was nothing but darkness. "Do you think they'll follow us soon?"

"No." Silas hefted a small box in front of him, then tossed it overboard, making room for himself to sit down inside the rowboat. He leaned against the flat stern with a chuckle. "It'll take hours to get new boats to the dock. And since no boats are floating down behind us, the three you loosed must be blocking the Drain. I'd say it'll be at least five or six hours before anyone can clear it enough to mount a chase."

Venn made space for herself between a barrel and the side, where she propped her feet up, frowning into the bottom of the boat. "Is there a way to get the pool out of the bottom?"

"It's just a little water." Silas glanced up at the wire running above them. "The Drain was the choppiest part of the trip. Now we float downstream, and the cable will keep us on track." As he said it, a metal pole came into view, jutting out of the rocks to their left, rising to clamp tightly to the bottom of the wire.

Kate opened her mouth to point out the obstacle, but the hook attached to their boat merely bumped over the clamp with a metallic click and continued sliding down the cable.

"Next stop," Silas said, "the White Wood."

"Should call it the Black Wood," Tribal muttered.

Venn turned to look at him. "Why?"

"There's a darkness there," Silas explained. "Saw it in the trees when we were investigating a landslide. 'Twas unnatural."

"A shadow as dark as the Drain." Tribal motioned behind them. "Except it moved."

Kate glanced at Venn, then back to Silas. "Will you show me?"

He considered the question. "We can take you to the rockslide, but I can't imagine the shadow will be there again. Last we saw, it had disappeared."

"No." Kate unbuckled the side pocket of her pack. "I have a serum that will let you share the memory of it with me."

"I doubt either of the Feral Weasel Brothers has the capacity to use *iza* to place their memory into it," Venn pointed out.

Kate paused with her hand in the pocket. "That's true." She took out the serum and unwrapped it, considering the dwarves. "I might be able to help with that."

She held up the vial, and the sparkles inside reflected the dim mosslight.

Tribal pulled away from it, his brow creased in suspicion.

Kate turned to Silas. "All you do is put your finger in the liquid and think of the memory. I'll give it a path to come out of you. Once it's done, I'll be able to watch it as though I were seeing it through your eyes."

"You want to steal my memory?" he asked.

Kate glanced at Venn. "That seems to be a common fear, but no. You'll just be sharing it with me. It will take nothing away from you."

Silas considered the vial for a moment before looking up at Venn. "Have you used it?"

She nodded. "It's painless and simple."

He hesitated another breath before holding out his hand.

"Do *not* touch her sparkly potion!" Tribal said.

"Serum, not potion." Kate climbed over a crate and squeezed

into a seat close to Silas. "There's a difference." She pulled the cork out of the vial, taking in the dwarf's thick hands. "Your smallest finger should fit. Just dip it into the serum and think of the memory."

"If you turn into some sort of toad," Tribal said, "I'm tossing you in the river."

Silas ignored him and held out his littlest finger, which barely fit into the vial.

Kate set her hand on the back of his and fed a trickle of *vitalle* into him as he watched her suspiciously. "Go ahead."

The serum pressed against his skin, searching. She snaked some *vitalle* through his fingertip, and with that path, the thread of memory poured out in a line of golden light.

Silas's eyes widened before he squinted in concentration.

When the thread cut off, he pulled out his finger, and Kate quickly set hers in.

> She stood on a hillside, surveying the remains of a wide rockslide next to her, choked with dust and mud and drying dirt. Evening sunlight streamed from behind her, casting Silas's shadow on the undisturbed ground at the edge of the slide. The motionless line of boulders and stones lay all the way down to the bottom of a narrow gorge, shouldering into the river that ran at the base, dyeing the water downstream a gritty brown.
>
> Tribal stood a few paces uphill, studying the rock-strewn slope.
>
> "Obviously not natural." Tribal pointed to a thin ridge snaking across the hillside. "Human, I'd say. Caused just below the road."
>
> "Seems that way, but it's odd. The initial shift must have been over that whole area," Silas said, motioning to a wide stretch of rockslide. "Looks like a bit of mining at the far edge."
>
> "True." Tribal turned downhill. "The humans must've worked hard to do several stupid things across that section at the same time

—" His eyes snapped to something behind Silas, and his hand reached for the knife at his belt.

Silas spun around.

Across the river, on the other side of the gorge, the slope was gentler and covered with trees. Just under the edge of the forest, a spot of darkness gathered between two trunks.

"Scared of shadows?" Silas asked.

"That shadow just moved."

Silas's gaze swept the woods, taking in the branches shifting in the wind. "All the shadows are moving."

"Not like that one."

The two dwarves stood still, but the darkness didn't change. The top of it reached up into the lowest leaves, easily twice as tall as a dwarf. That entire side of the gorge lay shadowed, but the evening sun lit the valley enough that every part should have been clearly visible. That particular spot was darker than a shadow. More like a bit of night caught in a hollow. Its edges bled into the common shadows around it with inky tendrils.

There was a strange motion to its stillness. A churning that couldn't quite be seen. A sense that if the sunlight hit it, its surface would roil like boiling pitch.

"Why does it feel like it's watching us?" Silas asked quietly.

"Because I think it's watching us."

"Think it's elven?"

"What else stays in trees so determinedly?"

Silas scanned along the rest of the woods but found nothing like it. He looked up the rockslide. The earth coating the rocks baked in the last light of the day, brown and dusty and cracking as it dried. The only shadows lay in the crannies between them. Everything was perfectly still.

Tribal glanced over his shoulder as well. "There's something off about this entire gorge."

Silas nodded. "Is it strange that the something feels...old?"

Tribal gave a grunt of agreement and turned back to the forest. He stiffened, his gaze raking across the trees. "It's gone."

There was nothing but perfectly normal trees. The evening light shifted innocently where the shadow had been, the now-visible strands of grass bobbing in the breeze.

The edge of the sun dipped behind the mountains rising nearby in the west, and Silas searched the forest for the darkness. Nothing stood out to him, but in the dying light, every shadow under the trees was deepening.

"You've seen enough of the rockslide?" Tribal asked, his voice tense.

"Yep." Silas started down the slope, keeping his eyes on the forest. "Humans being stupid and breaking things."

Tribal's quiet tread followed him. "Sometimes it's impressive how big the things are they break."

Silas crossed the river, jumping along a path of boulders that sat in the water like enormous stepping stones, and headed downstream on the other side. He skirted the trees, his gaze probing the forest. He reached a barely visible trail and paused, glancing at Tribal.

His brother's hand still rested on the hilt of his knife. "Let's get back to where pitch-black shadows are natural."

Silas moved into the woods at a brisk pace. Evening gathered around them, and the woods felt unnaturally quiet. Silas broke out of the trees into a clearing that butted up to a rock face at the base of a mountain. A fissure rent the cliff, and a swift stream flowed out of the dark gap. Silas hurried toward it, glancing over his shoulder at Tribal. "Let's hope Runnren isn't guarding the—"

The forest hung muted in the blues of dusk, except where the path behind Tribal entered the woods.

There, every bit of light had been sucked away into nothing.

Tribal swung around, his knife drawn and hurtling through the air before he'd fully turned. The bright metal blade ripped into the darkness, where it was swallowed up without a sound.

The shadow crept toward them, and Silas grabbed Tribal's arm, pulling him back. The two ran for the cleft in the rock. Silas reached it and skidded in, his feet sliding on the layer of gravel at the mouth of a large cavern. He looked back and found the blackness lingering near the tree line.

Tribal stopped next to him, their breaths coming fast. Slowly, the darkness sank back into the trees, dissolving into deep blue shadows along the underside of branches, draining into the hollow under gnarled tree roots, sliding into the crevices of a rotting stump.

The forest sat still and empty.

Tribal's knife lay on the path, just inside the trees, and the two stepped forward at the same moment, shifting apart enough for Silas to draw his own knife and Tribal to slide his axe from his belt.

Moving silently, Tribal's motions a mirror of his own, Silas crept toward the knife, his gaze searching the shadows.

They reached the trees, and Silas stepped past the knife, keeping his eyes on the woods.

"Marked him," Tribal said quietly, holding up the knife. Blood glinted along the blade, dark and wet in the dying light.

Silas gave Tribal a grim smile. "Then next time, we throw knives first instead of running."

Kate's eyes flew open, and she stared at Silas. "Venn!" She shoved her finger into the serum, pouring the memory back in and holding it out to the elf.

Venn took it and closed her eyes. Her brow drew down a moment later, and when the last of the thread had sunk into her finger, she looked at Kate. "Same shadow."

Kate nodded. "And it bleeds."

CHAPTER THIRTY-FIVE

TRIBAL SHIFTED in the front of the boat. "You two know the shadow?"

"Venn's talked to trees who've seen it." Kate worked the cork back into the tenea serum. "How close were you two to the White Wood?"

Silas shrugged. "Not sure where the creepy elven death wood starts, but probably within a few hours."

"Death wood?" Venn asked. "The White Wood has trees that—"

"Are white like bones," Tribal interrupted, "and regularly contain monsters."

"Those creatures come from the north," Venn said. "And the elves keep them from making their way into the human lands."

"So the story goes," Silas said. "And yet we only have the elves' word for that."

Venn gave him a flat look. "They don't care what you think enough to lie to you."

"Can you take me there?" Kate asked Silas. "To where you saw the shadow?"

"We already are. That river is where we'll come out."

"And the rockslide?"

"We're not giving you a tour of the north," Tribal objected.

Kate crossed her arms. "Because you'd rather stay in Rullduin and face the governor?"

The two dwarves exchanged looks.

"Maybe a trip out under the sky isn't a bad idea," Silas admitted. "And we did lose our last shipment of human goods."

Tribal scowled at Kate. "Fine, but just to the rockslide. Then you're on your own."

"It was over a month ago," Silas added. "I doubt you'll find signs of anything now."

Kate studied the dwarves. "Do you always investigate rockslides?"

"Vibrations travel a long way through rock," Silas answered. "We felt that all the way back in the gov'nor's house in Rullduin. He sent us to check it out."

She turned to Venn. "There was a rockslide when Bo found that weapon, after his men were killed."

Tribal leaned forward. "You know the humans who caused it?"

"I have a journal from my brother, who was at a rockslide in that area. He says a monster ripped apart the hillside."

"A monster?" Silas asked. "So, an elf?"

"He says it was like a tree that moved."

"Then definitely an elf."

"Elves don't turn into trees and rip up hillsides," Venn said.

"Well, no dwarf would cause such a useless, messy rockslide," Tribal answered. "Only humans do things so recklessly."

"Humans don't turn into moving trees either." Kate tucked the tenea serum back in her pack.

"Are you sure he really saw a tree?" Tribal asked.

Kate nodded. "He explores and finds strange things and sends me reports or sometimes the odd thing itself."

"But she's only seen him four times in the last fifteen years," Venn pointed out.

"Ah," Silas said. "So an estranged brother."

"We are not estranged," Kate said firmly, "and I know him enough to know he didn't make up a walking tree."

"If you're going to search for him, you need to base it on more concrete things than the unfounded belief that you still know him well," Venn said. "Trees don't walk."

"I don't care if none of you think the tree is real." Kate buckled the pocket of her pack. "I bet the rockslide is where Bo was working." She rubbed her hands over her face to banish her irritation and attempted to give Venn a smile polite enough for her next question. "I know I said we'd go straight to the clearing where he disappeared when we got out of here, and you'd be done with me, but if the rockslide is near where we come out of the tunnels, can we see it first?"

"Only if it's not out of the way." Venn rested against a crate and closed her eyes. "And if you linger, I'm giving you directions to the clearing and leaving you there."

"Agreed." Kate shifted, propping her feet up on the side of the boat, mulling over the idea of the rockslide and the shadow and the walking tree.

Besides the three mosslight lanterns that cast their dim glow over the nearest crates or bits of the hull and the occasional patch of moss on the rocks, the river was steeped in darkness. The walls around them were wider than the tunnels of the past few days. Three boats could have floated down side by side with room to spare. The stone slid by silently, and aside from a lapping of water on the boat and the soft hiss of the hook sliding down the wire, the cavern was quiet.

Kate shut her eyes.

A steady breeze blew past, and after days in stagnant tunnels, the feel of air moving across her skin was utterly refreshing. There was an emptiness around her, too, as the motion and expanse of the space let the remnants of her companions disperse. She could sense each dwarf and Venn, but mildly enough that her senses began to take in the physical world.

After a few minutes, she opened her eyes and discovered mottled oranges and greens glowing on the cave wall, interspersed with brighter yellows. A flash of blue light caught her eye from the river, and she sat forward to see it. Beneath the surface, through what must be perfectly clear water, tendrils of river grass glowed as they bobbed and swayed with the current.

"Venn!" She pointed at the water. "Plants!"

The elf opened her eyes and looked over the side.

"That's nothing," Silas said. "Give it a few minutes."

More blue plants slid beneath them. The river was far shallower than she'd expected. Maybe only waist deep. They floated over a stalk of pinkish flowers tucked between two rocks, then a field of glowing green clover.

Ahead, at the next turn in the river, dim light suffused the walls.

Tribal steered the boat around the corner, and Venn drew in a breath.

The walls of the next cavern were drenched in delicate, subtle colors. Partially from the lush blankets of moss that covered rocks and sprouted out of crevices, but mostly from the wavery light coming up out of the water itself.

Faintly glowing plants carpeted the riverbed. Shimmery scales darted through a swath of turquoise grass so tall the rippling tips brushed the surface. Green ribbony tendrils surrounded short clusters of purplish florets. Tiny fish blushing a delicate pink nibbled at the edges of a buttery yellow plant that bloomed in a circle of flat leaves, like lettuce.

Venn reached into the tall patch of grass and dragged her fingers through the blades. She let out a quiet breath of relief and touched a green stalk sliding alongside the boat.

"So...slimy river in the dwarven deadlands, huh?" Tribal asked, sitting down and laying the pole across his knees.

Venn left her hand in the water, reaching for any plants she could touch. "I may have been mistaken," she murmured. "It's beautiful."

Tribal studied her, looking for the insult, but Venn merely leaned closer to the water. Finally, he grunted. "Glad to see you're not always stupid."

The boat drifted in the crystal-clear water, hanging above the riverbed as though it were flying over an incandescent landscape.

Kate cast out and, for the first time in days, found glimmers of life all around her, spreading under the boat, creeping up the moss-covered walls. She settled her elbows on the side of the boat, watching the luminous plants drift past, enjoying the emptiness of the space, the relief from the crowded remnants of the tunnel. The breeze wafted through the cave with a gentle shushing sound. The water lapped against the side of the rowboat and rustled in wavelets against the rocks at the river's edge.

And underneath it all rolled a distant rumble of thunder.

Kate shoved herself up.

Not thunder. Waves crashing on a rocky shore.

And not ripples of river water, but massive ocean waves.

"Venn! The thunder's back!"

Venn pulled her hand out of the water. "The hive/toad/squirrel/moth thunder?"

Kate nodded and closed her eyes. It was quiet but close. Somewhere to her left. She looked sharply at Silas, but he was too far away, lounging at the stern, looking at her curiously.

She shifted toward her pack, and the sound grew louder.

Lifting her lantern, she searched for the moth, but there was nothing there.

Venn shifted closer. "It's in your pack?"

Kate cast out, and a little knot of *vitalle* sprang up, tucked in a crease under the flap of the side pocket where her serum was stored.

She pulled it open, and something black and shiny clung to the underside of it.

A small beetle.

She leaned closer. "Hello, there."

CHAPTER THIRTY-SIX

THE BEETLE WAS the size and shape of her thumbnail, with no separation between its glossy rounded back and its shorter rounded head. Six skinny, spiny legs stuck out from its sides. Two antennae, thin at the base and fatter at the ends, wiggled in the air.

"Is that a spider?" Tribal asked, his voice tight.

The beetle's back split apart, and black wings vibrated before stilling. Two tiny black eyes fixed on her.

And the sound of crashing waves on a distant shore rolled out of it.

"Your thunder animals keep getting smaller," Venn said.

The boat jostled as Silas came over. "Just a mud beetle, Tribal." He leaned closer to Kate. "He's a little scared of spiders."

"Of course I'm scared of them!" Tribal peered at the beetle suspiciously. "A scarlet banded spider took down Hathor the Thick precisely because he wasn't smart enough to be scared of them. Spiders kill people!"

Venn rubbed her smallest finger. "They do," she agreed.

Silas peered down at the beetle. "Don't see those in this

deep. You must have picked him up when we first got to the caves." He frowned at the beetle. "Not sure why he didn't go back out, though. They burrow in dirt. He must be unhappy to be here."

Kate cast out toward the creature. It felt like a regular insect, just a tangle of *vitalle* with the fleeting sort of feel that creatures who didn't live long always had. Although…

She cast out again and found…something. An extra brightness, no more substantial than the brush of a feather across her skin. The remnant was as full as any person she'd ever met, but distant. Or muffled.

"Who are you?" she asked quietly. The beetle's wings twitched again, but it stayed still. "You've followed us through the forest, and now for days in the tunnels. You're not a beetle, or a toad, or a squirrel, or a bird, or a hive, are you? You're something else entirely."

I…was never…in the hive.

Kate jerked back at the whispered voice in her mind. Next to her, Venn flinched and whipped a dart out of her quiver.

Silas straightened, and Tribal swore, shoving himself forward and jostling the boat to see the insect better. "Did that thing just talk in your head?" Tribal whispered to Silas.

A hive…is not…an animal. It was the voice of a man, thinned with old age, halting and raspy, as if long unused. His tone was scholarly, though, as if he were explaining something to a slightly dense student.

"Ahh," Kate said. "You were the fox. Not the hive."

"Am I losing my mind," Tribal whispered loudly to Silas. "Or is the beetle talking and the twig spewing nonsense?"

There was no more voice from the beetle, and Kate glanced at Venn. "We saved him from the vimwisps."

The elf rolled her dart slowly between her fingers. She examined the beetle, and her mouth curled up into a smile that held no warmth. "And now you owe us a life debt, don't you?" Her tone held an underlying twist of bitterness.

Kate spared a moment to study the elf. "A life debt?"

'Twas the fox's life in danger, not mine. I owe no life debt.

The dart in Venn's fingers stilled, and her smile evaporated. "And yet here you are."

"What does a life debt involve?" Tribal asked, peering over Venn's shoulder. "Because we just saved Kate and Venn from murderous dwarves."

Venn gave him a scathing look. "You drew a Snare to our campsite, then brought us into tunnels where our lives were at risk, and you haven't gotten us out yet. If anything, you owe us."

Tribal considered the words, then shook his head. "I'm pretty sure Silas and I are the heroes here."

Kate waved at him to be quiet and held out her hand to the beetle. Slowly, almost reluctantly, he climbed onto her fingers. She lifted him up until she could see him clearly.

Your talent of hearing remnants is intriguing. His voice sounded a bit smoother in her mind, as though he were remembering how to speak.

Kate narrowed her eyes at him. "You have been listening for a while, haven't you?"

You talked loudly. Is my remnant how you found me?

"That, and I felt your *vitalle.*"

The beetle shifted in what might have been some semblance of a nod. *It has been a long time since I heard that word.*

"What's a remnant?" Silas asked. "And what's *vitalle*?"

Venn motioned him to be quiet. "Your remnant is what Kate mistakenly thinks smells trustworthy, and *vitalle* is life."

The dwarves exchanged glances. "Clears it right up," Tribal muttered.

Kate let out an annoyed breath. "Will all of you be quiet and let the beetle speak?"

I am not *a beetle.* His voice was slightly exasperated. *My name is...* The insect turned and scuttled toward the nearest crate. *Absolutely not!* he scolded the beetle. *Turn around! Face the woman!* It wavered for a moment, then turned slowly back toward Kate. *The creature insists on turning toward any dirt it can find,* he grumbled. *What is in those crates? Potatoes?*

"Probably mushrooms," Silas answered. "We grow them up near the city."

Well, you don't need mushrooms, the voice said sternly.

"We don't?" Tribal asked.

I am speaking to the beetle, he said primly. After a few halting attempts, the bug finally faced Kate completely. *Now, what was I saying?*

"You were about to tell us your name," Kate said.

Ah, yes, he said, with an air of formality. *My name is Crofftus.*

"Hello, Crofftus. I'm Kate, this is Venn and Silas and Tribal."

Yes, yes. I know your names and what you're doing. Even though his voice sounded smoother, he still spoke slowly, as though picking out each word. *You are a strange group.*

"See many groups as a mud beetle, do you?" Silas asked.

This creature is merely my current vessel. I do not expect you to understand. I was once trapped in a single body as you are. There was a note of sympathy in his voice, *I'm sure you think your world rather large, but you cannot imagine the places and people I've seen.*

Kate's mind sorted through possibilities. Keepers were tremendously rare. People born with the ability to sense and manipulate *vitalle* were only born every five to ten years, but there were gaps when no Keeper had appeared. "Crofftus, are you human?"

Am I human? he said, sounding surprised. *What else would I be?*

"I'd honestly have guessed 'beetle'," Tribal said with a grin.

Crofftus let out an indignant huff, but before he could answer,

344

Kate continued, "If you're a human who knows about *vitalle* and can clearly utilize it…should you be a Keeper?"

The beetle's huff turned to a snort. *No!*

Kate raised an eyebrow at his affronted tone.

I avoid Keepers.

"Except Kate," Silas said, "who you've been stalking."

Crofftus ignored him. *I knew a Keeper long ago. That was enough.*

"Really?" Kate asked. "Who?"

His name was… Crofftus's antennae waved about for a moment. When he spoke again, it was even slower, and sounded distant. *I don't remember his name. I can see him, though. Sitting on the dock of the lake. His palms were burned, and he was so proud of it. Magic never burned my palms, of course. I was never foolish enough to use too much. He never pointed it out, not out loud, but he always thought that made him better than me. He was an ill-tempered, arrogant man.*

Kate felt a flicker of amusement. "I only know one Keeper who could be described that way. Was his name Mikal?"

Mikal? he said as though testing the name. *Yes, that sounds right. Such an unfriendly person. Uppity for no reason at all. Can he transfer his mind to an animal?* he asked, and Kate almost expected the beetle to puff out its chest as it continued, *Can he soar through the sky with the king of the eagles? Can he dive into the depths of the oceans with the great whales?*

When he'd finished the long, drawn-out words, Silas lifted a finger as though making an important point. "Can he crawl into a pack and stow away for days as someone carries him through dwarven tunnels?"

Kate bit back a smile. "I've never heard of a Keeper who could put their mind into an animal," she admitted.

The beetle turned toward the crate again. Its legs ended in sharp, stiff segments that tickled her palm. *Now is not the time!* Crofftus grunted in an effort to make it turn back.

Kate studied him. Beyond Keepers, there were other people scattered around Queensland who could sense *vitalle* in living things, although not many. Even fewer had minimal control over it.

Putting his mind into the body of an animal felt like more than minimal control, though. Which was a troubling thought. She had never heard of Keepers doing such a thing, but she'd read of something vaguely similar among the Shade Seekers, a loosely connected group with varying degrees of magical capabilities and little to no moral restrictions on how to use them. They took their enemies and trapped them in monstrous, bestial bodies.

She set the back of her hand down on her pack, and the beetle crawled off. "How long ago did you know Mikal? He just turned ninety-two."

Ninety-two? Crofftus scoffed. *Impossible.*

"Why? How old are you?" Kate asked.

"In human years," Tribal added, "not beetle years."

Old enough to not bother counting years anymore. Do you know what really matters? How much one has learned.

"Mikal would agree," Kate said, "and he's definitely ninety-two. We tried to celebrate his birthday last summer." Kate smiled at how appalled he'd been at the ridiculously ornate cake Gerone had baked for him. "You might like him now. He's lovable, in his own crotchety way. But if you remember any stories from when he was young, before he knew everything and was the most demanding tutor to ever live, I would love to hear them."

Crofftus sniffed. *There was no time before he was that way.*

"Burned hands are a common ailment among Keepers, then?" Venn asked, her eyes on the bandages wrapping Kate's palms.

"More common than we'd like." Kate studied the beetle. There was no overarching creed of the men and women who joined the Shade Seekers. They were too loosely organized for such a thing, but they tended to believe that the ends always justified the means. "Crofftus, how do you take control of these animals?"

I control nothing. I am able to inhabit these creatures as a temporary guest because I dedicated dozens of years to study and exerted a great deal of effort to learn how.

She considered the answer. "Can you inhabit anything?"

Tribal pointed at the bug. "You'd better not try to inhabit me."

The beetle turned to look at him. *I could, but I would not choose to. It would lead to a battle of our wills, and most likely end with your mind fracturing into madness.*

Silas frowned.

"A small animal wouldn't have a strong will like Tribal, though," Kate said. "A squirrel or a toad or a moth would allow you to direct it without much of a fight, wouldn't it?"

"So you take control of animals," Venn said, her expression distasteful, "and make them obey your will?"

They are a vessel, like this boat. They carry me from place to place, but I do them no harm.

"Except bringing a mud beetle days away from where it can survive," Silas pointed out.

The beetle is fine, Crofftus said with a note of impatience. *He's perfectly happy. Or what passes for happiness in a beetle.*

"What is it you want, Crofftus?" Kate asked.

For a long moment, there was nothing but the lapping of the water against the boat.

You saved the life of the fox. Had you not, I would have found myself in a difficult position. While I owed you nothing on the level of a life debt, I followed you to see if I could be of assistance. Thus, when the dwarves were robbing you, I woke you.

"Stupid toad," Tribal muttered.

"Then your debt is repaid," Kate said. "Why did you continue to follow us?"

The beetle shifted, looking almost uncomfortable. *It has been a very long time since I encountered one who can manipulate* vitalle, he said, his voice still slow and measured. *Even if you are a Keeper, I admit to having some curiosity about you. A wish to be around someone else who understands how the power of living things moves. And then...* The beetle's legs twitched.

"You eavesdropped on us," Venn finished for him, "and heard something that interested you?"

'Eavesdropped' is an ugly word. I was following you to see if I could assist you, and you speak loudly. He shifted to look at Kate. *I saw your treasure box in the campsite before the dwarves came. I saw you drip a blue liquid in, and...What did it show you?*

Kate studied the beetle.

"That box is a treasure box?" Tribal asked.

Kate ignored him. "It amplified the remnants of the people who had touched it."

Crofftus hummed as though she'd confirmed his guess. *I suspected as much. And then you have your sparkling memory serum. It even manages to catch light while wrapped securely in the pocket, you know.*

The thought of the scratchy beetle legs scrabbling over the two vials made her want to flick him off her pack.

"So you're sneaking around, coveting Kate's possessions?" Venn asked. "You're more like the dwarves than I'd expect from a beetle."

I am not covet—argh! The beetle took off in a buzz of wings and bumbled toward the crate. *Stop this instant!* The bug faltered in the air, then turned in an erratic circle near Venn.

She leaned back, and it landed on her leg. "Get off," she said icily.

My apologies, Crofftus muttered, making a short flight to the bench beside her. *Beetles are not the nimblest of fliers. They're not eagles, you know. Or hummingbirds—now those can fly. Up, down, backward. And fast! Did you know—*

"Crofftus," Kate interrupted. "What is it you want?"

The beetle walked toward the crate again, and Crofftus gave a grunt of annoyance. It stopped and faced Kate squarely. *Yes, right. Well, you see, I used to spend a great deal of time studying potions and serums and the interactions between ingredients,* he said, his voice attempting to regain its dignity. *I admit to a curiosity about yours. Perhaps I could help you with them, if you need any assistance in the future.*

"What sort of help?"

That depends entirely on what you want to do. Distill them? Strengthen them? Refine them? Combine them?

Kate twitched at the last question, and the beetle's black eyes seemed to fix on her with more intensity. *Ah. Such a combination would be challenging, but not impossible.* He made a sound like clearing his throat. *But also,* he said, with a slightly forced casualness, *you said you were traveling to the White Wood. You speak of monsters and shadows.*

"And?"

When he finally answered, his voice was guarded. *I've been to the White Wood, though it was long ago. There, you...* The beetle wavered, as though trying to shake its head when it had no neck. *You may need more assistance than you have.*

CHAPTER THIRTY-SEVEN

KATE SANK BACK AGAINST A CRATE, considering Crofftus's words. The glow from the water lit the faces on the rowboat with a soft greenish light as she gauged their expressions. Silas nodded in agreement.

"The trees are bone white," Tribal said. "What do you expect besides danger and death?"

When she looked at Venn, the elf was frowning at the beetle. "The White Wood isn't as bad as these people want you to think."

"There are monsters," Tribal said with a shrug. "Everyone knows it."

True, Crofftus agreed. *And ancient troubles that linger. Even among the elves themselves.*

Kate glanced at Venn questioningly.

The elf let out a breath and kept her eyes on Crofftus. "There are creatures, yes. They come out of the mountains in the north, and the elves have, for centuries, taken it upon themselves to drive them back, keeping them from the human settlements." Her eyes flickered up to Silas. "Or the dwarven caves. Some would gladly delve underground."

"And are there troubles with the elves?" Kate asked.

Venn finally looked at her, her expression conflicted. "The elves have lived there for centuries upon centuries. There have been times of peace and times of unrest."

"And right now?"

Her eyes shifted to the water, following a school of silvery fish that rippled through the plants like a flock of birds. "There is a good deal of peace. The king is respected, and the elves follow him willingly."

Kate waited for her to continue. "But…?"

Venn gave a humorless smile. "His royal highness, King Thallion, and I have differing opinions on some matters."

"But he's not your king, right?" Kate asked. "He's the king of the White Wood, and your people live at the lakes."

Venn shook her head. "It's more complicated than that. Strictly speaking, he is not our king. We have our own elders, but Thallion's line is ancient. His blood is intrinsic to the Wood. The elders of the lakes are, by comparison, from very young lines, and it's been merely three hundred years that we've lived there. Barely enough time to wake the trees and begin to weave ourselves into the land. King Thallion is the greatest elven king alive, barring the ancient elves who live across the eastern seas in the forests of the Old World. Were Thallion to order the lake elves to do anything, they would obey."

"What do you disagree with him on?"

She gave Kate a pointed look. "Humans. Thallion and my aunt Evay have held differing opinions on how elves should interact with humans for centuries."

"Wasn't she banished from the White Wood?" Kate asked. "In the old stories, it seemed that way."

"Not banished. But if she had any desire to return, which she does not, her welcome would be…complicated." She paused, as though considering her next words. "King Thallion firmly believes elves should protect the land from the dangers that might stumble in from the north, and he has done so for centuries. But he also believes elves have nothing to gain from interactions with humans. Evay, on the other hand, has long held that humans are as complex as elves and that connections with the human world can provide valuable knowledge."

"Like the knowledge of runes and how they can harness *vitalle*?" Kate asked, trying not to glance at Venn's covered forearm.

She gave a wry smile. "Among other things. When I grew to agree with Evay, the king was displeased."

"Did he order you to stop talking to humans?"

Venn let out a short laugh. "If he had, I would not be here right now. It is not our way to command each other, and so a command from the king, in the rare instances when it is given, is binding in a way you might not understand. So no, he did not command me to stop talking to humans. But our differing opinions have led to more than one disagreement, to the point where I try not to enter the White Wood." She shrugged. "It is no great loss to me. My family lives at the lakes, as does Evay."

"What do they think of dwarves?" Tribal asked.

Venn let out a short laugh. "They consider dwarves so much lower than humans that they wouldn't even imagine anyone would want to interact with you."

Tribal glanced at Silas. "I'd be offended if I thought elves were worth talking to."

"Or if there was anything of interest in the Wood itself," Silas said. "All the interesting things are outside of it."

"Like what?" Kate asked.

Treasure, Crofftus answered as though the answer was obvious. He climbed off Kate's pack and toward the side of the boat. *Dwarves are always after treasure.*

"What do you know of the treasure?" Silas asked.

"The stories of it in those parts are very old," Tribal said. "And no trace of any has ever been found."

Kate looked between the two dwarves, who were looking a little too intently at Crofftus. "What treasure? Something from the old Kalesh Empire?"

Silas smirked. "Not unless the old empire made an amulet that offered immortality."

"Immortality?" Kate repeated.

It is rumored that centuries ago, a great mage created the Oziv Amulet, which grants eternal youth to the wearer of it. Crofftus reached the side of the boat and looked out over the water.

"Renault the Mad," Tribal agreed.

"He was mad?"

"He was half-elven," Tribal said, by way of explanation.

"There are a good number of local tales about Renault," Venn said. "He was obsessed with the idea of immortality. The elven side of his family found the pursuit pointless. Once you've lived for centuries, immortality loses some of its draw. But his human family, after first supporting his work, eventually decided his research was growing twisted and dark."

"So he murdered them all," Tribal finished.

Kate looked at them all. "Is the story true?"

"Renault Half-Elven did exist," Venn said. "He sowed strife among the humans and elves and died while the Kalesh Empire was still at its height, although no one knows how or where. No one in the White Wood believes he created anything of value, never mind an amulet that could extend life forever."

Renault is said to have left many treasures hidden in the area, perhaps in caves or perhaps buried in the forest, but his creation of the immortality amulet is the greatest.

"You sound like you believe he created things of value," Kate said to Crofftus.

Perhaps. He was a man utterly dedicated to an idea. I admire dedica-

tion. He crawled along the side of the boat, as smooth and shiny as a wet black stone.

"Even in murderers?"

I suppose that depends on the reason for the murder.

Kate glanced at Venn, who was watching the beetle with growing suspicion.

"The fact that Renault died makes the story less believable," Kate said.

Tribal shrugged. "Some say he didn't die but still haunts the area."

Kate glanced between the dwarves. "You two know a lot about the human and elven history of the area."

"We know a lot about the treasure of the area," Silas corrected her. "Renault's amulet is said to have been made from an alloy of steelstone and gold. Apparently it's such a light gold, it's almost translucent. The center is hollowed out to hold some liquid that glows like moonlight."

She considered both of them, a connection forming between two parts of their incomplete story. "And let me guess. The rock-slide was near enough to where you think the treasure is that you went to investigate it."

Silas grinned at her. "The exact location of the Oziv Amulet has been lost to history."

"So you didn't really investigate for the governor."

Tribal let out a chuckle. "It was a bit of both."

Venn looked at Kate with a thoughtful expression. "Bo is the sort of person who knows about the treasure of an area as well, isn't he?"

"He is," Kate agreed. "Did he mention the amulet to you?"

She shook her head. "But do you think he would have been in the area for a few weeks and not heard of it?"

"No, he would have discovered there were tales of a treasure that big." She looked around the cramped boat. She needed a desk, and space, and good lighting.

Her fingers itched to write out a story map of Renault the Mad and rockslides and moving trees. To lay out Bo's letters and journal. To see everything at once. There were connections there —she could almost feel them taking shape.

With a sigh of irritation, she peered ahead through the dim cavern. "How long until we're out of these caves?"

"We show her glories that most humans can't imagine," Tribal said, waving his hand at the luminescent life around them, "and all she wants to do is get back out to the boring outside."

"It takes about a day," Silas answered. "You might as well get comfortable."

CHAPTER THIRTY-EIGHT

KATE TUCKED Bo's journal into her pack, and the back of her hand hit the corner of the aenigma box. She could only see the corner of the lid, but the mosslight hit it at such a shallow angle that the carved runes were full of shadows, standing out starkly against the smooth wood, calling to her to study them.

She pulled the box out and held it so the light from the lantern just skimmed the top, plunging every carved symbol into blackness.

The triangle created by the three main runes was readily visible. The topmost one reading *a king brought to his knees* connected strongly to *the battlement cannot stand*, which sat on the left. And both intertwined with the strange runes on the right.

Her eyes traced those carvings, moving past ideas of sorrow and loss and brokenness before getting caught up in something that reminded her of hope and life.

She set her finger on the edge and funneled a little *vitalle* into them. They blazed into warmth, the web of thin lines carved around the lid lighting up.

Not a web—a net.

The thin lines crisscrossed around the larger, bolder rune, containing it. Holding it together.

She leaned closer.

Once she started to separate the net-runes from the central one, she noticed it wasn't a single rune. It was two. The first and most obvious rune was *loss*. Not a small loss. A huge, gaping loss.

It took a moment to decipher that the second was one smaller rune embedded in the center of a larger one.

The root of the outer rune was *hold*, but the modifiers spoke of unending desperation. Clinging with all one's might and never stopping.

The smaller rune tucked inside it said *broken*. No, more than broken. *Shattered.*

The net wriggled around these runes, wreathing them with a repeated series of symbols made of smaller, thinner lines. She poured a little more *vitalle* into them until they brightened, and she separated them out.

Starlight.

Waiting. Or waiting with the slightest hint of hopefulness, so more like *anticipation*.

Something that meant beams of light, like *sunbeams*, with the idea of them emerging from darkness.

And finally, one that was repeated even more than the rest, *healing*. A short symbol twisted above it each time, and she considered the shape of it. *Complete*, maybe. *Complete healing.* There was a little more to it, though. She was tapping her fingers on the side of the box, trying to draw out the real meaning, when she noticed the thin tail wrapping around the rune.

Restore.

She sorted out the different ideas. Her thumb rubbed over a metal strap along the edge, the feel of the delicately carved runes oddly soothing against her skin.

This spoke of something shattered being held together desperately by the one who had suffered the great loss of it, all enveloped in bits of distant starlight and the anticipation of the broken thing being restored.

All the darker parts—the brokenness, the desperation, the interminable feel of the holding—were stronger than the rest, and Kate ran her fingers over the *waiting* rune.

Her gaze traveled the constellation of symbols, drawn continually back to cycle through them again. This she understood. The waiting and hoping and clinging and loss, churning endlessly.

Her locket hung heavy on her chest. She cut off the *vitalle* she'd been trickling into the runes. Their warmth and light faded, and the box slid out of focus as she tried to push back the surge of impatience and endless waiting that roiled in her. Everything she'd tried to contain for Evan over the last twenty years, the fear, the worry, the dread, the itch of hope she couldn't ignore. And now, she finally had the box, and everything was worse. All the fears for Evan were matched with ones for Bo.

She squeezed her eyes shut and kept rubbing her thumb against the side of the box, fighting against the rising restlessness inside her.

Another whole day would be wasted floating downstream in forced idleness, then a search through a forest where Bo's remnant would have disappeared from weeks ago.

It had been so long already, and she was stuck here, still so far away from all the things she needed to see.

Her thumbnail caught on a ridge, and she ran her nail along it, itching to search for any trace of where Bo had gone.

Her thumb stopped, and her eyes flew open.

There were no ridges on the side of the box.

She pulled her hand away, and there on the right-hand side was the outline of a deep drawer.

She shoved herself up and wedged her fingernails into it. It slid easily open to reveal a drawer that held two pieces of paper.

359

"It has another drawer?" Venn asked, sitting forward. "How'd you open it?"

Kate shook her head. "I'm not sure. Not with hope. This time, I felt restless." Her fingers were already reaching for the papers when she paused.

The drawer was deep enough and wide enough to cover almost the entire right-hand side and so long that when closed, it would fill up half the box.

Which would mean it was taking up at least half of the space that the Hope Drawer should sit in.

She tried to slide it all the way out of the box, but it only moved so far before it refused to come further.

"That doesn't seem right," Venn said. "Doesn't that drawer take up the same space as the first one?"

"It seems to." Kate took out the two papers and felt around inside the Restless Drawer. All the walls were continuous. Curving her fingers up, she felt a solid piece of wood above it too, which might have been the inside of the top of the box, although it was lower than she'd expect. "Aenigma may be an even more fitting name for it than I thought."

She pulled out her hand, and a breath of remnant rolled out too. Dry and brittle. It reminded her of the fragile edges of old scrolls. Or the dry whispery feel of feathers.

The first paper appeared blank but felt thick. She turned it over and discovered it wasn't a single sheet but a handful of very thin pages glued together. The back was a rectangle, the next toward the front a cutout of mountains glued high on the page. The next held a lower range, the next rolling hills, then a low-lying range of trees. The frontmost paper was the cutout of tall pines on the edges and some brush along the bottom.

The entire scene was like a detailed, three-dimensional view of mountains framed by pines.

The other paper was covered in a slanting, narrow hand and written in an older dialect of Kalesh.

> *People keep trying to separate light from dark as though one exists without the other.*
>
> *They want my art.*
>
> *They want my light but feel betrayed when the shadows linger at the edges. Why does no one see that he who sheds light causes darkness by his very nature?*
>
> *How can we see anything without the dark? The play of the light on the top of the tree and the darkness beneath its boughs. The difference between the sunlit distant mountains and the gloom of the forest where we stand.*
>
> *It is impossible to bring the light without casting shadows.*
>
> *What is runelight besides separating the light from the dark?*
>
> *If you think to find only light, you are a fool.*

"Where'd you get the shadow art?" Silas said.

Kate glanced at him. "The what?"

He pointed to the thick paper still in her hand, which sat between him and the lantern. "I'm sure it looks better with a real light behind it instead of mosslight, but it looks well made."

She shifted the page between herself and the mosslight, and the artwork brightened. The mountains in the back let through the most light, with each layer blocking more and showing up darker, until the trees at the front were nearly black.

Tiny details appeared along the top of each ridge—rocks and trees—and individual needles were visible on the foremost pines.

"It was in the box." Kate brought the paper closer to the lantern, finding more and more details as she did.

"From Bo?" Venn asked.

Kate shook her head. "I don't recognize the remnant, and the note with it is in Kalesh." She translated it for them.

Venn frowned. "Sounds like a cheery fellow. His isn't one of the remnants you found in the other drawer?"

Kate shook her head. "It feels old, though. The way some of the others did. And the language is old." She glanced at Venn. "What's runelight?"

"An older term. A way that elves once anchored magic to things with runes."

Crofftus buzzed over and landed on the crate nearest Kate. *I've seen shadow art like that before. A wealthy woman in Greentree had it on a screen that sat in front of her fire. Hers was a wolf moving through a forest and was made of thin screens of metal overlaid on each other. She claimed it was a family heirloom that came from what had once been the Kalesh Empire.*

"The only place I've ever seen things like it is weeks east of here," Silas said. "In lands that still speak Kalesh. The High Dwarf bought one once, and for a few years, all the wealthy dwarves were clamoring for them."

Tribal gave a grunt of agreement. "If that's the sort of treasure in your treasure box, Twig, the box itself is worth more."

The tunnel grew tighter, and he went back to the bow, using his pole to navigate. Venn leaned over the side, dragging her fingers through the water, and Silas situated himself in the stern.

Kate pulled out the remnant amplifier and let a single drop fall into the Restless Drawer. The papery remnant flared stronger, and she tilted the box until the bead of liquid rolled into the back corners. There was nothing except the single remnant.

She let the liquid sit against the tightly formed seam in the back corner.

Just before the last of it evaporated, the bell sound tolled. Rich and deep and distant.

What do you hear? Crofftus's voice was right beside her, and she flinched.

The beetle was sitting on the very edge of the nearest crate, peering at the box.

She twitched, pulling the box a little farther away from him. "A bell. I hear it deeper than all the other remnants. I think..." She closed her eyes and focused on the joints in the back of the drawer. The bell was there. Faint, but there. "I think that's the person who made the box."

Interesting.

She glanced at him. "Why?"

He made a noise that sounded noncommittal. *Always nice to get more hints of the whole story.*

Kate looked at him cautiously. "I agree."

He spread his wings and buzzed over to the side of the boat.

They floated downstream quietly. Silas kept one hand on the rod connecting them to the wire, watching Tribal and pressing down on the pole to slow their progress occasionally, although Kate never saw a signal pass between them.

She pulled out her own journal and copied the words from the drawer into it, as well as she could in the dim light, and tried to sketch out what the shadow art looked like.

When she was done, she tucked the papers back into the Restless Drawer and pushed it slowly closed. It slid perfectly into place, then disappeared into the surface. She ran her thumbnail across where the edge of the drawer had been, but there was nothing except smooth wood.

She was about to tuck the box securely back in her pack, but she set it on her lap instead. It felt more secure to hold it. Kate's mind circled from the box, to Crofftus, to Bo, to Evan before starting again.

The boat rocked gently, and she watched the beetle walk along the side of the boat until her eyes grew heavy and closed.

CHAPTER THIRTY-NINE

"How do the boats get back upstream to the dock?" Kate asked Silas as they floated swiftly around a bend and into one of the darker sections of tunnel. The luminescent river plants seemed to prefer certain parts of the river. The first glowing stretch had lasted for nearly an hour, sometimes near the surface, sometimes plunging deeper enough that the riverbed was too far for Tribal to reach with his pole and the boat merely drifted slowly along with the current. "A full day floating downstream is a long way back upstream."

"Paddle wheels." He pointed to some holes drilled into the top of the stern. "We don't bring the boats down often. Only a handful each week. We dock them at the exit, then string them together in groups, and a few cousins spend a day and a half paddling upstream."

"That sounds less fun than floating downstream," Venn said from where she still sat along the side of the boat.

"It is considerably less fun. But the alternative is a three-week walk through tunnels that aren't used often enough to be well stocked."

Venn straightened and looked ahead of them. "I smell forest."

Kate drew in a breath, but the air was only filled with the wet, mossy smell the tunnels had had since the lake.

Tribal glanced over his shoulder. "It's close. Just one narrow stretch, then we'll hit the lake with the dock. There'll only be two cousins there guarding the way out."

"Will they want to kill us?" Venn asked.

"They shouldn't," Silas said. "And since we stole a boat before it was ready, they won't be expecting us yet. It was fourth watch when we started, which is about midnight to dawn in the outside world. Shipments usually leave closer to midday, so we're hours and hours ahead of schedule." He glanced at Tribal. "We should reach it during fourth watch again. We may catch them sleeping."

"They still aren't going to be excited to see a human and an elf float up to their dock," Kate pointed out.

"No, they won't." Silas looked at Tribal. "You could share your log mead."

"Absolutely not!"

"You did it the time we took out the fire salts. And you know it became a legend."

"And nearly got me thrown in jail."

Silas waved away his words. "But it didn't. The gov'nor couldn't prove anything. These cousins sit here at a boring, thankless job, just hoping you'll show up with some log mead to bribe them into silence."

Tribal threw up his hands. "They never stay silent!"

"Maybe these will."

"I am not sharing my log—"

"Tribal," Silas interrupted. "We are currently wanted for harboring an elf and a human, who we've brought all the way from the Slide Door to the North Lake."

Kate nodded. "You are in a bit of trouble."

Silas waved her words away. "It's not that. We need someone

to finish the story. Brustol will tell everyone where we started, the worthy cousins at the dock will tell them how we got the boat, and these lucky boys down here will be famous for knowing how we escaped. You'll be doing them a favor."

Kate looked at him. "You're proud of all this, aren't you?"

Silas grinned.

Tribal, though, crossed his arms and pointed a meaty finger at Kate. "You owe me a bottle of log mead! A big one!"

Kate paused. "I have no idea what that is."

"I do," Venn said. "It's disgusting."

"They brew it in the human town of Home," Tribal said, "and it's like gold in a bottle."

"It does taste like metal," Venn agreed.

"I'm planning to go to Home," Kate said. "And I will happily buy you a bottle of log mead, assuming you can get us out of these tunnels without us having to do anything antagonistic toward any dwarves."

"Deal," Tribal said quickly. "A *big* bottle." He turned back around and jabbed his pole down into the water, propelling the boat forward. "You two stay in the back behind the crates. I'll go talk to these fine cousins, and when I've brought them inside, Silas will get you two out of the cave."

Crofftus crawled back onto Kate's pack and headed toward the flap of the pocket with the vials.

Do you know what gelesen is? he asked.

Kate paused. "Purified sap from a rennen thicket."

Smart girl! he said with a note of pride that made Kate's eyes narrow. *Your remnant amplifier could be stable in sunlight if you added some gelesen.*

She frowned at the suggestion. It was one she'd only found in an obscure note from a physician from Coastal Baylon. "I tried. It clouded the fluid and its potency dropped to a tenth of what it had been."

Clouding is the risk, of course, he answered, sounding pleased that she knew as much. *Gelesen is hypersensitive to thermal changes. There are ways, though, if you're ever interested in trying again.* He wriggled under the flap and into the pocket.

Venn watched him disappear. "Did that make sense to you?"

Kate nodded slowly. "If he's right, it would solve a problem I've been working on for a long time." She tapped the pocket. "Don't mess with my vials, Crofftus. If you damage them, I will be very angry."

How would a beetle get a cork out?

"Well...don't chew on it or anything."

Chew? I'm insulted.

Still frowning, she picked up the pack and moved to the stern of the boat, while Silas clambered up next to Tribal.

Venn sat down beside Kate, a small smile on her face. "Can you smell it now?"

A bit of cool air blew past, and Kate took a breath. There, woven through Venn's remnant, were the real smells of a pine forest. "I do."

Venn opened her bag and pulled out the last of the patches of moss that she'd stored. They'd grown brittle and brown, and she tossed them overboard. "Your metaphorical forest was a good idea. The last few days have not been terrible."

"Good." The water here held almost no plant life, and Kate's eyes scanned the barely visible rock ceiling above them. "Despite the unexpected beauty of the river, I am very ready to be out of mountains and return to places with actual light."

"And trees," Venn agreed.

"Shh," Silas said from the front of the boat. "Almost there."

The ceiling above them suddenly rose higher, and the walls fell away to the side. A new sort of light filtered through the air, catching on the tiny ripples on the surface of the water with silvery glitters and turning the walls to muted greys.

The air grew colder, and Kate pulled her cloak more tightly around herself. They floated into a small lake, barely a quarter the size of the one they'd started from. Through a tall, narrow gap in the far wall, spiky tops of pines were etched in moonlight against a dark sky. Embedded deep in the black were glittering stars.

Just that sliver of the outside world held such a vastness that she sank against the crate, unable to take her eyes off it.

The boat moved closer to the shore, and the glowing moss on the shoreline pulled her attention to the little wooden hut situated at the end of a handful of docked boats. As their hull slid over the gravel, Tribal jumped out and splashed in the last few inches of water. He tugged the boat up onto the shore and tossed a rope around a nearby post.

A stocky figure detached itself from the hut and started toward them. "There were no shipments expected tonight."

Tribal turned, his boots crunching on the rocky shore. "'Morning, cousin. This is a special shipment. Lucky for you, it's so special that there's no need for record-keeping. Silas and I would never want a cousin to have more busy work."

The dwarf peered at the boat. "Special how?"

"Special in the way that should be celebrated with a bit of log mead," Tribal said.

The dwarf's eyebrows rose, and he turned his attention back to Tribal with a wide smile. "Well, if there's no paperwork to be done, then I have time for a drink."

"Excellent." Tribal patted the dwarf's shoulder as he turned him toward the hut. "Silas lost a bet and has to do the unloading. But if you have some cups inside, I'm more than happy to share while he does all the work."

"Not just cups—I have big cups."

"Even better!" Tribal held the hut door open for the dwarf, then followed him in.

"Quietly now," Silas whispered, motioning Kate and Venn out of the boat.

They followed him onto the shore and close along the boats to the hut. Tribal laughed loudly from inside as they ducked below the windows and hurried toward the outside world.

Air from outside the cave blew in with the cold bite of winter lacing its edges, even as it carried the fresh scent of pine trees. She breathed it in, and the chilly air filled her lungs, stretching them as though she hadn't breathed deeply in days. Beside her, Venn did the same. They reached the edge of the cave and moved quickly outside into the night.

They stood in a clearing cut through by the river that flowed out of the cave and downhill. Above them, the sky was shifting to blue with the approaching dawn, but it still held a spattering of stars. Kate's back straightened, as though finally released of the weight of the mountain. Behind her, a line of peaks rose tall and jagged against the sky, heading north. To the east, the land rippled away in hills to the horizon, where a hint of purple washed out the lowest stars.

Without stopping, Silas hurried down a small path, and even in the predawn darkness, Kate recognized the trail as the one where Tribal had thrown his knife at the shadow. Silas led them into the pines, directly where the shadow had stood, and Kate's eyes fell on pockets of blackness everywhere. A shiver of uneasiness dragged its fingers along her neck.

Silas finally stopped at a large rock, placing his back to it and scanning the forest around them, glancing back often toward the cave. Venn moved to the nearest tree and sank down against it, closing her eyes.

Kate set her pack down by Venn, and Crofftus flew off of it toward the center of the path where bare dirt was visible.

Wait! Not there! Over by the tree! Do you want to be stepped on by a dwarf? The beetle shuddered in mid-air and turned toward the tree. The moment it landed, the black head burrowed into the earth.

"Does it understand you?" Kate asked.

No, it— The back of the beetle disappeared into the ground.

"Crofftus?"

How far are we from the White Wood?

"We could be in the frost pines by nightfall," Venn answered without opening her eyes.

I can feel it. His voice grew faint.

The forest stretched out around Kate, and she left him to his digging. She stepped a few paces away from Venn's remnant until it faded, then kept moving around the first curve in the path until she was surrounded by only the stillness of the cold, damp morning air and the scent of the pines. The sky above was lightening to blue, and the shadows were settling into the shapes and textures of tree trunks and fallen logs. Her breath clouded in front of her, misty white against the gloom. She cast out, just to feel the life flare up around her. The warm brightness of grass and brush spread along the ground as her wave rolled over them. Tree trunks rose from them like a crowd of solemn, steady pillars of heat, and a lattice of pine boughs shimmered into light above her, each needle glowing with *vitalle*.

After so much barren rock in the caves, the forest around her blazed with life. She unwound the bandages from her hands. The blisters were healed enough that when she set her palm against the tall pine next to her, the rough bark gave only a prickle of discomfort. She pulled a trickle of *vitalle* out of the tree. It flowed so easily and so freely that she just stood there for a moment, reveling in the abundance of life around her, letting the warmth of it seep into her flesh and warm her bones.

She tilted her head up to look into the branches. "I was only in the caves a few days," she said quietly, "and yet it feels like I've never touched a tree before." Pressing her other palm to the tree, she closed her eyes and pushed some of her own *vitalle* into it, feeling it swirl into the threads of life running beneath the bark.

The pine flared brighter, and her eyes snapped open.

She cast out again, and the tree in front of her shifted back into a pillar of heat. The current of *vitalle* moving between them was clearly visible, like a stream of molten gold. Brighter than she'd ever seen from any tree. She stopped pulling at the energy of the tree, and yet it continued to flow, gentle and steady.

Venn's brightly burning figure lit up behind her as the wave rolled away. "You should try that on an older tree." She stepped up beside Kate and set a hand on the tree. The *vitalle* of the tree shifted and surged.

"The Wildwood where I grew up didn't feel like this."

"My people only lived there for a few hundred years." Venn rubbed her thumb over a jagged piece of bark. "That's not long in the life of a forest. The elves have lived here for a millennium."

Kate's palms tingled with the energy moving through them, but she kept them against the pine. "What does the White Wood feel like?"

Alive, Crofftus said from the direction of her pack. *The White Wood feels like the forest is alive.*

Venn's eyes traveled over the bark. "I'll take you to the edge of it, and you can see for yourself."

Kate glanced over at her. "You will?"

Tribal's voice rumbled from the path behind them, and Venn turned to pick up her pack and Kate's from where they sat a few paces away. She held out Kate's. "They only promised not to steal our things while we were in the tunnels."

Kate shrugged on her pack. Crofftus's distant rumbling remnant lay under the sounds of Venn's and the rest of the forest. "Good point."

The two dwarves rounded the curve, Tribal swaying and

humming a rousing tune in a rich, deep voice, his arm slung over Silas's shoulder.

Silas grinned at them. "See? Easy as that." He strode past them, patting Venn—who twitched away from him with a slightly indignant look—on the shoulder. "The rockslide isn't far." He waved a hand. "This way!"

Kate wrapped her hand around the strap of her pack and took a deep breath. Bo had been in these woods. Weeks ago, but still, whatever trail was left would be somewhere relatively close.

Falling in behind Venn and the dwarves, she cast out again. She let a little hope pour out with the wave that rolled around her, because if she found Bo, maybe they could use the aenigma box to find some clue as to where Evan was.

The chilled mountain air blew against her back, nudging her forward. It tugged the hope into strands, spooling them out among the trees, creating a tangled tapestry of *vitalle* and light that spread throughout the forest.

CHAPTER FORTY

THE SUN HAD RISEN by the time Kate followed the dwarves out of the trees and onto the bank of a quick-flowing river at the base of a narrow ravine. The air was still crisp and cold, the sky a bright, limitless blue, but the gorge lay in early morning shadows.

The pine forest behind her rose away to the west, covering the base of a long range of mountains. The rocky tops that stuck up above the trees were dusted with stark white snow against the cloudless sky.

The slope ahead of her, though, was barren except for a few low, scrubby bushes. The river rushed along the bottom of the ravine with foaming swirls and white caps dotting the surface as it crashed around rocks. Shockingly smooth sections sat among the rapids, and the water itself was so clear that the rocky riverbed was perfectly visible. The stones that looked grey and brown on the shore were revealed in purples and blues and yellows where the river wet them, and Kate stared into it for a long moment, stunned by the beauty of it.

Silas stopped beside her and gestured upstream. "Your rockslide."

A swath of huge boulders and smaller stones scarred the opposite hillside not far away. Dozens of paces wide, it started high on the slope and reached down into a huge pile at the base that had tumbled into the edge of the river, leaving the water to churn and crash around it.

Venn stepped up next to them, her brow drawn as she looked up at the hillside. "It's this ravine?"

"Don't you recognize it from my memory?" Silas asked.

Venn merely frowned at the slope.

It *was* the hillside from Silas's memory, and Kate faced the forest, matching the trees to what he'd shown her. "The shadow was there?"

Silas nodded, and she walked over to the two pines where the shadow had watched the dwarves. The forest floor was strewn with old needles and small branches, exactly like every other place under the trees. She squatted down and set her hand on the ground, but there was no remnant.

She stood and considered the rockslide. "What do you see when you look at that?"

"An accident." Tribal sat heavily on a boulder next to the water and closed his eyes before swaying again and resuming his humming.

"It looks like it was caused around that height." Silas pointed to a spot two thirds of the way up the rockslide. "You can tell by the edges."

The edges looked exactly like the rest of the rock, and Kate glanced at Venn to see her reaction, but the elf was facing uphill, studying a small road cut into the slope a bit above where Silas pointed. A road that ended abruptly at the rockslide.

Tribal let out a shout, and Kate spun to see him scrambling off his rock. He brushed something wildly off his sleeve and staggered back a few steps, then looked up the hillside, still swaying slightly. "There was a spider," he said, outraged. "On my arm!"

Kate turned her attention back to Silas. "You were saying? About the rockslide?"

"The instigating event was wide. Nearly as wide as the rock-slide, which is unusual. Generally, a slide is set in motion at a single location." He shifted his finger to point a little higher up. "There are some small caves at that level. I would imagine the humans were doing something near them and destabilized the slope. But it's impressive how perfectly they had to do a lot of somethings at the same time to cause this." He waved at the entire side of the gorge. "That's a stable slope. If they'd disturbed a single point, they might have caused a few rocks to tumble down, but nothing of this magnitude."

"Caves?" Kate headed upstream. "Bo was in a cave when the rockslide started." She found the stepping stones across the river she'd seen in Silas's memory. The river swirled past the first one, spraying a cold mist up, and she jumped to the second. It teetered to the side under her weight, and she froze. When it didn't move anymore, she jumped to the next stone, and the next, until she reached the pile of rocks on the far bank.

Venn and Silas followed, and Tribal crossed last, looking over the rocks near the base of the rockslide carefully before picking one to sit on.

Silas moved uphill past Kate, taking his remnant with him. In a few moments, there was nothing around her but the dusty, earthy smell of the hillside, the sound of birds in the forest, and Tribal's singing, which had grown into a bawdy tavern song.

She climbed off the rocks and followed Silas to the edge of the rockslide. "The first part of this story is sort of straightforward. Bo's part. He was here working, and some creature that looked like a tree came and killed his men and tore apart the mountain."

"Straightforward?" Silas asked. "That sort of thing happen often where you're from?"

"Well, it's strange, I admit, but it would explain the distur-

377

bance that happened in more than one place. The tree tore up several parts of the slope. It makes a coherent story. Until we try to add in the shadow that followed both you and Bo after the rockslide. Because how do both a moving tree and a shadow fit into the same story? Unless they're somehow the same thi—"

Tribal hit a note so discordant she flinched. He sat on his rock, eyes closed, merrily singing in his low, rumbling voice.

"…thing," she finished, frowning at the dwarf.

The dissonant sound stabbed into her ear again, and she turned to the slide. It wasn't part of Tribal's singing.

She jumped onto a boulder on the edge of the rockslide, and the sound grew louder.

A remnant. From under the rocks.

The idea of someone trapped under the crushing stone dropped her to her knees. She cast out.

There was nothing below the rocks.

No signs of life at all.

The few clumps of brush that had been torn up by the crashing rocks were long dead. There were the tiny flickers of life from insects, but none nearby. Something mouse-sized scurried under the rocks higher up the hill, and a long strand of warmth that was probably a snake slithered away toward the river. But the dissonant remnant was coming from directly below her, and there was definitely nothing alive right there.

She teased out the sound from the background noise. It was almost a tune made up of burbling water and coos like doves, but every sound had jagged edges that grated against her mind like broken glass.

"This is where the humans died," Venn said quietly from behind her.

Kate turned to see her standing at the edge of the rocks, her eyes still fixed uphill.

Silas nodded. "The people of Home say five men died in the avalanche."

"No." Venn pointed up the slope. "Three hundred years ago. That's where the humans died." She held her hand out toward Kate. "Give me the serum."

Kate climbed over the rocks toward her.

"When we first came here from the Wildwood," Venn said, "there was an...incident. Right here."

"Right here?" Silas said, a note of disbelief in his voice. "No offense, but humans can barely tell one rocky hillside from another. Elves must be even worse."

Kate pulled the tenea serum out of her pack.

Venn shook her head and took the vial. "It was here." She glanced behind them. "It was that forest." Pulling out the cork, she set her finger inside. A long stream of glittering silver flowed into the serum before she handed it back.

Kate plunged her finger in, and the image of this ravine burst into her mind, crystal clear through Venn's eyes. Kate could feel the wind blow past and a rotten stench that made her gag.

Venn glanced behind her, across the ravine, at a tall mountain that rose high above the tree line. She walked up the hillside among a line of elves, all slightly taller than her, all somber, murmuring quietly to each other and looking warily ahead. They crunched up the rocky ground between tufts of tenacious plants striving to survive in pockets of dirt.

She could feel all the plants without effort. Snips of life tucked among the stone.

Higher up the slope, a road cut along the hillside. The scent of death wafted by again, and she covered her nose.

The voices around her quieted. The edge of the road came into view, along with the pointed tops of tents lined up on the far side, small and grey and utilitarian. Farther down the road, they grew larger and more colorful. At the very end, the gaudy gold fabric of a partially collapsed pavilion fluttered in the breeze.

As she climbed out onto the road, her eyes caught on an arm splayed out over some sharp rock, crawling with flies. It belonged to a young man dressed like a soldier. There was no sign of blood, but his eyes stared unseeing up at the sky.

Next to him lay another. And another.

The road in front of the tents was littered with death, human bodies sprawled out as though they'd fallen while running. They held swords or bows or work hammers. Everywhere, flies buzzed through the stench of decaying flesh.

The grass along the edge of the road glowed with life, but the bodies were empty. Pockets of cold on the hot day.

Unnaturally empty.

There was no blood anywhere. No sign of struggle at all. Just dead bodies.

"Mother?" Venn whispered. "What happened?"

The elf next to her shook her head, her eyes scanning the slope warily. "I don't know."

Venn took her mother's hand. "There are no trees to bury them under."

"Humans don't need trees. They cover their bodies in dirt or stone."

One of the older elves waved a hand, and a wind blew down from higher up the hill, pushing the stench away and driving off most of the flies.

Silently, the elves began to move the bodies, lining them up along the road, piling rocks on them to keep away the scavengers. Venn took the feet of a man in a soldier's uniform and helped her mother lift him. His stench made her gag, and the limpness of his body made him feel like a sack of rocks.

They moved him into line with the others. One of the older elves pulled a small pin off the human's collar. A dull circle of metal stamped with a leaf. He placed it carefully on a stone set above the dead man's head.

"What's that for?" Venn whispered to her mother.

"Other humans will come searching for these. This perhaps will help them identify the fallen."

The sun sank behind the tall mountain while they worked. When the last cold body was covered, Venn walked along the line, feeling the emptiness of the human husks beneath the rocks. Her eyes traveled over the little trinkets set above them. Metal tags from their uniforms, pieces of jewelry, a leather patch with some foreign writing on it.

As she neared the crumpled pavilion, the trinkets grew more impressive. Thick coins, glittering rings. Next to the second to last body, a large medallion on a chain had slipped partway off the side of the stone. Venn picked it up, and the heavy yellowish metal filled her palm, the surface stamped with a dragon coiled around the blade of a sword.

"That's gold," her mother said quietly. "Humans value it. To have this much…Whoever this was, they were important."

The artwork was interesting but violent, and Venn put it back down, arranging it in the center of the stone before stepping back and looking down the long line of bodies.

"That's all we can do," her mother said, wrapping an arm around Venn's shoulders. "Hopefully there won't be trouble when the other humans come looking for them."

The memory faded away, and Kate blinked, staring at Venn. "That was the Kalesh Imperial seal! Worn by the emperor's top ministers!" She spun to look up the canyon. "One of his personal ministers was here? Maybe Bo was right. Maybe that was Emperor Sorrn's entourage you found."

Venn shook her head. "The men we found were mostly soldiers and servants. That man with the medallion you saw

381

appeared to be the highest-ranking person. Unless the emperor was a subdued sort of man or was dressed like a commoner."

Kate laughed. "Sorrn was known for his lavish tastes and wearing an inordinate amount of gold jewelry, which he refused to take off because he believed it was protecting his life. He even slept in it."

Venn shook her head. "There was no one like that."

"Bo's notes mentioned an advisor with Sorrn. Maybe that was the minister."

"Then where was the emperor's body?"

"Taken, maybe?" Kate looked around the canyon again. "What happened when people came looking for them?"

"No one ever did."

Kate turned back to Venn. "Even if Sorrn wasn't part of this group, the owner of that seal was among the top men in the Empire. Someone would have come looking."

"The graves lay undisturbed for years. The tents and supplies deteriorated or were destroyed by the autumn winds and the winter snow slides. Within a hundred years, the road had worn away to the point where even horses wouldn't have been able to navigate it. But no one ever tried."

"The elves must have just missed it."

Venn gestured to the hill across the ravine. "We are within the range of White Wood patrols. They know of any humans who come near. I assure you, no one ever came for those men's bodies."

"That makes no sense." Kate looked up the slope. "Wait—there were no injuries on those men."

"I know. I was too young to realize the significance of that." Venn studied the thin line above that was the only sign of the road that had once been carved into the slope. "It was like they'd all died of old age at the exact same moment. Without aging at all."

Kate turned to look at her. "In Bo's journal—the men who were killed by the tree just fell. They weren't wounded. They just died."

Silas stumped down next to them, one bushy black eyebrow raised. "You think a moving tree killed Bo's men and did the same to an emperor three hundred years ago?"

"The two stories are too related to not have some connection, but that does sound far-fetched." Kate looked around the ravine. "I suppose we're assuming that this rockslide is where Bo was, and we don't really have proof of that. Were there other rockslides around the time of this one?"

Silas glanced at Tribal. "Not that we heard."

Kate considered the hillside. "In Bo's journal, he said the ravine he was working in was prone to rockslides, and the people of Home said it was cursed because of that. But if this slope is normally stable, maybe this isn't where he was working."

"It is stable," Silas said. "But there have been other slides here. You can't see them now. They're buried under this one. They were small, though. Caused by foolish human mining around the caves, not natural causes."

"Then maybe this *is* where Bo was." Kate let her eyes run over the hillside. "He mentioned something somewhere about caves. He didn't like them, said they felt odd." She couldn't quite place where he'd mentioned it, except that it had reminded him of the old mine from years ago.

She shifted her shoulders to dispel the swirl of complicated and unpleasant emotions that rose at the thought.

"These caves aren't odd," Silas said, "just poorly mined by humans."

"Can we get into them now?"

The dwarf shook his head. "All of them were covered by the slide."

Kate took in the wide path of rocks that had slid down the slope. "A lot happened in this single small ravine."

"This could be the cursed one," Tribal called from where he sat below.

Silas scratched at his beard and looked at the hillsides and mountains around them. "That's true."

"Cursed?" Kate asked.

"Haunted, by Renault the Mad."

"This canyon?" Kate asked the dwarves

Silas shrugged. "No one's sure exactly where, but somewhere around here."

"Is that why you're familiar with the caves here? Because you were looking for Renault's treasure?" The dwarf just smiled at her, and she moved back over to the rockslide. "Is this safe to climb on?"

"A twig like you won't disturb it," Tribal called.

She climbed up on a boulder, then moved from stone to stone until she stood far enough in that she couldn't feel the dwarves or Venn. Kneeling down on a large rock, she sought the remnant again.

A trace of it sounded from her right, deep in a gap between two boulders. Another harsh note rang out downhill. From uphill, the hoot of an owl drifted by, overlaid with the scraping of rusty metal.

They were subtle and faded to differing degrees, as though whoever had left them had come there often, until the rockslide.

"This happened about six weeks ago?" she called to Silas.

"Just about."

Kate moved until she was above the strongest remnant. It was not faded enough for six weeks. Even Venn's remnant wouldn't feel this strong after six weeks. And there was nothing similar between Venn's remnant and the discordant one.

"It may not have been a curse," Silas said, surveying the slope. "But something definitely went wrong in this ravine."

Kate stood and stepped away from the dissonant sounds. "I think the some*thing* is a some*one*." She stepped to the edge of the crumbled old road, and the first flat stone wobbled loosely beneath her feet. She moved quickly off it, away from the steep barren slope behind her. What had been a wide, flat roadway in Venn's memory was now just a narrow shelf along the ravine. A few paces to Kate's left, it ended, smothered under the edge of the rockslide.

"Someone was working here." Silas knelt near the tumbled boulders a little downhill.

Tribal peered over his brother's shoulder. "Excavating," he agreed.

Kate looked down at the wobbly paving stone. It was light grey, marbled with darker lines and cut with squared-off edges.

"The bodies we buried long ago would have been under where the rockslide is now," Venn said, stepping up next to her. She glanced down at the stone. "See something interesting?"

"A paver stone from the quarry at Elheim, perhaps." Kate motioned downhill where three similar stones had tumbled. "Or so Bo would tell me. This is where he was working, and those excavations are what his men were doing. They must have been uncovering the Kalesh bodies."

"Can you feel any of his remnant?" Venn asked.

"No. But I wouldn't expect to after all this time. I'm surprised that whatever I feel under the slide still exists. It's certainly not human."

"The walking tree?"

"Seems like the best guess." Kate looked at the forested slope across the ravine. "And based on the remnant, I hope we don't meet it."

"That bad?"

Kate rubbed the back of her neck, trying to banish the thought of the scraping sounds. "There was something wrong with whoever it was. They were…" She shook her head. "I don't know. Just wrong."

Tribal stood and stretched. "You owe me log mead, Twig. And the Blind Pig in Home is still hours away."

Kate looked sharply at him. "The Blind Pig?"

"The local tavern—the *only* local tavern, but thankfully the mead is excellent."

"And the coffee," Venn added.

Silas grunted in agreement.

"Bo mentioned staying at the Blind Pig, so I definitely want to talk to people there." Kate turned to Venn. "But I promised you we'd go see the clearing where he disappeared as soon as we left the caves, and we already put it off for this. Do you think we can get to the clearing and meet the dwarves in Home by tonight?"

"No." Venn started downhill. "But we might as well take the Weasel Brothers to Home first. The shortest route to the clearing requires us going almost to town anyway, and it'll be nice to get rid of these two for good."

"Are you sure?" Kate asked.

"We'll get all this done faster if everyone actually walks," Venn said over her shoulder.

Tribal rubbed his hands together. "Excellent. And you owe me an amulet, Twig."

"I'll fix it as we walk," Kate said.

At the stepping stones, Venn paused, letting Silas cross the river first. She turned to look back up at the rockslide, one of her fingers tapping thoughtfully on her quiver.

"What's wrong?" Kate asked, searching the hill above them.

"This place feels strange."

"Dangerous? Because that remnant under the rockslide feels incredibly dangerous."

Venn shook her head. "No. It feels...the opposite of dangerous."

Kate turned to look at her. "The ravine where a lot of people have been killed feels...what? Safe?"

Venn's gaze scanned the slope as she let out an annoyed breath. "No. Just familiar."

"Well, you have been here before."

"Not that sort of familiar. More like wearing your favorite cloak on a cold day. It's familiar in a comfortable sort of way. Except..." The tapping on her quiver grew faster. "It's very faint."

Kate considered the elf for a long moment. "I wouldn't expect you to feel that way about a rocky hillside."

Venn spun on her heel and jumped lightly onto the first stepping stone. "Neither would I."

CHAPTER FORTY-ONE

EVENING SUNLIGHT LANDED WEAKLY on Kate's face, unable to warm her through the chill of the air as she followed Venn out of a stand of trees and onto the floor of a flat valley. She pulled her cold fingers into the sleeves of her cloak, folding her arms to ward off the chill that had lingered all day long and grown stronger as the sun dropped into the west.

The river, which had flowed swiftly past them on their left since the rockslide, hugged the western edge of the valley. Ahead lay a snug lowland covered with pastures and fields, surrounded on all sides by forested hills. A cluster of timber-framed buildings sat nestled together just past the first field, their walls rough and bowed like the sides of wooly sheep, the stucco between the thick wooden beams tinted a warm honey yellow. Their steep roofs were layered with dark grey slate, and chimneys rose from nearly every steep peak. Several dozen thin trails of smoke rose straight up into the sky.

"The Blind Pig will get busy soon," Tribal said, striding past them. "No dawdling."

He led them into Home, past the small houses on the edges

and the clanging open workshop of a blacksmith, who looked up and gave Tribal a friendly wave before returning to his work.

A young woman sat on the stoop of the next building, shelling nuts. When she saw the two dwarves, she pulled her bag closer to her side. "Just keep moving, boys," she said with a wry smile.

"Nice to see you, Pren," Silas greeted her.

The woman's eyes widened when she caught sight of Venn. "What are *you* doing with these two?"

"Just dropping them off at the Pig," Venn answered.

Pren grinned. "Good. Let Yellow deal with them." Her eyes strayed to Kate with mild curiosity, but she merely gave a polite nod, which Kate returned.

"How often do all of you come to Home?" Kate asked as the dwarves led them into a town square formed around an enormous pine tree.

"The Pig has log mead," Tribal said, as though that explained everything. He headed toward a long two-story stucco and timbered building taking up a whole side of the square. A sign hung above the door with a poorly painted blindfolded pig dancing and holding up a dark bottle.

"Home is the town nearest the White Wood." Venn returned the nod of a passing white-haired man then jutted her thumb over her shoulder. "The road east connects to the two nearest towns. I come through a couple of times a year." She glanced up at the tavern sign. "Don't drink the log mead. He makes an excellent rosemary bread, and the rest of the food is good as long as you don't go near the overcooked, stringy pork."

"Are you saying that because elves don't eat meat?" Kate said.

"No. Meat isn't my favorite, but this pork is especially bad. Although the bacon is surprisingly good."

"Find me bacon that isn't." Tribal pushed open the front door, and the scent of bacon and rosemary rolled out into the square. "Yellow! Your biggest bottle of log mead!"

"Weasel Boys!" a deep, accented voice boomed.

Silas held the door open.

Kate stepped past him into a long room that swelled with warmth. "Why is it called log mead? Are they fermenting wood?"

"It's not mead at all." Venn moved inside and raised a hand in greeting to the huge man behind the bar. "It's some sort of beer the color and thickness of mud."

"Twig!" Tribal called. "Come pay Yellow for the mead!"

The tavern owner was a bear-sized man with shaggy brown hair and a red beard thick enough to impress a dwarf. He paused at the sight of Venn but gave her a wide smile. "When'd you stoop to traveling with these two?" His accent drew out the o sounds in the words and made the t's harsher.

Silas let the door swing closed. "We just heroically saved her life." He strode across the room to the bar, nodding a greeting to a few of the men hunkered down at tables and nursing goblets of a very dark drink.

A huge fire burned in a fireplace at the end of the room to their right, and lanterns hung in enough places that the whole place was well lit.

To each side, the common room's low ceiling was held up by rows of stout wooden posts, but the area between the door and the bar was open above to thick dark timbers that crisscrossed each other and held up the steeply peaked roof.

"Didn't expect you back until spring, Venn." Yellow set a steaming mug on the bar. "And I can't imagine these two could save you from anything but the trouble they caused themselves."

"That's exactly what they did." Venn breathed in the scent of the drink, then smiled and took a sip. "We're here because we need a place to dump them."

"We're here because they owe me log mead," Tribal corrected her.

Kate stepped up to the bar and caught the scent of roasted almonds. She glanced around for a bowl but found none.

The wall above the bar stretched up to the vaulted ceiling and held nothing but a yellow door mounted higher up than even the enormous bartender could reach. The paint must once have been bright but was now peeling off in long strips. There was no frame or handle, just a door, hung like a piece of art.

"Did you name the door," she asked Yellow, "or did it name you?"

Yellow grinned. "A bit of both." He motioned to the two dwarves. "You're forgiven for associating with these two, on account of knowing Venn. Can I offer you some coffee? Or log mead? And we do make the best pork this side of Poluntchun."

"I'll pass on the pork," Kate answered quickly, "and the log mead, but I hear your coffee is good. And I do owe you for Tribal's mead."

"Is that one Tribal?" Yellow said, peering at the dwarves. "I never can tell them apart."

"Apparently you have to smell them," Venn said. "Kate and I will take some rosemary bread and that sharp orange cheese if you have any. And a little bacon."

"Right away." He turned and ducked through the kitchen door.

The scent of almonds left with him, and Kate let out a laugh, taking the stool next to Venn's. "I've been surrounded by the remnants of you and the dwarves for so many days, a normal human one is hard to recognize."

Yellow returned with plates of bread and cheese, each with a fat slice of crispy bacon, and a steaming cup of coffee for Kate.

She wrapped her hands around the ceramic mug, and the heat of the coffee seeped into her hands, almost painfully hot. It smelled rich and nutty and comfortable. She took a sip, and the earthiness was laced with just enough bitterness to perfectly balance out the sweet. The warmth flowed down her throat, and she took another sip. "This is delicious."

"Try the bread," Venn said, pulling a chunk for herself off the loaf that was short and golden brown and filled the entire plate.

Kate tore off a piece, and her fingers sank into the soft bread. It smelled of butter and rosemary, and the first bite was even better than the smell. "Oh, that is good."

Yellow leaned his elbows on the counter and gave her a smile. "What brings you to Home? Aside from wanting to dump the Weasel Brothers on us?"

"I'm looking for someone who's gone missing."

Yellow's smile shifted to a troubled look. "Who would that be? Staven or Rye?"

Kate paused. "I don't know either of those names. More than one person is missing?"

"Two. As of yesterday." Yellow pushed himself off the bar and started cleaning a mug with a damp rag.

Kate stared at him. "You have *two* people missing? Just from this small town?"

"And the surrounding farms." He finished one mug and picked up the next. "You've visited during troubled times."

"It's the curse," an old woman's voice crackled from a table near the front window.

Kate faced her, along with all the other patrons in the tavern. "The curse?"

"Renault's curse." The woman pointed a spoon at Kate. "Get out of Home before you're taken. Or killed." The woman's accent sharpened the k, and Kate drew back from the ferocity of her voice.

Yellow set a mug down on the counter with a thunk. "Stop trying to frighten my customer, Maven. She's not gonna be killed."

"Tell that to Durg's boy. Or Ronan's."

Kate's grip tightened on her piece of bread, and she glanced at Venn. "People have been killed?"

"Two local boys," Yellow said quietly. "They went missing a little over a month ago. Their bodies were found in the woods. Looked to be ravaged by wolves."

Venn tensed. "Where?"

"Over on Reston Ridge. A couple of hunters found them. They'd been missing for nearly a week, but the wounds were fresh."

A patron called for Yellow, and he headed toward their table.

Venn gave her a troubled look. "Reston Ridge is just above the clearing where I found the box."

Kate stared at her. "They found bodies near where Bo disappeared?"

Yellow stepped back behind the bar, and Venn turned to him. "The boys had wandered the woods for a week? And then were attacked by wolves within sight of this valley?"

Yellow shrugged. "That's what no one can figure out. Neither were the type to run off. The next week, three men went missing, but all of them were found."

"Found addled," Maven added.

Yellow gave her an annoyed look. "Their minds are a bit confused," he admitted. "Two of them can't remember the last several months. The other has no memories from the past two years."

"And you have two more missing now?" Kate asked.

"A young farmer named Rye last week. Then three days ago, Staven the butcher disappeared."

"They're probably dead," Maven muttered, and Kate flinched at the words.

"Maven!" Yellow's voice cracked through the room. "You'll not speak bad omens under my roof. Quiet your tongue or take it elsewhere."

"Did the men have anything in common?" Kate asked.

"They were stupid enough to go to the ravine," Maven said.

Kate turned to look at her. "What?"

"That place is cursed. It killed some of them quick with a rockslide and tracked down the rest to make them pay for disturbing it."

No one in the common room objected to the sentiment. Even Yellow just frowned but said nothing.

Venn set her hand on Kate's forearm. "Bo's not dead."

Kate looked at her. "You can't know that."

"Bo?" Yellow asked, his voice growing harder.

Kate nodded. "He's my brother. He came here a couple months ago looking..." She trailed off at the dark look that crossed the innkeeper's face.

He pushed himself off the bar. "Ain't no one seen Bo in well over a month. Which is probably best for him."

Kate looked over her shoulder to find the rest of the tavern glaring at her.

Tribal slowly scooted one stool farther away from Kate, and Silas followed.

Maven pushed herself out of her chair and stood, her back hunched, her knobby finger jabbed toward Kate. "You know Bo?" she demanded.

Glares from every face bored into Kate. "He's my brother. He came here a few months ago..." An ominous rumble rolled through the room.

"He woke Renault's curse," Maven hissed. "Dragged our men to that ravine, and now they're dead or hurt or gone. If he ever comes back, we'll kill him."

PART IV

THE MOTIVE

It was easy to attribute simple motivations back then. To think of the obvious reasons for someone's choices and feel like I'd been clever about it.

But humans and dwarves and elves are endlessly more complicated than that, and the surface reasons are rarely the real ones.

Our real motives—the things that truly drive us—those are harder to see. Invisible at first glance, or second glance. Or thousandth glance.

They're invisible until we can see past all a person appears to be and understand what has shaped them.

Even then, they're hard to see.

I wish I'd known that back then.

Kings aren't always after power.

Elves love more than trees.

Dwarves search for treasure that isn't gold.

Yes, the real motives, the true ones, are very hard to see.

And not just in others.

Why do I really do what I do?

CHAPTER FORTY-TWO

KATE GLANCED around the tavern and met nothing but unfriendly faces.

She turned back to Yellow, but the innkeeper made no move to correct the old woman.

"It's not a curse," Venn said. "There must be a creature in the woods doing all this, and the elves will find it and root it out."

"They haven't yet," someone muttered.

"There's some that think the elves might be responsible," Maven said darkly.

Venn gave the old woman a dismissive look. "The elves have no interest in hurting humans."

The old woman snorted. "So say you."

"Venn has been a friend to our town for generations, Maven," Yellow said. "If she says it's not the elves, it's not the elves."

Maven snorted. "Because it's the curse."

The door swung open, and an entire family trooped in, moving to a table where an older man sat and calling out greetings to some of the others. The common room, including Maven, quieted at their entrance. The older man at their table said some-thing to the mother. Her expression curled into anger, and she glared at Kate.

The door opened again, and an elderly couple entered, followed by a young family with two babies.

"Busy place tonight," Silas noted.

"Town meeting," Yellow answered. He moved away, greeting people and lighting a few more lanterns hanging from the rafters.

A young man of maybe eighteen stood near the table where the first family sat, staring vacantly at the yellow door hung on the wall.

"Sit down, Gerren," his mother said, taking his hand and pulling him toward a seat. He followed her command numbly, keeping his eyes on the door.

Yellow came back behind the bar, and Kate leaned forward. "Is that one of the boys who was missing?" she asked quietly.

Yellow nodded. "His father's got weak lungs, but the boy's a sturdy lad. Carried the farm for years, but now…"

Despite the continual glares from Gerren's mother, Kate watched the young man. He seemed mostly unaware of the room around him but responsive to any direct command, moving obediently any time his mother spoke. His gaze slid from the yellow door to a blank spot on the wall, where it stayed.

"How long has he been like that?" Kate asked.

"Since he was found a fortnight ago, wandering the woods on a cold night without his shoes." Yellow met Kate's gaze, all friendliness gone from his expression. "I dunno if it's the curse or something else, but all this trouble started with Bo taking people to that ravine. You won't get a kind word from the people here. Probably best if you move along."

More of the town crowded into the room, and Venn motioned toward the far end of the room. Kate, Venn, and the two dwarves settled into a small table in a tight corner. Tribal took a long drink of his log mead, and Kate caught a metallic scent. "That smells awful."

Tribal took another drink. "You have no taste."

Silas tapped his fingers on the table as more people filed into the tavern. "Interesting about the curse," he said

Venn rolled her eyes. "There's no curse."

"But if there is," Tribal said, "you know what that means."

Silas smiled. "If the curse on the ravine is real, maybe the treasure's real, too."

Kate jabbed him with her elbow. "These people are suffering, and you are focused on rumors of an amulet that can bring immortality? Maybe this isn't the time to be obsessed with treasure."

Silas's smile faded. "It's not just treas—"

Tribal kicked him hard under the table and glanced around the room, taking another drink.

"It's not?" Kate asked.

Silas turned his attention back to his drink and said nothing more.

The room filled until it nearly burst with townsfolk, and Kate sipped her coffee, the drink warming her. There were more disappearances than Bo's, and if Yellow was right, Bo's was the first. She leaned toward Venn. "If all these people went missing after being in the ravine like Bo was, someone must know something we don't. Maybe we can talk to the families of the others who have gone missing."

Venn gave her an incredulous look. "You think they're going to talk to you?"

"It can't hurt to ask."

"Unless they take their hatred toward Bo out on you," Tribal pointed out. "That could hurt."

An older man with slate grey hair climbed up on a chair near the big fireplace at the far end. He wore a black robe with red embroidery around the collar and down the sleeves. The fabric, which looked as though it had once been stiff and formal, was worn at the edges, and the cuffs were frayed.

"My friends," he called out, his voice thin and nasal. Despite the worn condition of his robe, he wore it with the stiff-backed decorum that only minor officials seemed to master. "My friends!" he called louder.

A ripple of shushing rolled through the room.

"Any sign of them?" a man called out from somewhere to Kate's right.

The man on the chair shook his head. "Not yet, but—"

The room burst into angry shouts. Both dwarves stilled and took in the commotion. Their postures stayed relaxed, but Silas made a series of hand signals to Tribal.

Venn shifted closer to Kate. "We might not want to linger here."

Yellow pounded his hand on the wall just above the kitchen door, and it boomed out like a drum. "Let Magistrate Mirrow speak! Or get out of my tavern."

The room settled into angry mutters, and the magistrate gave Yellow a stiff nod.

Mirrow looked over the room from his chair, his face pinched in disapproval. "We have three hunting parties out each day. I'm sure we'll find them." He raised his hands to ward off the next round of grumbles. "The elven ambassador will be here shortly."

Venn straightened in her chair.

"The elves have ambassadors?" Kate whispered.

"We will carry ourselves with dignity," Mirrow continued, "or I will speak to him alone and convey to you what the elves have to say."

Yellow spoke again over the discontented grumblings.

"Everyone's worried," he said to the room, drawing the angry glares toward him, "but we won't get the boys back by fighting with each other. The elves offer assistance, and we should be grateful."

"Unless it's the elves that took 'em," someone muttered loudly from near the door.

Kate shifted to see who spoke, but they were blocked by too many others.

"We've lived next to the White Wood for hundreds of years," Yellow said. "And the elves have never been a danger. Don't let your fear for our boys make you stupid, Tom."

"Yes," the magistrate said, peering toward Tom. "If there's trouble in the woods, the elves are more likely to find it than we are. I ask that you all remain quiet so we can hear the—"

The door of the tavern swung open, revealing two elves. The square behind them was colored in dusky blues, but the elf just outside the door was lit as though he stood in front of a bright fire. His tunic was light green, threaded with silver that shone like moonlight, in sharp contrast to the warm coppery glow of his skin. His long dark red hair was interlaced with threads of brightness like strands of burning coals.

Venn gave a hiss of surprise just as the familiarity of his face snapped into place for Kate. He was older, but it was unmistakably the same elf.

"That's the elf from your memory!" she whispered to Venn. "The one who saw the city with you!"

Venn's eyes grew hard, and she stared at him.

He gave the room a small but polite smile, but his gaze jerked to a stop when he saw Venn. For a moment, his skin flared brighter. His smile shifted, almost imperceptibly, into something genuinely pleased.

Venn sat back in her chair and folded her arms, meeting his eyes with so much hostility the air almost crackled around her.

The edges of his smile turned pained, and he nodded to her, the motion holding more resignation than greeting.

"You said he was dead!" Kate said quietly.

Venn's eyes drilled into the back of the elf's head as he moved toward the fireplace. "No, I didn't, but he is dead to me."

CHAPTER FORTY-THREE

MAGISTRATE MIRROW GAVE the elf a stiff, formal bow. "Welcome, Prince Faron," he proclaimed in his nasal voice, as though welcoming him to some royal court.

"Prince?" Kate whispered, but Venn just continued her glare at the other elf.

His head was nearly at the same height as the magistrate standing on the chair, and he looked over the room with a small smile. "Thank you, magistrate."

The short, older man gave him another stiff bow and stepped down from the chair.

Faron looked over the room, his expression growing serious. "The recent circumstances are troubling, and I wanted to assure you that I am personally organizing the search parties from the White Wood. I came here tonight to get as many details as we can from you. Whatever is happening, it is not something our own rangers are aware of, which is…" He glanced at the other elf, who had remained near the door. "It's unheard of," he finished.

Kate glanced over at the other elf and straightened. "That's the ranger from your memory of the clearing!" she whispered to

Venn. "The one who seemed to be searching the area where the shadow was."

Venn gave a curt nod without taking her eyes from Faron. "Ayen."

"The good magistrate," Prince Faron began, his voice grave, "has given us the dates and descriptions of those who have disappeared, as well as the locations where the survivors were found. And he has told us where the bodies were discovered. We have doubled our patrols near the ravine. As of dawn tomorrow, two ranger units will be doing an exhaustive search of the woods to complement your own search efforts."

Kate leaned closer to Venn. "Your childhood friend, who happens to be the prince of the White Wood, is the ambassador to the humans—something I didn't know existed, since the elven king doesn't seem fond of humans—and is working with the one elf who might have insight into the shadow Bo was running from? And you didn't think that was worth mentioning?"

"There has never been an ambassador to the humans." Venn's fingers clenched. "Certainly not Faron." Her attention flickered to Ayen for a breath. The ranger captain met her gaze and inclined his head. She looked away without responding. "And you know everything I do about Ayen's involvement."

"It's Renault's curse!" someone called out.

A flicker of surprise crossed Faron's face, and he opened his mouth.

"Could the monster from the ravine be a trullen?" a wiry young man yelled before the prince could speak.

Faron's eyebrow twitched at the question, but he took a moment to consider both people. "We haven't found signs of any creature from the ravine."

A ripple of mutters and snorts of disbelief rolled through the room.

"Then what hurt my son?" the mother near him demanded, pointing at Gerren, who still looked vacantly across the room.

Faron took in the young man. "My rangers will find out," he assured her.

"It's a trullen," the wiry man repeated, sullenly. "It moves in shadows and destroys the minds of its victims."

No one objected, and Faron glanced around the tavern. "You all think this?"

"Lark was fishing on the river and saw a shadow that moved," the same man said. "Moved unnaturally."

Faron's brow drew together. "Where?"

The room turned to look at an old man seated at the bar.

"Past the sharp turn with the three rocks," he said, fixing the elf with an accusing look. "On your side of the river. In your trees."

"We'll investigate there, too. Has anyone else seen it? Or anything else unusual?"

"It's not a trullen," Maven said from where she still sat at the door. "It's a traptyr. You can't find it in your forest because it blends with the other trees. Until it finds a victim, steals their minds, and draws them in for the kill."

Faron hesitated before he answered. "We don't believe trap-tyrs are real. They seem to be a story created by the mixing of two different creatures, a borrey, which is very real, and thankfully very rare, and a forest troll, who does, from a distance, resemble a tree. Both creatures have a humming call that can confuse the mind—"

"My grandmother saw a traptyr!" Maven snapped. "Are you telling me she's a liar? Or she saw...what? A borrey?"

"If she'd seen a borrey," Faron said calmly, "she would not have lived to tell of it." He cleared his throat and turned to look at Ayen. "We will mention the idea of a traptyr to the rangers."

Ayen kept his face unreadable and gave a nod of acknowl-edgment.

"How long until you find our boys?" someone called. "You're supposed to be patrolling those eerie woods of yours."

"Curtis," Yellow said, a note of warning in his voice, "the elven prince is here as our guest. Mind your tongue."

The prince gave Yellow a nod of thanks and turned back to Curtis. "I cannot say how long it will take, but we have been patrolling regularly and will increase our search at first light. Our patrol will continue to search every day until they are found."

"And what if more go missing?" someone else asked.

"Maybe we should question her!" Gerren's mother shoved herself to her feet and jabbed a finger at Kate. "She knows Bo!"

Every face in the room swung around.

Kate held the mother's gaze and cleared her throat in the sudden simmering silence of the room. "I'm afraid I know nothing more than that my brother is missing as well," she answered. A rumble of mutters filled the room, and Kate found the prince's sharp eyes gauging her. His attention moved to Venn for a breath before settling back on Kate.

"I knew Bo too," Yellow said over the noise. "He came here often and sat at my tables. Plenty of us knew him."

The magistrate stepped back up onto his chair. "We will explore every avenue of investigation," he said loudly, slowly drawing the eyes of the room back to himself. "Human and elven. For now, the good elves are helping in every way they can, and we are grateful. I will stay in communication with Prince Faron and keep everyone appraised of the progress."

"If anyone sees anything else that may be of use," Faron said, "please notify the magistrate so he can get word to me imme-diately."

Kate leaned toward Venn again. "Do the elves usually help this much?"

Venn looked between Faron and Ayen. "Not without a reason."

Prince Faron cleared his throat again. "I hate to bring up another topic when your town is dealing with such trouble, but the Surn continues to sour."

"The river?" Kate whispered.

Venn nodded.

"I wanted to inform you," Faron said, "that four elves will begin a cleansing ritual a league upstream from Home, and we would ask that any washing or dumping into the river be moved downstream, past the narrows." There were some grumbles throughout the room, and he raised his voice to speak above them. "This will ensure that the water reaching your town cistern is clean."

"A fair request," the magistrate announced. "Thank you for your help with it. Do we know the source of the souring?"

"Not yet, but when the cleansing is done, we will know more."

"Why do the elves care about the river?" Kate asked quietly.

"There are wellstones in it," Venn answered.

Kate turned to look at her in surprise. "There are?"

"Uncut ones. They form in the northern mountains, but they flow down the river. Not a lot of them, but enough that we like to make sure the river stays clean and free-flowing."

"What's a wellstone?" Silas asked.

"A clear stone," Kate answered.

"Valuable?" Tribal asked.

"Not to you," Kate answered. "Unless you have some magical aptitude we don't know about and a need to store research and information."

Tribal glanced at his brother. "Sounds valuable."

The magistrate cleared his throat. "That concludes our meeting. All washing and dumping are to be moved past the narrows.

409

Thank you, Ambassador. We will let you go about your preparations for tomorrow's search. And hope it is a quick one."

The room broke into dozens of individual conversations as people rose and began to leave. The glances they cast toward Kate varied from suspicious to threatening.

Tribal leaned toward her. "Might be a good idea to head out of Home sooner rather than later, Twig."

"This is where Bo was," she answered.

"This is where Bo disappeared. From the looks of things, the town would like the same fate for you." He gestured to himself and Silas. "We've found it's always better to disappear on our own terms."

Faron headed for their table, and Venn let out a low sound that was almost a growl.

The prince gave a polite nod to the dwarves and a more curious one to Kate as he stopped. His remnant flooded the air, drowning out both dwarves and even overwhelming Venn's forest sounds and scents, although it was similar enough that Kate had to work to tell the two apart. While Venn's forest was the Wildwood of Kate's childhood, with birches and oaks mixed with the pines, the soft leafy smell of ferns and the scuttle of small creatures, Faron's was more crisp.

The resinous, almost lemon scent of pine trees rolled around her, and she drew back slightly at the strength of it. The vast bracing blue of mountain skies. Her fingertips tingled as though they touched the brittle crystals of hoarfrost, spiked along the edges of dark green needles, catching the sun in brilliant glitters of light.

She gripped the arms of her chair to banish the feeling in her fingers, focusing on the coppery shimmer of Faron's face, which at least seemed to be actually visible, instead of part of his remnant.

The prince met Venn's eyes. "I…" He swallowed and gave a

pained-looking smile, stuck somewhere between nervousness and curiosity. "I didn't expect you back. How long are you here?"

Venn stayed back in her chair, her arms crossed. *"You're* the ambassador?"

His smile faded. "I have always only wanted what was best for both the Wood and the humans."

Venn gave him a flat look. "Your father approved this?"

The elf prince's shoulders stiffened almost imperceptibly. "The king is in full support of my actions."

Venn let out a huff of disbelief. "You expect me to believe there's something hunting humans near the White Wood and you don't know what it is?"

Faron glanced at the dwarves and Kate, then lowered his voice. "Whatever has taken these people, my rangers can find no trace of it." He paused. "We could use your help, Venn."

"I'm not helping you," she said flatly.

"Even if it's for the humans?"

"It's time you got back on your side of the river, your highness," Venn said curtly.

The prince shifted, irritation creasing his brow. "We should talk, Venn."

"I have nothing to say to you, and you can say nothing I want to hear."

He let out a sigh. "You have to come eventually."

"We're not staying in Home," Venn said, as though he hadn't spoken, "so there's no reason for us to meet again. Go do your father's bidding, Faron, and stay away from me."

CHAPTER FORTY-FOUR

PRINCE FARON GAVE Venn one last aggravated look before striding toward the door. Ayen held it open, and Faron stepped out into the darkness, glowing like molten copper before he disappeared from view. Ayen gave Venn a slight nod, which she did not return, and left as well. The door swung closed with a thunk, shutting out the night.

Venn let out her breath and rubbed a hand across her face.

"What was that about?" Kate asked.

Before she could answer, Yellow came to the table, picking up their empty plates. Most of the tavern had emptied, but the few who remained gathered in small knots, occasionally sending dark looks toward their table.

"Thank you for the food," Kate said to him. "Tell me what I owe you, and we'll be off."

The innkeeper gave a reluctant sigh. "It's too late to find something else tonight, 'specially with all the trouble around lately. Take some rooms here, and you can head out in the morning."

Kate glanced at Maven, who still glowered at her from near the door. "I think the town would rather see us gone."

"Well, this ain't the town—it's my tavern and my rooms. No one'll bother you here." He pulled two keys out of his pocket and pointed his thumb over his shoulder at the stairs running up the wall past the bar. "Your room's available, Venn, and the one across the hall, Weasel Brothers. Don't steal anything out of it."

"Steal?" Tribal asked, sounding offended.

"We would never, Yellow," Silas said. "And thank you. It's been a bit since we had a bed to sleep on."

Tribal turned to Venn. "You have a specific room here?"

"Don't you?" she asked.

Yellow pointed his dishrag in Kate's direction. "Tomorrow, you need to find somewhere else, though."

"Thank you," Kate said

"The beds have thick blankets, but there are always extras down near the fireplace if you get cold," Yellow offered as he took their dishes toward the kitchen.

A thin man with hunched shoulders pulled out a chair at the bar, and Kate lowered her voice. "Isn't that the father of the boy who was in here earlier? Gerren?"

Silas glanced over. "That's Nevin. A man who appreciates a good drink of log mead."

Venn's eyes narrowed at Kate. "Why?"

The table where his family had sat during the meeting was empty, and Kate shifted. "His boy was one of the ones missing, so he might know something that could help us."

"No." Venn shook her head. "Whatever you're thinking, don't do it."

The few paces between Kate and the bar stretched out uncomfortably far, and she could still hear the hatred in Nevin's wife's voice. Her husband was bound to feel the same.

She pushed the thought aside and kept her attention on the

man himself. His elbows rested on the bar, his shoulders hunched forward and his head hanging down over a dark bottle of log mead. "I'm going to talk to him."

Tribal stared at her. "Are you trying to get yourself killed?"

Silas pulled his amulet over his head. "At least take this."

Tribal batted his hand down. "What are you doing? Don't give her that!"

"I'm going to feel a sense of obligation to step in when the man attacks her, but that puts us against the town, which I don't want, so I'd rather it didn't happen. Maybe this will help her convince him."

"We have no obligation to her," Tribal said. "And if you help her and we lose our access to log mead, I will personally knock you out."

Silas snorted. "You could try."

"I hate to agree with the dwarves," Venn said in a low voice, leaning her elbows on the table, "but this is a terrible idea. If you have a question, see if Yellow can answer it. Or find someone less directly related to this mess. Someone whose wife doesn't clearly want to make you pay for everything."

Kate looked at Nevin. "That poor man lost his son, spent days terrified he was dead, and now, instead of waking up from that nightmare, he's trapped in a different form of it. Nevin is not our enemy, and Bo isn't his. I'm not walking around this town as though either of those things are true when they're not."

Venn shook her head with a tight, urgent motion. "You will never get him to trust you, Kate."

The thought of walking over to the man and bearing the brunt of the anger he would turn on her almost kept her in her seat, but she repeated the Shield's words to herself. *The only key I've ever found for getting someone to trust me is to trust them first.*

"I got you to trust me." Kate pushed back her chair and stood.

"Who says I trust you?" Venn asked.

Kate kept her focus on the exhausted bow of Nevin's shoulders, the air of defeat that hung heavily on him, the endless feel of waiting that he had. She latched on to the familiarity of that pain. "There's enough fear and blame to go around without imagining it where it doesn't exist." She started across the room toward him.

"When this goes badly," Tribal muttered to his brother, "you stay out of it."

Kate reached the bar and hesitated by the stool next to Nevin. He didn't look up.

"Hi," she said quietly. "I'm Kate."

He twitched and looked at her, his eyes rimmed with red. When he recognized who she was, his expression hardened.

Kate held up her hands. "I know you don't want to talk to me and that everyone blames Bo for what happened. And maybe he did cause all this, but I just want to find my brother the way you wanted to find your son."

His face didn't soften, and his hand clenched around his bottle.

"Head up to your room," Yellow said quietly from behind Kate. She hadn't heard him approach, and she twitched at his voice. "Or find somewhere else to sleep."

Nevin's eyes were filled with anger and disgust, and words defending Bo and herself rose to Kate's lips, but she pushed them back. "My younger brother, Evan," she said quietly enough that only Nevin and Yellow could hear, "disappeared when I was twelve. Two men came and chased us and…" She swallowed. "I tried to stop them, but I lost consciousness. When I woke up, Evan was gone."

Nevin's eyes narrowed the slightest bit.

Kate closed her hands against the pain that had ripped through her palms that day. "Bo and I have spent twenty years looking for him," Kate continued, her voice low. "Maybe he died that day and they tossed his body in the river. That makes more sense than strangers taking him, and yet I can't stop looking. I..." She met Nevin's angry gaze, forcing herself to continue. "It would be easier to believe he was killed. It would be less painful to just accept that he's been dead all this time. Then I could stop the endless hoping that I'll find him."

Nevin's face twitched, but he didn't speak.

"It's the hope that's the painful part," she whispered. "Because if I hope he's still alive, then I can't escape the fear that he's still trapped and still in pain."

Nevin's hands gripped the bottle. His eyes grew wet, but he didn't look away.

"I have no reason to believe my younger brother is still alive, except that I can't accept that he's not." She paused. "Neither could Bo."

Yellow set a huge hand on Kate's shoulder. "That's enough."

"And now Bo is gone too," Kate continued, the words coming faster and sounding more desperate. "And I don't know why or where. I have no idea what happened to him or if he's..." She tried to take a step closer to the man, but Yellow's hand tightened and held her back. "You found Gerren. Maybe, if we can find Bo too, we'll get more answers. Find a way to help your son."

Nevin's face was etched in fury, but a tear slipped out of one eye.

Kate blinked back the wetness in her own eyes. "Bo would never have intentionally put any of you in danger. Whatever hurt your people hurt him too."

"Enough," Yellow repeated, pulling her away.

"Please." The word came out in a whisper as the huge man dragged her back. "I just need to know if Bo's alive."

"Wait." Nevin's voice was hoarse.

Yellow stopped but didn't release his hold.

"What do you want?" Nevin asked, his face still hard.

417

"Will you just tell me about when your son disappeared? I'll tell you everything I know about Bo before he went missing. Maybe we can help each other."

Nevin studied her for a long moment through weary, red-rimmed eyes, then nodded to Yellow.

The barkeeper released his hold. "Best be careful," he warned Kate, and then returned to cleaning tables.

Kate shifted her shoulder against the ache his hand had left. "Thank you," she said to Nevin.

He turned back to the bar without answering.

Kate glanced back at her table. Silas watched her with concern, Tribal with disapproval, and Venn sat back in her chair with an unreadable expression. Kate took the stool next to Nevin. "Does Gerren remember anything about while he was gone?"

Nevin ran his thumb over the side of the bottle of log mead. "He don't remember anything since the harvest." His voice was guarded, but there was a note of desperation in it. "Like the last few months didn't even happen. But ain't that so much as... He's..." He stared at the bottle. "He's still gone. He's not in his own head anymore. It's like he's always asleep."

Kate almost asked where Gerren had disappeared, but the pain in Nevin's face was too raw. "I hear Gerren helps you on the farm. Seems like you raised a good young man."

Nevin didn't answer.

"It's been a fortnight since you found him?" she asked instead. "Have any of his memories returned?"

"His younger sister got him to remember a day when they found a bird with a broken wing." Nevin's voice was dull. "For a few minutes, it almost seemed like he cared, but then...Remembering one day out of a hundred ain't enough."

"He remembered the bird?" Kate glanced back toward the table where her pack sat. Venn, Tribal, and Silas were all still

418

watching her closely. She turned back to Nevin. "Have you shared other memories with him?"

"We tried. Can't just stick a memory in someone's head, though."

Kate ran her fingernail along a groove in the wood of the bar. Among talk of monsters and curses, a magical serum that transferred memories might not be well received. "My home is on the other side of the mountains. I'm part of a group of people called Keepers." She watched his face for any recognition, but he stayed looking dully at his drink. "I have spent a lot of years researching memories and how they work. If you'd like, I can take a look at Gerren. Maybe there's a way to help him remember."

He turned toward her, his expression suspicious. "What do you want with my son?"

"Nothing but to help him." A candle flickered in a dish just across the bar, and her fingers itched to pull a bit of flame off it. "In the ravine, Bo was looking for signs of the last Kalesh emperor who died mysteriously three hundred years ago. He'd followed clues to that place, and he and the men from here were just trying to dig up old relics." She looked at Nevin. "Do you know anything about an old emperor?"

He shook his head and took a drink of his mead, returning to staring at the bottle. "Don't know nothing about that ravine except that it's cursed. Folk bring trouble down when they meddle in magic. Ain't nothing good in any of it."

She folded her hands together and ignored the flame. "You think there's magic involved?"

He gave her a sidelong look. "Don't you?"

She gave a small shrug. "Bo sent me a message after the rockslide. He thought a monster had caused the slide, and a shadow was tracking him in the woods."

Nevin turned to look at her, his eyes narrowing dangerously. "Shadow of what?"

"I don't know, but I plan to find out."

Nevin pushed himself up from his stool. "You should go back home and stay away from all this." He dropped a coin on the counter. "Stay away from my boy. My wife'll kill you if you come close, and I won't stop her." He turned and headed for the door.

"What did Gerren do in the ravine?" Kate called after him.

Nevin's hands rolled into fists, and he turned to glare at her. "My boy didn't go to the ravine."

Kate stood up. "What?"

Nevin shook his head. "Bo bought some eggs from us once, and he and Gerren got to talking, and he discovered my boy's good at drawing pictures. He invited him to help map the ravine, but Gerren's not that stupid. He never went close to that place. He helped Bo one day here at the Pig, organizing some papers and redrawing some maps, but that's all." His jaw clenched. "Guess that was close enough." He turned and shoved the door open and disappeared into the night.

Kate stared after him for a moment, then crossed to where Venn and the dwarves sat. "If Gerren never worked in the ravine, then…"

"It's not the ravine that really connects everyone," Venn said.

Kate sank into her chair. "What if it's Bo?"

CHAPTER FORTY-FIVE

"Wait," Tribal said quietly. "All the people here who've gone missing or ended up damaged or dead…You're saying your brother's the reason why, not the ravine itself?"

Kate glanced at Venn. "Maybe?"

"Let's change tables," Tribal said to Silas.

His twin gave him a confused look.

"We need to distance ourselves from this woman quickly." Tribal pushed his chair back.

"Too late." Venn looked toward the bar. "Yellow! How much do we owe you for the log mead for our good friend Tribal?"

Tribal shushed her, but Silas leaned forward, his face concerned. "If it's true that Bo is the cause of all this, you two might actually want to leave town soon."

"We're leaving tomorrow morning," Kate said, standing. "Venn'll show me the last few places she knew Bo was, and we'll see what that turns up." She held a hand out to Silas. "Thank you for the shortcut through the tunnels."

"Don't shake her hand," Tribal whispered.

Silas reached out with a smile. "Our pleasure. It's been a while since we ruffled so many feathers. We'll be staying around Home for another week or so, if you run into trouble anywhere. Gonna give the gov'nor a little longer to cool off before we head home."

Kate held her hand out to Tribal, but he shook his head. "If you run into trouble, solve it on your own."

"And if we discover any treasure in the ravine?" Kate asked.

He narrowed his eyes and took her hand for a quick shake. "Then we'll be here drinking log mead."

Venn wrinkled her nose and stood. "Disgusting." She started for the stairs along the wall by the fireplace. Kate picked up her pack and followed.

The upstairs hall was narrow and lit only by a couple of small lanterns on a shelf at the top of the stairs. It held only four doors, one of which was open, allowing moving lantern light to spill into the hallway. Kate reached the doorway in time to see Venn sink down onto one of two very small beds.

Kate pushed the door closed behind her before sitting on the other. The window was cracked open, and the trailing end of a branch from a skinny pine outside had been pulled through, hanging within arm's reach of Venn.

Kate took in the branch and the cold air sneaking in around it and pulled her cloak around herself. "Another night of camping, I see," she said with a tired smile.

Venn frowned at her. "Yellow said we could stay here."

Kate gestured to the window. "I didn't mean literal..." She shook her head. "Never mind. I see why this is your room. Yellow knows you need the branch?"

Venn lay on her back and threw an arm over her eyes. "I'm the only elf who ever stays here. He probably thinks we all want the room closest to the tree."

Kate watched her for a moment. "What happened downstairs?"

There was no answer.

422

"Your very alive childhood friend is the prince of the White Wood?"

Still no answer.

"His remnant is..." Kate shook her head. "It drowned yours out before he was even at the table. I've never felt anything like it. I could *feel* the frost in it."

"Because he's cold and heartless." Venn's voice was tinged with anger.

"No," Kate said slowly. "If it weren't for your reaction, I would think he was a reasonably good person. Or elf. Or whatever. He is the embodiment of an alpine forest. Much like you embody a forest more like the Wildwood."

Venn made an annoyed growly sound.

"Is it because he's a prince that he's so...bright?"

"Irritating, isn't it?"

"I was going to say impressive." Kate shifted on the thin mattress. It smelled faintly of wool and had some well-defined lumps. "Care to explain why the prince of the White Wood believes you'll have to come to him at some point?"

"No."

Kate dropped her pack on the floor. "How about yes? Who is he to you?"

Venn didn't move.

Kate sat forward. "Venn—"

"He's my betrothed."

Kate straightened. "What? You're betrothed to the prince of the White Wood? You were close to him long ago but now have an intense hostility toward him, even though he doesn't seem to share it?"

Venn grunted in agreement.

"No grunting. Explain. You obviously don't want to marry him now. Why not?"

She let out a long sigh. "I would love to explain, Kate, but I can't." She cracked one eye open. "Not I *won't*. I *can't*. Don't bother asking again. The royal house has too much authority."

"Too much…" Kate stared at her. "He swore you to silence?"

Venn closed her eye again.

"Is he…" Kate paused. "Is he sincere in his offer to help these people? Or did he just lie to them all?"

"I'm sure he's sincere."

"But should they trust him? What if he's part of the—"

"He's not killing humans, Kate," Venn said, finally looking at her. "He's too honorable and likes humans too much to knowingly hurt them."

"But what if—"

"If he says his rangers can't find any trace of a creature, he's telling the truth. He, himself, was never particularly adept at speaking to the trees, but some of his rangers are. Ayen is particularly good."

"That's why he wanted you? Because you can speak to the trees better than the rest of them? Even the elven rangers?"

Venn turned to look up at the ceiling but didn't disagree.

"Could you get more information from the trees than they can?"

"I intend to. Just not while working with Faron." She sighed. "These people are right. This mess began with Bo in that canyon. If we can figure out what happened to him…"

Kate lay down on her bed. The pillow was thin and filled with barely enough feathers to differentiate itself from the lumpy mattress. The top of the lantern had been pierced with star-shaped holes, and the flickering light made stars jump and tremble on the ceiling.

Kate ran over everything they knew, and the dark worry that had been holding back pushed its way forward.

"The first people from the town to go missing were found dead," she said quietly. "And Bo was taken before them…"

"He's not dead," Venn said, her voice firm.

"How do you know that? We don't know anything except that, one"—she held up a finger—"someone caused that rockslide, their remnant was all over that hillside, even now, so they weren't human. Or even elf. As strong as your remnant is, Venn, it wouldn't linger six weeks later. And two"—she raised another finger—"whatever that shadow is, it's real, it bleeds, even the elves don't know what it is, and it was definitely after Bo."

Venn looked pointedly at Kate. "Do you think he's dead?"

Kate breathed out an aggravated sigh. "No. But what is that aside from desperate hope?"

"It's an intuition of a Keeper." Venn lay back. "And the intuition of this elf says the same thing. Bo is somewhere. We just need to find him."

Kate pushed herself up to her elbow. "We?"

"You'll hardly find him on your own."

"What happened to not wanting to be around me or the box?"

Venn looked over at Kate. "I thought Nevin was going to…I don't know what. At the least get Yellow to throw us out. I don't know what you said to him, but it took a lot of courage to do it."

"He wasn't dangerous, just hurt."

"Those two things often overlap. Regardless, I admit there's something going on here, and this town isn't going to figure it out on its own. And neither will you. But I admire that you'd try."

Kate sat up. She pulled her journal out of her pack and spread it open to the story map she'd started before the tunnels, the web connecting between Bo and the shadow and the rockslide. She wrote "Renault the Mad" in an empty spot, then glanced up at Venn. "You don't trust Faron to figure it out either, do you?"

"I told you not to ask. For once, quell your insatiable desire to know everything. I can't speak about it."

"Can you give me a hint?"

You don't understand how elven authority works.

425

Kate glanced down to see Crofftus crawl out from under a flap in her pack. "I know it's more binding than human authority."

It is. If an elf in authority gives an order, the elves are compelled to follow it.

"It's more complicated than that," Venn said.

"You can't resist a command?"

If the elf has enough authority, their commands are only resisted at great personal cost.

Venn didn't argue with the clarification.

"And Faron commanded you to be silent about something?"

Venn shook her head but said nothing

Since the situation involves the prince, it is safe to assume whatever command was given to Venn came from the king or queen. Such a command is deeply binding to any elf in their community.

"What happens if they break it?"

The command is wrapped up in the threads that bind the elves together. If the command is broken, the threads are broken.

Kate turned to look at Venn. "You'd be cast out from your people?"

Venn let out an annoyed breath.

Not cast out, not the way a human would be. Crofftus flew with a buzzing of wings to the table. *Elves are intrinsically connected to each other—and all life, really. That is the source of the intuition they have, most powerfully into the minds and hearts of other elves, but to a limited extent also with humans. They gain strength from each other. Much like they are connected to the forest, their very life, their* ael'iza, *is intertwined with each other's.* He paused. *There is a simplicity to the idea that pleases me. A hearkening to the true meaning of community.*

Venn's brow creased even deeper. "Said by a beetle who wanders the animal world alone."

Breaking trust breaks community, Crofftus continued, his voice slightly airier and more scholarly, as though her objection wasn't worth addressing. *An elf alone is considerably weaker than an elf among their people.*

Kate glanced at Venn and tapped her fingers on her leg. "So you don't trust Faron because you're not sure what the king has really commanded him."

Venn just closed her eyes and sighed.

"This doesn't give me much faith in the assistance of the elves," Kate said.

Nor should it. Crofftus climbed to the back of the table, then spread his wings and buzzed up to the windowsill. *The townsfolk are similarly skeptical. I moved among their tables. More than half of them are leery of Faron, and many outright suspect the elves of duplicity.*

Venn shifted to her side. "The elves have no reason to hurt humans. They take their role as protectors very seriously."

Are you saying elves have never hurt humans?

Venn's expression hardened. "These two groups have lived near each other for centuries. They've both hurt each other."

Crofftus crawled to the windowsill and turned to look at Kate. He twitched as though he was going to speak, then crawled a little closer. *What are you writing?*

Kate glanced down at her journal. "I'm attempting to map out how this story fits together."

He made a thoughtful sort of hum. *Maybe it's not a web. Maybe it's a tree. Maybe the shadow and the emperor and Renault are all different branches, and they're merely connected by the trunk of everything happening in this area.*

Kate considered the page, tracing the connections between the different sections. "If it weren't for Bo, I could see that. But somehow he connects them all."

Or maybe Renault does. He's a bridge between the elves and humans. He lived outside the Wood, like a human, but supposedly was adept at elven runelight.

Kate looked between the beetle and Venn. "Runelight? The way elves anchor *vitalle* to objects?"

Indeed. Renault is rumored to have had greater success with runelight than most elves. It was runelight that supposedly allowed his amulet to store life itself.

Kate glanced at Venn. "I had no idea elves used runes so extensively."

"They don't anymore," Venn said. "They haven't for centuries."

You use runes, Crofftus pointed out.

Venn covered her sleeve with her hand. "I forgot you were eavesdropping when I told Kate about my tattoo."

I wasn't eavesdropping.

"You were sneaking around and listening," Venn said. "Which is eavesdropping. And these aren't runelight. Runelight is a specific sort of rune, and it's created and fueled by the elf themself. Mine were created by my aunt and are fueled by things outside of me. And mine don't light up when they're activated."

"That explains the 'light' part of 'runelight,'" Kate said.

"It's an antiquated sort of magic that's fallen out of use." Venn looked at Crofftus. "And Renault was never a bridge between humans and elves. He barely had anything to do with the elves at all."

Crofftus hummed again. *Everything in this part of the world has to do with elves. You should never leave them out of the story. The White Wood is old and has secrets that bleed into every story that happens in these parts. Be careful of them, Kate.*

"Are you telling her to be careful of me?" Venn asked mildly.

He crawled through the opening in the window next to the tree branch, his black form disappearing into the night, his voice drifting behind him. *Are you part of the White Wood?*

Kate watched the open gap in the window, but he didn't reappear. "Crofftus?" The sound of his remnant faded away. She glanced at Venn and lowered her voice. "What do you make of him?"

"With my intuitive connection to all living things?" Venn asked, looking after him into the darkness. "He's pompous and strange, but he does seem to have a decent amount of knowledge about things."

"His description of the elves was accurate?"

"Reasonably, but more negatively worded than the ideas deserve." She glanced at Kate. "And that's saying something, because I feel negatively about them."

Kate listened again for his remnant, but she could only hear Venn's. "He doesn't seem to hold elves in very high esteem."

"Or Keepers." Venn looked thoughtfully out the window. "He also feels lonely."

"Even now that he's attached himself to us?"

"Not that sort of loneliness." Venn frowned. "He feels like he's far away from us. From everyone. Not physically, but somehow still alone."

Kate nodded. "His remnant is...distant."

"Is it dangerous?"

Kate considered the question. "It's not thunder. It's ocean waves crashing against something huge. A cliff, maybe. It's strong. Relentless, but not dangerous or malevolent. It has an impersonal feel, though."

Venn considered the words. "Do you believe he's with us just because he's intrigued by your serums?"

"Maybe. He definitely has some knowledge of the field, and life as an animal must get dull. He could just be looking for something interesting to do."

Venn let out a snort. "You don't believe that."

Kate smiled. "No. I think he wants something from us."

"I think he wants something from you."

Kate squinted out the window. "I think you're right. I'm just not sure what it is yet." She turned back to Venn. "Do you think the elves are hurting people?"

Venn met her eyes. "I don't know, but I honestly cannot think of any reason they would."

"All right." Kate flipped through the pages of her journal. "Then tomorrow we'll start figuring out who is."

CHAPTER FORTY-SIX

ON A FRESH JOURNAL PAGE, Kate listed out everything she knew of Renault Half-Elven and his Oziv Amulet. He connected to the rockslide and the shadow and a curse. He connected to the caves the dwarves said were under the rockslide, which were the same caves Bo had been in and where the tree creature was supposedly buried.

For a mage who lived hundreds of years ago, he had a remarkable number of connections to things happening today. "I don't think it's a tree, Crofftus," she said quietly. She let her eyes wander around the connections on her map for a bit longer, but nothing important stood out to her.

Setting it aside, she pulled Bo's journal out of her pack. It fell open to a page filled with his small writing. Kate opened the door of the lantern and stretched a strand of *vitalle* over to the flame, pulled a bit of it onto her fingers. The snip of flame danced above her hand like a little knot of warmth. She fed *vitalle* into it until it brightened, and she moved it out to her fingertip.

She held her finger out over Bo's journal and smiled. "I have missed fire and enough light to read by."

Venn stretched her own hand toward the flame in the lantern, her brow creased in concentration. "I don't know how you move the fire. I can feel it, not alive, but almost alive. But I can't take hold of it."

"Well, I don't know how you talk to trees." Kate glanced up at the elf. "Do you want me to show you what I do?"

Venn's eyes stayed fixed on the lantern. "I don't think it will do any good. I can sense your *ael'iza*, and it flows like water. You push it into things or draw it out. Mine is like…the way sap moves in a tree. Or the way sunshine warms your skin."

"That make sense. When you touch a plant, the shift of *vitalle* between you is very subtle. More like communicating with it than acting upon it "

Venn watched the flame thoughtfully. "That's a good description. Elven *ael'iza* grows from our connection to the forest. We can communicate with each other and sense things through it. We can even heal each other through it. Well, others can. I've never been able to. Mine seems to only work well with trees."

"But runelight is different?" Kate asked.

"It was a way to affect the world outside of our connection to it. It was never used widely, though. Most elves don't have the inclination to learn. We are content with our community and the way we are intertwined with the forest. Runelight has always felt more…" She looked up at Kate. "It's always felt more human. Do Keepers all have similar magic to yours?"

"Most of us can do a core set of things, like pushing *vitalle* into things to make them hot. We each seem to have different strengths. Gerone and Mikal are older—they can do surprising things like move water or air. Will can use it to sense people's emotions and even share his with them. Alaric is good at moving it with nuance and in ways no Keeper has ever tried. Sini can actually feel the energy in the sunlight and harness it." Kate shook her head. "The amount of power she can wield is dizzying, but she can't use it without help from someone else."

"And you?"

Kate glanced down at her book. "I don't know. I have very middling skills. I can heal and move energy like the others. I'm better with fire than most, though."

"The shell you made around us to keep out the vimwisps was impressive."

"I'm better at that too, actually. It's just a wall of *vitalle* that absorbs what hits it instead of letting it pass through, and I've never used it for anything like the wisps before."

"What do you usually do with it?"

Kate let out a little laugh. "This." She spread a shield of *vitalle* over the top of the lantern, then shaped it into a tunnel that led to Venn on one side and herself on the other. The heat from the little flame rolled up against the shield and spread to the sides until the warmth washed over her, along with the subtle smell of her own remnant.

Venn gave a small smile. "That I can do."

Kate let the shield dissipate, and Venn closed her eyes. A wave of heat pressed against the side of Kate's face nearest the branch, then moved slowly across her like a bubble of warm air. "Is that from the tree?"

"They absorb a lot of heat from the sun and the ground, even in winter."

"Is it hard to keep up?"

Venn shook her head. "Once I create it, it stays almost on its own."

"Mine too. Other Keepers have to work hard to keep their shields, but the hard part of mine is the creation of it."

Kate shifted closer to the branch until she was fully inside the sphere of its warmth. It wasn't hot like the candle flame. This was like a mild spring day. "Well, at least we shouldn't freeze to death if it takes a while to find Bo."

"Do all Keepers do that?" Venn pointed to the story map.

"Things like it. We spend a lot more of our time deciphering, recording, and sharing history than we do using magic. I like this part, sorting out the complex pieces into a cohesive story."

"That looks more like a mess than a story."

Kate's eyes traced the connections. "It's not a mess—it's a map. I just have to figure out how to follow it."

"If you say so." Venn lay back down and reached her hand out to rub her fingers over the end of the branch.

"If I don't understand the whole story, there's no way to know the best decisions to make about it. If I know how or if Renault connects to Bo, it can help me decide how best to look for him."

Venn gave the page a sidelong glance. "You can never understand every detail."

"I can try."

The elf gave a little huff of laughter. "Sometimes you have to act before you know the whole story, or it will be too late."

"What do you hear when you touch the tree?"

Venn was quiet for a long moment. "The life of the entire forest." Some of the irritation that had creased the elf's brow since she'd seen Faron smoothed away.

Kate flipped through the pages of Bo's journal until she caught sight of the word "Emperor." The entry was dated nearly two months ago, on the 13th of Zemny.

Home is a cozy little town, Ria. You'd like it. I'm staying at an inn called the Blind Pig, which also happens to be the only inn. For a place named after a pig, the pork is awful, but the rest of the food is homey fare. Which I suppose is fitting in the town of Home.

I'm sitting in a small room with nothing but a lantern, feeling oddly unhappy. I've been in town a day and learned the local legend of the great emperor who died in a cursed ravine nearby. I even finally got directions to the ravine out of the blacksmith. No one was willing to take me there. Apparently, they never go there at all. This whole corner of the world holds their superstitions close. Of course, if rumors are true, an unsettling number of monsters come south into the White Wood and are held at bay by the elves.

I'm rambling because I don't want to admit my real trouble.

I can't open the box again, and I am unreasonably frustrated by this. I have tried every day since I first did it. It's been eight days, and I've only managed to open it twice. The last time was five days ago, when I realized keeping my journal in it was a stupid decision.

It calls to me. I keep fiddling with it, wanting to open it again. Except I feel more…something than hope. Something I can't name. A sort of hunger, maybe. What secrets is it holding?

Kate paused at the words. *Calls to me.* She looked toward her pack. The box did call to her, very subtly.

But it's more than the box…

I searched, Ria. I really did. I went to every town near the monastery where I discovered the box, talked to every person, interviewed every town gossip I could find, and found nothing. They knew the monastery had burned. It was three springs ago that the fire happened, and there were two very old men who escaped imprisonment there and made their way to the nearest town. They both died of injuries soon after. The people who cared for them in their last days said the other prisoners at the monastery were a young cook, no older than eighteen, who'd served the head cleric bad eggs, and a young woman accused of witchcraft. They'd heard nothing of a foreign man in his thirties.

And so I'm here in Home, following the trail of good old Emperor Sorrn, but my heart isn't in it.

I can't help fearing that I missed something. Some sign that

Evan was there. Some indication as to whether the clerics at this monastery were the ones who took the box from us.

I've spent my life searching for clues to different mysteries, and yet in this one, I have utterly failed.

Were you with me, I would never say it, but here, in a dark night in a foreign land that is growing closer to winter by the day, it feels as though even you may not be real anymore.

Were you here with me, I'd never say it, but I must. I must put out the thought that keeps haunting me.

I think Evan is dead. I think my search for him will never end because there is nothing to find.

And I cannot stop wondering how my brother died and whether he suffered, all alone among strangers.

I hope you never read this, Ria. And I hope that wherever you are, you still have a way to believe he's alive.

Kate let the flame on her fingertip flicker out and touched the locket at her neck.

I think Evan is dead.

She heard the words as though Bo had whispered them in her ear, and she squeezed her eyes shut against them.

But they sank into her until they echoed somewhere vast and hollow and dark. The place deep inside that she skirted every time she didn't quite catch Evan's remnant in the locket and every time the box reminded her of the day he was taken. The words dragged her down into the blackness with them and then faded to a dull, heavy silence.

Bo's voice was gone. If it had ever been real. If it hadn't been just another echo. She stood alone, surrounded by the vast emptiness that should have held so much. In the space that should have held the memories she would have shared with Evan. The moments stolen from her.

Something rustled in the darkness behind her, the merest whisper of sound.

She didn't turn to face it. That was always here. Starving, but not dying. Doggedly crawling on scraped and bleeding knees toward something it could never reach. Following the barest threads forward, grasping at thin air, surviving on the last crumbs of hope.

It wasn't the wretched part of herself she couldn't face. It was the hope she couldn't bear to look at. The painful hope.

Kate tried to shove herself out of the darkness, but a new emptiness pushed the edges further away. One that had been teased at before, an idea that had lurked in her fears, but that she'd firmly refused to accept.

It had been six weeks since Bo had disappeared.

Six.

The poor men of Home who'd vanished near that time were dead. The hollowness where Bo's voice should have been widened with that truth, growing with every breath she took.

It grew into the space that her fears had carved out for it long ago, then past that, stretching out so far she couldn't even feel the end of it.

Everything in the darkness fell silent. Even the crawling piece of her stilled for the first time in years, and Kate covered her face, shrinking back from the endless nothing.

You have nothing left, the crawling thing whispered, her voice cold and, for the first time, utterly devoid of hope. *They are both dead.*

Kate's eyes flew open to the lantern light of the small room, and she fumbled with her bag, pulling out the aenigma box. Her fingers gripped it so tightly that the edges jabbed into her skin. She cast out toward it, searching for…

There was nothing alive about the box.

She cast out again, blinking back tears.

The usual glow of *vitalle* spread across the runes on top of the box and shimmered along the metal bands protecting the edges.

She stopped herself from casting out again.

There was nothing else to find. It had been twenty years since Evan had touched this box and six weeks since Bo had done the same. Whatever clues it had once held were long gone.

Closing her eyes, she let the box fall to her lap and heard Bo's journal flip closed.

The emptiness of the room sank into her, and her fingers sought out her locket again, as though that could drive back the truth.

"What is the box to you?" Venn asked quietly from the other bed.

Tears squeezed out of Kate's eyes, but she didn't open them.

"It's a bit of a puzzle, certainly," Venn continued. "But it was more than that to Bo, and it's more than that to you."

Kate opened her eyes.

Venn had rolled onto her side and was considering Kate's hand clenched around the locket. "What are you looking for when you search it?" There was none of the early animosity from the Stronghold in the elf's face, and she watched Kate with curiosity tempered with sympathy and concern.

The hollow space inside of Kate gaped open like the dark night outside. Wind blew outside, and the branch creaked where Venn had it pinned with the window. The elf leaned over and pushed the branches outside, then shut the window against the night. "Should be fine until morning."

Her sleeve hid the tattoo, but Kate imagined it funneling *vitalle* into Venn's arm, holding back the venom that should have killed her.

Slowly, Kate pulled her hand off her locket and reached for the tenea serum in her pack. Ignoring the pang of vulnerability that rose in her, she pushed her finger into the serum.

Closing her eyes, she drew up the memory of that day. The red flag at the mine, Bo's excitement, Evan's laughter, the strange beginnings of her magic. The box...

She pushed on as Evan fell into the river, and she shoved him back out, only to have the men grab him. She pushed on as all her efforts failed and the world went dark, and she woke to nothing but Bo on an empty shore.

The thread of memory glowed brightly for such a dark day, and she handed it to Venn without speaking.

Venn took it, and when the last of the strand of light had slipped into her finger, she looked up. "That was your younger brother."

Kate nodded.

"And those men wore the Kalesh symbol."

Kate sank back. "The insignia of the last emperor, who died mysteriously somewhere near Home."

"Which means they brought the box here." Venn paused. "Did they bring Evan too?" At Kate's silence, she sighed. "Bo found the box, but no Evan." She shifted, her expression torn.

Finally, she held out the vial, but when Kate took it, Venn kept a grip on it for just a breath, opening her mouth but closing it again before she let go.

Kate wrapped the vial and tucked it into its pocket.

"Tomorrow," Venn said. "I'll take you to where Bo disappeared. With your skills, maybe we'll find a new clue as to where he is."

Kate sank back on her bed, staring up at the ceiling.

Venn was quiet for a moment. "Bo is alive, Kate."

Kate watched the lantern flicker its wavering stars across the ceiling but didn't answer.

439

CHAPTER FORTY-SEVEN

THE FAT DEW drops clinging to the grass and ferns on the forest floor soaked through Kate's boots, chilling her feet. The uphill trek had made the rest of her hot, and she kept her cloak unclasped, even as her breath clouded in the air.

She'd woken with the heaviness of last night still lingering, but the cool morning air lifted it a little. The sun had risen as they crossed the river and now slanted down into the forest in long beams of light that glittered when they landed on the dewy ferns and the tall tufts of grass.

Venn strode ahead of her with a troubled expression. She brushed her hands on the tree trunks they passed, moving swiftly uphill.

"The elves are patrolling," she said over her shoulder. "They're beginning near the river where that fisherman saw the shadow."

When Kate didn't answer, Venn glanced back at her. "Not far now."

Venn continued up a steep slope. When it leveled off, Kate stepped into the shadow of a large tree, and her boots crunched onto some low-lying leaves that were white with frost. Venn turned south, leaving dark footprints in the frozen shadows and sending water droplets flying when she passed through patches warmed by sunlight.

She stopped at a small clearing, and Kate came up beside her.

The three aspens and the juniper where Venn had found Bo's box were just to the left. The aspens, which had been still green in Venn's memory, now had mostly bare branches. The remaining leaves were more brown than gold and shivered in the slight breeze, as though they held on by the merest thread. Straight across from them, the game trail wound into the clearing between the two tall pines where the shadow had been.

"Will you wait here?" Kate asked. "Your remnant will over-power any others that might still be around."

Venn nodded, and Kate stepped forward gingerly. She cast out, but the wave rolled over nothing more than grasses and pine trees and assorted small animals. Eyeing the juniper where Bo had hidden the box, she crossed to where the shadow had threat-ened Bo and squatted down. There were no remnants at all.

A curious smell came from her right, and she moved over to it. A jumble of forest sounds and smells clung to a few leaves on a low bush. Elven, and almost worn away.

Moving back to where the shadow had lingered, she pulled the remnant amplifier out of her pack, and, holding it close to herself to keep it from the sunlight, she dripped two bright blue drops onto the widest leaves of some brush growing along the game trail before corking it and shoving it back into her pack.

The fluid rolled into the seam of each leaf, tendrils of blue mist floating away as the fluid evaporated.

A hint of forest again. Mossy and rich. Definitely elven, but not malevolent or vicious. Not particularly strong, either.

There was no sign of Bo at all.

The amplifier drops faded away, and the scents did as well.

She stood, looking over the trees as though some sign would still be here, weeks later. She crossed to the juniper bush where Bo had hidden the box and searched again, but she found neither Bo's remnant nor Venn's. She dripped out two more drops of the amplifier but still found nothing.

She sank back on her heels, the last of her hope disappearing like the glittering frost in the sunlight. "It's been too long."

Venn hesitated. "Can I ask the trees what they remember again?"

"Do you actually think there's anything new to find?"

"Perhaps." Venn set her hand on the nearest tree, then moved slowly around the clearing.

Kate knelt in the juniper bushes, staring at the empty ground in front of her.

Venn completed the circuit of the clearing and shook her head. "A few elven patrols." She glanced toward where the shadow had appeared. "Ayen came through twice but didn't linger. Faron once, headed uphill. The two of them often scout on their own, though."

"This is pointless," Kate said quietly.

Before Venn could answer, a flash of brown soared over the top of the clearing, accompanied by the rumble of ocean waves. Kate looked up to see a hawk circle over them.

"Crofftus," she said quietly to Venn.

He dove down and landed on a low branch of the aspens. *There is nothing large in the forest other than you two,* he reported. *The elves are down near the river, and no humans are in the woods.*

Kate gave a hum of acknowledgment.

Venn tilted her head at the hawk. "The trees already told me that."

His voice in Kate's mind gave a barely audible huff. *And above the tree line, nothing moves. Nor has anyone disturbed the ravine with the rockslide this morning.* The feathers of his chest were speckled with whites and light browns that turned darker on his wings. His black pupils were ringed with yellow, and he fixed his unblinking eyes on Kate.

She went back to searching the ground around the juniper branches. There was nothing but old pine needles and the remains of the fallen aspen leaves. She pushed clumps to the side, searching for any sign of anything.

Beside her, she heard Venn shift her weight. "I see you've taken a step up from inhabiting the beetle."

The hawk twitched, shaking the aspen branch and dislodging a few leaves. Kate looked up to see his body tense, his eyes trained on the ground at the edge of the clearing.

Crofftus let out a grunt of impatience, and the bird slowly relaxed. *This is only an upgrade in flight. Hawks are terribly distractible. Do you have any idea how many mice are in this forest? The beetle at least moved slow enough I could keep him where I wanted him.*

Venn glanced at Kate, as though waiting for a response. When none came, she turned back to Crofftus. "No strange shadows around?"

No. He was quiet for a minute. *It is too cold for your amplifier to work.* He stared at her with his round eyes. *The blue is from lissium powder, is it not? Dissolved lissium crystalizes at a slightly higher temperature than water. It's not going to react well unless you warm it up.*

Kate pulled the vial of remnant amplifier out of her pocket. Instead of a clear blue liquid, it was slightly grainy. "I..." She wrapped her hand around the vial. "How did I not think of that?"

A lack of focus, if I had to guess.

A flicker of irritation cut through the despondency that had settled on her, and she gave him an annoyed look.

Put it in your armpit, he suggested. *That should warm it in just a few minutes.* He shifted on the branch.

The fact that the suggestion was a good one was the only thing that kept her from snapping at him. She tucked the vial in through her collar and put the cold glass in her armpit. It was painfully cold, but she pressed her arm down over it.

I'll head toward the rockslide and see if— The hawk snapped its head back toward the spot. *No!* Crofftus commanded it. *You don't need—* With a flurry of wings, the hawk dove off the branch, snatched a mouse from the grass, and shot away through the forest.

Stop! Crofftus protested, his voice growing fainter as the hawk soared up above the trees. *Stop!*

His feathers disappeared into the forest while the vial warmed against her skin.

Venn moved to a tree and set her palm on it. "He's headed toward the ravine." She dropped her hand. "It's odd that he's so helpful, isn't he?"

The vial had grown a little warmer, and Kate pulled it back out. The solution was clear again, and she shook her head. "Yes, but this was a good idea. Where exactly was the box?"

Venn stepped over and surveyed the ground. "Between those two branches."

Kate dripped two drops onto the ground where Venn pointed. Blue mist rose as it evaporated, bringing with it the scent of wild windswept hills. She took a deep breath, as though it really were a smell. The aroma of dry leaves and juniper mingled with Bo's remnant, and she froze for a moment, just trying to draw it in.

The drops of amplifier shrank, and the remnant began to fade. She tried to draw out anything else. She smelled Venn's forest, strongly, and it took a heartbeat to realize that she was sensing the old remnant, not the elf standing next to her.

"Only you and Bo were here." She shoved herself up and

crossed the clearing. Reaching the game trail where the shadow had stood, she used two more drops.

The mingle of elven remnants rose stronger now, and through them all, she couldn't find any trace of Bo.

"Anything?" Venn asked.

"Just elves. None of them recent or distinct from each other." Kate glanced around. "Too many elves have traveled on it for me to feel Bo or…whatever remnant a shadow should leave."

She wrapped the amplifier carefully and tucked it into an inner pocket of her cloak to keep it warmer. The forest stretched out endlessly around them, and the futility of tracking anything through it descended on her.

There was nothing left to track.

Venn watched her with a troubled expression. She said nothing, though, as she moved across the clearing to lean against the largest tree and close her eyes.

Kate shifted her pack, and the hard side of the aenigma box jabbed into her. She pulled it out, and the act of just touching it sent a ripple of reassurance through her. Not as reassuring as if she could rustle up enough hope to open the drawer on the front. Even knowing it was empty, somehow opening it sounded… hopeful. She held the box like a talisman and searched the trees as though she could look back in time to see where Bo had gone.

There had to be something. Her eyes swept along the trail, finding nothing but low brush and hard-packed dirt.

There had to be *something*.

She was shifting the box so she could grab the amplifier again when a sharp edge jabbed her finger.

She froze.

Across the bottom of the front face, bumped out just a hair, was a new, shallow drawer.

CHAPTER FORTY-EIGHT

KATE PRIED the drawer open with her nails, and the toll of a deep, resonant bell poured out.

This wasn't a Hope Drawer. It sat lower on the front, although not low enough to clear the Hope Drawer, and everything in her quivered with fear and desperation. The toll of the bell rose and fell, still distant, still set in some empty, vast space, but so vibrant that it took her a breath to notice paper inside. It was tightly rolled and tied shut with a dirty, tattered bit of cloth.

She pulled it out and untied the fabric. Every part of it held the bell sounds. There was more to it too, a richness she couldn't put a name to. The writing was in ancient Kalesh, and written in an elegant hand.

> *They call me a king. If so, I am one who has been brought to my knees.*

She blinked at the words that mirrored the runes on the lid so clearly.

I have the world—the entire world—except the ones I want. The ones who give me life and strength.

How long can they stay safe? How long can the walls hold? Are they cold? Alone? Frightened?

Do they know I am the one who left them there? The thought chills my soul, but they must stay safe. I cannot risk losing them all.

But are they really safe? Will the walls hold? The idea of their failing haunts me.

Has the end come for them so far from me that I didn't even know it?

No. I refuse to entertain the idea.

They are safe.

I can save them—the thought cannot be dismissed. Will not be dismissed. I can save them.

That is all there is to cling to.

Kate read it again. A king on his knees, the battlements failing, the hope and the fear all tangled together.

Except…She looked it over.

Except this man knew.

He acted like he didn't, but it was there, between all his words.

He knew that his loved ones were gone—he just refused to admit it. Refused to stop whatever he was trying to accomplish.

She let her hands fall into her lap. It was longing she heard in the bell. He was doing nothing but longing for something he did not have.

She swallowed and looked at the path. The trail was empty. The hillside equally so. The next mountainside as well. The sky above an uncaring, vacant blue.

The man's words were too close, too understandable. The hint of madness in his words was unnervingly close to a thousand thoughts she'd entertained. He clung too hard to something he knew was gone, and she recognized the despair in it.

Kate rolled the paper slowly and picked up the fabric. It was a faded green with what might have once been tiny flowers dyed onto it. But it was ragged and dull. She tied it around the little scroll and tucked it back into the Desperation Drawer, pushing it closed.

It was futile to search for trails when there was nothing left to find.

She pushed herself to her feet. "You were right, Venn," she said quietly. "I shouldn't have expected to find anything."

Turning, she crossed the clearing, heading out the way they'd come.

Venn stayed where she stood.

Kate reached the far trees before Venn's voice called out, a note of desperation in it, "Wait!"

Kate turned to see her standing stiffly next to the juniper.

"I..." Venn cleared her throat. "I first met Bo up the slope. Above the trees." Every line of her body was tense as she gestured up at the bits of rocky mountaintop visible between the trees. "It's not terribly far."

Kate let out a tired breath. "What's the point of going there, Venn? Because we'll find so much out in the open, where remnants will have faded even faster than here, and there are no trees for you to talk to?"

Venn shifted her weight, her expression torn between frustra-tion and...something else. "Just come." She started up the hill.

Kate didn't move. "What if I don't care where you met Bo?"

"You care." Venn's bright hair disappeared around a wide trunk.

"I do not," Kate called back, her tone sounding annoyingly childish. Shifting her pack, she followed the elf.

After a walk that was certainly longer than "not terribly far,"

449

and steep enough that Kate's breath came hard and fast, the trees ended and she stepped out onto a rocky slope speckled with low, scrubby brush. The tree line stretched across the mountain and continued onto the rest of the range lined up to the north. Above her, thin patches of snow clung to the crevices. By the peak, the entire mountaintop was brilliantly white.

Kate's breath blew out in a cloud that was dragged away by a breeze.

"This way." Venn traveled along the trees for a quarter of an hour before she turned uphill into the open. She climbed the steep slope, stopping when they reached a spot that was unremarkable compared to the rest of the slope. She motioned to a handful of rocks nestled in crusted old snow. "Right there."

The midday sun poured down on Kate's hair and cheeks, warming them against the chill as she climbed up into the crunchy snow lacing the top of a flat rock, and her foot slid forward across an icy patch, hitting a fist-sized stone and sending it rolling downhill. She caught her balance as the rock plummeted down, skipping over outcroppings until it disappeared into the trees. Past that, the forest rippled down all the way to the river.

"Bad place for a wrong step." The wind shoved against Kate, blowing unhindered across the bare slope. The ground would have been washed by rain and melting snow, scoured by wind every day, but she squatted down anyway and touched the rock.

"There are no old remnants here." she said, pushing herself back to her feet. "They'd fade faster than usual in a place like this."

Downhill, the river glittered in the sunlight, winding north past the cluster of buildings in Home and south into the ravine with the rockslide. To the east, hills and valleys rolled away, shrinking and flattening until they smoothed out into a great hazy plain that stretched to the horizon.

The vastness of the view swirled around her. She stood like a tiny speck in the boundless landscape. It was soothing, somehow, to be so small. Even the emptiness that plagued her was nothing to this. She let the sun warm her face and the view dull the edges of everything swirling inside her. "This is pointless, Venn."

The elf shook her head. "He's alive, Kate. We just need to find him."

Kate kept her eyes on the distant plains. "You don't know that," she said quietly. Before Venn could argue, she added, "I see why you came here, though, and I can see why Bo did, too. It's beautiful."

Venn let out a frustrated breath but stepped up next to Kate and took in the view. "It was in the middle of an early winter storm. The rain turned to snow, and it was falling fast. The wind picked up, until I couldn't even see the trees."

Kate turned to her. "Why were you up here in that?"

Venn was quiet, then held out her hand. "Give me the serum."

Kate paused before she dug it out.

Instead of uncorking the vial, Venn rolled it between her fingers, watching the glitters swirl. "Bo—in your memory last night, from when you were young—that's just what he was like when I met him."

She stared into the vial, and Kate couldn't bring herself to come up with an answer to such a statement.

Finally, Venn nodded, as though some decision had been made.

"I am betrothed to Prince Faron," she said quietly, "because my great-great-grandfather was a prince of the White Wood."

Kate straightened at the unexpected topic.

"I am the only unmarried elf among the lake elves with a direct line to the White Throne. Our marriage will solidify a bond that has been lacking between our two groups for hundreds of years." Venn turned and looked north.

Kate followed her gaze to a wide valley that cut deep into the mountains. Pines filled it, but they looked different from the rest of the forests. Snippets of white peeked out between the dark needles. "The White Wood?"

"It's full of frost pines. Their wood is white like moonlight. They almost glow." She still rolled the vial between her fingers as her eyes traced the valley. "When the lake elves settled here, I was betrothed to Faron, and from that time on, I lived in the White Wood, was educated with him, and was trained by the royal guard. I am more of a White Wood elf than anyone I was born among." She sighed. "Except in one way."

She turned back to Kate, her chin raised. "You asked me once if I could step the way Evay did in the old stories. If I could, in a single step, cross a wide distance. It's a fair question. All of the White Wood elves can, and many of the lake elves." She walked over to a wide, flat rock and stepped onto it. "But I cannot. I can speak to the trees in more detailed conversation than any living elf, and yet I cannot step even five paces. A child can do such a thing with ease." Her eyes lost their focus. "There are times when I can almost feel it. Times when I can almost fold the space between myself and my goal. Almost push through it like it was just a mist. But..."

She blinked and looked around at the rocky slope, her eyes lingering on the patches of old iced-over snow. "It was foolish to stay here practicing when the storm arrived. But it's flat, and while my mother insists that makes no difference, how can it not? Up here there were no White Wood elves to point out how 'simple and natural' stepping should be. No humans to gawk. It was cold, but that was a small price to pay to be far enough from the trees that even they wouldn't notice me."

Her eyes grew distant again. "I heard the wolves, just like I heard the dozen deer nearby, and the alpine rabbits scuttling through the brush. There are always predators if the forest is healthy." She spared a glance at Kate. "I am not usually prey."

Venn moved to the edge of the rock and considered the next large stone, a handful of paces away. A gust of wind blew across the mountainside. "The attempted stepping did not go well. Once, I thought it might have almost worked, but by then the snow was building up and my feet were numb." Her hand curled around the vial. "Five paces. That's all I wanted. And so, despite my exhaustion and the growing cold, I tried again."

Her eyes dropped to a smaller rock just in front of her. The grey stone was shaped like an oversized arrowhead lying on its side, the top edge sharp and jagged.

"This rock was hidden by snow. And so when I stepped, landing merely one pace away instead of five, my foot slid down the side of it and my shin slammed into the edge." She grimaced. "I was exhausted and furious. When I stood, even the shock of seeing the snow red with blood wasn't enough to make me stop the next insanity."

Wind shoved at Kate, dragging even colder air across the hillside and teasing stray bits of hair out of her braid.

Venn pushed her own hair back and shook her head. "I don't know why I decided that if five paces was impossible, I should try twenty-five." She nodded her chin toward an outcropping at least twenty-five paces away. "I remember pouring every bit of *ael'iza* I could gather into the effort and aiming for those rocks."

Venn sighed. "I don't remember hitting the ground. All I know is the world went dark, and it was still dark when new pain ripped across my leg and the air was filled with snarls. It was night. I tried to crawl away, but everything was too cold, except the pain in my leg where something was tearing at it.

"Then there was a man's voice, and a lantern, and the snarls ended but the pain grew until everything went black again."

Venn didn't look at Kate but twisted the cork out of the vial and dipped her finger in. "When we reach Bo's camp, we're likely to not find anything more than we've found other places, so here's what it looked like while he was there."

She closed her eyes and fed her memory into the tenea serum.

When she finished, she handed it to Kate and turned to look out over the distant plains.

Kate dipped her finger into the vial.

Her eyes opened to speckled daylight coming through a leaning wall of branches, their pine needles dark green against the light outside. The memory of a waving lantern shifted into the glow of a campfire burning merrily between herself and the exit of the makeshift shelter.

It was warm. Almost hot. Venn moved, and pain shot up her leg like a knife. She let out a groan and sat, pushing aside a blanket to see her calf wrapped in a wide bandage.

A weight bore down on her, and she rolled her shoulders, trying to shake off the feeling.

Something moved outside the shelter, and a man's face came into view as he squatted in the doorway, offering a crooked smile. "Ah! She lives!"

Something painful jabbed into Kate at the sight of Bo. He looked…tired. His smile was familiar, but something was missing. *Because he's gone*, the wretched crawling thing inside her whispered.

She shoved the thought away and grabbed the memory for another view of his familiar face.

CHAPTER FORTY-NINE

"Where am I?" Venn's voice was rough.

"In my beautiful home. Not as fancy as an elven house, I'll wager, but it's warm and dry. Which isn't too bad for someone who can't speak to trees." Bo crawled into the shelter, keeping back to give her space. "Are you warm enough?"

She nodded, listening past his voice. The trees murmured of sunshine and sap. There was no snow on the ground outside, although the forest floor was muddy. "How far down the mountain are we?"

"Only a few minutes from the river. I'm not sure how long an elf can bleed out and freeze in the snow before it actually hurts them, but you looked like you had a good head start on both counts. So I brought you down to my basecamp, since I figured a bandage and less snow might help."

The heaviness coalesced into her head, and she shifted, trying to shake it off, but pain tore across her leg again, and she gasped.

He grimaced. "The wolves left a mark. I thought elves could heal themselves, so I just cleaned it and wrapped it, but I can find you a healer if you need one."

Venn blinked at him, trying to make sense of his words. "Wolves?"

"Only three, thankfully. And apparently not terribly hungry, since they let me run them off without much of a fight."

"You…" Venn stared at him, understanding of what had happened finally dawning on her. "You had the lantern. You…" The truth of the situation slammed into her like a blow. "You saved me from the wolves."

"And probably the cold," he said lightly, "but I think the wolves would have killed you first."

He sat against the far edge of the shelter with dirty pants and cuffs caked with dried mud. There was an independence about him, the vaguely solitary feel of someone who spends a great deal of time alone. But he felt honest and trustworthy and curious.

His jaw was square, his short beard cut into a slightly roguish point. His dark hair fell just to his humanly broad shoulders.

"You're…" She swallowed. The weight pressed on her mind. He'd saved her… "You're human."

He laughed an easy sort of laugh. "Is it that obvious?" He picked up two small pieces of wood from a stack near the wall and laid them on the fire.

"Yes."

He laughed again and set a pot over the fire. "There's soup from this morning. Just fish and a few turnips, but you're welcome to some."

"I…"

He paused. "Oh, do elves eat fish?"

She nodded, her mind spinning. How could she have been so stupid? She reached down to touch her leg. Her arm felt heavy, and around a surprisingly large wound on her calf, the ael'iza tingled and burned, spending itself in an effort to heal all the damage. The voice of a large tree murmured behind her, and she looked over her shoulder to find the wide trunk that the human had built his shelter

456

against. She shifted until she sat against it, closing her eyes and biting back a groan at the pain.

Heat eased out of the tree into her back like a gentle wave of warm water, washing through her. Aches in her back, and a thin pain in her hip that she hadn't even noticed, eased as the tree fed iza into her. It pooled down into her leg. A thousand little sparks of heat worked against the edges of the ragged wound, mending torn muscle, renewing tattered skin, knitting it together into wholeness. The warmth from the tree swirled around it, bolstering each spark, pouring the steady, massive strength of the pine into her, fueling the work with the nearly infinite life of the forest.

She opened her eyes to see the man watching her with a pained expression. "I'm Bo, by the way. And since you're the first elf I've ever met, I apologize if I've done anything…" He gestured at her leg, and then the whole shelter. "Wrong. I couldn't leave you in the snow, but I don't know how to find other elves."

Her breath came out in a tired, pained sort of laugh. "You saved my life," she whispered. The other words crowded to the front of her mind. The vow.

He waved the sentiment away. "It was nothing. I was there and heard the wolves. I have some ginger and nettle for tea, if you'd like, but I wasn't sure if that only helped with pain in humans."

The ancient words filled her mind, thrumming. Insistent.

She pinched her mouth closed against them, staring at his open face, his rather plain brown human eyes.

The vow was difficult enough. But not to a human. That was the path to nothing but pain.

He shifted, watching her with a worried crease in his brow. "I'll leave you in peace, then. I'm working just outside if you need anything." He turned and started out of the shelter.

"Wait!" The word ripped out of her against her will, and he stopped.

The vow burned in her throat, and she gasped for breath, trying to hold it back.

But it was done.

The bonds were already clamped around her like a vise, locked in place before she'd even seen his face. Regardless of the pain that would come, regardless of the short futility of human life, it was already done.

The first words clawed up her throat.

"All I have is yours," she whispered.

He drew back slightly and began to shake his head, but the rest of the vow shoved its way out.

"Ask for my day, it is yours. Ask for my aid, it is yours."

He shook his head faster, holding out a hand to stop her from speaking, but the vow was not complete.

"Ask for my blade, it is yours. Ask for my blood, it is yours."

"No," he said, "Stop. What are you saying?"

"Ask for my life, it is yours."

"Wait." He held up his hands. "You don't owe me anything. I ran off some wolves. Anyone would have done the same."

The heat of the vow spread out of her chest, burning away something she couldn't name, until it reached her skin and raced across it. The last of the words slipped out. "I vow this to you, until one or both of us lie beneath the trees."

Bo stared at her, his expression wary. "What did you just do?"

She let out a tired laugh, shifting against the weight of the vow. It settled inside her, across her shoulder blades, wrapping through her ribs, molding into the bones of her body. "You saved my life. I owe you a life debt."

"I…" He leaned back. "I release you from any obligation. Really, it was nothing."

The corner of her mouth twitched up. "My life is nothing?"

"That's not what I meant." He ran a hand through his hair, leaving it unruly. "You don't owe me anything."

"It is not something you can dismiss. It is done. The debt began when you saved me and will be repaid if I ever save you."

He opened his mouth again, but she held up a hand.

"I know humans speak of vows as something that can be chosen. Something that can be broken. This is not such a vow. The debt has been incurred. It cannot be removed. Not by me, and not by you. It can merely be paid."

He stared at her, his mouth working, but no words came.

"My name is Venn." She let her eyes close. "If you ever are in need, call me."

"Call you? I…I am from Queensland. Once I return home, you won't hear my call."

"I will hear."

He was silent for a long moment. "Because you'll hear me from far away? Or because now you're compelled to follow me?"

She opened her eyes. "I don't know. Life debts are rare. Ones with humans are almost unheard of. I know of one, and they stayed near each other until…for the entirety of the human's life."

Bo shifted. "I'm more of a 'travel by myself' sort of person."

Venn let out another snort of laughter, this one tinged with defeat. She settled back against the tree, drawing in the warmth, feeding it down to her wounded leg as exhaustion washed over her. "So am I."

KATE OPENED her eyes and stared at Venn.

The elf nodded. "So yes, I know Bo is alive. I owe him a life debt. It weighs on me every minute of every day, and it will until I repay him, or he dies."

459

CHAPTER FIFTY

KATE CONTINUED to stare at Venn as the ramifications of the oath to Bo fell into place in her mind. "A life debt," she said slowly, "and so when he called for your help and asked you to bring me the box, you really had no choice."

Venn turned back to look at the distant plains. "He asked for my help. I could not refuse."

"And this is why the box feels heavy to you." Kate pressed the cork back into the vial. "It's not the box. It's the oath."

"It was only two days later when he called for help." Venn shook her head. "I had stayed in the area, trying to figure out how to navigate a life debt to a human. The only one I'd ever heard of was one my aunt Evay had once."

Kate tucked the serum back into her pack. "With the human Melia. I know the story."

"Human lives are so short. When Melia died, my aunt wasn't there to protect her. The debt ended unpaid, but it did end. To this day, she doesn't like to speak of it, and now I found myself in the same situation." Venn let out a long breath. "I had finally decided to go find her and talk to her, and I was hours away when Bo called."

"And by the time you got here, he was gone."

Venn rubbed her hands over her face.

"Well, that explains a lot." Another gust of cold air shoved at Kate, this one stronger than the last. Piles of clouds rose up over the peaks just north of them, and the trees farther along the ridge shifted in the coming wind. It chilled her fingers, and she rubbed them together. "You could have just told me that from the beginning."

Venn dropped her hands. "I've told no one. My relationships with both the White Wood elves and the lake elves are...complicated. The betrothal to Faron stands, as it will unless King Thallion ends it. The lake elves would have me be their ambassador to the White Wood, and the White Wood would have me settle there. But..."

"If you're bound to a human who doesn't even live in the area..."

Venn nodded. "You see the problem."

"You're..." Kate studied her face. "You're sure he's alive?"

Venn let out a humorless laugh. "I'm sure."

The relief that had been creeping up finally washed over Kate, and a smile spread across her lips, despite the fact that they still had no idea where he was.

"Then what we really need to do," she said, giving Venn a pointed look, "is find Bo and have you save his life."

The edge of Venn's mouth twisted up as well. "Agreed."

Kate turned back toward the ravine below them, and her attention caught on the rockslide. "Where was Bo's camp?"

"This side of the ravine, a bit south of the rockslide."

"Well, let's go see what we can find there."

The sun dropped behind yet another of the clouds quickly filling the sky, plunging the forest into cold shadows, and Kate's foot slid down yet another steep bit of slope, sending pebbles and clods of dirt trickling downhill ahead of her. Among the trees this low on the slope, there was no wind, and despite the fact that downhill treks always seemed like they should be easier than uphill, Kate unclasped her cloak.

The path from where Venn had been hurt by the wolves to here hadn't been a path at all. It had been only steep, wild forest, and Kate tried to imagine Bo carrying Venn this entire way in a snowstorm.

"He's not human," she muttered.

Venn stopped and turned. "He's not? What is he?"

Kate stumbled to a stop beside her. "Metaphorically, Venn. Literally, of course he's human. But he carried you all the way down this in a blizzard with wolves nearby? I can barely carry myself down in nice weather."

Venn scowled at her. "Are you sure he's human?"

"Yes. And what difference would it make?"

"I have a life debt with him. What if he turned out to be a dwarf? Or a troll?"

Kate stared at her. "He's my brother! Did he look like a dwarf or a troll?"

Venn waved her words away. "You can't blame me for taking that literally. You're the only actual human around, outside of Home. Even the historical wizard blamed for the curse is only half-human." She started downhill again, moving smoothly over the rough ground, not even disturbing any pebbles. "There are very few humans in this story you're trying to sort out."

A stick twisted under Kate's boot and jabbed into her other ankle. She kicked at it, snapping it in half. "It's annoying how light you are on your feet."

Venn glanced over her shoulder. "You should steal the dwarves' boots."

"Those are just quiet, not light." Kate considered the idea but shook her head. "I understand what's happening to make them quiet. I don't think I could alter them to make me lighter on my feet, though."

"Then you should adjust theirs to make the dwarves' steps extra loud. Make them sound like trolls."

Kate laughed as she jumped off the loose rock onto the grass next to Venn. "Might help keep them honest."

Venn peered through the trees at a sliver of the rocky wall across the ravine. "Bo's camp isn't far."

Sunlight rolled across the trees around them for a brief moment before being swallowed up by the clouds again. Venn squinted up at the sky. "I think we'll get snow today."

"Then let's get to Bo's camp before that happens. I don't need snow covering whatever faint remnants are still there." Kate glanced around. "Are the elven patrols nearby?"

Venn set her hand on a pine. "No elves or humans anywhere close to us."

Kate cast out but found nothing brighter than a tree and the occasional squirrel. "Too bad you can't tell if there are any shadowy monsters. Do you think you could teach the trees to look for it?"

"I don't even know what makes that shadow different from any other. I tried to get the trees back in the clearing to focus on it, but they didn't understand what I meant. Not that I can blame them. I don't even understand what I'm looking for."

Venn led them swiftly through shadows and sunshine, brushing her fingertips along the trunks they passed, until she stopped at the edge of a stand of large pines. Each trunk was wider than Kate, and they stood in a lopsided circle, their lower branches nearly touching each other.

Against a tree to their right, two slanting walls of branches leaned against the lowest bough, creating a small triangular shelter. An old fire pit sat at the entrance with a tea kettle beside it and a small log pulled up close like a bench. Kate stepped past the blackened pit and looked inside.

It was the little shelter from Venn's memory, although the walls were no longer green pine boughs but brittle and brown. The floor was strewn with dead needles and pine cones, and one side near the trunk had fallen in.

"This is a good camp." Venn's voice floated in from outside. "Since staying in Home seems out of the question, I say we expand this a bit and use it for shelter while we're finding Bo."

Kate turned slowly, searching for any remnant of Bo, but there was nothing. "These walls are not in great shape."

"We can do better than this." Venn's footsteps moved across the clearing.

Kate knelt and crawled toward the trunk, pushing the fallen branches away. All the way at the back, Bo's pack lay knocked over, its top chewed through, and some of his clothes pulled out and frayed by tiny teeth. She pulled the fabric out of the way. Beneath it, a neatly rolled cylinder of maps was tucked down one side of the bag, surrounded by more rolls of clothes.

The faintest scent of Bo's remnant floated out, and she leaned closer to the bag. The smell was so feeble it faded immediately, but she moved some more clothes aside and caught another hint of summery wind.

The oddness of Bo in Venn's memory clicked into place. He hadn't looked strange—he'd smelled strange. Of course, in Venn's memory, there had been no remnant. It had left him feeling hollow.

From the other side of his pack, she pulled out a leather-wrapped stack of papers. She unwound the rough twine that bound the stack and opened the leather cover, revealing page after page of neatly written script, meticulous notes, and sketches.

His official records. She flipped through them, pausing at the name "Renault the Mad."

Renault is said to be a half-elven mage who inhabited the area around four hundred years ago. The people in the region treat him like a historical person, although the stories of him are sensational enough that he may be merely a myth or a combination of several historical people.

His legend says he was attempting to create an amulet that would gift eternal life to the bearer, but whatever methods he employed to do so were horrific enough that the human side of his family begged him to stop. The story says he murdered them all.

The Spire Library in Morrow holds two interesting documents. One by a historian written five years after Emperor Sorrn, the last Kalesh emperor, disappeared, and the other written by a scribe who had been employed by the emperor himself but had narrowly escaped execution in one of the emperor's rages. The scribe's accounts are especially interesting and contain enough detail that they appear genuine.

These two references note that late in his reign, Emperor Sorrn grew increasingly withdrawn from his responsibilities and obsessed with the idea of immortality. He discovered the legend of Renault and traveled in secret, with only a small retinue of soldiers and his most trusted advisor, a man who was accused of filling the emperor's head with dreams of eternal life, to find either Renault himself or his amulet.

The closer a person comes to the area where Renault lived (the current town of Home is the nearest modern settlement), the more signs there are that the emperor really did come to this part of the world.

In a ravine south of the town, finds have included metal signets

466

from soldiers of the last dynasty and a medallion that would have been worn by one of Sorrn's closest advisors.

It is my belief that with more excavation, we may find signs of Emperor Sorrn himself, who not only did not find immortality but perhaps died in such secretive isolation that he was lost to history for hundreds of years.

The next page held a drawing of the ravine with the remains of a road marked two thirds of the way up the slope and several cave mouths a bit lower down. Detailed notes filled the edges, but the sun dipped behind clouds again, and the small writing grew too difficult to make out under all the branches.

"Venn!" Kate grabbed the papers and the map rolls. "I know why no one ever came looking for those humans you found dead so long ago."

She climbed out and stood, pausing to stare at the side of the clearing next to Bo's shelter. The lowest branches of the two large trees near it, a blue spruce and a thick fir tree, were bent down until their tips brushed the forest floor. The area sheltered beneath it was four times larger than what Bo had built. The walls were solid pine needles, blueish branches from the spruce intertwining with the green of the fir.

Venn stepped out from a small gap between two branches. "Why?" Above her, a branch from the spruce lowered itself slowly until it lay on top of the sloping wall below it.

"I..." Kate pulled her eyes away from the trees. "This is impressive."

Venn squinted up at the shelter. "I need to close off the top, or all our heat will pour out, but it's coming together. What about the humans?"

Kate held up Bo's papers. "I think it *was* Emperor Sorrn, and he never told anyone he was coming here. No one knew to come looking."

"If the emperor was in that group, he was probably killed. But…" Her eyes grew distant, and she shook her head. "There was no one there fancy enough for an emperor."

Kate sat down on the log, rereading Bo's notes. "The timeline matches, though. You found those men right at the end of the Empire."

"My parents might remember more." Venn ducked back inside the shelter. "Or Evay. I was young. There's a good chance they noticed more than I did."

Kate watched another branch of the fir bend down. "How far is it to the lakes?"

"It would take nearly a day to—" Venn stepped out of the shelter, dragging her hand along a branch. "There's someone nearby! A human."

"Where?" Kate wrapped the leather cover around Bo's papers and pushed them into her pack.

Venn pointed north along the hillside, her other hand still on the needles. "A man."

Kate froze, the roll of maps halfway into her pack as well. "Bo?"

"No." Venn closed her eyes. "Younger. With brown hair and dirty clothes." She frowned. "I think there's something wrong with him."

CHAPTER FIFTY-ONE

KATE CAST out in that direction. At the very edge of her range, a person flared up. His movements were irregular and hesitant. "Not a human encased in shadows, right?"

Venn shook her head. "Looks utterly plain."

Kate started toward him. "Where did he come from?"

Venn fell in beside her, snapping a dart into her crossbow. "I'm not sure. There was no one around us, and then he was there. He just walked out of a clearing, but none of the trees saw him walk into it."

Kate's eyes searched the forest for unusual shadows as she headed toward the man who seemed to be barely moving. He'd stumbled a few paces downhill, then stopped. She cast out every few steps, making sure there was no one else nearby, but he appeared to be alone.

They stepped past a row of low pines and found him. He turned, blinking blearily at them. He shivered in a thin short-sleeved tunic, his arms wrapped around himself.

Venn set one hand on a tree. "Hello," she said, the words sounding more cautious than welcoming.

The man stared at them, his expression blank.

Kate took another step toward him, but he didn't move. "I'm Kate, and this is Venn. Are you from Home?"

The man nodded, shivering.

"Do you have a cloak?" Kate asked.

"I..." He looked around. "I don't know."

Venn scanned the woods around them.

Kate caught the scent of his remnant. Grassy, with a touch of damp earth and an echo of something sharp. Or maybe bright. Like the flare of a candle flame. It made her pause, and Venn glanced at her questioningly. Kate didn't step any closer. "What's your name?"

"Rye."

Another cloud blocked the sun, this one large and dark on the bottom, and he hunched in on himself. His voice and posture didn't fit his remnant. The bit of brightness would have led her to expect someone quick and engaging. Witty. Maybe impatient.

Instead, the man stood numbly, his expression vacant.

"Wasn't Rye one of the names Yellow told us?" Venn asked quietly. "One of the missing men?"

Kate nodded.

Rye started to wander uphill. "My cloak...by the blackberries."

"The blackberries?" Kate asked.

"Near the....ridge." His voice was sluggish.

Venn's eyes narrowed. "Blackberries ripen during the Fire Moon," she said to Kate. "Near midsummer."

"Yes," Rye said. "They're early this year..."

"Rye," Kate said slowly. "You're a farmer, aren't you?"

He looked at her, his face too dull to be curious. "Do I know you?"

"We haven't met," Kate said, giving him a smile that felt strained. "Yellow, the tavern keeper, mentioned you." She motioned to Venn. "We're headed back to Home. Want to walk with us?"

Rye blinked at Kate. "Yes. Home. I should go to Home."

Venn grabbed Kate's arm. "But should we?"

"We can hardly leave him here. Something is wrong with him."

Venn gave her an incredulous look. "Noticed that, did you?"

Kate sifted through the impressions from his remnant. "How long did Yellow say he's been missing?"

"Since last week."

Rye showed no curiosity about their conversation. His gaze wandered to the treetops around them.

"Showing up in Home with one of the missing men, who's"— Venn waved a hand in Rye's direction—"in this condition, after they already hate us for knowing Bo, who's apparently to blame for..." She waved her hand at Rye again. "Everything..." She sighed. "They're hardly going to greet us like heroes."

The man stared at a passing cloud.

"Probably not," Kate admitted, "but I want to talk to his family."

"I'm sure they'll be thrilled," Venn said dryly.

"Who else should I talk to, exactly?" Kate knelt down and pulled her blanket out of her pack. "Him?"

"At least he doesn't hate you yet."

"He thinks it's still summer. He's lost months. He knows nothing we need to know." Kate shook out the blanket and wrapped it around the man's shoulders. He took it without any response, pulling it tightly around himself.

"Rye," Venn asked, "have you ever met a foreigner named Bo?"

"Bo?" he repeated blankly.

"Did you ever work for him in the ravine?"

"What ravine?"

"The one with the big rockslide."

His brow creased. "What rockslide?"

Kate sighed. "Can we go talk to his family now?"

"We can try, but it's not going to go well."

"Don't you trust me?"

"I sort of trust you." Venn started down the hill. "It's the people of Home I don't trust."

Kate followed, but Rye merely stood still, staring at a rock on the ground. "Come on, Rye," she called. "Let's get you home."

"Home," he agreed, and walked toward the rock.

"Yes, this is going to go great," Venn muttered.

"Rye…" Kate pointed after Venn. "This way."

"Home," he repeated, and headed downhill, his eyes fixed on Venn's back.

Kate fell into step next to him. She cast out, and his body lit with *vitalle*, as bright and active as Kate's own. "Rye, how long is it until Midsummer?"

"A fortnight?"

"Can you tell what's wrong with him?" Venn asked over her shoulder. "Either the memory loss, or why he's so…lifeless?"

Kate pulled out the tenea serum. "Rye, would you help me with something?"

He stopped and faced her.

She uncorked the vial. "Could you put your finger in here?"

Without question, he pushed his finger into the vial so quickly that Kate grabbed his hand before he could shove the serum up and over the edge. "Just your fingertip." She fed some *vitalle* through his hand. "Can you remember where you were just before Venn and I met you?"

His expression remained vacant, but a thin silver thread spooled out into the serum. When it ended, Kate pulled the vial away and dipped her own finger in.

The morning was hot, the sun bright. The steep, forested hillside stretched up toward a rocky peak that was dry and brown through the gaps in the branches. Fat bumblebees buzzed along the wild-flowers as Rye moved uphill.

He stopped to examine deer tracks in the dirt. He surveyed the hillside, then searched the ground nearby, but found no more prints.

A smudge of darkness clouded the edge of his view.

Kate drew in a breath, but it wasn't a shadow. It wasn't anything.

The darkness spread from every direction, as though the forest were burning away, leaving nothing behind.

In moments, there was only the ground directly in front of Rye's feet, and then that was swallowed up, too.

He stood somewhere different. Still in the woods, but it was cold and the summer grass had turned brown. He stared at the husk at the top of a tall blade. He ran his finger over the little brown pockets left from where the seeds had long since blown away. Their brittle, pointy edges crumbled at his touch.

There were more brown blades of grass next to it, and more beyond that, and he raised his eyes to the trees around him. The pine needles jumped out in stark relief. Short and dense on the fir trees, longer and spiky on the pines.

He spun slowly, wandering downhill, pausing every few steps to pick a different direction.

Motion through the trees made him turn. Two figures moving out of the trees, cautiously. A female elf and a woman.

Kate pulled her hand from the serum. Venn waited a few paces downhill. Kate shook her head. "There's nothing. It was summer, then his memory just…burned away, and he was here where we found him."

"What was he doing when the summer memory ended?"

"Looking at deer tracks."

"Do you think whatever is wrong is permanent?"

Kate took in the man's vacant expression. "Without knowing what happened, I don't know how to tell."

Venn led them downhill again, and Rye followed along mindlessly. He stepped over obstacles that were pointed out to him and tripped over ones that weren't.

The sun had started sinking into the west when the tall slate roofs of Home came into view. Venn moved around the outskirts of town, heading for the Blind Pig. She rounded a low half-timbered home with golden candlelight in the windows and turned down the street that led past the side of the tavern and into the square.

They'd reached the back corner of the Blind Pig when a cry rang out.

Two women came running toward them from the square.

"Get away from him!" one of them shouted. The other grabbed Rye's arm and pulled him away.

"We found him in the woods," Kate said. "He thinks it's midsummer."

One of the women pulled the blanket off his shoulders and threw it at Kate. "Stay away from us!"

Kate took a step forward. "Can I speak to his family?"

"Get out of our town," the other woman hissed.

Faces appeared in the square and down the nearby streets, pausing to watch the commotion as the women pulled Rye away.

A woman flung open a nearby window. "Where did you have him?" she demanded.

"We found him," Kate said, holding her hands up as though that might calm everyone. "He was just wandering in the woods. He doesn't know how he got there."

"Where in the woods?" a man demanded. "Near the ravine?"

"Yes," Kate answered. "In the trees on—"

"They were in the ravine!" someone shouted.

Angry muttering peppered with the word "curse" floated down the street as the women guided Rye into the square. The gathering crowd closed behind them like a wall.

"I assume that's a no to talking to his family," Venn said quietly.

CHAPTER FIFTY-TWO

"AND I THOUGHT WE CAUSED TROUBLE." Tribal's voice rumbled from the alley that ran behind the Blind Pig. He leaned against the back of the tavern, his face amused.

"I don't think we've ever gotten an entire town to hate us so fast," Silas agreed from where he rested against the rickety building across the alley.

"Maybe we should try harder," Tribal said.

Kate started toward them. "Have you two learned anything about the missing people?"

Silas gave her a blank look. "Well, they're missing." He motioned after Rye. "Except that fellow, I guess."

"We find it's better not to interfere with situations where everyone's angry." Tribal took a drink from a brown bottle.

"Thanks," Kate said dryly.

"It has gotten a bit dull around here though," Tribal continued. "You two need help with anything?"

Venn looked at the two of them suspiciously. "From you two? Since when do you want to be helpful?"

J.A. ANDREWS

"We're bored," Silas said. "It's too soon to return to the gov'nor, but there's nothing interesting happening here."

"Right," Kate said. "Shadows stalking people in the forest, men going missing, people being killed, others being found with their minds damaged. Nothing interesting at all."

"That seems more like your sort of 'interesting' than ours." Tribal gestured in the general direction of the ravine. "Have you heard any new rumors of Renault or his treasure?"

Kate paused. "Actually, I have. Bo believes that Emperor Sorrn snuck away from his capital to search for that Oziv Amulet that Renault supposedly made."

Tribal raised an eyebrow. "Where was he looking?"

"I think in the ravine where the rockslide happened."

The dwarves exchanged looks, and Tribal's fingers flickered in a series of motions.

"What is that?" Kate asked, pointing to his hands. "What do you two say to each other when you do that?"

"Hm?" Silas said innocently. "Just wiggling fingers. What did Bo learn about the amulet?"

"Why are you so interested in it?" Venn asked.

Silas's eyes widened a little too far to look purely innocent. "It's treasure—what's not interesting about that?" He turned to Kate. "I tell you what, you tell us all the details you know about anyone's search for that amulet, and we'll tell you everything we've heard about the missing people."

Venn crossed her arms. "You just said you didn't know anything."

Silas frowned at her. "I did not. I just said they were missing."

"So far," Kate said, "everyone we know of who searched for anything in that ravine is either dead, missing, or seriously damaged."

Tribal shrugged. "But those were all humans."

"Who are far less likely to get themselves into trouble than you two are," Venn pointed out.

"You wanted to talk to that fellow's family," Silas said, pointing in the direction Rye had disappeared, "which they didn't seem too keen on. How would you like to talk to one of the other families?"

"Which one?" Kate asked.

"Remember Nevin? He came by to deliver some eggs to Yellow this morning, and we got to talking, and I think we could get him to talk to you. He even brings his boy half the time. The one who was missing for a bit and isn't quite right in the head now. You could talk to them both."

Venn grimaced. "The wife doesn't come, does she?"

"Nah," Silas said, "she'd probably punch Kate in the face, but the father likes us, and he doesn't completely hate you anymore, Kate. Yellow says he shows up each evening for a quick drink. In exchange for access to whatever information you have on the Oziv Amulet, we'll hang around here until he shows"—he tapped his own amulet—"and convince him to talk to you again."

"All right," Kate said slowly, "but I don't know much."

Tribal gave her a wide smile. "Even tiny bits of knowledge improve the mind. Isn't that the sort of thing you Keepers think?"

Kate looked between the two dwarves. "You two realize that there is no Oziv Amulet, right? You can't bottle immortality into…anything, never mind a piece of metal. That's not how life and death work."

"If Renault's amulet doesn't exist, then there's no curse on it and no reason we shouldn't explore the area," Silas said. "Unless you really believe a ravine is cursed."

Kate studied him for a moment, but he just smiled easily at her. She glanced at Venn. "Do you think it's cursed?"

"No," Venn said.

"I agree with Venn," Kate said. "But just because the curse is a legend doesn't mean there's nothing dangerous going on."

"Your concern for our safety is adorable," Tribal said.

Silas grinned. "Do we need to also promise to be careful?"

"Yes."

He raised one hand, still grinning. "I swear we will be models of prudence and judiciousness."

"No, you won't," Kate said, "but let's go find a table. I'll show you Bo's notes and the map he drew. You find a way to get Nevin to trust me enough to talk to his boy."

Silas rubbed his hands together and spun, waving for them to follow down the alley to the other side of the building. "This way's less unfriendly," he called over his shoulder. "And we have a table already!"

Kate glanced toward the square, where a few people still milled around. The sun had fallen behind the tall peaks to the west, and a candle flickered in a window across the square.

Venn stood watching the two dwarves disappear around the corner of the tavern. "What do you think they're really after?"

"I'd be surprised if it's an amulet that brings immortality. Neither of those two seem particularly scared of death. Was Renault supposed to have other sorts of treasure?"

"I have no idea."

Kate sighed and started after the dwarves. "Maybe we should look into that as well."

They rounded the building and found Silas at the door of the Blind Pig, motioning for them to hurry. "Come along before all your new friends decide to follow you."

A few glares were directed their way as he opened the door and a burst of warm air rolled out. Kate stepped inside into the warm glow of a huge fire blazing in the fireplace and a dozen lanterns hanging from low hanging beams.

Yellow paused at the bar in the act of opening a bottle of log mead. Venn gave him a small smile, and he sighed, waving her in.

"You!" the grey-haired Maven snapped from a table right next to the door. "What are you doing back here?"

"We're over by the fire," Silas said, ushering them forward. "Let's not dawdle."

Tribal was pulling a fourth chair around a small table near the fireplace, and Kate started toward it. A man drinking log mead at the bar gave her a bleary look, and an older couple eating at a table near the middle of the room squinted at her. Maven leaned back in her chair and settled for a glare.

Kate dropped into a rough chair on the side of the table nearest the fire. The flames crackled loudly, and a wave of heat rolled over her. She tucked the blanket Rye had used back into her pack, then pulled off her cloak and turned her chair to face the flames, holding out her hands.

Yellow stepped up to the table, his face not entirely friendly. "What brings you two back to town?"

"We found Rye wandering in the woods," Kate said. "And he wasn't in any condition to find his own way back."

The innkeeper studied her for a moment. "How's his mind?"

"Troubled," Kate said.

Yellow's thick eyebrows drew together. "That's the second man who's been found today. Staven, the butcher, was found wandering near the river. In the same condition as the others. Where did you find Rye?"

Venn paused. "Not far from the gully that drains Reston Ridge. A little south of it, down closer to the river."

Yellow frowned. "That means everyone's been found down-hill from Reston's Ridge. Including the bodies of the two men who were killed."

"Where's Reston Ridge?" Kate asked.

"The whole slope," Venn answered. "From where we were above the tree line all the way down to the river."

"So Bo's camp is there too?"

Venn nodded.

Kate glanced around the room. "No more people have disappeared, have they?"

Yellow shook his head. "Look, if you're here, at least order some dinner." He lowered his voice. "I don't know how long you're planning on staying in town, but nothing here is growing more friendly toward you."

"We need to find out what happened to Bo," Kate said.

The innkeeper tapped his rag against his palm as he glanced around their table. "I liked Bo. A lot. He stayed here several times, met with men here. Spread out big maps on my tables and did who knows what for hours. But..." He sighed and looked Kate in the eyes. "It's been, what? Six weeks since he disappeared?" He shook his head. "That's a long time."

"He's still alive," Venn said.

Yellow raised his hands. "If you say so. Who wants some pork?"

"No," Tribal said. "Anything but your pork."

Yellow frowned at him. "You travelers never know what's good." He turned and headed toward the kitchen.

Silas looked at Kate expectantly, and she pulled out Bo's official notes, spreading his map of the ravine on the table. "He says that Emperor Sorrn came here, searching for Renault's amulet. The records say he was looking for a cave, and Bo marked these cave entrances on the map."

The dwarves exchanged looks.

"There's nothing in those caves," Tribal said.

Kate shrugged. "All I know is that Emperor Sorrn thought there was. Of course, he was old and possibly going mad himself. He snuck away from all his responsibilities, searching in secret for an amulet to bring him eternal life, instead of just living."

Tribal tapped his finger thoughtfully on the table, studying the map.

"And Bo was exploring these caves too?" Silas asked.

Kate pulled out his journal. "He says there were signs that they were mined long ago. He was in one when the tree attacked. It came into the cave where he hid. It was wounded, and the creature kept trying to collapse the cave until some large rocks fell on it. He presumed it was dead and barely escaped before the rest of the cave was lost behind the rockslide."

Tribal looked up at her, his brow creased in confusion. "A monster, who was like a tree, caused a rockslide, then…went into a cave during it? Not back into the forest?"

Kate gestured to Bo's journal. "That's what he said. It was making some sort of noise, like speech. It climbed into the cave and collapsed, then tried to tear down the ceiling."

Silas frowned at her. "It was trying to kill itself?"

"So it would appear," Kate said.

"Which cave was he in?" Tribal asked, looking at the cave mouths surrounded by notes on the map. "What does all this say?"

"It describes what the caves were like. Dry, rocky walls, signs of mining, but the only tools he found were rotted and rusted from age. Some signs of animals, but nothing recent." Kate glanced back at his journal. "He never marked what cave he was in. Aren't all these covered by the rock slide?"

"All it'll take is a little excavation." Silas studied the map again. "They're all connected. We've been in them before." He tapped the cave on the left side of the map and glanced at his brother. "That's the one that dropped down in the back before it met the others?"

Tribal nodded.

"If you've been in them before," Kate said, "you know there's no treasure."

"We know there's a tiny bit of copper in the walls, and few gems in the rock," Silas corrected her. "But we were studying the caves themselves, not looking for places an old mad wizard would hide his goodies."

"You really think you'll find an amulet that brings immortality—an amulet that's been lost for hundreds of years?" Venn asked.

"Anytime something is being protected as fiercely as that ravine is, it's worth investigating." Tribal grinned. "We'll start tomorrow."

Kate sighed. "Well, be careful. I don't want to add you two to the list of people we're looking for."

CHAPTER FIFTY-THREE

SCENTS OF ROASTING pork and potatoes filled the tavern while Kate pulled herself off a generous piece of the rosemary bread Yellow had brought to their table. "Are you sure the pork is bad?"

Tribal shuddered. "We're sure."

Kate glanced over at the few tables that were filled. "The people here seem to eat it."

"I have no idea why." Venn blew on her bowl of creamy potato soup.

"It's not good." Silas gave Kate a probing look. "You're tempted to try it, aren't you?"

Tribal shook his head. "It's smarter to go treasure hunting in a cursed canyon than to try the dry stringy pork you've been warned against."

The tavern door opened, and Nevin walked in, holding Gerren's arm. They headed for a table near the bar, and Silas rose and followed them.

Venn sipped her soup and peered over the bowl at Gerren. "He's just like Rye."

485

Nevin turned to look at them. Kate gave him a smile, but he just turned back to Silas.

"I've been thinking about their memories," Kate said quietly. "If we could use the serum to share a memory from someone who was right there with him during the time he lost, maybe that would trigger some sort of connection? If his sister got him to remember a wounded bird, maybe we can get him to remember enough pieces to unlock…whatever's locked up inside him."

"If it's locked," Venn agreed. "What if it's just…gone?"

"Nevin said his son almost seemed interested in the bird when he remembered it. I think somehow everything is locked together. The memories and the…autonomy. Almost like his mind is afraid to remember."

Venn paused with the spoon halfway to her mouth. "Then it might not be a kindness to help him remember."

"Even if it gives him back his mind?"

Venn looked back at the young man, who stood listlessly looking at the yellow door mounted on the wall above the bar. "I guess that depends on what he remembers."

Silas patted Nevin on the shoulder and pointed toward Kate. The three came to the table, and Tribal stood and offered his chair to Gerren while Nevin took the other empty seat, and the dwarves pulled chairs over from the next table.

Gerren stood numbly beside his chair until his father reached up and took his hand. "Sit down, son. This is Kate, and she'd like to talk to you for a few minutes."

Gerren looked obediently at Kate but said nothing.

He was younger than Kate had realized. He was as tall as his father, but his height was from the lanky arms and legs of a boy shooting through his teens.

She offered Nevin a smile, then turned to his son. "Hello, Gerren." She held out her hand, and he shook it numbly.

His remnant was a combination of dry autumn grass and the

warm smell of animal fur. A hint of wind blew past, reminding her of the vast farmlands of southern Queensland. Not a wild wind, but a strong one that pulled up dust and seeds and strewed them across the land. It felt complex and robust and utterly undamaged.

She cast out toward him, and his body flared into warmth and brightness, slightly brighter than that of his father, who was watching with narrow eyes. "How do you feel, Gerren?"

"Fine," he answered without hesitation.

"You're not tired?"

He blinked at her for a moment. "Is it time to sleep?"

"Not yet," his father said, setting a hand on his shoulder.

Kate offered Nevin a tight smile. "I told you last night that I'm a Keeper. I know that doesn't mean anything to you, but where I'm from, we're known for several things. We have a very large library and spend most of our time recording stories and histories. We travel among the people of our land offering our help to them."

He glanced at Venn.

"It's true," she said.

Silas nodded. "She's among the most respected people of her land."

"Why are ya here?" Nevin asked.

"Because Bo really is my brother, and I really am worried about him." She swallowed. "The other thing Keepers are known for is magic."

His eyes narrowed, and his gaze flickered to Silas, who nodded again. Nevin looked back at Kate. "Did ya use magic on me t' get me to talk t' ya last night?"

"No," she answered with a smile. "Unless you count the magic that exists in the shared humanity we have. But Keepers are, in general, opposed to using magic to make people do things they don't want to."

"What do ya want with Gerren?" he asked.

"I have a serum," Kate said. "It's for sharing memories. I would like to have Gerren share with me what he remembers about being taken."

The man's eyes narrowed.

"It just takes a copy of his memory and lets me see it," she said.

"That's all it does," Venn agreed. "I've used it myself."

"What will it show ya?"

Kate paused. "I don't know. I saw Rye's memories of when he was taken and when he came back. The little he had of them. Maybe if I can see Gerren's too, I can get a clue as to what happened with them both."

Nevin swallowed, then gave a small, jerky nod.

Kate pulled the tenea serum out of her pack, holding it up to show Gerren. The sparkles in the fluid caught the firelight and glittered gold, and the boy's eyes locked onto it. "Set your fingertip in this." She guided his hand into the serum and trickled some *vitalle* through his finger. "Can you remember where you were the day that they found you wandering the woods?"

"Hunting rabbits," he said with no inflection in his voice.

The thin stream of light seeped out into the serum, and when it ended, Kate pulled his finger out and put in her own.

He knelt behind a large rock, a pebble locked into the slingshot in his hands. Ten paces away, the tail of a fat rabbit was visible from the side of a red-leaved bush. His eyes scanned the trees, noting the wind and the motion of a squirrel farther away. The rabbit twitched, and his attention locked back on it.

There was a rustle behind him, and he started to turn.

The edges of his vision turned black. There was the impression of trees and splotches of shadow. Before he'd turned all the way around, the darkness collapsed upon him.

Yellow light filtered through the darkness. He opened his eyes slowly, but there was no rock. There was just the pale sky of an early dawn and a birch tree barely clinging to the last of its golden leaves.

He stared at a quivering leaf for a moment until it snapped off and fluttered away. When he sat up, the breeze blew over him, cold and crisp. He wrapped his arms around himself and stared at the browning birch leaves littering the ground. Each serrated edge was curled. Each bleeding their color out into nothing.

His eyes searched for nothing else. He didn't look around the forest to find himself or at his own body to see if he was injured. He merely sat staring at the leaves until a voice called out from somewhere nearby, and he looked up to find the shocked face of a man running toward him.

"Gerren? Is that you?"

Kate opened her eyes and looked at Venn. "He's just like Rye. His memory goes black, and then instantly it's months later." She corked the serum and studied the boy. "Gerren, could you think about that day again?"

He nodded and she cast out, focusing on his brain. It lit up, bright and warm, except for a more muted section deep inside.

She switched her attention to Nevin. He watched his son with a troubled look, and his brain was uniformly bright. Possibly even brighter, deep in the center. She closed her eyes, sending small waves into Gerren's, searching for anything that seemed damaged or blocked. But there was nothing. Just a slightly subdued section.

She set her hand on his and fed a stream of *vitalle* into him, guiding it up to his head and funneling it toward the dim section. She searched for any sign that his body was trying to heal. The tiniest glimmer of *vitalle* lit up along the base of the shadowed part, and it pulled in a little of her energy. But it was so small that it barely took anything from her.

She sat for a few minutes, feeding the section the smallest dribble of *vitalle*, and when she cast out again, there was a little divot of brightness into the dim section.

She opened her eyes. "His mind is healing, but very, very slowly."

Nevin's hand twitched on his son's shoulder. "So he'll recover?"

"I don't know." Kate tapped the vial of serum she still held in one hand. "His last memory before the gap, he was hunting a rabbit. Can you think of anything you did together with him between then and when he disappeared?"

"We finished the new barn." Nevin gave a wan smile. "After tying down the last o' the thatch, we sat on the roof and watched the sun set." He took in a wavering breath. "He told me he wanted t' raise more pigs next summer. Asked if he could work for our neighbor in exchange for piglets from the next litter. We planned out where we'd build the pen." His smile faded. "He doesn't talk about the pigs anymore."

"Would you mind using the serum? If you put your finger in and think of the memory, I can share it with him. Maybe if he sees something he forgot, something significant like that, it'll waken his mind a little more."

Nevin swallowed again and set his finger into the serum. When his memory swirled in it, Kate gave it to Gerren. The thread sank into his fingertip, and the boy's eyes widened. He sat up, staring unseeing as the memory spooled into him. Kate cast out toward him, watching his mind, and a small flash of light appeared in the dimmer part.

A smile twitched up the edge of his lips. "The piglets."

Nevin grabbed his shoulder. "Yes! The piglets! Remember the holes ya dug for the pen the next day, after I left?"

Gerren's smile faded. "Holes?"

Nevin's wide eyes flashed between Kate and his son. "Yes...
the holes for the posts..."

Gerren merely stared at him.

"The memory did something." Kate cast out again, and the
new bright part in Gerren's mind was still there. "But just a little.
Do you have more we could share with him?"

Nevin paused. "That was a month before he went missing, and I
left the next morning for a trip t' buy southern wheat. I only
returned right before he disappeared. My wife will have more.
I'll..." He squeezed Gerren's shoulder. "If it'll help him, she'll do it."

Kate tapped her finger on the side of the vial. "That memory
elicited an emotion from him, and that's when I saw his mind
wake a little. Maybe you and your wife can think of more memories that he'd have an emotional connection with? Or some of his
friends or a sibling? Maybe if we can give him several at once, it
will help him grab on to that missing time."

Nevin nodded, and Kate gave him a smile. "I promise you,
that woke a tiny part." She cast out toward Gerren's mind again,
and the spot was still bright. "And it's staying awake. Is anything
else different about him since he came back?"

Nevin lowered his voice. "He's afraid of the dark. Won't sleep
away from the fire. Won't even walk into the barn without a
lantern."

Kate met Venn's eyes before looking back at Nevin. "So he's
scared of shadows?"

Gerren flinched at the word.

The man swallowed. "I think it's th' shadow that people seen
that's done this to my boy." Gerren twitched again, and Nevin
rose, urging his son up as well. "I'll talk t' my wife. If there's
anything we can do that'll help our boy, we'll do it."

He glanced at Venn with a nervous look. "I remembered
somethin' 'bout Bo. Somethin' no one else might know."

Kate's fingers tightened on the serum.

Nevin shifted. "Just before the rockslide happened in the canyon, the day I came back from the south, I passed a field at the edge of town, and I saw Bo there. Arguin'." He swallowed again and flicked his eyes to Venn. "With that elf prince fellow."

Venn's mouth fell open. "Faron? Are you sure?"

Nevin nodded. "Couldn't make out what they was saying, but the prince looked angry. All shiny and coppery, like he was gonna burst into flame." He gave the serum a sidelong glance. "I could show you."

Venn leaned forward. "Please!"

He dipped his finger in the serum and poured out a very short memory. Venn drew it in then turned to Kate. "That was definitely Faron, and he was definitely mad."

"Could you tell what they said?"

Venn shook her head, looking puzzled. "Bo looked insulted."

Nevin gave a small shrug. "If I remember anything else, I'll let ya know, but I didn't know Bo much myself."

"Thank you!" Kate said, rising.

He gave a short nod and took his son's arm. "C'mon, Gerren. Your mama'll be worried if we're out too long."

CHAPTER FIFTY-FOUR

Before the tavern door closed, Yellow reached over Kate's shoulder to pick up empty plates off their table. "I'm impressed. Nevin didn't look furious at you when he left."

"We made a tiny bit of progress helping Gerren." Kate took the last piece of rosemary bread from her plate and handed the dish to him.

"You think you can heal all the men who lost their memories?" he asked.

She paused. "I don't know. Maybe. I'll need help from their families, and I don't know if it will fix everything."

"It was brave of you to come back to town and kind to try to help these folks." He glanced out the dark window. "Feels like snow tonight. Your room's available, if you two want a roof over your head."

"Thank you," Kate said, and the innkeeper left. She turned to Venn. "What do you think Faron argued with Bo about?"

Venn gave her a lost look. "I've never heard of Faron being anything but excruciatingly polite to humans."

"Are you sure it was him?"

493

"No other elves glow coppery like that when they're agitated. But...even after seeing it, I find it hard to believe."

Kate looked at Venn expectantly.

The elf's face darkened. "No."

"We need to talk to him."

"He's just going to lie."

"You said he was honorable."

"Honorably bound to keep the secrets of the White Wood. It is *not* in the Wood's interest for him to fight with a human. So he'll never admit it happened."

"That is a very loose definition of honorable."

"He's utterly bound to obey the king."

"Can you imagine if we were bound to obey the gov'nor?" Tribal whispered loudly to Silas.

"If he talked to Bo..." Kate said. "Heatedly..."

Venn crossed her arms and glared into the fireplace. "He will lie. I promise you."

Kate leaned into Venn's field of vision. "If he's going to lie, let's see what he lies about."

"It will lead to nothing but frustration."

"Which we already have. So what's a little more? How do we contact his royal highness?"

Venn glared at her for a moment, then shoved her chair back and pointed at Kate. "This is a bad idea." She spun on her heel and stalked toward the door.

"Is it me," Tribal asked quietly, "or is she glowing a little bit?"

"Maybe all elves glow?" Kate answered.

"You should ask her," Silas said.

Venn stepped outside and the door shut behind her with a bang.

"Maybe another time." Kate pushed herself up. "I do want to see where she's going, though."

Outside, the night had grown dark, and an icy wind whipped

Kate's hair across her face. Venn stood at the massive pine that grew in the center of the town square with her hand against the trunk. Kate had just reached her when Venn dropped it again and started back toward the inn.

Tiny droplets of ice-cold rain spattered Kate's face, and she looked between Venn and the tree. "That's it?" She hurried after Venn. "Is that tree connected to the ones in the White Wood? I thought trees had to be in the same forest to speak to each other."

"All trees are connected." Venn shoved the tavern door open.

Kate stepped in after her, pausing to look back into the dark square. "Is he going to come?"

"I'm not standing in the cold waiting for him," Venn said, striding toward the table. "I told him to come in the morning."

Kate pulled the door closed, keeping in the heat of the common room. The townsfolk stared at her with looks varying from curiosity to mistrust. "Is he going to?"

Venn dropped into her chair. "He'd better."

Tribal smirked at her through his black beard. "Or what?"

"How come you can boss around the elf prince?" Silas asked.

Venn stared moodily into the fire.

"Because they're betrothed," Kate explained.

"Ooooh," Tribal said. "Then...yes. He'll come."

Venn pointed at the dwarves. "Not because of *that*. Because the First Ranger is beholden to the elven people. If he is called, he is duty bound to come, no matter where he is in the Wood. And Faron never shirks his duty."

The dwarves eyed her finger warily. It did seem to be glowing faintly.

"He's duty bound to come...even if you're not in the Wood?" Silas asked.

Venn glared at him.

"Maybe only if he's betrothed to you," Tribal whispered loudly.

Venn shoved herself to her feet. "I'm going somewhere less dwarven." Ignoring the stares of the common room, she stalked toward the stairs.

Yellow walked over, holding a key out to Kate and watching Venn with a concerned look. "Can you take this to her before she breaks my door trying to get in?"

Venn lay on her bed, running her fingers along the end of the pine bough wedged under the window, glowering at the ceiling.

"Could you have called Faron from this tree?" Kate asked.

Venn gave a hum that might have been a yes but certainly didn't invite more conversation.

A cold breeze trickled in, and Kate wrapped the blanket from her bed around her shoulders before pulling her pack closer. It tipped, and both Bo's journal and the aenigma box tumbled out. She reached for Bo's journal but paused. Picking up the aenigma box instead, she examined the side where the drawer had opened in the woods.

The desperation for any sort of clue that she'd felt in the woods had faded with finding Rye and the conversation with Nevin. She still didn't have much to go on, but at least there was something. And if Faron had talked to Bo, that was another person who might know...something.

Her desperation had settled into the long process of waiting and following clues, and that would never get the drawer to open. She contemplated trying, from memory, to record the words from the scroll, but it would be better to wait and copy it. Although she wasn't looking forward to feeling desperate enough to open the drawer anytime soon.

She set the box down, keeping it close against her leg, and picked up Bo's journal, drawing a bit of flame from the lantern into her hand. She'd read everything from the end of the journal, so she skipped back to a random page earlier. It was dated from late summer and held a sketch of a hillside topped with a ruined city.

> *Ria,*
>
> *This is one of those places I wish you were here to see. My sketch does not do it justice.*
>
> *That is the pink ruins of Blessrechen.*
>
> *There was a mine in the next hill to the west that produced some rare salt, but they exhausted the supply, and there is absolutely nothing else here to support anyone, so the population deserted the area fifty years ago.*
>
> *The salt was mined from deposits mottled with pink cerrion, which is a useless mineral that crumbles easily. To extract the salt, the chunks from the deposit were broken and shaken and tossed in the air, where the powdery remains of the crushed pink cerrion would be carried off by the wind. A bit like wheat and chaff.*
>
> *But the powder didn't go far. Instead, it coated the western side of every single building in town (and the hillside itself) with a thick layer of crystalized strands that look like pink fur.*
>
> *Apparently, if I wait until the sun sinks low in the west, the fur will sparkle.*
>
> *So here I sit, staring at a ruined city, waiting for the pink edges of it to sparkle in the setting sun, and pondering what an odd world this is—and laughing at myself for all of it.*
>
> *And no, before you ask, I did not get you your own sample of pink cerrion. Yes, I know you would be interested in examining it, but the crystals are supposedly infested with wasps. You know how I feel about wasps.*

"Yes, Bo," she said with a smile. "I know how you feel about wasps." The day they'd found a hive in the tree fort near the river was the day they'd abandoned it. Bo had flat-out refused to even go close.

She could almost hear his voice declaring the fort fallen into enemy hands and see him striding off to find a different place to carry on their daily adventures.

She shifted the blanket and knocked the aenigma box onto its side. She reached down to put it back into her bag and stopped.

Along the top of the lefthand side of the box, a drawer was visible.

"Venn!" Kate pulled it open. It was shallow enough to only sit in the top third of the side and so narrow it barely filled the middle third, but it was nearly as long as the entire box.

"Another one?" Venn sat up. "How did you open that one?"

"I don't know. Wasps? Or maybe nostalgia?" Kate held her bit of flame over the drawer, and a thousand lights glittered back at her as a faint, tattered remnant filled the air with the sound of a tinkling stream.

Venn drew in a breath. "What is that?"

"Shattered glass, I think." Kate brought the light closer until she could see the shards of colored glass filling the bottom of the drawer. She reached in and picked up one of the bigger pieces. It was no longer than her fingernail and a quarter as wide. The edges were sharp, and she held it up gingerly. Streaks of blue and green colored the glass, and she searched for another piece that matched it. The drawer was a chaos of colored slivers, most no wider than a blade of grass. "I have no idea what it used to be."

She dropped the piece back in and nudged the other slivers around, sending glints of light reflecting off them. She gave the box a little shake, and the shards shushed against each other as they tumbled around the drawer. "Why can't we hear these when it's closed?"

Venn stretched out her hand but stopped before she reached the box. She rubbed her thumb across her fingertips before touching the edge of the box. Her fingers twitched, but she held them there for a long moment.

Finally, she nodded. "When I first picked it up, it felt solitary. Isolated, even. Thought it was because it was Bo's, and he'd been a bit lonely when I met him. But, honestly, it doesn't feel like him. This feels utterly solitary. More so than anyone I've ever met."

"That matches the bell I can hear in it. That sounds like it's ringing in some huge empty cavern."

"Does the broken glass have a remnant?" Venn asked.

"It sounds like a stream." Kate straightened. "Or maybe like glass shattering." She pulled the amplifier out of her cloak pocket and dripped some into the drawer. The sound, like an endless shower of crystals falling to a stone floor, grew louder. She looked up. "It sounds like breaking glass."

Venn raised an eyebrow. "That's very..."

"Odd." The amplifier dissolved into a light blue mist, and the sound faded. Kate glanced up at Venn. "Unless this person who filled this Nostalgia Drawer knew what their own remnant sounded like. Then this is like...signing their name."

"Do you know what your remnant sounds like?"

Kate nodded. "The river near where we grew up. And the smells of the wheat field in spring. I just hear it and smell it all the time, so it's easy to ignore."

"Have you ever heard of anyone else who can sense remnants?"

Kate shook her head. "None of the Keepers even knew it was possible." She moved the glass around gently again, but there was nothing else in the drawer as far as she could see. Slowly, she pushed shut the drawer until it blended into the side of the box. She gave it a shake, but there was no sound at all.

Venn lay back on her bed again. "That is a very strange box."

Kate tried to generate the hope to open the first drawer, but nothing appeared. She fiddled with it for a few minutes, attempting to open any of the drawers she had before. But nothing moved.

"It's a finicky contraption." She pulled out her journal and flipped to the page where she'd drawn the aenigma box. She sketched the Nostalgia Drawer along the top left side and jotted down a description of its contents. "This drawer should definitely take up the same space as the Restless Drawer and probably the top of the Hope Drawer as well. The only one it doesn't overlap with is the Desperation Drawer, but that takes up space that should be in both the Hope and the Restless Drawers." She shook her head. "Who made this thing? And how many different people put things in it?"

She was opening her pack to tuck both the journal and the box back when she caught a glimpse of a brown cover. Curious, she reached in and found the little book the Shield had given her in the Stronghold.

"I forgot about you," she said, flipping it open to see the blank pages. At Venn's curious look, she held it up. "The Shield found this for me just before you showed up. Said he'd been looking for it for weeks because the library wanted me to have it."

Venn let out a short laugh. "Does your library want people to have books often?"

"This was the first I'd heard of it. The Shield is…different, though. If he says the library talked to him, I actually believe him."

"He's an elder," Venn said, as though that explained talking to libraries.

"He is?"

Venn tilted her head curiously. "Isn't he?"

"That depends on what an elder is."

"You don't have elders?"

"Clearly not. Are they just the oldest elves?"

"Usually, although some become elders younger than others.

They have…insight. More than just the wisdom of their years. Something happens, and they aren't just elves anymore. They're…" Venn looked at the ceiling, as though searching for a way to explain it. "When elves die, we're buried among the roots of a tree. Our spirit joins the forest. But for an elder, their spirit begins to join the trees while they're still alive. They are connected to the forest in a way we don't really understand. Even they don't understand it, I think. But speaking with them is a bit like speaking to the trees."

"I've always thought the Shield seemed to live in more than one place. He's somehow sitting in his chair in the library but also somewhere else. Or he can see into somewhere else and make out a little of what's going on."

Venn lifted her head to see the page of the book. "That's an odd book. I can feel that it is full of…something. But are those pages blank?"

"It's called *Monsters of the North*." Kate pulled the lantern closer and blew it out, plunging the room into darkness. "And it's written in *verus* ink."

"…Is it going to glow?"

Kate laughed. "Sort of." She set her fingertip next to the smoking wick and pushed a surge of *vitalle* into it. "*Verus elucida*." A silvery blue flame burst into life, and silver writing glimmered on the page.

Venn swung her feet down. "That's an interesting trick."

"It's true light. The ink isn't terribly hard to make, but it's a bit finicky and takes enough *vitalle* to write with it that it's mostly reserved for secret messages added onto something else. I've never heard of an entire book written in it." She smiled. "Except Kellen is in the process of making one in the Stronghold purely to irritate Mikal."

Venn peered at the spidery-thin writing on the page. "I can't read that."

"It's in an old dialect of Kalesh." Kate set the book down next to the lantern. "I think the entire book is children's rhymes, but look." She turned to the inside of the cover to show the map of this area. "I'm guessing the *Monsters of the North* are all from the White Wood."

"What do the poems say?"

Kate flipped to the first page. "This one is called...I don't know this word. *Rööks.*" She ran her finger down the page. "Oh, there's a translation at the bottom into...well, a very old dialect of the local common tongue, I think. Looks like they didn't know how to translate *rööks* either. The translation reads:

Watch the shadows, watch the cracks,
Fill your pock's with lime and *rööks*,
Claws'll gouge,
Jump the S'yern
Teeth'll bite,
Dodge the holt
Race the shadows, flee the cracks
Copper's blue, so mind the *rööks*."

Venn frowned. "Holt? Like forest?"

"I would guess. In Queensland, that word fell out of use hundreds of years ago. What's the S'yern?"

"I have no idea." Venn paused. "Read it again."

Kate did, and Venn nodded. "It has the cadence of a jumping rhyme. The human children here have a game where they set a rope on the ground in some shape, then they chant little rhymes like this while jumping over and around the rope."

"Children in Queensland have a similar game involving sticks." Kate flipped to a drawing of a mouse-like creature with broad antlers.

"That'd be cute if it's the size of a mouse," Venn said. "Less so if it's large enough to hold a full-sized rack of elk antlers."

The next page held a very short poem. "This one's alarming," Kate said.

"Shadows crawl from dark to dark,
Wailing, wailing in the dark,
Dry the bones and stop the heart,
Wailing, wailing in the dark."

Venn gave an interested hum. "Almost rhymes."

"In Old Kalesh, the rhyme is nearly perfect. *Sartkovy* and *tretmovy*."

"Do you think these shadows are literal?"

"Normally, in a poem like this, I'd say obviously metaphorical, but…"

Venn nodded. "Either way, they're ominous."

"I agree." Kate turned the page and paused. "The next one is actually called *The Shadow*. It doesn't have a translation, though. It might take me a bit to sort out."

Venn lay on her bed and kept a suspicious eye on the book. "Is it too much to hope that one of these poems will just tell us what the shadow is?"

"Probably." Kate scanned the third poem. "There are a lot of words I don't know in this one, but the first line reads 'Darkness seeps into your mind…'"

Venn drew back slightly. "Maybe I don't want to know what it is."

PART V

THE RIVERS

Maybe we're like rivers. We begin as a trickle, moving over the ground. We grow into the world around us. Affect it. Shape it.

But it shapes us as well.

We come up to something hard, something solid and immovable and implacable, and we bend around it. It defines our course, and the longer we skirt it, the more deeply we carve ourselves into that path.

But we continue on, affecting and being affected by the world we encounter. Sometimes finding low, gentle places to slow and rest. Sometimes finding places so low we pool there and cannot rise high enough to leave.

Sometimes rockslides tumble into us, shoving us in a new direction.

There are aspects to the metaphor I like. The river's path is the path of my life. I could map it out for you. Name the things that molded it.

But somehow, I am also the water. All of the water.

Even here, when I know I'm reaching the end, when I can smell the sea, feel the vastness of the unknown I'm flowing towards—even here I am still in every stretch of the river I've passed.

Or maybe it is in me. Particles of silt from the valleys. Slivers of stone I broke off over the rapids.

I suppose it's both.

It has formed me, and some part of me is still back in every turn.

I'm still twelve years old, staring at the empty patch of ground where my brother had just been.

Still thirty-two, looking for the push from something outside of myself, something I love, so I can take that one step into the darkness that I can't yet define or understand looming ahead of me.

I can see it all. I can still feel every curve and obstacle.

I would imagine everyone else is the same. Still living all the disparate parts of their lives. Still mired in bogs, still celebrating victories, still forging the path ahead. All at once while also living through today.

What complicated creatures we are.

CHAPTER FIFTY-FIVE

KATE SCRAMBLED around a thin pine and stumbled, crashing to her knees on the hard ground. She twisted to see the blackness looming in the trees behind her.

A massive shifting shadow slithered closer with edges that bled into the dark crevices of the forest.

It oozed around the needles of the pine tree, swallowing entire branches.

She shoved herself back, but sludgy, wet mud wrapped around her legs, gluing her to the ground.

A tendril of shadow stretched toward her with a hiss of icy cold air.

Kate jolted awake with a gasp.

A silvery patch of moonlight lay on the floor. Around it, the room was steeped in darkness, every corner black with shadows.

Freezing cold air pressed against her, and she pulled her blankets tighter. Venn's breath came slow and steady from the other bed, and Kate tried to slow her own.

The pine outside was etched in moonlight against the night sky. The book of poems sat under the window, and Kate rubbed her face. It might have been a mistake to read eerie shadow poems before bed.

She sat up and checked the window latch. It was closed, with Venn's branch shut outside. The center of the tree was lost in shadows so black that she leaned closer, trying to see into them.

A shadow along the corner of the windowsill shifted and slid toward her. Kate yanked her hand back and cast out.

Venn burst into light and warmth so brightly that for a moment Kate couldn't make out anything else. She focused on the tree, and it resolved into its slow, steady flow of *vitalle*. It ran thick along the trunk and dwindled to thin strands in the needles.

There was nothing else there.

The shadow on the windowsill sat as innocuous as any night-time shadow. Kate stretched her fingers out to touch it and found only the worn wood.

She blew out a breath, and it clouded in the moonlight.

Yellow's pile of extra blankets called to her from downstairs. Shivering, she grabbed her cloak and wrapped it around herself. When she pushed open the door, it let out a faint squeak, but Venn didn't move. Aside from the elf's breathing and some muffled snoring from the dwarves' room next door, the inn was quiet.

Kate peered down the hallway. Far at the end, a dim red light filtered up the stairs. The hallway itself was filled with inky black shadows crouching along the floor and skulking in the recessed doorways.

A creeping uneasiness clawed its way up her back. The same feel the gaping door of the root cellar had given her as a child. The nagging sensation that the darkness wasn't empty.

She shifted her shoulders and cast out. There was nothing in the hallway.

Ignoring the lingering uneasiness, she padded quietly down to the common room.

The banked coals in the fireplace glowed with a rich red light. A welcome heat pressed against her cheek from it, and she paused to soak it in.

The pile of blankets sat on the nearest table. She pulled a heavy woolen one off the top, then sorted through the pile, looking for a second for Venn.

A brush of uneasiness slid across her neck again, and she twisted around.

The front of the tavern faced away from the moon, leaving the windows dark and filling the room with shadowy columns and bulky dark shapes of tables.

Nothing moved. She shook out her hands, trying to banish her nerves. Grabbing a second blanket, she headed back toward the stairs.

A heavy thunk shook the floor.

She spun toward the kitchen, her fingers digging into the blanket.

Through the door, she could see the edge of the cooking fireplace, glowing with the same reddish light as the common room.

She almost called out to Yellow, but the uneasiness kept her quiet, and she cast out instead. Someone lay on the floor, sprawled in an awkward position. A large, Yellow-sized someone.

Beyond him was…nothing.

She crept forward.

A rustling sound slithered out of the kitchen, and her feet froze.

With the fading end of her wave, she could feel Yellow on the floor, unmoving.

There was something strange about the space past him. It was too empty.

She gripped the blankets and strained to hear anything else.

Bo's words came back to her. *It was one of those moments that always feels too big for me. I'm paralyzed by my own weakness. By all the times I've failed before...*

That's always what those One Step moments need. Not a huge goal or feat of strength or brilliant answer.

They need a small push, a real push. Driven by something outside of me. Something I love.

And then I can see the best decision, and I can take one step. And then I can take another.

Kate drew in a wavering breath.

Something outside herself.

Yellow was obviously not just sleeping on his kitchen floor. He was lying there at the mercy of...something. She set the blankets on the bar and moved a step closer to the kitchen door. Then another. She placed her hand on the door frame, steadying herself, and peered around it.

A wide-mouthed fireplace took up most of the visible lefthand wall, and a huge table took up the right.

Yellow lay sprawled on his back on the floor in the open space between them, small and vulnerable in the face of the void that filled the room beyond him.

Kate's hands clenched on the doorframe. The shadow was impenetrable. Its surface shifted and churned. Its edges leaked into the rest of the room, merging with the shadow of the table and the lines of darkness hiding along the thick beams of the ceiling. It wasn't a figure or a creature. It slid forward like a mass of liquid night.

A tendril extended out of it toward Yellow's head.

Kate shoved herself into the kitchen. "Get away from him!" She flung *vitalle* toward the fireplace, and the coals burst into flame. Light poured into the room, making the physical shadow of the table flicker and jump.

The looming darkness pulled back like a wall of roiling pitch.

The tendril disappeared into it, and though there was no face to be seen, she felt its attention shift from Yellow to her.

Fear coursed through the bones of her arms and legs as she scanned the kitchen for a weapon. Every surface was meticulously clean. There were no knives, and the heavy pots hung all the way across the room by the fireplace. The table next to her held nothing but a rolling pin.

She grabbed it and stepped closer to Yellow, reaching toward the fire. Ignoring how her hand shook, she lashed out with a finger of *vitalle* and snatched a tongue of flame into her palm.

The massive shadow shifted closer to Yellow's unprotected body.

Kate crossed the room and stood above him, pouring more *vitalle* into her flame until it grew to the size of a torch. "Stay back."

The darkness slid closer. A tendril emerged from the surface, stretching toward her like an inky snake.

She hurled the rolling pin at it.

It disappeared into the blackness and smashed into something on the far wall, shattering glass and sending some heavy object crashing to the floor.

She cast out again, but there was absolutely nothing in the kitchen but herself, Yellow, and the fire. "What do you want?"

The edge of the shadow spread across the front of the fireplace, smothering the light. She kept her handful of flame raised, illuminating the space around herself and Yellow as the shadow crept closer.

Three more tendrils reached out toward her, and Kate threw up her free hand, flinging a shield of *vitalle*, even as she knew it wouldn't stop a creature without any sign of life.

But the shadow flowed against it like water against a glass.

The darkness spread to the side, searching for the edges, and she widened her shield, staying just ahead of its grasping tendrils.

She sank to her knees next to Yellow's shoulder, enlarging the shell, trying to encompass herself and the huge innkeeper. Her palms burned with the effort to cover Yellow. A chill crept up her arm as she leeched more *vitalle* from her body.

The flame in her other hand burned more *vitalle* than she could spare, and, with a grimace, she snuffed the light, plunging the kitchen into darkness.

She threw both hands up to feed the shield. In the blackness, she yanked the shell shut behind her, locking herself and Yellow into a cocoon. With the shield in place, she reined in her *vitalle*.

The shadow pressed against it, wrapping over and around her, probing the shield. A small tear formed above her head, sending a ripping pain across her hands.

The shadow shoved inside, and she ducked. An icy stream of blackness poured onto her skull.

She twisted to look at it and slammed the rent closed. The finger of shadow trapped inside her shell dissolved with a gust of air as cold as the snowy night outside.

The cut left a hole at the end of the tendril. Inside, a hazy grey light shone before the shadow sealed itself shut.

The darkness crashed against her shield again, shoving at every surface. All the way down at Yellow's feet, tiny holes formed, and the shadow pounded against the weakness.

Kate closed tear after tear, making her palms burn.

Suddenly, the shadow drove a spike of blackness through the shield—not at Yellow's feet, but directly at his head.

Kate shoved *vitalle* toward the gash, but the shadow surged in, ripping the hole wider.

Blackness flooded onto Yellow, covering his face like someone had poured pitch over him, drowning him in darkness.

A distant ripple of *vitalle* washed over her, and Yellow's body shuddered.

The shadow tore at the hole in her shield, shredding the edges.

Pain seared across Kate's hands. She lost her grip on the shell, and it unraveled like smoke in the wind.

Icy cold air slammed into her skull with the weight of a mountain.

"No!" She squeezed her eyes shut and threw a shell up inside her own mind.

The darkness pummeled at it. She vaguely sensed another flash of *vitalle* from near Yellow's head, and she tried to stretch the shield to cover him, but the shadow was like a wall. She curled forward, gripping her head, desperately trying to push the flood of darkness and cold back.

The floor under her knees vibrated with footsteps. Distant voices came muffled from behind her.

The pressure from the shadow lightened for a moment, and Kate hurled her shield outward, heaving the shadow away.

It fell back—almost stumbled back—and she lashed out at it, filling her hand with the last of her *vitalle*.

Her fingers dug into the darkness, gouging out a thick, cold, viscous chunk.

The shadow recoiled, and the writhing piece of void dissolved in her hand with a hiss.

"Kate!" Venn's voice called.

"In the kitchen!" Kate yelled. "The shadow!"

Dwarven voices shouted over each other, and the footsteps ran closer.

The shadow pulled toward the back of the room, sliding away from the fireplace. Light flooded back into the kitchen.

Footsteps pounded through the kitchen doorway.

A dart shot into the roiling black surface.

The darkness drained into the cracks of the floor and the deep shadows hiding beside the fireplace. It drew farther back, sinking down until it revealed a counter crowded with baskets and bottles and crates and casks.

Tribal hurled a knife at the last of the darkness.

The void tore apart into countless tattered bits, dissolving down into the dark side of every object, and the knife sank uselessly into the thick wood of the wall.

CHAPTER FIFTY-SIX

"WHERE IS IT?" Silas jumped over Yellow's legs, rushing toward the far wall, brandishing his axe.

Venn followed him, her crossbow held up in front of her. "Kate?" she asked over her shoulder.

"I'm fine." Kate spun, searching every shadow. "It got Yellow more than me."

The innkeeper groaned and opened his eyes before squeezing them shut again. His hands moved up to cradle his head. "Why am I on the floor?"

Kate leaned closer. "Do you know who I am?"

He cracked an eye. "You're staying in my inn, Kate, and the whole town hates you. How would I not know who you are?"

"Because the shadow was here."

His eyes flew open. "The shadow! I remember! I heard something in the storeroom and thought it might be one of you looking for something." He pointed toward a door at the back of the kitchen, next to the crowded long counter, watching it warily. "Darkness poured out of there."

Tribal and Silas moved through the storeroom door.

515

"Room's empty," Silas called out.

A dark shadow along the edge of the fireplace caught Kate's eye, but nothing moved there, and she dragged her attention back to Yellow. "What did it do?"

The innkeeper pushed himself up to sit. "It filled the room and then...I was in a cave." He shook his head. "That doesn't make sense, but there was definitely a cave."

Kate reached into the pocket of her cloak. "Would you share your memory of tonight with me? The way Nevin and Gerren did?"

His eyes widened, and he grabbed her arm. "Gerren—he was in the cave!"

She held out her vial of tenea serum. "Please show me. Just put your finger in here, and think about what happened."

Yellow swallowed and nodded.

When his memory swirled in the liquid, she drew it in and found herself looking out of the eye of someone very tall, moving through the dark common room.

> Yellow stepped into the dim kitchen. "Hello?"
>
> A wall of shadows poured out of the storeroom door and flooded the room, washing around him until he drowned in the black.
>
> Something shoved him, and he fell backwards. His head cracked onto the hard floor, and there was a moment of nothing. Then the world turned foggy and grey. A flicker of images raced across his mind.
>
> The rocky floor of a cave.
>
> A set of hands gripped a twisted wooden latticework, peering through it as though trapped in a cage.
>
> A shadowy shape at the far side of the cave drew back, revealing Gerren's body lying senseless.
>
> A dark arm stretched out.
>
> A flash of light.

Shouting voices rang out, and the image of the cave shattered.

Yellow opened his eyes into the brightly lit kitchen, looking up into Kate's face.

Kate looked at Venn, who was peering into the shadows just outside the kitchen door. "The shadow had Gerren in a cave."

Silas strode across the room to them. "What was the cave like?"

"All I saw was a piece of rocky floor," Yellow said, rubbing his hand across the back of his head.

"That does not narrow it down," Tribal said.

Venn eyes still scanned the room. "How could Yellow see that?"

Kate shook her head. "I don't know. Maybe the shadow was connecting to Yellow with…whatever it uses to steal memories when we interrupted it. Maybe Yellow caught some other memory trapped in it."

"What did it want Yellow's memories for?" Silas asked.

"I don't know." Kate surveyed the kitchen and the bit of common room she could see. "We've been thinking it's attacking people who knew Bo, and during the town meeting Yellow said he knew him. Maybe that's why."

"Did it try to get your memories?" Venn asked Kate.

"It was trying to get something," Kate said. "It would have, too, if you three hadn't come when you did."

"We heard crashes." Silas held out his hand.

Kate grasped his wrist, and he pulled her to her feet.

"What is the shadow?" Venn asked. "Could you tell?"

"It was…" Kate shook her head. "It was like a huge piece of nothing. I couldn't sense anything about it. I couldn't see it or hear it or sense any life at all in it. But not like an empty room. Like less than an empty room. But when it tried to reach me, I could stop it. My shield held it back." She paused. "It's not solid, though—I cut off a piece of its…arm, or tentacle or whatever it has. Inside was a murky, hazy grey."

"You cut it?" Venn asked.

"And at the end, just before it disappeared, I…" Kate flexed her fingers, trying to find the words to describe it. "I pulled a piece off. Not a piece—it was like…mist. Or sludge. It was icy cold and empty."

Everyone in the kitchen stared at her.

"So," Silas said slowly, "what is it?"

Kate wiped off her hands to banish the feel of the gooey nothing. "I have no idea."

"Whatever it is," Tribal said, extending a hand to Yellow, "it's cowardly enough it only preys on people when they're alone. I say you come upstairs for the night, Yellow. Take a room near ours. We'll share a watch."

Kate stood with Venn at the edge of the woods in the early dawn light. Snow soaked through her boots, and she flexed her toes, trying to bring a little warmth to them. Fat snowflakes fell, muffling the world in silent whiteness. Behind them, the chimneys of Home let out thin trails of woodsmoke that dispersed through the trees.

Kate's eyes were gritty with exhaustion as she and Venn searched for any bit of darkness in the woods. But the snow scattered the bits of early light filtering through the clouds, leaving nothing but diffuse blue-grey shadows.

Venn rested against a large tree trunk, looking steadily toward the White Wood, the reds and oranges of her hair stark against the snow. Her arms were folded, her fingers tapping an impatient beat on her arm. She showed no sign of weariness, despite the fact that Kate knew she had barely slept after they'd returned to their rooms.

They'd divvied up watch between themselves, the dwarves, and Yellow, but Kate was fairly certain no one had actually slept.

With no shadows to be seen, Kate shifted to searching the trees around them for signs of the elven prince. "Are you sure you can't tell me what happened between you and Faron?"

Venn's fingers stilled. "Stop asking." The tapping resumed.

"Right. No talking about your prince."

"He is not my prince."

"Well, in a purely literal sense, no."

"Not literally, not metaphorically," Venn said in a firm voice. "Not my prince."

"You say that, but if King Thallion can order the lake elves around, it seems like Faron probably can too, meaning perhaps he's not your prince in name, but he is in any practical sense of the—wait!"

Venn glanced over at her.

"You said your great-grandfather was a prince. Doesn't that make you a princess?"

Venn narrowed her eyes. "No."

"How can it not?"

The elf turned away again.

"Is there some sort of rule about how distant you have to be from the throne to not be a princess?"

"Yes."

"Really? How far?"

Venn gestured to herself. "This far."

"That doesn't sound official at all. Do the other elves know what it is you object to about the betrothal?"

Venn grew still but kept her eyes on the forest. "Enough of them do."

"Even your parents and Evay?"

"They understand. More than most."

"But they still want you to marry Faron?"

Venn let out a long breath. "I will marry Faron. Unless King Thallion changes his mind about it, which he won't. I just…" She looked up into the falling snow. "Just not yet."

Kate took a step closer and lowered her voice. "If we told Thallion about everything with Bo, would that make him end it?"

Venn shook her head quickly. "Whatever solution he'd come up with for that problem wouldn't be to end the betrothal."

Kate stared at her. "What are you saying? He'd kill Bo to get you out of it?"

"Maybe not kill him. Maybe keep him in the White Wood, somewhere 'safe,' so his life was never in danger and I never had to do anything for him."

"For the rest of his life?"

Venn let out a laugh that held no humor. "Thallion would reap the added benefit of tying me more closely to the Wood. Traveling to distant cities would be less appealing if any problem with Bo would just draw me back."

"Well, we'll just have to make sure Thallion doesn't find out, then, won't we?"

Venn didn't answer.

"We'll find Bo," Kate said, trying to put more certainty into her voice than she felt. "Between the two of us, we'll find him. As long as you can feel him, as long as you know he's alive, I won't stop looking."

Venn was quiet for a moment. "And if I stop feeling him, do you want to know?"

The words sank into Kate like a blade, cutting into the knot of fear that had sat inside her since she'd first held the box. "Have you?"

Venn shook her head. "But I could, at any moment." She paused. "Your younger brother has been gone for twenty years.

You have no reason to think he's still alive, and yet you still hope to find a trace of him every time you pick up that box." She looked over her shoulder. "If the life debt ends because of Bo's death, I need to know if you want me to tell you. Or do you want to keep holding on to hope?"

Kate opened her mouth, but Venn held up a hand. "I have been holding out hope for more than a century that things with Faron will heal. That things which I know to be utterly unchangeable will...change." She looked down at Kate's pack where the edge of the aenigma box was visible. "It is not a bad thing to live with hope. Even if everything around you says that hope is..." She shrugged. "Hopeless."

Kate swallowed down the fear that rose in her. "If he dies," she said, forcing her voice to be firm, "tell me. And then I'll keep looking until I figure out what happened."

Venn studied her. "I'll help you until you do." Kate's eyebrows rose, but Venn held up a hand again to stop her from speaking. "Whatever is happening here needs to be brought out in the open. Secrets just keep the guilty safe."

Kate moved under a tree, sheltered from the snow. Her pack lay heavy against her, and the corner of the aenigma box dug into her hip. She set down her pack, pulling the poem book out before fishing out the box.

The box felt a little warm in her hands, and in the silence of the snowy woods, she could hear the bell without even trying. She turned it over in her hands, searching for any sign of a drawer, but there was nothing.

She prodded at the sides for a few minutes, but she only felt a general exhaustion. She couldn't stir up enough hope or nostalgia or desperation to open any drawers. She set it down on her pack and stretched.

Venn still stood watching the woods ahead of them, and Kate cast out in that direction.

"You won't feel him coming," Venn said. "He'll step from a ways away."

"Is he good at stepping?"

"He's good at everything. Stepping, history, languages, tracking. It's annoying."

"What languages?"

"All sorts of runes, a little Dwarvish. He spoke Old Kalesh when we were young. When I left, he was learning Kendish, which is a human language from farther east. It's not entirely fair. He's good at learning things, while also good at most everything requiring *iza*."

"Ah," Kate said. "Does stepping use *iza*? Is that why you're bad at it?"

Venn gave a grunt of agreement.

"How does it work?" When Venn didn't answer, Kate added, "I know you know. I don't understand the mechanics of it. Kobolds can do something similar. I read an account of one who said she just folded the world up and stepped to the other side."

"That's not far off. The other elves speak of bringing a distant place close, somehow using *ael'iza*."

"Melia, the human who your aunt had the life debt with, could step. So theoretically, I could learn, too."

"Not from me." Venn's head twitched to the space between two trees, and her shoulders straightened.

Kate cast out in that direction but found nothing. Until a figure flared up where Venn was looking, and, with a small gust of *vitalle*, Faron stepped out of thin air.

CHAPTER FIFTY-SEVEN

KATE CAST OUT, more out of surprise than anything. Faron and Venn blazed into pillars of *vitalle*.

Faron glanced around at the trees that had lit up around them, then looked at Kate. "That's an interesting trick." He stayed under the trees at the edge of the clearing. In the diffuse blues of the snowy morning, his skin shone like warm copper. His hair, hanging loose past his shoulders, was a smoldering dark red, like coals ready to blaze up with the slightest breeze. His expression was guarded, but there was something in his eyes that looked almost eager.

"Funny." Kate gave Venn a smile. "That's exactly what Venn said the first time I cast out near her."

"It's not funny," Venn said.

"It's a little funny." Faron gave Kate a wry smile. "She and I have always been more alike than she'd care to admit." He looked curiously at Kate. "Can you do it again?"

She cast out again, and his eyes followed the wave through the forest, lingering on a spot high in a gnarled pine where a knot of *vitalle* was nested, large enough to be an owl, or maybe a hawk.

Kate studied the same spot but caught no sense of a thundering remnant from it.

"I've never met a human who could do that," Faron said thoughtfully.

"Hardly surprising," Venn said.

Faron's expression tightened almost imperceptibly before he turned to face her. "What is surprising is that you're not usually this indecisive, Venn. First you order me to stay away, then command me to come?" His voice stayed easy, but there was something in his tone Kate couldn't quite name.

When Venn didn't answer, Kate cleared her throat. "We wanted to ask you some questions." Faron didn't pull his eyes away from Venn. "We thought you might be able to help us."

"She thought you could help." Venn tilted her head toward Kate. "I know better."

Faron took in a deep breath and pointedly turned away from Venn to face Kate. "I have been commanded by my father to help the humans, as far as it doesn't harm the White Wood. So I'm beholden to help you, Kate. Although I have no such command regarding Venn."

"Good enough for me," Kate said. "What were you arguing with Bo about?"

Faron eyebrows shot up. "What?"

"Bo," Venn said. "The human foreigner you were seen arguing with. What were you arguing about?"

"It was hardly arguing," Faron said. "It was merely a passionate discussion."

"I saw it," Venn said. "It was an argument."

Faron's eyes narrowed. "Saw it from where?"

"You were standing at the edge of the field with a line of apple trees along the side, arguing."

He searched her face but didn't disagree.

"My brother is missing," Kate said, pulling Faron's attention back to herself. "And we're trying to figure out where he is."

"Maybe he just left. Went back home."

Kate shook her head. "I assure you, he did not."

"How do you know?"

"He left all of his belongings," Kate said. "His work, things of great value to him. Things he would never leave without."

Faron considered her words for a moment. "Bo and I argued about his work in the ravine. There have been rockslides there before, and when they happen, they can block the river. This causes flooding upstream, and at least once in my people's history, it was very difficult to clear. That ravine is within sight of our regular patrols, and my rangers had raised concerns about his work. I went to ask him to stop disturbing the ravine. He... refused. Rather rudely."

Kate crossed her arms. "Bo isn't rude very often."

Faron shrugged. "Perhaps he was having a difficult day. Regardless, I tried to persuade him to stop, and he was adamant that he would continue. The conversation grew heated, and we both left unsatisfied by the exchange."

Venn gave him a probing look but said nothing.

"Does a rockslide in the river make it harder to find well-stones in it?" Kate asked. "Or do you care about the river for a different reason?"

Faron stiffened and cast a reproachful look at Venn. "Not many humans know there are wellstones in the Surn."

"So that's the reason you care?" Kate pressed.

He turned his attention back to Kate. "We care because the river is essential to the life of the Wood. But yes, we find wellstones there as well. In fact, it's not the white pine trees that give the White Wood its name. It was originally named for the white wellstones that were found in the streams that run into it from the mountains.

We call them soul keepers, and they hold recollections of the lives of our ancestors back for thousands of years. We rarely find them in the smaller streams any longer, but there are still some in the river."

"A good reason to keep the river safe." She paused. "How long after your argument with Bo did the rockslide happen?"

Faron squinted up into the falling snow. "A couple of days? Maybe three at the most."

"Did you see Bo after that?"

Faron shook his head. "I left the next day to patrol the northern border."

"He was being followed by the shadow others have seen," Kate said. "He was convinced it was after him for some reason."

Faron frowned at her. "We've found nothing to track at any of the locations where the shadow was supposedly seen. Most of my rangers are questioning whether it actually exists."

"It was in the Blind Pig last night," Venn said. "It attacked Yellow, and then Kate when she stumbled onto them."

"What?" Faron looked between the two of them. "Do you know why?"

"It's not just targeting people who worked in the ravine," Kate said. "I think it's targeting people who knew Bo."

Faron considered the idea. "That actually makes the search for it more difficult. I was hoping it had just settled itself in the area near the ravine. Most of the creatures from the north leave quickly. Contrary to human myths, they're not usually after blood. They live isolated in the mountains because they like it that way. If they stumble into our lands, we can usually root them out and convince them to go back home." He paused. "This shadow has been here longer than most."

He rested his hand on the hilt of his knife, tapping his fingers. "Why was Bo here? The townsfolk say he was looking for Renault's treasure but found nothing of consequence."

"He was looking for the remains of the last Kalesh Emperor.

The man disappeared three hundred years ago, causing the fall of the empire, but no one knows where he went. Bo followed the trail here."

"The empire?" He glanced at Venn. "We had some contact with them before they crumbled. We never knew what happened. Did Bo find anything?"

"A creature he described as a walking tree attacked him and his men before he could find much," Venn said.

Faron let out a short laugh. "A walking tree?"

"He said it looked like a tree," Kate said, "but walked on its roots. It had a sort of face, and it used its branches to rip up the slope and start the rockslide."

Faron turned to Venn. "What sort of creature is that?"

"They're your woods—you tell me."

"Yes, they're my woods, and I know what moves through them. But there are no walking trees."

"Bo has been missing for six weeks now," Kate interrupted before Venn could respond. "Have you found any trace of him?"

Faron shook his head. "There are no humans wandering the woods for weeks at a time either, if that's what you're asking."

"We found one doing just that yesterday," Kate said.

He straightened. "Where?"

Venn turned to Kate. "Clearly it was stupid to think he might know more than we do."

"What exactly is *your* interest here, Venn?" Faron said, the control in his voice slipping into frustration.

Venn gave him a small smile. "I'm looking for Bo too."

Faron stared at her for a moment. "Why?"

"Are you saying a missing human isn't worth looking for?"

He looked up at the sky for a moment, as though begging for patience. "You are the most irritating elf I have ever met. Why are you looking for *this* human, in particular?"

Venn shrugged. "I'm interested in his welfare."

A muscle in Faron's jaw twitched. He stood still for a moment, studying her. "Well," he said finally, "he's lucky to have both of you so concerned for his safety." He squinted at Venn. "Or possibly unlucky."

His gaze caught on Kate's pack, sitting against the tree. "What's that?"

The aenigma box sat on top of it.

"A puzzle Bo was trying to solve," Venn answered.

The box suddenly felt exposed to the cold. To the world. Something inside Kate tensed, and she shifted uneasily.

"It feels…unusual." Faron took a step toward it.

The uneasiness flared into something almost like fear.

He took another step. "It has a strange—"

"It's nothing." The words rushed out of Kate as she squatted down and shoved it into her pack in such a rush that the poem book fell out. She grabbed the book and rose back to her feet, brushing off the snow.

Both Venn and Faron stood watching her with curious expressions.

Kate squared her shoulders and forced a smile, trying to shake the strange anxiety. "It's just an old box," she said, half to Faron, half to herself.

"All right," Faron said slowly, his eyes lingering on her pack. "Keep your secrets."

Kate fought the urge to step in front of her pack. Instead, she looked down at the book in her hand, focusing on wiping off the last of the snow, which was so dry and fluffy it didn't even wet the cover.

He looked between the two of them. "Is there anything else I can help you with?"

Kate shook out the book and flipped through the pages, keeping her eyes down as the strange feeling faded.

"I don't think so, Faron," Venn said.

He hesitated, then gave them a slight nod and turned to leave.

The apparently blank pages of the poem book flipped past. "Wait!" Kate held it up. "Venn said you speak Old Kalesh."

He paused and looked curiously at the book. "I did once. It's been a long time."

"Could you help me translate some poetry? It's written in an ancient Kalesh dialect, and I can translate parts of it, but some words are...odd."

"No," Venn said. "He's too busy."

"It's written in invisible ink," Kate said, trying to make it sound enticing, "and at least three of the poems in it talk about shadows."

A look of interest crossed his face.

"But not literal shadows," Venn said.

"Even metaphorical shadows might be related to our current troubles," Kate countered.

The curiosity in his expression grew.

"I could really use your help," Kate said. "If you're not busy, we could go to the Blind Pig right now and look at it."

"But we don't need to," Venn said with a pointed look at her.

Kate waved her off. "But we could."

Faron's gaze shifted between Venn and Kate before it settled on Venn, along with a small smile. "I would love to help."

CHAPTER FIFTY-EIGHT

"SO THIS IS FLANK?" Kate asked, tilting the book toward where Faron sat beside her.

The cold blue-white flame of the *verus* light lit the table tucked in the darkest corner of the Blind Pig's common room.

Faron bent over the silvery writing. "They're all military terms." He studied the paper between them. "*Hold, charge, guard,* and *flank.*"

Venn looked on in silence, as she had all day, only chiming in with ideas occasionally. Mostly she'd watched Faron with a gauging expression.

"So," Kate said, "this reads:

> *The lord will hold, though broke and bent.*
> *Anguish holds the footing firm.*
> *Impatience fills the righthand flank,*
> *but faith, as always, leads the charge.*
> *Fondness stands o'er essence's vault*
> *and guards the heart from time and death.*
> *The lord will hold, though broke and bent.*

His treasures safe, the lord will hold."

Faron gave a small smile. "Those are the words. I have no idea what it means."

"Neither do I. But now that it's translated, I can work on that."

The day had disappeared quickly. Faron had an excellent grasp of ancient Kalesh, including some idioms that Kate hadn't known. They'd translated two dozen poems in the book. Some clever and whimsical, some dire warnings against monsters, some seemingly utter nonsense.

Faron had seemed relaxed and amused by the project. Venn, while staying mostly silent, was watching closely, and had settled more comfortably into her chair as the hours passed.

Kate turned the page and picked up a slice of apple from a tray Yellow had brought. "This next one is about a family of pirate pigs. I know everything but these two parts here." She took a crisp bite.

Faron shook his head. "I don't know what *risca* is."

"It's a cake," Venn said. "At least, in the larger cities that used to exist in the south, they had something called *riscalin* that were tiny sweet cakes baked with cinnamon. The *-lin* part meant they were small."

"Like…what were they called?" Faron looked at Venn with a small chuckle. "Pinlin tarts."

The edge of her mouth twitched up, and she nodded.

"What's a pinlin tart?" Kate asked.

"Little fruit pastries we used to buy in a human tavern a few towns east of here." Faron gestured at the book. "And cake makes sense here. As much sense as anything makes when talking about pigs on sea voyages."

Kate looked at the two elves. "You two are very helpful."

Venn's smile faded. The ire that usually lurked around her

eyes when Faron was near had faded, replaced with something that looked sorrowful. "And my help didn't even need to be commanded by the king."

Faron stilled and kept his eyes on the book.

Kate studied him, searching for anything that felt insincere, but he seemed genuinely interested in the poems.

With a slightly forced smile, he looked up at Kate. "Seeing as my father never commanded me to help any human decipher old texts, you can be assured my help is sincere. Which Venn is perfectly aware of, even if she pretends to not know me."

Venn watched him with a serious expression. "There was a time I thought I did."

Faron almost looked at her but brought his gaze back to the book instead.

He reached out to turn the page, revealing linen wrapping around his wrist, held in place by a leaf-shaped metal pin that glinted in the *verus* light. Venn's eyes caught on it, and she froze. Faron cleared his throat and tugged his sleeve back down.

"It looks like you translated the next poem already," he said to Kate with forced casualness.

"The next two. Both sort of morbid poems about death and brittle bones. If these are children's rhymes, they're dark. But this one you might like. I've only managed to sort out the first line, but it says 'The elven king of sun and light.'"

Faron looked mildly surprised. "That's Glendir, my grandfather." He looked at the page and moved his finger along the lines, translating it slowly. "'The elven king of sun and light bestowed a gift of great...' I'm not sure what that word is. *Wealth*, maybe. 'He fluttered in on streams of sunshine and gifted the Dragon the fruit of...' something about long-lived food? *Eternal sustenance,* maybe?"

"So the next line is 'The emperor feasted and basked in the light,'" Kate said, "'until Glendir flung beams into the sky and rode away on the...' Wings of light?'" Kate glanced at Faron. "Could he fly?"

"I don't think so. Glendir had unusually strong control over *ael'iza*, and he used runelight extensively to help him harness it." He motioned to the poem. "Like that says, he was skilled at controlling light. He could gather starlight and brighten a clearing at night, but I've never heard anyone say he could fly."

"Why did runelight fall out of use among the elves?" Kate asked. "It sounds powerful."

"Practically," Faron answered, "very few have the aptitude, and most elves are more drawn to the subtle connections they hold with the world. Runelight draws power from the wielder, not the forest. It rubs many elves the wrong way."

"And King Thallion doesn't approve of it." Venn selected a slice of apple for herself.

Faron hesitated. "That's true. My father has discouraged its use. It's a more human use of magic than the traditional elven use."

"And no one can control someone else's runelight," Venn added. Faron gave her an exasperated look, but she pointed her apple at him. "If an elf is capable, whatever magic they create with it would come out of their own essence. Any other elf—including Thallion—would have a very difficult time stopping someone else's runelight or affecting it in any way."

Faron spread out his hands in exasperation. "Why would he want to affect someone else's magic?"

"I don't know." Venn sank back in her chair. "But can you honestly tell me that's not one of his reasons?"

Faron gave her a complicated look that Kate couldn't sort out. "I don't know all his reasons," he said finally and turned to Kate. "What I do know is that my father expects me soon, but we have time for one more poem if you have one in particular you want to look at."

"Right." Kate flipped to another page. "How about this one? It has Renault's name in it."

Faron straightened. "The half-elf? That name keeps coming up."

"What I can translate says, 'The home of Renault where his madness rests, and the walking...'" Kate looked at Faron. "*Ubov?*"

Faron hesitated. "You're going to read into this."

"I am?"

"*Ubov,*" he said with a slight grimace, "is a tree. An oak."

Kate raised an eyebrow. "So this says, 'The home of Renault where his madness rests, and the walking oak haunts his grave'?"

Venn leaned forward. "That's admittedly odd. What does the rest say?"

Kate moved her fingers along the Kalesh words. "'Lift your feet and jump the hill—'"

"The mound," Faron corrected her. "Or a very small hill."

"Like...a grave?" Kate asked.

He paused. "Yes."

"All right. 'Lift your feet and jump the mound. Don't disturb the...*trev koset?* Does that literally say 'blades of grass'? I didn't think Kalesh used *blades* to describe grass. I thought they called them stems or something. With no knife references."

Faron frowned at the words. "You're right. It means the grass with knives." He pulled the book closer. "Actually, it's ambiguous. It can be read either as 'the cut grass' or 'the grass that cuts.'"

"So we should try not to disturb either the cut grass or the grass that cuts? I'm inclined to think the latter is the sort of thing to be warned against." She looked at the poem. "Unless someone's caring for grass on a grave. Then maybe they just want no one to disturb the grave."

"Actually, *koset* has to do with harvesting." He tapped the word almost absently. "Scythe may be the best translation. Yes, I think this is *scythed grass*."

"As in grass that has been scythed? I'm right in assuming that scythes here have as many connotations revolving around death as they do in Queensland, right? Harvesting crops and harvesting souls? That sort of thing?"

Faron nodded but his eyes were trained on the poem.

"All right," Kate said. "The rest says, 'Darkness lines the only path—*lest vêt* and *rok* break every bone—to the home of Renault where his madness rests.' What's *vêt and rok*?"

Faron blinked and looked up at her with a slight grimace. "Branch and root."

Kate stared at him. "So this entire poem says Renault's grave is haunted by a walking tree who will break anyone who steps on it?"

Faron shook his head. "You took all of this metaphorically except the tree. The tree is probably just his gravestone with a tree carved on it."

Kate jabbed a finger at the page. "We're looking for a walking tree, and it says walking tree!"

"The last poem was about pirate pigs!" He ran his fingers through his hair. "Trees don't walk!"

"One did," Kate said.

Faron blew out a slow breath, as though trying to regain his calm. "I'm not trying to be offensive," he said slowly, "but are you sure that's really what Bo saw?"

"Why would he make it up?" Kate asked.

"He..." Faron shrugged then spoke in a slightly apologetic tone. "He sounds like a man who sought the sensational. Sometimes we see things and our mind...expands them into what we expected instead of what's real."

"Are you serious?" Venn asked.

"There was a rockslide happening *right* where he was," Faron said. "It must have been chaotic."

"So…" Kate blew out the blue *verus* light. She set her finger on the wick and, with a little shove of *vitalle,* lit the candle with a normal flame. She pulled out the letter Bo had kept in the aenigma box. "While a rockslide was happening on a slope he knew his men were digging on, he didn't blame them but decided to instead make up this:

"*'I was deep in one of the caves when the ground started shaking. I wasn't even to the exit when I heard the first screams. By the time I reached the entrance, three of the men I hired lay on the ground not far away. The last two were facing off against…Ria, I don't know what it was. A tree? It moved on long, snake-like legs, its body was rough like a trunk, and there were branches…or arms that reached out with this horrific groaning.*

"*'Two knives were stabbed into it, farther than a knife should go into a tree, and a half-dozen arrows.*

"*'Ignoring the men, it shoved its branches down into the ground and twisted, making the whole hillside shake.*

"*'They shot at it again, and two more arrows sank into it before it stretched a branch with a dozen gnarled fingers toward them. There was a light and…*

"*'Ria, the men just collapsed.*

"*'Dead. In an instant.'*"

She looked up to see Faron studying her, working to keep incredulity off his face. "Does this sound like something Bo's just making up?"

"The tree thing killed his men without touching them?" he asked, his tone carefully neutral.

Kate turned back to the letter and read on, telling how the creature had climbed into the cave with Bo. "*It didn't move easily. Each shuffle forward on its roots seemed tortuous.*

"*'Something dark and wet dripped from each wound, leaving a smear on the ground behind it like blackened blood. It had a face, of sorts. A slash through the bark for a mouth, dark holes for eyes. A moan tore out of it, like some plea I couldn't understand, and it stumbled to the far wall where it crashed to the floor with its back to me.'"*

Faron listened closely as the creature tried to break apart the cave from the inside, and then was knocked senseless by a falling rock. When she finished, Faron looked at Bo's letter with a troubled expression.

"Still think he was just imagining something sensational?" Venn asked.

Faron shook his head. "No, that sounds real enough."

Kate pointed back to the page of poetry. "A tree attacked Bo in a canyon, supposedly cursed by Renault, and then we find an old poem that claims that Renault's grave is haunted by a walking tree. I'm going to go ahead and assume there's something to all this."

Faron looked between the two of them, his face vaguely apologetic. "Some of my rangers think all this might be a clever human pretending to be a monster." He gestured at Kate. "Some humans do have the ability to use magic."

Venn let out a laugh. "Are you saying Kate is doing this? She's the tree? And some mysterious shadow?"

"No," Faron answered quickly. "Not Kate in particular. I'm just exploring other possible answers."

"A skilled human could possibly wrap themselves in shadows," Kate said, "although I'm not sure exactly how that would work. I can't imagine them moving with such stealth they wouldn't leave any trail that the elves could find, though. And I've never heard of a human who can turn themselves into a moving tree. Humans can't really turn themselves into anything."

The thought snagged at her mind. She glanced at Venn, who met her eyes with a thoughtful frown.

There was one human who could...not turn into other creatures, exactly, but Crofftus could do something close to it.

Kate opened her mouth, but Venn glanced at Faron and gave a quick shake of her head.

"I'm expected at my father's soon," Faron said, looking curiously at the book. "Where did you find that poem book?"

She closed it carefully. "It was in the library at the Keeper Stronghold in Queensland."

He made a thoughtful hum. "Made it a long way from any place that would have cared about Renault."

She shrugged. "I have no idea how it got there."

He gave her a slight nod. He glanced across the table and swallowed. "Venn, you could come—"

"Please don't ask," she said quietly.

He looked almost like he would continue but instead merely nodded.

Kate cleared her throat. "Thank you for your help, Faron."

He pulled his eyes away from Venn and stood. With a puff of *vitalle*, he disappeared.

Kate flinched at the sudden empty space in front of her.

Venn let out a quiet sigh. "Show off," she said, her voice tinged with disappointment.

CHAPTER FIFTY-NINE

THE SMELL of Yellow's rosemary bread and the indistinct sounds of the common room flowed into the space left by Faron, and Kate sorted through them. Voices, the clank of dishes, the scraping of chairs on the floor. Faron's remnant lingered on his chair and in the air where he had stood, and Venn's emanated from her side of the table.

Venn lowered her voice. "Is Crofftus nearby?"

"I can't hear his remnant." Kate cast out. "And there's nothing near us."

Venn's eyes ran over the walls and the rough ceiling beams as Kate's wave faded.

"The tree creature can't really be Crofftus, right?" Kate asked. "Could he inhabit a tree? An animal is one thing, but a tree?"

"Inhabit it *and* make it move?" Venn shook her head. "That seems far-fetched. As much as I hate to agree with Faron, trees don't walk, no matter who's controlling them." She frowned. "It doesn't make sense anyway. If he was the creature, why would he have been all the way over in Queensland when we met him?"

"You had time to get there, and you can't fly with the king of eagles, or whatever he said he could do. But if he was the tree, why would he go to Queensland?" Kate paused in the act of picking up one of the last slices of apple. "Unless he was following you."

Venn narrowed her eyes. "Why would he? Because I had Bo's box?"

"I don't know, but…" Kate lowered the apple. "That would mean he was following Bo first."

Venn's mouth fell open. "You don't think…"

"Can he inhabit a shadow?"

"Maybe. Whatever the shadow is, we know it can bleed."

"This doesn't make sense, though. There are too many holes in the story. If he was some tree creature who killed people working in the ravine, then he was very calm about us being there too, and he seemed unbothered by the fact we're investigating the rockslide."

"Maybe we weren't close to whatever he's protecting." Venn turned to scan the room. "And there's something strange about Crofftus. He never really explains why he's here, and his responses to things are…off."

Kate took a bite of the crisp apple and chewed thoughtfully. "True, but his remnant isn't murderous."

"Maybe because he's not really human any longer," Venn pointed out. "A bear wouldn't feel murderous when it was just protecting its cubs. If he's lost his connection to humanity and become heartless toward them, that can be dangerous without intending it to be."

"I suppose if he's not involved with Bo's disappearance, I don't know why he's following us around."

"Is he? When was the last time you sensed him?"

"Not since he was the hawk in the clearing."

Venn looked thoughtfully out the window. "So instead of following us here, maybe he stayed close to the ravine."

"I guess we'll see when and if he shows back up again."

Yellow crossed the common room toward them holding a basket, bringing his remnant of roasted almonds with him. He reached their table and looked curiously at Faron's chair. "I didn't see the prince leave."

"Sneaky elf magic," Kate said with a smile, stretching her neck to see into the basket. "Did you bring us rosemary bread?"

Yellow gave her a wide smile. "You've been working so long, I thought a few apples might not be enough." He set the basket down, and the scents of butter and rosemary filled the table. "Do you need more? Is the prince coming back?"

"No." Venn pulled a chunk off the loaf and dropped it on her plate. "I think he's gone."

Yellow paused at the solemnity of her words.

"We would love some coffee," Kate said.

The innkeeper smiled again. "Right away."

He left, and Kate picked up the warm rosemary bread. It was soft and buttery to the touch. She pulled off a piece and took a bite, glancing around the common room.

There were only a few other patrons, the nearest being a pair of elderly men sitting at a front window, playing cards, enjoying the bright afternoon sun reflecting off the morning's snow outside.

"What was that leaf pin on Faron's wrist that made both of you so uncomfortable?" Kate asked.

Venn took her own piece of bread. "I gave that to him as a gift," she said slowly. "A very long time ago. I had no idea he still wore it."

No one was close enough to hear, but Kate leaned forward anyway. "You have to tell me what happened between you and Faron."

Venn looked up from her bread. "I *can't*, Kate."

"Because Faron forbade you to?"

543

"No."

"Because the king forbade you?"

Venn sighed. "Essentially."

Kate tucked the poem book back into her pack. "Can I guess?"

"I can't tell you if you're right."

"But you can tell me if I'm wrong."

Venn studied her as though weighing her choices, then nodded.

Kate lowered her voice. "All right, I'll stick to guesses, and you just tell me if I'm wrong." At Venn's nod, she continued. "The problem is more with King Thallion than with Faron."

Venn merely looked at her.

"I thought so. Does it also involve Queen Naevys?"

"No. The queen has never been anything but kind to me."

"Ah, so the king was not kind to you?"

Venn thought about the question for a moment. "The king has not been unkind to me."

Kate tapped her fingers on her leg. "Not the clearest of answers, but I'll assume whatever happened with Thallion didn't necessarily affect you directly, but you still disagreed with it."

Venn gave no response.

"Interesting." Kate thought for a moment. "Your problem with Faron is that he's following his father's orders."

Venn's expression shifted to one of annoyance, but she didn't disagree.

"Is this your main problem with him?"

There was no answer.

"I'm guessing, then, that Faron actually agrees with you about whatever this is but is obeying his father anyway."

Venn let out a breath. "The prince of the White Wood is very loyal," she said dryly.

"Right. To his father." Kate looked out over the common room. "Since the other elves seem content to obey the king," she mused, "I think the issue you have trouble with concerns humans, not elves."

Venn stayed quiet.

"Thallion doesn't really think humans are worth knowing," Kate said slowly. "Does he also think it's not worth telling them exactly what's happening?" Venn didn't answer. "Something with monsters?" No answer. "Is there some danger in the woods Thallion isn't telling the humans about?"

Venn opened her mouth, considered the question, then closed it with a conflicted look.

"All right, not exactly that...Are the humans in danger from something?"

Venn shook her head. "The elves really do take protecting the human lands very seriously." Her expression was slightly pained.

"How long have you been sworn to silence?" Kate asked.

"One hundred and fifty years."

Kate's eyebrows rose. "That's a long time. So maybe something particular happened in the woods then that Thallion didn't tell the humans about, and you've been mad ever since."

Venn just stared at her.

"Wow, you must have been really mad. Unless..." Kate paused. "Unless what he did there is just symptomatic of something. Sometime when he didn't value humans enough."

Venn sighed again and took a bite of bread.

"If he did something serious enough that you're still angry, I assume his actions hurt humans—"

Venn gave her a pointed look.

"Did he kill humans?"

"The king of the White Wood wouldn't kill humans. Unless they attacked him."

Kate's eyes widened. "Did they attack him?"

"No, and I wouldn't blame him for fighting back if they did."

"Oh, that makes sense." Kate took another piece of bread. "If he wouldn't kill humans....Would he let them die? If he thought the end goal was worth it?"

Venn closed her eyes, her brow creased with pain.

"But what goal would...ahh..."

Venn opened her eyes, looking resigned.

"It all involves humans. He was doing something that would protect them from a monster, but in the process, he let some of them die and figured the price was worth paying. But you disagreed. And since the humans around here don't think the elves are evil, I'm guessing no humans know that Thallion could have stopped those deaths but chose not to in order to...what? Stop more deaths later? While not exactly heroic, that's not the most awful thing he could have done."

"Do I look like I'd be angry for a hundred and fifty years because someone tried their best but couldn't save everyone?"

Kate studied her. "No. Which means he could have stopped it all, but he decided the human lives lost in whatever plan he picked were worthless enough to not care about."

Yellow approached with two steamy mugs, and Kate waited while he set them down. She wrapped her hands around the warm cup and breathed in the roasted, homey smell as the burly innkeeper headed back to the kitchen.

Venn took a sip of hers. "Do you remember when we first met Crofftus, and Tribal claimed he and Silas had saved us, when it was really them who'd brought all the trouble on us in the first place?"

Kate blinked at the change of topic. "Yes."

Venn narrowed her eyes. "That makes me mad."

Kate's mouth dropped open. "Thallion claimed he'd saved everyone? After he was the one who put the people in danger?"

Venn glared into the steam rising from her coffee.

"And Faron went along with all of it, even though he also disagreed."

"Faron always keeps his vows."

"Is Crofftus right? If an elf broke the command of the king, would they be cast out?"

"Yes. Not physically, but they'd be cut off from the community. I can sense the presence of other elves. When I'm home, it's always around me. Not invasive, but more like a warmth. Something to fall back on if I need it. But that sense, that connection, would be severed." Venn paused. "Depending on the strength of the command, it can affect their family as well. Their spouse and children if they're married. Their parents if they're not."

"Wait. If you broke one of the king's commands, your parents would be cut off too?"

Venn ran her thumb along the side of her mug. "You see why the commands are so binding. Whether or not I am willing to be cut off from the elves here isn't the question. My parents choose to obey the king in order to keep their community. I couldn't possibly make a choice that would steal that from them."

Kate stared at her. "That's…That power would be so easy to abuse!"

"It costs the king to make the commands, though. It's rare for him to order anyone to do anything. And the more people he ordered, the more it would cost him. His authority is wrapped up in the forest itself, which is bound to all the elves. He couldn't command any elf to harm another, or harm the wood, or harm themselves."

"But it's less picky about humans?"

"It seems to be."

Kate studied her. "But…If Faron is bound as tightly as you are, why are you so mad at him?"

Venn shook her head and took a sip of her coffee. "There are commands of silence about a topic, and those are very specific. Like not speaking of a particular thing outside the Wood. And then there are commands of action. Those cost the king a great deal, and he wouldn't use such a thing on his own heir. He wouldn't use it unless the need was very, very dire. But sometimes, elves do what the king wants, even if it goes against their own conscience, even without being commanded."

"Oh," Kate said quietly. "Faron helped him with a plan that sacrificed some humans, without a command, even though he didn't agree that it should be done."

Venn looked over the room. "I don't know what Faron agrees with or disagrees with." She let out a long breath, a flicker of pain crossing her face. "We told each other everything until that day." She turned to Kate. "We're only sworn not to share a specific story outside the White Wood, and yet he has never once told me why he did what he did. I asked him, I *pleaded* with him to explain it, and the only thing he's ever said is that his father made the right decision." Her eyes flashed. "And then he commanded me not to question him again."

Kate's mouth dropped open.

"So, if Faron would like our betrothal to continue as a real bond," Venn said with an icy cold voice, "then he must remove his command. Then he'd better explain what he did and why, and why it took him a hundred and fifty years to do so."

CHAPTER SIXTY

THE TAVERN GREW BRIGHTER, and Kate glanced around to see the front door open to the bright snow of the square. Silhouetted against the white was an elf. A wide smile broke across Venn's face, and she raised an arm. "Aunt Evay!"

Kate straightened. "Evay?"

The elf pulled the door closed and looked over curiously. She caught sight of Venn and strode over with an equally wide smile on her face.

"Welcome back," Yellow said from where he knelt stoking the fireplace. "Coffee?"

"Definitely," Evay answered.

Venn rose as Evay reached the table and gave her aunt a tight hug.

Evay's remnant flowed around Kate like a tide coming in. It was rich and complex. Not merely a sense of the forest like the other elves Kate had met but holding impressions of grasslands and coasts. Of rocky valleys and rolling hills. Nothing too overwhelming, just a sense of vastness and exploration.

"Aunt Evay," Venn said warmly. "This is Kate, a Keeper from Queensland."

The elf's eyes widened, and she glanced down at Kate's hands. "A Keeper?"

Kate flipped her palms out, showing the healing burns sitting on top of her old scars. "It's an honor to meet you!"

"Likewise. It's been a very long time since I've talked with a Keeper." Evay pulled out a chair and sat. Her russet hair fell over her shoulder in a thick braid with a few strands of grey woven through it. She glanced around the common room. "I was told Faron was here."

"He was." Venn offered her the plate of rosemary bread. "He left to see his father a little bit ago."

"Ah," Evay said with a slight grimace. "I'd hoped to catch him outside the wood."

"Why?" Venn asked.

"The lakes sent me to request that the queen come out for the ice blessing on midwinter. Faron told me he'd speak to me in his mother's place." Evay gave Venn a pained look. "I think he's going to offer to take her place."

Venn's expression turned incredulous. "He can't take her place."

"What's an ice blessing?" Kate asked.

"When the lakes begin to freeze," Evay explained, "it's tradition for a respected female elf to perform a blessing on the lakes. The queen's bloodline is intermingled with those of the lake elves, and she is currently the oldest elf who qualifies. For centuries, she's been an ambassador between the lakes and the White Wood."

"Faron isn't a female elf," Kate pointed out.

"He won't be chosen, obviously," Venn said. "It's a symbolic offer." She crossed her arms. "What excuse did he give for the queen?"

Evay gave a small grimace. "He said she was traveling, and he couldn't be sure she'd be back in time."

"Traveling?" Venn said flatly.

Evay nodded.

Kate looked between them. "She's not traveling?"

"She's old," Venn said, her voice harsh enough that Kate pulled back slightly. "And the king refuses to talk about it."

"Why?"

"Because she's not really that old," Evay said.

"She's eight hundred and thirty," Venn said.

"Which isn't terribly old for what's happened to her."

"Which is?" Kate said.

"She has spells of confusion," Evay said.

"King Thallion and Queen Naevys have a political marriage," Venn explained. "They have been unified in their leadership of the Wood but live in separate parts of it. Faron lives with his father, and after he and I were betrothed, the queen brought me into her house so I could be tutored and trained and see how the Wood was ruled." She smiled. "The queen is a determined woman, and I learned a great deal from her." Her smile faded. "The last time I saw her, though, she didn't recognize me. Or know where she was."

Evay sighed. "It's been worsening for years."

"And the king won't admit it to anyone," Venn said.

"Why not?" Kate asked.

"Because he doesn't want to look weak," Venn answered.

"Or," Evay said mildly, "because he's having trouble admitting it to himself."

"They barely see each other," Venn retorted. "He can't have any emotional attachment to her. He's just trying to preserve something for himself."

"I have seen many, many partnerships," Evay said, "and Thallion and Naevys love each other."

"If so, it is from a very great distance," Venn said, "and Thallion's love is usually self-preserving." She turned to Kate. "Regardless, she's not traveling. She's too ill to come do something like the blessing, and if Faron's not saying that, it's because his father has sworn him to silence about it." She pointed at Evay. "This is why I can't go back there."

"You can't change the Wood, Venn. Even if Naevys is aging, Thallion will still be king for a very long time. You need to find a way to make peace with all this."

"Or they could change," Venn said firmly.

Yellow came over and set a mug of coffee in front of Evay. "More bread?"

"Absolutely," Evay answered.

Venn watched him leave, then took a deep breath and smiled at her aunt. "Never mind King Thallion's shortcomings. I'm glad you're here. I need to talk to you."

"About the trouble at the ravine?" Evay asked. "It was Ayen who told me Faron was here, and he mentioned the humans have been having trouble there. Something about a shadow hurting and killing people."

Venn hesitated. "Actually, that's part of it. Remember the Kalesh bodies we found there when I was young?" Venn gestured to Kate. "Her brother Bo was exploring there when he disappeared, and Kate thinks the Kalesh emperor himself was among the humans we found. He would have been wearing a lot of gold, but I don't remember anyone like that."

Evay tapped her mug, looking thoughtfully up toward the ceiling. "No, they were mostly common men. Soldiers and workers. A few with slightly more elaborate clothes, but no emperors. There was one tent that was remarkably lavish, but that's all."

"Did you find any horses?"

"Not there, but there were horse tracks leaving along the road. It bothered me, because the humans looked like they'd been interrupted just going about a normal day, but if so, the horses would have been corralled or at least hitched somewhere. If all the humans died, who released the horses?"

"Were there any human tracks leaving?"

Evay shook her head. "I searched. I figured if there were any survivors, maybe they were wounded and needed help. But I found nothing. Any horses that left went farther than I checked, but I saw no sign of humans doing the same." She looked between Venn and Kate. "I get the feeling I didn't give you any new answers."

"It confirmed what Venn remembered when we were there," Kate said.

Yellow came over to the table and set another basket of rosemary bread down.

When he was gone, Evay waved her hand at Kate and Venn. "How did you two meet?"

Venn gave a slight grimace. "That's the real thing I need to talk to you about."

CHAPTER SIXTY-ONE

"A LIFE DEBT? TO A HUMAN?" Evay leaned forward in her chair, her voice low. "That complicates things. How heavy is it?"

"It was lighter at first," Venn said. "When he first saved me, it was just a persistent pressure. But ever since he called for help, it's been stronger. Heavier."

Evay looked at Kate. "And he wanted the box taken to you?"

"He and I found it—and lost it—together when we were children. We've been looking for it ever since." She paused. "Venn says if he were dead, she'd be released from the debt."

Evay shifted. "Yes. She would know."

"How long did you have the debt with Melia?" Kate asked. "The stories I know of you two aren't specific."

Evay's mouth twitched up in something far too sad for a smile. "Melia saved my life, and I was under the full debt for half a year before I saved hers. During those months, it sat on me lightly, unless she was in danger. Then it weighed on me like a mountain was crushing me."

Kate looked between the two elves. "So Bo's still in danger?"

"This is hardly a mountain," Venn said. "But it's not light."

Evay studied her niece. "If the pressure is mild, I would guess he's being held prisoner or something. In danger, but not immediate danger. By the time I saved Melia's life and repaid the debt, we'd been fighting against the Kalesh together for so long we'd become friends. She'd helped me, and I'd helped her. The fluctuation of the debt between us was complex enough it could never really be balanced. From then on, there was...not a weight. It wasn't heavy. She was like a sister, and the compulsion to keep her safe shifted into the same sort we feel for anyone we love." She looked out the windows at something Kate couldn't see. "When she was in trouble, though, there was still the pull. Less intense, but still there. The night she died, it dragged me from the campsite I was making and sent me running toward her. But she was weeks away, and before the sun was even fully set..." She let out a breath laced with sorrow. "It snapped. Gone, in an instant. I'd lived with it for so long, I..." She swallowed. "I knew she was gone. If Bo dies, you will know."

Venn stared into her nearly empty coffee. "Well, he's not dead, then."

Kate turned to Evay. "Did your bond help you know where Melia was? Could you track her through it?"

"Not unless she was in immediate mortal danger." Evay looked at Venn. "You feel no pull in any particular direction?"

Venn shook her head. "The only time I felt anything like that was when he first called for help, and it pulled me to the clearing where he'd left the box. But once I read the note from him, there was only the compulsion to go to Kate and fulfill what he'd asked. Since then, I just feel heavy all the time."

Evay rolled a piece of rosemary bread between her fingers. "Have you told Faron?"

"I've told no one but you."

"Are you going to?"

Venn shook her head and reached for more bread.

"Good." Evay considered Kate for a moment, then gave Venn a smile that seemed more sympathetic than anything. "It's a heavy burden, but I can't say I'm sorry you carry it."

Venn stopped with the piece of bread half torn off.

"I'm glad Bo was there to save you, obviously. But more than that..." Evay met her niece's eyes with a solemn look. "I raged against the idea that I was bound to a human at first, but Melia became my sister, not because of the debt, but because the debt kept us close to each other until we'd learned to depend on each other. Before Melia, I was as independent as you are. Which is how I liked it. But the more I got to know her..." Her mouth twisted up in a wry smile. "The more she got to know *me*...It changed me. For the better."

"But human lives are so short," Venn said quietly. "You knew it wouldn't last."

Evay dropped her eyes to the table. "True. I only knew Melia for twenty years, and I mourned her death more than almost any other I've known. I mourned her children's death, and her grand-children's." She looked at Kate. "I think we use that as an excuse to not grow close to humans. But it turns out it doesn't matter. The fact that a life is short makes it no less valuable. No less precious."

She reached out and set a hand on Venn's shoulder. "The other elves will not understand this, but I want you to hear it. Even with all the grief and all the loss. Even with the fact that now, four hundred years later, I still feel the hole Melia's death left in my soul, even with *all* that, I would gladly choose to bind myself to her again. Those twenty years of my life were among the best of the six hundred years I've had, not because of what we were doing, but because it is the other souls we connect with that make anything about life good."

Venn met her aunt's earnest look with one much more doubt-ful. "I doubt Bo will end up feeling like a sister."

Evay let out a short laugh. "Possibly not, but it's connected you to people." Evay glanced at Kate. "You just sat here and revealed every detail about the life debt you owe Bo, how it feels, what it means to you, how it affects your life, whether you will tell Faron...and Kate hasn't looked surprised once."

Kate stopped chewing as both elves focused on her. She swal-lowed quickly. "Am I not supposed to know all this?"

Evay laughed again. "How long have you known my niece?"

"About..." Kate tried to count the days.

"I reached the Stronghold less than a fortnight ago," Venn said slowly, giving Kate a puzzled look.

Evay straightened. "How are you possibly back here already?"

"Dwarves took us through some tunnels," Kate said, "and along an underground river. It only took a few days to get to this part of the world."

"You...?" Evay turned to Venn. "You were underground? For days?"

Venn stared at Kate as though she'd never seen her before.

"We fueled her tattoo with my *vitalle*," Kate explained to Evay when Venn didn't look like she was going to. "And then found some moss along the way for her to carry. Between the two things, it was fine."

Venn still looked puzzled, but Evay's face was etched in shock.

Kate shifted. "And there were these glowing underwater plants in the river that helped too..."

Evay turned her stunned look on Venn. "She knows about your tattoo?"

Venn spread her hands in a helpless shrug. "She's a Keeper. I was wounded, she saw it, she could read it enough to know it did something. She could even feel that it drew in *iza*." Venn dropped her hands to the table. "She figured out most of it on her own."

Evay grinned at the two of them. "Do you know how many elves know of Venn's tattoo?"

Kate shook her head.

"Six. Her parents, me, Faron, and the king and queen."

Kate turned to Venn. "What?"

"My niece," Evay continued, smiling widely, "is one of the most private, closed-off elves I have ever met."

"I am not closed off," Venn muttered.

Evay studied Kate for a moment. "Venn, why is Kate here looking for Bo?"

"Besides the fact that he's her brother?" Venn glanced at Kate. "She and Bo have been searching for their younger brother, Evan, who was taken when they were young. That locket she wears has a keepsake from him that doesn't do what it once did, but she imagines it does. And with some clues Bo found recently, for the first time she has hope that she might actually find out what happened to Evan."

Evay shifted a ring on her finger. It was shaped like a thin, knobby branch with a few small leaves fanning out. Nestled between the leaves, a sliver of stone glinted a flash of white light. "In the White Wood, when elves bond closely, they share a gift. Usually rings."

"For a wedding?" Kate asked.

"Yes, but for other bonds as well. Siblings share them. Or close friends. A mentor and apprentice might. We embed a sliver of a wellstone into each and put a tiny piece of our *ael'iza* into it before exchanging them. Melia's matched this one."

Kate leaned closer. "That's a wellstone? Did you store memories in them?"

"These are too small to hold anything more than a bit of

vitalle. Instead of memories, it carries a bit of the person. When I traveled, it was like a tiny piece of her was with me as well."

Kate cast out toward the ring. The bodies of both elves burst into light, but a spark of stunning brightness exploded from the ring. A tightly contained flurry of motion, like a bird launching into flight, or the way water smashed against rocks at the base of a waterfall. A fierce, wild fleck of *vitalle.* "That is not like the Wellstone in the Stronghold."

"No," Evay answered with a small smile. "Your stone is unique. I saw it once, not long after the Greenwood elves gifted it to you. It is among the largest I've ever seen, and it's...tame."

Kate let out a short laugh. "It doesn't feel tame when you step into it and try to sort through memories."

"It's tame compared to an uncut wellstone." Evay held her ring out. "This is merely a shaving. We save the full stones for the end of our lives. We hold on to it until we know the end is near, and then we allow it in. Once a wild stone is allowed into your mind, you can't disengage it until it has learned the memories of your entire life. Meaning you must relive them all as it replays them. So we save them until the end. And not all elves choose to use one. A wild stone is a powerful force. Not all elves want to grapple with that when they're already tired."

Kate glanced at Venn. "A wellstone can absorb memories."

"You think the shadow is using a wellstone?" Venn asked.

"Or something like it. My serum isn't strong enough to hurt someone's mind, but that doesn't mean something like it couldn't be stronger. Bo did say the tree that attacked him had a weapon like a gem."

At Evay's curious look, Kate explained the walking tree and the rockslide.

Venn shook her head. "A wellstone wouldn't take people's memories away. The bearer still retains their own mind. It's like your serum. It takes a copy."

Kate tapped her finger on the table. "True. The Keeper's Well-stone doesn't take our memories either, but if it's tame, and we're Keepers..." She shrugged. "Maybe a wilder one would damage a regular human mind."

Evay's eyes narrowed. "There's a chance it would be too strong for the human to handle well." She glanced around the common room, then lowered her voice more. "A wellstone would point to elven involvement."

"And since neither elves nor humans around here dabble in serums," Venn said, "a wellstone is a viable explanation for what's happening."

The door to the tavern opened, and Maven stepped in, taking her usual seat near the front window. "Yellow!" the old woman called. "Is the pork ready this early?" She glanced around the tavern, and her eyes landed on Kate. Her expression immediately darkened.

Kate looked back at the two elves. "Renault the Mad dabbled in serums."

"The half-elf?" Evay asked. "He's long dead."

"Is he?" Kate asked. "Because his name seems to be related to everything we find."

Evay considered the two of them. "I don't know for sure he's dead. He stopped bothering us centuries ago."

Venn's gaze searched the table and the nearby wall. "Crofftus also has dabbled in serums," she said quietly.

"Who's Crofftus?" Evay asked.

"A suspicious little friend of ours," Kate answered.

"Not really a friend," Venn added.

Kate studied the sliver of wellstone tucked into Evay's ring. "That still holds a bit of Melia's *vitalle*? Even after all this time?"

Evay ran her thumb over the stone. "Wellstones hold whatever you put in them for as long as you let them. Usually these rings are just a symbolic gesture, but I think because Melia and I shared a life debt, I've always been able to almost sense her in it. It's a totally different thing than the life debt was. That was just a weight. This is more like that secure feeling of being with a close friend. Familiar…in the most comfortable sort of way."

The phrase snagged at Kate's mind. "Familiar in a comfortable sort of…" She straightened. "Venn!"

Venn set her mug down so hard that coffee sloshed over the side. "I felt that in the ravine! From the rockslide!"

Kate stared from one elf to the other. "Bo's in the ravine?"

"Not necessarily." Evay raised a hand. "Melia has never been in my ring."

"I don't feel any pull toward it," Venn said. "No tug to go help him there. It's not the life debt. That feels exactly the same in the ravine as anywhere else."

Kate dropped her piece of bread to her plate. "But something of him is there? That's what you felt?"

"I…" Venn's hand tightened on her mug. "I don't know."

"Is Bo a Keeper?" Evay asked Kate. "Could he have put some of his *ael'iza* into something there?"

"He can't do anything like that. If any of him is in that ravine, all of him must be." Kate pushed herself to her feet and grabbed her pack. The square outside was still bright with afternoon light. "We can get there before dark!"

Venn sat frozen in her seat, her hands gripping her mug. "I've felt this before." Her voice was taut with alarm. "The day I left with the box to find you, I passed through the ravine, and I felt it then too."

"He's been there all this time? Where? In the caves?" The long stretch of weeks spooled out in Kate's mind, dragging at her like an anchor pulling her down into the terrifying blackness. She gripped the back of her chair. "Yellow said the shadow and Gerren were in a cave. It's taking people to the ravine, Venn! Bo must still be there! He's been trapped—for weeks!"

"Kate." Venn's voice was little more than a whisper. "That day... The feeling was so much stronger than it is now."

Kate's fingers tightened on the chair. "It's fading?"

Venn swallowed, her face drawn with fear. "Compared to that day, it's almost gone."

CHAPTER SIXTY-TWO

KATE PUSHED her burning legs faster down the dirt path between the forest and the river. The haunting feel of deep tunnels dogged her steps. The musty smell of stagnant air. The weight of the mountain pressing down, inexorable and silent. Her skin crawled at the feel of the darkness thickening the deeper you went.

The horror of it prowled through her like a restless creature, crawling its way up her throat. She sucked in a breath of cold air and forced the creature back down.

Weeks. Bo had been trapped there for weeks.

The trail, which had been wide enough for a wagon when it left Home, had shrunk over the past two hours to a thin scratch winding through the forest. It was rough with half-buried rocks and knotted roots. Patches of white from the morning's snow lingered in the shadowy edges. The path dipped downhill, drawing alongside a narrow stretch of river rapids, and she broke into a run. Her feet thudded against the damp, cold dirt.

"I still can't make this fit the story you've been trying to figure out," Venn called from behind her.

The creature inside Kate scrambled to life again at the words. "It could." Her words had a stubborn ring. "The shadow takes people and keeps them in caves. It must have taken Bo as well."

"The caves were already covered by a rockslide."

The path rose steeply again, slowing Kate to a fast walk. "There must be a way in." Ruddy evening sunlight slanted through the pines across the river. "Maybe Tribal and Silas have found it by now."

The river drowned out Venn's footsteps, and when she didn't answer, Kate glanced back at her.

Venn shook her head with an apologetic look. "Even I can see this doesn't fit. The shadow isn't keeping people. It releases them —no matter what state they're in."

Kate spun around, her breath coming fast. "Then what do you think is happening? You can feel something of Bo in that ravine. What is it, if not him?"

"I don't know. I just…It doesn't make sense."

"I know! I have been trying to fit this into everything else we know, and I can't make it fit. But what part of this story does?" Kate flung her hand toward the ravine. "Walking trees that cause rockslides? Shadows that steal people's memories, stalk humans and dwarves, and sneak into taverns in the middle of the night to attack innkeepers? None of this makes any sense. But we know something of Bo is in that ravine…" She dropped her hand. "He's nowhere else that he should be. Why not there?"

Venn held up her hands. "You're the one who's always trying to make the story make sense."

"Well, maybe this one just…doesn't."

Venn studied her. "You don't really believe that."

"Of course I don't. There's always an explanation. Things always make sense when you see the whole picture. When you know who is acting and why." She shook her head. "But I don't know who or what the shadow is, or why it's doing this.

"It takes people, does something with their minds, and lets them go. It has to be looking for something. But maybe none of the others had what it needs. And maybe Bo does. He's different from all the men from Home. He's not from here, not a farmer or a butcher. He's traveled the world and studied all sorts of strange things, and maybe he has what the shadow needs. Or knows something. Or..."

"You're grasping," Venn pointed out. "If he had what the shadow wanted, it wouldn't have taken anyone else."

"I know! But you're the one who told me I don't need to figure everything out before I act. So here I am. I have no idea what's going on, but I'm going anyway. There's something in that ravine, and you know it."

"I do." Venn brushed her hand against the nearest pine. "But just...temper your hopes."

"I can't lose another brother." Kate turned and pushed a low-hanging branch out of her way, starting down the path again.

A glimpse of grey rock flashed through the trees ahead, and she broke into a run again.

The path and the river spilled out of the forest into the northern end of the ravine. The rockslide marred the slope a hundred paces downstream, covering the hillside and piling up alongside the river, narrowing the water enough that it churned and foamed around the pile of rocks.

Kate scanned the steep, empty slope above her. "Tribal! Silas!"

There was no answer.

Venn stepped past her and closed her eyes.

"Can you feel Bo?" Kate asked.

Venn's brow drew together in concentration. "Uphill, I think."

Kate jumped over the thick patch of snow beside the trail and started up the hillside, angling for the edge of the slide. Her feet slipped on the loose rocks and slushy remains of this morning's snow, but she grabbed a tuft of brown grass still clinging to the hillside and moved higher.

"Tribal!" she called again. "Silas!"

A head of dark hair emerged over the top of a large rock at the edge of the rockslide. He was too far away for her to feel his remnant, and she wasn't sure which dwarf it was.

She waved. "Are you through to the cave yet?"

He shook his head. "This is a rockslide. Every single time we move a rock, it can shift another. We're trying not to bury ourselves—"

"No, Twig." A second head popped up. "Silas is trying to say no. It's gonna take time." Tribal turned back and disappeared.

Kate's foot slipped, and her shin slammed against a rock sticking out of the ground. The pain stole her breath for a moment. "How long?" she managed. "Bo's in there!"

Tribal's face reappeared next to his brother. "In this cave?"

"Some part of him is here in the ravine," Venn called. "Probably not all of him."

Silas glanced at his brother. "Like his arm?"

"No!" Kate climbed higher. "Like part of him trapped in something magical. Or maybe all of him buried too deep for Venn to feel well." She scrabbled up to where the dwarves stood.

Both dwarves had donned fur-lined vests against the cold and stood together in a hollow cleared into the edge of the rockslide like a small cave. The sides were braced with thick logs, but the back was just a wall of jumbled stones. The roasting meat and spiced ale of the dwarves' remnants filled the space, mingling with the dusty smell of the rocks.

"The cave is past that." Silas pointed at the wall. "But we're not sure how far."

"It could take days, Twig," Tribal said, "and that's if we can keep a stable path. If the rocks above us shift at all, we'll have to clear all those first." He gave her a grimace. "That could take weeks."

"No." Kate took a step closer. "It can't take weeks. Whatever Venn feels is already fading."

A frown peeked out from behind Silas's bushy beard. "How could he be in here? These caves have been covered since before he disappeared."

"I don't know." Kate stepped back and craned to see over the rockslide. The hillside was completely covered with a layer of rock so heavy it made her shift her shoulders in an effort to dislodge the weight of it. "Is there another way in?"

"Not that we found. There are several other entrances here, but they're all covered with more rock than this one."

"Kate!" Venn called. "It's lower down!"

Kate scrambled out of the hollow. "Where?"

Venn stood on a large rock a dozen paces into the rockslide, her eyes closed and her head bowed. "I don't know, but it's lower than the caves."

Kate headed down toward her and cast out over the slope. Aside from Venn and the two shapes of the dwarves watching her from above, there was no one.

A grating, scraping sound scratched against her mind. The whisper of wind through the trees interlaced with a rasping sound. The taste of rust coated her tongue. "That corrupted remnant is here. Very strong. Under the rocks."

Venn nodded. "So is the feel of Bo."

"What's under this part of the slope?" Kate called to the dwarves.

Silas gauged the distance to where Kate stood. "I'd say the cave system goes that far down."

How had she missed this? This was where Bo had worked. This was what he knew. If he'd been scared and hadn't gone to

Home, of course he'd have come here. She'd wasted time searching the forest.

All of his meager supplies would be long gone. The air would have grown stale. She could feel the weight of the rocks pressing down, sealing him in like a coffin.

Kate ran back up toward the dwarves. "I need to get in there!" She pushed past Silas and climbed into where they'd been working.

The dusty air caught in her throat, and she coughed as she dropped to her knees.

"Don't touch anything!" Tribal yelled, following her in.

"Let me help you!" Kate's fingers scrabbled at the edge of a rock, trying to find purchase and pull it from where it was wedged.

Silas's thick fingers wrapped around her arm. "Stop!" She tried to pull away, but he lifted her to her feet and dragged her back. "You'll pull the mountain down on us!"

She grabbed him. "I have to get in there!"

He took both of her shoulders in his hands. "We'll get you in. But you need to let us work."

She shook her head. "I have to do something. My brother has been trapped in there for…" Her legs trembled, and she dug her fingers into his arm to brace herself. "Silas, he's dying."

"We'll get you in, Kate," he repeated. "Just give us space to do it."

Tribal stepped past them. "The sooner you move, the sooner we can work."

She forced her hands to loosen their hold on the thick fabric of Silas's sleeves. She nodded, the motion feeling stiff. "I'll look for another way in."

Tribal squatted next to a large rock, examining how it lay. "There is no—"

"Yes," Silas interrupted him. "You and Venn look for another way in. Maybe we missed something."

Tribal let out an annoyed breath, but Silas's heavy hand patted Kate on the shoulder. With a tight smile, he pushed her away.

She climbed out and took in a breath of fresh air. "We're coming, Bo," she whispered.

CHAPTER SIXTY-THREE

Kate moved to the level where Venn still stood and knelt on the rocks. Setting her hands on the ground, she cast out. Not with a wave of curiosity, but with a desperate surge of fear. She thrust the wave into the earth, searching for any sign of Bo. Instead of spreading out in a ripple, it stabbed down, brushing past the traces of life on the surface, plunging through the rocks and dirt that made up the hillside.

It reached a dozen paces deep but found nothing before it faded away. She almost turned away before the faint flutter of lattice-like webbing just along the surface caught her notice. As slim as if it were made from single strands of grass. The threads of *vitalle* spread across the slope as far as her wave reached.

She stood and shoved out a stronger wave, sending it rippling out in every direction as though she'd hurled a heavy stone into a still pond.

"Venn!" Kate spun around.

But the elf's gaze was already racing across the slope, following strands of *vitalle* as they twisted and snaked across the ground. "What is that?"

"A web! A shield! Over the whole hillside!"

Kate stood and cast out one more time, this time funneling all her desperation into the wave. It poured out like a flood.

The hillside lit as though the entire surface had caught fire.

A burst of light exploded from downhill, along the side of the rockslide.

She met Venn's eyes for a heartbeat before they both scrambled toward it.

A huge, flat rock stuck out of the hillside below like an enormous shelf, creating an overhang filled with prickly bushes. The lines of *vitalle* lingered here, still glowing and vibrating, even after those on the rest of the slope had faded.

Venn stopped beside her, staring at the bushes. "I can feel Bo here." She turned slowly, looking over the slope. "Kate, I feel him in the *vitalle*." She looked back at the rock. "Stronger here, though. Everything is stronger here."

The evening sun painted the rock shelf with a golden glow, and something glinted from the shadows beneath it.

Kate shoved aside two bushes. Tightly packed needles tore at her sleeves as she pushed forward. The ground dropped away, and she stumbled in, tumbling down a small incline and landing hard on her shoulder. Lines of *vitalle* glowed over the rock above and spread across the hardened dirt beneath it.

A few paces away, the edge of a wagon wheel stuck out of the ground.

"Venn!" Kate called.

One of the bushes shuddered and lifted out of the ground, revealing Venn holding the fat, twisted trunk. The roots hung below it, showering down bits of soil. Venn moved it away and set it down. The roots wriggled back into the earth again.

Kate stared at the newly planted bush. "How did you do that?"

"You just convince the roots it's time to grow, and they swell a little, which loosens the dirt. Then they shrink, and you can pull them out. Planting them again is just...a little more of the same."

"Like making it walk?"

Venn straightened. "No, just some swelling and shrinking. There are no muscles in its roots to make it walk." She looked around. "This is bigger than I thought it would be."

"Look at this wheel." Kate knelt and pushed loose dirt away from it. Scoops of earth had been shoveled away from where the wheel disappeared into hard, clay-like dirt. "Someone was digging it out."

Venn squatted beside her. "Bo? I thought he was looking for ancient things? This looks new. The wood isn't even rotten."

"And the metal is still shiny, but I'd wager anything this was Bo. Look at how carefully the earth has been removed." Kate brushed a layer of dust off the central hub of the wheel and drew in a breath. "That's the imperial stamp!"

"As in Emperor Sorrn's stamp?"

Kate nodded and shoved more dirt off the wheel. Everything was fine particles that must have been blown into this protected space by the wind. A deep gouge marred the surface of the hub, and Kate looked closer. A hint of windswept hills escaped it. "It's Bo's remnant!"

Something prickled at the back of Kate's neck, and she glanced back through the hole in the brush at the forest across the river. A tangle of large pines near the water sheltered a cluster of shadows so dark they looked solid. She opened her mouth to point it out to Venn, but a bird darted up from the water and through the shadows, shifting from grey to black to grey again as it winged through the darkness and down the river.

"There are more markings around the imperial stamp," Venn said.

Kate cast one last look over the forest before turning back to the wheel. The metal hub around the seal was scuffed and

575

dented, and she knelt closer and recognized a few symbols. "You're right. This is Kalesh writing."

"Who put this here? Barely anyone in this part of the world knows Kalesh anymore. Can you read it?"

Kate shifted around the wheel, rubbing at a smudge of dirt. "I think this one is dragon. The end of it is damaged, but I don't know any other word it could be."

"Dragon?"

"Kalesh emperors called themselves the Dragon. The next symbol is too faint to read—but the third looks like..." Kate stared at the symbols. There it was. Clear as if the blacksmith in Home had stamped it on. "It says Sorrn!"

"So someone stamped a wagon wheel with a three-hundred-year-old imperial symbol and buried it in the ravine where the last emperor is said to have died?"

Kate nodded and picked up a sharp piece of rock. She began to dig the hard earth away from the part of the wheel that was still buried, catching hints of Bo's remnant as she did. "Bo was here, Venn!"

Venn's eyes searched the sheltered space. "Do you...Do you think he's still here?"

Kate's hand slowed in its digging. "No." The fear that he was trapped nearby began to lessen, replaced by an aching need to know what had happened. Evan had left no clues when he'd disappeared, but here was something that could lead to Bo. Something tiny, but still something. "These are old traces. Just the trail he left behind after working here."

Venn was quiet for a moment before she returned her attention to the wheel. "The empire has been gone for three hundred years. Who would care about stamping a wheel with that symbol today? Everyone who cared about it is gone."

"Not everyone." Kate dug down into a side pocket on her

pack and pulled out the medallion with the same stamp. "This was on the aenigma box."

"Which is also very old." Venn sat back on her heels.

"Yes, but the men who came after it—the ones who took Evan —they had this embroidered on their clothes." Kate ran her thumb over the dragon on the medallion. It was identical to the one on the wheel. "Who today cares about this symbol? And what does it have to do with a box found in Queensland?" She scraped away another chunk of earth from the rim of the wheel. "What connects a long-dead emperor to all this today?"

Venn nodded absently. "The web of *vitalle* finally faded here, but this place feels...strange." Her gaze ran over the ground sheltered under the overhang, and she straightened. "There's something else here."

Venn knelt a few paces from the wheel and brushed dirt away. "It think it's..." She scrubbed at a particular part. "Kate! It's a carriage!"

Kate clambered over to see a few inches of smooth wooden surface. She stood, her head nearly brushing the overhanging rock, and took in the shape of the ground. "You can see the outline!" A large, flat shape like the side of a carriage was covered with earth and a few scraggly patches of grass. "That is definitely the shape of an imperial carriage."

Venn glanced at the wheel. "The wheel does not sit right compared to the rest of it, so it's clearly not in one piece." She moved more dirt from the edge of the flat surface. "This wood is painted black, and it's in nearly pristine condition." She shook her head. "How did it get here? The road above hasn't been fit for a carriage in fifty years. And whatever time it takes to let this much dirt build up should also have rotted the wood."

Kate shifted to the other side of the carriage to find the edge covered with soft, loose dirt. "Bo was digging this out too." She scooped out the shallow channel that was dug into the ground along the edge of the carriage. "But hadn't made much progress."

Less than a hand's width had been dug out, but the paint on this side was just as flawless as the paint on the side facing up. A flat rock was wedged along the side of the wood at the bottom of the channel, and she tried to work it loose.

"There's gold paint along the edges," Venn said. "A vine, I think, and the paint is still shiny."

Kate met the elf's puzzled look. "So either this is very new, and someone worked hard to make it look like it's been buried for a long time, or it's very old and very well preserved."

The rock came free in Kate's hand, and another shiver of disquiet rolled across her shoulder blades. She twisted to look behind her, but there was nothing in the ravine. She rubbed the back of her neck, but the feeling remained, just the slightest tingle under her skin.

"Did someone say gold?" Tribal's voice rang out from the edge of the overhang.

Kate jumped at the sound.

He gave her a little smirk as he stepped through the bushes. "What's got you so nervous?"

She glanced around, but there was nothing unusual to see. "Nothing. Did you reach the tunnel?"

"No." He gestured at her. "You shouted and ran here, and we thought that warranted checking out. But I'm glad we scrambled to stabilize what we were working on so I could rush down here, seeing as you're totally safe." He turned away. "Next time, don't shout unless you're in danger."

Kate stretched out and caught hold of the cuff of his trousers. "Wait! Could you help us dig this out?"

Tribal gave the wheel a sidelong glance. "Is Bo in a buried carriage?"

The idea sent a chill down Kate's back, but she shoved it

away. "I...I don't think so. But something about him is connected to this."

Venn nodded. "Definitely."

Kate tightened her hold on Tribal's cuff. "We have to unearth it and find out why."

He hesitated.

"There's gold!" Kate said quickly, not letting go.

A shadow fell over them, and Kate looked up to see Silas kneeling in the opening.

"What about gold?" he asked.

"She wants us to dig up a carriage," Tribal explained.

Kate turned her appeal to Silas. "It might hold a clue to where Bo is."

He leaned farther in. "That looks like it's been buried for a very long time. Longer than Bo's been gone."

"Except it still looks brand new." Venn pointed to the fresh paint.

"You two always say if something is well protected, it's probably valuable," Kate said. "There is magic all over this, protecting it." Both dwarves squinted at her dubiously. "And this is just what Emperor Sorrn would have ridden in. An emperor who was as obsessed with gold as you are."

Tribal studied the bits of visible carriage. "This feels like a long shot."

"Please, Tribal," Kate said, desperation creeping into her voice. "I need your help. *Something* here relates to Bo."

He crossed his arms.

"This is a perfectly preserved carriage in a cursed ravine!" She stabbed a finger toward the ground. "You should be itching to dig this out."

A smile twitched behind his beard. "Move out of the way."

Kate dropped her hand with a breath of relief. "Thank you. Start with the wheel. There are markings on it I need to see."

The two dwarves moved over to the hub. Tribal took the pick-axe, considered the earth around it, and jabbed the tip under the wheel, twisting it sharply.

"Don't hurt it!" Kate said.

He gave her an insulted look. "I'm going to pretend you didn't say that."

"Tribal has never damaged anything that could prove to be valuable," Silas assured her, kneeling on the other side of the wheel and pulling what looked like a fat chisel out of his belt.

Venn moved to the bushes and relocated them one by one, letting in the evening light. The two dwarves leaned over the wheel, muttering and pointing at different places before Tribal let out a yell and smashed his axe against the wheel.

Silas yanked his hands back.

"Tribal!" Kate snapped. "I said *don't* hurt it!"

His eyes flickered up at her. "Sorry," he muttered. "There was a spider."

Kate stared at him. "A dangerous spider?"

"All spiders are dangerous," he grumbled.

"Better safe than sorry," Venn agreed.

Silas gave Tribal a shove in the shoulder. "You're embarrassing us. Put your axe away and use something smaller." He looked closer at the wheel. "Huh. You barely marked it. Maybe something *is* protecting this thing."

Tribal muttered something under his breath but set the axe aside and pulled out a small chisel.

Silas glanced around. "Speaking of bugs, where's the beetle? He could try to climb into any small crack we find."

"He changed into a hawk," Kate said, wiping dirt off the glittering paint. Intricately painted vines climbed up the corner of the carriage box. The work was highly detailed with shadows and shading and thin dragons crawling among the leaves. "Is there anyone near Home who could paint like this?"

"I haven't seen human art like this since..." Venn shook her head.

Kate looked up. "Since the Empire?"

Venn frowned at the carriage. "This *can't* be hundreds of years old."

"Unless..." Kate left her hand on the corner and cast out.

A flicker of *vitalle* ran along the gold paint, then a skin of burning heat flared over the entire surface, mapping out the box. The carriage top was smashed in, but Kate could feel the shape of the rest of the body, the axles underneath, and three wagon wheels still attached to it. The fourth, broken off, flared into brightness where the twins were working on it.

Aside from the crushed roof and the broken wheel, everything else seemed to be unharmed.

"Maybe I can find a gap in what's protecting it." She pushed a little *vitalle* into the surface.

A burst of heat exploded under her palm and raced across the wagon.

Kate yanked away from it, and Venn scrambled back with a hiss, shaking out her hand. Both dwarves jumped back and dropped their tools.

"What was that?" Venn demanded.

Kate rubbed her palm. "It's...shielded, somehow."

"That was not a shield." Venn looked at her hand where a red welt was rising. "That was an attack."

CHAPTER SIXTY-FOUR

KATE EXAMINED the corner of the carriage. There was some sort of gouge in the wood, like it had been scraped by a rock, but the wood itself showed no sign of age. At the edge of the dirt, another narrow scratch cut through the paint, looking like part of a small spiral. She carefully reached out and wiped at the dirt near it. Nothing happened.

"Is this wheel going to shock me again?" Tribal asked.

"No." Kate continued to clean off the scratch. "It didn't like me messing with its *vitalle*. Doesn't seem to mind if we brush it off, though."

The dwarves exchanged looks, but Silas set his chisel gingerly against the hard earth covering the wheel and chipped away at it again.

More of the scratch in the paint grew visible. It wasn't just a spiral. It was a curl at the edge of a larger symbol. "Venn, there's writing scratched onto this. It looks almost like Kalesh runes."

A rush of wind sounded at the opening, and everyone twisted toward it. The dwarves raised their chisels like weapons.

A golden eagle flew into view, spreading its wings nearly as wide as Kate's arm span and landing next to the replanted bushes. Its bronze feathers caught the evening sun as it settled and cocked its head to the side.

Elvish runes, Crofftus's voice floated through the air.

He hopped a few paces to a half-buried rock at the edge of the overhang. A dead mouse was skewered on his talons. The bird bent down, ripping off a bit of fur and flesh. *I told you to drop the mouse*, Crofftus snipped, but the eagle tore off another bite.

"Hello, Crofftus." Kate probed at the distant ocean remnant. It felt the same as she remembered it. Powerful but far away. Not malevolent or dangerous. Just...distant.

Venn turned until she faced him squarely. "*You* read Elvish runes? I don't even read them."

Elves should educate each other better. Runelight is an excellent way to bind power to things.

"Maybe we aren't fixated on binding power."

Crofftus gave a fairly derisive snort.

"Didn't you two say he was a hawk?" Silas interrupted. "That's a lot bigger than a hawk."

Kate exchanged looks with Venn. "Exactly how wide is the range of your ability, Crofftus? Can you inhabit any animal?"

I've never met one I couldn't.

"Can you inhabit things that are...less than animals?" Kate asked, keeping her voice merely curious. "Like a plant?"

Crofftus gave a little snort. *Plants aren't alive in the same way. They don't move or think.*

"Trees think," Venn said.

The eagle turned his yellow eyes on her. *An elf would think that*, he said, a note of disdain in his voice. *There is a difference between awareness and thinking.*

"The trees in the White Wood can think," Venn said.

His voice hummed in what sounded like an agreement. *But you elves keep those trees to yourselves.* He spread his wings slightly and shifted on the rock before peering down at the carriage. *These runes look like some I read in a book once.*

Kate paused at the abrupt change of subject, and Venn crossed her arms, watching the eagle as he stepped closer to the carriage.

I don't remember what book. Something about endings. His voice was surprisingly solemn. *The ending of everything.*

Tribal looked up. "This work would be more pleasant with less gloom and doom from the bird."

The eagle snapped his attention to the dwarf. *I'm not here for your entertainment.*

"Why *are* you here?" Venn asked.

Because I— He stopped, his yellow eyes locked on the hub. *There are runes on the wheel as well.*

"We know," Kate said. "How much of this can you read?"

The eagle spread his wings and launched into the air, arcing out from the outcropping and circling around with a long, wide-winged glide.

Tribal and Silas leaned out of his way with annoyed expressions as he landed on the rim of the wheel, his head tilted to the side. *Shadow of death.*

"What?" Tribal moved back farther.

Silas glanced across the river at the trees. "Kate, you said gold, not shadows and death."

Brush off the rest of that sharp rune.

"Me?" Silas looked from the eagle to Kate.

She nodded. "Gently."

Silas grimaced and bent over the wheel, gingerly scraping the dirt away from a symbol that resembled half a star.

Continue...or stay...or persist. Something about that and the shadow of death.

Venn straightened. "Silas, clean off the runes just before that one."

The dwarf let out an unhappy grunt but took his chisel to the hard-packed dirt until the next set of runes was visible.

Venn looked at Crofftus. "'Those who seek you out shall never find you'?"

The eagle's head twitched sharply toward her. *That's exactly what it says.* His voice was low and cautious.

"You know these words?" Kate asked.

Venn pushed herself to her feet and took a step back from the carriage. "It's a curse. It's *the* curse."

Kate pulled her hand off the carriage. "Renault's curse?"

"No. The one used when an elf is cut off from their home for an act of treason."

"Or for disobeying the authority of the king?" Kate asked. Venn gave a tight nod. "What does the whole curse say?"

Venn kept her eyes on the wagon.

> *"You are cast out, isolated, left in outer darkness.*
> *You shall remain as you are, forever.*
> *Locked away, unseen, unfound.*
> *Those who seek you shall never find you.*
> *If they persist, the shadow of death shall come for them."*

The dwarves drew back from the wheel.

Crofftus stayed, though, peering down at the runes with his inhuman eyes. *A real curse! Fascinating!*

Kate stared at Venn. "Why would anyone put an elven curse on a human carriage?"

Venn shook her head slowly. "It wouldn't mean anything to a human. It cuts an elf off from other elves." She looked over the carriage. "I didn't even think it was a real curse. It's more… symbolic. It describes what already happens when an elf breaks the trust of the woods. They lose their connection to the community, but they're not physically cast out."

Silas shifted his weight. "What was the beginning part? You shall remain as you are, forever?"

Tribal's pickaxe handle rested on the wheel, and he nudged it off with his foot. "Like a three-hundred-year-old carriage still looking brand new?"

Kate cast out, and the entire buried carriage lit again with *vitalle*. This time she noticed the lattice of runes glowing along the edge nearest her. "I think it may be more than symbolic, Venn."

Locked away, unseen, unfound, Crofftus said with an ominous tone. He tightened his talons on the wagon wheel and stared at Kate with his yellow eyes. *Nice to see a curse that cleaves to its dark, classic roots, don't you think? People don't give enough weight to tradition these days.*

Kate met his emotionless stare. "It's unsettling more than nice."

"And it's safe to say"—Tribal clasped his hands behind his back—"that this isn't *unfound* anymore."

"No, it's not." Kate looked at the disturbed ground around the carriage. "It hasn't been for a while. Bo found it and was followed by a shadow"—she glanced at Venn—"just before he disappeared."

Venn turned to study Crofftus. "That shadow followed Bo and the Weasel Brothers, all of whom were interested in this ravine."

Silas cleared his throat. "Would you say, right now, all of us are seeking to find what's locked away?"

Kate nodded. "I believe we are."

Crofftus's voice echoed in her head with a low chuckle. *Classic and ominous.* He took off again, soaring out from under the rock shelf. *Perfection.*

CHAPTER SIXTY-FIVE

"Anybody else not entirely trust the bird?" Tribal said as the eagle spiraled higher.

Venn gave a hum of agreement and stared toward the river.

"There's something off about him," Silas agreed. "It's suspicious that he claims to be an old wizard who's familiar with this area while being very interested in supposed curses left by some other old wizard who used to live in this area. A wizard people *think* is dead, but no one knows for sure."

Kate turned to look at both dwarves. "You think he's Renault?"

Tribal shrugged. "How many crazy old wizards live in the world, really?"

Venn nodded. "He does know a lot about the White Wood."

"He's not old enough to be Renault," Kate said. "If he grew up in Queensland when Keeper Mikal was young, then Crofftus is no older than a hundred. Renault disappeared while the Empire still existed. Crofftus is at least two hundred years too young."

"I don't know," Tribal said. "If a couple-hundred-year-old

half-elf decided he'd caused too much trouble here and was hiding out in Queensland, he'd still be mistaken for a young man, don't you think?"

"Maybe," Kate admitted.

"It is a little troubling that he doesn't like Keepers," Venn said, brushing more dirt off the side of the carriage. "You people are well respected everywhere."

"Also true," Kate agreed. "But he said he was human when we first met."

Tribal scratched his beard. "No, he didn't. You asked if he was human, and he said, 'What else would I be?'"

"That's…" Kate frowned at him. "I didn't notice that."

"Not answering a question while making someone think you did is a skill Tribal and I have dabbled in from time to time," Silas said. "Once you've done it enough, it sticks out when other people try."

"He also didn't answer the other question," Tribal said.

Silas nodded. "You asked if he could inhabit a tree, since the ones in the White Wood could think. He answered that the elves keep those trees to themselves."

Kate looked out at the empty bit of sky she could see outside.

"I say we keep a close eye on the bird," Tribal said, chiseling at the edge of the dirt.

Kate went back to doing the same on the side of the carriage. "Did you find anything interesting while you were excavating?"

"Not really," Silas answered evasively.

Venn glanced at him. "They're not excited enough to have found something like the Oziv Amulet but too smug to have found nothing."

Tribal smiled. "The rockslide might have churned up a few sparkly things."

Silas pulled a reddish stone that was cloudy and irregular from his pocket.

"What's that supposed to be?" Kate asked. "A ruby?"

"A garnet," Silas said. "Don't bother looking for more—you'd miss them."

"Miss seeing a dull reddish rock?" Venn said turning back to the carriage. "How will we cope with the disappointment?"

"You have no imagination," Silas said. "This is going to be a beautiful stone. And the gov'nor's daughter loves garnets. A little shaping, and we have the beginnings of a gift to sweeten our return to Rullduin."

"If you say so," Venn said.

Kate continued to chip at the dirt along the edge of the carriage.

Bo had been in those caves. She glanced at the dwarves. Maybe she should have left them working on getting into those. But then the carriage…

She had no answer. Wherever they dug, the other would be left, and more time would be wasted. But there were too many unknowns. Too many clues that made no sense.

The old lingering doubt breathed into the back of her mind. *When you don't understand the whole picture…*

She shoved away the memory of Evan on the riverbank, but she couldn't banish the truth. She hadn't known the whole story, hadn't known what had been happening, hadn't been strong enough or smart enough or fast enough.

The more she tried to organize the pieces into a coherent story, the more disconnected they felt.

Twenty years later, and she still didn't know.

The uncertainly of it flooded into her mind, eroding away her confidence in what she was doing. When you didn't know the whole picture, how could you pick the right choice? She rolled her neck, stretching against the tightness that locked into her back and shoulders.

What am I supposed to do, Bo? she thought.

His words from the monastery came back to her.

That's always what those One Step moments need. Not some huge goal or feat of strength or brilliant answer. They need a small push, a real push. Driven by something outside of me. Something I love.

And then I can see the best decision, and I can take one step. And then I can take another.

She took a deep breath, drawing in the bits of his remnant she kept uncovering. They were merely on the surface of the carriage, but they were here, because he had been here. She nodded. *All right, Bo, I have no good goal, no unusual strength, and definitely no brilliant answers, but somehow you're connected to this. So I'll continue and figure out what you found.*

She read the runes carved into the surface. *And hopefully not end up just as missing as you are. But I think it's time to take the one step forward, even not knowing.*

Tribal cleared his throat. "Not to be the doomsayer here, but are we about to call a shadow of death to come find us?"

"Maybe." Kate glanced at each of them. The two dwarves gave her matching frowns, and Venn met her look with the slightest smile. Kate straightened her shoulders. "But I think we should draw it out."

Venn nodded. "We know it bleeds. Between the four of us, I think our odds are good against it."

Five of us, Crofftus said, gliding back under the rock shelf and settling on the ground.

The others exchanged looks, but no one answered.

"I promise I won't push any *vitalle* into the carriage," Kate said. "We'll just work carefully, cleaning it off and not damaging anything."

"Revealing the carriage that was cursed to remain unfound?" Silas asked.

"If you're scared," Venn said, stepping up to the edge of the carriage, "you don't have to help."

Tribal shook his head and pulled out his pickaxe. He knelt back next to the wheel and looked at Silas. "This is all wrong. How are *we* the ones pushing to be cautious here?"

Kate took her hunting knife out of her belt and set it against the hard dirt packed onto the side of the carriage. A chunk of it snapped off, revealing a stretch of black-painted carriage wall. More runes were scratched across it in a long line. She pried up the next bit, and it popped off to reveal a ridge of wood. On the far side, the surface was perfectly smooth. Kate wiped the dirt away from a cold pane of glass. "A window!"

She climbed up on the side, digging the tip of her knife into the dirt caked over the glass. A bit more of the clay-like earth broke off. Rubbing her sleeve on the glass to clean it, she peered inside again. "There are a lot of papers! I think they fell out of a box of some sort. It's all fallen to the other side."

The others moved closer, blocking the little evening light and dropping the carriage into darkness.

"Clean off more dirt." Kate yanked a blade of dry grass out of the ground and set her finger on it, pushing *vitalle* into it. It lit like a candle wick, and Kate pulled the fire off into her hands, dropping the charred bit of grass. She fed the flame until it grew bright and held it over the window.

Venn snapped off a section of dirt that had hardened on the window, but the two dwarves sat back, watching the flame warily.

Kate wiggled her fingers and making the fire dance between them. "I'm not going to burn you."

Both dwarves stayed back.

Venn gave them an amused look then made an exaggerated show of looking through the window. "By my scraggly beard," she said in a slow-witted dwarven voice, "is that gold I see in there?"

The twins twitched closer, craning to see inside.

593

Silas pointed at the fire. "Keep that away from our beards."

"And you do a terrible imitation of a dwarf," Tribal said to Venn, crawling forward to help clear more earth.

"Are you kidding?" Venn worked at the next section. "It sounded exactly like you. "

Kate held the fire over the window and dug her other fingertips under the cold, hard earth still covering the window. A part as broad as her hand split off.

The light fell on a vibrant blue pant leg and a leather shoe.

Kate hissed in a breath. "A body!"

Tribal moved around the carriage to look into the window. "What shape is it in? Bloody and new? A three-hundred-year-old skeleton?"

Venn jabbed him with her elbow. "Is it Bo?"

A moment's fear caught in Kate's throat before she saw the hand of an elderly man, limp and grey but covered in perfectly whole flesh. "No." She shifted the fire to see the hand more closely. "I see a man's hand, but far too old for Bo's. It looks perfectly preserved—" A fat ring sat on his smallest finger. Kate breathed on the glass and rubbed it again until it was perfectly clear.

The firelight hit the ring, and it shone with a warm gold glow, the metal untarnished. It flared out into a shield with a perfect engraving of a dragon coiled around a sword.

Kate stared down at the ring. "I think we found the emperor."

CHAPTER SIXTY-SIX

THE INTERIOR of the carriage was in complete disarray. While Tribal and Silas cleaned off the last of the dirt from it, Kate and Venn lay on their stomachs, their faces pressed up against the cold glass.

"There are maps up in the corner," Venn said. "And a surprising number of shoes. How many feet did he have?"

Aside from the leather boots that the man wore, which were seamed with bright red threads, there was a rich purple slipper stuck among some of the scattered papers and the red leather sole of what might be another boot.

"Who cares about shoes?" Tribal asked. "Can you see any gold?"

"At least three gold rings," Kate said, "a cuff around his wrist that is partially covered by his sleeve but looks thick, and…I can't see his head, because there are too many papers scattered on top of it, but there are several thick gold chains around his neck."

The two dwarves finished cleaning off the window, which was wide enough across that Kate's arm wouldn't quite span it.

There was no opening for a door on this side of the carriage, just a window, and Kate peered in to see if she could see the door on the side facing down.

"If this isn't your emperor," Silas said, "it was someone pretending to be one. Look at the sapphire in that chest." He tapped the glass, pointing to the blue stone set in the side of an open, overturned chest. It was easily two fingers across and glittered with a deep, vibrant blue. "If that's real, it's worth a fortune."

Tribal fished a small bit of curved polished silver out of a pocket and held it next to Kate's fire. It reflected a bright circle of light down into the carriage, and he angled it down onto the gem. Flashes of vivid blue sparked from the center of the gem, throwing glittering blue lights on the inside of the carriage.

"Ooh!" Silas said. "Promising."

"Can I borrow that?" Kate held out her hand for the silver. Tribal handed it to her, and she reflected some light into the darker corners of the carriage. A pile of gold coins lay where the ceiling met the far side, the hilt of what looked like a decorative sword glittered in elaborate gold filigree from under where the body was sprawled, and a handful of scrolls were crushed under the box with the sapphire.

"Look on the wall!" Venn said.

Kate shifted the light and found a red and gold painted symbol of the dragon and the sword. "That's…"

Tribal tapped the window with the hilt of his knife. Instead of the clink of glass, it thudded as though he'd hit stone.

He hit it harder, and the top of the carriage vibrated. He let out a little gasp and dropped the knife with a clatter, rubbing his palm. "Doesn't seem to want to be disturbed."

Kate looked over the visible surface. "The runes are just scratched into the surface." She cast out, and the skin of *vitalle* that spread across it was paper thin. "If we could remove them, whatever defense is built into it should unravel as well."

Tribal picked his knife back up, scraping the point against the rune nearest to him. It made no mark at all. He dug harder, but the blade still left no mark.

A lock with magical runes needs a magical key, Crofftus said.

The others looked at him with varying levels of suspicion, then every eye turned toward Kate.

She shook her head. "I tried that already, and it shocked us all."

"Maybe try it more gently." Tribal pushed away from the window and moved back. "As soon as we're all at a safe distance."

Silas followed his brother, and the two of them took several steps back before watching Kate expectantly. She glanced at Venn.

"Do we really want to follow the bird's advice?" the elf asked.

I am hardly giving advice, Crofftus said with an insulted sniff. *I am merely pointing out the obvious since no one else is.*

A dissonant sound scraped across the back of Kate's neck, and she froze. The chirping of birds and wind rustling forest across the river were overlaid by a hair-raising creak of trees rubbing against each other.

"Kate?" Silas took a step forward.

"No!" Kate held up her hand. "Everybody move back."

The dwarves backed away quickly.

"The remnant is here." Kate pressed her hands to the carriage. The chilliness of the wood seeped into her palms. "The one I could feel beneath the rockslide."

"On the carriage?" Venn asked.

Kate nodded, concentrating on the remnant and tightening her shoulders against the harsh grating sound of it.

"Inside it?" Tribal asked.

"Maybe. It almost feels like a solid sheet of it wrapped around the outside. But maybe it's inside as well." Kate pulled her hands off and shook them out. "Let's find out."

Venn let out a groan and backed up.

Try something subtle, Crofftus offered, flapping his wings and moving farther back on the rock he sat on. *But effective.*

"Thanks for that helpful advice," Kate said dryly, moving off the carriage. The line of runes ran along the edge of the wooden wall, and she searched until she found the one that seemed most like the Kalesh rune for *cast out.* "This is the beginning of the curse?"

Crofftus shifted his wings and stretched his neck to see without coming any closer. *Yes. It appears to repeat all around the edge of the carriage.*

Kate rubbed her hands together and cast out toward the runes. *Vitalle* trickled along each rune, pouring from one into the next along hair-thin scratches. That would be the easiest point to overload. She focused on the line connecting this rune to the final rune of the group before it and set her fingertip on the scratch.

Carefully, she funneled the tiniest bit of *vitalle* into it.

A burst of the corrupt remnant exploded into the air, and the line of runes blazed up in a blinding light. A wave of force exploded out of the carriage, knocking Kate onto her back. Loose dirt tumbled down the sides of the gaps they'd dug out around the carriage and showered down from the overhanging rock.

Kate scrambled back as the ground rumbled slightly.

The very real, very horrible grating of rocks shifting against each other sounded from under the rockslide.

Everyone stayed frozen as a few pebbles dislodged from the rock shelf above the carriage, clattering down onto the pristine side. The ravine quieted, and Kate cast out toward the carriage. The runes were perfectly intact.

"Well," Tribal said, picking up a sharp rock. "Let's see if that did anything."

He strode forward and lifted the rock above his head.

"Wait!" Kate shoved herself to her feet and lunged away from the carriage. "I didn't—"

Tribal slammed the rock down onto the window.

A thunderclap rang out, and a shockwave exploded from the impact, smashing her back to the ground.

Tribal flew backward through the air, slamming onto the ground a half-dozen paces away from the carriage. Silas and Venn fell to their knees, and Crofftus toppled off the rock, flapping his wings to get control before shooting into the cloudy sky.

"Tribal!" Silas ran over to kneel by his brother. Tribal groaned and held his head as his brother helped him sit up.

The surface of the carriage blazed with markings. Not just the ring of curses they'd seen around the outer edge, but countless more, scratched in thread-thin lines covering every visible surface.

Deep under the hillside, the ground vibrated with a low groan.

Venn turned slowly to look warily up at the rockslide. "What was that?"

Silas moved around the outcropping until he could see up the slope. "That is the sound of an unstable hill."

Kate crawled to her hands and knees. The ground shook again, and she tensed until it stilled.

Everyone waited, eyeing the rockslide.

When a dozen heartbeats passed, Kate's shoulders relaxed, and she climbed to her feet. "Tribal," she said, glaring at the dwarf. "Are you all right?"

"His head's harder than the ground," Silas answered, although he held out a hand to steady Tribal as he got to his feet. "Can't hurt him quite that easily."

"In that case"—Kate pointed a finger at him, raising her voice —"that was the stupidest thing I've ever seen! I didn't damage the curse at all. It's still perfectly intact!"

"Well..." Tribal blinked blearily at the carriage. "The window isn't."

A gaping, jagged hole sat where the window had been. She moved forward and peered down into the interior. The evening light illuminated it enough to see shards of glittering glass covering everything inside.

A biting metal stench poured out of the window, so sharp it scoured the back of her tongue and stung down her throat. She coughed and threw her hand over her nose and mouth, stumbling backwards, but her whole mouth tasted of metal.

She turned and spit, trying to get rid of the taste, and caught the others looking at her warily, all of them looking unaffected.

"Kate?" Venn said cautiously.

"His remnant." Kate spit again, even though she could tell now it wasn't a physical taste. "It's like eating metal."

A cold breeze blew by, dragging the initial burst of remnant away. The rest of it faded into a normal remnant strength. Kate stepped forward, moving closer to Venn and letting her forest scents outweigh the emperor's metal.

Silas craned to peer into the window without getting too close. "What sort of metal? Gold?"

Kate looked at the dwarf. "I can't imagine metals taste very different from each other."

Tribal gave her an incredulous look. "You need to taste more metals." He and Silas sidled up to the carriage.

Venn hung back, her arms crossed. "Don't get too close. Its curse *is* still intact."

Silas clapped his brother on the back. "Who needs a magic key to open a magic lock?"

Crofftus flew under the overhang and landed near the window with a new mouse in his talons. *Look at that.* His voice was tinged with awe. *All perfectly preserved.* His beak tore into the mouse.

Every bit of paper was intact, the fabric of the seats still a vibrant red. The body, which was covered from the waist up by papers and boxes and something that looked like a cloak, was also perfectly preserved. Kate breathed in carefully, expecting to smell the actual physical stench of a decomposed body, but the air was merely stale.

Silas knelt down. "The explosion blew the papers around. Look. That gold hilt is attached to a knife." He leaned closer. "The workmanship isn't even terrible."

Use caution. The eagle swallowed the end of the mouse. *I do not think this is as open as it looks.*

Tribal picked up a stone and dropped it through the window. It clattered into the carriage, bouncing off the sapphire box and landing amidst the slivers of glass. "Looks pretty open to me. Can you reach the hilt?"

"Do *not* stick your arm in there," Venn warned.

"I'll have to dip most of the way in." Silas held out one hand to his brother, and Tribal grabbed his brother's forearm and set his feet.

"Silas," Kate said, reaching out to stop him. "Don't!"

Stupid dwarf! Crofftus snapped, stepping forward as though he had arms to grab him.

Silas shoved his arm down through the jagged hole, his fingers stretched wide, reaching for the gilded hilt of the knife.

His elbow had reached the level of the window when a surge of *vitalle* shot out from the walls of the carriage. An icy blue arc of light stabbed into Silas's arm, and he let out a cry of pain. A blast of wind swirled through the carriage, sending papers and fabric flying. The muscles of his arm seized up, and his hand clamped shut, snatching a tangle of papers out of the air.

Kate cast out and felt a rush of *vitalle* surge into the dwarf.

The grating, scraping of the corrupt remnant scratched against her like sand grinding across her skin.

Silvery blue lightning lanced up his arm, enveloping his shoulder in a cage of light and stabbing into his neck. He threw his head back, and a hoarse scream ripped out of his mouth just as the light raced across his chest, down his other arm, and slammed into his brother.

Tribal collapsed to his knees, and the flow of *vitalle* twisted back the other way, syphoning energy out of the brothers like a rushing river.

Venn ran forward but skidded to a stop at the side of the dwarves, her eyes wide.

"Don't touch them!" Kate flung out a shield of her own *vitalle*, forming a shell around her hand. She lunged forward and grabbed Silas's just below his shoulder. Stretching the shield lower, she wrapped it down his arm, cutting off the arcs that pierced into him. The light smashed into her shield, and she poured more *vitalle* into the barrier, extending it down around Silas's forearm.

The emperor's metallic remnant gusted out, coating her tongue again, while the corrupt remnant flowed around her, cutting and abrasive.

The curse stabbed at the shell, crackling and hissing against it. A thick knife of light shot from the side of the window and slashed through the shield into Silas's arm just below Kate's hand.

He gave a strangled shout.

Vitalle ripped out of Kate's palm, gushing through Silas before it was sucked into the carriage.

Her own body heat bled out of her fingers. A knife of cold slid slowly up her arm, leaving her muscles and bones like ice.

Vitalle drained out of her chest in a flood before she wrestled the hole in the shield shut.

She gasped at the hollow chill that filled her and gripped

Silas's arm tighter as she shoved the shield farther down his arm. It reached his fingertips, and she sealed it off like a glove.

The blue light crackled between the carriage and her shell like a lightning storm, but the net of blue surrounding Silas winked out.

He gave a gasp and toppled forward toward the window, pulling Kate with him toward the swirling mess of paper and silks and biting metal stench.

"Tribal!" Kate gasped. "Pull him back!"

But Tribal's eyes were glazed, his body limp.

Venn leapt over Tribal and grabbed Silas by the shoulder, dragging him away. When his arm was free of the window, his hand still clamped around the papers, Kate released her hold on him and fell back, crashing down onto her side.

Venn staggered under Silas's limp weight and lowered him to the ground. "Kate?"

A wave of exhaustion rolled over Kate as she watched the last of the crackling light flicker out around the window. Her palm blazed with pain from two long blisters running across it, but her fingers were white and numb. Icy cold filled her arm almost to her elbow. Her breath came in gasps, and her chest felt strangely hollow. "Are those two idiots still breathing?"

Venn knelt between them. "Yes."

A thunderous rumble shook the ground. Small stones pelted down on Kate's side from the overhang, followed by a shower of dust.

Kate tried to throw an arm over her head, but it was too heavy to move. "Venn," she said, the word thick. "I think the curse pulled a bit out of me."

"Are you saying 'a bit' literally?" Venn asked, shoving Tribal onto his back so she could peel one of his eyes open. "Or do you mean it took a *lot* out of you?"

A crack rang out, and Kate twisted her head enough to see a

rock larger than her head crashing and spinning down the bit of rockslide she could see, bouncing off the slope of stones that still managed to hold their places.

The ground heaved, and Venn swore. "I think we need to move."

CHAPTER SIXTY-SEVEN

"I CAN MOVE." Kate cradled her palm to her chest and struggled to her feet. One of the dwarves groaned. "Can those two walk?"

Venn shook Tribal's shoulder. "Get up, you ridiculously heavy creature."

He pushed himself to his knees.

"Crofftus," Kate said, moving around the window to help Venn, "get in the air and tell us what you see." She reached Silas and smacked him on the cheek with her good hand. "Wake up, Silas! We can't carry you!"

The ground vibrated again, and she crawled toward the edge of the overhang in time to see another stone twice as big as the last careen down the rockslide until it hit the stones at the bottom, bounce high over the river, and crash through a line of young pines growing on the bank, leaving a trail of smashed trunks and limbs.

The sight cleared a little of the fog in Kate's mind. "Crofftus! Get in the air and—"

The eagle was perched at the edge of the window, his body rigid. Arcs of blue light crackled up the one talon that curled down into the window and up his leg, racing under thick golden feathers.

His yellow eyes were glassy as he stared forward, unmoving.

"Crofftus!" Kate cast out as she scrambled back around the window. The eagle was almost dark, the last of his *vitalle* draining quickly into the carriage.

She threw a shield up around herself and lunged for him, diving through a cloud of the metallic and the corrupt remnants, grabbing the eagle and shoving him back from the window. He didn't even flinch. She tried to cushion his fall with her arm, but they landed hard on the ground, and something in the eagle gave a sickening crack.

She cast out again and found barely a flicker of *vitalle* beneath the feathers.

Another shockwave made the ground tremble, and Kate shoved herself to her feet, trying to hold the eagle carefully as she stumbled forward. Tribal made an effort to stand but crumpled again, and Silas still lay senseless on the ground.

The ravine shuddered, longer and louder than before, and Kate looked up.

Venn met her gaze with a bleak expression and pointed to the far end of the ravine, where the slope flattened slightly and the pine forest resumed. "Maybe together we can drag one of them to the trees." The ground trembled, and Venn reached up to the rock overhang to steady herself, even as more dust and pebbles rained down on them. "But we'll never get both of them away."

Kate cast out toward the dwarves. Tribal was in better shape than Silas, and she forced herself to hurry over and kneel next to him, placing her good hand on his forehead. She pressed some *vitalle* into him until his eyes flickered open. "Get up! Rockslide!"

His eyes flew wide, and he clambered to his knees. "Silas!"

"We'll get him." Kate gave his shoulder a push toward the

line of trees at the far end of the slope. The distance seemed impossibly far. "To the trees. Hurry!"

She glanced down at Crofftus, who was still rigid. Venn grabbed one of Silas's legs, pulling him over onto his back, and pointed to the dwarf's wide chest. "Put the bird there and grab his other leg!"

Kate opened the front of Silas's fur-lined vest and tucked Crofftus inside. She grasped the dwarf's foot with her unburned hand, wrapping her other wrist around his boot. Even lifting just his leg was heavy.

"Pull!" Venn shouted over the sound of more stones clattering down the hillside, and Kate pulled. At both their efforts, the dwarf slid a foot across the ground. "Again!"

Step by step, they dragged him out from under the rock. Tribal was still crawling across the slope, shaking out his head and occasionally trying to stand.

"Again," Venn said, breathing heavy.

Kate braced her legs and heaved Silas one more time. He moved barely half a step. The world spun as Kate tried to catch her breath, and a drip of sweat rolled down her back despite the coldness of the air. They hadn't even moved ten paces, and the tree line was a hundred more away. Her hands and arms were so cold, she could barely feel Silas's foot, and black spots dotted her vision.

A noise uphill made her look up, and one of the black spots shifted, rolling downhill. She blinked and saw it was a handful of rocks rolling down just above the overhang, skipping and jumping, knocking loose more as they went. They hit the huge rock above the carriage and snapped off a section of it as they tumbled down the hill.

Kate tried to tighten her grip on Silas, but her legs buckled, and she fell to her knees. "Venn, I can't..."

"Venn!" a voice snapped out of the air next to them as a gust of *vitalle* blew against Kate.

She spun to see Faron appear steps away, his face thunderous.

"What are you doing? Bringing down the entire—"

Another quaking groan sent a spattering of stones skittering down the slope, and he stopped short, taking in Silas and Kate. His eyes flicked to Tribal, still crawling toward the trees, then back to Silas.

"Help me get him up!" He reached down to grab Silas's shoulders and yanked his hand back. "Why is there a dead bird on his chest?"

Venn grabbed Crofftus and tossed him toward Kate before pushing her shoulder under Silas's arm and shoving him higher.

Kate caught the eagle, barely, and stumbled to her feet. His remnant thundered even more faintly than usual.

Faron wrapped his arms around the dwarf's chest and glared at both Kate and Venn with a furious expression. "Get her off this mountain, Venn!"

And then he and Silas disappeared.

Venn grabbed Kate's arm and dragged her after Tribal.

"Where'd Faron go?" Kate asked, squeezing her eyes shut to banish the floating black spots. The slope shifted strangely under her feet, either from the shaking of the mountain or the dizziness in her head, but she tried to focus on the point ahead where the rocky slope ended at the line of trees.

Before Venn could answer, Faron appeared again with a burst of *vitalle* next to Tribal.

"Up you go," he said to the dwarf.

"Faron!" Venn called. "Stop! You can't take both of them that far!"

The prince ignored her, squatting down to help Tribal to his feet.

"Hello, Your Highness," Tribal said blearily. The dwarf only came up to Faron's chin, but the elf pulled Tribal's arm up over his shoulder.

"Why are you dwarves so heavy?" Faron grunted. "Keep your arm on my shoulder. Now, take just one step."

"Faron!" Venn yelled, but the elf and dwarf disappeared.

Two figures appeared at the tree line ahead before they both dropped to their knees.

"Idiot!" Venn hissed, pulling Kate along faster.

"I didn't know you could take someone with you when you step," Kate said, concentrating on moving her feet, which felt like they'd been encased in stone.

"Most can't, and even someone who can"—she raised her voice to a shout—"shouldn't!"

They were close enough to the trees that Kate could see Faron on his hands and knees, his head hanging down in exhaustion.

The entire world shuddered, and a deep rumbling rolled out from behind them.

Kate twisted to see over her shoulder. Everything spun, and for a moment, she couldn't make the ravine stop swimming in her vision.

She blinked.

It wasn't her vision.

The entire slope at the outcropping with the wagon was sliding downhill.

"Venn..."

"Come on." Venn pulled Kate's arm over her shoulder and half carried her forward. "Pick up your feet a bit. I mean that literally. Just high enough to step, Kate."

The rumbling grew louder, like a never-ending thunderclap so close it reverberated in Kate's chest and vibrated along her bones.

She forced her feet faster, and the two of them stumbled over the shaking ground.

They reached the trees and staggered to a halt, turning to see a massive stretch of rock churn up out of the earth and roll down-hill, raising a huge cloud of dust. It smashed down into the base of the ravine and crashed into the river.

The billowing dust obscured everything near the bottom, and Kate leaned on Venn's shoulder, her body heavy and cold, watching the slope crumble.

It lasted another ten heartbeats before the thundering stopped.

They stood in silence, staring at the cloud of dust being slowly blown away on the wind.

"Venn," Faron said from where he'd crawled to slump against a tree. "What did you do?"

Kate pulled her eyes away from the slope. Tribal was sprawled on his side, squinting at the ravine, Silas lay next to Faron, unconscious, and Crofftus was still stiff in her arms.

Kate knelt and set the eagle on the ground. He was shockingly light for such a large bird. She cast out a tiny wave and found the bird still alive, but barely. Setting her unhurt hand on his chest and the other against the tree beside them, Kate pulled *vitalle* from the trunk and funneled it gently into him.

Venn took several steps until she loomed over Faron. "Why would you possibly do something that stupid?"

"Me?" Faron glared up at her. "I didn't bring a *mountain* down. You're welcome for saving your friends."

Venn took another step toward him. "You shouldn't have stepped even one dwarf this far! Never mind both."

"You have no idea how much I can or can't step," he snapped.

"Oh, really?" Venn crossed her arms. "Stand up."

Faron's expression grew darker. "I don't want to. I'm tired."

"You mean you can't. Kate!"

Kate looked up from Crofftus.

"Cast out at the good prince, will you?"

Kate sent a wave toward Faron. It rolled past Venn's towering brightness, but when it hit Faron, he was substantially dimmer. His legs, especially, were not even bright enough for a human's, never mind an elf's. The tiniest trickle of *vitalle* flowed out of the tree into him, so small Kate almost couldn't see it.

"You are such an idiot." Venn dropped to her knees next to him and slapped her hand onto his chest. "What if you'd died trying to save the lives of two dwarves?" Kate felt a thick stream of *vitalle* begin to flow from the tree into Faron's back.

He frowned up at her. "You know you are terrible at healing."

"I'm not healing you—I'm convincing the tree to give you enough *ael'iza* that you don't die right here for your idiocy."

"Hey, Prince," Tribal said slowly. "Don't listen to the angry elf woman. We appreciate what you did."

Faron looked up at Venn, his face pale, and gave a faint smile. "Somehow I imagined you'd be impressed with an act of nobility expended on someone who wasn't an elf."

Venn stared at him, incredulous. "You are the prince of the Wood. You can't run around doing stupid things."

He leaned his head back and closed his eyes. "You're the princess and you do stupid things all the time."

Kate cast out at Crofftus, who was now slightly warmer. The eagle's breaths were a bit deeper. She could hear the faint thundering remnant. A bit of *vitalle* knotted in the bird's leg around one of his bones. She cast out and found the small break. It was clean, but the eagle was too weak to begin healing it yet.

"Why isn't Silas moving?" Tribal asked blearily.

Kate turned to Silas. He lay senseless on the ground where Faron had dropped him. Her limbs felt heavy, but she crawled over next to Silas and cast out at him. His arm was cold, with barely any light at all. His chest was dim, his neck and head only faintly warm.

"Is he…" Tribal's words trailed off.

"The curse drained a lot of his *vitalle* away." Kate cast out again, and Tribal flared brightly next to her. "The trees will work too slowly. Can I give him some of yours?"

Tribals cheeks drained of color, his skin looking stark white against his black beard. "Is he dying?" he whispered.

"Not yet. Put your hand over his heart."

Tribal set his wide hand on Silas's chest, and Kate put hers on top. She pushed some *vitalle* into them, working to open a path, but a channel opened up so easily between the two dwarves she had to draw her own back before her energy was dragged into the flow. Tribal's *vitalle* slid smoothing into his twin's, as though they were a single person.

"That's...good." She left her hand on his, keeping the channel between the two dwarves open. "Just stay like that. Tell me if you start feeling too tired, and I'll stop the flow."

A cold wind brushed past her, sneaking around her neck to freeze the back of her collar, which was still damp from sweat. She shivered and pulled her cloak tighter.

Tribal's eyes crinkled with something like regret. "I'm sorry, but I don't think we can reach the carriage again without a lot of work."

A frozen river of rock covered the area where the outcropping had been, smothering every sign of it.

It was gone.

The world spun, and Tribal leaned closer, pressing his shoulder against her to steady her.

"Thank you," he said without looking at her. "I know you saved our lives."

His arm was like a solid wall, and she sank against it.

"We'll help you dig it out again," he offered.

Kate relaxed against him, feeling the weight of the rocks imprisoning the carriage and everything it could have told her.

The same weight settled on her, taking the little hope she'd found and crushing it into the ground.

CHAPTER SIXTY-EIGHT

FARON FROWNED TOWARD THE ROCKSLIDE. "You found an ancient carriage protected with runelight so powerful it tried to collapse the hillside when you disturbed it?"

Kate nodded. "Who could have created that?"

He looked at her blankly. "Three hundred years ago? Not me, if that's what you're asking. I was a bit young to know how."

"How many elves would have the authority?" Kate asked. "Your father? Your mother?"

Faron shook his head. "My father wouldn't do something as imprecise as a vague curse. And my mother wasn't the type to curse anyone. Of course, if she did..." He looked out over the ravine in the direction of the White Wood.

"She won't remember it now," Venn finished quietly.

Faron didn't disagree. "But whoever wrote that wouldn't need elven authority if they were putting it on humans."

"That's true." Kate thought for a moment. "What about Renault the Mad?"

Venn's gaze flicked to Crofftus, then back to Kate. "That's an idea. He was half-elven, lived in caves, and knew elven magic and enough Kalesh that I'm sure he knew runes."

Faron's brow creased. "That's a possibility. I can't imagine he's still alive, though. If he is, he hasn't bothered us for centuries."

"Would he need to still be alive for the curse to still work?" Kate asked.

"I have no idea," Faron said. "I've never even heard of it used on something like this." He looked out over the ravine. "Maybe that's evidence that it was Renault."

Kate glanced between him and Venn. "You think it's more likely it was some mad half-elf, even though there are hundreds of elves in the area who could have done it?"

Faron looked at her as though considering his next words. "Renault makes more sense," he said slowly, "because I don't know why an elf would bother with this for a human. No offense, but you're not that threatening. Even your emperors." He waved a hand toward the ravine before dropping it tiredly back into this lap. "Why would an elf care about this ravine? There are no trees anywhere on it."

"Then why were there elven tracks in the caves?" Silas said, his voice hardly above a whisper.

Tribal let out a quiet breath of relief at the sound of his brother's voice but cleared his throat and looked at Faron. "He's right. We explored those caves years ago. There were footprints too narrow to be human."

Faron shook his head. "Elves don't go in caves."

"Unless they have to," Venn muttered.

"These were probably elven." Tribal glanced at the newly widened rockslide. "We didn't study them too closely. We weren't really there looking for tracks."

"What were you looking for?" Faron asked.

"Has nothing do with trees," Tribal said. "Just some sparkly things you wouldn't care about it."

His head bobbed, and Kate pulled her hand off his, cutting off the *vitalle* between the dwarves. "That's enough for now."

Tribal's brow dove down. "We can do more."

Kate patted his hand. "Silas will be all right. Just needs rest. Let's not make both of you too weak." She sank back against the tree. "What else do you two know about those caves?"

"There's something strange about them," Silas said quietly.

"Strange?" Kate asked.

Silas nodded without opening his eyes. "Creepy."

"All caves are creepy," Venn said.

"No." Tribal pointed at her. "Caves are homey and cozy. Like a warm blanket."

Venn raised an eyebrow. "A smothering blanket of death, maybe."

"These caves aren't cozy," Silas said, his voice still quiet. "They feel...conflicted."

"How can caves feel anything?" Faron asked.

Tribal shook his head, but Silas continued, "They feel both sad and like they want to kill us."

Tribal dropped his head in his hands, but Venn's and Faron's surprised looks matched Kate's feelings.

"The cave was sad?" Kate said. "And murderous?"

"I told you that was a stupid way to describe it," Tribal muttered.

Silas cracked one eye. "How would you describe it, then?"

"There is no other way. Which is why I wouldn't have brought it up."

"You didn't find a cause for the creepy feeling?" Faron asked.

Tribal scanned the hillside. "No, but something's in there. When things are strange, there's always a reason. Often that reason is very valuable to someone, and we like to figure out what those valuable things are."

"They want to steal whatever it is," Venn explained to Faron.

The prince's expression turned slightly distasteful.

"Twig," Tribal said, his voice a little reluctant. "Did you learn anything about Bo from that carriage?"

Kate looked over the rockslide. "He'd been around it, but there was no sense of his remnant inside. I could feel the emperor's once the window was broken, but whatever it is of Bo's that's on this hillside, it's not actually him. It's more like…"

Kate paused. The corrupt remnant had been enmeshed in the magic around the carriage, which meant it was probably a part of the net of *vitalle* protecting the entire slope and the caves. And Evay felt the closeness to Melia only through the wellstone in her ring, which held a sliver of Melia's *vitalle.* "I think somehow Bo's *vitalle* was used to fuel the shield protecting this whole hillside."

Everyone looked at her with varying degrees of confusion or skepticism.

"I don't know how that could have happened," she admitted. "But that's what it feels like."

Faron squinted at her and opened his mouth as though to object, but he closed it again. Instead, he gestured to where Crofftus lay. "Why is there an unconscious eagle here?"

"It's not really an eagle," Venn said. "It's a…"

"That's Crofftus," Tribal said. "Or the animal Crofftus currently inhabits."

Kate explained the mage and his skills. "So he can inhabit animals and talk…in your mind."

"That's…" Faron's eyes shifted among them, as though trying to gauge if they were joking.

"Weird," Tribal said, nodding. "It's really weird."

Setting her hand on Crofftus, Kate pressed *vitalle* into him.

The eagle's body was small and fragile, and half the energy she sent in trickled through him and into the ground.

The eagle twitched, and a spasm ripped across his wings. A raw cry ripped out of his throat, and he rolled to the side, convulsing.

Kate grabbed him, pressing his wings closed, trying to hold him still as he thrashed. "Crofftus!"

The eagle's head flailed from side to side, and Faron scrambled over to it, taking his head in both hands. The eagle twisted, and his beak bit deep into the flesh near Faron's thumb, but he didn't let go.

"Shh," he whispered, and Kate felt a wash of *vitalle* pour through the bird's head. "*Yesilla*," he said quietly, and the eagle stilled, his body going limp.

Kate held him, but he appeared to be peacefully sleeping.

"Its leg is broken." Faron let go of the eagle's head and moved his hand to the eagle's leg.

A sprinkling of *vitalle* like a spring rain fell from his hand and through the feathers. Unlike Kate's attempts, this soaked into the muscle and bone, warming them, setting the edges of the bone to healing.

Faron shifted his hand until it hovered above the bird. In a moment, his skin glowed a bright copper, and he gently moved the feathers aside to look at the leg. "It'll take a while to heal fully, but that's a start. When he wakes next, the pain should be less."

"How long will he sleep?"

The light from Faron's hand dimmed and disappeared. "Until tonight at least. It's a kindness to let him, at this point." He tried to stand but fell heavily to his hands and knees.

"Get against a tree," Venn said, stalking over to him and helping him scoot back against a trunk. His head thunked back against it as she put her hand on his chest. Kate felt the *vitalle* of the tree begin to seep into him again.

617

"I don't need your—" he started.

"Shut up." She shifted until she was sitting next to him, her hand resting on his chest. "And this time, you don't decide when you've had enough. I do."

He lifted his hand and set it over hers. "Was I supposed to let the eagle suffer?"

"You're supposed to not be an idiot," she answered.

He patted her hand. "And here I thought you didn't care anymore." His eyes shut. "Maybe your friend's no longer in the eagle," Faron said in an exhausted voice.

Crofftus's remnant still rumbled quietly beneath all the remnants around them, and Kate shook her head. "He's still here."

"How can you tell?"

"She can smell your soul," Tribal said.

Faron frowned and opened his eyes. "Is that supposed to mean something I don't understand?" he asked.

Venn shook her head. "Literally. She can smell you. Says you smell like an alpine forest."

Faron drew back slightly. "You are a very strange group." When no one objected, he looked around at all of them. "Now that you tried to destroy the ravine and choked the river to the point that it's going to be a real trial to clear it, what disastrous adventure are you planning to embark on next?"

"I plan on lying here." Silas lifted his hand, which still held a wad of papers. "Maybe Kate will read to us. Show us what's being protected so fiercely."

Kate grabbed the pages. "I forgot you had those!" She spread them on her lap, smoothing out the crumples. The sun had nearly set, but there was enough light to make out the writing. It was five handwritten pages that didn't look as though they should be stacked together.

"They're records of a journey." She flipped to another page

and stopped. "The date!" She held up the page. "'17th of Resuent'—that was a Kalesh month in late summer—'54th year of the reign of Emperor Sorrn'!" She looked up at Venn. "This really is three hundred years old!"

"So," Silas said, pushing himself to sit up, "the part of the curse about 'remain as you are, forever' seems to be true. Do we assume the 'shadow of death shall come for us' part is also true?"

"Maybe it really meant 'shadow of deadly rocks,'" Tribal said. "Because that came for us."

"I still don't understand why anyone would curse the carriage like this," Kate said. "I could feel the outline of the carriage underground. The top is smashed in. I think it rolled down the hillside. Sorrn probably died in the crash. What's the point of cursing him after he's dead? It's not like he knows he's been there for three centuries."

Silas shook his head. "Had nothing to do with cursing him. It's about keeping anyone else from finding whatever he found."

Tribal gave a grunt of agreement. "Classic treasure protection. Hide the evidence that the treasure even exists."

"Except they didn't hide it," Kate said. "They preserved it for centuries."

"In an unreachable place," Venn pointed out. "If you hadn't been there, Silas, Tribal, and Crofftus would all be dead. And I certainly wouldn't have reached into that window to find what it holds."

Faron looked at all of them. "But what did he find?"

A splatter of snow landed on Kate's pants, and she pulled the papers up, quickly tucking them in her pack. "Silas, can you walk far enough to reach camp? Maybe we'll get some hint to what he found on these pages, but I think we need to get to somewhere dry."

CHAPTER SIXTY-NINE

FAT, fluffy snowflakes floated through the darkening air as Kate trudged into the clearing with their shelter and breathed an exhausted sigh. She shifted Crofftus in her arms for the hundredth time.

The snow landed in little clumps of wetness on her lashes and forehead, feeling cool after the effort of walking up the hill.

Behind her, Faron grunted from under Silas's arm as the dwarf took shuffling steps.

"C'mon," Venn said to Tribal, who'd stumbled to a stop and stood swaying slightly. "Get inside. We'll get a fire going, and everyone can rest."

Kate made it the last few steps into the shelter before dropping to her knees and setting Crofftus down on the far side of the fire pit. She let her pack fall to the ground and arranged some of the wood they'd left stacked nearby.

Venn pulled Kate's pack over by her own and glanced at Tribal. "Do you boys have any food?"

He flipped open the bag he'd dropped on the floor and tossed Venn a bundle. She opened it and gave a hum of approval.

Faron angled Silas in through the narrow entry and helped the dwarf over until he slumped down next to his brother.

Kate stuffed a wad of dead pine needles into the bottom of her stack of wood and poked her finger into it. "*Incende.*" The *vitalle* flowed out of her finger sluggishly, but a wisp of smoke rose from the needles, and she blew on it. The motion made her dizzy again, and she pressed her eyes shut against it while the world spun.

Tribal's hand grabbed her shoulder and pulled her back just as a tall tongue of flame flared out of the wood right where her face had been.

"Mind yourself," he said in a low, tired voice.

The shelter swam in front of her eyes, and he kept his hand on her shoulder while it settled.

"Thank you." She patted his hand.

Faron brought in an armful of firewood and then, in the first show of uncertainty Kate had seen from him, stood awkwardly near the spruce trunk as though he wasn't sure whether he should sit or leave.

Venn didn't acknowledge him but looked resigned enough that Kate offered the prince a weary smile. "Any chance you have anything to contribute to whatever meal Venn is assembling?"

"Choke roots wouldn't go amiss," Venn said. "We'll let them simmer for a few hours while everyone rests." She glanced up at him. "And some juniper berries for flavor."

Faron stared at her for a moment, his eyes slightly wide, as though she'd asked him for something shocking. The expression passed quickly, and he ducked out the door.

Kate gave Venn a questioning look.

Venn let out a sigh and went back to crumbling some dried meat into the pot of soup. "I have no idea what was surprising about that."

"Maybe he didn't like being treated like an errand boy, being a prince and all." Silas looked out the door after Faron. "Actually, this might be a first for Tribal and me. Don't think we've ever dined with royalty."

The shelter was beautifully dry, and the warmth from the fire pressed against Kate's face. She lay down on her side, curling toward the flames. "Venn's a princess." She let her eyes close.

"Oh," Tribal said, a note of disappointment in his voice. She heard him rustling as he lay down near her feet. "Who knew royalty was so uninteresting."

The world spun slowly beneath Kate, and if Venn answered, it was lost in a haze of sleep.

A nutty smell spiced with a piney, peppery scent dragged Kate from sleep. She opened her eyes to find the interior of the shelter warm with firelight. The sliver she could see of the clearing through the entrance was a dusky blue, made somehow brighter but hazier by the thick snow still falling outside. The ground at the entrance was totally white, and snow was piling up on the few branches she could see outside.

Her exhaustion had receded to a dull tiredness behind her eyes. Venn sat against the trunk of the fir, flipping through a small book. The two dwarves, Faron, and Crofftus were all fast asleep.

Kate sat up and rolled her neck, and Venn looked up. She lifted the book, showing the cover of Bo's journal.

Venn held it out, open to a page. "He knows you better than I gave him credit for," she said quietly. "And I think you still know him too." She glanced at Faron, curled on the ground with his back to the fire. "I may have been talking more about me than you."

Kate leaned forward and took the journal. "Maybe yours isn't as unknown as you think it is either."

"What's the point in trying to know someone who lives their life ruled by someone else?" Venn asked. "I might as well just marry his father. It will amount to the same thing."

Kate looked down at the page in Bo's journal.

It's raining again, Ria. Four days. Nothing but rain.

Not just rain, but Rain. The stream downhill from me is flooded, and the hillside is a muddy mess. I'm essentially trapped in this small dead-end cave until it subsides.

I have never been so bored.

If you were here, what would you do?

That's a stupid question.

You'd have your notes out, and you'd be organizing them into a story map. You'd probably be thrilled with the uninterrupted time to structure your thoughts and be able to flesh out the story into something even more interesting and entertaining than whatever the original event really was. You'd be drawing in threads from other stories, finding patterns I'd never see, doing the story weaving you're so good at.

And you'd be shooting me looks of veiled impatience every time I interrupted you.

But, as you're not here, I challenge you to come up with a story that isn't utterly boring and tedious of a man trapped in a small cave while the world does nothing but rain on him for days and days and days.

I think that would defy even your skill.

At the bottom of the page was a sketch looking out of a cave mouth at hazy hills while lines of rain obscured everything else.

"He always hated staying still," she said quietly. The thought stirred the fear of what he must be enduring right now, and the thoughts she'd been trying to stifle rose to the surface. "If he's been held somewhere for all these weeks, he may have driven himself mad already." She looked up at Venn, who didn't disagree. "Unless he's too hurt or weak to think that much."

Venn was quiet for a moment. "He seems like a resourceful man. He'll have thought of something." Her voice wasn't particularly convincing.

"Twig," Tribal said from where he lay, a note of reluctance in his voice. "I know you don't want to admit it, but it is starting to feel unlikely that your brother is still alive."

Kate glanced at Venn, who shook her head.

Tribal caught the motion and sat up, giving Venn a disapproving scowl. "What point is there in drawing out hope when there's no evidence for it? I want her to find him too, but you have to admit that we don't really have any reason to believe he's still alive."

Both Silas and Faron stirred.

Tribal turned to Kate, looking apologetic. When he spoke, though, his voice was firm. "For your sake, Twig, I'd like to believe he's just being held somewhere and we'll find him, but chances are he's died somewhere in these woods. And..." He shrugged. "The elves probably know where."

Faron pushed up onto an elbow, frowning. "This is a forest. Things die here every day. Plants, animals. We don't keep a list."

"He's not dead," Venn said flatly, stirring the soup.

"You can't be sure," Faron objected.

Her hand stopped, and she turned the slightest bit toward him. "I'm sure."

Faron's eyes narrowed. "What is this human to you, Venn? I thought you were just searching for him for Kate's sake."

"She is helping me," Kate said.

"Nah," Tribal said, looking into the soup. "Venn's soul is connected to his or some such thing."

Faron stared at the dwarf, then turned slowly to Venn. "Explain."

Venn went back to stirring. "No."

"Andovenn," he said, a note of command in his voice.

She spun to face him, whipping the spoon out and sending a spray of soup through the air. She pointed it at his face. "Don't you *dare* even *think* about commanding me to do something. You, of all people, cannot blame others for keeping secrets. You have no right to ask anything of me."

He snapped his mouth shut but glared at her as though he were trying to rip the truth from her thoughts.

She turned away and picked up a small bowl, scooping out some soup and thrusting it at Silas. "Eat this. And don't do anything else stupid like shoving your hand in a cursed carriage. Next time, we're leaving you to be smashed by the rockslide you started." She picked up a wide piece of flatbread and threw it at the dwarf

Silas caught the bread against his chest. "It was Tribal who started it," he grumbled.

"Doesn't matter." Venn shoved a second bowl toward Tribal. "You're the same person."

Kate took the bowl Venn offered her. It had bits of bacon and small chunks of some root that looked like potatoes. Even through the mishmash of remnants filling the shelter, the soup smelled remarkably good. Tribal handed her a chunk of the flat bread, and she dipped it in. The broth was nutty and warm, and she dunked and ate the entire piece of bread before bothering to use a spoon for the rest.

The shelter settled into a brittle silence as Venn and Faron did not speak to each other. Tribal and Silas finished their soup and dug a pouch of unremarkable-looking stones out of Silas's bag, leaning their heads together and discussing each quietly.

Kate finished her soup, and she flipped through Bo's journal again. The mention of a cave caught her eye.

Ria,

The sun is setting earlier each day. I climbed the mountain again just to get some perspective. The cave looks dark in the fading light, and I'm trying to ignore the way it looms. I feel the need to justify my fear of it to you, even though I know that you know that I don't dislike caves. Interesting things are often preserved well in caves. But this feels...It feels like it doesn't want me to enter. I wish you were here. You'd probably see in an instant what's going on with it. Then work your magic on it and break whatever strange spell lingers in it and we could explore.

I realize if you ever get ahold of this journal, you may think I'm crazy for talking to you all the time. But the truth is, I couldn't do any of this without you.

On nights like this, I need to believe that the messes I send to you are useful. That you can draw something of value from them. I wish I could do what you do—take the pieces and see how they fit together. I wish I could see the whole picture the way you can.

I hope it's helpful to you, the way I dump everything I find in your lap. I hope you think we make a good team.

You're not here to tell me whether you do, and I'm too cowardly to ask you in a letter, but I hope you find me a partner worth having. In...whatever it is we're trying to do here.

Kate reread the last paragraphs, feeling nearly as stunned as she had when she'd realized he'd found the emperor. *He* was worried about not being the useful partner in this endeavor?

She had started reading it again when Silas's voice interrupted. "What did the papers from the carriage say?"

Kate blinked and looked up. "I..." She straightened. "How did I forget about those?" She flipped Bo's journal closed and tucked it in her pack, pulling out the pages from the carriage and spreading them on her lap.

The first page was just a formal record of the emperor's movements a few weeks away from Home. She turned to the second page. It was unconnected to the first and began partway through a dull description of weather and travel.

The third page was in a different hand and began mid-sentence. It was messier, and it took a moment to translate the ancient Kalesh.

...the entire complex seems to be connected. There are signs that it was used, although my scholars disagree about how long ago. The workers will be mobilized tomorrow to begin searching each cave.

It's close. I can feel it. I have not made this trip in vain, and when I return home with the amulet, every whisper of dissent will be silenced. There will be no talk of lacking heirs. No scheming to break away from the throne. The Empire shall enter a thousand years of peace, and I shall form the shape of it all.

She looked up. "These are Sorrn's personal notes! He found the caves and was about to send his workers in to search them. He thinks he's close to finding an amulet that will let him reign for a thousand years."

"Told you the Oziv Amulet was real," Tribal said.

Venn shook her head. "This only means an eccentric emperor thought it was."

Kate turned back to the page and slowly translated his next entry, letting the others return to their own devices.

The woman returned tonight, cloaked again so I could not see her face. I would say she is merely a figment of my mind, except she speaks in a thick accent I cannot place. Would my mind invent such a thing? She waited again until I was alone in my tent before appearing. She stayed in the shadows, and if she hadn't spoken, she might have stayed there all night and I wouldn't have known.

She bid me take my men and leave. Warned that only the blackness of death walks this canyon.

I told her she was rather smaller than I'd pictured death, but she merely laughed and told me that death knows no size.

Then she was gone. She has a chilling way of delivering her warnings.

Tomorrow I shall station men outside to capture her. Her audacity in coming to me twice should be curbed.

Although I admit I am curious to see her face.

There is a town nearby named Home. I sent men to speak to the townsfolk and discovered that this whole area is shunned. They say it is inhabited by a wild woman who guards his remains.

They call him Renault the Mad here.

I am finally in the right place.

Today, the men discovered a tunnel in the cave that had been partially blocked. The scholars say it was purposefully closed.

The workers are nearly done clearing it. I have them working through the night.

Witch or no, tomorrow we search.

The next page was another excerpt of the formal records, mostly distances traveled and weather encountered.

The final one was again in Sorrn's hand, but only a few lines were scrawled across the top.

...so I had Reslon run him through. No guard of mine will let one small woman escape. I am surrounded by incompetence.

If she returns, I shall gut her myself. Insolent, arrogant woman. Reslon admires her—I can see it. If he breathes the opinion aloud, I will gut him too.

She is plain and small and ugly, and if she dares to come near me again, I'll rip her condescending head off.

The amulet is in my land. It is mine. Anyone who contests that will die.

The line beneath it was scribbled through with heavy strokes.

Below that, words dashed across the page, written so fast the scrawl was nearly illegible.

Kate studied them, working out the messy letters until she suddenly caught the meaning.

She drew in a deep breath and turned the page over but found nothing else. She flipped through all five pages, checking the fronts and the backs, but there were no more words.

She looked up to find four sets of eyes staring at her. Behind them all, the far edges of the shelter were steeped in impenetrable shadows.

"What is it?" Venn asked.

Tribal leaned closer. "Did he find the Oziv Amulet?"

Kate looked back at Sorrn's writing. "I don't know. A local woman warned him away, said death walked the canyon." She held up the page and read his last line.

"'It comes! We cannot flee! Death is here—'"

CHAPTER SEVENTY

No one in the shelter moved.

Something snapped outside, and Kate flinched.

In less than a breath, Venn's crossbow was loaded and aimed at the entrance and both dwarves were on their feet, knives drawn. Faron disappeared from his seat and reappeared in the doorway, a long, thin blade in his hand.

Kate cast out, and light blazed outside the shelter in the shape of two deer, moving slowly through the clearing.

Kate set her hand on Tribal's arm. "Just deer." His fingers relaxed.

Faron had already lowered his blade, but he kept looking outside into the falling snow. Light from the full moon trickled through the clouds, showing the snow falling in lazy grey flakes.

"If something comes," Venn said icily to the prince, still pointing her crossbow at the door where he stood, "and you step into my way, you're going to get shot."

Faron returned to his seat. "You wouldn't hit me by accident," he said calmly. "You have better reflexes than that."

She stalked away from him. "Maybe it wouldn't be an accident."

"Kate," Silas said, "does your emperor happen to mention what death looks like?"

She glanced back at the papers. "The woman called it *the blackness of death.*"

"At least everyone is staying consistent," Tribal muttered. "Shadows and death. Death and shadows."

Faron looked at them all. "You think the shadow killed the emperor? Hundreds of years ago? The one that people are talking about today?"

"Do you have a better reading of it?" Venn asked.

He didn't answer.

Kate cast out again. A few deer, along with the surrounding oaks and pines, flared brightly as the wave rolled over them. "We're all exhausted," she said, "but I think a double watch is in order again tonight."

"I'll take first watch with Tribal," Venn said. "You and Silas sleep for a bit."

"What about me?" Faron asked.

"No one trusts you enough," Tribal said bluntly, moving over to settle himself next to the door.

Venn's expression was slightly amused as she joined him and set her hand on one of the thick branches making up the wall.

When Faron turned to Kate, she shrugged. "Take whatever shift you want. A third set of eyes and ears can't hurt anything." His expression stayed annoyed, but he backed up and sat against the trunk of the spruce, glaring at Venn's back.

"There's nothing nearby," Venn said over her shoulder to Kate. "Get some sleep while you can."

Kate massaged the muscles at the back of neck, turning her head side to side in a gentle rocking motion. She covered her mouth to stifle a yawn. The eagle twitched, and everyone turned to look at him warily.

Kate glanced at them. "Does anyone object to having Crofftus sleep until morning?"

"Nooooo," Tribal said quickly.

Kate glanced at Faron. "Would you mind? Your *iza* seems better received than my *vitalle*."

The prince moved over next to the eagle and set his hand on its neck. "The eagle is a creature of my woods," he said quietly, his eyes twitching just the slightest bit toward Venn.

"So you can command it easily?" Kate asked.

Faron's eyes tightened. "The creatures in the wood are as much a part of it as the trees and the elves. And just as much under our care."

The same sensation came as the last time Faron had touched the eagle. From his hand, a shower of energy sprinkled into the bird, soaking in and gently pushing it toward deep, untroubled sleep.

Kate studied Faron's face. There was a gentleness in how he touched the eagle, but he looked tired and troubled. Something she couldn't quite untangle was wrapped up in his expression.

"So humans are at the bottom of your list?" she asked. "Of things that need protecting?"

He looked at her sharply.

"Your father had to command you to help the people of Home," she said. "But you helped the eagle on your own."

"I would have helped Home on my own too." He pulled his hand away from Crofftus and gave Kate a gauging look. "But there was no need. My father has a long history of helping the humans who live near the woods."

His face was serious, almost belligerent.

Kate gave a small nod. "I know he takes his role as protector seriously."

Faron studied her as though looking for something hidden in her words. After a moment, he returned her nod and started to turn away. His eyes caught on the corner of the aenigma box, which was visible inside the open top of her pack. "Can you read those runes?"

A flicker of uneasiness tickled her mind, and she flipped the pack closed. "Yes."

Faron raised an eyebrow. "I wasn't going to take it."

The urge to push it farther away from him, farther from all of them, made her shift toward her pack. Venn caught her eye with a questioning look, and Kate cleared her throat. A sharp pain from the blisters on her palm made her realize her hands were balled into fists. She forced them to relax.

"Sorry." She rubbed her face with her unharmed hand, trying to banish the strange sensation. "My brother left this for me, and it's the closest connection I have to him."

His words from his journal came back to her. *It calls to me. I keep fiddling with it, wanting to open it again. Except I feel more...*something *than hope. Something I can't name. A sort of hunger, maybe.*

Kate slowly opened her pack and looked critically at the box. The runes scratched into the surface pulled at her, and she picked it up with more caution than she'd ever used.

Faron's expression grew more curious, and she tilted the top toward him.

She watched his hands, unaccountably nervous that he'd reach for it. He did nothing but look. "These speak of a king brought to his knees behind crumbling battlements, and some deep sorrow," she said.

"Sounds depressing." Faron's gaze ran over the lid. "Any idea who made it?"

Kate shook her head. She could almost feel the weight of his scrutiny on the box, and she slipped it back into her pack, then wiped her hands on her pants, trying to banish the desire to pick it up again. "I'm still trying to figure out what it really is."

Faron's eyes lingered on the bag for a moment before he returned to his seat across the fire.

She added a few more thick branches to the fire and sat for half an hour, letting the strange possessive feeling fade. When she lay down, though, she shifted her pack until she was leaning against it before letting her eyes close.

She drifted toward sleep with the edge of the box pressed reassuringly against her. The shelter was filled with the dwarves' rich, welcoming remnants and the wild forests of Venn's and Faron's. Even Crofftus's ocean wove its way into her mind as she floated into dreams of carriages and shadows and women speaking ominous omens.

A distant thud shouldered its way into a dream of sliding rocks and dark trees.

Kate struggled to open her eyes and banish the darkness of sleep, but they were so heavy that she merely managed a groan. Something moved, and she dragged her eyelids open to see the flames of the fire shrouded, as though she were looking through a dark curtain.

A scuff sounded from near her, but the blackness only thickened. A featherlight touch brushed across her face. *Vitalle* seeped into her and dragged her toward darkness.

She fought against it, trying to rise, but she couldn't move. Every part of her was pinned down by an immovable weight.

She cast out—and found nothing.

Something whispered near her, and her mind scrabbled at it, trying to grab on to it. Trying to grab on to anything.

But the heaviness dragged her down. She cried out, but there was no sound.

Wings rustled, and a gust of wind hit her face. Then even that faded.

Silently, she slipped into a black, endless pool, and darkness closed over her.

Light trickled in from somewhere, ruddy and flickering.

Kate groaned and opened her eyes.

The fire burned low, its heat mostly spent, and cold air blew across her from the entrance.

Her mind crawled sluggishly away from the darkness. She struggled to sit up to prod it into some kind of action.

Something hard held her in place.

She blinked and saw a tangled net of roots stretching over her, holding her arms against her chest and pressing her body against the ground. Her legs were bound too, and she could do nothing more than shift against them.

The sleep evaporated from her mind, and she twisted to see around the shelter.

Silas's space near her feet was empty. Tribal was nowhere to be seen. Faron's spot by the tree was vacant, and there was something wrapped in roots near the entrance.

Venn.

The rest of the shelter was empty.

Her wave rolled out into the forest and found no one.

Straining her neck to see where Crofftus had slept, she saw nothing but bare earth.

"Venn!" She shoved her arms against the roots, but they didn't budge. "Venn!" she called louder.

She could hear nothing over the pounding of her own heartbeat in her ears.

The shadow.

It had been here, in the shelter.

Filled the shelter.

Kate pinched her eyes shut and focused on the remnants around her. Venn's was still strong, filling the space with the scent and sounds of trees and streams and rustling leaves. Silas's spiced ale warmed the back of her throat, lingering in the space beside her. He must not have been gone long. Beyond it, she could still smell Tribal's roast pork. Faron's alpine forest was crisp and crystal clear.

She stopped.

There was something near the door. A sharp puddle of bright-ness that poured out Faron's remnant.

Kate shoved against the roots, trying to see. It felt like the way fresh-spilled blood smelled so strongly of someone's remnant.

"Venn!" she cried again before realizing the one remnant she didn't feel was Crofftus's.

Venn didn't move, and Kate blew out a deep breath, trying to slow her heart. The air was cold in her lungs. Snowflakes swirled in through the door, landing on a growing patch of white in the entry.

The roots. There had to be a way to release the roots.

The thickest parts were anchored into the ground on her right side and stretched over her, thinning until they burrowed into the earth on her left.

She closed her eyes and forced her sluggish mind to remember what Venn had done to uproot the bush near the carriage. "Convince the root it's time to grow." She opened her eyes to look at the strange pale wood wrapped around her. "All right." She slid her hand across her stomach until she could touch a root near her elbow and pressed *vitalle* into it. "Time to grow," she murmured, pushing the idea of stretching into it.

Nothing happened.

She pushed more *vitalle* into it, imagining rain-soaked soil and sunshine falling warm on the ground.

The root shifted.

Kate shoved at it, and it came loose.

Squeezing her hand a little higher, she grabbed the next piece of wood. Slowly she loosened the roots around her arms and shoulders until she could shimmy up out of it and sit up. The low bed of coals tilted to the left. She set her hands on the floor and blinked away the vertigo. There were shadows everywhere. Throwing a handful of sticks onto the hot coals, she scrambled over to Venn.

"Venn!" Kate shook her shoulder, but Venn gave no response.

The moon was high in the sky, and the wind blew through the trees, sending flakes swirling. The snow drifting into the shelter obscured any tracks.

She worked on Venn's roots, loosening them one by one until she could pull her free.

The fire had flared up, brightening the inside of the shelter. Where Silas had lain the ground was scuffed from some sort of struggle, and between it and the door was a wet patch of earth that radiated Faron's remnant.

She touched it, and her fingertips came away red.

Swearing, she dragged Venn closer to the fire and set her hand on the elf's forehead, funneling some *vitalle* into her. Slowly, Venn's mind brightened, but she didn't move.

Snow crunched outside.

Kate spun, casting out and ripping a piece of the flame off the fire and into her hand.

Her wave lit an enormous form stepping toward the entrance.

Kate registered the huge shape of a bear just as she heard the thundering remnant of the ocean.

CHAPTER SEVENTY-ONE

THE SHAGGY MUZZLE of a brown bear pushed into the shelter, his nostrils flaring as he sniffed the air.

Kate's eyes fell on the crossbow still strapped to Venn's arm, but it had taken two darts to bring down a dwarf only half as big as this bear. She stepped between Venn and the bear, funneling *vitalle* into the flame in her hand. It swelled larger, and the bear's head swung toward her.

He took another step inside the shelter, and a branch at the edge of the doorway cracked against the press of his shoulder.

Kate held the fire forward and saw the flames reflected in the creature's small brown eyes. "Stop, Crofftus."

The bear swung his head to the side and sniffed.

His head was as wide as Kate's torso, and behind it, thick, grizzled fur covered shoulders that were even wider. His back was as high as Kate's ribs. She poured more *vitalle* into the fire in her palm, growing it until the flames lashed up like a blazing torch.

It is gone. Crofftus's voice was low and angry. He turned to face her and moved one huge paw closer. Long claws reflected firelight off their smooth surfaces as the sharp points dug effortlessly into the ground.

Kate planted her feet and braced herself, scanning the area for an escape. Her hand quivered under the flame. "What's gone?"

The emotionless face stared at her for a moment. *The voice.*

"What voice?"

The bear sniffed again, swinging his head back and forth. A growling noise sounded from his chest, so low that Kate felt it in her own. *The voice that roused the eagle.*

"What do you mean?" Kate demanded.

I didn't hear it, but it woke the eagle. The bear lowered his head and shook it, stepping forward in agitation.

"Crofftus! Stop!"

He hesitated. *Everything was dark.*

Kate stared at him, the fear inside her curdling into anger. "I *know* everything was dark. What did you do? Where did you take them?"

Everything was dark except the entrance, he said, as though she hadn't spoken. *I didn't like the voice. It terrified the eagle.*

"I heard no voice. I woke to darkness, heard your wings, and that's all."

We were in flight before... He stepped forward, his body snapping branches at the entrance without him seeming to notice, until the entire front of his body was inside. *The eagle saw only darkness.*

A raging anger grew inside her. He'd taken more people. The dwarves were gone, and Faron. Venn still lay senseless. "Crofftus," Kate said between clenched teeth, taking a step toward the bear and holding the fire toward him. "Explain yourself. Now."

The bear shied away from the flame and, for the first time, focused on Kate.

"What did you do with them?"

I did nothing.

"Explain better than that," she said, hating the slight quiver in her voice.

I'm no threat to you.

"Tell me where they are!"

The bear didn't even flinch at her tone. *I don't know. The last thing I remember is the dwarf reaching into the carriage, then I was here, and it was dark, and the eagle was flying toward the exit. It was wounded and in pain and crazed. It was afraid of the voice. I couldn't get it to stop. I finally got it to land near the bear, but the bear was sleeping. It took me time to wake him and return.* He put his nose to the ground. *I thought the bear could smell the source of the voice.*

Kate didn't lower her fire. "Can you?"

There is only you two and the dwarves and the prince. He took another step in, and his nose hovered above the blood on the ground. *The prince has been hurt.*

"Tell me where they are," she repeated.

He looked at her with the bear's eyes. *Their trail goes up the mountain.*

"What have you done, Crofftus? Why be the tree and the shadow? Why all the mystery?"

The bear stared at her. *You think I am the monsters?*

"I don't know anyone else who can change their shape. Can you inhabit a tree—one of the awakened elven ones?"

He considered her. *Yes. But trees don't move.*

"Some seem to."

I do not know how.

"And the shadow?"

How would one inhabit anything as insubstantial as a shadow?

"Don't answer me with questions. Are you the shadow?"

The bear's head tilted to the side. *No.*

She probed out toward him, finding his remnant as distant and ceaseless as ever. The continual rise and fall of the waves, the continual crashing against something immovable. "Are you Renault?"

Something like a huff of laughter echoed in her mind. *Am I a dead half-elven mage?*

Fury rose in her at the evasive question, but before she could say anything, he dipped his head in something like an apology. *No, I am not Renault. I am a human, born in southern Queensland.*

Kate studied the bear. "Why are you here? What is your interest in the ravine and the emperor?"

His head tilted again, as though curious. *I have none. I was merely assisting you.*

"Why?"

I... The bear shifted. *I need your help. The Keepers have powers beyond most others, and you won't harm anyone in using them.*

"So?"

He didn't answer for a moment. *I lost my human body long ago and want to return to one. I miss having hands and moving where I want without a struggle. I miss human food and human companionship.* He was silent. *I miss being human. But if I inhabit one, I will drive them mad. Destroy them. And...I cannot do such a thing.*

"You think the Keepers can figure out a better way?"

The bear twitched in what might have been a shrug. *Do you know anyone else better to ask?*

Kate kept the fire raised. "No."

Crofftus lowered his nose to the ground. *I cannot smell the source of the voice or what brought the darkness. The prince bled, and the dwarves struggled.* He shifted his head to where Venn had been bound in the roots. *Venn did not move any more than you did. I can smell her scent here on the ground, and then the trail of where you moved her.*

"I can't feel any other remnants either." Kate turned to look over the shelter. "Of course, I've never found any remnant from the shadow." She turned back to Crofftus, gauging the bear.

He looked at her for a moment, then moved closer, and she stiffened, trying not to look at the huge paws that could kill her with a single swipe.

The way his claws slid effortlessly into the ground as his paws rolled with each step made it impossible to ignore how easily they'd slice into her flesh.

He moved closer until he was within arm's reach, and he looked up at her. The bear flinched away from her fire, but Crofftus made a soothing sound at him, and he relaxed slowly.

I am no danger to you, Katria.

His voice was slow, as always. Measured and careful. But the name reminded her of the way the Shield said it. Or Mikal and Gerone. "How do you know that name?"

You told it to Venn the night you saved the fox, when you explained why Bo calls you Ria.

Kate didn't move.

I have had a hundred chances to do you harm and have never done anything but help you. There is nothing near for you to be afraid of.

Kate stared at him, weighing his words. "I need to wake Venn."

Is she wounded?

"Not that I can tell." Kate glanced down at the dark spot on the ground. "That is a lot of blood."

Crofftus was quiet for long enough she thought he might not answer. *There is more outside on their trail. You should prepare your-self—and Venn when she wakes—for the worst possibility.*

Kate tried not to think about the size of the bloodstain or how strongly Faron's remnant filled the space around it. "If the shadow kills the prince of the White Wood…"

There was a low grumble that vibrated through the bear's

back. *I tremble to think what King Thallion would do.* He was quiet for a long moment. *Katria, if the prince is dead, you should leave.*

"Leave?"

You were among the last with him.

Kate shook her head. "I didn't kill him."

Do not expect reason from Thallion if his heir has been killed.

CHAPTER SEVENTY-TWO

"Until it's proven otherwise," Kate said, "I'll keep believing that Faron is still alive. Will you show me the trail?"

The bear lowered his nose and backed out of the shelter. Kate followed. At the door, she held the bundle of fire into the clearing. Wind shoved at her flame, making it dance and almost gutter out. The clouds above were thick and dark grey, barely lit by something above, whether the full moon or a coming dawn, it was impossible to say.

The snow on the ground swirled and shifted with the wind, already wiping away even Crofftus's huge prints leading out of the trees. He nosed along the ground, pushing aside the soft powder, following a trail that led around the side of the shelter. *They went uphill.*

"Uphill? Away from the ravine?"

Something dragged them. One at a time. Silas first, then...I'm not sure. Perhaps Faron's blood smells stronger than Tribal's trail, but blood always holds its scent longer. I do not know which was taken next.

"Then whoever took them will be coming back for the rest of us."

Shall I follow it?

"We'll all follow it as soon as I wake Venn. Will you keep watch?"

Crofftus gave a grunt and positioned himself over the trail leading uphill.

Kate moved back inside, dropping her flame back onto the campfire, flaring it brighter. She knelt next to Venn and set a hand on her forehead. Slowly, she funneled *vitalle* into Venn, brightening her mind and warming her.

Venn groaned and sat up. She swayed, blinking at the fire, and Kate put a hand on her shoulder to stabilize her.

"It was here, wasn't it?" Venn dropped her head into her hands with another groan.

"Hold still for a minute." She put both hands on Venn's head and eased more *vitalle* into her. The energy stopped at the edges, as though the energy hit some sort of barrier. "Something's blocking me."

Kate probed at the blockage, mapping it out. It was anchored to Venn, drawing *vitalle* out of her to hold the barrier in place, keeping her body from fueling her mind.

"It's like what I used against the vimwisps." Kate paused. "Hold on, I need to make a little stinger."

Venn turned enough to look incredulously up at her. "Into my head?"

Kate gave her a short laugh. "A metaphorical stinger." She focused her *vitalle* to a very sharp point just under her left palm. With a flick, she jabbed it into the barrier, and a tiny tear opened.

Venn gasped and started to topple to the side, but Kate caught her, leaning the elf's head against her shoulder.

Around the tear, the shield unraveled, fizzling away as Venn's body pushed its own *vitalle* past it, warming her mind.

"That," Venn said, her body limp and her voice muffled against Kate's cloak, "did not feel metaphorical."

Kate patted her back. "Sorry."

Venn sat up, blinking and rubbing her hands against her face.

"Better?" Kate asked.

Venn nodded. "Felt like my head was stuffed with...wool or something." She shook her head again. "Thank you." She glanced around the shelter. "What—" Her eyes locked on the huge bear head sticking through the entrance. "Kate..."

"It's Crofftus," Kate explained. "And he's not Renault or the shadow or the tree."

Venn's eyes narrowed. "Are you sure?"

"He wants the Keepers' to help him regain a human body."

Venn studied the bear for a long moment. "That fits. You feel lonely and out of place."

The bear shifted but didn't object.

Venn glanced at Kate. "You trust him?"

Kate shrugged. "I think so. That fits his remnant more than being a heartless murdering mage. You?"

The elf pushed herself to her feet and stepped up until she was directly in front of him. "Not until he explains how he knows this area so well and why he distrusts the elves."

The bear made an aggressive snort, but Crofftus shushed him. *I distrust the elves because I met King Thallion once. I can give you all the details, but it is a long story.*

Venn gauged the answer.

"You can tell us later," Kate said, stepping toward the entrance. "Venn, the dwarves were dragged out, but Faron was bleeding."

Badly.

She motioned to the dark stain on the ground, and Venn froze for a moment before crouching down next to it and touching it with her fingertips. A shudder ran through her. "He was...desperate."

Kate looked between Venn's face and the red on her finger-tips. "You can read people's blood?"

"Only Faron's. A betrothal is not just a formality." She tilted her head and pressed her fingers into it again. "He was...torn about something. He didn't want to fight."

"What would he be torn about?" Kate asked. "He was fighting off the shadow that's been..." She stopped, understanding dawning. "Oh."

The shadow was an elf, Crofftus said quietly. *And the prince realized it.*

Venn stared at the bloodstain but didn't disagree.

"Crofftus said it had a voice."

"What did it sound like?" Venn asked. "Male or female?"

The bear shifted. *Neither. Or both, maybe. It was...strange.*

Venn pushed herself up. "Where did they go?"

"Their trails lead uphill." Kate stood with her. "There's more blood along it. Are you all right to go?"

Venn's face was set in a grim look. "C'mon." She started toward the opening but lost her balance for a moment and grabbed one of the branches in the wall. Suddenly her head snapped up, and she pointed at the side of the shelter. "Shadow!" she hissed. "The trees see the shadow! Just outside!"

Kate cast out. Venn and Crofftus flared into light, then the walls of the shelter. Beyond that, there was nothing but the towering trees of the forest. Kate searched through them, looking for the unnatural emptiness she'd felt in Yellow's kitchen.

Along the side of the shelter, where the trail of remnants had led uphill, existed a pocket in the world utterly devoid of *vitalle*.

Crofftus let out a growl and was out of the shelter in a breath, rushing toward the emptiness. In the remaining trail of her wave, his blazing form crashed into the nothing and his *vitalle* blinked out of existence.

The sound of his remnant cut off so suddenly Kate flinched.

Venn's mouth dropped open. "Where did he go?" She stumbled forward.

Kate grabbed her arm to keep her from staggering into the fire pit. Together, they moved toward the door.

The world outside was silent. They stayed at the entrance for a moment while Venn touched the nearest branch.

"The shadow is still there," she breathed. "Around the side of the shelter."

Venn raised her crossbow and inched along the side of the shelter. Keeping close to the wall, Kate crept along with her until they could see around the side.

A handful of paces ahead of them, between the shelter and the nearest tree, an inky patch of blackness filled the air and covered the ground.

Kate cast out toward it, and the weak traces of *vitalle* that still lived in the winter grass lit the ground. The trees near the shelter shifted into pillars of light—and then everything abruptly stopped, like a rent torn open in the forest. A black void that puddled on the ground and pressed against the trees around it. Shadows snaked up between the boughs and fused with the inky darkness tangled in the thickest clusters of pine needles.

A roar ripped through the clearing, and the bear burst from the darkness. It barreled out, its huge teeth bared, its eyes wide and wild.

Kate grabbed Venn's arm. "No remnant!" she whispered. "That's not Crofftus anymore!"

The bear caught sight of them and stopped. There was something different in his expression. The curiosity was gone, replaced with nothing but menace.

Venn raised her crossbow. "This is not going to put a bear to sleep," she said grimly.

He paced to the side, his head lowered, his gaze fixed on Venn.

Kate glanced back, but the campfire burning inside the shelter was too far for her to reach.

"Venn!" She reached toward the knot of *vitalle* embedded in Venn's dart.

Venn's brow creased, but she moved closer to Kate while keeping it pointed at the bear. He shifted his weight, rocking from side to side, pacing and trampling the snow until the brown winter grass was visible again.

He opened his mouth and bellowed, the sound so loud that it shook the branches of the shelter.

Venn tensed.

"Wait!" Kate pushed her palm onto the *vitalle* in Venn's dart and shoved more into it.

The tiny bit of energy definitely wasn't fire. It was more subtle and smooth than the feel of flames, but Kate funneled more *vitalle* in until it pressed against the edges of the space, swirling and jostling against itself.

The bear bellowed again and shifted toward them.

Kate pulled her hand away. "Shoot the grass by his feet!"

Venn dropped her aim. The twang of the crossbow was lost in the roar of the bear.

The dart landed just in front of him as he started forward.

The *vitalle* exploded out of the tip with a surge of energy, and Kate flung more toward it, catching the bit of warmth and fueling it until a flicker of flame burst out from the grass.

The bear twitched back, and Kate stepped forward and sent more *vitalle* through the air and into the small flame. It surged up into a blaze of light, and the bear twisted away and plunged into the woods.

Venn had another dart loaded, and when the back of the bear disappeared through the trees, she swung it around to the shadow.

Kate took a step toward the burning grass, pushing more *vitalle* into it and lighting the clearing.

The shadow was changing. Shifting. Rising.

The edges began to tatter.

Venn's crossbow twanged again, and a dart shot into the heart of it just as the darkness leeched away, pooling into a hundred natural shadows in the forest.

CHAPTER SEVENTY-THREE

KATE STARED in to the forest. "It's gone."

Venn stepped slowly forward, her crossbow reloaded and raised. "So is my dart."

"Do you think your darts put shadows to sleep?"

"Depends on how big it is."

"The shadow was pretty big."

Venn nodded. "Why did it leave?"

Kate moved over to the patch of forest that had been steeped in darkness.

Whether from the coming of dawn, or in contrast to the blackness that had just been here, the space seemed relatively bright. Snowflakes fluttered down from the dark grey sky, landing on trampled snow riddled with bear prints.

"Maybe Crofftus hurt it."

Venn came over and knelt among the prints. "I see nothing but bear."

"No remnants besides Crofftus's either," Kate said. "How can it be shot but leave no sign it was here?"

Venn shook her head.

Kate moved past the trampled ground to where Crofftus had found the trail of the two dwarves and Faron. The prince's remnant was easy to pick out, the alpine forest smells fitting perfectly with the wintery night. She could smell it stronger a dozen paces uphill. Brushing the top of the snow away, she found a red stain. The homey scent of the two dwarves wafted up from below it, as though they'd been dragged along the ground.

Venn came and looked over her shoulder. A flicker of something crossed her face at the sight of the blood.

Kate peered up the hill. "What's up there?"

Venn shook her head. "Beyond two dwarves and an elf prince? I have no idea."

Kate moved through the snow, sending little puffs of powder up ahead of each step.

It was unsettling how often she found spots of Faron's blood. She'd considered moving past the first few, leaving the snow above them undisturbed so Venn wouldn't have to see it, but what was the point in hiding how badly he'd been hurt?

And so, far more often than she wanted to, she bent down and brushed the snow off the drops of blood along the trail.

The path led up the slope and through the trees, all three remnants following essentially the same path.

She watched the shadows under the trees warily, but nothing moved or spread or did anything unnatural.

As they climbed, the snow tapered off and the sky brightened. The shadows faded away, and Kate picked up her pace, merely pointing to where Faron's blood had dripped instead of brushing them off.

Venn strode quickly without speaking, her eyes fixed uphill as though she could see whatever destination they were headed for.

By the time they reached the tree line, dawn had definitely come. The remnant trail twisted away from the tree line, up toward a low ridge of rock. Kate continued along it, scanning the hillside around her.

"What's up there?" Kate asked over her shoulder. Venn merely shook her head.

As they moved up the slope, the clouds in the east thinned and the snow grew brighter until they were the only bits of color moving across a blindingly white slope. They neared the rock ridge, and Kate looked downhill and stumbled to a stop.

Because of a dip in the hillside below her, the face of the ravine was perfectly visible across the valley. Where she and Venn stood was still gloomy with clouds, but the sun had broken through across the valley and landed on the snow-covered slope of the ravine, etching the surface in stark whites and shadows. The rockslide was a long line of irregular lumps. The remains of the road where Emperor Sorrn's men had been killed was a slash of pure, smooth white, cutting horizontally across the slope.

Venn stopped next to her. "What's wrong?"

Kate stared across the valley. "I've seen this before."

"The ravine?"

Kate slid off her pack and rummaged through it, pulling out the letter she'd found in the aenigma box the first time she'd opened it.

She flipped to the second to last page and held it out for Venn to see.

I'm sitting on an outcropping of rock and losing the light. I can see down the ravine to the rockslide that now covers the caves. A bit of the work we did along the road is still unharmed, but without

*help, I'll never make progress on it. At this moment, it doesn't feel
like the work will ever continue.*

The sketch that interrupted his writing was a perfect match to
their current view. The thick pines covering the hillside below
her, the rocky slope visible across the ravine, the center scarred by
the rockslide.

> *The White Wood is to my left, filling the long, wide valley with
> a ghostly aspect. Bone-white suddenly feels like a fitting description.
> The world feels large and lonely, if I'm being honest.*
>
> *I can see a few lights from the outskirts of Home, but I can't go
> back there.*

Kate glanced over and saw the snowy spread of the White
Wood, and off to the northeast, past the river, smoke rose from
the chimneys of Home.

> *I'm high above my camp. It's on this side of the valley, but not
> terribly far from the bottom of the rockslide. Right now, that feels
> like a long way to go, and I can't shake the feeling that the shadow's
> somewhere in the woods.*
>
> *There's a cave along the rocks I'm sitting on, and I contemplated
> staying in it tonight, but—maybe it's everything else that's happen-
> ing, but it feels…wrong.*
>
> *Actually, do you know what it feels like? It feels like the old
> mine. There's a thick timber set over the opening and…*
>
> *There's nothing else really. Nothing I can put my finger on. But
> I stood at the entrance and all I could think of was Evan.*
>
> *Tonight does not feel like the night to recall such dark memories.*

Venn glanced over her shoulder, and Kate turned, searching
the hillside above them. The ridge of rocks was only twenty paces

away, and it was riddled with shadows from nooks and overhangs.

Kate's eyes caught on a square opening topped with a rough, thick piece of timber. "Look. Is that dwarven?"

"Maybe. The elves don't patrol above the tree line. There's nothing up here but the barren peak."

"Tribal and Silas never mentioned it, and I…" Kate paused. "I just assumed any cave Bo was talking about was in the ravine."

"Does the trail lead toward it?" Venn motioned to the nearest opening.

"I think so." Kate tucked Bo's letter back in her pack and followed the trail at an angle until it drew near the ridge, directly toward the opening of the cave.

Bo had been right. There was something similar to the old mine. Even though the opening looked natural, a rough beam had been braced into the top of the opening. The morning sun streamed weakly through the heavy clouds, only lighting a few paces of the uneven rocky ground within.

She set her hand on the rough beam and stepped cautiously in.

The walls were rugged and oozed shadows from a dozen crevices. The floor swelled and dropped before it rose again, dimmer and farther away, where it met the mouth of a tunnel thick with shadows. For a moment she was twelve again, scrambling through the utter blackness with Bo, racing for the entrance of the mine.

She took a step back and gulped in a breath.

Venn stood at the entrance, one hand gripping the thick timber beside her. "I don't want to go in there," she said quietly.

"Neither do I," Kate agreed.

A hint of stubbornness narrowed Venn's eyes. "Why? It's just a cave."

Kate shifted her shoulders. The cold morning air stretched around her like freedom and light. "You hate caves."

"But you don't."

"I hate this one."

Venn tilted her head. "Why?"

"Because it's just like the mine that..."

It wasn't really like the mine. The morning sun lit the walls enough to make it evident that there were no tool marks. Aside from the timber at the entrance, there was nothing similar. The shadows in the nooks weren't even particularly dark. "It's not like the mine..." She stepped forward, her eyes falling on a drop of blood a few paces in. "What's happening?"

She took a few more steps into the cave. The dust on the floor was cleared away in a long line as though something heavy had been dragged along it, and the remnants of the dwarves and Faron hung in the air. "I was so frightened, I didn't even notice the trail."

"Something didn't want you to," Venn said.

The baleful feel of the room grew again, but Kate hunched her shoulders against it and knelt down. She focused on the floor and caught a jumble of other remnants. "Venn! There are more trails. Human." She dragged her fingers along the edge of the dwarves' trail and found hints of leather and turned earth and—

Her hand twitched at a very vague familiar scent. Dry autumn grass and animal fur.

"Gerren was here!"

"Nevin's son?"

She nodded and pressed forward along the trail. The sense of foreboding increased, and she cast out. There was nothing living around them. "He went the same way, although a while ago. There are at least two other very faint human remnants too. People I don't know."

Another impression flitted across her mind, so light she

almost missed it. Grass again, but green this time, and damp earth. With a touch of something sharp or fiery.

She drew in a breath. "Rye was here too!"

"So two of the missing men from Home, a few humans we don't know, and now Tribal, Silas, and Faron," Venn said.

Kate crawled forward, searching for any hint of windswept hills. The ominous feel of the room wrapped around her, pushing her back toward the entrance, but she moved farther in.

There had to be something here of Bo's.

A looming dread dragged its fingers across the back of her neck, and she snapped her attention to the black tunnel again. The shadows seemed to ripple and pulse in a darkness so solid it was like a living thing.

For a moment she smelled windswept hills and felt Bo's hand, gripping hers as they rushed through the absolute black of the tunnels.

She dragged her hands over the floor, searching for it again, but it was gone. If had even been more than a memory in the first place.

There was no sign of Bo, and she was alone.

The echoes of the terror from that day long ago crowded around her. She opened her eyes wider, trying to pierce the blackness of the tunnel, even as she stood and scrambled backwards.

She backed up into Venn's hand.

"I'm not *this* scared of caves," the elf said, a note of irritation in her voice. "And neither are you. Someone's making us." She blew out a long, controlled breath. "I don't like people making me do things."

Kate shook her head, trying to dislodge the fear. "You're right." She swallowed, but the terror remained, curled in her gut, making her heart pound. She cast out, and a very thin web of light lit the walls. Little pockets of something in the rock held trace amounts of *vitalle*, but the thin lines connecting them created a net around the entire room.

Kate cast out toward the nearest pocket of *vitalle* in the rock, and the shape of a small rune burst into light.

"There are runes all over the walls. Stay close, and keep your hand on my back." Kate funneled some *vitalle* out of her hands and spread it like a shield between herself and the black tunnel. She closed her eyes and stretched it back over her head and around Venn, extending it down toward the ground.

The moment it anchored to the floor, the terror snapped out of existence.

Venn let out a relieved breath, and Kate's shoulders relaxed.

"How long can you hold this?" Venn asked.

"With no vimwisps or carriages attacking it? For quite a while."

"Good." Her voice was tight. "The elves protect the White Wood from humans by enchanting the border. When a human enters it, they want to leave. It begins subtly, with merely a suggestion that they turn aside, but if they continue, it grows frightening, until they flee."

Kate looked over her shoulder. "You think this is elves?"

Venn's expression simmered with anger, and the lighter orange strands in her hair began to glow. "You and I were bound with roots in the shelter. And Faron did not want to fight the shadow."

"Both of which point to elves," Kate agreed. "Are you sure you want to go in there?"

"I am tired of not standing up against the things the elves have done." Venn's eyes narrowed. "This has gone too far." The red in her braid had begun to glow too, as though the morning sun had managed to break through the clouds and land only on her.

Venn kept her eyes on the tunnel. "Whatever this shadow is, it's wounded and took the First Ranger of the White Wood."

"Being the First Ranger...that means he's probably a good fighter, doesn't it?"

Venn gave a curt nod.

"Better than the dwarves?"

Venn gave her an insulted look.

"All right. Better than you?"

"By a wide margin."

Kate turned back toward the tunnel. "Great, so we're tracking something into its lair that is strong enough to best two dwarves, and a good enough fighter to beat Faron."

"Or command his obedience," Venn said quietly.

Kate twisted around to stare at her. "You think King Thallion is in here?" she hissed.

Venn's face stayed grim, the skin across her cheeks brightening as though hot coals sat underneath. "You're the one who connects clues into a full story. I'm just pointing out the possibilities."

"Fantastic." Kate considered the solid wall of blackness. "How long can you keep glowing like that? I can't hold a fire and keep the shield up."

"Long enough. The elves only protect the borders with magic like these runes. If you can keep someone from entering, you don't need the protection farther in than that."

"You think this will end soon?"

"Most likely as soon as we step through the unnaturally dark tunnel."

Kate swallowed. "I legitimately do not like unnaturally dark tunnels."

Venn shifted her hand to Kate's shoulder, and the skin on her fingers shone with a faint golden light. "Then we'll make it light."

Kate was taking a step forward when Venn's hand tightened on her shoulder.

"In the remnants…is there any sign of…?"

Kate glanced down at the floor where the jumble of remnants trickled up toward her. "None of them were Bo."

Venn let out an almost inaudible sigh. "We're getting closer, though." Her words held more stubborn resolve than actual conviction.

Kate glanced at the blood on floor and stepped over it, into the shadow.

CHAPTER SEVENTY-FOUR

KATE STEPPED into the blackness of the tunnel. Venn glowed behind her, but even so, the floor and walls were barely visible. The darkness hummed gently against her shield, but it was more like water on the hull of a boat than something trying to break through.

The dim shape of the tunnel turned to the left, and Kate shuffled forward. There were no sounds beyond the scuffing of their feet and the snippets of Faron's remnant that drifted out of the drops of his blood whenever they encountered one.

After a dozen paces, the darkness receded and the glow from Venn's skin and hair reached the walls. Kate moved forward until they were out of the strange darkness. "I'm going to lift the shield a little." Slowly, she pulled the shield away from the floor and waited. No rush of fear rose up in her. Nothing but the tense wariness that was all her own.

She flicked her fingers, and the shell dissolved into the air.

The tunnel around them was irregular and rough. At the widest point, she'd barely be able to touch both walls, but ahead it narrowed to a point where her shoulders would brush both. The ceiling was so high that Venn's meager light didn't reach it.

"Tell me you have some sort of light in your pack," Venn said quietly. "I can only stay mad for so long."

Kate knelt and pulled flint and a small bundle of kindling out of her pack. With a quick strike, she lit the kindling, then swept the fire into her hand and stood. Cupping the flame, she held it up, and the flickering light lit the path ahead. Behind them, the light ended at the ragged edge of a shadow that filled the tunnel.

The floor was still marred by the drag lines from the dwarves, and Kate cast out ahead of them.

Nothing lit up.

They'd moved a half-dozen paces before Kate spoke quietly. "I was thinking about all this pointing to the elves, but maybe there's another answer. Would Faron be reluctant to fight a half-elf?"

"You think this is Renault?"

"Just because Crofftus isn't him doesn't mean the half-elf isn't involved somehow. He comes up too often for me to discount him."

Venn gave a hum of agreement. "I guess it would depend on how obviously elven he looked whether Faron would consider him an elf. Of course, Faron has also been commanded to work with the humans, so he'd be reluctant to fight one of them too."

Kate glanced over her shoulder. "You don't really think all this is a human."

Venn's skin brightened. "No. I think it's elven."

The tunnel twisted to the right, and suddenly the walls fell back to either side at the edge of a long cavern.

Only a few paces ahead, the ground turned to dirt and rose to the height of her knee. There it leveled off to a flat surface paved in cobblestones before it dropped back down to dirt again at the floor level. It was like a very short, very artificial plateau. The strange little rise reached from one side of the cavern to the other. At its widest point near the left-hand wall, the cobblestone top was nearly five paces across. As it meandered toward the other wall, it narrowed to only two paces, and then widened again before it reached the right-hand wall.

Venn stopped next to her, considering the chamber. The dwarves' scuff marks traced a trail to the narrowest point of the rise.

"The shadow dragged the dwarves a very long way," Venn pointed out. "They're not light."

"And why to here?" Kate took a step forward, holding up her fire. On the far side of the plateau, the floor was covered in what looked like tufts of grass, which continued to a distant wall. "Doesn't this room feel a little...odd?"

"More than a little." Venn moved to the left and peered at the little rise. The top was old and dusty, but the neatly placed cobblestones formed a relatively smooth surface. "Some of these stones are missing. Could you bring the light over here?"

Kate came up beside her, and the firelight flickered across the dusty stones. Except near the edge where three cobblestones were gone, leaving a gaping hole. "Why is it so dark?" She moved her flame closer.

Underneath the missing stones was nothing at all, just a black hole.

Venn reached out and pushed down on one of the cobble-stones next to the hole. There was a small crack, and the firelight showed the stone tumbling down into blackness for several heartbeats before it smashed onto an unseen ground.

Venn peered into the hole. "Let's not step on the cobblestones."

Kate brought her fire up close to the remaining stones. "They're held up by a lattice of thin...it looks like roots."

Venn reached into the hole and brushed her fingers along the bottom of the stones. "Not alive any longer." She snapped off a little piece, and the stone above it wobbled. "So brittle it would never hold any weight."

Kate held her fire up again and looked over the room. "So if the fears generated by the entrance didn't drive someone away, and if they were brave enough to go through the pitch-black tunnel, they would fall to their death the moment they stepped across this." She looked at Venn. "Someone went through a *lot* of work to keep people away."

Venn walked back to where the dwarves' trail ended. "So the trail goes here because this is where we could jump over the mound, and then…why are there blades of grass in a pitch-dark cave?"

Kate looked up at her. "What did you say?"

"I said we jump over the mound into what looks like—but can't possibly be—blades of grass."

"Jump the mound!" Kate swung her pack off and used her free hand to rummage inside it. "We don't want to touch the grass."

Venn squinted into the dim cavern. "That's going to be hard."

Kate pulled out her journal and flipped to the page where she and Faron had translated the children's rhymes. "Maybe it's not unreasonable to connect this place with Renault. Listen to this:

The home of Renault where his madness rests
 and the walking oak haunts his grave.
 Lift your feet and jump the mound.
 Don't disturb the scythed blades.
 Darkness lines the only path
 —lest branch and root break every bone—
 to the home of Renault where his madness rests."

Venn stared at her. "You think your book of invisible children's nonsense from the Stronghold tells us how to get through this random cavern?"

"Normally, I'd say that was a ridiculous idea, but…" She moved over to the narrow part of the mound. "'Lift your feet and jump the mound' certainly sounds like good advice. And some of that grass over there is shorter than other. 'Don't disturb the scythed blades…' so we keep away from the cut grass and stay in the long ones."

"Why?"

"I don't know! But the mound advice is sound, so I'm willing to at least consider the grass advice could be too."

Venn pointed at her. "You said this was all metaphorical. Jumping over the grave was disrespecting the dead."

"Well, I hardly expected this!" Kate flung her arm out, encompassing the entire cave and tunnel. Her voice echoed in the cavern, and they both froze. She cast out again, but there was still nothing else in the cavern but them and the low carpet of grass. There was an odd pattern to the grass. Swirls of brighter and dimmer swaths that wound through the cave. There were even a couple of ribbons with no grass at all. "It's not a far jump to the other side."

"I can make it," Venn said. "You never stole the dwarves boots to make you light on your feet, though."

"Well, you go first, and if I misjudge and land on the cobblestones, you can catch me before I fall to my death."

Venn shook her head. "The grass is right up to the edge of the stones. Are you sure I should land in the tall grass, not the short?"

Kate shrugged. "'Don't disturb the scythed blades.' If that doesn't mean to avoid the cut grass, I don't know what else it's saying."

"A few days ago, you thought the scythed blades were metaphorical weapons that brought death."

"Which I still hold to be a decent translation," Kate hissed, "but given that we are faced with actual scythed blades, let's not disturb them."

"Fine." Venn turned to face the far side of the cobblestones. "If the tall grass kills me, I'm coming back to haunt you."

Without waiting, she leapt easily across the mound and landed lightly on the very edge of the tall grass.

She stood perfectly still for a moment before pulling up one of the long blades. She swiped it through the smaller grass and held it up.

It had been sliced cleanly in half.

"The short grass has some very sharp blades hidden in it." Venn took a step away from the mound, giving Kate room to land, and held out her hand. "You may be right about the literal translation."

Kate stood at the edge, looking across the stretch of cobblestones, which suddenly seemed longer than two paces.

"Stop overthinking," Venn said, motioning her to come. "You can't research your way over it. Just jump."

Kate moved back and took a single step, then jumped across the mound.

She landed hard on the far side, her heel just missing the cobblestones. Venn grabbed her arm and pulled her forward a step into the tall grass.

The rest of the cavern was a patchwork of taller and shorter tufts of grass, the vast majority of which were short.

Kate stared at it all. "There are easier ways to protect something than creating a swath of grass embedded with knives."

"I agree. This doesn't feel elven any more. The cobblestones feel like a human trap, and the grass is…Well, aside from tedious, it's overdone. Either someone knows to keep to the tall grass, or they get their feet sliced open. Seems like a quick lesson to learn. What's the point of filling the rest of the cavern with the same threat?"

Kate pointed to a few paces ahead of them where the path of tall grass split and headed in two separate directions, surrounded on both sides by low grass. A bit farther on, it split again. "It's a maze."

"Well, which way do we go? I don't feel like trying a half-dozen paths while Faron bleeds somewhere farther in and the dwarves... Who knows what shape they're in?"

"Faron and the dwarves!" Kate searched the floor for any of their remnants. She turned slowly. "There's nothing here."

"Where did they go?"

Kate shook her head. "No one's been right here but you and me. There's no trace of Rye or Gerren or anyone."

Venn studied the grass. "Then which way do we go?"

Kate raised her fire. The stream of *vitalle* she was pouring into it was beginning to sting her palm, but she added more until it lit the far side of the cavern. The wall was rough and uneven, but there were no openings to be seen. "I don't know."

"What's the next line of the obviously non-metaphorical poem?" Venn asked.

"'Darkness lines the only path—lest branch and root break every bone.'"

"Charming." Venn kept her feet planted. "Douse the light."

Kate closed her fingers, snuffing the flame, and the cavern fell into absolute darkness.

"Ahh," Venn said, just as Kate made out a dim diagonal line on the wall.

"Ahh what?"

"There's a door." Venn rustled as though she might be pointing.

"I see a line, but not a door."

"It's a door, but I can't see the path of the tall grass that gets us there. Occasionally the blades in the short grass catch the light, but not enough to show a safe path."

"Wait, darkness *lines* the only path." Kate cast out. The tall grass lit with a dense, feathery *vitalle*, the shorter showed up dimmer, and along the edge of the tall grass they stood on was a strip of darkness.

Venn reached down and touched the grass that wasn't lit with *vitalle*. "It's fake. Just very thin strands of wood painted green."

Kate pointed ahead. "It goes all the way through the maze. C'mon." She followed the ribbon for a half-dozen steps, then cast out again when the *vitalle* around them faded.

"What did your children's poem say comes after this?"

"That we're going to the home of Renault where his madness rests."

Venn sighed. "Wonderful."

CHAPTER SEVENTY-FIVE

KATE SHUFFLED her feet through the tall grass, staying close to Venn. She kept her eyes wide, waiting for them to adjust, but all she could make out was the dim grey line on the far wall.

Venn turned to the right for a few paces, then the left, moving deeper into the maze of grass. They wound slowly through the room until the grey line on the wall became more obviously the entrance to a tunnel.

"If we need to leave in a hurry," Venn said quietly over her shoulder, "this room is going to be challenging."

From the dim light, Kate could finally see the end of the path of tall grass, and she dropped her hands from Venn's shoulders. "I've been trying not to think about that."

They stepped out of the grass onto plain rock, and Kate looked behind them. Their footprints had flattened a path that was clearly visible. "Maybe it won't be as hard as we thought. We are obviously the first people to cross that in a very long time."

"I still don't understand how it's growing here at all," Venn said.

The tunnel leading deeper into the mountain was lit by a faint grey light, like the very first hint of dawn on a cloudy day. Kate took a step toward it and caught the alpine scent of Faron. She searched the ground until she saw a smear of blood on the floor. "I think the shadow had a better way across the grass than we took," she said quietly.

Venn pointed ahead to where the trail of the dwarves cut through the dust again.

Kate put her hand on Venn's arm to stop her and cast out very gently ahead of them. Bits of thin *vitalle* lit up farther down the winding tunnel. "There are more plants ahead," she whispered.

Venn checked the dart in her crossbow, and they started forward, shoulder to shoulder. The tunnel grew brighter as they moved, shifting from grey dawn to the greenish light of a dense forest. Before long, the trickling of a small stream echoed around them, accompanied by the smell of moss and plants.

They reached a corner and peered around into a room bright with light.

After a heartbeat, they stepped around the corner, Venn with her crossbow raised. A cavern spread out in front of them with a trickle of sunlight coming in high in the ceiling. To their left, huge stair steps of rock rose toward the ceiling, with streams of water cascading down them, pooling at the different levels where clusters of plants grew.

Not just thin blades of grass, but flowering bushes and small trees. Thick green moss covered the top and sides of much of the rock, blooming with tiny flowers in pinks and whites. The entire room buzzed with the low hum of fat bees bumbling through the flowers.

The cavern was unseasonably warm.

Off to the side sat another pool, this one with no plants growing around it. Steam rose from the surface, along with the faint scent of sulfur.

Kate cast out, and the plants burst into light and warmth. The wave crossed the room and flowed into the three openings on the far side, none of which were lit with sunlight.

Her wave faded out before she could see if anything was alive in them.

Venn stepped out carefully onto the moss beside the clear pool. She squatted down and dragged her fingers over the green carpet.

"This is surprisingly beautiful," Kate whispered.

"I don't recognize these plants," Venn said quietly. She ran her fingers over a fern with thick blueish leaves. "I've never seen any of these before." She brushed off her hand, and, after a frown at the plants, she stood. "Which way do the remnants go?"

Kate pointed to the doorway on the right. The moss on the floor muffled their footsteps as they moved toward it. Beside the trickle of the stream, there were no sounds at all. Kate cast out repeatedly with tiny, gentle waves, hoping that sentient shadows couldn't feel waves as well as elves could.

They were nearly to the opening before her wave rolled over a bright form collapsed on the floor.

"Those are the right size for dwarves," Kate whispered.

Venn moved silently to peer around the side of the opening. "Cages," she whispered. "The rest curves to the right, though, and I can't see all of it."

Kate cast out again, this time sending a strong enough wave that it flowed in and mapped out the entire room.

Around the corner to the right, a dozen small points of warmth flared up, more like plants or small animals than people. At the far end of the room, though, another form was sprawled on the floor.

A hint of an alpine forest remnant lingered in the air, and Kate caught sight of a drop of blood on the way into the room.

"Faron," she said quietly. She felt the rest of the room before the wave faded, trying to see any abnormality that might hint that the shadow was there. "I don't feel anyone else."

Venn crept into the room, her crossbow raised.

Kate stayed next to her. The room quickly widened to their right into a long, low-ceilinged chamber.

Enough light trickled into it from the cavern behind them that Kate could easily make out the row of domed cages set along one wall. Each was made of pale gnarled branches knotted together and anchored to the ground.

The top of the cages reached almost to Kate's shoulder. Tribal and Silas were slumped senseless in the first two.

A long table made of the same roots ran along the wall to the right. The top was knotted together so tightly that the surface was almost solid and held a variety of little chests and bottles and flowering plants growing out of mounds of dirt. A few bees bumbled around them.

At the far end, Faron was curled up on the floor. His back was to them, the side of his shirt torn and bloody. A dark stain colored the rocks where he lay.

Venn ran across the floor toward him.

"I expected the shadow to be here too." Kate tossed her pack toward the table. It hit the edge and toppled off, but she left it and rushed to Tribal's cage. She ran her hands over the cage, but the web of tangled roots had no door or opening of any kind.

"Then let's hurry," Venn said, dropping to her knees next to Faron. "It's a long walk out the front door, and I'm not going into any other tunnels unless you discover another poem."

Kate shoved her hand through one of the gaps between roots. "Tribal!" She grabbed his shoulder and cast out. He looked unharmed, but when she shook him, he didn't wake. She shoved some *vitalle* into him, but he didn't move.

She glanced over at Venn, who'd rolled Faron over onto his

back. His face was pale and slack, and the whole side of his shirt was wet with blood.

Tribal moved, and Kate turned back to him to find his eyes cracked open. He gave a groggy moan and squinted at her.

"Tribal! Get up! We need to get you—"

His hand snapped up so fast Kate didn't have time to move. He clenched his fist around her arm and yanked her forward until her shoulder and the side of her head slammed into the cage.

"Silas!" he bellowed. He rolled to his knees and wavered slightly but kept an iron grip on Kate's arm, wrenching her harder into the unyielding wood of the cage.

"Tribal!" she snapped. "Let go!"

He dragged her closer until his breath washed over her face. "Who are you?" he snarled.

CHAPTER SEVENTY-SIX

KATE STARED AT TRIBAL, stunned by the hostility in his face. "You don't know—"

"Silas! Wake up!" he yelled again. "What did you do to my brother?"

Venn's arm swung over Kate's shoulder, leveling a crossbow dart at Tribal's face. "Let go, dwarf."

His black eyes locked on the dart. With a growl, he released Kate, and she fell back, scraping her arm along the rough roots as she pulled it out.

"What did you do to my brother?" he repeated, his voice low and ominous.

Venn kept her crossbow raised. "Can I shoot him?"

"He's too heavy to carry out." Kate rolled her shoulder. "Tribal, what's the last thing you remember?"

His eyes narrowed. "How do you know my name?"

"Answer her question," Venn said.

His brow creased slightly as he took in the cave. "We were at the gov'nor's party."

Kate let out a breath. "What's the date?"

"You wouldn't understand our calendar, human," he sneered.

"I bet I would. How about you just tell me what season is it?"

"Mid-autumn, in your outside world."

Kate sat back on her heels. "Tribal, it's not mid-autumn. Winter begins next week. Must be near the end of Drustlenntide in the dwarven calendar." He snorted in derision, but she raised a hand to quiet him. "Shut up and listen. This is Venn. I'm Kate. I'm a Keeper from Queensland. I'm going to wake your brother so I don't have to repeat the rest of this twice. As unbelievable as it sounds, we're friends of yours, and we've all been traveling together for a couple of weeks now. So just shut up and don't give Venn a reason to shoot you."

"They're remarkably lucid for having their memories stolen," Venn said.

Tribal glared at her. "How'd we get here?"

"A shadow took you." Kate moved over to Silas's cage.

"Can you handle this one on your own?" Venn asked.

"Now that I know what we're dealing with." Kate glanced at Faron. "How is he?"

"Not good." Venn strode back across the floor.

Kate reached into Silas's cage and took hold of his leg, far from where he could grab her. "Silas!" She shoved *vitalle* into him, ignoring how much it stung her palm, and continued to feed it into him until he groaned.

She pulled her arm out as he rolled to his feet.

"Tribal?" he said warily, his eyes darting around the room.

"What's the last thing you remember?" Kate asked before Tribal could answer.

Silas studied her. "Buying reddseed powder from some humans in Queensland. Who are you?"

"I'm Kate."

"We never bought reddseed powder from anyone," Tribal said with a suspicious look.

"If reddseed powder caught fire, would it put off poisonous fumes?" Kate asked.

Silas nodded. "Where am I?"

"I think this is Renault's cave," she answered. Both dwarves straightened. "Yes, that Renault." She pointed at Silas. "Your memory is newer—that's right before Venn and I met you. You two led a Snare to our camp, and we had to make a run for it. You brought us through Rullduin—"

"We did *not* bring a human and an elf through Rullduin," Tribal said.

"You did. You're actually in a lot of trouble for it and lying low here in the White Wood. But I had information about Renault, so you've been entertaining yourselves digging down to caves buried under a rockslide, looking for the Oziv Amulet."

Both dwarves grew very still, but neither said anything.

"Until last night," Kate finished, "when the shadow captured you and dragged you here."

"Literally," Venn said over her shoulder. "It literally dragged you up a mountain and into these cages."

Both dwarves stared at them, looking torn between incredulity and curiosity.

"We're going to get you out," Kate said, "but first I'll need an airtight promise from you that you won't hurt either of us. I swear to you, we are friends."

"Friends is pushing it," Venn said.

"You don't really think we're stupid enough to believe this," Tribal said.

Kate let out an annoyed breath. "You both wear amulets around your neck that make you barter better, except they were cheap and rough and barely worked. So I fixed them." When neither dwarf moved, she made an impatient motion at Tribal's chest, and he pulled his out.

"That looks…"

"Better. It actually works now. You did take us through Rullduin. The river on the way to the White Woods has all sorts of luminescent plants." She spun to point at Silas. "You have an uncut garnet in your pocket. It looks like a stupid, boring reddish rock, but you think if you cut it, you can give it to the gov'nor's daughter as a peace offering since he's *very* angry with you for bringing Venn and me through your tunnels. And for going out into Queensland, unsanctioned, where you could have been seen by Duncave Dwarves."

"And we know why they call you Weasel Brothers," Venn added.

Tribal made a series of hand signals at Silas.

"Yes," Kate said, pointing at the hand signals, "you do that a lot too. Check your pocket. The other day it was in your right-hand pocket."

Silas reached in slowly and pulled out the garnet. "All right," he said slowly, "I believe you."

"Good." Kate looked at the two dwarves. "Swear you won't harm either of us in any way if we let you out."

"Or take our stuff, even if we happen to set it down," Venn called. She was hunched over Faron, her hands splayed out on his chest.

Silas gave the hint of a smile.

Kate spit in her hand and held it out.

His smile widened, and he spit in his own.

"Don't you dare swear me to that!" Tribal sputtered.

"Until we're out of these caves, we promise not to harm you two in any way or take any of the things you now possess." He shoved his hand out one of the holes.

Kate grasped his forearm and let him wrap his thick fingers around hers, ignoring the warm sliminess on his palm. "That's very short-term, but good enough for now." She let go and wiped the spit off on her pants. "Let's get these cages open."

Unlike the roots that had imprisoned her and Venn in the shelter, these didn't go down into the solid rock beneath them. Instead, they twisted together to form a floor, totally encasing each dwarf. Silas's had no obvious weaker spots. She moved to Tribal's and found the same.

There was no visible sign of life on the gnarled wood. No leaves or shoots or even bark, but when she cast out, a dull, languid *vitalle* lit along every limb. She set her hands on either side of one of the larger gaps and drew the *vitalle* out into herself. Beneath her palm, the wood dried and withered, and she moved to the next portion.

"Kate!" Venn's voice cut across the room, laced with fear.

Kate twisted around. The pool of blood next to Faron was growing. She shoved herself to her feet.

"Wait!" Tribal reached out, grabbing for her. "Get us out of here!"

Kate avoided his hand and ran over to kneel next to Venn.

"I moved his arm." Venn's face was drawn and pale. Her hands were pressed against Faron's chest, and Kate could feel *vitalle* flowing into him. "And it started bleeding. So much!"

The wound cut deeply across Faron's waist and into his stomach.

The *vitalle* from Venn poured into his chest but had no direction. It merely swirled around, pooling in useless places.

"Let me direct it." Kate funneled some of her own *vitalle* into him, providing a path that gathered Venn's and guided it toward the wound. The damage reached deep into his gut. "How is he alive?"

Venn's breath came fast. "It's not working!" There was a note of panic in her voice, and she pushed more *vitalle* into him, shredding apart the pathway.

"Venn!" Kate grabbed her arm with her free hand. "Stop!"

Venn met her gaze, her eyes wide with fear. "He can't die." She swallowed. "The prince of the White Wood—he can't die!"

"I know." Kate tightened her grip on Venn's arm. "Let me help."

Venn's arm trembled, but she gave Kate a twitch that was almost a nod.

Kate closed her eyes and opened up a wide channel between the two elves. It reached the deep damaged parts of Faron's gut and began knitting the gashes in his organs together as it squeezed out fouled blood and bile.

It moved unbelievably fast. In a matter of minutes, the wound was just a shallow cut through the skin and the muscles right below the surface.

Faron gasped in a breath, and Kate's eyes flew open. He stared at the ceiling for a moment before he caught sight of her. Pain and panic filled his face, and he moved his arm sluggishly to grab her wrist.

"Faron!" Venn said, her voice full of relief.

"Do you remember me?" Kate asked.

"Kate?" Faron's voice was weak, but he kept his hold on her wrist, and his eyes locked on her face.

Kate leaned closer to him. "Yes! Do you know how you got here? What happened?"

"I..." His expression wavered between frustration and something that looked almost hungry. *Vitalle* still flowed from Venn into him, and his skin regained its normal coppery undertones.

"I can tell you what happened to him," Silas said from his cage. "Looks like he got hit with an axe."

"That was an axe wound," Tribal agreed. "From a good dwarven axe."

Venn's brow creased. The flow of *vitalle* out of her hand slowed. "You were attacked by an axe?"

Kate took in how he was lying on the floor. "Faron... Why aren't you in a cage?"

He let out a sigh and gripped Kate's wrist more firmly. "Stupid dwarf got the jump on me while I was tying up his brother."

Kate stared at him.

"You're the shadow?" Venn's voice was barely above a whisper.

He met Venn's eyes with an expression tinged with guilt. "You weren't supposed to be here."

Venn started to draw back, but Faron's other hand grabbed her arm. Regret twisted across his face, and his fingers tightened. "I'm sorry, Venn. I wish..." His gaze shifted to Kate, and his eyes hardened with resolve.

A floodgate opened between Venn and Faron, and a torrent of *vitalle* ripped out of her, pouring into him.

"Faron!" Kate shoved her own *vitalle* out, trying to shut the channel he'd ripped open, but it was like trying to stop a raging river.

Venn's breath turned to shallow gasps, and her head sagged toward him.

Faron's skin began to glow with a faint copper brightness.

Kate worked a sliver of shield between the two elves, blocking the flow. "Faron! Stop! What do you want?"

He released her wrist and pushed himself up to a sitting position. His skin exploded with light and his face contorted into a snarl as he leaned toward Kate. "I need Bo!"

Shadows bled out of his hand, wrapping around it with a blackness so complete it was like a rent torn in the world itself.

The giant raven-colored fist shot out and plowed into Kate's chest, hurling her into the air.

CHAPTER SEVENTY-SEVEN

KATE CRASHED onto the table on her back. Her head slammed down on the hard wood. Flashes of light burst across her vision, and a deafening ring filled her ears.

Glass jars shattered and shot in all directions. A foul-smelling liquid sprayed across her cheek.

The ceiling above her shifted in and out of focus. She coughed, and pain shot across her chest as she rolled to her side, her motions as slow as if she moved through mud. Shards of glass cut into her arm, and the sharp sting cleared her mind a little.

Faintly, over the fading ringing in her ears, she heard Venn's voice sounding weak and desperate.

Kate heaved herself to her feet, and the world spun. She braced herself on the table, focusing on the broken glass speckled with dribbles of her blood. Bees, disturbed from the plants at the far end of the table, resettled themselves on the flowers.

Frantic motion near her hand caught her eye.

In one of the unharmed glass jars, a spider with bristly legs scrabbled against the cork. Its back was striped with the distinctive black and white markings of the tundra spider. Two large fangs curled from below its numerous eyes, needle-sharp and full of venom strong enough to paralyze a grown man.

She yanked her hand away from it and spun to see Venn topple forward.

Faron knelt in front her and caught her. His skin glowed with a warm copper light, and his face was torn with remorse. "I'm sorry," he whispered into her hair.

With a small groan, Venn went limp, and he lowered her to the ground.

"Venn?" Kate pushed herself away from the table. She cast out. At the feet of Faron's blazing form, Venn's own *vitalle* was barely warm.

Faron stood and faced Kate. The room behind him shifted, growing darker as tendrils of shadows from every crevice in the cavern wall flowed toward him. His skin brightened against the gathering darkness. Around his wrists, lights began to glow through his linen wrappings, forming bright runes.

The shadows reached him, rippling around his feet and covering Venn's unmoving body with a pool of nothingness.

He stepped over Venn, holding out his hand. A small white gem glittered in his palm, and Kate forced herself not to step back. Flashes of erratic light shot out of the stone, and she felt something hungry and wild brush against her mind.

A wellstone.

He walked toward her. "I need every memory you have of Bo."

This time, she did take a step back.

"Don't fight me." He gestured to the dwarves. "I figured out how to take your memories without damaging your mind like the men from Home. If you fight me, though…" A flicker of reluctance crossed his face, but he shook his head. "Don't fight me, Kate. I can't leave without every memory since you met Bo."

The wellstone grew brighter, and she felt it lap up against her, snagging on the edges of her mind.

The extent of Faron's words sank into her. "Since I met Bo? He's my older brother! I met him the day I was born!" The idea of losing every memory she had opened like a gaping hole in front of her, and she shrank back. "That's my entire life, Faron!" Every memory of her childhood, every day spent in the Stronghold, everything she'd ever learned as a Keeper. "Just ask me what you want to know."

His expression steeled into something implacable. "If it were that easy, I would have just asked everyone." Shadows poured into the air around him, churning and shifting. The edges bulged and stretched, reaching out toward her with long tendrils like liquid soot. "I'm sorry. You won't know if you've seen what I'm looking for."

Kate threw a shield around herself. The scent of her own remnant filled the air. The rush of the river from her childhood. The rich, earthy smell of the wheat field.

Strands shot out of Faron's shadow, swirling and crashing against her shell like a wild, blustering wind.

It thrust her to the side, and she staggered against the table. Next to her, the spider flung itself against the wall closest to Kate, and she flinched back. It was unnerving how much it looked like it wanted to get out.

A sharp onyx blade slashed against her shield, and she funneled *vitalle* against it.

The spider stilled and stared at her.

Amidst everything, she caught a trickle of *vitalle* leaking out of the spider's jar.

Kate pulled one hand off her shield and picked up the jar.

"Is that a tundra spider?" Tribal asked, his voice slightly panicked. "Don't let it out!"

"Faron!" Kate grabbed the cork. "What did you do?"

"Silas!" Tribal yelled. "Stop the twiggy human!"

"What am I supposed to do?" Silas demanded.

"Kate!" Faron's voice whipped through the air with a snap of command. "Don't!"

Kate ripped out the cork, and a thundering remnant poured out. "Crofftus! Bite him!"

Faron stood glowing in the midst of his writhing shadows, and she hurled the vial at him. It tore a hole in her shield, but she snapped it shut again.

The darkness around Kate shrank back, coalescing into a single solid arm that knocked the jar to the ground. The glass shattered, and Crofftus's bristly legs scurried over the shards toward Faron's feet.

The shadow arm shifted to a column and plowed toward the floor.

"Crofftus!" Kate yelled.

Darkness smashed onto the spider, and the sound of ocean waves cut off so abruptly Kate stumbled forward into the silence it left behind.

The black slithered away, leaving only a smear on the floor.

Kate stared at it.

"Stop fighting." Faron's shadows surged out again. This time wrapping behind her and pulling her in as he enveloped them both in a cocoon, blocking out every bit of light except from Faron himself.

"I like you, Kate." His voice was conflicted. "Venn likes you. She trusts you, and she doesn't do that easily." He stepped closer, his hands curled into fists. "I didn't want it to go this way."

Shadows rippled under his skin, darkening it to a seething bronze.

He clenched his jaw, and the cocoon collapsed around her, barreling into her shield with the weight of a flood.

"Where are your runes?" he snarled, stepping closer and

holding out the wellstone. "I can feel your essence in the shield. How do you control the runelight?" His shadows dragged her closer.

Kate planted her feet, but she slid forward as her mind struggled to grasp his question. "It's not—"

There was a crack of splitting wood and heavy footsteps, and Tribal barreled through the wall of darkness, slamming into Faron.

The two of them crashed to the ground.

Faron's shadow separated into distinct strands, and the natural light of the cavern streamed in through the gaps.

Kate staggered back as Tribal straddled the prince, holding him down. Silas shouted something, but her eyes locked on the writhing end of the nearest shadow.

The pieces of a story map snapped into place, creating a clear picture.

The carriage had been protected by runelight, and it had felt like a solid remnant.

"Runelight is fueled by remnants!" She stared at the tendril that still thrashed against her shield—

Her shield that smelled like her own remnant.

The truth washed over her.

It smelled like her remnant not because the shield was trapping it, but because it was *made* of it.

Faron shoved Tribal off of him, and Kate's eyes locked on the glowing runes she could see clearly through the fabric on Faron's wrists.

His shadow was made of runelight.

So...His shadow was made of his remnant.

And in Yellow's kitchen, she'd cut some of it off.

Kate stretched her shield into a sharp point and sliced it through the end of the tendril nearest her. It dissolved into smoke.

Tribal bellowed at the prince and pulled back his huge fist to strike.

Shadows raced out of Faron, hurling Tribal into the air and flinging him across the room. His body crashed into the wall with an explosion of broken stone, and the dwarf fell, unmoving, to the floor.

Faron leapt to his feet and spun to face Kate. He reached both hands out, his fingers curved as though digging into the very world. Huge walls of blackness filled the room on either side of her.

He slammed his hands together, and the shadows hurtled down, smashing into her and crushing her shield.

Kate fell to her knees as the light around her choked out. The dark drove against her like a wild, battering storm. Her shield collapsed until her legs were outside it, their warmth being leached out faster than if she were kneeling in snow.

"You can't stop me, Kate." Faron's voice was only paces away, but she couldn't see him.

She wrestled against the pressure, her mind grasping at the idea of runelight and remnants. "If my shield is my remnant," she said through clenched teeth, "then I can do more than just sense it. I can affect it." She started to form a spike out of part of her shield. "And I can affect yours too."

She jabbed the spike deep into the shadow.

It flinched, then the storm raged back to life. Deafening. Crushing her into a smaller and smaller space.

Each tendril grew more solid in her mind, though. She could almost feel the shape of them pouring out of Faron.

She lashed out with thorns of her own remnant, cutting into his.

The assault on her shield redoubled, driving it back until it only covered her head. The rest of her body grew numb with cold, and her strikes against him weakened.

The shield took too much to hold.

She couldn't keep it up and fight back.

The shadow scraped against the edges of her mind, grasping and hungry, and a stab of fear shot through her.

The dark fingers snagged on bits of memories.

Running along the river with Bo and Evan as a child.

Stepping into the Stronghold for the first time, feeling the remnants of the building wash over her.

The quick smile and bushy eyebrows of the Shield.

Venn, Tribal, and Silas on the boat, surrounded by luminescent plants.

She shoved the shadow back, and the thought of every memory of her life being torn away kept her shield in place for another heartbeat.

But the memory of Venn floated to the surface of her mind, pointing an apple at Faron. *No one can control someone else's runelight.*

The shadow battered against her like a maelstrom. Kate stared into the abyss, seeing nothing with her eyes, but she could almost feel the shape of his remnant around her.

I can feel his runelight.

She gritted her teeth against the coming onslaught.

She clenched her hands into fists and dropped the shield.

His darkness rushed in, and she tilted her head back, opening herself up to everything around her.

The roiling, shifting shape of his remnant sprang into being like a living creature, as easy to feel as her own shield had always been.

The shadows burrowed into her mind, but she wrapped her will around them, holding them back and expanding her thoughts until she held every bit of his remnant with her own. Until she held every ripple of blackness that filled the room like a feral creature.

With a surge of *vitalle*, she formed her remnant into a thousand jagged claws and slashed into his.

It tore into shreds.

The darkness in the room splintered. Light poured, in and the tattered bits of shadow fled.

But Faron's remnant continued to flood out of his body. Kate closed her own around him, digging into his, grabbing handfuls and tearing them off, pulling his essence away as it flowed out of him, chunk by chunk, until it slowed and he sank to his knees, his face pale.

"How…?" He fell forward onto his hands, his arms shaking.

The shadows dissolved, revealing Venn still lying on the floor near him. Her body was limp, but she met Kate's look with a weak smile. "That human just ripped up your runelight, Faron."

The room was crowded with tangible remnants. Faron's was frail and small, like a mist, but Venn's was a thick cloud filling the air around. Each dwarf had a knot floating around them like thick yarn.

A shimmering glow emanated from Kate's hands, and she could feel the extent of it in the air around her. She stretched her fingers, and the glittering remnant flared out into claws.

Faron looked up at her, and she felt him gathering *vitalle* to step.

Her remnant was so solid she merely flicked some of it at him, and it obeyed, thinning and enveloping him in a shield. "You aren't leaving," she said. "You have a lot to fix and—"

From behind her, another tangle of remnants caught her attention. Strong and terribly complex.

She turned.

The aenigma box lay on the floor by her spilled pack, a new drawer cracked open.

Multiple remnants snaked out of it, jostling against each other.

The toll of the bell sounded, louder and clearer than she'd ever heard it. An aching loneliness seeped out into the room.

She fell to her knees next to it, sorting through the remnants.

A toasted pungent spice. Frost-laden wind. The sense of endless, empty space—

The impression of windswept hills.

She snatched up the box and yanked the drawer open. "Bo?"

The drawer was empty, but a sound tickled her ears.

Voices, muffled and far away.

"Bo!" She leaned closer, casting out, but found nothing.

Amidst the crowd of remnants and the tolling of the bell, his distant voice came back to her. "Ria!"

"Bo! Where are you?"

Among a handful of remnants she didn't recognize, she caught the scent of pine trees after the rain.

"Evan!" She scrabbled frantically at the drawer, but it wouldn't open farther, and there was nothing inside it.

Something tore through the shield she'd put around Faron, slicing a sharp pain across Kate's mind. Venn let out a hoarse yell as Kate spun.

Faron knelt beside Venn, his arms stretched through the shield, gripping her shoulders, holding her upright on her knees as she swayed. Her hair began to glow with an angry, sullen red.

Kate threw a hand out toward them, expanding the shield until it encompassed both elves, and healing the rent he'd created.

"Enough playing with humans and dwarves, Venn," Faron growled. "I need you. Come home."

Kate scrambled to her feet. The drawer hit against her arm and almost closed. She wrenched it all the way open, keeping the threads of remnants from both brothers trailing out.

Venn tried to jerk her shoulder away from Faron, but the motion was weak. "You and I are finished."

His eyes narrowed. "You'd stay here? Claim her"—he jerked his head toward Kate—"over your own kin and friends?"

"Over you? In a heartbeat. I'd even take the dwarves over you."

Kate set the box down carefully on the table, making sure to leave the drawer open. "Give me the wellstone, Faron, and show me everything you know about Bo and the ravine. Tell me how to heal the humans you hurt, and I'll let you crawl back to your father."

The corner of his mouth twisted up in a pained smile. "That's impossible."

"She has you beat, Faron," Venn said. "You can't step, and you can't fight her. Stop all of this." Her voice dropped to a whisper. "Please."

Faron closed his eyes, and his brow creased in pain. "You know I can't. You'll come back to me, Venn, because it's not up to you. It's not up to either of us." He opened his eyes, and the expression in them was utterly broken.

"Until then," he continued, his voice anguished, "I forbid you to speak of this to anyone outside this cave."

A wave of *vitalle* rolled out of him at the command.

Venn's mouth dropped open.

"As you've claimed this human," Faron continued, holding Venn's gaze with a tortured expression, "and these dwarves, they are under you and bound by the same oath."

Her face curled into a livid mask. "You pathetic coward!"

His hand shot up, and he grabbed the crossbow on her arm. With a smooth motion, he ripped it off. "Drop the shield, Kate," he said, still looking at Venn. "You can't hold me here and heal Venn too."

Faron's remnant was trapped inside her shield, but she could see wisps of shadows beginning to reform around him as he strengthened.

694

Kate stepped closer. "Venn, do you need healing?"

"I need a lying, spineless elf out of my face." Venn tried to pull away from him, but her head lolled to the side. "What are you going to do, Faron? Shoot me and put me back to sleep?"

He pulled her forward until her head rested on his shoulder and pressed his face into her smoldering hair. "It can't go this way, Venn. You know it can't. I'm so sorry."

He drew a knife from his belt, pushed her away, and brought it down in a sharp slash.

Venn let out a gasp and fell back.

She turned to stare at Kate, her eyes wide, her hand wrapped around her forearm.

Blood streamed between her fingers from a slice ripping straight through her sleeve—and her tattoo.

Kate stood in shock for a heartbeat, then dropped the shield and ran to her, grabbing her arm.

Faron staggered to his feet and pointed the knife at Kate's face. "She'd better be right about you."

Something small streaked toward him.

A bee, roaring like a distant ocean, slammed into Faron's neck.

The prince slapped his hand down on it with a hiss of pain and stumbled toward the table.

He snatched up the aenigma box.

His copper fingers wrapped around the metal straps and covered the runes.

The drawer slid shut

The faint sounds of Bo's and Evan's remnants cut off.

With rush of *vitalle*, Faron disappeared. ·

CHAPTER SEVENTY-EIGHT

KATE STARED at the spot where the box had been, its absence a gaping hole torn into her. The absence of her brothers' remnants was like a fragment of Faron's empty blackness still lingering. Invisible but more real than the table the box had just sat on.

Her fingers slipped on the warm blood, and she looked down at Venn's forearm and cast out with a shiver of fear. The cut from Faron's knife sliced through Venn's arm like a sliver of night in the brightness of her *vitalle*.

It wasn't terribly deep, and her body was already working to heal it, but Faron had drained so much *vitalle* out of her to heal himself that the activity wasn't as fast as it should have been. Not nearly as fast as her body had healed from the vimwisps.

Kate shoved Venn's torn sleeve out of the way and pressed her own *vitalle* into the wound, pouring it into the deeper edges and knitting it back together.

"He..." Venn's voice was weak. "He..."

"I can fix this." Kate's words came out short and desperate. She shoved more *vitalle* into the cut. Her arm was numb with cold, and the energy flowed slower than it should, but she pushed it in anyway, which spread the chill up toward her own shoulder.

The interior of the cut was healing. Kate wiped the blood off the top of the tattoo so she could see the edges. She cast out again. There were little knots of *vitalle* trapped in different runes, stagnant and fading.

A patch of darkness in Venn's hand caught Kate's attention. Venn's smallest finger was withering, a pool of blackness inside it spreading out into her hand.

Kate leaned over the tattoo. Starting at the top, she healed the skin, drawing it back together, making sure the lines of the tattoo met again, sealing them with a little *vitalle* when they connected.

The process was terrifyingly slow. Kate's *vitalle* moved sluggishly.

"Kate," Venn whispered.

Kate glanced up to find Venn's face deathly pale. Her eyes were wide with fear but growing unfocused.

"I can fix this," Kate repeated, the words still sounding frightened. The skin of Venn's smallest finger was turning black. "This is too slow." She cast around the cave, but there were only the few small plants on the table. That would never give her *vitalle* fast enough. "Tribal! I need something big and alive! Or fire!"

"No fires in caves!" Tribal squinted at her. "We're really friends?"

Kate shot him an annoyed look. "You let me rest on your shoulder yesterday after you two almost killed us all trying to get gold out of a three-hundred-year-old cursed carriage."

Tribal's mouth twitched up in a smile. "Sounds about right." He looked at Venn. "I'm big and alive."

Kate stared at him for a moment. "Put your hand on her, right next to the tattoo."

Tribal shifted closer, and his huge hand wrapped around Venn's arm. Kate cast out and felt the rich, dense power of the *vitalle* that filled the dwarf. She opened a pathway between his arm and Venn.

Energy poured out of him, and Kate funneled it toward the cut, sewing it back together, slowed only by the precision needed to reconnect the tattoo.

"He cut it..." Venn's eyes were closed, her body limp on the floor of the cave. "And left me in a cave."

Kate pressed *vitalle* into the next stretch of wound, knitting the edges of the tattoo back together. "Remember when I asked you why you didn't want to marry him? I take the question back."

Venn let out a little huff of laughter. "Kate." She swallowed, not opening her eyes. "Even if you can't fix it, thank you for trying." Her voice was barely a whisper. "Not your fault."

"Is she turning black?" Tribal asked warily.

Venn's hand twitched. "Growing colder." Withering darkness lined the side of her second finger and crept up toward her wrist.

Kate dragged her eyes back to the wound. "I'll fix it. Stop talking, and let me work."

"When you find him," she said, her voice so low Kate could barely hear, "tell him I always hoped he was better than this."

"You can tell him."

Venn let out a faint groan. "And tell him I hate him..." Her voice trailed away, and her head sank to the side.

"Is she dead?" Tribal whispered.

"No." Kate was past the middle of the cut. Tribal's *vitalle* still flowed into Venn, but slower than before. "You all right?"

His skin was pale, but he nodded.

There was too much left to do. Kate swallowed back a wave of fear and glanced back at Silas, who was pressed against the walls of his nearby cage. "Can you reach Silas? If you two are touching, I can use you both."

Tribal lay down and stretched out a leg, and after a moment of watching them suspiciously, Silas shrugged and grabbed his brother's foot.

Kate spared enough attention to connect the path through Tribal and tap into Silas's full strength.

With the surge of energy, she pushed through the healing of the rest of the cut before pulling her hands off both Venn and Tribal.

Each stroke of the tattoo looked whole and smooth. Each rune complete. She wanted to shove *vitalle* into it, but she forced herself to study every piece of it to be sure it was undamaged.

She traced each line with her eyes, verifying the tattoo touched across the thin red line where the cut had been.

She reached the bottom of the tattoo, and her gaze caught on the dark bluish grey that now covered two of Venn's fingers and the side of her hand all the way to the wrist bone.

Kate dragged her eyes away from the withering flesh and set a single finger in the middle of the runes. She opened up a new path, and the tattoo immediately pulled in a trickle of warmth from her. She prodded it to take more, and it did.

Casting out into Venn, she found threads of light running along every rune and seeping into Venn's arm with a complex flurry of activity that stretched down toward her blackened fingers.

Kate sank back, shifting to rest her palm on the tattoo while it continued to draw trace amounts of *vitalle* out of her.

Tribal still lay on the floor, watching her. "Is she…?"

"I think it's fixed."

When the tattoo stopped pulling from Kate's hand and Venn's arm was a warm bustle of activity, Kate pulled her hand off, and her head sank forward. Both arms felt cold and heavy. Her ribs and back were achy with cold.

Bo and Evan were in the box.

The truth hit her with a weight as heavy as if the whole mountain had collapsed on top of her.

They'd been right there in her hands the whole time.

And now...

She stared at the empty spot on the table.

"That prince is gone, right?" Tribal asked in a tired voice.

Kate cast out toward the other cavern but found no sign of Faron. She nodded.

They lay quietly for a long moment.

"Did we get the gold?" Tribal asked finally.

Kate glanced at him. "What gold?"

"The gold from the three-hundred-year-old carriage."

She let out a huff of laughter. "No. We got a few papers."

"Hmm." He lifted his head and looked at his brother. "We'll need to try again."

"I would love to," Silas said, "as soon as someone lets me out of this cage."

Tribal sat up. "Right. The cage." He moved over to the twisted net of branches holding Silas and studied it. "This branch looks brittle."

He grabbed one, and it snapped in his hand.

"That's where I was leaning when that human pulled our souls out," Silas said, "or whatever she did."

Kate crawled closer, each movement feeling like she was wading through sand. "I just took a little of your life energy. You'll be fine. Move back and I'll weaken some more branches." She set her hand on a tangle of thick limbs and drew the *vitalle* out of them. It slid into her arm gently, warming her fingers and palms, then her forearms. The branches withered before the warmth even reached her shoulders. "Try that."

Silas grabbed the branch and broke it apart, shoving himself quickly through the gap. When he was out, he peered at her. "Who are you again?"

"I'm Kate. That's Venn." She glanced at the two dwarves. "We need to get her to the forest. She needs to be touching the biggest tree we can find."

Tribal looked around the cave. "Where are we now? This isn't Rullduin."

"A cave up on the western slope of the same ravine where you two saw the shadow in the trees."

Both dwarves stared at her.

She sighed. "The elf prince who left us in this predicament was the shadow."

Tribal's eyes narrowed.

Kate sank against the wall of the cage. "I'll tell you everything. I just need help getting Venn to the forest." She grabbed a branch and started to pull herself up. Her legs refused to hold her, and she sank back down. "It can't wait."

The two dwarves looked at each other, and Tribal made a short hand motion. Silas trudged over to Venn. Bending down, he scooped her up. "Which way is out?" He swayed slightly on his feet.

"Through that cavern. Then there's another with tall and short grass. Follow the tall grass, then you'll have to jump over the mound, then there's a—"

Tribal wriggled one arm under Kate's back and another under her legs and lifted her up.

"Tribal," she said wearily, "you're too tired. You two take turns carrying Venn out, and I'll follow."

He snorted. "Your sad little human brain would just get you lost, then we'd have to spend hours looking for you." He took a staggering step toward the exit.

"Tribal, put me down."

He shifted his shoulders and started forward again, more steadily. "The more times I have to tell you to shut up, the more energy I'm wasting. Besides, even like this, I have more strength than Silas. I could carry all three of you out."

"Looks like Tribal's lost his mind as well as his memories," Silas said from behind them, his voice slightly strained. "But don't worry, Kate. I'll come back for both of you when he inevitably collapses."

They started out of the room, each dwarf scooping up a pack.

Kate looked over Tribal's shoulder until she finally lost sight of the empty table.

CHAPTER SEVENTY-NINE

THE DWARVES' banter lasted all the way through the winding path of tall grass, until they reached the mound.

"We have to jump that?" Silas asked, looking at the surface of cobblestones stretching two paces wide in front of them.

Kate stared dully at the stones, which now looked unreasonably far across. "The stones won't hold you." Her mind felt foggy, and her limbs still felt cold and heavy.

"This won't be comfortable for you, Twig," Tribal said.

"You remember you call me Twig?" Kate asked.

He looked down at her. "No. You're just scrawny like a twig."

With a grunt, he heaved her up, making the world spin. She landed over his shoulder, her legs hanging down in front of him, her hands scrambling for purchase against the back of his vest. One of his huge arms wrapped around her legs, and he took a long step and jumped.

Kate clamped her hands on a fistful of his shirt and tried to hold back a cry of surprise.

He landed hard on the far side, and his shoulder shoved into her gut as he stumbled down the short slope.

Kate let out a groan as the world tilted erratically.

"Time to get down for a minute," Tribal said, swinging her off his shoulder and trying to stand her on her feet.

Kate's legs shook, and he frowned at her, helping her down to sit against the wall.

"You're a mess." He turned back to his brother and motioned him to come.

Venn, unconscious, was carried over his shoulder already, and he stood looking at the cobblestones. "You sure they won't hold?"

"Push on one," Kate said, leaning her head back.

Silas touched one of the first cobblestones with his toe. The quiet snap sounded, and the stone plummeted down into whatever lay below the mound. He glanced back at his brother. "Seems they won't hold."

Tribal gauged the distance with a troubled look.

"Can you jump it?" Kate asked.

"Of course I can jump it," Silas answered. "This is not a problem."

"It is a problem," Tribal said. "He has an old injury. Doesn't jump as far as he used to."

"Shut up, Tribal." Silas shifted Venn on his shoulder.

"You could toss me the elf," Tribal offered.

"She weighs nothing." Silas took a deep breath and made a quick hand signal.

Tribal positioned himself at the edge, holding a hand out.

With a low rumble like a growl, Silas took two quick steps and launched over the mound.

His jump was too short. His leading foot slammed down on the last cobblestones. They broke off, and his foot plunged down into darkness.

Tribal grabbed his outstretched arm and yanked him forward, wrapping his arms around Silas and Venn's legs, and dragging them past the stones.

Silas's foot caught on the edge of the mound, and the three of them toppled over, crashing onto the slope in a tangle of arms and legs.

Kate shoved herself forward as the dwarves groaned and untangled themselves.

"See?" Silas said, pushing himself to his knees and putting Venn back over his shoulder. "No problem at all."

Tribal sat for a moment longer, slumped on the ground. "Exactly. No problem."

Kate cast out toward Venn. She was still weak and dim, but even the jolting of the jump hadn't roused her.

Tribal stood and came over to Kate. His shoulders were slumped, but he held out a hand to her. "Up we go, Twig."

"You need to rest," she said.

"When the elf's in the trees," he answered, pulling her up and scooping her back into his arms. "What other irritating things does this path hold?"

"Just a tunnel of absolute blackness," Kate said.

"Not a problem," Silas answered. "Tunnels should be black."

"And the cave at the exit will use magic to terrify you. It won't do anything but make you frightened."

Tribal squinted at her. "Can you stop it?"

Her head sagged against his shoulder. "Probably not. Just move through it fast."

Tribal started toward the next tunnel with a grim determination.

"Did that elf prince make all this mess?" Silas asked. "Because I already didn't like him."

"I think he made the dark tunnel and the fear, but I think the rest of this was made by Renault."

Tribal glanced back at Silas. "So this cave was protected by Renault. That's interesting."

Tribal's trudging pace was surprisingly soothing, and Kate's eyes closed.

He stumbled, and her head bumped against his shoulder.

She opened her eyes to find trunks rising around her and the sun shining down through patchy clouds.

"She needs a big pine?" he asked, his voice blurred with exhaustion.

Kate looked around and pointed to a reasonably thick trunk. "That one will work "

Tribal grunted and headed toward it. When they were close, he dropped to his knees with a half-stifled groan and set her down.

Silas knelt by the pine and pulled Venn off his shoulder, sitting her against the tree. He lay down not far away and threw an arm over his face. "Now what?"

Kate crawled over to another tree and leaned her back against it, drawing *vitalle* out of it. The energy flowed slowly and gently, like a seeping warmth, slowly filling her. "Now you sleep, and Venn heals. I'll keep watch."

"You fell asleep while we walked," Tribal said from where he lay, his own eyes closed.

Kate drew some *vitalle* up toward her mind, and the haziness began to lift. "I can stay awake now. You all sleep for a bit. When you wake, I'll see about giving you back some of the memories you lost."

Tribal cracked an eye open. "You can do that?"

"I can share my memory of times I was with you."

He was quiet for a moment, then met Silas's gaze. Tribal made a few hand signals, and Silas nodded.

"Sounds good," Tribal said, closing his eyes. "Are you at all qualified to keep watch?"

"I can tell if any living thing approaches."

He considered the words for a moment. "That works."

"Will you teach me your hand signals sometime?" Kate asked.

"No," Tribal answered.

"Maybe," Silas said. "If you make us a good enough deal."

Tribal pulled his finger out of the tenea serum, his bushy black eyebrows high on his forehead. "It's been a busy few weeks."

Kate took a bite of the dried meat the dwarves had shared. "It has." She turned back to the journal spread out on her lap.

It was open to a new page, with the word *Faron* written in bold in the center.

Spiderwebbing out from it in all directions were lines and notes connecting the shadow to the men from Home who'd disappeared, to the dwarves, to the ravine with the rockslide on one side of the valley, to Renault's cave far up on the opposite hillside.

Venn groaned from where she sat slumped against the pine and opened her eyes.

"Welcome back." Kate handed her a piece of the dried meat.

Venn reached for it but stopped, staring at her hand.

Her smallest finger and the one next to it were grey and thin, the skin withered around the bones. She flexed her fingers slowly, and those two didn't close completely. The heel of her hand was greyish blue all the way to her wrist. She pulled her eyes away from her hand and studied the tattoo. "You...fixed it," she said quietly.

"I think so. The poison hasn't visibly spread since I finished." Kate glanced up at Venn. "I'm sorry. It took me a while to... The venom spread so fast and..." She clenched her own hand at the painfully shriveled fingers on Venn's. "I'm sorry."

Venn let out a little huff of laughter. "For saving my life?"

"For losing you another finger."

Venn gave her an incredulous look. "It's a finger. I thought I was dead." She looked at the two dwarves. "You two remember us yet?"

"Kate's showed us what's happened since we met you," Silas said. "We're willing to agree that we're…if not friends, acquaintances working toward some mutually beneficial plans."

"I never would have called you friends," Venn said.

Silas smiled at her. "Then we're all at the same place."

The elf narrowed her eyes. "In the cave, you only promised to not hurt us or rob us until we got out."

Tribal made a dismissive sound. "My brother already agreed to extend that indefinitely, or at least until we find that coward of an elf prince and make him pay."

Venn looked at Kate. "Did Faron—" Her voice faltered on his name, and she cleared her throat. "Did Faron take the aenigma box?" This time the words were firm and almost emotionless.

The question jabbed into Kate like a needle. "He did."

Venn closed her eyes, and flickers of fury and pain chased themselves across her face before she quelled them. "Why would he?" The question was far too complex to merely be about the box, but Venn opened her eyes and met Kate's gaze with a fierce look. "For a moment, just when I was waking up, I felt a pull toward the box. You sensed Bo in it, didn't you?"

The surge of anger Kate had been trying to keep under control flared up at the memory of Faron's fingers wrapping around it. "And Evan. I felt their remnants," Kate said. "I heard Bo's voice."

Venn's expression hardened. "We'll get it back," she said, a note of steel in her voice. "I promise." There was a moment of silence before she gave a hum that sounded like she'd solved a problem. "Maybe you could always sense them in it. You were more protective of the box than it deserved."

Kate paused at the thought but shook her head. "Bo said it called to him, and…I think he was right. I think it called to me

too. Made me protective of it. Made me want to keep it close."
Kate could almost feel the edges of the box on her fingertips. It
was a greedy feeling. A hunger. Something utterly different and
less wholesome than her drive to get to her brothers. It was
somehow tainted. She rubbed her fingers together to drive away
the feeling. "I think the box has its own goals. And it wants to be
wanted. Until that drawer opened, I had no sense of Bo from it at
all. Or Evan."

They sat in silence for a few moments.

A distant rumbling sound caught Kate's attention. A squirrel
scurried out of the trees and spiraled up a nearby trunk. It
perched on a branch and looked down at them with bright eyes.

Kate looked up. "Crofftus!"

The prince entered the White Wood, he said, his voice irritated.
And three elven rangers noticed me and cast me out of the bee.

"I thought Faron killed the bee," Kate said.

He almost did.

"Wait!" Tribal said. "I know I'm not completely caught up yet,
but don't we think the beetle-bee-squirrel thing is the walking
tree?"

"I thought we thought he was Renault," Silas said.

"He's just a human mage," Kate said, "trapped in animals."

"How exactly did that happen?" Tribal asked.

That is a long story.

"I think it's time you shared it," Kate said.

The squirrel scampered to the end of the branch and coiled as
though ready to jump away, but Crofftus made a calming noise,
and it relaxed. Reluctantly, the squirrel returned to the nearer part
of the branch and looked down at them.

*I lived in southern Queensland, where I studied for years until I
finally learned how to enter the mind of an animal. I spent even more
years perfecting it, traveling with all sorts of creatures, until finally I
entered a raven.* He was silent for a long moment. *Ravens are highly*

intelligent, and I could not convince it to do anything. It flew me far to the south. So far that we found the ocean. The squirrel's tail twitched. *I could not find any creature capable of bringing me back quickly, and so days passed.*

"Ahh," Tribal said. "I see where this is going."

I had been pushing my human body to the brink of exhaustion and malnutrition through my studies and... His squirrel eyes stared into the branches of the pines. *It took five days before I felt the connection to it sever.*

It took a week more before I found a vessel that could return me home, but...

"There was no body to go back to," Kate finished for him, "so now you're stuck inhabiting only animals."

I do not think of it as being stuck. I have traveled as far in any direction as they can take me. I've explored the ocean, slithered as a snake across the Roven Sweep until we reached the lifeless desert beyond. I've wandered the entirety of Queensland and everything here that was once the Kalesh Empire. I've explored elven woods and dwarven realms. I've been a bug on a wall in the room of great scholars, watched the most skilled artisans work. I have explored the wonders of the world at every turn.

The squirrel spun and faced into the woods, its body tensed to run.

Kate cast out, and the shape of a fox lit up in a small hollow. It was moving away at a trot.

Tribal slid his knife out of its sheath. "Elves?"

"Just a fox," Kate answered.

His brow creased. "How do you know?"

"I can do something called casting out," Kate said, "and sense living things."

I can feel when you do that. Crofftus's voice was quiet. *It makes me miss...everything.*

Kate straightened. "Could you cast out? Before you..."

No, but I made a potion that did something similar. Let me sense anything nearby holding vitalle.

There was a tinge of nostalgia to his voice that softened it more than she'd ever heard. He gave a very quiet sort of laugh. *It was unstable in sunlight until I found a way to add gelesen.*

She considered his words for a moment. "I need you to show me how to do that."

Of course, Katria. And you can show me how you made your memory serum, because that is an impressive concoction.

"Tenea serum from Napon."

Tenea... He was quiet for a breath, then a chuckle sounded in her mind. *Very clever.*

Kate looked down at her journal. "We need to decide where to go next."

"We should go back to Home," Silas mused. "Tell them that Faron is the shadow."

Venn shook her head sharply. "You can't!"

"Faron commanded her to silence," Kate said, "and put us under her. If any of us speak about it, Venn will be cast out from the elves, and her family will as well."

Tribal blinked at her. "If the elves are like Faron, that doesn't sound too bad."

"Swear to us you won't speak of it," Kate said.

Both dwarves frowned at her.

"Please." Kate spit into her palm and held it out to Silas.

He shook his head.

Tribal, though, spit in his own palm and held it out. "I swear we won't speak of anything that happened in that cave to anyone but you two."

Silas's mouth dropped open. "What?"

Kate grabbed Tribal's forearm before he could take it back. He wrapped his hand around hers and squeezed.

"I can*not* believe you just swore me to that." Silas stared at him. "What's wrong with you?"

Tribal let go of Kate's forearm, and she surreptitiously wiped the sliminess onto her pants.

He shrugged. "She knows how to get past the traps in Renault's cave."

Silas gave Kate a thoughtful look. "True. How exactly do you know that?"

"I have a poem that talks about it."

Venn frowned at her. "There's more to the poem than the mound and the grass, though. Wasn't there something about a tree that would break your bones if you disturb it?"

Kate gave a small smile. "Maybe that part is metaphorical?"

Venn rolled her eyes.

"We're not going to Home." Kate looked at the group around her. "We need to go talk to Thallion."

"The elven king?" Silas asked.

"We know Faron wasn't working on his own," Kate said. "We need to know what the elves want. Faron is the shadow, but we still don't know what he was doing. Why was he stealing memories?"

"King Thallion is key," Venn said. "Faron was obviously obeying his orders."

Crofftus made an unhappy noise. *I'm not anxious to see Thallion again.*

Venn looked at him in surprise. "When did you see him before? He doesn't usually meet with humans. He sends Faron."

I wasn't in human form. I had been traveling this land, exploring all sorts of interesting things, when a hummingbird flew me up here into the White Wood. I'd never been in an elven wood, and the trees are so…

"Alive," Venn offered.

Yes, alive. Well, the hummingbird flew close to a huge old spruce, and...I can always sense nearby animals, but I could sense the tree too, so I joined it.

"You inhabited a tree?" Kate asked.

Yes, but it didn't move. It was a tree, after all. It did think, though. Slowly and ponderously, but there were thoughts. I stayed there for quite some time. It was lovely, really. Peaceful.

I admit I lost track of...everything for a while. Until someone was talking, in Elvish. It took me some time to realize he was the king, but he was pacing through the trees, looking up into the branches, pleading with...someone.

"I need your help! I know you can hear me!"

He was desperate, crazed almost. He began going to each tree, setting his hands on them, imploring them for help.

He reached a tree not far from me and it...I don't know what it did. It started groaning, this dreadful noise. It was horrifying, and in my fear, I shook the branches of my tree. King Thallion spun to face me and...somehow, he knew I was there. He began shouting, asking who I was, screaming things at me in Elvish, half of which I didn't understand. He grew brighter and shouted, "Get out! You are bound to secrecy and silence!"

He slammed his hand onto my trunk and somehow shoved me out of it. The entire forest went blurry except him, and he was this blazing tower of light.

I was flung away. There were no animals nearby, and I felt myself begin to spread out. The edges of me started to dissolve away. I thought the end had come, and then a dragonfly flew near.

"You don't seem bound to secrecy and silence," Tribal pointed out.

I'm not an elf. Crofftus paused. *I don't know what the king was talking to in that forest, and I don't know what was wrong with that tree, but whatever it was, he didn't want it seen.*

Venn frowned at him. "The tree groaned?"

715

Screamed, almost. The squirrel's body shuddered. *I have never heard anything so ghastly.*

Kate scanned the branches surrounding them. "Do trees scream?"

Venn shook her head slowly. "Not that I've ever heard."

"Well," Kate said, looking back at her journal. "Thallion making trees do things that trees don't usually do seems like another reason to talk to him."

"What I can't figure," Silas said, "is what the prince wanted with Tribal and me."

Kate studied the two identical dwarves. "Me neither. I thought all this was about Bo, but neither of you ever met him, so Faron has to be looking for something else."

"The only thing these two have in common with the others whose memories Faron stole," Venn said, "is that they were interested in the ravine with the rockslide."

Silas glanced at his brother. "We care about the caves, not the ravine."

Kate considered the idea. "Why would Faron care about those caves?"

"Why was he trapping people in Renault's cave over here?" Venn asked. "I think it's safe to say that we don't understand what Faron's up to." She shifted against the tree.

"When we find him," Kate said, "he's going to explain all this."

"When we find him," Venn said, "I'm going to kill him."

"I'll help," Tribal offered. He held out a jumble of leather straps.

It was Venn's crossbow, its harness in tatters.

"We're not going to kill him," Kate said. "We need him to tell us how to heal the people whose memories he took."

"Fine." Venn took the broken harness. "I'll kill him after that."

We're not going to get into the White Wood, Crofftus said. *Their borders are too protected.*

"Venn could get in," Kate said. "You are still betrothed to the prince, after all."

"Maybe," Venn admitted with a distasteful look. "But they're not going to let me bring in two dwarves, a human, and a..." She waved at Crofftus. "You."

"Well," Kate said, turning back to her journal, "we'll go give it a try as soon as you're up for a walk, Venn. We have a lot of questions still to answer. Like what does Faron want with Bo?"

"And what's hidden in Renault's cave?" Silas said.

"Whose corrupt remnant is all over the ravine and the carriage?" Kate added.

"And why is that carriage cursed?" Tribal said. "And how do we get the gold out of it?"

"And why is Faron stealing memories?" Venn added. "And why does he care about a rockslide and some caves?"

Kate tapped the big question scrawled across the bottom of the page. "And where did he take the box?"

EPILOGUE

I had truly believed, while I was walking up that slope, following those trails, that I was about to find my answers. I was about to find Bo and understand everything that had happened. About to assemble all the missing pieces and have the story fall neatly into place.

I had thought there were simple reasons. Maybe greed. Maybe envy. Maybe the age-old desire to protect what is yours.

I suppose, in the end, some of those were part of it.

But I knew so little about the souls involved. So little of what actually drove them. Almost nothing of the fears that kept them up at night. The fears they would do anything to ward off.

And maybe I knew too little about myself to even understand my part in it.

I had truly believed that I'd fought through mysteries and monsters and secrets and curses and was about to find everything I was looking for.

But it wasn't nearly that easy.

THE END

ACKNOWLEDGMENTS

Thank you to you for taking the time to read an indie author! It means more to me than you know.

Thank you to Constance Lopez and Karyne Norton for your invaluable critiques.

Thank you to Dalton, for being willing to stick your neck out and offer critiques to your own mother.

And most of all, thank you to my husband. This book would still be a hot mess without you. Thanks for always encouraging me to work out the best way to write these stories. I love you.

ABOUT THE AUTHOR

JA Andrews lives deep in the Rocky Mountains of Montana with her husband and three children.

She is eternally grateful to CS Lewis for showing her the luminous world of Narnia.

She wishes Jane Austen had lived 200 years later so they could be pen pals.

She is furious at JK Rowling for introducing her to house elves, then not providing her a way to actually employ one.

And she is constantly jealous of her future-self who, she is sure, has everything figured out.

For more information:
www.jaandrews.com
jaandrews@jaandrews.com

facebook.com / JAAndrewsAuthor
twitter.com / JAAndrewsWriter
instagram.com / jaandrewsbooks

Made in the USA
Middletown, DE
22 August 2024

59571525R00435